THE
HILL WITCH

by James Christopher

Rev. 11/10/20

There was an intense looking man in a suit and tie with receding brown hair standing by the trucks, his hands on his hips. He was wearing a flabbergasted expression behind his spectacles. The father pulled up next to him and rolled down his window.

The man stooped over, frowning. "Are these your trucks?" he asked.

The father cleared his throat. "I own the carnival, yes," he replied. He smiled. "My name is Carson Downing."

The man in the suit wasn't impressed. "There must be some mistake," he said. "This is a hospital, not a fairground. We can't have a carnival here."

"And you are?" Carson asked, his smile intensifying.

The man straightened up. "Dr. Cameron Sativa. I'm the hospital administrator."

Carson said, "We left messages for you."

Dr. Sativa replied, "I returned them, but the church in Harrisburg said you'd already left." He shifted uncomfortably. The old woman in the back seat dressed in Gypsy attire was glaring at him. "I tried to warn you. We cannot have a carnival on hospital grounds. The noise, the lights… we have patients to consider. I'd like you to tell your trucks to move on."

Carson looked into the rearview mirror. The old woman rolled her window down. She crooked her wrinkled finger beckoning the doctor to come closer. He gestured with his head. When she didn't speak, he went to her. Mickey smiled, warm and friendly. Dr. Sativa was compelled to smile in return. His gaze fell on the old woman and his breath caught in his throat. The irises of her eyes were glowing with a midnight blue light.

"We need to set up the carnival, doctor," she said.

Dr. Sativa felt her words as much as heard them. They echoed around him and within him, ricocheting inside of his skull. His eyes rolled back.

"Time is short. Of course, we have your complete support. The compensation we offered is more than adequate."

Her eyes dimmed. Her hazel irises returned.

Dr. Sativa stumbled but caught the trunk of the Chrysler. He moved back to the window. "As I said," the doctor smiled. "Time is short. I'll let you get back to your work." He smiled at Mickey again. "You have my complete support. The compensation you offered is more than adequate."

Carson said, "Thank you, Dr. Sativa. You won't be sorry."

Dr. Sativa walked confidently toward the hospital. In the back seat, the old woman gripped her temples and grimaced in pain.

"Grandma?" Mickey asked, touching her forearm. "Are you all right?"

"It will pass, love," she said. She touched his cheek. "Have you had any more dreams?"

Mickey nodded. He took her hand. "Death is here, grandma," he said. "He's been waiting for us."

The old woman glared at her son-in-law with an urgent expression.

The Downing Family

It was early, not yet noon, but it was already hot outside. They could feel the heat burning through the dark blue Chrysler sedan's air conditioning. Waves of distortion radiated from the hood. The woman in the passenger's seat glanced at her husband with concern. He caught her expression and nodded. He looked into the rearview mirror. His mother-in-law met his gaze. Determination blazed in her hazel eyes. They needed her strength and the Lord's guidance. Their family was coming full circle. Destiny was upon them. A whispered prayer escaped his lips. His wife took him by the hand and joined him as they prayed to the Lord for protection.

An albino boy with closely-cropped platinum blonde hair and crystal blue eyes was lying in the back seat with his head in his grandmother's lap. He sighed, "Are we there yet?"

His father tilted the rearview mirror down so his son could see his smile. "It won't be long now, Mickey," he replied. "Just rest." He paused at a stop sign and signaled a right turn. "We've waited this long. Patience is a virtue."

Mickey looked up at his grandmother. "Is there anything we can do?" he asked. "Can we warn them at least?"

His grandmother shuddered. She lifted him up. He was ten years old and as thin as a rail.

"No," she said, her German accent strong, "and you must learn this, my love. You cannot alter Fate. To do so…"

"… could make things worse," the boy finished. "I remember."

"Please," his grandmother said, kissing his hand. "Do not learn that lesson the way my mother did."

The father flipped on his right turn signal again. He slowed to enter the hospital's parking lot. He eased the car over a speed bump. He pointed to a row of trucks at the far end of the lot lined up side by side. They were carrying carnival rides neatly taken apart and waiting to be reassembled. He drove toward them.

"They found their way here."

They usually led their carnival to each stop, but this time they sent the trucks ahead. They had been forced to cancel two days of their Harrisburg, Pennsylvania commitment. The family remained behind to smooth things over with Bishop Maris of St. John's. It couldn't be helped. They needed to be in Connecticut. After so many years of desperate searching, they had found their quarry. The Lord was guiding them. He would see them through this evil. Their faith in Him was unshakable.

"Who's that?" Mickey asked, pointing out the front windshield.

"We'd better get started," Carson said. He pulled the Chrysler into a parking spot and shut down the motor.

Mickey looked out his window. The temperature increased as the sun grew higher in the sky. He focused on a figure shimmering in the distance. It became more defined as it moved closer to the car. No one else could see it except him. He watched as it took the shape of a familiar man. This ghost had spoken to him before.

"I told you we'd come," Mickey whispered.

"Aye, lad," the ghost replied, with a heavy Irish accent. *"I just hope I led ye t' th' evil in time."*

His sad expression stayed with Mickey long after the ghost faded away.

DAY ONE
Monday

The Dougan Family

There was a crash, the sound of breaking glass, of splintering wood, and the dull thud of a coffee table leg landing on the throw rug in the downstairs hallway. Craig Dougan awoke from his uneasy sleep. He always slept that way when his father was out drinking. He lay there with his eyes closed, breathing evenly, his ears refusing to turn off. They searched for the barest whisper of Jack's presence. It was a common occurrence. His father was always out drinking, so Craig always slept that way. It was why the dark circles under his eyes never faded away.

Craig was too young to look so tired. He was fourteen, fifteen in a few weeks – July twenty-third – but he felt like he was going on fifty. His smile was wan whenever anyone saw it as if there was nothing in the world to be happy about. His face was soft but worn, drawn in and sad, his expression dulled by years of dreading his father might reach up and pull the string that lowered the stairs to Craig's attic bedroom. There was only one reason he ever did that.

To punish me, Craig thought, his thin eyebrows furrowing. The sadness in his expression was profound.

His eyes tried to open but Craig kept them locked shut. There was a cold feeling in his heart. The sound of the destruction downstairs echoed in the attic, but then the house fell silent. Craig tried his best to stay asleep. The silence lasted a whole minute. It was the calm before the storm. A loud explosion of glass jerked him upright and Craig's eyes shot open. It was the sound of the front picture window smashing out. He could hear the shards tinkling down on the front walkway. Craig scurried backward against his window. He drew his knees up to his chest and hugged them, rocking back and forth.

"Please, God," he whispered. His cheeks faded to pale white. "Not again. Please? *Please?*"

"No good little bastard!" his father screamed, in the living room below.

Craig jumped, startled. His father's words were slurred and running together. He wasn't just drunk, he was really drunk. Craig shut his eyes. His first tear of the day ran down his cheek. He was in trouble and there was nowhere to run. The attic window was twelve feet above the asphalt driveway. If he jumped, he might break his leg, or worse his neck. If he ran, Jack would catch him. He didn't even want to think about what would happen then.

Craig inhaled sharply. He counted to five before he let it whoosh out trying to calm down and stop his legs from shaking. The attic air was dank and musty. No matter how hot the Connecticut summer got, or how cold the winter was, the attic humidity never left. The mildew never vanished from his sparse furnishings, like the fear that never left his chest, or the pain that never faded from his memory.

What did I do? Craig wondered, his mind searching.

He shook his head. It didn't matter. He might not have done anything at all. It was like that sometimes. His father blamed him for everything. His mother ran out on them when he was a baby. *Craig's fault!* Jack lost his job at the battery mill for being drunk on duty. *Craig's fault!* Misty's Café closed before Jack was good and hammered. *Craig's fault!* Even the war in Afghanistan – *Craig's fault!* An excuse was all his father needed to beat him. When Jack didn't have one, he made one up.

Craig rested his head on his knees and whispered a Hail Mary. Church was a refuge for him, like going to work at his Uncle Mike's grocery store, or the hours his father spent at the bar. Craig went to St. Peter's on Sundays with his grandmother, aunt, and uncle. He knew his prayers well even though God never answered them. He shivered more forcefully. The vibrations grew up his bare legs into the rest of his underdeveloped body. He was a late bloomer. That's what his grandmother always said. She assured him puberty would come, but Craig was convinced he was doomed to be childlike for the rest of his life.

Sometimes Jack placated himself by tearing the house apart before stumbling off to bed. Craig hoped that's how it went this morning. New bruises would cost him another gym class, the last one of the year. The other kids would stare at him, too, *like always,* as if there was something wrong with him for refusing to change into his gym clothes. The coach would send him to the office for another insubordination detention and a referral to the counselor's office. How many would that make for the year? Two dozen?

Craig didn't know and he didn't care. It was a joke. The counselor would stare at him with her all-knowing contempt as she prodded him to tell her why he didn't want to undress with the other boys.

"Do you have strange feelings of excitement in the locker room?"

Like I'm gay, or something.

Then the subject would turn to his father. There were rumors of his abuse. Lancaster was a small town. Craig would adamantly deny them and storm out, refusing to go back even under the threat of child services.

Which never happened.

The counselor obviously believed Craig was gay. She needed no further explanation. His withdrawal from Lancaster High School's social circles and his odd behavior in gym class were conclusive. Craig had no idea if he was gay or not, but if that's what she wanted to believe and it kept her from prying into his life at home, he was fine with that.

Like I care what she thinks? I could be gay if I wanted...

Craig suddenly gasped hearing the squeak of the folding stairs as they opened. The sound heralded his father's decision to remember he was up there.

He cried, "Oh, God... no... *please!?*"

Jack climbed the rickety steps. There was an open bottle of whiskey in his left hand. A black leather belt dangled from his right. Silhouetted in the hatchway, Jack rose up from the floor as if passing through it like a malignant spirit. Shadows obscured his face. His breathing was shallow as he approached Craig's bed. Spittle exited through his clenched teeth.

Craig whispered, "Daddy... no... *please...*"

Jack stepped into the pale light beaming in from the streetlamp outside. His deep green eyes were like flames raging in his skull.

"No *what?*" Jack spat, saliva spraying through the air. "Did you think you were going to get away with it?"

Jack shifted from side to side. He was a tall man, six-one, wiry, with a boyishly handsome face and a firm grip. His red-brown hair was past his shoulders. His face was darkened by five o'clock shadow. Craig's mind whirled with the events of yesterday. He desperately tried to figure out what he had done wrong. The severity of the offense determined the severity of the beating. The belt lashed out with a loud snap in the middle of that thought slicing into his smooth thigh. Craig screamed in pain. He squirmed away pulling into a ball. Jack lunged, grabbed him by the back of his underwear, and yanked, only Craig didn't move as his father had intended. His underwear tore instead.

Jack went into a frenzy. *"Didn't I tell you to put the dishes away before you went to bed!?"* he screamed, his voice cracking with mania. *"Huh? Didn't I!?"*

Craig's beating began in earnest. His father's arm rose and fell, the strikes so fast against his buttocks, legs, and back that Craig lost count after fifteen. He felt welts rising on his skin. The pain rippled through him as he wailed hoping God might hear him for a change. At last, his father stopped and stood there panting.

"Don't... *mess* with me, Craig!"

Craig sobbed and shook. He didn't look up. He'd seen the rage in his father's eyes more times than he cared to remember.

"You're going to obey me, Craig... even if it kills you!"

Jack observed his handiwork. Satisfied, he shuffled to the hatchway. His utterances became unintelligible through an alcoholic haze. Craig couldn't make out what he was saying over his loud forceful sobs. He thought it had something to do with cleaning stuff up, but he wasn't sure.

The mumbling ended as the ceiling stairs closed with a slam. Jack stumbled through the hallway to his room. Craig heard him fall onto his bed. He lay down but immediately sat back up. His welts were on fire. He held himself, warm tears dropping onto his forearms. His legs ached. He ran his fingers over the welts. He could feel the heat where the bruises would appear, black and purple reminders of his father's wrath.

The dishes, Craig despaired. *I forgot about the dishes.*

He supposed he deserved the beating this time. Jack was right. He had become so distracted by the TV, he neglected his chores, forgot about them, and went to bed. He needed to try harder, be more focused. If he was a better person, a better son, his father wouldn't beat him anymore. All he had to do was think. People made mistakes, but when God designed him why did He give Craig more imperfections than anyone else? Like Jeremy McKee, for example. Why couldn't he be more like Jeremy? Craig was willing to bet that his classmate had never been beaten in his life. Craig wanted that life. He felt so desperate and hopeless.

Am I a just worthless screw-up? Is that why dad hates me so much?

When his sobbing subsided, he wiped his face with his sheet. Despair reached into his soul like a cancer. Craig forcefully blocked it out. He wasn't letting it go that far. Giving in meant giving up and he couldn't do that. Not yet. He had a dream. He kept it in a secret place in his mind where no one could go and no pain could touch him. He had built it out of hope when there really wasn't any, but sometimes his fantasies were more real to him than reality. He could dream and be wide-awake. This dream in particular was special. In it his father loved him as much as he loved his father. Craig wanted that dream to come true. It was only a matter of time and a lot of work.

Craig slipped off his torn underwear. He sat up and put his feet on the boards that made up his floor. He set them down carefully since the boards were unfinished and gave killer splinters. He stood holding his underwear out in front of him. He crossed the room to his wastebasket. He raised them high, following them with his eyes, and then dropped them. They floated down light as a feather into the plastic can.

Craig stared at them for a long time. There was something behind his father's rage, something he knew instinctively, but was unable to fully comprehend. There was sorrow in his anger, but it was more than that. It was as if Jack was ashamed of something.

Does he hate me or himself?

It confused Craig. His relationship with his father was cloudy at its best, savage at its worst. It was the only part he ever shared, and only with his grandmother, even though Nancy's answers weren't very enlightening.

"Your father wasn't always like this, lad," Nancy would sigh, her Irish accent thick, her voice deep for such a small rotund woman. "I blame me'self mostly."

"Why's that, grandma?" Craig whispered, into the attic shadows. He was in the memory, standing naked above his wastebasket.

"Your father had a grim childhood."

"Grim?"

"Aye," Nancy said. He imagined her appearing out of the darkness in front of him. She was blurry, a phantom, but she was as real as Craig could imagine her right then. "Times were tough. Jackie was th' eldest. It fell on him t' help support th' family."

"Dad worked when he was a kid?"

"Craig," Nancy replied, "your father left school at twelve years old an' worked full time over at Milliken's farm."

A chill ran down Craig's spine. He knew the farm. It was by his uncle's house although he never got too close to it.

Nancy said, "I'm not sure th' boy took a day off more'n once or twice afore he left for Afghanistan. By then, he was eighteen."

"That's a long time," Craig replied. He cringed and covered his mouth. He had spoken out loud with the memory. He shook his head. "I have to be more careful."

"He worked hard, too," his phantom grandmother continued.

Craig imagined her standing over him only it wasn't by that much. He was nearly as tall as her and he had just recently reached five feet. He could almost smell her lilac bath soap.

Phantom Nancy moved around him, her hands clasped behind her back. "Some nights he cried himself t' sleep."

"Dad cried?" Craig whispered.

"Aye, lad, he cried," Nancy replied. "I could hear him through th' wall, although he never copped to it. Your grandfather wanted t' make Jackie quit and go back t' school, but I wouldn't allow it."

"Why not?"

Nancy sighed, "Your grandfather had a bad heart, lad. I wasn't goin' t' lose him for workin' himself into an early grave by takin' two jobs. Talk o' me takin' a job just started his blood boiling."

"He didn't want you to work?"

"Not an iota," she frowned, her image fading in and out. "It was for th' men t' win the bread, th' women t' prepare it, and so it went."

"That's sexist."

Phantom Nancy vanished.

Craig glanced around. "Grandma?"

"Here, lad," she replied. She was sitting on top of his dresser across from the foot of his bed.

Craig said, "Oh, there you are." He asked, "How hard did dad work?" although he already knew the answer. This was an old conversation.

Nancy put her hands on her hips. "Sunup 'til sundown and beyond most days. He lived at the farm more'n he did at home." She paused, considered, and then said, "Th' only night he came home was Saturday. Your grandfather insisted he come to church with th' family every Sunday."

"Dad lived with the farmer?"

"Aye, for th' most of it."

Nancy faded away again. She reappeared sitting upside-down on the ceiling. Her gray and black hair was in its usual bun, but her bangs dangled comically. Craig smiled. Imagining her like this was very funny since his grandmother was so stern.

"You said he wasn't always this way?" he asked. His smile faded. "Mean... like he is?"

"No, lad. He was, perhaps, a lot like ye."

"Like me?" Craig asked. He found that hard to believe.

Nancy smiled. "Sweeter. He was a loving, kind, and gentle boy."

"That's hard to believe."

There was a hint of anger in his voice. This was the father he thought about, the Jack who should have been. It was so unfair. There was so much he didn't understand.

"Why did dad change so much?"

Nancy shook her head, shrugged, and disappeared.

Craig knew she wasn't coming back. The conversation always ended there. Nancy didn't have any more answers. Working for Hiram Milliken had changed Jack.

Was it the hours dad worked? Was sacrificing his childhood and his education for his family a resentment that festered until it burst all over everyone?

Nancy didn't know, or at least she wasn't saying. She told Craig his father got ferociously angry with his Uncle Mike whenever Mike ventured anywhere near the farm. Nancy believed it was jealousy. He treated Hiram like his own private property. He even ran off other kids who came to the farm looking for work. She said she partially understood. Hiram was young, strong, and very charismatic back then. Wade Dougan was no slacker, but his heart condition left him little strength to keep up with a growing boy.

Hiram took Jack places and did things with him. Nancy was grateful, she supposed, but sad that Hiram had replaced Wade so completely as Jack's father figure. Wade had regrets, too, but he never voiced them. Jack was his favorite, but Hiram was the one who was always there for him, which puzzled Craig. As far as he understood, his dad hated the farmer's guts. Jack had repeatedly warned Craig what would happen to him if he ever went near the farm especially after Mike and his wife, Sandra, built their house down there.

His imagination came to life again. It was vivid, inspired as usual by his memories. The attic room distorted and twisted. The faded rafters changed into the clear blue sky of three summers ago. The unfinished floor took on the softness of his grandmother's lawn beneath his bare feet. Craig looked down and frowned. He decided to find some clothes before he let this memory go any further. He didn't relish the thought of standing in the open stark naked even if this was just a fantasy. He wasn't going to get any more sleep, so he figured he would just get dressed for the day.

Unless I sleep standing up, Craig thought. *Sitting in class will be hard enough. These welts are stinging like crazy!*

Craig walked across the lawn to his dresser. It was old, rickety, and covered with mildew stains around the legs, but it was all he had. He needed to keep his clothes somewhere. He wasn't about to get new furniture with his father out of work. They were barely squeezing by on his unemployment check. His car wasn't dependable either. It knocked and blew black smoke like a factory. Jack only drove it when necessary, usually to the unemployment office in Manchester or to Misty's Café.

Lancaster was a stone's throw from Stafford, but it was an economically depressed area, and too far from Willimantic to walk. It was a good thing his grandmother bought them food or Craig was sure he would starve. He passed a frozen image of his Uncle Mike at the barbeque grill preparing to flip a burger. Mike was a big man with almost black hair and brown eyes, but he was a full head shorter than his older brother. What he lacked in height, he made up for in muscle. His arms burst forth from his half-shirt which appeared painted on him.

Craig glanced over as he dressed marveling at his uncle's bulk and washboard abs. He hoped they shared some genes. Craig didn't know anyone on his mother's side of the family – or his mother either for that matter – but he hoped for something from them, too. All he knew, and this came from his relatives, was that his mother was beautiful. She had the same deep hazel eyes as him, and the same soft, fair skin. It wasn't much, but it was better than not knowing anything about her at all.

Craig reached into his drawer. He chose a pair of blue jeans and a faded Red Sox tee shirt. He hated the jeans. They were too tight. He would end up with wedgies all day, the worst kind of wedgies, too. He would have to pull his pants down to pick them out which meant several trips to the bathroom.

People will think I'm diabetic.

They were his only clean pants, so he was stuck with them. All of the other kids would be wearing shorts today since it was June, but his bruises made that impossible.

Another reason for them to stare, Craig thought, as he dressed. He let the memory go forward.

Craig had turned twelve that summer. It was a hot and muggy Sunday sometime after his birthday. His family had gathered at his grandmother's Bog Dancer Drive home for a cookout after church. Jack still went to Mass with them then. Craig was the only kid in the family since Wade and Nancy were only children, and Mike and Sandra had yet to conceive. Craig was trying his best to keep out of the way of the grownups. Jack came out of the house and sat at the picnic table next to the grill. He was swilling his third Budweiser even though he and Craig had only arrived twenty minutes before. Mike was flipping burgers and humming.

Nancy and Sandra were slipping in and out of the house bringing condiments and bowls of picnic essentials to the table. Nancy looked comical as her stout body bounded up and down the back stairs, but Craig held in his giggles. Nancy Dougan was not a person to laugh at even in jest. She ruled over her family with an iron fist. Even Jack didn't cross her. She had to become this way to keep the family together after Wade died, especially after Jack returned from Afghanistan. Sometimes Craig wondered if it had been worth the effort. This was one of those days.

Jack asked Mike, "Did you have any luck finding land to put a house on?"

The Lancaster Savings and Loan had approved Mike and Sandra's mortgage, the same bank that financed Mike's grocery store. Craig had worked at Mike's Market as the stock boy every day after school since he was ten years old. Mike and Sandra had been searching for a plot since February. They were determined to settle in Lancaster, but there were complications.

The town owned some of the land they liked, but it wasn't for sale to private families for housing development. Jerry Copeland was one of Lancaster's primary private landowners. His mill, Copeland Industries, made batteries under contract with NASA and the military for the space program, satellites, and missile targeting systems. Prior to his death, Wade had worked at the mill. Jack had, too, until his drinking got the best of him. Nancy was still there working in Wade's old position as the Dayshift Production Supervisor. Unfortunately, the plots Jerry was willing to part with were near the swamp behind Misty's Café and not well suited for residential construction. Mike wouldn't have lived near there anyway even if the plots had been good. They were too close to the bar for his taste. Besides, Jerry, true to form, wanted way too much for the property.

Margaret Adler was the next largest landowner. She was Craig's science teacher this year. She refused to even discuss the matter with them. She had inherited her land from her father, and although she leased some of it on occasion, she would never sell any. She claimed her father wouldn't have approved. Mike and Sandra were disappointed. She had some beautiful spots up in the hills, but even so, they were glad to get away from her house. Ms. Adler unnerved Sandra. She never blinked the entire time they were with her, not even once.

Sandra told Craig about it during one of his weekend visits back in September when school started after he mentioned being in her class. She said it had felt like his teacher's staring eyes were burning into her brain, digging through her thoughts. It sounded ridiculous, she knew, but it seemed so real when they were sitting in her parlor. Mike had Ms. Adler, too, at Annie Potts Elementary when he was in the eighth grade back when Lancaster had only one school. She moved to Lancaster High School when it was built to teach Ninth Grade Science. He told Sandra he knew exactly what she meant, and so did Craig. Ms. Adler creeped him out, too!

The only person left to speak with – and the single largest landowner in town – was Hiram Milliken. Mike wasn't going to ask him. He knew Jack would be furious if he did, but he had little choice. He and Sandra had decided on a brand-new modular home. They weren't going to settle for buying a house from someone else. They wanted it to be theirs from the beginning.

Mike rationalized that this crap between Jack and Hiram had gone on long enough. When Hiram said yes to their plot request, Mike took it. He figured he would tell Jack when he could shield the family from the resulting explosion sure to follow. The moment Jack asked the question, Sandra and Nancy froze in mid-step. Mike was struck dumb and said nothing. Craig immediately knew something was wrong.

Jack stared at his brother. "It was a simple question, Mike. Did you find some land, or not?"

Mike's expression suggested Jack had asked him to explain the meaning of the universe. Craig looked at his uncle with the same blank expression as his father, but with a twist. Craig had caught the reactions of his aunt and his grandmother. Jack hadn't.

"Well?" Jack asked, leaning toward his brother.

Mike nervously cleared his throat. "Sure, Jack," he replied, flipping the rapidly charcoaling burgers. "We found… something."

Nancy and Sandra inched closer.

"Hey! That wasn't so hard!" Jack exclaimed. "Congratulations, little brother. Where are you moving?"

Nancy walked over next to Craig and put her hands on his shoulders. He knew there was trouble on the horizon feeling her grip.

Sandra went to Mike and slipped her arm around his waist. Something like this was bound to happen sooner or later. The plot they purchased from Hiram had closed two weeks ago. She bit her lower lip.

When they called him, Hiram said he would be happy to see them right away. He told them to follow the driveway around the old Milliken family Victorian to the trailer home behind it. Hiram said he moved there to make remodeling the Victorian easier. It seemed to Mike this remodeling job had started when he was a boy. They arrived a short time later. Jerry Copeland's youngest son – Dabney they thought his name was – greeted them at the door as he was leaving. He wore an angry look on his otherwise handsome freckled face.

"Dabney does some feeding for me," Hiram volunteered. "He's learning to milk, too, but under the table. He isn't fourteen yet." He winked.

Sandra watched the boy with the chocolate brown hair and eyes walk to the road. It struck her as odd he would wear white soccer shorts and a green fishnet shirt to work on a farm. His sneakers probably cost a mint, too. They were Balenciaga's. They looked brand new.

Sandra shook her head and tossed her long raven dark hair back. She thought, *Jerry's rich. The kid probably throws his dirty clothes in the trash.*

She wondered what a rich kid like Dabney Copeland needed a job for in the first place. He didn't look much older than eleven or twelve judging by his height and features. She was sure he was Craig's age.

Aren't they in the same grade?

Hiram called Sandra in off the porch. Two minutes later, she had completely forgotten about Dabney.

The inside of the trailer denied its outward appearance. It had looked small when they pulled up, but the place was huge inside. There were two bedrooms, one on each end, with a full bath, kitchen, dining room, and a living room in-between. Sandra asked why he had two bedrooms when he lived alone. Hiram replied it was coincidental. The two-bedroom trailer had been the better bargain when he bought it. He said the second bedroom had proved invaluable. Sometimes in severe weather he allowed his employees to spend the night. It also served well if an employee had to work late and then milk early the next day. Mike agreed it was convenient. Sandra nodded, her eyebrow flickering.

Hiram led them to the dining table. "I'll tell you, Mike," he began, sitting across from them. He was a husky man, six-two, with large hands, light blue eyes, and curly gray hair. "If it were anyone else but you, I would have said no. Your brother worked for me for six years before he left for Afghanistan. No one's worked as well since. I feel like we're family."

"I appreciate that, Hiram," Mike said, shaking the farmer's sweaty, callus-encrusted hand. He looked old for fifty-something. He was weather worn and grubby, a far cry from the youthful Hercules Mike remembered from his childhood. "Hiring Jack when he was only twelve was one of the best things anyone ever did for our family."

"I knew things were tough," Hiram said. "Wade was a fine man. I was only trying to help. Jack helped me a lot, too, especially with all the hours he put in. Can't do that nowadays."

"Honey?" Mike said to Sandra, laying his hand on her forearm. "Jack spent so many days and nights here as a kid we rarely saw him."

Sandra nodded. Dabney came back into her mind for a moment. Her eyebrow flickered again.

"Jack slept here more often than he did at home," Mike added.

Hiram said it was only the two of them running everything back then. Wade and Nancy appreciated all the hours Jack was able to get.

Mike agreed.

"Now, about the land…," Hiram began.

Sandra interrupted, "Would it help if we told you what we were interested in, or…?"

"I have a better idea," Hiram said, holding up his hand. "You can have any five-acre plot you want as long as it's on this road. I own every acre down here all the way to the Tolland-Stafford town lines. They're in residential zones. I have a map that shows the property boundaries. I'll let you borrow it."

Near the farm? they thought together.

Mike and Sandra considered this carefully. They rationalized that Milliken Road was as long as the width of town. Surely they could find a spot far enough away to not be overwhelmed by the reek. The smell went everywhere in town anyway. They accepted his offer. They choose a plot closer to the farm than they had wanted, but it had a stream out back. Mike wanted to build Sandra a goldfish pond.

"Well, now," Hiram said, sporting a wide smile. "You guys go ahead and look around." He patted Mike on the back. "Plan on having babies?" he asked, hopefully. He continued before Mike could answer. "I hope so. It would be nice to bring some life into this corner of town."

Mike didn't have the heart to tell him they had decided not to have any kids until the store was paid off. That would take another five years. He was sure it didn't matter.

Why would Hiram care if we had children? Mike wondered.

"What's wrong with you, Mikey?" Jack asked, interrupting Mike's train of thought. "You sniffing glue?"

"No," Mike answered, but a tad too slow.

Jack was getting suspicious. His brother was keeping something from him. When Nancy interrupted and suggested they eat – a blatant attempt to change the subject – Jack stood up.

Craig slipped behind his grandmother.

Nancy sighed, "Oops."

"Okay," Jack demanded, his green eyes catching fire. "What's going on here? Somebody want to give me a straight answer? Where are you guys moving? It's not like I asked a national secret, or some…"

"Milliken Road," Mike replied.

"… thing. Yeah? Impossible. Hiram owns every stitch of…"

Jack never finished his sentence. His jaw fell open. His face turned bright red.

"You… dirty…"

"Now, Jack," Sandra said feeling Mike's arm stiffen. "Calm down."

"… rotten…"

"C'mon, Jack," Mike said.

Jack stepped toward him with each word.

"… *nogoodsonofa…!*"

Craig cringed as Jack went off. He had never seen his father so angry. Jack screamed that he had told Mike to stay away from Hiram. He accused Mike of going behind his back and betraying his trust. Craig made a mental note never to go anywhere near the farmer. If his father was this angry with his Uncle Mike who was a lot bigger than him, he would positively kill Craig.

"Jack...," Mike said, controlling his temper.

Mike didn't appreciate being made to feel like a child again. Until Jack met Hiram, he and Mike had been best buddies. Jack showed his baby brother nothing but love and affection. He became cold and distant after he began working at the farm. Mike still loved his brother, but in a minute he was going to punch his lights out.

"No!" Jack yelled. "You knew I wasn't going to like this, but you did it anyway!"

Mike had an Irish temper of his own. He snapped having heard enough.

"Give me one good reason why I shouldn't have taken Hiram's offer!" Mike cried, walking over to his brother. "C'mon, loudmouth! Tell me!"

Jack stood there, his mouth moving, but no sound came out. Mike suddenly looked very big to him. Craig saw his father's fist clench and feared the punch he was about to throw. Fortunately for Jack, Nancy spotted it, too.

"I'd like t' hear that reason me'self, boyo," Nancy said.

Jack whirled around his eyes raging.

"Spit it out," she demanded, sliding her glasses to the edge of her nose. "Why is it ye've always insisted on keeping Hiram Milliken t' yourself? Michael's no child, bucko. I want an answer."

Jack's gaze shifted from Nancy to Mike, back to Nancy. They had him cornered. Even Craig wondered what his father's reasons were now. He never talked to the guy. It wasn't like they were friends.

Jack turned to Mike. "Fine!" he spat. "You move wherever you want, but *Craig's* not going over there, and that's the end of that!"

Craig burst into tears at this point although in the memory vision he merely stood there observing. He knew the feeling well enough. Being with his Uncle Mike was a safety zone. The thought of not going to see him ripped his heart out. Nancy looked down at her grandson and her temper went over the red line, too. She stormed over to her eldest son poking him in the chest as she spoke. Mike moved next to Sandra getting out of the way.

"Ye listen t' me, Jack Dougan!" Nancy yelled, shaking her small fat fist at him. "Your petty jealousy has hurt this family for years! I'll not allow ye t' hurt th' wee lad. He'll see his uncle as he chooses and ye'll do nothing t' interfere, or by Jesus Himself, ye'll have more'n a pimple on your eye t' be sure!"

Jack stormed to his car and tore out of the driveway leaving two neat strips of rubber on the concrete.

Nancy sat down at the table as if nothing at all had happened.

Craig nodded as the memory closed. The images faded and he was back in his attic room. He shook his head. He was tired of thinking. He was glad the summer was here and his freshman year of high school was over. He was tired of being the butt of so many jokes. His peers were even crueler now than they had been in grammar school… well, except for Jeremy. He was always nice. Craig wondered why.

He crouched down and went to the window. He knelt on his bed and peered outside. He looked toward Wickett Avenue – Lancaster's main street – toward the Ramirez family's house. It sat directly across from Craig's Gator Road home, directly across from his attic window.

Craig gasped and ducked down. He thought, *Someone's sitting on Ramirez's roof!*

A shadowy figure stood up and slipped into Max and Ricardo's room through the upstairs window. They were José and Marianna's teenage sons. Craig went to school with them. He was in the same grade and classes as Ricardo. Max – who Craig believed had been the shadowy figure – was a year older. Their window was over the roof of their front porch. They sat out there a lot during the warm weather. Max must have been out there this morning despite the early hour.

Was he drawn out there? Craig wondered. *Did he see anything?*

He lowered his head and rested it on the windowsill. He regretted his screams, his unanswered wails as his father beat him. He had probably woken Max up and lured him outside, an eyewitness to his private hell. Craig usually had a fan in his window. It was an old fan, very loud, but last night there was a cool breeze blowing over the heat. He had taken the fan out and left the window open without thinking. He was usually more careful than that. His family life was his problem. Besides, what if they took him away from his father, or worse, put him in prison? He would never win his father's love after that. Who would he have and what would happen to his dream? Jack would hate him only now it would be forever.

No! Craig thought, balling up his fists. *You're not taking my dad away from me! You're not!*

There were only two houses on Gator Road. The Dougans lived in one as their mailbox proudly proclaimed and Mrs. Turner lived in the other next door. Mrs. Turner was as old as dirt and deaf as a post. Craig could scream his lungs out on her front step and not wake her up. At this end of town – in the wee hours of the morning and within hollering range – there weren't many people. Gibbons' Garage was on the corner of Gator Road and Wickett Avenue. José Ramirez worked for the owner, Lyle Gibbons. The Ramirez house was across the street. The garage closed at five and Lyle usually left by nine. He always hung around after closing to play cards or chat with whoever dropped in. Often it was Arthur Kelly, the owner of the hardware store, or Hiram.

They play cards a lot, he thought, *poker maybe.*

Craig should've thought twice before removing the fan. He should've run through the list of *What Ifs* he had memorized. *What if* someone heard him screaming?

Keep the fan in the window. Duh. That was simple.

But he hadn't. He was sure Max had heard everything, too. Craig heard the Ramirez brothers arguing clearly enough whenever they did, or their mother hollering at them in Spanish. There was no doubt about it. Max knew. Craig looked up. There was a light on in Max's room. Craig could see him standing in the window with his arms crossed staring at him.

Craig jumped back and tugged at his window. It was stuck, swelled up from the heat and humidity. He stood up and yanked on the pane. It slammed shut rattling the whole room. He cringed at the noise and froze. His ears searched for the sound of his father stirring, but all he heard was the low growl of Jack's snoring. Craig slumped down on his bed and leaned back against the wall ignoring his bruises' objections. He grabbed his forehead between his left thumb and middle finger. He massaged his temples feeling very afraid.

Will Max tell anyone? Craig wondered. *Yup, Ricardo most likely who'll tell everyone else in town. I'm doomed.*

Craig almost cried again, but the sob caught in his throat. If it came down to it, it was his word against Max's. His father could deny it with ease. He wouldn't remember doing anything. Jack wasn't deliberate like that. When he was sober – the rare instances that he was, usually when he was out of money – he isolated and ignored Craig. There was only reason to fear him when he got drunk.

Craig wasn't alone in this fear. The entire town avoided Jack when he got loaded. He was dangerous and quick to get into it with anyone who dared cross his path. He never backed down, not from twenty men. Craig had only ever seen his father's temper falter once. It was at the town meeting concerning Hiram's proposal to sell Lancaster the land they needed to build the high school and middle school a few years back. Jack almost looked sad when the motion passed. He glared at the other men who had objected with him – Peter Rollins, George Skinner, Donald Barry, and Hugh Kreeger – as if thinking, *You chickenshit bastards. You pussies.*

Craig walked over to the stairs and lowered them. *It's time to get ready for school,* he thought. He closed his eyes and sighed. *This is going to be the longest day of my entire life.*

*   *   *

The Stone Family

Sam Stone, Jr. stretched out in the driveway of his home on Annie Potts Road preparing for his daily five-mile run around Lancaster. His legs were spread out straight to his sides in a straddle split. He could feel the cool tar against his red jogging shorts. He rested his forehead on one knee and then the other, his long dark hair tickling his kneecaps. He closed his bright blue eyes. They were his mother's eyes, her hair, traits he shared with his brother and sister. He stretched low, proud of his flexibility. He was the only sixteen-year-old in town who could do any split whatsoever. It was a lot of hard work, but he had the determination to succeed. Sam had been the first sophomore in the town's history to make the Varsity track team at Lancaster High School. He once feared running cross-country would be the death of him, but he was still breathing the last time he checked.

Sam rose and walked toward the end of the street. He breathed in the damp morning air deeply, steeled himself, and began to run. His red New Balance running sneakers tapped an even rhythm on the blacktop as he met his pace. He turned left at the end of his road and headed down Route 41. In the dim light of the rising sun, fog lingered above the ground. It was chilly against his arms and legs and lowered his visibility to a foot. He stuck close to the shoulder. Few cars traveled this early, but it was better to be safe than squished. He wasn't ready to die. If he were, it would've been easier to play football or baseball where a solid hit in the chest could put his lights out for good.

Only Sam's family, his doctors, the school nurse, and administration knew about his heart condition. He intended to keep it that way. He wasn't going to let anyone treat him like he were *coronarily* challenged, or whatever. Hypertrophic Cardiomyopathy was an inherited cardiovascular disease that resulted in a thickening of the muscle wall in the left ventricle. Sam's heart couldn't pump enough blood to the rest of his body. He had experienced shortness of breath and dizziness as a youth, but his condition had gone undiscovered until a spectacular fainting spell playing little league when he was twelve. Sam stole home and fell unconscious on top of home plate. He got the score and the diagnosis on the same day.

The condition ended Sam's contact sports career. HCM was called the *Silent Killer* for a reason. High-intensity workouts or a substantial impact on his chest could cause ventricular fibrillation – light's out for Sam Stone, Jr. Sam wasn't allowed to play any sports at all following his diagnosis. His mother was adamant. He wouldn't even be running right now if she hadn't passed away. Sam often thought about her when he ran.

Don't push yourself, Sammy, she whispered, her spectral voice concerned. *Don't overdo it. Mommy's afraid for you.*

"I'm afraid, too," Sam said, speaking out loud. He jogged a little faster. "Afraid I'm going nuts and you need to go away."

Terrified Sam was going to die, Jeanette Stone kept him out of public school to protect him from the roughhousing boys do. She educated him at home. She was a fair teacher. Sam stayed ahead of the other kids his age. He was a diligent student and loved her for the attention. His father diagnosed Jeanette's breast cancer around Sam's ninth birthday. She had ignored the lump and the cancer spread to her lymph nodes, liver, and brain. She didn't tell her husband until the symptoms had become more than she could bear. It was too late to save her. She died two months later.

Sam was crushed. His rage at his father's failure to save her – *He's a doctor! It's his job!* – resulted in grief counseling for him, his younger brother, and his sister. Stephanie and Steven couldn't understand why Sam was so angry with their dad. God took mom away, dad had said so. He was the one to be mad at not their father. Sam didn't care. God had nothing to do with it.

So what if mom never told anyone? Sam thought. *Dad's a doctor! He should've known what was happening and he should've cured her!*

Stephanie and Steven came to terms with their mother's death. The grief counselor suggested Sam continue one on one therapy sessions. He suffered fits of temper often aimed at his father. His adjustment to public school wasn't going well either. His tantrums and outbursts of foul language had caused severe disruptions in class. The middle school eventually assigned him a temporary home tutor.

During one of his counseling sessions with Dr. Anderson – the psychologist the grief counselor had recommended – the doctor had suggested Sam participate in sports to burn off some of his frustration and anxiety.

Sam laughed, but then he got angry. He had no idea people could earn college degrees in stupidity. "I can't do sports with my bad heart!" he cried, his face turning red.

Dr. Stone said, "That's not true, Sam. There are…"

"Liar!" Sam spat, his face contorting as tears fell. "I wanted to play *baseball,* remember?"

Dr. Stone reached out but Sam pulled away from him.

Dr. Anderson suggested he give his father a chance to finish his sentence. Sam quietly sobbed. After a minute, and with some coaxing, he nodded.

Let him say whatever he wants, Sam thought. *I'll hate him anyway. I'll always hate him.*

His father calmly explained, "No, you can't play baseball, or football, or hockey, but there are plenty of other sports you can do."

"Like what?" Sam asked.

Dr. Stone replied, "Swimming?"

Sam said the chlorine bothered his sinuses.

"Golf? We could play together."

Sam looked at his father in disbelief. *Is he serious? What kind of geek does he think I am? I'd rather be dead than wear those stupid shoes.* He shook his head.

"Basketball?" Dr. Anderson suggested.

Sam rolled his eyes. "Too short."

Dr. Stone agreed. He crossed his arms and added that one solid elbow in the chest and everyone at the game would get a live demonstration of cardiopulmonary resuscitation and a defibrillator.

Dr. Anderson nodded.

"Horseback riding?" Dr. Stone asked.

"Hurts my ass."

"Buttocks," Dr. Anderson corrected.

Sam frowned and thought, *I'll say ass anytime I feel like you gray-haired quackosaurus.*

"Tennis?"

"Dad? Are you trying to make me gay?"

Dr. Anderson said the magic words when it seemed their destiny was to get nowhere.

"How about running?"

Sam's eyes lit up.

Dr. Stone wasn't sure, but his son's excitement was growing. He agreed to discuss the matter with Sam's cardiologist.

The runner's high Sam enjoyed started to take effect. He checked his *Omron HeartGuide* fitness watch for his heart rate and blood pressure, and then picked up his pace. He passed Satchell Hill and then Owen Road on his left. To his right through the fog, he made out the sign for Lead Sinker Road. It was a half-moon shaped street that ran off Crescent Drive behind Mike's Market.

He used to take a left here, follow Owen up to where it met Satchell Hill, and then run Satchell Hill to Adler Road on the cliffs. That was until he spotted Ms. Adler watching him from the rocking chair on her front porch two weeks ago. It was the last morning he went that way. Ms. Adler was his freaky freshman science teacher from last year. Her house was perched near the edge of a sharp cliff overlooking Lancaster. Residents could see it from any point in town. Sam was afraid of her, but it caused him no shame. Everyone was and for a good reason.

Ms. Adler was a witch.

Dr. Greenblatt, Sam's cardiologist, had initially said no to running as an activity. Sam pitched a fit that nearly destroyed her office. She agreed to allow him a chance after he broke an heirloom vase her grandmother had given her. She told Dr. Stone to purchase the *Omron HeartGuide* watch and to make sure he knew how to operate it. She said Sam needed to keep his heart rate below one-fifty. She made him promise to stop if it went higher, if he felt lightheaded, or experienced any pain.

Dr. Stone agreed and said he would monitor him. They purchased the watch and clocked a one-mile route in the car that afternoon. It went from home to Satchell Hill and then Adler Road all uphill. Sam ran it the next morning without incident, and then walked home. His father had tried to give him a ride, but Sam refused. He didn't like getting up so early in the morning, but it had been necessary. Dr. Samuel G. Stone, Sr., Internal Medicine, was the town doctor. His office hours began at eight-thirty.

Sam didn't notice the early morning hour after the first couple of days. Dr. Stone had given up following him with Dr. Greenblatt's approval and Dr. Anderson's support after a month. By the time he turned fourteen, his route went all the way up Satchell Hill, down Adler Road to Wickett Avenue, Wickett to Route 41, and then back home to Annie Potts Road. Sam eventually came around. The solitude of running did wonders for his attitude. It became easier for him to forgive his father. Sam ran that same route every morning, too, until the day he encountered Ms. Adler.

Sam had reached the top of Satchell Hill when he spotted her out of the corner of his eye. She was sitting in a rocking chair on her front porch, her legs and arms crossed. A cup of coffee rested on her knee despite her movements. She stared at him over the top of her glasses. A chill ran down his spine and Sam froze.

That's the same look she had on her face every day in last year's science class! he thought. He checked his Omron watch. *One-sixty! Calm down, Sam! Breathe in, out...!*

Her expression bordered between hate and disgust. She looked strung out. Her long dark blonde hair was streaked with gray. It went in every direction except neat. Her aura was evil. Her deep brown eyes never blinked. They fairly glowed above her glasses.

Sam got lost in her stare, paralyzed with fear like a deer in headlights. His heart pounded in his chest. He thought he was going to die right there.

Then he heard her voice.

"Better move along, young Master Stone, before you have a heart attack."

Sam panicked which in turn gave him the strength to move. He ran back down Satchell Hill and didn't stop until he was in his yard. He collapsed onto the grass terrified, his chest heaving, his heart pounding.

I heard her voice, Sam thought, *but her lips didn't move! How does she know about my heart? Is the administration gossiping about me? The nurse? They wouldn't do that! Would they? It felt like she was talking directly into my brain!*

Sam made his father clock out a new route for him that afternoon. He vowed never to go near her house again.

It's true! She is a witch! There's no other explanation!

Sam shivered at the memory. He could still feel her words inside his head. It was like fingers had reached into his brain and put them there. He shook his head and tried to get his bearings in the fog. He nodded when he realized where he was. After Legion Avenue, which was named for the American Legion hall there, came Milliken Road both on his right. Hiram Milliken, the local farmer, owned all the property down here on the northeastern edge of town except for one plot. Hiram lived at the opposite end of the road named for his family. His farm took up most of the eastern corner of Lancaster, but Sam would've bet it was more like half judging by the stink. The fog was thicker on Milliken Road than on Route 41. It was the lowest point in Lancaster, a town dominated by hills. Sam slowed his pace so he didn't trip over anything. He followed the slap-crunch noise his sneakers made as one foot hit the pavement and the other the sand on the side of the road.

The only other house near the farm besides Hiram's empty old Victorian and his trailer home stood on the only plot of land the farmer had ever sold to a private family, Mike and Sandra Dougan. Sam knew a lot of people who were mad about that, especially his father. Dr. Stone wanted to build a house down here, but the fat old farmer wouldn't sell him a plot. The area around Milliken Road was breathtaking with its thick hardwoods and ample cedars. The area on the cliffs was better, their height offering a staggering view of Lancaster, but Ms. Adler owned that property. She had inherited just like Hiram and was even more adamant about not selling any.

Sandra Dougan came out of her front door and closed it behind her. She slung her heavy canvas bag onto her left shoulder and walked to her car. The Dougans' house was a yellow modular two-bedroom ranch on the left side of the road just before Grady Lane. It was the halfway point of his run. Sam waved to her. Mrs. Dougan was the only early riser on his new running route. He wished there were more, but at least he wasn't alone the entire way.

Thank God, Sam thought, feeling Ms. Adler's voice in his head again.

Sandra called out to him. She smiled her usual morning pleasantness. She was dressed a woman's business outfit. Her raven dark hair shined. Her hazel eyes were bright and aware.

"I can barely see you, Sam!" she cried, half-laughing.

"Yeah," Sam puffed, jogging past. "The fog's mighty thick this morning, Mrs. Dougan!"

"Well, it's the last day of school, right?" she asked, unlocking her black Honda Accord. "I'll bet you have one heck of a summer planned."

"Absolutely!" Sam replied. "I'm going to stay home and do absolutely nothing!"

Sandra told him to be careful and warned him that next time it was this foggy he'd better have a flashlight. She suggested a reflective vest, too. Sam promised her he would have both as he disappeared. He was glad the Dougans lived down here regardless of what his father and others thought about Hiram's selfishness. Running was lonely sometimes. Seeing Mrs. Dougan charged him up for the rest of his route. Sam would go a little past Grady to Hiram's farm, turn around, and come back. The extra distance made his run five miles. Sam gagged at the scent of manure as it strengthened. He was sure it was the sweet reek of money.

Hiram's rich, Sam thought. *He has to be. He lives alone, owns tons of land, and has all kinds of dairy cows. I wouldn't be surprised if the old man was a millionaire.* He breathed through his mouth. The stench of cow crap, although profitable, was rank. *He has a generous nature, too, from what I've seen. So? He doesn't want houses built around his farm. Is that so bad? It doesn't make him the slimeball dad says he is. He can't be that bad of a guy. He gave up the land for the schools, didn't he?*

Hiram sold Lancaster some land at a substantial discount for the construction of the middle and high schools when Lancaster outgrew being a one school town. Annie Potts Elementary near Sam's house used to be kindergarten through the eighth grade. The older kids had to be bussed to E.O. Smith High School in Storrs before the new schools were built. Lancaster Middle School was constructed near the American Legion hall off Legion Avenue, on School Street. Lancaster High School was built on the other side of town on Lancaster Hill Road off Wickett Avenue. It was a lot more convenient having a high school in town and the new middle school solved the overcrowding issue at Annie Potts, but again some people grumbled about it.

Sam, his father, and most of Lancaster had attended the town meeting where they voted on Hiram's land proposal for the schools. It had become a shouting match. Sam didn't understand what all the fuss was about. His father couldn't explain it either. Jack Dougan, Peter Rollins, Hugh Kreeger, Donald Barry, and George Skinner were vehemently opposed to building the middle school by the farm. In their opinion, the land off Lancaster Hill Road was more appropriate. Hiram insisted they build the high school there.

Lancaster's First Selectman, Ronald Morris, pressed the men to explain their reasoning. He was a short bald old man with thick glasses and an intense glare. He wasn't at all intimidating, so Sam didn't understand why the opposing men were struck dumb. They were unable to explain why the town should go against Hiram's wishes. Sam thought that was odd after the heated words exchanged. The tension between Jack and Hiram in particular was tangible. They clearly hated each other.

Hiram had several reasons for not wanting the high school near the farm. The first was the isolation, the potential for partying and other adolescent activity on the property. The land surrounding Lancaster Hill Road was densely populated and more easily supervised. It also placed the high school at the other end of town where football games and other school functions wouldn't disturb his peace.

Hiram won the vote. The objectors couldn't offer any reasons to refuse him and the town was getting the land cheap. There wasn't much choice. Margaret Adler declined to sell any of her land, Jerry Copeland, Lancaster's largest employer, wanted an exorbitant amount of money for anything he was willing to part with, and the town didn't own any plots large enough that were suitable.

Sam's father commented it was the strangest town meeting ever. Jack Dougan had never attended one before or since. All of the men who objected had worked for the farmer at one time or another, too. He assumed it was a vindictive attitude toward an ex-boss. Working on a farm wasn't easy. Perhaps they resented Hiram for something. He had a reputation of being a tough boss.

Henry Schwartz, an upperclassman with the same lunch period as Sam, had recently quit working for Hiram. When Sam asked him why he had left, Henry refused to talk about it. The subject seemed to make him uncomfortable. He was angry about something, too. Sam wondered if anything was wrong with the farmer, but then he remembered that Chris McKee, a sophomore like Sam, had worked for Hiram for over a year and he'd never complained. Dabney Copeland and Todd O'Connor worked there, too.

Sam shivered thinking about them. Dabney and Todd were two of the worst kids he knew. Dabney was a conceited rich brat, the mill owner's younger son, and Todd was just trouble. Sam might have considered working at the farm if not for them. He liked Chris though, at least until he heard the rumors about him. Now, he wasn't sure if he should.

Totally haunted.

Sam looked up the driveway. Chris might be doing the morning milking. Sam needed to ask him about what he had heard, but if Todd was there?

No way! Sam thought.

Todd didn't like him. Sam had turned in Todd and his buddy Frank Garrison for smoking weed in the boys' room when he was in seventh grade and they were in eighth. Sam would quickly move on if Todd was working. Todd didn't understand. It wasn't like Sam had any choice but to rat. Principal Hogan was going to suspend every student that got a pass that period for suspicion of drug use. No way was that going on his record.

Todd hadn't caught up with him yet, but he swore he would. He knew Sam was the only one who had seen him and Frank getting high. As far as Sam knew, Todd got suspended, but that was it. Frank, however, lived on the same street as Sam. He got his butt whooped by his father, Francis, who Sam thought was an incorrigible yuppie. Francis owned a clothing store at the Buckland Mall in Manchester.

What's it called again? Sam wondered. *Clothes for Queers?*

Sam felt bad about Frank's beating, but nothing more. There wasn't anything Frank could do about it. Sam wasn't afraid of him like he was Todd. Frank was a skinny kid with a tremendous amount of body hair as intimidating as Bugs Bunny in a dress. Sam could whoop him, but he avoided Todd. Todd was a good-sized kid who liked to fight. Sam would be the one whooped if Todd ever got a hold of him.

Sam heard Todd griping at the cows and he took off running.

Nope, no Chris McKee, Sam thought. *It must be his day off or he's working the night shift. Oh well, I'll see him in school.*

Sam wanted Chris to ask out one of the girls in their class. He thought it was a good idea after the rumor he had heard in Mike's Market the other day. He hoped it wasn't true.

It would suck if Chris is gay, Sam thought. *I won't associate with any homos.*

"No… *way!"* Sam puffed, turning left on Grady Lane.

Sam stopped and crooked his head toward the farm. He strained his eyes trying to see through the fog. He swore he had heard someone running across the cow pasture to his left, and was sure that's what it was when he heard it again. His heart nearly stopped dead in his chest. The sound was headed right toward him. He steeled himself controlling his breathing. If it was Todd, he would take off toward the trails and go home that way. Sam could outrun him. Todd smoked cigarettes while Sam was bursting with health, weak heart and all. There was no way Todd could keep up. He tried to zero in on the sound, but it abruptly stopped.

Sam waited, sweating, but after a minute spent scared out of his wits, he thought, *False alarm. I must be hallucinating. I'm so worried about Todd I'm hearing things.* He jogged in place to keep from cooling down. *Whatever it is, I need to get moving. I'll be late for school if I mess around much longer.*

Sam heard the sound again and a rush of anxiety shot through his body. It lasted a few moments and stopped, but it was closer this time. Sam's pulse quickened. He moved away from the pasture to the soft grass on the shoulder of the road. His sneakers were making too much noise on the tar. If Todd wanted to jump him there was no sense announcing his presence. He tried to see through the fog, but it was too thick. Every second was agonizing.

A voice in the back of his mind whispered, *You're not alone! You're in danger! Run, Sam! Run away!* It sounded like his dead mother.

Is Todd waiting for me to make the first move? Sam wondered. *Did he lose me in the fog? It could be a cow.* He shook his head. *No, it was the sound of two feet, not four.* He danced on the grass like the blades were made out of rice paper. *Don't give yourself away!* A bead of sweat ran down the inside of his nose. *If it's Todd, he'll kick your handicapped ass!*

It took another full minute for Sam to convince himself his paranoia had gotten the best of him. Relieved, he laughed out loud and continued on his way home. He was feeling wholly foolish as someone raced up behind him, grabbed him around the waist, hoisted him up, and slammed him sideways onto the road. Sam's head hit the pavement with a loud crack. Pain shot through his skull as the entire world went black.

＊　　＊　　＊

The McKee Family

The alarm clock app on the computer went off with the blasting sounds of heavy metal. It was a live stream of *iRockRadio.com*. The song was Rob Zombie's *Living Dead Girl*. It grooved through the room. Startled awake, Jeremy McKee reached toward his desk and slapped the spacebar on the keyboard, the app's snooze button. His room fell silent. He lifted his head. His deep blue eyes strained to see through the blur of half-sleep. He looked for a landmark, something to tell him where he was. He wasn't sure. He focused on his TV. The screen shone a pale green light.

Jeremy groaned and slumped face down on his pillow. His wiry black hair felt matted. He needed a shower. He knew where he was, in his room at home. He had fallen asleep with the TV on again. He hoped his mother hadn't noticed. She would ground him from it for a week if she had. He didn't think so. He had turned his light off last night when he heard his parents coming up the stairs. He didn't want them to see that he was crying. He should've thought about the TV then, but he had fallen asleep once his room was dark. She might have seen it flickering under his door. Jeremy could hear her chastising him already.

"We don't own stock in the electric company, buddy."

Jeremy rolled to his side and grabbed the remote control. It was on his nightstand next to his iPhone and his TOS Starship Enterprise model. He pressed the off button.

He thought, *I need to remember to set the sleep timer on that thing.*

The screen went dark. Jeremy dropped the remote on the floor. It landed on top of a comic book sealed in a protective bag. They were a common find in Jeremy's messy room. It was cluttered with other comics, mostly X-Men, his clothes – some dirty, some clean – and scattered CDs his father had given him, all rock and roll, no pop or rap music for him. Jeremy wasn't into the violence of most rap and pop music just sucked. He enjoyed movies though.

Jeremy rubbed his eyes. He stretched and groaned feeling the blood flow through his muscles. They tingled as if aware it was the last day of school. He smiled and thought, *Thank you, God!* He let his left foot dangle off the end of the bed. He looked out the back window. The bright sun promised a super afternoon. He was glad. It meant the night would be warm, too. Jeremy was camping out with his older brother, Chris, and their friends tonight. Good weather made the activity more appealing, and it needed all the appeal it could get.

Jeremy hated camping. The mosquitoes were blood-sucking storm troopers that came in divisions to stab him and partake of his tasty plasma. They thrived in the wet and heavy night air. The humidity made Jeremy sweat like mad, too, which would attract them by the millions. He preferred cool air-conditioning to a muggy summer night outdoors. Despite this, Jeremy had given in to his brother's relentless prodding and promised to go. If he backed out now, he would never hear the end of it.

Jeremy felt the gentle touch of a padded paw batting playfully at his dangling foot. Mishmash, his calico kitten, was under the bed. She had discovered this new toy hanging in the air. His wriggling toes were demanding prey. Jeremy could feel her excitement. It invited him to play. He welcomed the distraction. Anything to delay getting out of bed. His freshman year of high school was over, his grades were good, and he was sure to pass into the tenth grade, although he wished he had Chris' discipline. His brother was a year older and a straight A student despite working full time. It was one of the many things Jeremy envied about Chris.

Except the fact that he's gay.

Jeremy shook his head. He didn't want to think about that. Not yet. He supposed that's what was keeping him under the covers. He was usually up after the first blast of the alarm clock app. Well, maybe the sixth blast. He had a weakness for the snooze button which he hit again. He wriggled his toes some more. Mishmash's attack intensified. He could feel her claws now.

Jeremy thought about the camping trip. It was his first outside of Scouts. It was Chris' nine-millionth. Jeremy had tactfully been able to avoid going until now, but this time something was different. Chris wouldn't take no for an answer. He swore if Jeremy didn't go, he would wish he had, but he refused to elaborate. He simply insisted his brother join them. Jeremy's curiosity got the better of him and he relented. He could always leave and go home if he didn't like it. He supposed he should. Chris practically lived in the woods. They shared some genes, right?

Just not the gay one.

"Oh, be quiet!" Jeremy hissed.

Chris camped in the winter, too only not as often. The only person who would go with him then was Ricardo Ramirez, but Ricardo couldn't go every weekend. Ricardo worked at Gibbons' Garage with his father. He was fifteen like Jeremy. Both of their birthdays were in October, the tenth for Ricardo, the sixteenth for Jeremy. Despite his age, Ricardo could already rebuild an engine blindfolded. Lyle swore he would put together the fastest car Lancaster had ever seen one day, even better than the '69 Chevelle Lyle built for his daughter. The Chevelle was called *Lisa's Baby* but the only thing about it resembling an infant was its baby blue color.

Jeremy was jealous of Ricardo, too. Ricardo was a freshman like him, friends with Jeremy since kindergarten, but Ricardo liked Chris better.

Well, 'better' might not be the right word, Jeremy thought. *Maybe preferred?* He sighed. *The feeling's still the same.*

Jeremy was popular and his friends liked him, but Chris was more outgoing and fun. Jeremy thought that's why their friends, even the ones his age, spent more time with Chris than with him. He wondered if he had some failing he didn't realize. Too many freckles on his nose? Not quick enough with a sarcastic snap when the occasion called for wit? Jeremy didn't know and it made his heart heavy. Part of him believed everyone just tolerated him. It wasn't true, but that's the way it felt. There were just some things they enjoyed that Jeremy found boring or inane, like fart tag for example. If he got a nickel each time one of them passed gas, he could leave for college tomorrow. They were too silly especially Derek Mellon. Derek was only an eighth grader, but he was part of their group. Even he relished Chris' company more.

Jeremy could bet it was Derek dropping by every time the doorbell rang. He would be on the porch, his fiery red hair wisping in the breeze. "Chris home?" he would ask, leaning over and looking around Jeremy. Jeremy would step to the side and sweep his arm as if presenting the McKee abode to the Mellon family's paragon of hyperactivity. Derek would grin, slip inside, and charge upstairs to Chris' room. Jeremy would retreat to his room and shut the door, iRockRadio.com on his computer drowning out their laughter.

Jeremy groaned as Mishmash licked his big toe. Her distraction was failing him. His mind was racing. He closed his eyes and counted to ten trying to slow his thoughts. It wasn't working. He was drowning. If it hadn't been for the phone call he'd gotten from Ricardo last night…

Jeremy rolled onto his back and stared at the ceiling. Mishmash clung to his foot until she was sure he wasn't trying to escape. She hung there like a furry Christmas ornament. She let go and went back to batting his foot once it settled. Jeremy sniffed for the scent of coffee. It was missing which meant his mother wasn't up. He was glad he had fallen asleep quickly last night. If his mom wasn't up, it meant his parents probably had sex last night. He shivered. Parents making love was gross. He shared a wall with them and heard everything, too. The way they went at it, their headboard banging against the wall, his mother moaning, you would think coupling was an Olympic event.

If it were, they'd win the gold medal.

The house phone rang. It was set loud and shrill since his mom slept like the dead.

Who's calling this early? he wondered, but decided he didn't care.

He turned toward his TOS Starship Enterprise model. Star Trek was the best and Captain Kirk was the man, but looking at the model didn't make him feel any better. Neither did his iPhone. He knew he should've turned it off before lying down last night, but he hadn't until after Ricardo called. Jeremy looked up at the ceiling. He didn't want to think about this now, but he couldn't avoid it. He had to face it even if it meant watching their lives fall apart.

Jeeze, Chris, Jeremy thought. *What were you thinking?*

Ricardo had called last night just after ten. Jeremy was half-asleep watching Star Trek TOS on CBS All Access through a link from his computer to his TV. He couldn't help it. James T. Kirk was the coolest guy on the planet. Jeremy's mother, Virginia, was downstairs demanding that Chris strip off his clothes in the laundry room out in the garage. Chris worked at the Milliken Farm and reeked of cow manure after every milking. Virginia had just returned from picking him up.

Chris didn't have his driver's license yet even though he was sixteen because he hadn't bothered to take the driving test. He wasn't in a rush. He planned to do it over the summer. His mom had to pick him up as long as he didn't have it, unless he rode his bike, and Chris got a kick out of listening to her complain about the smell. According to her protestations this evening, they had driven all the way home with the windows down.

Jeremy shook his head. *How can Chris stand the stink? He's such a queer about his looks, and his clothes, and his hair...* He scowled. *He spends more time in the bathroom than ten women!*

Chris said, "Yeah, yeah," coming in from the garage.

Jeremy chuckled when his mother hollered, *"Christopher! Get back in there and put your underwear on!"*

Jeremy could picture Chris standing naked in the kitchen with his hands on his hips. "Why? They're only getting thrown in the laundry later."

"Now, young man!"

"Sheesh!" Chris cried. "Like it matters?"

"Streak in your room, not through my house!"

Jeremy heard his mother snickering. He answered his iPhone. The ringer was the theme song from Star Trek TOS.

"It's your quarter," Jeremy quipped, laying the phone on his ear. He was engrossed in the episode. It was *The Doomsday Machine*.

"Are you alone?" Ricardo whispered.

"Why are you whispering?" Jeremy asked, yawning.

"My mom's close," Ricardo replied. "She's making a late dinner. My dad just got home." After a pause, he added, "He works for a living."

"So does mine," Jeremy said, with some irritation. *So?* His dad was a lawyer. *So?* He and Chris had the latest iPhones. *So?* He asked, "Are you jealous?"

"No, dude," he whispered. "I'm irritated that's all."

"Forget it," Jeremy replied. He lowered his eyebrows. "And don't call me *dude.*"

"Whatever."

Jeremy sat up and put his feet on the floor. "Do you want Chris?" he asked. Ricardo hardly ever called him, only when he was bored and Chris wasn't around. "He just got home."

"No!" Ricardo exclaimed, but then shushed himself. After a few moments, he continued. "I have to be careful, man," he stated, whispering again. "If my mom catches me on my phone this late, she'll whoop my butt."

"Then why call?" Jeremy asked. "It's not like I won't see you tomorrow. We're in the same classes."

"This can't wait."

Jeremy lowered the volume of the Star Trek episode. Ricardo had his undivided attention. Jeremy hadn't noticed before but something in his voice wasn't right. His usually detached Puerto Rican demeanor sounded concerned.

"What's wrong?" Jeremy asked.

Jeremy's bedroom door swung open before Ricardo could answer. Chris stood in the doorway wearing only his Hanes and a big smile. His scent carried into the room.

Jeremy gagged. "Hang on," he coughed, into the phone. He glared at his brother. "God, Chris!" he whined, waving his hand in front of his nose. "Take a shower, will you? You're polluting my atmosphere."

"Yeah, I'm pretty ripe, huh?" Chris said, but didn't move. A good reek was best shared with someone you love. He had more for his brother, too. He nodded at the phone.

Jeremy covered the receiver. "Ricardo," he said. "Want me to tell him to call your cell?"

"I can't talk tonight. I need a shower."

"Really?" Jeremy asked. He defiantly crossed his arms.

Chris rolled his eyes. He turned, stuck his butt into the room, and farted. *"Ahh!"* he proclaimed, waving it in. "How's that for pollution?"

Jeremy scowled. "Gross, Chris." He sneered, "I'm surprised it made any noise."

Chris' voice trailed down the hallway. *"Wouldn't you like to know?"* he sang, and closed the bathroom door.

"Not particularly," Jeremy said, returning to his phone call. "All right, what's going on?"

"Is Chris gone?"

"Yeah. He said he couldn't talk tonight."

Ricardo scoffed, "I didn't call him, did I?"

"You usually do," Jeremy challenged.

It was a shot. Ricardo picked up on it quickly as intended.

"That's going change, amigo."

Again there was silence. Jeremy heard the sound of the Ramirez's front screen door closing as Ricardo stepped onto the porch.

He asked, "Are you still going camping?"

Jeremy replied, "Chris made me promise. He won't tell me why though."

"You'll see."

"You know?"

"Sure," Ricardo said. "I just can't talk about it now."

"Who else is going?"

Ricardo took a deep breath, "Matt Gardner, Derek, Sandy and Ian Sturgess, me and Max, and you and Chris."

Great, Jeremy thought. *They're probably going to Nair my head when I'm sleeping or put my hand in warm water.* "So, what's wrong?"

"Are you sitting down?"

"Just tell me," Jeremy said. "Did I miss some hot gossip?"

"This isn't a joke, okay!?" Ricardo snapped.

"Jeeze, chill out, will you?" Jeremy cried. "I didn't mean it that way!"

"No, amigo. I'm sorry. I shouldn't have snapped like that."

"It's okay," Jeremy said. His paranoia was growing. "What the heck is going on?"

"Remember when Chris went camping with Dan Mellon?" Ricardo asked, whispering again.

"Sure," Jeremy replied.

It was two weeks ago. Dan was Derek's older brother, a junior at Lancaster High School. Chris had been pretty irritated after that campout now that Jeremy thought about it. Dan had called Chris a bunch of times since then, but Chris was ignoring him. When he called Jeremy's cell, Chris told him to say he wasn't home. Dan seemed nervous. He made Jeremy promise to tell his brother he called and to have him call back. Jeremy did, but Chris replied, "Fat chance." He guessed Chris and Dan got into a fight or something. Jeremy figured it wasn't his problem since Derek still called.

Jeremy overheard Chris tell Derek only to call him when Dan wasn't home. It seemed strange, but he'd forgot about it until now. He was sure his mom brought home a written message for Chris when she went shopping, too. Dan worked at Mike's Market and practically everyone in town bought their groceries there. Chris crumpled it up and tossed it in the trash without reading it.

"I went shopping at Mike's Market with my mom today," Ricardo whispered. "Dan took me aside."

"Did he get into a fight with Chris, or something?"

"Jeremy, dude," Ricardo replied, "you haven't got a clue."

He filled Jeremy in. Ricardo's words echoed in his mind as his heart sank. Dan was telling the whole world the night he and Chris slept out, Chris came out of the closet. Ricardo believed it. Jeremy wasn't sure even though he had often wondered about his brother. It was the way Chris acted and the fact he'd never had a girlfriend that made Jeremy suspicious. He didn't want to believe it. He loved Chris, but God, how was he supposed to deal with this? Gay people made no sense to him and everybody hated them, right? Lancaster was a small town. There wasn't even an LGBTQ club at the high school. What was he supposed to do now? Hate his brother?

"I don't believe it," Jeremy said, his words sounding hollow. *Denial. That's a good choice.* "Dan's lying."

"Jeremy," Ricardo said, "we've talked about this before, dude." He checked to make sure his mother hadn't heard him. "Neither of us wanted to believe it, but you know as well as I do that Chris is gay."

Jeremy's unease turned to anger. "Hey, screw you, Ricardo! You're talking about my brother! What's your problem, anyway? Chris has always been good to you!"

"Maybe he just wanted to get me."

Oh, that's it, you just crossed the line! Jeremy thought. He ended the call and turned off his iPhone. *No one talks about my brother like that! I don't care who it is! Where's Ricardo's loyalty? If Dan told me something like that about Max, I would've punched that redheaded loser in the face! And saying Chris only wanted to get him? Grr, GRR, **GRRRRRR!**

Chris peered into the room, his wet bangs hanging over his eyes. They dripped water onto Jeremy's dark blue carpet. Jeremy didn't look at him, and just shook his head when Chris asked if Ricardo had wanted him for anything important.

"Better get some sleep, bro," Chris said, with a smile. "It's going to be a busy day tomorrow."

Jeremy nodded.

Chris closed the door.

Jeremy wanted to tell him what Ricardo had said, but he couldn't, not yet. He needed time to think. He lay on his bed staring up at the ceiling. He heard his parents coming, so he shut off his light. If it was on, they would stop to say goodnight. Jeremy didn't want them to see him especially since he had started crying. The tears were warm rolling down his cheeks. If Virginia saw him, she wouldn't let the matter drop until she discovered why he was so sad.

Only my life is over, mom. That's all.

Now, resisting the need to get out of bed with his third strike at the snooze button, he wondered if he should confront his brother. Jeremy wasn't sure. He decided to stay in his bed until he was. He wondered if anyone would miss him for the next two years.

*　　*　　*

Thomas McKee was half-asleep in the room across the hall from Jeremy. He groaned after the third ring of the phone.

Thomas thought, *I hate Mondays.*

As usual, the phone was ringing at six-thirty a.m. on his day off. He wondered if it was Thurman Millner calling again like last week. He was Thomas' boss, the head of Connecticut Legal Associates in Hartford. He had called to ask Thomas to take his caseload for the day. Most were simple continuances, but Thurman wanted to spend some time with his daughter, Madelyn, who everyone called Millie. She was home from college for a visit. The week before it had been Thomas' mother, Amanda, calling to wish him a happy birthday.

Doesn't the world know there's no court for me on Mondays? Thomas thought. He felt fatigued. *Even I need a day to sleep in and be left alone. If there was some emergency I'd understand, but there never is.*

It made him mad which said a lot. Thomas rarely got angry. He liked to sleep sometimes though. Virginia was lying beside him, her long brown hair spread out on her pillow. She breathed evenly, her breasts pressing against his stomach as they rose and fell. Her warm breath hit his sternum. Her hand rested on his hip just above his pelvis where it had remained after their lovemaking last evening. Thomas smiled. The boys surely heard them, especially Jeremy. No doubt it would be a hot topic at the breakfast table.

Christopher won't hold anything back, Thomas thought.

He would remind his oldest son that his day was coming. McKee men were nothing if not virile. Frankly, considering what he believed his sixteen-year-old's sexual orientation to be, he hoped Chris would wait, or at least take care. There was so much to worry about in the world nowadays. Sex was the one thing that could cause more harm than good if discretion failed to rule over desire.

Thomas adjusted his position. He leaned over and kissed Virginia's cheek. The ninth ring caused her to stir. Thomas kissed her on the cheek again as she woke. She smiled, sliding her arm along his side to his face. Her eyes snapped open on the tenth ring.

Virginia looked at Thomas with a puzzled expression. *That stupid phone's ringing on Monday morning again?* she thought. *And he's smiling rather than giving me that 'We put the phone on your side of the bed so it wouldn't wake me up' look that he usually has?*

"I'm sorry, sweetheart," Virginia said, reaching behind her for the receiver. "I know, I sleep like the dead. We should get voicemail."

"You know I'm on call twenty-four-seven," Thomas reminded her.

"Hello?" Virginia said, answering the phone. Her voice was more than a little annoyed.

"Hi, Mrs. McKee," a chipper voice said. "It's Matt. Is Chris there?"

"Hi, Matt," Virginia replied, advancing to fully annoyed. Matt went to school with Chris and Jeremy. He lived up the street. *How many times do I have to tell these guys…?*

"Hello?" Chris asked, picking up the hallway extension.

He had a towel around his waist. He had just finished his morning shower. Working on the farm required taking two, one after shift, one in the morning.

"Chris?"

"Yeah. Hi Matt."

Virginia cleared her throat.

"Mom?"

"Yes, Christopher Robin McKee," Virginia replied. "It's your mother. Remember me? The one who allowed you and your brother to get iPhones?"

Chris thought, *I sense another long lecture on the horizon. It's not like I haven't told my friends a thousand times not to call the house phone.*

"*Matt...,*" Chris sang.

"Sorry, Mrs. McKee," Matt replied.

"I'll sorry you in the head, Matthew," Virginia said. "How many times do I have to tell you guys, Chris and Jeremy have iPhones so we don't get calls on our line?"

"But I called Chris' phone first!" Matt whined.

"I was in the shower," Chris said.

"Well, where's your brother?" Virginia asked.

"Sleeping, I guess," Chris replied. "Jeremy turns his phone off at night. Hiram called his line by mistake once and woke him up at four in the morning. He was pretty pissed."

"Dude, don't say *pissed* in front of... *oops!* Sorry, Mrs. McKee!"

Virginia shook her head. As if *pissed* was a word she worried about considering some of the other choice words she had heard come out of Chris' mouth.

"Don't call me *dude*, asswipe!" Chris exclaimed.

"Hey, buddy," Virginia said. "I find *dude* a lot more acceptable than *asswipe.*"

"Who are you talking to?" Thomas asked.

She covered the receiver and told him, "Matt and Chris."

Thomas thought, *My lovely wife carries on such enlightening conversations with the neighborhood youth.*

"That's because you don't know what it means," Chris said.

"Oh?" Virginia asked. "Educate me."

"A dude is a horse's dick, mom."

"*Chris!*" Matt cried. He couldn't believe the way he talked in front of his mother. If Matt had ever said that in front of his mother, Linda would've grounded him for a century.

"Are you boys still camping tonight?" Virginia asked, assuming that's what prompted this phone call. "It couldn't wait until the bus stop?"

"I guess, but...," Matt began, feeling foolish. *Stupid, stupid, stupid! I can't tell her why I'm calling, so why did I call on this phone? Duh!*

"It's that teenage instant gratification thing, mom," Chris replied, coming to Matt's rescue. "And yes, we're camping. Jeremy's coming, too."

Virginia raised an eyebrow. She thought, *Jeremy isn't much for camping, not like Chris. It's a wonder he didn't stay in Scouts. At least Jeremy stayed until he was twelve. By thirteen, he was too 'mature' for that kid's stuff. Still, if Jeremy's going camping, I guarantee the boys are up to something, probably partying. This is a new one for Jeremy. Chris, however…*

Virginia was sure Chris was drinking with his friends whenever they camped out, but she let it go. He hadn't gotten into any trouble and whoever was buying the liquor was staying well behind the scenes. She monitored him closely though. If his drinking became more than social, she would intervene. She respected his space, his right to make his own decisions, yet she tried to guide those decisions without a lot of direct interference. The camping trip was a first for Jeremy. She supposed it was time for him to experiment. Most teenagers did. She wondered if alcohol was all they were using, but unless there was some modern way to cover the signs – or the smells – she believed the boys were clean. She gave them room to make their own mistakes, but there was a limit to her Liberalism.

She even stayed out of the way when Chris decided to take a job. That had been a tough one. Virginia thought the idea ridiculous. Thomas made plenty of money. Besides being an excellent lawyer, he handled the firm's probate and estate matters, too. The thought of the boys working was ridiculous, but Chris was adamant. Virginia tried to dissuade him. She graphically described what he would be in for working on a farm – the long hours, the rough weather, and being up to his knees in manure. She figured that would be the clincher considering Chris and his obsessive attitude toward his appearance, but he wouldn't hear any of it. He wanted his own money. Virginia elected to wait him out. She figured he wouldn't last a week. There was no way he could stand it. That was a year ago. She had to admit she was surprised.

Hiram Milliken was an older gentleman with a quiet manner and an honest face. He had won Virginia over five minutes into their conversation on Chris' first day. They sat on lawn chairs next to the front porch of his trailer sipping coffee. He had given her a tour of the barn, the grounds, brought her inside the mobile home, but stopped her from going into the Victorian. He said there were rats in there. Virginia was glad for the heads up. She hated rats.

The Victorian was beautiful even though it was old and its paint was peeling. Virginia was jealous. She would've loved a house like that. It would be like living in a castle. Hiram told her there was no electricity or running water. He had them shut off since he didn't use the house for anything anymore except storage. She looked in through the front window. The Victorian was empty. Hiram explained that the attic was huge. He had everything stored up there except for his grandfather's furniture which he kept in the barn. When she asked why, he cringed. "More rats," he mumbled. Hiram had grown up in the Victorian. His grandfather died in one of the upstairs bedrooms. It was a family place, too big for one person. The trailer was good enough for him.

"It has two bedrooms," Hiram remarked, "which is convenient in bad weather. Sometimes I need a farmhand to work late, and then milk the next morning, too. I let them stay in the guest room." He leaned in confidentially. "A lot of parents thank me for that the next day."

Virginia agreed with the concept. Chris had stayed there once, but he said the guest bed hurt his back, and he refused to sleep on the floor or the ratty old sofa. Virginia had offered to drive him even if it was early, but Chris insisted on making his own way. His self-reliance frustrated her, but she accepted it as being in the McKee genes. Chris had some of his grandmother in him. The only reason he was letting her take him to work now was because of his learner's permit. He got to drive her Camaro both ways, but he still rode his bike to the farm when the occasion called for it.

"Matt?" Chris asked.

"Yeah?"

"Call me on my iPhone, okay? I need to get dressed."

"No prob. Sorry about calling so early, Mrs. McKee."

"Don't worry, Matt," Virginia said, motioning to Thomas. "Mr. McKee will kill you later."

"Yeah!" Thomas growled. He leaned his ear toward the receiver.

Chris said, "Right dad. You can bore him to death with one of your *'Guess what happened at the office today?'* stories."

"Hey! Screw you, junior!" Thomas laughed.

Virginia slugged him.

"Eat me, butt-muncher!"

Virginia hung up the phone. *That's enough of that. I'm up now and coffee's top on my list of things to do.*

*   *   *

Chris stepped into his bedroom and locked the door. He was at the opposite end of the hall from Jeremy. His room faced the backyard like his brother's did. His mother's sewing room was across the hall.

Not that she ever sews, or anything, Chris thought, *but I'm not complaining. It's better than what Jeremy has across from him, Mom and dad's nightly sex-o-rama? Eew!*

Jeremy shared a wall with them, too. Chris had a window between him and the sewing room at his end of the hallway. His brother always whined up a storm the morning after another McKee sexcapade. It was hilarious!

Did Jeremy hear them last night? Chris wondered. *I sure did. I finally put on headphones so I didn't have to listen.*

Chris was only five-foot-seven. He hadn't reached puberty until last September. He hoped to get a little taller, but if he didn't, so what? He was happy with the way he was. He had his father's dirty blonde hair, but it was straight like his mother's. Chris wore it shaved in the back and on the sides but grew the top out long. His bangs hung down over his face whenever he didn't wear a baseball cap, which was hardly ever, except for church and school when he pulled it back and wore it in a ponytail. He didn't really care much for sports. The cap was a fashion accessory. He wore it because it looked cool. He had an assortment on a rack in his closet. As long as he didn't develop his father's receding hairline everything would be great.

Brr, Chris shivered. *Baldness would not be cool.*

Chris' eyes were a deep shade of green. His face was unblemished by a single zit or blackhead and sported a few light freckles. His body – which he looked at in front of his full-length mirror, posing GQ-ish – was smooth, even feminine. He liked the way he looked and fought to keep himself that way. Chris exercised every night before bed and washed his face faithfully. He avoided the sweets and things said to cause acne.

Screw that, Chris thought, as the phone rang. *No acne for me.*

"Matt?" Chris asked, snatching up his iPhone. He lay down on his waterbed.

"I got it," Matt said.

Chris smiled stretching out. He wanted to go back to sleep. He didn't see much sense in going to school today. It was a half a day with nothing to do except turn in books.

They're not serving lunch and they're mailing everyone's report card home, so what was the big deal?

They could've turned in their books last Friday, but he figured it was because of snow days. They had a lot of them this year.

Everyone loves them until they have to pay for them.

Chris kept his room simple, not cluttered like his brother's. The less he had around him, the less he had to clean. His double-sized waterbed took up a lot of space, so there wasn't much room left anyway. His desk was next to the back window. He had his computer on it, his iPhone charger, and a small lamp. There was a bulletin board on the wall to his front and left. In the upper right-hand corner, it had Mr. Hot Shit in big red letters.

Pictures of Chris and his friends lined the bottom – him and Max Ramirez in the first one, him and Sanford Sturgess in the next. Then there was one of the whole crew including Jeremy in a shot at Lancaster Pond. Derek Mellon was proudly displaying his butt in that one having mooned the camera as Virginia snapped the picture. That was Derek. He had no shame. The last one was of Chris and Keith Keroack, a kid they knew from Scouts. He was a pothead. They didn't hang out with him much. He was funny though. He had a way of making you laugh at just the right moment. Chris didn't have any pictures with girls, but that was okay. Chris didn't like girls, not romantically anyway.

The wall-to-wall carpeting was a soft shade of light green like his curtains. A black beanbag chair sat on the floor next to his desk. The window on the other side of his waterbed had a single Wandering Jew hanging in a green crocheted plant hanger. It was the only thing Chris had that even resembled a pet.

Jeremy's kitten is getting flying lessons the next time she kneads a hole in my mattress, Chris thought. *She's done it twice already. I hate waking up in the morning thinking I pissed the bed.*

Chris had a large closet with sliding wooden doors across the room from his bed. He owned tons of clothes just like his mom. He would have more, but his space was limited. Virginia's wasn't. Her closet and the sewing room closet were jam-packed with all kinds of crap.

Half the outfits she only wore once, too, Chris thought, *and she has more shoes than Mariah Carey!*

Chris had six pairs of sneakers, one set of Hush Puppies for church, and a pair of beige Timberland hiking boots. He'd bought them with his own money. His walls were plain except for a few posters, one of the K-pop group EXO, one of Jimi Hendrix, a blacklight poster of a dragon, and one of Dave Mustaine from Megadeth. Chris thought he was a fantastic guitarist.

"Chris?" Matt asked. "Are you still there?"

Chris shook his head. "Sorry, Matt. I was thinking about something. So, you got some beers?"

"Some blackberry brandy, too."

Chris grinned. He didn't drink that often, but when he did he liked to drink brandy. It made him feel warm inside. Matt's cousin, Phil Anderson, was the best. He was a Psyche major at UCONN in Storrs. He always bought liquor for them.

"Cool," Chris nodded. "I don't have to work again until Wednesday either. It's the morning shift though."

"Yes!"

Now they could camp for two days. Chris worked so much he rarely ever had two days off.

"Who else is going?" Chris asked.

Matt took a deep breath and rattled off the names, "Max and Ricardo, Sandy and Ian, Derek, you, and me. Jeremy, too, if he's still going."

"He is. He promised."

"Who's got a tent besides you?" Matt asked. He knew Chris' three-man wouldn't be big enough for everyone.

Chris said Jeremy did. So did Sandy. They were both two-man tents.

"I hope we have enough room."

"I hope we have enough stuff," Chris said. "Ricardo has a tent, too, but it's crappy."

"No problem. We have enough. Phil's getting a quart of brandy."

Whew, Chris thought. *That will do it.*

"Call Sturgess' house and make sure they're good to go," he said. "I'll call Ramirez." He cautioned, "Remember, we can't talk about this in school. If word gets out, the whole town will show up."

"Okay," Matt replied. "What about Derek?"

Chris frowned. Derek would have him on the phone all morning. He couldn't risk texting him in case Dan intercepted it. Chris had nothing to say to him except, *"Jerk!"* He wasn't going to call Max until after breakfast either. That didn't leave a lot of time to get ready for school.

"Call Derek, too. I'll meet you at the bus stop."

"Okay," Matt replied. "This is going to be great!"

"We'll meet at the pond after school," Chris added. "Is Phil putting the stuff where we talked about?"

"You bet."

"All right. I'll see you soon."

"Later," Matt said, and hung up.

Okay, Chris thought, digging out some clothes. *First, I need to get dressed, and then I need to get Jeremy moving. I guess he thinks he's sleeping late? Hah! Just wait!*

Chris made sure the spray bottle for his plant had nice cold water in it.

*   *   *

Sam's head swam as he woke. He wasn't entirely sure what happened. He tried to reach up and touch where his forehead hurt. It was bleeding. He could feel the warm blood running down his face. It pooled in the corner of his mouth. Dread enclosed his heart. He couldn't move either of his hands. They were bound. He was gagged, too. A tightly tied string of rawhide held a foul rag in his mouth. It tasted like sour milk and manure. It made him retch. His opened his eyes into a vision of madness.

Rawhide bonds secured him to a tree in the farmer's pasture out of sight of Grady Lane. A large man in a ski mask was standing in front of him manically grinning. His light blue eyes burned. He held his hand out. It was rough with calluses and wrinkled with age. He gripped Sam's throat. Sam tried to pull away twisting his hips against the rough tree bark.

Holy Jesus! Sam thought. He was terrified. *Please help me!*

The man's eyes turned cold as he held up the largest hunting knife Sam had ever seen. The edge was keen like a razor. It glinted in the risen sunlight. He waved the knife in Sam's face turning it from side to side. Sam's heart sank and he began to cry. The man growled, drew his hand up, and slapped Sam across the face with the flat of the blade. The tip caught the skin under his left eye tearing the flesh like tissue paper. Sam screamed into the gag as more blood ran down his face. The man leaned into him, took him by the hair, and jerked his head back. Sam's heart raced. He'd never been so frightened in his entire life.

The man reached around him and cut the rawhide holding his hands and feet. He tried to force Sam onto the ground the knife firmly against his throat, but Sam panicked, thrashing. He stunned the man with an elbow to the side of his head. He reached up, tore off the ski mask, and threw it away. Horror rose in him as his outraged glare met the startled face of someone familiar. It was the farmer.

It's Hiram Milliken!

Hiram dropped the hunting knife. Sam was enraged. He tore off the gag and kicked the farmer in the shins. He broke free of Hiram's grip and turned to run away, but his foot caught on a tree root. Sam fell face first landing hard. Fresh black earth filled his mouth and nose as his face sank into the dirt. Hiram pounced on him. He flipped Sam over and punched him in the face. He knelt over his midsection, his white tee shirt soaked with sweat. He arched back and put his weight on Sam's hips, pinning his flailing hands under his knees. He went into a rage, screaming at the top of his lungs.

Sam wept again, blood and dirt coming out of his mouth.

"You stupid…!" Hiram raged. *"You've spoiled everything!"*

He slammed his fist down on Sam's chest accenting his words as he yelled. Sam's eyes filled with surprise and fear as pain shot down his left arm. He gasped for Hiram to stop, begging for mercy. Sam had never wanted to live so desperately as the moment he realized he was going to die. A sharp pain stabbed into his left breast heralding the end of his life. He felt the cool damp pasture beneath him. A wave of sadness and despair washed over him as his heart stopped beating. Shock invaded his face. He convulsed, his chest heaved, and his legs shook.

Hiram cried, "Hey! Cut it out!"

Please, God, Sam thought, fading away. *I don't want to die like this.* His eyes rolled back into his head. He shuddered, they closed, and he was gone.

Hiram held Sam's limp body by the shoulders and glared at him. His head lolled back and forth.

"Not yet!" Hiram growled. "You won't cheat me, you hear?"

Hiram grabbed the knife and raised it high into the air. He stabbed Sam's corpse repeatedly until he had spent his rage and his clothes were covered in blood. He took a moment to regain his composure. He felt like he was coming down from a high. It was always that way when he killed. He stroked Sam's cheek in awe of his peaceful expression. He picked up the body and carried it to a spot a few feet away.

Perfect! So worthy of the Gift.

Hiram tossed Sam's corpse into a hole he had dug with his backhoe. The carefully cut grave lay neatly alongside the final resting places of the other boys buried in his pasture. Hiram had saved them from the trials of growing up, the ravages of age and adulthood. He had given them the *Gift* of being young forever. Now, they were his. Pain was a rite of passage, although Sam had gone a little too easily into the abyss.

Hiram frowned. *Someone else has to die today,* he thought. *Someone I can vindicate properly like the others.*

His victims dotted the pasture hidden beneath the thick black earth and fresh green grass. He glanced at the nearby backhoe before heading toward his Victorian. The killing was over. Hiram needed to record the details of Sam's death in his *Ledger*. It was the only way he could ensure Sam would be waiting for him on the other side. *The Ledger* was Hiram's book of life. When he died and went to paradise, the boys recorded within it would be waiting for him, forever his.

Hiram felt an eerie sensation. Someone was watching him. *She's here*, he thought and ran toward the barnyard.

*　　*　　*

Ms. Adler

Ms. Adler was parked on Grady Lane in her black Mercedes Benz next to the spot where Hiram had grabbed Sam. She had arrived just as Hiram was carrying Sam to the tree, only she hadn't revealed herself until now. No one ever saw her unless she allowed it, but she saw everything. Nothing happened in the Lancaster town limits that escaped her notice. She was all-knowing. The domain of the mind was her territory, every thought, every dream, and often every nightmare. She had waited until Hiram's madness was sated before she reached out and touched his mind. She watched him run toward the barnyard when he realized she was watching him.

She tilted her head to the side, concentrating, and the backhoe's engine roared to life. She didn't have to strain. She merely imagined it happening and it did. Thick, black diesel smoke reached for the sky. The smell reminded her of another place, another time. Her finger traced the outline of the steering wheel's cover. It was black leather. She liked black leather. There was a sense of power in it not unfamiliar to her. It was like the sense she got from the farmer, his thrill as another boy was laid to rest in his field. Hiram was looking at himself that very instant, excited about the blood on his hands. The sticky feeling on his skin filled him with euphoria. He intended to wear Sam's blood all day. If anyone saw him like that, he would tell them he had slaughtered a calf. It was common practice on the farm, not that anyone ever saw any of the meat.

Ms. Adler waited until Hiram was over the crest of the hill before she got out of her car. She crossed the road to the shabby barbed wire fence that bordered the pasture. She focused her power and rose off the ground, gently floating over it. She landed silently on the other side. She walked across the pasture and stood over Sam's grave, her hands in the pockets of her flowing black skirt. She lowered her head, closed her eyes, and gathered her strength. Her eyes snapped open, her irises exploding with bright midnight blue energy. Their radiance burned with power.

"Come, Master Stone," Ms. Adler said, her voice distorted by the power. *"You have one last thing to do in this world before you move on to the next."*

Sam's corpse obeyed, clawing its way out of the grave. She wasn't raising the dead. She didn't possess that power. She was manipulating his corpse with her telekinetic ability. It pulled itself up, jerking and writhing, and collapsed at her feet. Ms. Adler withdrew a large syringe from her skirt pocket. She held it up, removed the cap, and nodded at it.

The syringe flew out of her hand and stuck into Sam's temple. The plunger pulled back filling the reservoir with a pinkish-colored fluid. The needle withdrew when it was finished and floated back to her, hovering in front of her face. She plucked it out of the air, replaced the cap, and slipped it back into her pocket. She turned and walked toward her car.

"Time to sleep, Master Stone," she said, waving her hand to the side.

Sam jerked up and fell backward into the grave. Ms. Adler waved her hand at the backhoe next. It moved in response, its claw hand wrenching into the ground, covering Sam's body. It finished its task quickly and the motor died.

Ms. Adler sailed over the fence and got back into her car. Her eyes dimmed and returned to normal. She started the engine and drove up Grady Lane. She turned right on Wickett Avenue and went through town. She turned right again when she reached Route 41 and made an immediate left onto Annie Potts Road. She pulled over and parked in front of house number seventeen. The mailbox was an elaborate wooden post office. It had the name *Stone* on its side in golden stickers. She set her head back and closed her eyes. Invisible fingers reached out from her mind as an ominous glow appeared beneath her eyelids.

The fingers stretched forth clawing through the air. They slipped through the walls of the Stone family's residence. Ms. Adler could see inside the house now. Her astral fingers expanded into a ghostly duplicate of her physical form as she completely left her body. She was nearly transparent. Steven Stone stirred as she floated past his room, the air in the hall giving way to her evil presence. His sudden movement caught her attention and she stopped. She probed his mind, easily maneuvering through the thoughts of the ten-year-old. She found what she had assumed would be there, confusion and a sense of danger. Steven sat bolt upright and looked right at her, his eyes wide with terror.

He is very sensitive, she thought, grimacing at him.

It was true more people were than ever knew it, especially children. She smiled a malicious grin.

"Go back to sleep, Steven," Ms. Adler mentally commanded, thrusting the words into his brain. *"You have seen all you are going to see this morning. I was never really here. This is only a dream."*

Bad dream! Steven thought, scared to death. *Real bad dream!*

Steven was about to scream when his body betrayed him. He fell back on his bed and was fast asleep a moment later. It would seem like nothing more than a fading nightmare to him in the morning, exactly the way she wanted.

Ms. Adler's astral form passed through Dr. Stone's door, her feet floating several inches above the floor. She settled at the end of his bed, hovering above the brass footboard, eerily rising and falling as she allowed his mind to perceive her. Adults, unlike children, rarely possessed the ability to see the unseen. For the young, it was as natural as breathing. The bright light from her irises illuminated the room and caused him to stir. He looked sleepily toward her, shielding his eyes from the glow. His expression became confused.

"What is it?" Dr. Stone croaked, somewhere between awake and asleep.

Ms. Adler latched on to his mind with her telepathic power. Dr. Stone's features went blank. His eyes rolled back into his head.

"I came to remind you about your son, Sam, doctor," Ms. Adler whispered. Her voice echoed everywhere inside him.

"Sam?" he asked, his heart sinking. "Oh, Sam… I love you…"

"Yes, you do, doctor," Ms. Adler smiled. *"That is why you had to send him away."*

"No… I… sent Sammy… send…?"

"It is a special place, remember?" She pushed him harder, digging deeper into his mind. *"Somewhere he can learn to move past his weak heart and be more like other children. A place he can be strong… a camp, doctor. Sam's gone to camp."*

"Strong… yes, my Sammy…"

Ms. Adler locked him in the false memory. *"You will remember, doctor. Sam is unavailable but will be back sometime soon. Everyone just needs to be patient."* She smiled as she faded away. *"This will all be over before you know it."*

"Sammy? I… love you."

Dr. Stone fell back to sleep.

The black Mercedes roared to life a moment later. Ms. Adler drove away, the psychotic titter of her laughter carrying on the breeze.

*   *   *

Jeremy heard his parents' door open. It was his mother on her way downstairs to make coffee. His father followed her a minute later. The morning was advancing regardless of his feelings. Jeremy groaned. He pushed everything out of his mind and concentrated on Mishmash. Her attack on his feet had become more brazen. It was bad enough she had clawed his waterbed to shreds forcing him to get rid of it. He wasn't in the mood for this now that her distraction had grown painful. Jeremy pulled his foot up careful not to take the sheet with it. He turned his head and watched for the kitten. Mishmash's paw reached under the covers searching.

Jeremy thought, *Gotcha! Time for my next move!*

He rolled over and slid his foot to the opposite side of the bed. He did this without alerting Mishmash of his intention to catch her. Jeremy hoped to snag her with his hand while she was lost in her zeal to catch his foot.

I'll show you who the hunter is in this picture!

Jeremy eased onto his side. He slipped his leg into position, dangled his foot over the mattress, and rubbed it against the bedframe. She took the bait batting at him in earnest. He pulled his foot back. Mishmash followed it under the sheet, squinting in the daylight.

Yes! Jeremy thought. *You're mine!* and lunged at her.

His door flew open in the same instant.

Chris exclaimed, "Jeremy! Time to get up, dude!" He had his plant's spray bottle in his hand ready to fire.

Jeremy was startled in mid-lunge, lost his balance, and tumbled out of bed onto the carpet. He landed with a dull thud. Chris roared with laughter. Mishmash disappeared down the hall in a flashing streak of calico. Jeremy laid there with his butt in the air and sighed. Chris doubled over in the doorway and dropped the spray bottle.

I have to remember to lock my door, Jeremy thought. "Are you going to help me up?" he asked, feigning anger. "What was the water bottle for, Chris?"

Chris held out his hand. "Here he is, ladies and gentlemen! *Mr. Coordination!"*

Jeremy took his brother's hand and groaned while he rose. "Brave words from the guy about to become *Mr. Unconscious!"*

Jeremy moved to tackle his taller sibling. *He was going to squirt me? He thinks he's funny!? I'll show him something funny!*

That's exactly what he did. A bagged copy of X-Men was under his foot as he dove. He slipped on it and his legs went out from under him. He slammed face down onto the carpet. Chris exploded with laughter. He stumbled against the doorjamb and slid to the floor. Tears rolled down his cheeks as he struggled to catch his breath. Jeremy scrambled to his feet. Chris gasped and jumped up, still laughing, and raced to his room.

Well, Chris thought, *Jeremy's up now!*

"Wait!" Jeremy cried. He grabbed the spray bottle. "I want to show you something *really* funny!"

Virginia glanced up from her newspaper and coffee when she heard the boys racing along the upstairs hall. She gave Thomas *The Look.* He was cooking bacon and eggs. She was at the dining room table with her feet on another chair. Thomas looked at her and shrugged, swishing his hips back and forth. *Slave* by The Rolling Stones was playing on the tiny radio on the windowsill above the sink. He was wearing Virginia's white apron with the pink ruffles.

Virginia thought, *Wait until the boys get a load of him.*

Jeremy caught Chris by the ankle inside his room and knocked him to the floor. He got on top of him and locked his brother's hands under his knees. He sat on his chest and crossed his arms. His wiry black hair fell over his striking blue eyes. He smiled as Chris struggled. He aimed the squirt bottle at his face. This was the first time Jeremy had ever gotten the best of his brother in a physical altercation. They were close, but they fought occasionally. It was never serious, only some pushing and wrestling, no punches thrown, but Chris always came out on top.

"No way, buddy!" Jeremy cried, holding on tight. "You're mine!"

"Are you going to let me up?" Chris asked, still laughing, gasping for breath.

"No," Jeremy replied. He leaned over and touched his brother nose to nose. "Not until you and I talk."

"Aw, c'mon Jeremy…"

Jeremy sat up, tossed the squirt bottle on the bed, and then shook his head. Things needed to be said, questions demanded answers. Part of him didn't want the answers, the part that already knew, but there was another part that needed to hear the truth. It was the same part that almost wished Chris would lie to him.

"Ricardo called me last night," Jeremy said. His eyes narrowed. "He said Dan Mellon told him you were gay."

Chris rolled his eyes. *Here it comes*, he thought. He wasn't looking forward to this conversation. He feared it. *Can Jeremy handle the truth?*

"So?" Chris asked.

"Well?"

"Well, what?"

Jeremy cried, "What do you mean, *'Well, what?'* you geek!"

He grabbed Chris' sides and tickled him. Chris thrashed trying to get free, but it was no use. Jeremy was stronger than he had been a few months ago.

"Tell me," Jeremy said, poking Chris in the stomach.

Chris laughed.

"Tell me!"

"Okay, *okay!"* Chris cried.

He regained his composure with two deep breaths. His smile faded at the sad expression on Jeremy's face. Its pleading look broke his heart.

God, Chris thought. *He's hoping it's not true.* He realized something then. *We're at a crossroads. Something's come along to test our friendship, our brotherhood. Should I tell a nice painless lie? Deny who I am and spare Jeremy the pain? Is this what I have to look forward to in school today from my friends?* He set his jaw. *I'm not going to lie, bro. I can't.*

"Yes," Chris said, his eyes searching. "I'm gay."

Jeremy moved off of his brother and sat on the floor. He drew his legs up and put his arms around them. Chris came up on his elbows his chin resting on his chest.

"So, Dan's telling the truth?" Jeremy asked.

"Yes," Chris replied. "He is."

He knew the rumor. Dan had told Max at the grocery store a week ago. Chris couldn't lie to him either. Max stood by him. He looked at Jeremy and suddenly wished they lived in a bigger city with more acceptance of gay people. He loved Lancaster, but there were more people like him in a city. If they lived in NYC, he could go to youth group meetings in the Village. Why wasn't there one in every town and school district in the country? Why weren't they teaching tolerance instead of fear and prejudice?

They have a weapon, Chris glumly thought. *Ever seen a televangelist pull his Bible out of the holster? The .44 magnum scriptures, the most powerful fag-bashing tool on the planet. It can blow your self-esteem clean off. Tell me, punk... do you feel swishy?*

"It all started because of Doug...," Chris began, looking away. He didn't want to risk seeing a look of disgust or disapproval in his brother's eyes.

Jeremy nodded. *Dan and Derek's little brother. He's ten with ADHD.*

"He water-ballooned us, the little creep," Chris said. "He waited until we were settled in, opened the tent flap, and *pow.*"

"He's a brat," Jeremy agreed.

"Yeah," Chris replied. He grinned. "Cynthia caught him."

"Oh?" Jeremy asked. *If it was Douggie's father, Kevin? He's a grounder not a spanker, but their mom?*

"I bet he didn't sit for a week."

"No doubt."

"Anyway, we were soaked, but we had clothes for the next day so we changed. I was going crazy wanting to tell someone."

"Why not me?" Jeremy asked.

Chris frowned. "I had only just admitted it to myself. Telling the person I love most in the world wasn't my first thought, Jeremy."

Jeremy smiled.

"So, I blurted it out," Chris continued. "I thought we were friends, but Dan glared at me and covered up like I was peeking, or something."

His eyes met Jeremy's.

Chris crossed his arms. "I was *not* peeking."

"I believe you."

"Jeremy, I wasn't peeking!"

"I said I believe you."

"Anyway... Dan got dressed and left. He said he wasn't sleeping in the same tent with a fag. I wished I'd kept my mouth shut. In the morning, I walked home feeling like crap. When he started calling here, I got mad."

"Why, bro?" Jeremy asked.

Chris saw curiosity in his eyes, but that was it. Relief washed over him. He sat up resting his forearms on his knees.

"It made me mad because Dan made me feel guilty," Chris said. "I didn't like that. No one should make me feel guilty for being who I am."

"Why would he tell everyone though?" Jeremy asked.

"I don't know, to be a jerk? Or to try and get popular? A hot rumor can get someone a lot of attention. Dan isn't going to be Prom King."

"You could be Prom *Queen!*"

"Maybe," Chris winked. He shrugged. "I thought what Dan did was low."

"Screw him," Jeremy said. "We should give him a beat down."

Chris shook his head. "It'll only make things worse. Besides, you're not a fighter."

"True," Jeremy replied. He smiled. "Max is though."

"What happened to *we* should give him a beat down?"

"It's not the same thing?" Jeremy asked.

Chris scowled at him.

Jeremy relented. "Okay, you're right. What are we going to do then?"

"I could just tell everyone," Chris said. "They're going to hear about it anyway."

"It'll ruin your reputation," Jeremy replied. He lowered his head and whispered, "Mine, too."

"Not with the ones who matter."

Jeremy guessed so. Max would stand by them, and so would Sandy Sturgess. Sandy's brother, Ian, would be a punk about it. Derek didn't get along with Dan anyway so he would be okay, but Ricardo?

He'll be a tough one, Jeremy thought, *but I'm mad at him anyway, so forget him. If he can't handle it, I don't want him around.*

"Ricardo's angry," Chris said.

Jeremy stared at him. *How does he know that?*

Chris said Max had already warned him. "I'm going to talk to him at the campout," he said. "I want Ricardo to understand."

"He might not."

Chris nodded and closed his eyes appearing to pray.

"Man, Chris," Jeremy whispered. "This is like... I don't know." He bit his lower lip. "What am I supposed to do, bro?"

Chris took Jeremy by the chin and turned his head so they faced each other. Jeremy searched Chris' eyes and saw the strength in them, the strength he always lacked, the conviction he needed.

Chris said, "You love me, that's what. I'm your brother and I love you."

Tears welled up in Jeremy's eyes. "I love you, too, Chris," he said, a sob catching in his throat. "I always will no matter what."

They hugged each other. Chris felt their bond strengthen. Jeremy held his face against his brother's and pulled him close.

No one's going to hurt you, Chris. No one. Ever. I promise.

The clearing of a masculine throat startled the boys and they let go. They wiped their eyes and looked up into their father's concerned face.

Thomas was standing in the doorway with his arms crossed. "Your mother said I should make sure you guys were still alive," he said. "Anything going on here I should know about?"

Chris looked at Jeremy who looked back. They turned to their father.

"No," they replied in unison.

Thomas thought, *Whatever happened between them, I missed it. Judging from their embrace, they solved whatever it was themselves.*

Jeremy leaned over and whispered something into Chris' ear. They snickered.

"What's so funny?" Thomas asked, his hands on his hips.

His sons laughed, pointing at him.

Thomas remembered the white apron with the pink ruffles. He blushed.

Jeremy headed for the shower, his laughter echoing in the hallway.

Chris put a hand on his father's shoulder. "My dad the cross-dresser," he said, and burst out laughing.

Virginia looked upstairs wondering what the heck was so funny.

*   *   *

The Ramirez Family

José Ramirez was surprised to find his son Max awake and dressed already. Most of the time he had to come into the boys' room three or four times before they stirred. Even then, it took Marianna's commanding voice to get them moving. When he opened the door, he saw Max staring out of the front window. He grew concerned. He stepped in, sat next to his oldest son, and slipped an arm across his shoulder.

Max gave him a half-smile. "I'm okay, papa," he said, but looked away too quickly.

"Hey!" José exclaimed, pulling Max against him. "Do I look like I just got off the banana boat, chico?"

Max chuckled, "No, papa." He leaned into his father's shoulder. A scene flashed into his mind. It was Jack's hand, the leather belt descending, and the sickening sound of the crack it made against Craig's flesh. He said, "I saw something this morning that I wish I hadn't seen."

José looked out the window. Directly across from them and a little to the right, down on Gator Road, stood the Dougan residence.

José's face fell. "The Dougan boy?" he asked.

Max's expression answered for him.

"Be careful, Max," José cautioned. "Jack is a dangerous man."

Max asked, "Are you afraid of him?" He couldn't imagine that.

"Would you be afraid of a rabid dog?" José asked in return. His expression went stone cold. "That's what Jack is, Max."

Max lowered his head. "I almost went over there. He was beating Craig so badly."

"I know," José said. He patted Max on the shoulder and stood up. He walked to the door. He asked, "Do you know how many tears your mama's cried for that boy? Lyle sent the police over there once. Ask him what happened before you take this too far. You can't help someone who doesn't want your help, Max."

José walked into the bathroom and closed the door. Max didn't move until he heard the shower come on. When he did, he reached across to the twin bed on the other side of the room and shook his brother awake.

Ricardo pulled the covers over his head. "Five more minutes, mama, please?"

Max cuffed him. "Get up, dude."

"Ow!" Ricardo whined, uncovering his face. He pulled the blanket around his head. He looked like an old Chinese woman. "That hurt, Max!"

Max looked out the window toward the Dougan house. "You don't know what hurt is, hermano," he whispered.

Ricardo sat up and put his feet on the floor. "What's going on, man?" he asked, brushing his long black hair out of his eyes. "You look like you saw a ghost." He glanced around. *I hope that's not it!*

Max ran his fingers through his neatly cropped black hair. He said, "I wish I had."

"Shh!" Ricardo hissed, crossing himself. "They can hear you!"

"Don't be stupid, okay?"

"Then tell me what's wrong," Ricardo said, "or did you just wake me up to be a dick to me?"

Max opened his mouth, but then shut it. *Should I tell Ricardo what I saw? I love my brother, but Ricardo has a big mouth. If I tell him, it'll be all over school before the end of the day.*

"Well?"

Max chose a different conversation. He said, "I heard you talking to Jeremy last night. You were out of line, Ricardo. You know that, right?"

Ricardo scowled. "I don't know anything." He lay back down and turned away. He didn't want to talk about this. It hurt too much.

"C'mon, Ricardo!" Max cried. "Chris is our friend."

"He's not my friend," Ricardo said. "Not anymore."

"What kind of two-faced crap is that?" Max asked. "We've been friends with Chris since we were little."

"He wasn't a fag then, Max," Ricardo replied, rolling back over so Max could see the anger on his face.

"I can't believe you. This is no way to be, dude."

"People think you might be, too," Ricardo continued, going on the offensive. "Matt and Sandy, too. You guys are always together."

"Let them say it to my face!" Max exclaimed. He asked, "We find out Chris is gay because of a stupid rumor and now we have to hate him?"

"So it's true," Ricardo said, lowering his eyes. He closed them. "Chris is gay."

"Dude…"

"I didn't want to believe it," Ricardo whispered. A tear ran down the side of his face.

Max thought, *Ricardo never cries!* He asked, "Does it really matter?"

Ricardo nodded.

"Why, man? He's still Chris."

Images flooded Ricardo's mind. He was six years old again, lost at The Big E Fair in Massachusetts. It was hot and he was crying. His family was nowhere in sight. They had gotten separated by the Budweiser Clydesdales when they came prancing by and Ricardo followed them. A man knelt in front of him. He had a friendly face and curly brown hair. He told Ricardo everything would be all right. He promised to help him find his mommy. Ricardo was relieved.

"First," the man said, taking his hand, "let's wash your face. You don't want your mommy to see you acting like a cry baby."

Ricardo didn't care about that, but he didn't want Max to see him crying. The man led him to a bathroom marked *Out of Order*.

Ricardo read the sign and said, "Broken."

The man replied, "It's okay. We only need the sink."

They slipped inside. The man locked the door behind them. Ricardo's fear returned as they passed the sinks and went into one of the stalls. Everything Ricardo had ever known about life came crashing down in the minutes that followed. When it was over, he was in shock. The man washed his face at the sink, dropped him off at a security booth, and then disappeared into the crowd. The guards paged his family once Ricardo was able to blubber out his name. The man was long gone when his crying mother scooped him into her arms. Ricardo never saw him again. He never told anyone what happened to him. He was too frightened.

"Why does it matter so much, Ricardo?" Max repeated.

Ricardo almost told him, but he couldn't. "It just does."

Max wanted to press the matter. *He's hiding something,* he thought.

"Max?" Marianna called up the stairwell. "Ricardo?"

Max went over to the door. Before he exited, he turned back. "He's still our friend, Ricardo. You don't turn your back on your friends."

Ricardo said nothing. After the door closed, he wept. He loved Chris, and that was the truth. Max was right. Chris was his friend.

But how can he be my friend when he's everything I hate in the world?

Ricardo lay on his bed searching for answers. They weren't forthcoming.

At the top of the stairs, Max paused and looked down at his mother.

"Teléfono," Marianna said, pointing toward the kitchen. She was a round Puerto Rican woman, five-six, with tan skin and black eyes. Her pretty face wore an expression of authority. Her straight black hair was tied in a ponytail that went to the middle of her back. "Chris McKee."

It sounded fine to Max when she said Chris' name, but non-Hispanics would've probably heard *Magee* instead of *McKee*. He smiled and thanked her. He zipped down the stairs to his cell phone. It was on the charger in the kitchen. They hadn't been allowed to take their phones to bed with them since Ricardo got caught texting at one a.m.

"Chris?"

"Hey, Max," Chris said. "We're in business."

Max jumped for joy inside but kept his emotions under tight rein. Marianna would never let them go camping if she even suspected they might be drinking.

Chris picked up on Max's silence. "Your mom's there?"

"You got it, amigo."

Chris said, "Okay, listen. Make sure Ricardo brings his tent. I know it's a piece of crap, but we're tight for space."

"Are we good about supplies?" Max asked, using the code phrase they had agreed on yesterday.

"Yes," Chris replied. "Bring some food. We're meeting at Lancaster Pond after school."

"We'll be there."

"Cool."

"Uh, Chris?" Max asked, moving out of his mother's earshot. He decided he had better remind him about Ricardo.

"What's up?" Chris asked.

"Don't forget, you need to talk to my brother about you being...," he stopped. There was silence.

Chris finished his sentence for him. "Gay, Max. It's only a word."

"Not to mi madre it's not!"

"I will. We knew this was coming."

"I know," Max said, lowering his voice. Marianna walked to the stairs and started to go up. She had José's coveralls from the dryer. "I warned you, though. Ricardo has a problem with..."

"Gay people," Chris offered, helping him along.

"Right. It's even worse than I thought. He probably already told Jeremy."

"He did, but it's cool. I talked to Jeremy this morning. Dan's working pretty hard at screwing me over."

Max volunteered to beat him up.

Chris said no. He suggested telling people the truth.

Max shrugged. "Whatever, I got your back." He thought about it, and then added, "I said your *back,* not your *backside.*"

"Oh, funny," Chris said. "Like you do anything at all for me, Ramirez?" He hung up.

Max smiled.

Marianna returned to the kitchen and made a cup of espresso. Her favorite coffee was Bustelo. Max slipped in behind his mother and kissed her on the cheek. She smiled wryly, stirring some sugar into her cup. He noticed a large plate of fried plantains. He eyed them, hungrily.

"I heard ju arguing with jour brother, ¿entiendes?" Marianna said. Her stirring became more pronounced. "I don' know about what. I couldn't hear over jour father's shower. Jou're lucky."

Max lowered his head. *Uh, oh.* He said, "I'm sorry, mama."

"No, mi hijo," she replied, facing him. "Jou're not sorry."

"But I will be?"

"Sì," she smiled. It was a coy smile that said she hadn't decided what to do about it yet. "Only not today."

"Yes, mama," Max said. He thought, *Oh, great. She's going to dog us the next time we want to do something.* He kissed her again.

Marianna sat down at the kitchen table. She slipped on her reading glasses and opened the Hartford Courant. She couldn't read English very well, but looking through the paper was her way of practicing. She had a *Spanish to English* dictionary on the table so she could look up words she didn't know.

Max grabbed a handful of fried plantains and stepped onto the front porch. He was glad his mother had heard their raised voices. Of course, if she'd caught any of their conversation, he and his brother would've been consigned to the family room under her scrutinizing gaze until she got to the bottom of the fight. It reinforced in him just how screwed up Craig's life was.

He didn't put the dishes away and got beaten? Max thought. *¡Ay Dios mío! Mi madre is strict, but Jack's way out of bounds.* He frowned. *I wonder how Craig sees the world. The word bleak comes to mind.*

Max looked out at the rapidly brightening day. It was eighty-five degrees already and promised to hit the mid-nineties before lunchtime. The heat felt good through the large weeping willow trees on either side of their walkway. He smelled his mother's roses. There was a large red rosebush under the window facing Wickett Avenue. They were the envy of the town. Denise Copeland had once asked Marianna if she could work the same magic on her flowers, but his mother politely declined. She had enough to do in her own house raising two teenage sons.

Gibbons Garage was across the street. There were two gas pumps outside – unleaded and super – two repair bays on the left side of the building, and an office on the right. A seven-foot high chain-link fence covered with green opaque plastic enclosed the scrapyard out back. It went all the way down the length of Gator Road to the front of the Dougan's house. The fence had cost Lyle a fortune, but there was a town ordinance that insisted the public didn't have to look at all the wrecks he had saved.

Max used to wander the scrapyard when he was younger. Sometimes he sat inside cars brought in from accident scenes. Lyle and José split the wrecker work during the week. Lyle did it four days, José three. Sometimes the wrecks were from fatalities. Whenever Max came across one that was stained with blood and gore, he would show Ricardo. He loved the way his brother went, *"Eeeeewww!! Eeew! Eeeww!"* The way he scrunched up his nose like that? It was hilarious.

They had learned about cars and engines there. One of the jobs the boys shared was going into the scrapyard to retrieve used parts for customers. They learned how to rebuild master brake cylinders and grind down rotors. Over the years, they had become quite adept at overhauling engines. Ricardo was better at it than Max. Max was a people person. Ricardo worked best on his own which Max found isolating.

Ricardo gets along better with inanimate objects than human beings, Max thought. *He's building a pretty sweet car even though he won't get his license until he turns sixteen in October. I'll be seventeen in September. It's a 1968 Barracuda. Lyle sold it to him bit by bit for working the last three summers. By the end of this one, the title is his.*

Max daydreamed about his car. He hadn't decided what he wanted to build yet. He supposed he should get his license, too, but why bother? He didn't have a car and he couldn't have afforded the insurance even if he had. He worked at the garage on the weekends but only part time. It wasn't enough and he didn't want to work more. It would mean pumping gas which he loathed. He had considered working at the farm with Chris once, but Chris talked him out of it. Max was glad. He knew Hiram Milliken from the garage. He was a friend of Lyle's. Max thought he scored way high on the creep-o-meter.

He chewed his plantain as one of the cars he was considering roared into the garage. It was a 1966 Mustang convertible, candy apple red with a white top. It bore the vanity plate *GIBS 66*. Max watched it swing into the space reserved for its owner. It purred low, but then growled as Lyle stomped on the accelerator. It was for the benefit of Max, and he knew it, but the way the motor hummed? It made his heart skip. Lyle let up on the gas and shut the car off. Max swore the Mustang rose six inches when the big man stepped out of it.

Lyle Gibbons was six-foot-two with curly dark brown hair and a beard. His forearms looked like phone poles graced with the tattoos he had acquired in the Marines in Afghanistan. His dark brown eyes bore a maddening stare. He had gained some weight over the years, but it was food weight. Lyle appeared to have a beer belly, but people who knew him knew better. He hadn't touched a drop of alcohol since the day his wife, Marjorie Steele-Gibbons, died giving birth to their only child, Lisa Ann.

Lyle squinted toward the house he had once owned. He crossed his arms over his massive chest. "Where's your old man?" he asked. He glanced at his watch. "He's going to be late."

"And?" Max replied. He crossed his arms to mock the big man. "It's not like you're ever on time!"

Lyle snorted, "I own the friggin' place." He laughed a hearty, heavy, fat man's laugh. "You're something else, Max." He furrowed his brow. "What're you doing out here anyway? I don't usually see you this early."

Max considered that. "Actually," he said, "I guess I was waiting for you. I need to talk to you about something."

Lyle leaned back. "Broads?" he asked, closing one eye. He looked like a pirate, like his next words should be, *"Arrggghh, matey!"*

Max replied, "Nah. Don't need any help there, tubby."

Lyle dismissed him with a wave. "Is it serious?"

"It's serious."

"Come over. You can talk while I get the shop open for business."

Max told his mother where he was going. Marianna heard him, but she was too busy putting her foot in Ricardo's behind to reply. He was in slow motion this morning. To her chagrin, so was her husband. She chewed both of them out in Spanish. Her words were coming so quickly even Max – who was fluent in his native tongue – had trouble understanding her.

She's getting mad though. It's the only time she ever talks that fast.

Max jumped over the three steps from the porch to the walk. He crossed Wickett Avenue to the gas pumps. Lyle unlocked one and checked its readings. Max didn't know where to begin.

Lyle opened the conversation for him. "What's on your mind, kid?" he asked, donning his glasses. He only wore them long enough to read the pump, and then they disappeared into the pocket of his overalls. He didn't like people to know about them. They were only for reading. They were thick, too. "Did you talk to your old man about this first?"

"Sì," Max replied. He grinned at Lyle's scowl.

"You know that Spanish crap drives me nuts," he complained. "I'll never forgive your parents for teaching it to Lisa. I got the only white daughter in town that sounds like Ricky Ricardo."

"That's what you get for letting mama take care of her when she was a baby."

Lyle reflected on this scratching his chin. His eyes were sad, but only for a second. "Yeah, it was tough when Marge died, Max. Here I was with this little pink thing in my arms and a dead wife on the birthing table. I never felt so lost in my life, not even in the desert." He shook off the memory. He asked Max what was bothering him.

"I got woken up last night," Max sadly said. "It was Jack Dougan. He was beating the crap out of Craig."

Lyle stopped fighting with the pump lock on the second pump and closed his eyes. Max thought he was counting to ten.

"Your dad told you to talk to me?"

"Yeah. I'm not sure what to do about it."

Lyle shook his head and went back to fighting the lock. It was old, the same lock his deceased father used to battle with. He promised to buy a new one today for sure. Of course, tomorrow he would be right back here fighting the lock again. He had every day since his old man passed away and he inherited the garage. As much as he hated the lock, it was a small piece of his father. Carl Gibbons was gone, but he had put his heart and soul into this place. Lyle kept it as original as possible while still being competitive.

"It was late one Saturday," Lyle began, his hand on Max's shoulder. "We were playing poker, Kelly, Milliken, and me. All of a sudden, we heard the kid screaming like he was right in the room with us. Craig was probably ten. It was the week your family took off to NYC, remember?"

Max nodded remembering the trip to his Aunt Zoe's house. She was his mother's younger sister, but she had come to the mainland first. She married a soldier named Matías Ortiz from the Bronx. Matías had been killed in Iraq. He left behind his wife and Max's cousins, Elena, who was Ricardo's age, and the twins Matías, Jr. and Miguel. The twins turned eleven on April Fool's Day. Max smirked. Matías, Jr. and Miguel called each other "Fool!" all the time because of their birthday. Max shook his head.

Lyle continued, "I threw open the garage door and there they were, Max, in my lot! Jack had the kid by the hair as was whipping his legs with a leather belt."

Max's eyes widened. He bit his lower lip.

"I tell you, Max, I was going to plant Jack right there, as Jesus is my witness." Lyle held up his right hand as if swearing in for testimony. "I snatched up that skinny prick, slammed him onto the pavement, and do you know what happened?"

"You beat the crap out of him?"

Lyle shook his head. "I was going to, but as I raised my fist, the boy grabbed hold of it…"

"Craig?" Max asked.

"That's right, begging me not to hurt his daddy. I couldn't believe it."

"What happened then?"

"I called the state police. They went over there…," – Lyle gestured with his chin toward the Dougan's house – "… and they didn't do squat! Craig said he got the bruises falling down the attic stairs. Can you believe it?"

Max said he couldn't. *How could the cops be so blind?*

"Jack even threatened to bust me for making a false report. Milliken and Kelly weren't any help either. They *declined* to get involved." He grumbled under his breath, "Couple of pussies…"

"What kind of crap is that?" Max asked.

"This kind," Lyle replied. "As long as the kid loves his father – and he does even if the man's a piece of garbage – no one's going to be able to do squat."

Max's expression darkened. *Oh?* he angrily thought. He set his jaw in a determined expression. *We'll just see about that!*

*   *   *

Craig slipped quietly out the front door side-stepping the broken glass on the living room floor. The dishes didn't need to be put away any longer. As for the broken front window, Craig spotted a large cast iron cooking pot in the middle of the front lawn.

Another mystery solved, Craig thought.

He hoped his father hadn't meant for him to clean up the mess before he went to school. There was no way he could do that and still make it in on time. It was a double-edged sword. If he stayed to clean the mess, the school would call home when he got there reporting his tardiness. That would buy him another whooping when got back from working the market tonight. It was a cardinal sin to wake Jack up in the morning after a night of boozing. On the other hand, if he didn't clean it up, his father would slap him around a bit when he got home and make him clean it then. It was the lesser of two evils. The latter would involve a lot of angry hateful words, but the beating would be less. Waking Jack up into a hangover was never the best choice.

Craig walked to the rear of the house and unlocked his mountain bike from where he kept it chained to the back porch railing. It had been an early birthday gift from his grandmother. Even though he was just far enough from the high school to warrant riding the bus, Craig didn't like the way the other kids looked at him, so he rode his bike. He was the son of the town drunk to them. That's all he would ever be.

One day that'll change, Craig thought, *then you'll all see.*

He hopped on his bike and started to ride, slinging his backpack onto the handlebars. Halfway down the driveway, he saw the Ramirezes' house. He screeched to a halt. A clammy feeling spread through his chest.

I forgot about Max.

When Craig had come down from his attic room, he went to the bathroom, took a leak, washed his hands, and then went to the kitchen for breakfast. He'd forgotten all about his lone witness. If he had paid better attention, he would've known where Max was before leaving for school. He had a sinking feeling Max was going to say something to him about what he had seen. Craig wanted no part of it.

I'm getting along just fine, thanks. No need for concern. Careful, that bruise on my shoulder is still tender.

Craig cringed. He didn't need this. He just wanted to get through the last day of school and fade away into obscurity. He could hide all summer avoiding his neighbors like he always did. By the fall, they would've forgotten all about him. If he maintained a low enough profile, his worries would be over. People had short attention spans and even shorter memories. Craig wasn't remarkable enough to stay in anyone's thoughts for too long. There were advantages to being unpopular, especially when you didn't want anyone sticking their nose in your business. Of course, by leaving the fan out of the window, it had been an open invitation for Max to walk right in.

"How do you do? I'm the guy who's going to wreck your whole life."

Craig stared at Max's window hoping to catch a glimpse of him. If he was still home, he wasn't at the bus stop yet. Craig could ride quickly by and be on the trails before anyone was the wiser. The trails – old railroad tracks, footpaths, and unfinished roads webbing throughout Lancaster – were a blessing to anyone wanting to get around town without being seen. Practically everyone's backyard had a trail. Anyone who knew them well, like Craig did, could get anywhere in town from anywhere else in town with ease. He glanced at his Iron Man watch and ground his teeth.

"C'mon!" Craig whined, feeling a need to pee. "I'm going to be late!" He spotted movement in the Ramirezes' upstairs window. *Someone's getting dressed!* He strained his eyes. *It's Ricardo!*

Craig pushed off with his feet and peddled like crazy. If Ricardo was still home, chances were that Max was, too. They always walked to the bus stop together. Craig peddled as hard as he could. He appeared as a blur as he flew past the fence that marked Mrs. Turner's property line. He had his eyes locked on the Ramirezes' house struggling to make it past before anyone saw him. As he approached Wickett Avenue, picking up speed, he cut through Gibbons' Garage watching Ricardo instead of where he was going. As he came around the building, Craig crashed full speed right into Lyle.

* * *

Chris and Jeremy kissed their mother goodbye and walked out of the house. It was their routine. Virginia showed them to the door every morning. The other kids ragged them about it on occasion, but they didn't let it get to them. The bottom line on their parents was simple: practically every kid they knew wanted to belong to Thomas and Virginia. Having the coolest parents in town raised the McKee brothers' popularity. Virginia ruffled Jeremy's hair as he slid past her. He frowned and she was quick to apologize.

"I know," Virginia stated, chastising herself before he did. "It's hard enough to keep your hair under control without me messing it up, right?" She leaned against the doorjamb in anticipation of his response.

"Well, it is," Jeremy scowled. He looked at her with accusation. "Why did I have to get the wiry hair anyway, huh? Tell me that?"

He walked backward with his arms held out to his sides. He was confident he knew their yard well enough to keep going without incident. He hadn't counted on Chris stopping short. Jeremy collided with his brother in the middle of the yard and almost fell. He would have, too, if Chris hadn't grabbed him by his backpack. He swung his brother around so he faced the bus stop. Jeremy hung there like a side of beef about to protest this manhandling until he spotted what had caused Chris to stop short in the first place.

"Oh, nuts," Jeremy groaned. His eyes locked on a kid at the bus stop who didn't belong there. "What's he doing here?"

"I'll give you three guesses," Chris said, adjusting his glasses. They were transition-lenses already darkened by the bright morning sun.

"No, thanks," Jeremy replied.

There was only one reason Dabney Copeland would be at their bus stop when his stop was up Satchell Hill at the corner of Textile Road. He had heard Dan's rumor.

Jeremy growled under his breath.

Chris patted him on the shoulder. "No trouble," he said. "He's not worth it."

"No," Jeremy agreed. "He's not."

Their bus stop was diagonally across from their house where Satchell Hill met Points of Light Road. Matt Gardner was strategically standing on the opposite corner from Dabney. Henry and Herman Schwartz lived on Points of Light Road near Matt. They stared at Dabney as he spoke to them in hushed tones. It was evident by the way Henry was looking at Chris that Dabney was telling them everything. Jeremy had the sudden urge to punch him in the face. Dabney would see that the rumor got all over town as fast as possible just to be a douche.

Jeremy didn't think he had it in him to hate anyone. If he had, Dabney would be number two on his list of people to hate first, right after Dan for what he was doing to Chris. Herman was Jeremy's age. They were in the same grade and classes as Dabney. Jeremy and Herman also played on the same baseball team. Dabney, unlike his older brother, Dennis, the football star, didn't do sports. Herman looked confused at Dabney's words. Henry was a senior and Chris' ex-co-worker. In contrast to his brother, Henry looked positively disgusted. Dabney shut his mouth when he saw the McKees approaching. He stood there with his arms crossed in unrestrained arrogance. He was ready for them. There was nothing he liked better than a confrontation especially with the deck stacked in his favor.

Chris and Jeremy walked past him without saying a word. Herman broke away and followed them.

That's the ticket, Matt thought. *Screw Dabney. He's not worth the hassle. Even my mom isn't as annoying as he is.* He shook his head. *God, was I walking on eggshells around her this morning…*

* * *

The Gardner Family

A short while ago, at the Gardners' dining room table, Matt forced himself to eat his cornflakes slowly, methodically, as was his usual. He didn't want to alert his parents – seated on either side of him at the head and foot of the table – to his excitement. On the outside, Matt maintained a manner of bored disinterest, a calm and detached look as if it was just another ho-hum day in the life of the Gardners' only child.

Inside however, Matt felt like he was kneeling in the middle of Wickett Avenue, his long blonde hair flying, as he headbanged on the pavement. He wanted to jump onto the table and dance a jig around Randy and Linda, two of the stiffest parents any teenager ever had. They weren't mean or anything, just proper to a fault. Matt's life had a strict plan to carry him through medical school and beyond. There was no room in that plan for the kind of night he had set up.

Linda possessed parental radar like no one had ever seen before. If she caught a hint of Matt's excitement, two antennas would pop out of her head like *My Favorite Martian* and the third degree would begin. Matt shivered. That would be a disaster. Linda could ferret out any lie, and she would, too, until she had him cornered. He would have to accept being grounded for his silence or for coming clean about his plans. It would definitely be the silence. Regardless, Linda would call everyone's parents and tell them she had discovered the boys were up to something.

That would only cost Matt the camping trip. If he came clean about the partying, everyone – especially the Ramirez brothers – would be in deep trouble for weeks. Their mother was adamant about them not drinking. She didn't like Puerto Rican stereotypes. Not every PR was a drunk. She intended to make sure it stayed that way. Linda was already suspicious. She always was whenever Matt was out of her sight with his friends. He had been thirteen before she let him sleep over another kid's house. She preferred Matt to invite his friends to stay over with them.

That's so aggravating!

His house was a realm that lacked the main ingredient for a good time: privacy. Randy wasn't any help either. Linda's word was final on household matters. His father stayed out of her way. Matt vowed to be the man of his house. His future wife could like it or lump it.

He smiled at that thought, lifting his spoon.

"Something amusing, Matthew?" Linda asked, pausing her coffee midway to her lips.

Matt fought back a blush while his mind raced for a quick – but not too quick – answer. To his surprise, his father came to his rescue.

"You know adolescents, honey," Randy said. "Matt's probably thinking about sex."

Matt glared at his father. Randy covertly winked at him. Linda shook her head. Matt swore he could see the antennas rising out of her long, straight blonde hair, a shade lighter than his. Matt could've strangled his father for even mentioning the *s-word* and his name in the same sentence. Matt was a virgin. His mother intended to keep him that way if she had to confiscate his penis and lock it up until his wedding night.

"That's not funny, Randy," Linda replied, looking down her nose at her accountant husband. "Don't give Matt any ideas. He can wait until he's married."

Matt scowled. *As if thoughts of sex overran my mind all the time, or something, right? I'm not Sandy Sturgess!*

He was curious, however, but there was no way he was bringing the subject up with his parents. To his relief, Linda had thought his father's comment so absurd, she dropped the subject and went back to her coffee.

Thank God! The last thing I need is for mom to have any suspicions rekindled, especially after the grilling I got when I brought up the campout in the first place. It's a good thing we anticipated that and Sandy helped me come up with a backup plan. Sturgess is just too slick!

"No," Linda had flatly said when he asked her permission to camp out. She returned to throwing clothes from the washer to the dryer.

Matt was standing in the doorway to the laundry room holding a basket of dirty sheets. He'd helped her with the housework all morning, dusting, vacuuming, and cleaning his room to eliminate any obvious reason she would have to say he couldn't go camping. It was bad enough she would have a week to come up with something even if she said yes, but at least he would have a fighting chance. He hoped his enthusiasm for cleaning hadn't tipped her off that he wanted something, but it probably hadn't. Matt was good about helping around the house. He considered it building up credits.

Linda was right on him about who else was going and where they planned to be the moment he brought up the subject. Matt said they would be in Sturgesses' yard. It wasn't technically a lie since Alex and Susan owned the land next to their house, but he withheld the fact they would be a hundred yards away into the woods. If they decided to camp at Lancaster Pond, another possibility, they would be even farther away and nowhere near the Sturgesses' property. They were meeting there after the last day of school to go swimming. Matt chose not to mention that. It was going okay and she seemed on the verge of giving her consent until he rambled off the names of everyone going. That's when she said no.

"Why not?" Matt asked, holding in his anger. If he blew up, it would be all over.

Linda stopped tossing clothes and pushed her hair away from her face. The humidity left little droplets of sweat on her forehead.

"You know why, Matthew," she said. Her blue eyes bored into him.

Matt didn't look away. Doing so would suggest he felt guilty about something. At least, that's how Linda would perceive it. Matt – who at five-foot-nine was an inch taller than his mother – crossed his arms over his chest.

"Remind me," he said.

Linda considered whether or not he was being disrespectful. Satisfied he wasn't – although she'd caught the challenge in his tone – she went back to filling the dryer.

"Matthew," Linda began, bobbing up and down with the laundry. They had a stackable washer and dryer. The washer was a front loader. "You know how I feel about so many of you guys gathering together. There's always the potential for trouble. Besides, you must be up to something."

"How come you're always so suspicious?" Matt snapped.

Linda glared at him. "Mind your tone, young man," she scolded. "This conversation will end *toot sweet* if you speak to me like that again."

"Sorry," Matt said, lowering his head. *She's such a bitch sometimes, too overprotective.* He was losing the battle. It was time for an alternative strategy. "Have I ever given you a reason to not trust me?"

Linda paused when her son switched tactics. She came back with the old standby, "I like to think it's because I provide proper supervision."

Matt groaned. Proper supervision meant if there were friends over, he kept his room door open. It meant not being allowed to camp in the yard out of her sight and no swimming in the pool at night. Bedtime was her bedtime. No snacks unless she made them, no sleeping in the same bed, no phone calls after nine, no visitors of the opposite sex, no television except in the family room, and endless spot checks every time they were outside her line of sight.

That spells out a fun time! C'mon, guys! How about a game of Chutes and Ladders at the dining room table?

Matt crossed himself.

"Why don't you boys camp out in our yard instead?" Linda suggested.

Matt felt a wave of relief. *Predictable as ever, mom!*

He had known she would say that. She always did if it involved camping with anyone other than Chris, or being anywhere other than at Chris' house. This was where Sandy's slickness would come into play.

The day before, Chris, Matt, and Sandy were in the Sturgesses' kitchen well within earshot of Sandy's mom. Susan's long lifeless brown hair was tied back in a ponytail. She was watching TV in the parlor, but they knew her bionic ears were tuned in to every word they said. Sandy was a pro at getting around his mom. When they told him about the anticipated problem with Linda, he immediately knew how to fix it so Matt could go. Sandy put his finger up to his lips, his hazel eyes twinkling behind his glasses. Chris and Matt nodded following his lead.

"You guys want to camp out with me?" Sandy asked, acting like it was his idea. He made sure he had spoken loud enough for his mother to hear. "It's kind of an end of school get together. Max, Ricardo, and Derek are."

Chris nodded giving Sandy a thumbs up while silently laughing. "I will if I can get the day off," he replied. He turned to Matt, and asked, "What about you, Matt?"

"I don't know if I can," Matt sighed, feigning sadness. "You know how suspicious my mom gets when a lot of us are together. Maybe we could go to my house? She would say yes for sure then."

"Everybody else got permission to be here," Sandy argued. He lied, "It's my campout. Besides, my mom will be home."

"Yeah," Matt frowned, preparing the zinger. "It's just that… my mom doesn't think a lot of parents give good enough supervision. She lets me camp with Chris at his house because we're right down the street and she can check up on us, even though she doesn't anymore. I don't know if she trusts your mom to keep a good enough eye on us."

"What was that?" Susan cried, hopping off the couch. She clicked the mute button on her remote and strutted into the kitchen as if on cue. The boys nodded, but then acted surprised. "I'll have you know I watch my sons and their guests just fine, Mr. Gardner!"

Matt held up his hands. "It's not me, Mrs. Sturgess! You know how my mom is!"

"Well, where is she?" Susan demanded, placing a hand on her hip. "I'll fix it so you can go, Matt, mark my words. Linda doesn't even want to think I don't watch you guys."

Despite her posturing, it was no coincidence the boys had chosen to camp at Sandy's house. Alex and Susan would check up on them all right. They would call to the boys from the back porch maybe once and that would be it. If they went to Lancaster Pond instead, Susan would text Sandy to make sure everything was okay. Since there were so many of them, any other parent, even Virginia, would walk out to see how they were doing. If they weren't where they said they'd be, it would be a whole different layer of drama. Matt had told Susan the best time to catch his mother was Sunday after church since it was cleaning day. Susan said she would call his house promptly at one-thirty.

"Because it's Sandy's campout, mom," Matt replied eyeing the clock next to the dryer. It was almost time. "That wouldn't be cool. Besides, Sandy's mother might think you don't trust her to watch us, or something."

Linda smiled. She thought, *The kid is getting good.*

Matt knew how much she valued her standing in the community. She wouldn't risk any confrontations with other parents unless they'd screwed her over before. Susan Sturgess was her friend and within their parental circle. Their sons had been buddies since kindergarten. Thomas McKee, Alex Sturgess, and Kevin Mellon had been childhood friends themselves.

Randy and Linda were younger, but they were Lancaster natives, too. They started dating in the eighth grade and got married right out of high school. They had both been on the cheerleading squad back then which Matt begged they would keep strictly confidential. (*Dad was a cheerleader in high school!? Omg! Just let the Sturgess brothers learn that! Or Ricardo!? Oy vey!*) Susan was a little too outspoken for Linda's taste. It was an underhanded maneuver on Matt's part to use her as a bargaining chip and she could see right through it. She was about to call him on it and put the kibosh on the whole deal when the phone rang.

"I'll get it," Matt said. He darted past the kitchen phone to the one in the living room. *Thank you, God!* he thought. *Phase two is right on schedule!*

"Hello? Gardner residence. Matt speaking."

"Okay, Matt," Susan said. "Where's the bitch?"

Matt held back a laugh. Susan was a lot like Virginia McKee, but with a sharper edge. His mom – the world-class yuppie – was out of her league and in for it now.

"Are you going to yell at her?" Matt asked.

"Just watch my smoke," Susan said. "I'll show you how to get around Miss Smarty-pants."

Matt heard Sandy and his brother Ian snickering in the background. Susan ordered them to shut up. Matt put the phone to his chest, took a deep breath, and called for his mother.

Linda picked up the extension in the kitchen.

Matt listened in. *This is going to be great!*

"Hello?"

"Linda? Susan Sturgess."

"Oh! Hi, Sue," Linda began. "I was just going to call you."

"Good. I saved you a quarter."

Linda weakly laughed.

Susan continued, "I just wanted to make sure you knew the boys were camping out in our yard Monday the last day of school."

"Well, I…"

"You know I always check up on these things," Susan interrupted.

Matt's grin widened.

"Of course, I…"

"Can you imagine? The boys thought Matt might not be able to come because *you* might not think I watch them well enough."

"Oh?" Linda asked.

"I gave them a piece of my mind!" Susan exclaimed, a little heated. "I told them you were perfectly aware of how well I supervise my sons and their guests when they're at my house. I was insulted they would even think such a thing!"

"That's terrible!" Linda exclaimed, electing to defuse the situation immediately. "I wonder what gave them that idea? Of course Matt can go! We were talking about it only a minute ago."

Matt set the receiver in the cradle and went to the kitchen. He enjoyed watching his mother squirm for about ten minutes. There was no way he couldn't go now unless Linda came up with an ironclad reason to ground him. It meant walking on eggshells around her until the last day of school, but it was worth it. He crossed his fingers as his mother said goodbye to Susan. She stormed past him without another word.

Phil, Matt's cousin on his mother's side – her cousin Deidre's son – finally returned his voicemails last night. Phil was bad at checking his messages. Matt never sent texts or emails to him about party matters in case Linda had some way to recover his deleted history that he didn't know about. He wouldn't put it past her. Phil had lived with them for a few months while waiting for campus housing after coming down from Maine to go to UCONN. Phil got Matt, Max, Ricardo, and Chris drunk for the first time when Matt's parents had gone to Martha's Vineyard last summer and Phil baby-sat. Since then, he always bought for them whenever they camped out.

When Matt told him how many kids were going, Phil was a little wary. He didn't know Derek, Jeremy, Ian, or Sandy. It took some pleading, but Phil finally agreed to buy if he didn't have to get separate orders for everyone. Matt decided on brandy and beer. Phil said he could pay him back later. Matt directed him to the hiding spot they had scouted in the woods behind Lancaster Pond. Phil said he would leave the stuff there and would lend Matt his cooler.

"Just don't let anything happen to the cooler, okay?" Phil pleaded. "I need it for hell week."

Matt promised he wouldn't. Phil also told him to make sure they didn't get caught. As he scooped up the last of his cereal, Matt silently patted himself on the back. The time for the camp out was here and no one was the wiser. He had to call Derek and the Sturgess brothers after breakfast. He would do that from his room once his father had left for his Copeland Industries office and his mother was in the shower.

Water striders skipped along the surface of their in-ground pool. Matt watched them through the bay window that faced the backyard. The Gardners' house was a modern, light-stain colored menagerie of solar panels and a perfectly squared lawn that stood proudly on the right side halfway up Points of Light Road. Randy had it built when Matt was seven. They had lived in Glendale Apartments back then off Wickett Avenue diagonally across from Kelly Hardware. His mother had just opened her insurance business. Now there wasn't a family in town who didn't have a policy from her. Randy did some private accounting work for a few people from home, but his real money came from doing the books at Copeland Industries.

Matt didn't like Jerry Copeland. He had a superiority complex that wouldn't quit. His middle child, Dabney, was the only Copeland kid of the three he knew. They were in the same grade. Dabney was a conceited rich brat with a chip on his shoulder. Matt had tried to talk to him once in sixth grade. He had felt sorry for him because he always ate alone. Dabney had straight, thin, milk chocolate brown hair and eyes, freckles all over his cheeks, nose, and shoulders, a pale complexion, and a round face that was kind of sweet in a way. Physically, he had been a little boy with smooth features and high-pitched voice. He was the same way now only taller and his voice was deeper.

Matt began with, "Hey, Dabs. You're always eating alone, so I thought I would…"

Dabney nearly bit his head off. "What do you want, Gardner?" he asked, his milk chocolate brown eyes raging. "Do you think I care if anybody eats with me? Step off, okay? Copelands have real money. Your father plays with it."

Matt vowed not to bother with him again. Only Jeremy – who was cool with everyone – even talked to Dabney. He mostly got snotty one-word answers. Matt wondered what was behind Dabney's attitude, but he was so hostile it wasn't worth finding out.

Randy rose from the table and dropped his cup in the sink. Matt asked his mother to be excused. After a quick glance into her son's bowl, Linda nodded, her blue eyes satisfied. He elbowed his departing father in the side as he passed him. Randy continued into the hall and motioned for Matt to join him out of his mother's sight. Matt walked up to him. Randy was an inch shorter than his son, the same height as his wife. He had thin, light brown hair and eyes with a deeply receding hairline. He was a nerd but an awesome baseball coach. Whenever someone pictured an accountant in their mind, Matt was sure an image of his father appeared. He was a walking stereotype right down to his loafers and brown briefcase. Matt scowled feigning irritation. Randy held his arms out. After a dramatic pause, Matt hugged him.

Randy kissed his son on the cheek. "Don't get too drunk tonight," he whispered, into Matt's ear. "And for God's sake, don't let your mother find out about it." He let go of his son and stepped out the door.

Matt stood there his mouth agape, and then dashed up the stairs before his mother saw him. He took the steps two at a time. Inside his room, he closed the door, his heart pounding.

Dad knows! And he didn't tell mom!? Holy crap! What's going on?

Matt sat on his backpack in the middle of the floor in a state of shock. He put his hand over his chest struggling to catch his breath. His mind raced trying to figure out how his father could have known about the party. He hoped he hadn't made some colossal mistake that might alert his mother, too.

"No," Matt said, forcing a calm. "Dad said to make sure she didn't find out." It took five minutes for his hands to stop shaking. He picked up his

Droid and dialed Sandy's house. *A re-evaluation of dad is in order. How the heck did he…?*

"What's up?" a voice said.

It was Ian, Sandy's middle brother. He was a year younger than Matt and an eighth grader like Derek.

"Hi, Ian, it's…"

"Matt!" Ian exclaimed. "What-up, dude? Did you get the stuff, or what? You never called us back last night!"

Ian was strutting through the kitchen trying to convince the world he was Black, not white. He had said as much on many occasions. Ian was a die-hard rapper. He spoke the part, dressed it, and acted it so well that sometimes he almost convinced them. Matt guessed Susan and Alex were already gone. Alex was a UCONN English Professor and Susan taught Special Education in the Lancaster School District. Matt explained that when he was done with Phil last night, his mother said it was too late for any more calls.

"I didn't dare try to sneak a text, but I got it all taken care of."

"Sandy!" Ian hollered. Matt heard a muffled reply. *"Matt got it!"*

"Got what?" Sean asked his older brother.

Matt sighed. Ian and Sandy's younger brother had the biggest mouth for a ten-year-old. He was also the only Sturgess kid with brown hair.

"Don't tell him, Ian."

"Do you think I'm stupid?" Ian asked. "Besides, you kept us hangin' all week. You think I'd blow it now? Sean! Go away, you geekling!"

"I don't have to if I don't want to."

"See what I have to put up with?" Ian grumbled.

"Can't see through the phone, Ian," Matt replied.

"Ha… ha…," Ian said. "Skype me next time."

"No more Skype," Matt replied. "Not after Derek mooned me. Too much of a risk I'll see something else I can never unsee."

"Like you're the only one with Derek's butt imprinted in your brain?"

Matt told Ian to bring some food and to make sure they were at the pond after school. They would spend the afternoon there and maybe have a cookout in the barbecue pits. They could set up the tents later. Ian said that was no problem. Their mother had already packed a bag of edibles. Matt said his mom had, too, and added that Sandy needed to bring his tent.

"Sandy! You need to bring your tent!"

Matt held the Droid away from his ear and sat on the edge of his bed. Ian was five-foot with light blonde hair that parted in the middle and feathered back with no effort. He had a million freckles, steel-gray eyes, and huge dimples in his cheeks. He also had a mouth even bigger than Sean. Everybody told him so, but he was still loud.

The only place it ever served them was on the baseball field. Matt, Max, Ricardo, Jeremy, Ian, and Derek all played Babe Ruth League on the same team, the Kelly Hardware Wildcats. Ian's mouth was one of the greatest batter-distracters ever. Matt wished he would tone it down a little until their next game. Matt's dad coached with Kevin Mellon, Derek's father. They were close to making the playoffs.

Jeremy was an awesome pitcher. As long as he was healthy, they were going all the way. Ian played second base, Matt had first, and the Ramirez brothers played center and left. Derek was a fantastic shortstop. He was never afraid to dive after a ball no matter how chopped up he got. He was a walking bruise after every game. It was a wonder Cynthia could get his uniform clean. Billy Wilde, another ninth grader, played third. Herman Schwartz had right field, and chubby wise-mouthed Colin Skinner was the catcher.

Herman was okay for a brain. Billy was just weird with his blonde mop of huge curls, but Colin was someone who was always bucking for a beat down, especially from Max. Last season, Colin made the mistake of calling an opposing player the derogatory word for a Puerto Rican. It was all the team could do to keep Max from ripping his head off. Ricardo paid him back in the boys' room at the middle school just before the end of the year. He had dunked Colin's head in the toilet about ninety times. Matt had been there with Jeremy who tried to calm Colin down and save him from an even bigger problem, angering Ricardo worse than he already was. Matt laughed. Colin was dripping wet and cursing up a storm. Matt had led Ricardo out as Jeremy put his hand over Colin's mouth warning him of things to come.

"God, Ian," Matt complained. "Can you tone it down a bit?"

"Sorry, dude," Ian said, lowering his voice. "Sandy's in the shower."

"Duh, Sturgess!" Matt cried. "Can't you wait for him to get out?"

Ian explained that Sandy had told him to let him know the minute Matt called.

"Let him know about what?" Sean's small voice asked.

"Shut up, Sean!"

Matt sighed. He was glad he didn't have siblings. He wouldn't mind if they got along the way Chris and Jeremy did, or Max and Ricardo – most of the time, anyway. Matt was lonely sometimes, but whenever the Sturgess boys started to rumble, he just let that all go.

"All right, Ian," Matt said. "I still have to call Derek, and then I'm heading to the bus stop."

"Holy crap!" Ian yelled. Matt winced. "I just remembered! Wait until you hear what Dan Mellon told Sandy about Chris!"

"I heard it already," Matt said. He didn't Ian's tone, like he had the key to the city, or something.

"Oh?" Ian asked. "Do you believe it?"

"I don't know what to believe," Matt replied. "Chris is my friend. I think Dan's a punk for trying to ruin his reputation no matter what."

"Yeah, I guess you're right," Ian replied, deflated. Matt was sure Ian had told everyone in the eighth grade by now. "Sandy punched Dan in the gut as soon as he got done telling him, right in the middle of Mike's Market! Good thing nobody saw him. Mike Dougan's a big dude!"

Sandy belted Dan Mellon?

That was the best news Matt had heard on the subject. He wished he'd done the same. It was no big surprise though. Dan should've known better than to talk smack about Chris to Sandy. Sandy and Chris used to be together all the time until Sandy started dating Danielle Wolicki. Matt was glad he did. He had always liked Chris. With Sandy gone, it gave him the opportunity to hang out with him solo. Chris was good at taking suggestions about activities. When Sandy was there, they always did what he wanted to do, unless Max was there, too.

Matt told Ian he would see him at the pond later and hung up. He dialed Derek's house and the phone only rang once. Derek answered sounding depressed. Matt hoped nothing was wrong with him going tonight. Derek said that wasn't it at all.

"Dan told me if I went anywhere with Chris he was going to kick my butt," Derek sadly said.

"Did he say anything to your dad?" Matt asked, suddenly worried his whole plan was about to blow up in their faces.

"No," Derek replied.

Matt sighed relief.

"Dan doesn't know about... you know. Dad told him to mind his own business. He said if I wanted to hang out with Chris, Dan had nothing to say about it."

"Oh, yeah?"

"Yeah, dad thinks they had a fight, or something. He said if they did, it was probably Dan's fault."

Good for Coach Mellon, Matt thought. Derek didn't seem to know anything about the rumor. He guessed Ian hadn't called the whole eighth grade after all.

"So, Derek," Matt said, trying to sound cheery, "why so glum, chum? If your dad said you can go, what's the problem?"

"Oh, it's Dan," Derek replied. "He swore he would get me if I went. He will, too."

All of the Mellon kids had red hair like their father. Derek's was more intense than Dan or Doug's, and he had green eyes rather than his brothers' shared blue ones. Dan was mean to Derek sometimes with his temper. Considering Dan was older and bigger, Matt saw why he would be worried. Douggie was his little brother and inconsequential.

"Where's Dan now?" Matt asked.

"Walking to the bus stop."

"Do you want to go?"

"'Course I want to!" Derek exclaimed. "But Dan...!"

"Don't worry about Dan, dude," Matt assured him. "When I see Max, I'll tell him what's going on. Max won't let Dan lay a finger on you."

"Really?" Derek asked.

"Really," Matt assured him. "I have to get going so I don't miss the bus. Meet us at the pond after school."

Derek thanked Matt profusely and said he would be there once eighth grade graduation was over. It was starting at ten o'clock and might not be done before the high schoolers got out. As Matt hung up, he grabbed his backpack and prepared to leave. His excitement was building again. Being bad felt kind of good.

"Let's rock and roll!" Matt exclaimed, pumping his fist.

"What was that?" Linda called, from the hallway outside of his door.

Matt said it was nothing, and then he growled.

*   *   *

At the bus stop, Matt was grinning as he shook off his morning memories. "That was so cool," he nodded, as the McKees approached. He rubbed his temple. "You guys just walked by Dabney like he was nothing." He looked past Chris and smiled.

Dabney scowled back.

Chris set his backpack on the ground. It was heavy with all the books he needed to return. "He's a punk. We're not. End of story." He glanced at Dabney and furrowed his brow. *When did he become so cute?* he wondered, feeling an odd sensation in his chest. It was tingly all of a sudden. He shook his head. *It's a bad boy thing. It has to be. Great eyes though... omg, will you listen to me?*

Herman adjusted his yarmulke and his round-rimmed glasses. He cleared his throat and asked, "I guess you know what he's saying about you?" He seemed uncomfortable, but not with Chris. He was just in way over his head inside someone's personal life and Herman wasn't that kind of person.

"I have an idea," Chris frowned. *It's only the beginning, too.*

"I want to smack him one," Jeremy said.

"No," Chris insisted. "Don't even think about it, Jeremy."

"But Chris, he's..."

"... a loser and everybody knows it. Just let it go." He glanced at Dabney again. *Cute though.* He snapped his tongue. *When the heck did that happen?* He turned to Herman who was examining him like a newly discovered fungus. "What's your major malfunction, Schwartz?"

Herman shrugged. "I've never seen a gay guy up close before."

Matt and Jeremy burst out laughing.

Chris glared at them.

Jeremy held up his hands.

Chris lowered his eyes. *It's going to be a long day.*

74

"Herman!" Henry barked, his deep voice an insistent commanding tone. "Get over here. I don't want you anywhere near McKee."

Herman looked at Chris, sighed, and said, "Give me a moment." He stepped away from the boys and leaned in his brother's direction. "Henry?" he asked.

"What?" Henry replied.

Jeremy was amused. Henry and Herman looked so much alike, it was as if they were the same person. Herman was just the smaller version.

"You are not my lord and master," Herman stated, with all due respect. "So bite me."

Chris, Jeremy, and Matt laughed.

"Bite me?" they chorused, looking down at their small Jewish friend.

Henry flushed. "You'll be laughing out of the other side of your face when I tell papa."

"Henry?" Herman replied. "Don't be a schmuck."

The boys' laughter renewed. Chris held on to Matt to keep from falling over. Jeremy noticed Dabney eyeing them with an odd expression. He stepped away from Chris and Matt, and motioned for Dabney to come over to him. Dabney glared at him, rolled his eyes, and then stormed over. This action convinced Jeremy he had some influence over him otherwise Dabney would've ignored him.

"What?" Dabney demanded.

Chris and Matt stopped laughing.

"Uh, oh," Matt whispered.

"We're not friends, Copeland, right?" Jeremy said, more than asked. It wasn't something he had ever said before. Jeremy was friends with everyone.

"Hardly," Dabney scoffed.

Jeremy took this as a given. "We're not enemies either."

"What's your point, McKee?"

Dabney watched Matt and Chris out of the corner of his eye convinced they were going to jump him. Jeremy moved into Dabney's line of sight. They were the same height only Dabney was skinny. Jeremy worked out.

"My point," Jeremy replied, "is that everyone's talking about my brother, right?"

Dabney smiled. "You could say that."

Jeremy held him in his gaze. "Then don't you think it's pretty common of you to involve yourself?"

"Exactly what do you mean?" Dabney asked, crossing his arms. *Common* was not a word people used to describe him.

"I mean, if everyone's going to talk about my brother anyway, why would you, of all the people I know, join in with such trailer trash gossip? I never thought of you as the type of person who would sink so low."

Jeremy patiently waited as Dabney considered this. He could tell the statement had caught him off guard. He was used to confrontations, not logic.

Dabney was annoyed at how easily Jeremy had pegged him. He didn't like that, but he respected it.

"You know something?" Dabney asked, a hard expression on his face. "I'm surrounded by morons who think they're something when they're not."

"And?" Jeremy replied.

"Look, Jeremy," he said, almost smiling. "I get your point." He leaned forward and whispered, "I don't care if your brother's gay. I always thought he might be, but whatever." He smiled. "I just like the way people squirm when I tell them about it."

Jeremy bit back on his anger. "This is hard enough on us, Dabney. Isn't it a little too easy for you?"

Dabney nodded. "All right, I'll leave it alone. For now."

"That's good enough. For now."

"You know something?" Dabney said, seeing the bus making its way up Satchell Hill. "You're not stupid. I almost like you."

"Well, you know something, Dabs?" Jeremy replied, shaking his head. He laughed a little. "I almost like you, too, and you're the biggest dick I know."

"You bet," Dabney replied. He walked away toward the bus.

Chris and Matt met Jeremy halfway. They looked at him like they didn't know him.

"What?" Jeremy asked.

"You actually talked to Copeland?" Matt asked.

"Sure," Jeremy shrugged. "Dabney's not all bad."

"But he's such a prick!" Chris cried, but he thought, *Cute, though, for sure.* He smiled, discreetly examining him. *Love those freckles. They're like perfectly distributed, too. Would he let me count them? He acts so sour, but I bet he's cuddly as hell.* He blushed. *Thank God no one can read my mind! I mean, Copeland!?* He stifled a laugh.

"Sure," Jeremy agreed, approaching the steps, "he's a prick, but at least you know what to expect from him."

Chris and Matt supposed he was right.

Dabney heard the end part of that, but he didn't react. Weakness was the last thing he needed to show when he was surrounded by people who hated him. He pushed his thin hair away from his face and stared out the window at Chris. Henry was in the doorway waiting for Herman, but his brother had his arms crossed defiantly glaring at him. Dabney didn't understand how Jeremy could sway him from messing with his brother so easily, but it was just that, easy. No one had that kind of influence over him, not even his own family.

Perish forbid, Dabney thought.

Chris noticed that Dabney was looking at him. It was a probing look that lingered. Dabney caught himself and quickly looked away.

Chris lowered his gaze and smiled. *He seriously has some great eyes.* He snapped his tongue. *I can't believe it. He's making fun of me and spreading Dan's rumor, but I'm fawning all over the guy. I should be righteously pissed off, but what am I doing? Acting like a fangirl.* His heart skipped a beat when Dabney looked at him again. It was only for a moment as he got on the bus. *Do I have a crush on Dabney?* He shook his head. *Good God, is that it?*

Dabney looked at him again, but then looked away.

Chris smirked. *Okay, Dabs... you can stop being so cute now.*

Dabney felt he should apologize to Chris although he would never do it. That was so incredibly weak, he couldn't. He wasn't trying to hurt Chris though. There was something about him Dabney found intriguing, but making people squirm made him feel powerful. The rumors about Chris set them all aflutter. Dabney needed to examine his feelings. He had always thought Chris was gay. He felt drawn to him a lot this past year. He could think of a dozen different times he had caught himself watching Chris, but turned away before he noticed.

Dabney thought Chris was quite stylish. He wore nice clothes and he had a great haircut. Dabney thought an earring would look good on him. He might have wanted to talk to Chris a few times, too. He even showed up to work early on occasion with the intention of *accidentally* running into him, but he had been afraid of being rejected, so he never actually said anything. They shared a cordial nod in the barnyard, nothing more. He had hoped Chris might talk to him sometime, but he never had. Dabney didn't understand what was going on, but there was something about Chris that was different. If he had been gay, too, he would've said that Chris was really hot.

His eyes are an amazing shade of green, Dabney thought. He shook his head. *Just saying.*

As for Jeremy, he was slick like his father, Thomas. How many times had Jerry warned his sons to be careful around the McKees? Thomas was a smart lawyer and that made him dangerous. Still, there was something in Jeremy's eyes, sympathy, or empathy, for him. Most people hated Dabney. He was used to that. It was comfortable. Jeremy seemed indifferent. It drove Dabney up a wall. Jeremy was either becoming his friend or his worst enemy, and friendship involved trust. Dabney didn't trust anyone. At least, he didn't think he did.

Textile Road was near the top of Satchell Hill just before Adler Road. The Copeland Estate was nestled in the hills surrounded on two sides by the cliffs. It was the only house on the street. Above them to the left stood the house Colonel Timothy Adler built. His only daughter, Margaret – Ms. Adler, the science teacher – lived there. Dabney looked at her house. It was like he could feel her and knew she was watching him. It made him uncomfortable. Ms. Adler had that effect on everyone. It was one of the reasons they called her the Hill Witch.

They passed Textile Road where the bus driver backed up and turned around to avoid Adler Road which was unimproved. A familiar roar dragged Dabney's gaze from the Adler house to his own. His brother, Dennis, was leaving for school in his Mustang. The sleek green convertible charged out of the cul-de-sac, its tires screeching. Every kid on the bus turned to watch him. There was a chorus of *"Ooo!"* and *"Aaah!"* that made Dabney want to vomit. Dennis wouldn't even let him sit in the stupid car. He hated his brother so much it wasn't even funny. One day, him and their old man – who Dabney hated with equal venom – were going to wish they had been kinder to him. They all would, except Chris, and maybe Jeremy.

Dabney shook his head. *What is it with these guys anyway?* He glanced back at Jeremy, and then lowered his gaze. He felt very alone for an instant until he forced the feeling away. It returned when he looked into the driver's mirror and saw Jeremy smiling at him. He noticed Chris was looking at him, too, but his expression was different. It was curious like he was trying to answer a question. Dabney understood that. He was having the same difficulty. Their eyes met and locked in a searching gaze. They each could see something familiar in the other. When Chris smiled, Dabney thought he could get lost in his open friendliness. They both turned away at exactly the same time.

*　　*　　*

Craig glanced up from the pavement into Lyle's stern eyes. Max was standing next to the big man holding Craig's mountain bike. He had caught it before it hit the ground, too. In Craig's mind the words *stupid, stupid, stupid!* were repeating in an endless looping chorus. Luck wasn't with him today. Craig wondered what else could go wrong. He brushed his shirt off, Lyle assisting him some. He tried not to look at Max, but his eyes betrayed him. He glanced up and saw Max staring at him. His expression said it all.

I got you, Dougan. I know your secrets.

Craig cringed and looked away. Max didn't have him cornered, not yet. He could still get away before his life was ripped open. He needed to get back on his bike.

"Are you bleeding anywhere, Craig?" Lyle asked. The kid had hit him and sailed over the handlebars landing on the pavement.

Craig checked for scrapes. His left hand was a little raw but that was it. "I'm okay," he replied, clearing his throat. He looked up at the big man and asked, "What about you?"

"Me?" Lyle chuckled, helping Craig stand. "You couldn't hurt me if you rammed into me with a truck, boy."

Craig's face was even with Lyle's belly. "No, I guess not," he said, softly. He asked Max, "Can I have my bike?"

Max gave it to him. "Here. Are you okay?"

The question wasn't general and Craig knew it. From Lyle's expression, he knew what Max meant, too. His heart sank. It had started. Lyle had already called the cops on them once. Craig remembered that day. He had never been so frightened in his life as he was when Officer Robert Bigelow – a Lancaster resident – stepped into his house.

Craig reached for his bike. He mumbled, "I'm okay," and hopped on it.

"I want to talk to you…," Max began.

But Craig quickly peddled away. "I have to go," he said. "I have to get to school."

Max managed to say, "But I…," before Craig hit Wickett Avenue. "Oh, nuts," he mumbled, his hands on his hips. "What's it going to take, man?"

He wasn't asking anyone in particular, but Lyle answered him.

"It's going to take a lot, Max," he said. "You know, Jack was my best friend once."

Max looked at him stunned.

Lyle nodded. His eyebrows lowered. "What are you going to do about it?" he asked, his tone expectant.

Max looked at him, shook his head, and then took off after Craig.

"Hey, wait!" he called.

Craig looked back, saw Max running toward him, and peddled faster.

Ricardo stepped out of the front door in time to see Max tear across Wickett Avenue after Craig. Ricardo was about to follow. If something was up, he had to be there. Max was the epitome of the cool character. He didn't run after anyone unless something bad had happened.

Is he going to beat the crap out of Dougan? Ricardo wondered. *What could Craig have possibly done to make Max angry?*

Ricardo took a step in their direction prepared to run after them, but Lyle's bellow stopped him cold.

"Ricardo!"

Ricardo froze. He looked at the big man, confused. He gestured with his chin.

"Get on the bus, boy," Lyle said, motioning Ricardo to the bus stop. It was right in front of the garage.

Ricardo jogged over and asked, "What's going on?"

Lyle crossed his arms. "Craig needs to hear some things. Max is gonna say them to him."

*   *   *

Craig shot out into traffic causing motorists to screech to a halt.

A man in green scrubs blew his horn and cried, *"Watch where you're going, you idiot! Are you trying to get yourself killed!?"*

Max raced behind Craig. He leapt over a garbage can. His sneaker hit the sidewalk with a sound akin to the crack of the leather strap. Each time Max heard it, he moved faster, ran harder. He didn't know what he was going to do when he caught Craig, he just knew that he would. Something inside was pushing him. It was the beating he'd witnessed. He couldn't live with ignoring it.

They shot across Kelly Hardware's parking lot. Arthur Kelly was easing out of his white Lexus as Craig flew past him.

Arthur was startled and dropped his briefcase. "What in God's name…?" he managed, in a feminine manner.

Max almost slammed into him as he whizzed by.

"Jesus!" Arthur cried, holding his heart. His balding head flushed pink. "Are you trying to kill someone, Max!?"

They ignored him.

Arthur collected his briefcase and sashayed toward his store. "Kids," he grumbled, adjusting his glasses.

Craig raced around the building trying to go faster. He had to get to the trail and up the hill before Max caught him. He could lose him once he was inside the school. His life flashed before his eyes. It was a defining moment. He knew if Max caught him, nothing would never be the same again. He didn't know what scared him more, the shame of public exposure, or everything that would happen afterward. He knew he wasn't going to stop peddling. If God had finally heard him and was going to tear his life wide open, Craig decided he would rather the Lord stay deaf. He looked back to see that Max was only a few feet behind him.

Craig jumped the curb as he switched gears. He raced into the woodline. A small branch slapped the side of his face, but he ignored it. The trail began just past Kelly Hardware's lawn about six feet into the woods. It was very dry light brown dirt. Craig skidded kicking up some dust. The sudden shift in the terrain caught him off guard and he automatically slowed to compensate.

Max reached out and snagged Craig by the collar. Craig tried to pull away. Max dug in his feet and yanked backward. He pulled Craig off the seat and sent the two of them sprawling. Craig's shirt tore with a loud rip. His bike continued without him for a few feet, but then fell on its side at the base of the hill, its wheel spinning. Craig rolled over Max and sprang to his feet. His hands worked, his eyes filled with fear, but then he saw his shirt.

"Look what you did!" Craig cried. His face flushed as he held the ripped shirt out in front of him.

"You should've just stopped," Max panted. He was on his side on the ground wiping dirt from his lips. It tasted like the swamp behind Misty's Café.

"You should've left me alone!" Craig cried, storming over to his bike to make sure it wasn't damaged. He ripped his shirt off the rest of the way and fished inside his backpack for a replacement, the one that wasn't going to be used in gym class today.

Max looked at the bruises on Craig's back. They were thick, purple, and in half a dozen different spots. He gasped, "Holy Christ, Craig!" his voice shocked and dismayed. "Is that what he did to you?"

Craig froze, his hand touching the Lancaster High School gym shirt in his backpack under his books. The shirt came out as he turned. He looked at Max with a hatred in his eyes he never knew he possessed. He saw the expression of fear and pity on Max's face. It reached out and stabbed him in the chest. Craig fell to his knees as if someone had struck him. Before he knew what was happening, he was crying. They were long hard sobs, his tears running free as he clutched his shirt to his chest, vainly trying to cover up with it. He felt so ashamed. Guilt sucked the life out of him. Despair tore into his soul. For the first time in his life, Craig just wanted to die.

Max scooted over to him. He put his hand on Craig's shoulder and whispered, "It's okay, Craig," as Craig fell into him. He felt Craig's tears fall hot onto his wrist. He patted his shoulder, awkwardly. Craig gripped Max for dear life. Max dropped all his machismo and just held him. They slowly sat on the trail.

"My... *dad,* my...," Craig managed, but the words only made him cry harder.

Max looked into the clear blue sky. *Did it have to be like this?* he asked God. He shook his head, *No, it didn't.*

"Why didn't you... just *leave*... me alone?" Craig asked, trying to stifle his emotions.

Max stood and pulled him up, surprised at how heavy he was. He looked scrawny for his age, but under his clothes Craig was pretty solid.

"Because I can't, Craig," Max said, letting him go. He gripped him by the arms tighter than he'd wanted to, but then loosened up a little. "The rest of this stupid town might be able to ignore you, man, but I can't. Not after what I saw."

Craig sniffled. He wiped his eyes roughly with the backs of his hands. "So what are you going to do now?" he asked. "Ruin my life?"

"You call this a life?" Max asked, touching the bruises on Craig's back.

Craig winced and pulled away. He replied, "That's right, Max! It's my life!"

"It's not right, man," Max said. "Your dad..."

"I love my dad!" Craig exploded. It was so loud Max jumped. *"Leave him alone!"* He put on his gym shirt. He was crying again but fighting it harder this time. "You don't understand," he blubbered.

Max stood up and spun him around. "How am I supposed to understand this, Craig?" He pulled the shirt collar and pointed to the bruise on his shoulder blade.

"You're not!" Craig replied, slapping his hand away. "You can't! All you can do is murder my life! If that's what you're going to do, do it! Don't ask me to help you!"

"You'd rather live like this?" Max cried, lifting his shirt.

Craig snatched it back down. "What's other choice do I have, Max? Live without my dad?"

"Yes!"

"No!"

"I can't believe you!" Max exclaimed, throwing his hands in the air.

Craig crossed his arms. "Like you ever cared about me before now?"

"What?" Max asked, taken aback.

Craig nodded, "You heard me." His face wasn't showing any emotion at all now. "How long have I lived across the street from you? All my life?" He began pacing. Max's stunned gaze followed him. "In all that time, you're going to tell me you never knew what went on in my house?"

"Well, no, but…"

"But nothing, Max," Craig cut him off. "You don't know me, you don't talk to me, and now because you saw something you never should've seen in the first place and you feel guilty about it, you think you have the right to save me? I don't need your help, Max, and I don't need your pity."

Craig grabbed his bike and started pushing it up the hill. He stopped and looked back, his face blanketed in an expression of hurt.

"You could've just been my friend, you know. It's not like I have any."

Max watched as Craig resumed climbing the hill toward the high school. He cleared his throat, and asked, "You know who you remind me of?"

Craig stopped again and rolled his eyes. "Who?" he asked.

"Jeremy McKee," Max replied, smiling a little.

Craig laughed, "Oh, right! *Sure*, Max. Whatever!"

"I'm serious," Max insisted, jogging to catch up with him. "You remind me of Jeremy."

Craig pushed on. "Jeremy's probably the most popular kid in my grade, Max. I'm a loser. We have zero in common."

"Boy, you are so wrong it isn't even funny," Max whistled, helping Craig push. The bike was heavy. *Craig pushes this up the hill every day? Now I know why he's so buff!*

Craig said, "I don't see how I could be wrong. He's nice to me though. He talks to me a lot."

Max smiled. "I know. He talks about you all the time, too."

Craig was stunned. "He does?"

"Sure. He likes you."

Craig frowned. They were near the top of the hill. "Why would he like me?"

"You're a lot alike," Max said. "I think he knows that."

Craig paused before the crest. "Does his dad… you know? Is he like mine?"

"Does his dad kick the crap out of him?" Max asked.

Craig nodded. He seemed worried.

"No, man," Max replied. "It's not like that."

"Then what is it?" Craig asked. Max knew Jeremy a lot better than he did. If they had anything in common, Craig couldn't see it.

"I'm not sure," Max said. "It's like you both need somebody, you know? Like a real friend maybe?"

Craig snorted, "Jeremy has a billion friends."

"You think so?" Max asked, pushing the bike the rest of the way up the hill. "You might be surprised, Craig."

They stepped onto school grounds. Before Craig could say anything else, the first bell rang. They looked at each other knowingly. That bell meant they had five minutes to get to homeroom. Craig showed some visible relief. Max wet the corner of his shirttail with his tongue, and then wiped Craig's face with it. He was still a little flushed, but the tear streaks were gone. Max pushed the bike off the grass onto the road. They were on the left side of the school near the teacher's parking lot, but out in front where the buses unloaded. The bike rack was next to the building near the main entrance. Max stopped to let Ms. Adler's Mercedes pass. She scowled at him, and then glared at Craig with disgust. He felt a shiver go down his spine.

Man is she creepy, Craig thought.

Ms. Adler put her brakes on and looked back at him.

Craig moved quickly after Max, wiping his face some more with his own shirttail. They went over to the bike rack. Max pushed in the front tire. Craig slipped the lock on with a practiced motion. They walked together to where oceans of kids were filing into the school. They stood by the second bus in line, the one from Satchell Hill. Max knew this but Craig didn't. A few of the kids looked oddly at Craig. He could tell they were wondering:

Why's he standing there with Max Ramirez?

Craig decided not to rush to class. He was enjoying their confusion. He looked at Max who eyed the other kids expectantly. Dabney scowled at Craig as he disembarked but kept going without saying a word. Craig breathed a sigh of relief. Dabney was a jerk to him every chance he got. A hand fell on his shoulder and he spun around. It was Jeremy. Craig always thought his eyes were the deepest blue he had ever seen.

"Hey, Craig," Jeremy smiled. It was a warm smile. Craig decided he liked it. "What are you doing here?"

"I... uh...," Craig stuttered, but Max came to his rescue.

"He walked to school with me," Max said, and left it at that.

Craig looked at him and nodded. *Thank you,* he thought.

It was like Max heard him. "Yeah," he continued with a wide smile. "Craig's going to the campout with us tonight."

"What!?" Craig cried.

"Oh, cool," Jeremy said. "Do you want to tent with me? I got a two-man I've never used before." He whispered, "Please say yes, or I'm going to have to share it with Ian Sturgess."

"Sure he does, *don't* you, Craig?" Max replied.

"Well, I have to ask."

"No problem," Jeremy said. "We're meeting at the pond after school."

Craig's face turned white. He remembered the broken dishes and the mess at his house. "I have some chores to do first. I have to talk to my uncle, too. I'm supposed to work tonight."

"Dougan," Max groaned, "you work all the time. Your uncle can give you one night off, can't he?"

"I guess."

"You guess what?" Chris asked, stepping down from the bus. He looked at Craig puzzled. "Hey, Dougan."

Craig blushed.

"Dougan?" Matt asked. He was the last one off the bus. He saw Craig and smiled, "Well, look at this! Where did you come from?"

"He's with me," Jeremy said. He hoped Matt wouldn't say anything bad. Jeremy liked Craig.

"Whoa!" Matt exclaimed. "I surrender."

"C'mon, guys," Chris said, looking up at Lancaster High School. The building seemed huge today. "We'd better get going."

Ricardo ran up to them. He had seen everyone from his bus, the last one in the row. He looked at Craig, and then at his brother.

"Max?" Ricardo asked.

"What?" Max asked. He said to Craig, "See you later, man."

"C'mon, Craig," Jeremy said, walking toward the parking lot. Craig looked at him oddly, but then followed, his expression suddenly knowing.

Ricardo stood there looking lost. "Okay, what did I miss?" he asked, but no one answered. He walked quickly after his brother. "Max? *Max!*"

Jeremy continued around the side of the school. Craig walked with him in almost perfect rhythm. They moved across the lawn ignoring the *Keep Off the Grass* signs. The morning dew soaked into their sneakers. They felt a gnawing urgency to get to the parking lot as quickly as they could. They needed to do something although neither remembered what it was.

"We're going to be late to class," Craig said.

Jeremy shook his head. "She'll take care of it." He pointed toward the lot.

Craig saw Ms. Adler standing by her car with her arms crossed, an impatient look on her face.

"Indeed I will, Master McKee," she said, as they approached.

Jeremy wasn't sure how she had heard him from so far away. They walked up to her, their eyes glazing over, their expressions suddenly blank. Craig was fidgety and uncomfortable.

Ms. Adler turned to him, her eyes unnaturally bright. *"No need to fight me, Master Dougan,"* she whispered, her eyes narrowing. *"I need you to help me carry some things to my classroom."*

Her words came from all around them. They nodded in unison, and then stumbled like puppets whose strings had just been cut. Craig reached up and rubbed his temple. Jeremy shook his head feeling like he had just woken up.

"Whoa," he said, blinking.

"Yeah," Craig agreed. "Me, too."

"Come now," Ms. Adler said, walking to the back of her Mercedes. She opened the trunk. There were two cardboard boxes within. "We do not have all morning."

Jeremy grabbed one, Craig the other. They stood there looking at her. They had no idea how they came to be helping her.

"You are helping me because I am old," she replied to a question no one asked. "Does it matter how?"

"It's just weird," Craig said. "I don't remember…"

"Good!" Ms. Adler interrupted, slamming the trunk. Both boys jumped. *"You only need to remember that I asked you to help me yesterday."*

"Oh, right!" Jeremy exclaimed, a look of understanding on his face. Then he looked puzzled. "Craig? I…"

Craig struggled. "I'm not sure, I…"

Ms. Adler bent down and looked deep into his eyes. "You are strong, Craig," she remarked. Her expression darkened. "But I do not have time for strength. *You offered to help me yesterday."*

Craig smiled. "I guess I did. I'm sorry."

"Do not mention it," she replied, glaring at them as they walked together toward the school. She shook her head. *This bears watching,* she thought. *Together they are very strong. They each carry the missing pieces of the other. It is the formula for the perfect friendship. I wonder why they have not figured that out yet. It is the reason they are drawn to one another.*

Ms. Adler walked behind them watching the boys closely. She was six feet tall and stringy like she never ate anything, but Craig knew that she did. She got her food delivered from his Uncle Mike's market once a week. Lisa Gibbons usually brought it to her. Craig glanced back and she smiled. It was more like a grimace. Her gray-streaked hair was tied back in a bun. She had her glasses perched on the end of her nose. Her brown eyes never blinked. She looked like what the kids called her behind her back. She looked like a witch.

"Is this for the blood test?" Jeremy asked, nodding at the boxes as he reached the side door.

"Blood test?" Craig asked. *What does he mean?* he wondered, pulling on the door. It was locked. "It's locked," he said, tugging harder while balancing the box on his knee.

"No, it is not," Ms. Adler stated. She glared at the door handle. It made an audible click. "Try it again."

Craig yanked on it and almost fell over when it opened. He looked at Ms. Adler, queerly.

She strutted past him. "See?" she said.

Craig looked fearfully at Jeremy who only shrugged.

"Who cares, Craig? This box is heavy."

"What blood test are you talking about?" Craig asked, watching Ms. Adler get farther away. He suddenly liked that idea. *The farther away, the better.*

"My brother told me about it," Jeremy replied. "It's the last thing she makes you do. It's a blood sugar test. You prick your finger and…"

"Do come on!" Ms. Adler called from the stairwell. "School will be over before you make it to my class!"

Jeremy and Craig looked at each other. They shrugged and followed her wanting very much to be rid of her boxes and away from her. They could swear they heard her impatient words echoing inside their heads.

*   *   *

Chris stepped into the second-floor boys' room and closed the door. He gagged at the overwhelming pine smell from the urinal cakes. He stepped up to the first one in the row of four and unzipped his fly. He looked up at the ceiling as he peed. So far no one had said anything directly to him about the rumors Dan started. People only looked at him oddly, cupped hands covering whispered comments as he passed. They were talking about him and it was putting him on edge. He sensed a confrontation looming on the horizon. Chris felt it closing in on him.

Seeing Dabney at the bus stop should've been the harbinger of things to come, Chris thought. *I might've realized that if I'd kept my hormones under control. I can't figure out why Dabney's so attractive all of a sudden. There's no way he's gay, right? Why would he help spread rumors about me then? It's a pretty powerful story though and like any good rumor, it's making its way through the school like wildfire.*

It was especially prevalent among the girls. Many of them had considered him datable since middle school. Chris wasn't conceited. It was the truth. It seemed like an underground contest of a sort who would land Chris McKee first. Up until now, he had been tactfully able to avoid it. He used homework and his grades as an excuse, or he told them he worked too much. He said he liked them, but he didn't have the time to commit to a relationship. It wasn't fair to them if they dated and he didn't have any time to spend with them. He was thoroughly overscheduled. It was an excuse that had worked fine, only now there was another explanation. He could see it in their faces as soon as he walked into homeroom. This excuse was easier and it made more sense.

Of course Chris won't date us! He doesn't like girls! No wonder!

Chris cringed. There was no way to dispel the rumor now. He had two choices. He could lie about it. He would have to make a gesture to show he wasn't gay which meant dating someone. Chris shook his head looking down into the urinal. He aimed at the urinal cake.

I'm not going to do that. I'm not hiding behind a camouflage girl. Not only is it unfair to her, but it would also involve living the lie more than just telling it. That's not happening. I'm nobody's liar.

The alternative was dangerous. Lancaster was a small town. His revelation would not only damage his and Jeremy's reputations but possibly his parents' standing in the community. There were his friends to consider, too.

What will their parents think? Will I still be allowed to hang out with Derek or Ricardo if they learn the truth? Ricardo didn't say a word to me this morning. He didn't even look at me. If that's what Ricardo's going to be like, what about Derek? God, I hate this! Why is Ricardo so skeeved by the whole thing? We've spent two times twenty-dozen nights alone together in a tent!

The boys' room door opened. Chris cringed. He had hoped to be in and out before anyone else needed to use the facilities. He heard the unmistakable flick of a Bic lighter. The acrid scent of cigarette smoke hit his nostrils. Chris glanced over his shoulder. Two upperclassmen were standing behind him. He knew them. He also knew he was in serious trouble.

"We'll wait," Todd O'Connor said, nodding toward the empty urinals next to Chris.

Todd looked angry and disgusted. A Marlboro hung from the corner of his mouth. He was a stocky seventeen-year-old, five-foot-ten, with black hair cut short with a side part. He had angry brown eyes, huge hands, and a perpetually mean expression. He was wearing jeans, a jean jacket, and black Herman Survivors even though it was summer.

Frank Garrison was next to him. He looked stoned.

"Yeah," Frank laughed. His dark peach fuzz mustache trembled. He was five-eight, skinny but tone, with black eyebrows, brown hair to his shoulders, and light brown eyes. He had a mischievous smile and his teeth were stained with pot resin. His breath smelled like burned rope. He was also the hairiest teenager Chris had ever seen. "Can't be too careful nowadays with all the *fags* around here."

"Really," Todd said.

Chris worked with Todd at the farm. He had been Hiram's employee a lot longer than Chris. He didn't trust Todd and he didn't like him. He was a little too close to the farmer for comfort, and the farmer was… well, nevermind. Chris didn't want to think about that. He had enough problems right now without dredging that up. As far as Todd was concerned, the feeling was mutual. Chris' first confrontation from his new status as an out gay teenager was written all over Todd's face. Todd stepped toward him. Chris felt his breath on the back of his neck. It stank of stale cigarettes and pot.

"All the faggots around here," Todd whispered.

Chris shook off, tucked in, zipped up, squirmed around Todd, and went to the sinks. He washed his hands. His left leg was twitching. There was something in the air. He felt danger. He glanced down at the silver faucet. He saw Todd's grinning face in the reflection. He also saw Todd's fist raised, about to strike.

"No!" Chris cried, whirling around.

He shoved Todd with all of his might. Todd stumbled backward. He tripped over his feet, his black Herman Survivors scuffing the tiled floor. He fell into the first stall. His arm splashed down into a bowl someone had neglected to flush. His cigarette dropped from the corner of his mouth, but Todd hadn't noticed. He glared at his arm. The stench of old urine filled the air.

Frank pointed at him laughing even harder than before.

Todd looked up at Chris with death in his eyes. "McKee?" he asked, through gritted teeth.

Chris shrank back against the sink.

"You're not only a faggot, you're a dead faggot."

Todd shot forward and grabbed Chris by the shirt. He lifted him up and pulled him so they were face to face. The boys' room door opened and closed behind them. Todd ignored it. He didn't care if it was the principal. He drew back his fist, but when he went to throw the punch someone was holding his hand in a firm grip.

"O'Connor," Dennis Copeland smiled. He pulled Todd's arm back.

Dennis was the quarterback of the Lancaster High School football team. He was headed to college to play for UCONN. He was a senior who lifted weights regularly. He had the same milk chocolate hair color as Dabney, but darker eyes and no freckles. He was strong, handsome, and popular. He didn't use drugs and he didn't like people who did, especially if they picked on weaker kids.

"This just isn't your lucky day," Dennis said.

Todd opened his mouth to protest, but Dennis closed it with a solid punch to the jaw. Todd flew back into Frank who pinwheeled across the bathroom. He hit his head on the metal frame of the small prison-like window. There was a loud crack and Frank fell to the floor. Todd shook off the blow and held his fists at the ready. Dennis was on top of him in an instant. He grabbed Todd by the collar and slammed him against the last stall. Frank got up, stumbled to the door, and ran away.

"I guess it's just you and me, tough guy," Dennis said, pulling Todd's collar tighter. "How does it feel, loser?"

"Dude!" Todd insisted, motioning his head toward Chris. "He's a fag, man!"

"Yeah," Dennis replied, punching Todd in the stomach. He collapsed on the floor gasping for breath. "I heard about that."

Todd rolled over on the wet bathroom floor. He got to his feet wiping his mouth with his hand. He stared at the blood.

Dennis stood with his fists out ready to hit him again.

"Do you want to bleed some more?" Dennis asked, stepping forward.

Todd eased back toward the door. He shook his head, but then glared at Chris.

"You're dead meat, McKee!" he spat, balling up his fists. "You queer!"

"I don't think so," Dennis said, moving between them. He shoved Todd into the door. "You touch him and I'll break your face, got it?"

Todd threw the door open and stormed out. *"Screw you, Copeland!"*

The sound of his boots stomping down the nearby stairwell carried into the bathroom. The clank of metal followed it as Todd kicked open the outside door. He'd had enough school for today.

Chris leaned against the sink and let out a sigh of relief.

Dennis asked, "Are you okay, Chris?" genuinely concerned.

"Yeah, thanks," Chris replied, a little shaken.

Things were happening too fast. He was in awe of Dennis. He was wearing his blue and white letterman jacket from football. He was an Adonis with a friendly handsome face and a pleasant manner.

"Why did you help me?" Chris asked.

Dennis stepped over to the urinal to tend to the reason he had entered the boys' room in the first place. "Well, I could say it's because I can't stand punks like O'Connor," he replied, taking his leak.

Chris didn't look at him. He made a point not to.

"I wouldn't be lying. Not really."

"Not really?"

Dennis finished and moved to the sink. "Look, Chris," he said, washing his hands, "I heard what they're saying about you, and you know what?"

"What?" Chris asked. He'd never talked to Dennis before. Dennis was an unreachable God to the underclassmen.

"I think you have guts coming out." He reached for a paper towel. "You could've lied about it."

"Can't," Chris shrugged. "I don't want to live a lie."

Dennis nodded. "Yeah, you've got guts. I've never been that brave."

He leaned over and kissed Chris lightly on the cheek. It was a friendly kiss, not a romantic one, but it conveyed an unmistakable message.

Chris gasped. His cheek felt charged with electricity. "You?" he whispered.

Dennis held his finger to his lips. "Shh!" he said, and smiled. "You're not the only one, Chris." He handed him his Copeland Industries business card. It said: *Dennis Arthur Copeland, Supervisor*. It had his office, home, and cell phone numbers on the bottom. His email address was written on the back. "You call me if anyone bothers you. I promise, no one from school is going to lay a hand on you. I'm putting the word out, even after graduation. I'm only going to UCONN."

Chris held his hand against his cheek. "You…? *You're…!?*"

"Gay?" Dennis asked, finishing his sentence for him. He shrugged his shoulders. "So? It's one in ten right? Someone has to be. Of course, I don't have your guts. Keep a lid on it, will you? My dad would flip if he found out."

"Um… sure, I swear."

Dennis walked toward the bathroom door.

"Dennis?"

"Huh?" He stopped, the door half open.

"Thanks," Chris said. He folded his hands in front of him. "I mean it. I'm glad you're not like your brother." He thought, *Besides being cute to death. What is it with Copelands today? Dennis is gay!? Oh my God, could Dabney be, too? He's so cute, I mean, seriously. Is he?*

Dennis replied, "Yeah, Dabney's one of a kind. Just wait until he hears you and I are friends now. He's going to have a cow." He walked out. "Catch you later, Chris." He stuck his head back in. "You can call me Denny. Only my parents and my brother call me Dennis."

"Denny?" Chris asked, but it was too late. He was gone.

Chris walked over to the window. He had to get up on his toes to look outside. He could see Todd walking down Lancaster Hill Road toward Wickett Avenue. He shuddered. He wondered what would happen the next time he had to go to the farm.

Will Todd be waiting for me?

Chris had a gnawing feeling this wasn't over, not by a long shot.

*　　*　　*

Jack Dougan was at the CTWorks Office in Manchester near the end of a very long line. He was hungover. His foot throbbed with a dull ache. His anger was growing as he waited to file for an extension of his unemployment benefits. An hour had already passed. He swore the clock only moved when he looked at it.

These people are messing with me, Jack thought. Sweat beaded up on his forehead. *In a minute, I'm going to show them why no one keeps me waiting, not with the morning I'm having.*

It started at ten o'clock. Jack awoke from the same dream that had plagued him for years. He was bathed in sweat and screaming his head off. He scanned his bedroom like a crazy man, his heart racing, his blood thumping through his temples. He had no idea where he was. He leapt off the bed, hands groping, growling like a wild animal.

"Show yourselves!" Jack cried. *They're here! I can smell them!*

The fetid stench of undead zombie soldiers assaulted his nostrils.

Jack wanted to rip them apart with his bare hands, but he paused when he didn't feel the hot blood-soaked sand under his feet anymore. It was only his oval throw rug with the rainbow colors and the black border.

I'm home, Jack thought. *I'm in my room.*

The realization tore through him. He fell to the floor and curled into a fetal position. He cried, but he hardly noticed. His mind was drowning in pain and shame, paranoia and hatred, death, anxiety, guilt, and loss, the worst emotion of all. It tore chunks out of his soul, the pieces replaced by a hatred of everything that lived including himself.

Jack heard the VA counselor in his memory. "These are symptoms of PTSD, PFC Dougan," he said, his tone condescending. Jack thought the counselor might have been nineteen, but that was pushing it. "You need to be under observation. You need medication."

Pills? Jack thought. His face flushed as his anger grew. *Pump me up with drugs until I can't even remember my name?* He slammed his fist on the carpet. *No! That's not what I want!*

Jack wanted to be back at that no-named dune in Afghanistan lying dead with his buddies.

It's my fault! I failed them!

"I'm such... a loser," Jack whispered, under his breath. The unemployment line moved one person forward. He clenched his fists and closed his eyes. He thought, *It wasn't always that way, was it? I was human once, a good son, until that bastard... until Hiram Milliken. God, I don't want to think about him, not now... please?* He drew in a deep breath and let it whoosh out. *Dad, Jesus, do you know how much he hurt me?*

Jack was twelve when the world came crashing down on him. His father, Wade Dougan, had been the epitome of the strong Irish family man. He was sitting with his boys and their mother at the dining room table one afternoon. Nancy was troubled. Jack could see the pain in his parents' eyes. When Wade spoke to them, Jack could feel his shame. Wade was the best father a kid could have. Jack would've done anything to never see that look on his face again.

"I called ye here, lads, for what I've t' say involves th' whole family," Wade said, his thick Irish drawl full of quiet despair. "Jackie more'n anyone."

"What's wrong, daddy?" Mike asked.

Nancy pulled him into her lap. She hugged him, but told him to hush up and listen to his father.

"Just name it, dad," Jack said. He laid his hand on his father's on top of the table. His green eyes shone. "What's going on?"

"Ah, lad," Wade whispered. He patted his son's hand. "I'm afraid I have t' ask ye t' grow up afore your time."

Jack understood instantly. He had overheard his parents many times in the last year. They were in financial trouble. His father's salary wasn't cutting it anymore and they were in danger of losing their home. His mother said she would find a job. Everyone knew it was a two income world, but Wade vehemently refused. His stubborn pride wouldn't bear his wife toiling anywhere other than in the home he provided, and he refused to seek out any public assistance. Nancy knew better than to push him, but she also knew his intention to work a second job would end in disaster. His heart was too weak. Wade wasn't a young man anymore. Neither of them were, and Nancy was fifteen years younger than him. She was thirty when she had Jack. It was a stalemate, but then a different solution presented itself. She wasn't going to let her husband refuse this one.

Nancy had been in the market talking to the girl at the register. Hiram Milliken was standing behind her in line. He was a handsome young man who owned the farm not far from their house. He'd inherited it when his father passed away. He heard Nancy speaking of her husband's plans to work more. She lamented Wade taking a part-time job, but they were out of options. They needed a second income. She wished her husband would let her take a job, or that Jack was old enough to help.

"He'll work himself into an early grave, Lois," Nancy said, handing her coupons to the cashier. "Mark me words."

"Excuse me, Mrs. Dougan?" Hiram asked. His neatly combed dark brown hair accented his honest and open light blue eyes. "Did you say you had a boy who needed a job?"

Nancy stepped back, her hand to her chest. She recognized Hiram, of course. There wasn't a person in town who hadn't heard about the unfortunate young man. Hiram's father, Caleb, had accidentally drowned in the manure pit at the farm, a horrible death. A passing policeman found him. Hiram had been at school when it happened. His mother had died some years earlier, kicked in the head by an ornery cow right in front of him. She bled to death in his arms. Nancy had represented her family at both funerals. Her heart went out to Hiram as she watched the tears running down his cheeks.

"Hiram Milliken!" Nancy cried. "Ye scared th' daylights out o' me!"

Hiram took Nancy's hand. "My apologies, dear lady," he said. "I was only trying to be of service."

"Apology accepted," Nancy replied.

She pulled the last of her groceries out of the carriage. She smiled when Hiram helped her. "I only wish ye could," she sighed. "Times are a lot tougher than they used t' be."

"That's a given, Mrs. Dougan," Hiram said. "Since my father passed away, I've gone through more employees than I can count. So many people out of work, but all I can offer is minimum wage. They leave my employ when they find higher pay. Seems the trend. People want less work for more money."

"Aye, lad. Wade's a supervisor at th' battery mill. He complains similarly about his employees. 'Tis th' shame of it."

"I'm alone at the moment," Hiram said. "My last boy, Peter, left for military school. I've been trying to do everything myself. It's not easy."

"I'll wager it isn't," Nancy said. Her eyes lit up. "Ye were askin' about me boy?"

Hiram replied, "I was." He smiled. "I was going to put an ad in the paper today. Since Peter left, I've had no luck with adults. I was hoping a new boy might prove a more loyal employee."

"Well, Jackie's loyal," she said. "He's a hard worker, too. 'Tis a shame he's but twelve years old."

"Oh?" Hiram asked. "Why is that?"

Nancy stared at him.

Lois bagged the groceries. Hiram moved up with his. Nancy paid for hers, pushed her carriage by the window, and then returned to help him.

"Surely, Mr. Milliken…," Nancy began, laying his orange juice on the conveyer belt.

"Call me Hiram," he interrupted. "Every time I hear Mr. Milliken I start looking for my father. It's spooky."

"Surely, Hiram," Nancy continued, "a boy Jackie's age wouldn't be that much help t' ye."

"On the contrary, Mrs. Dougan…"

"Nancy."

Hiram nodded. "I started working when I was eight. Is Jack a sturdy boy?"

"Fit as a fiddle."

"Can he work whenever he's needed?"

"That he can," Nancy replied. She thought, *At minimum wage, a full-time job would have t' take th' place o' school. It'll be worth it if'n it keeps Wade from takin' another job. I can teach Jack at home. 'Tis sad it's come t' this, but it would be worse if'n Wade works himself into th' ground.* She crossed her fingers. *Lord, I can't lose me husband. I love him so.*

"Then," Hiram concluded, paying Lois and placing his bags into the carriage, "Jack's exactly what I'm looking for."

Nancy carried the offer of work home. Wade was against it. He had never dreamed Jack could find work when he entertained the idea. Nancy put her foot down then. She let Wade know her responsibility to care for the family wasn't limited to the children and rattling pots and pans. He wasn't working a second job. He had two choices: let Jack take the job, or let her find one.

Nancy proclaimed, "I'll not allow ye t' work yourself into an early grave!"

Wade's anger rose, but he knew she wasn't going to back down. "Ye drive a hard bargain woman. 'Tis not fair to th' boy, ye know."

"Oh?" Nancy asked, slamming a can of corn beef onto the countertop. "Tell me just what in life is fair?"

Wade only shook his head.

Jack listened as his father described the situation. The mortgage was behind and the taxes needed to be paid. Wade's wages weren't keeping up with the rising costs of everything. Jack understood his responsibilities as the oldest son. He agreed with his mother. Working on the farm would be tough, early mornings and late nights. School was out of the question for the time being. Nancy said she would homeschool him. Jack was glad to see an upside to this. He hated school. He didn't look forward to being bussed out of town for high school like his friend Lyle Gibbons would be next year. Jack liked animals, too, even cows.

"Ye don't have t' do this, Jackie," Wade said. "Despite your mother's crowin', th' choice is yours."

"I'll do it, dad," Jack replied.

He set his jaw in a manner that made Wade's eyes tear. There was no doubt Jack was on the road to manhood. He shook his son's hand.

Jack pushed the memory away as the unemployment line moved up another person.

I lost everything that day, Jack shivered. *Everything that mattered. Hiram picked me up the next morning. We barely made it past milking before… Jesus, I can't stand it.* He pinched the bridge of his nose. *I couldn't tell dad. I was so ashamed…*

The line moved again, but Jack didn't.

A short bald man behind him poked him in the back. "Hey, buddy! Do you want to move up with the line, or take a seat somewhere? I haven't got all…"

Jack whirled around and snatched the man's finger in his fist. He leaned over, twisting it, breathing whiskey halitosis into the stunned man's face. His eyes burned.

"Touch me again," Jack whispered, "and I'll kill you, right here, right now." He squeezed the man's finger hard before he released it.

The man shook it, backed away, and disappeared out the door. He didn't come back.

Jack looked up at the clock. *Two hours in this line, but at least I'm only three people from the counter.*

He slipped back into his memories. It was a long slide down a greasy slope. Jack didn't want to go. His thoughts would lead him from the farm to his military service. He didn't want to think about that any more than being molested by Hiram.

Afghanistan was as much a hell on Earth as the farm. Six years of my life I sacrificed to that son-of-a-bitch followed by four in the Army. I didn't go in the military first though. It was Lyle. He's the one who put the idea of the service in my head.

Lyle Gibbons had been Jack's best friend when they were kids. They palled around together before Mike was born and Jack began working on the farm. They lost touch, only occasionally running into each other in town.

Jack had been on his way to the supply depot in Mansfield for grain one afternoon. Hiram allowed him to take the truck even though he didn't have his driver's license. Jack spotted a massive banner over Gibbons' Garage on his way out of town.

It read: *Good luck, Lyle! Come home safe! Semper Fi!*

Jack pulled into the garage and stared up at the sign wondering what was going on with his buddy. A burly muscular young man appeared at his window. Jack was about to say something, but his jaw dropped open instead. This colossal fellow was Lyle. Jack could hardly believe it.

"Holy cow!" Jack exclaimed. "When did you get so big?"

Lyle laughed. "Well, Dougan, if you'd bothered to stop by once in a while in the last *five* years, you wouldn't have to ask! Besides, you're pretty tall yourself."

Jack had come into his own at sixteen. He grew like a weed reaching six-one in a year. He pointed at the sign and asked why Lyle needed luck.

A grim sincerity replaced Lyle's smile. "Afghanistan, buddy," he replied. "I enlisted in the Marines."

Jack shook Lyle's hand. He said he would be eighteen in a year. Maybe he would enlist, too.

"Hey!" Lyle proclaimed, slapping Jack on the shoulder. "Maybe I'll see you over there."

Jack said he might.

Carl Gibbons bellowed, *"Lyle!"*

Lyle jogged toward the garage. He waved back wishing Jack luck.

Jack watched every newscast and read every article having anything to do with Afghanistan after that. When he turned eighteen, he told Hiram about his plans to enlist in the Army. They had a heated discussion about it, but Jack remained firm. He was a man now and wasn't going to be bullied by his abuser any longer. Jack had endured years of Hiram's perversion. During that time, he had driven away other boys who had come to the farm looking for work. They didn't understand, but it was for their own good. Jack even beat up Mike once when he showed up at the farm to bring him some birthday cake. Images of Hiram doing to Mike what had been done to him flooded his mind. It was the only time Jack had ever raised a hand to his brother.

Wade returned the favor out in the woodshed when Jack wouldn't explain why he'd done it. How could he? How could Jack tell his father what had been going on all those years? Wade would die if he learned the truth! That's what Hiram had always told him. If learning the truth didn't kill his father, the extra work he would throw himself into to make up for Jack's lost income certainly would. Sacrificing himself was the only answer. He endured the shame of his father's disappointment to save his brother from a monster.

Jack had watched Hiram like a hawk, but as his enlistment day approached his vigilance failed. He stopped by the farm on his day off shortly after his eighteenth birthday to tell Hiram he had met with a recruiter. He entered the Victorian and walked in on Hiram with Arthur Kelly, the eleven-year-old son of the hardware store owner. They hadn't seen him. Jack threw his hands over his mouth and backed out. He ran away in shock, grief-stricken, traumatized, and guilt-ridden. There would be more victims, too. Maybe there already had been. He hadn't been guarding the farm twenty-four hours a day. Jack felt responsible for every one of them and he couldn't do a thing about it. His father was weaker than ever.

I ran away, Jack thought, shaking off the memory and forcibly shoving the images away. Finally, he was next in line at the counter. *I enlisted that day, got a train ticket to Georgia, and waited in a motel until I started basic training. I couldn't face my family. I was terrified of what I would see in my father's eyes. The years of abuse I suffered at Hiram's hands tore me apart, but not turning him in cost another boy his innocence. My fault, it was all my fault. Was that price worth saving dad's life? Dad wouldn't have thought so. Other boys followed after I left. Hugh Kreeger, Donald Barry... that day at the town meeting about the land for the schools?*

Jack clenched his fists. He squeezed his eyes shut trying to keep from screaming. He wanted to scream. He wanted to scream forever and never stop screaming.

They didn't say anything. None of us did even at the risk of the middle school being built near the farm and all of those kids in that son-of-a-bitch's reach. The way they glared at me, like they wanted me to speak up first. They knew Hiram had me before them. I could see it in their eyes. They blamed me for not turning him in. Peter Rollins was there, too. He had worked for Hiram before me. He was a victim, too, I'm sure. Why hadn't he said anything? If he had, Hiram would've been in jail and I would never have been hurt. None of us would've! I blamed him just like the others were blaming me!

Jack's hand shook. The liquor he drank when he woke up was wearing off, but it wasn't only that. Memories of the desert were in his head now. Without the liquor to make them go away, he would soon be overwhelmed.

Dale, Jack thought, remembering his nightmare. *God, Dale, I'm so sorry I didn't waste the bastard.*

Jack felt his memories dragging him away as his body inched closer to the counter. It was Bagram Airfield in Afghanistan. Dale Kerrigan had been the only friend Jack ever had besides Lyle Gibbons.

"What's your problem, PFC Dougan?" Kerrigan asked.

Dale slapped Jack on the shoulder. He was from Wisconsin. They had gone through basic training together. They shipped out for Afghanistan on the same day, were assigned to the same company, the same platoon, and then the same squad. Dale was an open-minded smiling individual whose cheeriness often angered the moody Jack. For some reason, Dale liked him. He stuck to Jack like glue, determined to pull him out of his shell. His persistence paid off. Jack opened a tiny crack in the wall he'd built and dared to allow a friend in.

"Back off, Kerrigan," Jack grumbled. He was wiping down his weapon.

"You miserable prick!" Dale exclaimed.

In the time they served together, they had killed more insurgents and walked away from more scrapes than anyone in their unit besides their platoon leader. Death came to someone every time they went into the desert, but never to them. Jack found killing didn't bother him after putting a bullet into his first Taliban. He had watched the soldier's skull open up like an overripe melon.

Dead bodies didn't bother him either even after a battle when blood soaked the sand and the heat made the corpses swell. The reek of death turned even the most seasoned soldier's stomach, but Jack waded through bodies without breaking a sweat. If they found an insurgent hiding under the dead or feigning death, Jack would coolly remove his bayonet and cut his throat. Dale was a different story. Where Jack was cold and unfeeling about killing, Dale killed with glee. He let out whoops of laughter each time he wasted one of them. Man, woman, child, Dale didn't care. He was determined to destroy the insurgents alone if necessary.

Their platoon leader appeared before them. He handed a letter to Jack who recognized the handwriting immediately. It belonged to his mother. Jack's color faded. Dale snapped to attention surprised Jack didn't do the same. Lt. Sweetwater, Dale, and Jack were the only troops from their original platoon still alive. The lieutenant, a West Point graduate, was the best combat leader a soldier could want. It paid to keep him happy.

"At ease, Kerrigan," Lt. Sweetwater ordered. "Bad news, Dougan? I can't remember you ever getting a letter from home."

"I'm... not sure, sir," Jack quietly replied, staring at the envelope.

"Well, it's the night for it," Sweetwater said. "Find me if you need me, Jack. We've been through some crap." He looked at Dale. "You take care of him, Kerrigan. That's an order. You're the closest thing Dougan's got to a friend."

"Yes, sir," Dale said, laying his hand on Jack's shoulder. "Dougan will be fine with me around."

"Make sure. I've got bad news for you boys."

"Are we going back out, sir?" Jack asked, sounding far away.

"Before first light," Lt. Sweetwater replied. "Be sharp. It's going to be hot. I'll find the others, although I don't know why we need those limp dicks. I'd take the three of us alone if it were up to me." He looked around. "Where the hell are my squad leaders? My platoon sergeant is missing, too. This is his job."

Jack held the envelope. He didn't want to open it. He had run out on them. He hadn't even called them before he left. They knew where he was, he assumed, since his most of his pay was being sent home every month.

Jack lived for regaining Wade's respect. He considered every moment he spent in the desert penance for what had happened. Jack had come here to purge his guilt and shame, to do something brave in his father's eyes. He opened the envelope and read the single page it contained. Everything he had hoped for came to a shattering end once again.

Jack dropped the letter and slowly walked away. Dale called to him, but Jack didn't answer. He was about to follow when he snatched up the letter and read it.

August 8ᵗʰ

Dear Son,

It's with a heavy heart I write these words knowing the pain they will cause you, but I believe it would be crueler to wait. I know of no other way than to be straightforward, although I wish I could be there with you. I'm sorry, son. Your father has passed away.

The day you disappeared, he combed the state searching for you. When he couldn't find you, he assumed the blame for your lost childhood. For weeks he couldn't sleep nor eat praying you would call so he could beg your forgiveness, as I must do now. I should have stood my ground and took a job myself. I realize now it was too much of a burden to place on a child.

When your checks began to arrive, he raved about your courage and how proud he was that you had chosen to serve your country. He was glued to every newscast. The more he learned about the Taliban, Al-Qaeda, and their atrocities, the more he feared for your safety. The worry took its toll on your father's health. As time went by, his doctor pressed him with increasing urgency to take it easy. He wanted him to stop working altogether and have surgery, but he refused. Doing so meant being laid up for months. Even though Mike volunteered to take your place at the farm – and although Hiram was perfectly willing, and indeed eager, to let Mike work for him – your father refused to allow another son to sacrifice his childhood.

He had his first heart attack two months ago. From that moment, once your father regained consciousness and came home, he spent his days in front of the television hoping to catch a glimpse of you on the news. I took over his position at the mill by the grace of Garfield Copeland who considered your father a personal friend. He ordered his son Jerry to train me in everything I needed to know to be a supervisor. I have to admit, Jerry is a young man who knows his business. There isn't a job he can't do in the mill despite being barely out of his teens, but it's no surprise. Charlie O'Connor, who works in production, told me Jerry's been working at the mill since he was a boy, learning the family business. I think you'd like him. The two of you are a lot alike – hardworking, determined, and loyal to family.

I was so busy training, I couldn't find the time to contact you although it had been my intention. To my eternal shame, I failed before your father's second and final attack. He was writing to you at the time, but he only completed a single line. I've kept it here for you when you return. It said simply: "I'm sorry, son, and I love you." I hope you can find it in your heart to forgive us, Jackie. Mike misses you terribly, but he's proud of you. Never forget that. Your father was, too, as am I.

Please be careful. We've lost too much already.

With love,
Mother

Dale caught up with Jack on the road outside the airbase. Tears were running down Jack's cheeks. He stared forward silently crying. Dale walked with him until they were away from the other troops. They sat on the sand where Jack mumbled to him his entire life story, all of the ugliest details included. Dale's anger grew with each word. Jack told him everything about Hiram and what the farmer had done to him. He told him how he felt the day his father whipped him after he had beaten up his little brother for coming to the farm, and his shame at walking in on Hiram with Arthur Kelly that drove him to run away.

He hadn't stopped the farmer when he had a chance, and Hiram had taken another boy into his nightmare. He should never have left the farm. He should've watched Hiram closer. He begged Dale to tell him his father forgave him now that he surely knew Jack's shame. He asked Dale's forgiveness for what he had done to his family, and how he broke his father's heart by leaving. Jack ended his confession and cried once more.

Dale put his arm across Jack's shoulder. "I swear to God," he said. "When we leave here, we're going back to Lancaster, and we're going to bury that scumbag. I swear to God we will."

It was a promise Dale couldn't keep. He died near the end of their fourth tour in the hottest fighting they had seen. A mortar blew him apart. Jack ran away with his remains toward the medics at the rear, ignoring Lt. Sweetwater's commands to come back. Taliban fighters swarmed through Jack's position and overran the platoon. The Taliban were wiped out by the airstrike Lt. Sweetwater called in just before he died. Jack stayed in the brush cradling his friend's remains. No one survived to tell that he had run away. They said he was a hero and discharged him for PTSD.

Some hero, Jack thought, the memory fading to black.

He walked up to the counter and placed his forms in front of the woman at the computer. He was deflated now and said nothing as she punched up his file. The alcohol had worn off. The ache in his foot had become a sharp stabbing rip. This morning when he realized he was going to be late for unemployment, he grabbed some clothes, dashed into the hallway, and stepped on a piece of a broken dish. Jack gasped. He held his foot, a deep cut bleeding onto the floor. He glared at it. His face darkened, and then twisted.

"Craig!"

Jack shifted his weight to take the pressure off the foot. *He was supposed to clean up the mess before he left for school!* He looked down at his throbbing foot. *If he'd put the dishes away like he was supposed to, this never would have happened. God, is he going to pay.*

"He's going to pay," Jack mumbled.

"Excuse me?" the unemployment clerk asked.

Jack shook his head. He told her it was nothing.

"You're here to file for another extension of benefits?" she asked.

"And for the last check of my previous claim," Jack said, pinching the bridge of his nose. His head was throbbing. He needed to get to the bottle he had stashed under the front seat of his Monte Carlo.

"Well, I can help you with your final check," the woman said. "Unfortunately, there's no longer an additional extension program to offer you. The President did away with that program a while ago."

Jack's stomach churned as his face flushed with fury.

*   *   *

"Uh… Ms. Adler?" Matt asked. He was in the aisle seat at the black lab table on the right side of the room, in the front row.

Each of the ten rows had two rectangular lab tables with sinks in the middle and three stools. There was a natural gas valve for connecting Bunsen burners in front of each stool. The narrow aisle between the tables had worn tiles from years of Ms. Adler's pacing while she lectured. There was a plethora of lab equipment on shelves around the room, microscopes, diagrams and models of the human body, and dissection pans from when they dissected pig fetuses…

Jason Carlander threw up on Andrea Lee's shoes that day, Matt thought, fighting not to laugh out loud. *Omg, it was hilarious!*

… as well as beakers, Erlenmeyer flasks, tubes, a real human skeleton, and chemicals. There was a poster hanging on the whiteboard behind Ms. Adler's desk – at the head of the class, in the center, facing them – of a DNA strand. Curiously, it displayed an additional branch jutting out from the top of the helix. The classroom smelled of bleach and formaldehyde.

Matt cautiously raised his hand. "You're not serious about this, are you?"

Ms. Adler closed her eyes behind her spectacles. Her hair bun seemed to tighten. *Is it the same every year?* she wondered. *Is it harder?*

She didn't know anymore. The years bled into each other. The children were faceless, nameless entities. She taught ninth grade Science so she could observe her subjects and get to *this* point, *this* test, on *this* day, the last day of the school year.

Is each generation destined to be more difficult than the last?

Ms. Adler opened her eyes. She sent Matt a look that made him swallow hard. There were times she regretted her decision to teach, times like this in particular.

"What part of my instructions did you not understand, Master Gardner?" Ms. Adler asked. "My B and C group classes had no trouble."

"Uh…," Matt struggled. He paused when Ricardo, sitting behind him, snickered. "Shove it, Ramirez!" he whispered, out of the corner of his mouth.

Ricardo snorted.

Dabney said, "Like it's Ricardo's fault you're a moron?"

"Dabney?" Ricardo asked. He was across the aisle from him. "Shut up before I crack you one in the mouth."

Jeremy was behind Ricardo next to Craig. Ricardo was serious. Jeremy could tell by his tone of voice.

"As if!" Dabney cried. He pushed his hair out of his eyes. "Like you have the nuts? My family owns Lancaster. You'd better remember that."

Ricardo clenched his fists.

Ms. Adler firmly tapped the top of her desk with the tip of her pointer. There were only twenty-five minutes left before the bell rang and she released her class on Lancaster for their summer vacation. She had a final task for them. This was infinitely more important than posturing.

"If you gentlemen are through?" Ms. Adler asked, glaring at Dabney. She ignored Ricardo altogether.

Dabney lowered his gaze from her unblinking stare. He wasn't sure why she disliked him so much, but everyone else did, so why not? It wasn't like Dabney cared.

I don't and that's all there is to it. Really. I don't. No fooling.

He glanced at Jeremy.

Jeremy returned a sympathetic expression.

Dabney looked away. He thought, *Why does he have to be so understanding? C'mon, I can hate him. I can! I… oh, nuts…*

Ms. Adler said, "Then let us begin."

She stood, adjusted her skirt, and moved in front of her desk. Her face was tight and drawn. She crossed her arms over her breasts and looked down at Matt who cringed.

"Yes, Master Gardner," she said, "I am serious, half of your final grade serious."

A collective gasp passed through the room.

"Half?" they cried.

Of the fifteen students in her class, only Brenda Pinkwell, the pudgy girl in the back row next to Andrea Lee, said nothing. Ms. Adler scowled reading her thoughts. Brenda had been building up the courage to say that no teacher could make her do what she didn't want to do.

Ms. Adler spoke first, "This is my class, Miss Pinkwell. I can do what I wish. And yes, I can make you."

"How did you know I…?" Brenda began.

Duh! Jeremy thought.

Craig looked at him. He nodded.

They don't call Ms. Adler 'The Hill Witch' for nothing, they thought.

"Any more questions?"

The room was silent.

Ms. Adler reached for her clipboard. It held a single sheet of paper broken into two columns: *Name* and *Reading*. She set it down next to a red Hazardous Materials Container labeled *Blood Products*.

She turned back to her class. "Fine then. Who is first?"

Craig squirmed when nobody volunteered. *What's wrong with everyone?* he wondered. He bit his lower lip. *Didn't we spend the last two weeks studying Diabetes? What's so hard about taking a blood sugar test? All we have to do is prick our fingers with the lancet, put a drop of blood on the stick, and slide it into the reader. How hard is that? Is it the pain? Are they afraid it will hurt? What's a needle prick compared to…?*

Craig shook his head as this morning's events intruded into his thoughts. He forced the memory away…

… the sound of the falling leather belt as it lashed against his back and buttocks, the pain of each strike… and the breath, his father's horrid breath, the stench of bourbon that was so familiar…

"No!" Craig cried, jumping up from his stool.

He gasped his face flushing. Everyone was staring at him. The stares melted into laughter. He blushed even more. They were laughing at him *again*. He'd made a fool of himself *again*.

No, Craig thought. *Not everyone.*

Craig's hazel eyes fell on the only person who wasn't laughing, the one who never did. Sympathy was the only emotion in his intense blue eyes.

Jeremy's always like that, isn't he?

"Are you volunteering to go first, Master Dougan?" Ms. Adler asked. She slid her spectacles down to the end of her nose and looked over them. "Or is this some new dance you would like to teach the rest of the class?"

Their laughter erupted once more.

Craig's face shone like a stoplight. He reached down, picked up his empty backpack, and slung it over his shoulder. He slipped through the tables to the front of the room and stood there looking at the floor.

Jeremy felt Craig's isolation, got up, and fell in next to him. He leaned over and whispered, "Forget them, Craig. They're idiots."

Jeremy took the test first. He signed his name on the line marked number one. Craig noticed Jeremy was left handed. He wondered why he had never realized that before. Jeremy put a drop of his blood on the stick and slid it into the reader.

Ms. Adler looked down at the result, disinterested. "Normal."

She pointed to the box next to his signature. Jeremy wrote in his result. Craig looked at it curiously and took the test, too. He was likewise normal. He filled in his reading. To their mutual surprise, Ms. Adler dismissed them. She deposited their numbered sticks into the Hazardous Materials Container.

"But...," Jeremy said, "... class isn't over for another twenty minutes, Ms. Adler."

"You are the dense one in your family, Master McKee?" Ms. Adler asked. "If I remember correctly, your brother took the test first last year, too. Did you know I barely finished saying, *'You may go'* before he was out the door and down the hall?"

Jeremy and Craig took off slamming the door behind them. Dabney dashed to the front of the room as everyone else shoved to get in line.

"Relax, children," Ms. Adler said. "You will all have the opportunity to bleed for me before this is over." Her smile was cold. She looked at Dabney. "Trust me," she sneered. She handed him the clipboard.

*   *   *

Jeremy and Craig speed-walked down the hall away from Ms. Adler's class. It was over, *at last!* Ms. Adler only taught freshmen. They would never have her again. They said nothing about it even though they were thinking the same thing. They shared a superstition. They were afraid that if they said it out loud, they would find themselves back in her class in the fall, primed for another year of hell. Ms. Adler's was the toughest Science class in Connecticut. She gave tons of homework and spent a phenomenal amount of time teaching them about DNA – of which she seemed to have information even the textbooks lacked. Ms. Adler possessed a detailed map of the DNA strand and claimed to know the exact purpose of every little letter. She gave no second chances when it came to late work or bad grades, and no one was allowed to fail her class.

She's so strict, Jeremy thought, *she has to be a Nazi.*

Today had been the biggest waste of time as far as school days went. They came in, spent half a period in all of their classes, turned in their books, and now they were leaving. The only exciting part of the day was when they got their yearbooks. Jeremy's was in his backpack. It had accumulated about a million signatures including Dabney's. He signed it in their English class, but not on the inside cover where everyone could see. Instead, he signed his class picture on the interior. Jeremy wasn't going to ask him to. He didn't think he would since he never signed anyone's, but then Dabney just walked over and snatched it from him. Jeremy watched with growing curiosity as Dabney brought it back to his desk. He considered his words carefully as he wrote. He returned it when he was done, dropping it in Jeremy's lap.

Jeremy said, "Thanks, Dabs."

Dabney walked away.

Jeremy opened the yearbook to Dabney's picture and read:

What is it with you? Why are you so perfect? It's making me mad. Everyone else in this town is so easy to hate. Why can't I hate you? I'm not even sure I want to which only makes it worse. If you're playing some kind of game, leave me out of it. If it's <u>not</u> a game...

Dabney's iPhone number was beneath his signature. There was also a postscript.

P.S. I trust you'll keep this between us. Yes, you can call me, but I don't know why I'm doing this.

An invitation? Jeremy wondered. *Who would've thought?*

Craig's yearbook was in his locker. They stopped to get it. He didn't see much sense in bringing it to class. He was sure no one would sign it. Jeremy grabbed it before he could slip it into his backpack. He whipped out a black Bic and wrote something on the inside front cover. He closed it and handed it back to Craig.

"Don't read it until later," Jeremy said.

"Why not?" Craig asked.

"How about because I asked you not to?"

Craig shrugged and put it away.

Graduation ceremonies for the high school were later that afternoon. The middle school commencement should almost be over if they started on time. Derek and Ian were graduating and would be freshman next year. A lot of people Jeremy knew likewise were like Teddy Bigelow and Andy Lee. Jeremy said he hoped all the seniors got home safely this year. Last year, some of the graduates had driven out to a Rhode Island beach to party. They headed back at dawn. One of the drivers had fallen asleep at the wheel and hit a utility pole. He died along with two of his friends. Even Virginia cried that day. She couldn't think of anything worse than losing one of her children. Craig remembered it well. He and his father went to the memorial service. Death it seemed touched everyone with equal ferocity.

Jeremy had made a point to check on Chris after every period throughout the day. He ended up late to two of his classes, but he wanted to make sure his brother was okay. He also wanted Chris to know he was there for him. It was a demonstration of unity that Jeremy intended to thrust in everyone's face, especially Dan Mellon. Dan was conspicuously absent from the sophomore hallways between classes. He was a junior. Juniors were on the top floor, but he usually made an appearance. From the expression on Max's face, it was safer for Dan to maintain a low profile.

Jeremy wasn't alone in his concern for Chris. His brother had an entourage between periods that included, to his surprise, Dabney, although discreetly. He was hovering in the background watching Chris closely. He wore an expression that Jeremy might have called longing if it hadn't been so absurd. *Why would Dabney feel that way toward Chris?* he wondered. Jeremy wasn't sure, but decided it didn't matter as long as he stopped spreading the rumor. Sandy was there, too, with Max, Matt, Ricardo – reluctantly – and Jeremy. One person's presence caught everyone off guard except Chris. Dennis Copeland was escorting him between classes. It caused a lot of commotion. When Dabney saw him, he rolled his eyes, scowling. Jeremy looked at Dennis like he was an alien. So did everyone else. They decided they liked him though. They liked him a lot.

Jeremy remembered something. Chris had been lingering in the hall just before last period after everyone had gone to class. Jeremy noticed him and walked over. He punched his brother lightly on the shoulder.

"What's wrong with you?" Jeremy asked.

Chris looked at him, confused. "Huh?" he asked, and then blushed. "Oh, nothing. I was just thinking about something."

"About what?" Jeremy asked, crossing his arms.

Chris replied, "Hiram had an ad posted in the Resource Room here and in the counseling office at the middle school for a part-time employee."

"What for?"

"The summer's here," Chris remarked. "He wants someone to work for a couple of hours during the day. He asked me, but I said no. Todd and Dabney must have said no, too. I noticed the ad last week."

"And?" Jeremy asked.

"The ad's gone now. The resource counselor told me Hiram had filled the position." His gaze became faraway. "Teddy Bigelow took the job. You know, the Altar boy from St. Peter's?"

"His dad's the cop, right?"

"Robert Bigelow."

Jeremy gripped his shoulder. "Well, it looks like you might get some time to yourself this summer. I have to go. I can't be too late. I have Adler this period."

Chris nodded, but stayed in the hallway for a long time after the bell rang. His expression was concerned. He shook it off and darkly thought, *I warned you, old man,* and walked into his class.

Jeremy and Craig made their way to the bottom floor. They went out the same door they had come in this morning.

"I'm glad it's over," Jeremy said, stepping into the hot sun. He shielded his eyes with one hand and sucked on the index finger of his other. It was still bleeding a little. "I wish they gave out report cards instead of mailing them home. Oh well, I won't miss school that's for sure. What about you?"

Craig shrugged. "If I'm not here, I'm at work, a relative's house, or at home. It doesn't matter much to me."

"Why do you work so much?" Jeremy asked.

"Nothing better to do," Craig frankly replied.

"That's going to change, Craig."

"Oh?" he asked, walking toward his bicycle. "How so?"

Jeremy followed him. "I don't know. I guess I was hoping you'd hang out with me this summer."

Craig said nothing. He didn't know if Jeremy was serious, but he didn't want to know if he wasn't. Each time he thought about hanging around with him and the other guys tonight he felt lonelier. He didn't like it. They had taken him into their company so easily, it made him feel paranoid.

Is Max up to something? Am I really welcome?

He looked at Jeremy, his eyes searching.

Jeremy looked back, curiously.

Craig shook his head. "It's nothing," he said, and knelt next to his bike.

"I'm used to my friends being a little more communicative, Craig," Jeremy said. "You're going to give me a complex."

"I'm the one getting the complex," he whispered, and cringed.

"What?" Jeremy asked.

"Forget it," Craig replied, climbing onto his bike. "It's nothing."

"I'll bet," Jeremy said, crossing his arms. He remembered the campout. "Oh, hey! Is it okay if I meet you at your house later? The other guys are going to the pond to swim, but I'm not into that yet. The water's too cold. I hate swimming when it's like that."

"Me, too," Craig agreed, not that he swam much.

He thought about what Jeremy asked. His father had gone to file for his unemployment check today. Jack would go straight to the bar afterward. He wouldn't be home when he got there. Still, it would be easier to meet Jeremy at the market. It was closer to the McKees' house. Then Craig remembered the mess he had to clean up and cringed. He needed time to finish before Jeremy got there. Of course, he hadn't even asked if he could go camping yet. He had to talk to his uncle about that and about getting out of work early.

"Okay," Craig finally replied. He was certain his uncle would let him go. He was always prodding his nephew to do something social. "It's twelve-thirty now. I'll try to get off work at two. Can you meet me at my house at three?"

"Sure," Jeremy replied.

"Do you know where I live?"

"Craig?" Jeremy asked. "Is there anyone in town who doesn't know where you live?"

Craig peddled away. He was starting to feel excited. He decided to trust Jeremy and take him at his word. *He's going to be friends with me? Whoo hoo!*

Jeremy watched until Craig disappeared down Lancaster Hill Road. He walked back toward the school, but paused outside the front door. He looked down the street again. Jeremy hadn't notice it before, but when Craig rode away? He suddenly felt very lonely. He opened the door and walked inside just as the final bell rang.

*   *   *

Ms. Adler watched as the last of her students, Herman Schwartz, exited the room. She let out a tremendous whoosh of breath as she slumped back in her chair.

"Thank the gods!" she cried, rubbing her temples. "Two more minutes and I would have wrung one of their necks!"

She picked up her clipboard and the black magic marker. She dumped the blood sugar test sticks out of the Hazardous Waste Container onto the top of her desk. She matched each stick by its number to the corresponding number on the list. If it belonged to one of the girls, she tossed it into the garbage can and crossed the signature off the list. If it was a boy's number, she carefully placed the stick back in the container and put a check mark after whose name it was. She saved all of the boys' sticks except for Herman's. She glared at it with undisguised contempt.

"Jew," Ms. Adler said, her voice suddenly deeper.

She tossed Herman's stick into the trashcan on her way out. The classroom door closed by itself a few moments later. Ms. Adler had nothing to do with it. She didn't even know they were there. No one did. They were invisible to everyone except themselves. They sat throughout the room, a dozen at first, and then more. A foul stench of death filled the air, but it was no surprise. They were the ghosts of Hiram's victims, and they were angry.

Sam Stone, Jr. appeared on top of Ms. Adler's desk. There was blood all over the front of his tee shirt. His expression was rife with sorrow.

"You were right," Sam said.

"Of course we were right," a young blonde boy replied. He appeared about eleven years old. Blood smeared his golden locks. *"More people are going to die you know."*

"I know."

"Do you understand now?" the blonde boy asked.

Sam glared at him. The other boys hissed at his threatening gesture.

"Back off!" Sam yelled. *"Or you can do this without me!"*

The janitor stopped outside the room. He opened the door and stuck his head in. He scrunched up his nose at the smell.

What was she doing in here? Burning cats?

The room was empty. He resumed sweeping.

"I must be losing it," the janitor said. "I thought I heard voices."

The blonde boy flashed a wicked smile. *"You should be more careful, Stone. If you stir up too many emotions, they can see you."*

"So what, Terry? Like they'll believe what they see anyway?"

"Are you with us?" Terry asked, clenching his fists. *"It's the only way you'll ever be free."*

"You either," Sam reminded him. His expression filled with regret. *"There's no other way?"*

The boys laughed as they disappeared. The janitor paused in the hall again. He shook his head and decided to sweep downstairs instead. He didn't go back to the second floor again until September.

Sam remained for a short time staring at the pile of textbooks on the shelf in the back of the room. He wondered if anyone would turn in his books. He closed his eyes, faded slowly, and then disappeared with the others. There was one ghost left. He was a little boy with jet black hair. He was sitting on the floor in the back of the room. He had gone unnoticed by Sam and the others. He was glad because he had tried hard to make it that way. He was as pale as a sheet, shivering, and covered in rich black earth.

"Bad things!" he cried. *"They're doing such bad things!"*

Then he vanished, too.

*　　*　　*

Craig eased his bike around the side of his Uncle Mike's store. He dragged his Reebok along the tar until he came to a stop in front of the bicycle rack. It was next to the shipping and receiving dock around the back of the building. He felt charged with electricity. Jeremy's invitation to hang out with him this summer sounded better the farther away from the school he had gotten. His doubts faded with the rush of the hot afternoon air.

Craig decided keeping his friendship with Jeremy away from his father was paramount. He knew he could do it. He had done the same with his uncle for years. Mike was Craig's only real confidant up until now. This wasn't much different. Trusting someone was a risk though, and he knew it. He decided daring to risk was the only way to tell if Jeremy was sincere. It was a price worth paying for the chance. He was so excited at the prospect, he thought he was going to explode.

Jeremy wants to hang out with me!

Craig had never realized just how lonely he felt until today. He knew when Max caught him this morning that everything was going to change. He never dreamed it would change for the better. Max didn't seem anxious to tell anyone what he had seen either. Craig kicked himself for being afraid. Of course, his father was still going to beat him, but at least he was making friends. It was the greatest day of his life. He wasn't going to let anything bring him down. He beamed happiness like it was radioactive.

The bicycle rack clanged as he popped in his front tire. Craig went up the stairs next to the dock taking them two at a time. The metal gate was closed over the shipping and receiving bay. He saw Mike's tan Buick Regal parked in the space labeled *OWNER*. Craig peered through the small square window in the back door. He could see his uncle in the office counting the money from yesterday. Craig smiled. His uncle was a creature of habit. He couldn't wait to tell him about Jeremy. Mike had always said he should make some friends.

Craig was too young to be working so much without time to be a kid. It bothered Mike as much as knowing Jack was taking all of his money. It was the only reason Craig hadn't gotten a raise the last time around and still worked for minimum wage. Mike knew enough not to say anything about it as Craig would likely deny it. It was frustrating the way he defended his father. Mike ran interference for him as often as he could, but he feared the day Jack went too far. God help Craig then.

Mike turned toward the familiar knock on the back door. He saw his nephew waving in the small window. Craig was wearing a big smile.

Mike breathed a sigh of relief. *I guess Jack didn't bother him today. Good, Craig deserves a break.*

Mike pressed the button on the wall next to his desk. Craig pushed on the door when he heard the electronic lock buzzing. The door opened with a click. Craig burst in and headed straight for his uncle. Words were pouring out of his mouth like a dam with its floodgates open. Mike stared at his nephew with a dumb look on his face. He couldn't understand half of what Craig was saying. He held his hand over Craig's mouth.

"Take a deep breath and slow down, kiddo," Mike said. He couldn't remember ever seeing Craig so excited. He didn't think he had ever been this happy.

Craig smiled. "I got invited to go camping."

Mike hugged him. *Thank God! Someone finally realized he was alive!* He knew it was hard. His brother's reputation caused most people to shy away from Craig.

Mike sat him on the desk. The cool metal felt good through his jeans.

"So," Mike said. He pushed the bangs out of his nephew's face. Craig's eyes shined. "Tell me what's going on."

Craig took a deep breath. He started with the condition of the house this morning strategically skipping over the beating. It was a necessary lie to keep the peace. His uncle would break his father in half if he knew how many times he actually got hit. Mike didn't understand his relationship with his father any more than anyone else, but Craig loved them equally. He couldn't stand the thought of them punching each other out on the front lawn. It was better this way. Mike rolled his eyes as the story progressed. He agreed his nephew would have to clean up the mess.

When Craig mentioned Max Ramirez, Mike went through his mental file of customers. *Oh, yeah. The son of the woman who made me order all the Spanish food.* Mike liked him and his brother, Ricardo. Any doubts about this sudden interest in his nephew went out the window. Max was a good kid. Mike had a sense for these things.

Excitement filled the office as Craig spoke. It was a welcome change from the way he usually looked when he came in. An eternal black cloud followed him, bloated with overwhelming sadness. How Craig could love his miserable father was beyond Mike.

It isn't a wonder Carol walked out on Jack, Mike thought, *but I'll never understand why she left Craig behind.*

He despised her for that. So did his mother.

Craig paused between sentences to catch his breath.

Mike saw an opening and asked, "Where are you guys going to camp?"

Craig opened his mouth to answer, but then closed it. A puzzled expression came over his face. He didn't know. His brow furrowed as he tried to remember if Max or Jeremy had said anything about it.

"I'm not sure," Craig replied. "Jeremy McKee is meeting me at my house at three though." He swallowed nervously. "If I can get out of working today."

Mike pulled out his mental customer file again. *Virginia's son? Nice kid. Craig's in good hands for sure.* He shook his head at his nephew's desperate expression.

"You can leave in time to meet Jeremy," Mike said.

"What about my dad?" Craig asked.

"I'll take care of that, too," Mike promised. "If he calls, I'll tell him I let you go. He can yell at me for a change." He watched relief wash over Craig's features. "Who else is going?"

Craig replied, "I don't know. Maybe Ricardo. Jeremy's brother, Chris, probably."

"Is there going to be any partying?"

"I don't know."

"Well, just be careful, okay?" Mike cautioned. "Partying can be all right, but only in moderation. Stay away from drugs if there are any. I wouldn't expect there to be. These guys seem pretty straight to me. Remember alcohol is a drug, too. If you're going to drink, don't get out of control."

Craig wondered, *Would I drink?*

Watching his father had convinced him a long time ago he should stay away from it. Craig always believed he would until now. He thought about it. He had finally got invited somewhere. If everyone else was drinking, how could he say no? Craig didn't want anyone to think he was a wuss, or anything. One thing was for sure...

"Whatever you do," Mike cautioned, "don't let your father find out about it."

"The camping trip?" Craig asked.

"No, you bonehead," Mike replied. He tapped Craig on the head with his fist. "The drinking."

"I'm not sure I would drink," Craig said.

Mike thought, *No lessons about the dangers of alcohol needed here.* "If you're meeting Jeremy at three, you'd better get busy," he said. "There's a lot of work I need you to do before you go."

Craig hugged his uncle. "Thanks, Uncle Mike," he whispered.

Mike rubbed his back. "Forget it, kid," he replied. "Whatever you need, you got."

Both Dougans turned toward the back door when the bell rang. One of Mike's cashiers, Beatrice Jones, was in the window. Craig hit the button to let her in. He hopped off the desk and met her by the time clock. Bea gave him his daily pat on the head and smiled. She was a middle-aged woman with Nice & Easy brown hair cut in a bowl. Her black rectangular glasses sat on a pointed nose between her brown eyes and green shadow. Her soft narrow face had pretty lips that made her look younger when she smiled. She was only three inches taller than Craig and carried a black leather handbag. She smelled like baby powder.

Craig liked Bea and the stories she told, but they weren't all happy. Bea's youngest son Bobby had disappeared a few years back. She was sure he had run away after an argument they had. It was a tough time for her. Craig remembered how sad she looked when she told him about it. Her other two children, Hannah and Allen, were away at college in California.

Old Ted Collins, an ancient WWII vet with white hair and a mustache, arrived next. Mike said Old Ted was the only Black man who had lived in the town of Lancaster when he was a boy. The market belonged to the late David Rosenberg then. No one knew how he could possibly have lived this long, but Old Ted was the best and only butcher around. Mike had offered him anything he wanted to stay on when he took over the market. He thought Old Ted would take him to the cleaners, but he hadn't.

"I don't need all that much, boy," Old Ted told Mike. His gravelly voice took on a tone of reflection. "A twenty-five cent raise might be nice." He scowled. "Oh, and one other thing."

"Anything!" Mike replied. He decided to pay Old Ted a lot more money than that. Mr. Rosenberg was pretty reserved when it came to payroll.

Old Ted looked on Mike with suspicion. "What do you know about meat, boy?"

"Well, actually," Mike replied, "I majored in business at college, so not a lot."

"Uh, huh," Old Ted sniffed. "Then you keep out of my butcher shop, got it? If you want to learn, I'll be happy to teach you, but in my own good time."

Mike agreed. He also gave Old Ted the raise, but it was the raise he had decided on, not what Old Ted wanted. When Old Ted got his first check from Mike's payroll, he demanded Mike write him another for less money. He owned his house, he had his veteran's pension from the Army, his kids were grown and gone, and his wife had passed away years earlier.

"What do I need so much money for anyhoo?"

Mike paid him what he had asked for. He put the difference into a savings account to give him when he retired.

Old Ted winked at Craig as he punched in and disappeared into the butcher shop.

"Bea?" Mike called, from the office.

Bea came back from her register where she had been setting up.

"Get the Adler order ready, okay?" Mike asked. "Craig's delivering it today."

Bea shuddered. Her face grew long and she paled. She seemed to be fighting something. Her left hand twitched.

Craig quietly groaned.

"Lucky you," Lisa Gibbons said.

She had come through the door a moment before. She ruffled Craig's hair as she reached past him for her time card. She had just completed her junior year at Lancaster High School. Lisa was five-eight with long blonde hair held in a ponytail by a peace sign clip. She wore jeans shorts and a Lancaster High School Eagles blue and white tee shirt. She had her father's brown eyes but her mother's pretty face and friendly smile. She wore makeup, but only enough to highlight her high cheekbones. Her round breasts stood firm without a bra. Her hips and smooth tanned legs curved down to her black Converse All Star Chuck Taylor high tops.

"Yeah," Craig muttered. "Thanks."

Going anywhere near Ms. Adler was the last thing Craig wanted to do. He'd had enough of her this year. He was curious why he was bringing her groceries.

"Don't you usually deliver to her, Lisa?" Craig asked.

"Usually," Lisa replied, "but daddy's having José service *My Baby* today, so I don't have her. He wants to make sure everything's working right. There are about a dozen graduation parties tonight. *My Baby's* got to make all of them, know what I mean?"

Baby indeed! Craig thought.

Lisa's Baby was a customized '68 Chevelle with a 454 engine, mag wheels, headers, dual exhaust, and a sound system that had earned the back seat the nickname *The Concert Hall*.

Craig frowned. He didn't want to do this delivery.

"Don't worry, kid," Lisa said, smacking her eternal piece of gum. She swished her ponytail. "It's usually only one or two bags and they're not that heavy."

"I wasn't worried about that," Craig frowned. "I just never wanted to go to her house. At least in class I was safe."

Lisa smiled. She sometimes forgot Craig was just a kid. "Don't let the stories about her scare you, Craig," she said. "You survived her class, right?" She punched her timecard. "Margaret Adler's just an eccentric old woman who lives in an old house. People make up crap all the time."

"Make up what?" Dan Mellon asked, his blue eyes shifting nervously from Craig to Lisa.

A pink hue appeared beneath the freckles he only had on his button nose. All of the Mellon brothers had the same nose, a gift from their father, Kevin, but they varied in freckles which they had gotten from their mother, Cynthia. Dan's were on his nose. Derek's filled his cheeks and covered his shoulders like his mom. He also shared her green eyes whereas his brothers and Kevin's eyes were blue. Douggie's freckles were exploded all over his face and body.

Craig was startled when he spoke. He hadn't heard him come in.

Dan looked oddly like a rat in a trap.

Lisa elbowed him. "Lighten up, Dan-O," she said. "We were talking about Margaret Adler."

"The Hill Witch?" Dan asked. He relaxed. *Oh, thank God!*

Craig wondered what was wrong with him.

Dan continued with, "I hear she killed her father."

"Her adoptive father," Craig corrected.

"Yeah, him."

"She did not," Lisa yawned, rolling her eyes.

"That's what I heard," Dan offered. "I hear she throws lightning bolts…"

"… and she can fly!" Craig added, his eyes widening.

Lisa sighed long and loud. She placed her hand indignantly on her hip. "Will you two give me a break?" she said, scolding them. "Colonel Adler died from a stroke, period. I know because my dad told me. My grandfather was there that day. I usually bring Ms. Adler's groceries to her and I'm still breathing. We've all had her class! You sat next to me that year, Dan, remember? Lightning bolts, indeed."

The last half of her sentence trailed off as she walked away. She paused in the office doorway to smack her gum at Mike and say hello. Mike smiled. He had been waiting for her. Lisa saw the look on his face and recognized it immediately. She tossed her head back and looked up at the ceiling. She knew what he was going to say.

"I know," Lisa said. She reached into her big cloth purse and withdrew her wallet. "I was short yesterday, right? Ten bucks?"

"Ten bucks," Mike echoed.

This was no odd occurrence. Lisa snatched a bill from her till now and then when she was short on cash. Mike figured she was simply too lazy to stop at the ATM. He'd told her a million times it would be easier to write him a check, but Lisa declined. If she needed cash, her father gave it to her. Since that never depleted her bank account, why should she spend her own money? Lyle Gibbons was a strong man, but he spoiled his daughter rotten. Lisa handed over the ten she had gotten from him before he left for the garage this morning.

"What was it this time?" Mike asked, snatching the bill from Lisa's hand. "Did you need gas, or something?"

"Gas?" Lisa declared, indignantly. "Do you think my father, the owner of the service station, would make a sweet and innocent girl like me pay for gas?"

"Sweet?" Dan asked.

"Innocent?" Craig added.

They laughed.

"Shut your pie holes," Lisa said, holding up a fist. "I'm going to come over there and rap you one in the schnoz."

Mike laughed.

Lisa strutted away with her drawer.

There's no doubt she's Lyle Gibbons' daughter, Mike thought. *Good thing she's got her mother's looks!*

Mike told Craig and Dan to start rotating the stock and went back to counting the money. He had overheard them talking about Margaret Adler. She had been his teacher, too, at Annie Potts Elementary. Ms. Adler taught for so long she was a local institution like the rumors about her. They had been around forever, too. Mike didn't blame the boys for being afraid of her. They were right.

Well, maybe she isn't a witch, per se, Mike thought, *but she's one scary woman.* The only time she had ever come into his store, opening day, entered his mind.

Mike scratched his head. "Yeah, that was something." He shivered at the memory.

He had been checking the aisles getting ready to open for the first time. Ms. Adler almost gave him a heart attack when she appeared in front of him. He stood there with his mouth open. He looked into her deep brown eyes and they drew him in. Mike felt naked. She was wearing a flowing black skirt and a sleeveless pink blouse. She had a black crocheted shawl over her shoulders. She looked downright menacing. He couldn't remember if it was him or Bobby Bigelow who first called her the Hill Witch. He only knew they were right.

"Mr. Dougan," Ms. Adler sighed. "Would you kindly pick up your jaw and invite me to your office? I have business to discuss with you."

'Mr. Dougan?' Mike wondered, scooping up his jaw. *It was always 'Master Dougan' when I was a kid.*

"Of course," Mike replied, gesturing to the back. "Right this way."

Ms. Adler followed him into the Plexiglas office and took the chair next to his desk. She exaggerated her movements in a manner that made Mike think she was trying too hard to appear feminine. She glared at him as if she had heard that thought. He chided himself for thinking such a thing, but it was difficult not to. The stories about her came back to him. Mike wasn't surprised when he noticed his hand was trembling.

Ms. Adler spoke about what she wanted after ordering him to take notes. Mike flashed a grin. It was a familiar line from her class. She was always telling him to take notes. Ms. Adler presently had her groceries delivered from a market in Tolland, but had decided to switch her account here. He was curious why she got her food from the next town over when Rosenberg had been here for years.

"Do you honestly think, Mr. Dougan," she said, her eyes narrow, "I would do business with a *Je...* with a man like Rosenberg? He was... dishonest."

Really? Mike thought. *I never heard that before. Didn't she almost say...?*

"I have a list of items I require weekly," she continued. "If there is a change in what I desire, I will phone you. I doubt there will be as I am a creature of habit. Deliver the items to my house no later than three p.m. each Monday. No exceptions, Mr. Dougan, including holidays."

Ms. Adler handed him an unsealed envelope. It contained a modest list of items and a check written to Mike's Market for a thousand dollars. Mike tried to give the check back. He said it was too much money up front. Ms. Adler refused to take it.

"Ms. Adler...," Mike began.

She held her hand up. "I am sure your service will be fine, Mr. Dougan."

How did she know I was going to say that?

"I expect a detailed receipt with each delivery. I will tip the delivery person accordingly."

Ms. Adler rose, walked out of the office, and headed toward her black Mercedes-Benz parked in front of the store.

Mike followed her. He asked, "Wouldn't you rather just come in and shop yourself instead of paying so much money in advance?"

Ms. Adler laughed, but continued walking. The sound chilled Mike. It was patronizing, a superior being mocking a troglodyte.

"Come now, Mr. Dougan," Ms. Adler replied. "You do not want *the Hill Witch* frequenting your establishment. It was you and your childhood friends who gave me that nickname in the first place, was it not? Bobby Bigelow? Dillon Pettipaw?"

Mike's mouth hung open again. Ms. Adler left the store. He knew there was something weird about her now. No one but him, Bigelow, and Dillon knew they were the ones who had first called Ms. Adler *the Hill Witch*.

Mike stood there for a long time after she drove away. *Is it true?* he wondered. *Is Margaret Adler a witch?*

He was in the middle of that thought when Craig knocked on the doorjamb.

Mike nearly jumped out of his chair. "Jesus!" he cried, holding his massive chest. "Don't do that!"

Craig chuckled.

Mike glared at him. "What?" he asked. He smiled, feeling foolish.

"Bea has the Adler order ready," Craig said. His laughter bled out of him. "She says you can check it anytime."

Mike could see that Craig wasn't too thrilled about making this delivery. Unfortunately, there was no one else who could do it. Mike had to count the rest of the cash from yesterday and finish last week's figures. There was a ton of pricing to do and Dan was the fastest with the tagger. He also walked to work, so that left him out. Bea refused to go to Ms. Adler's house under any circumstances. Mike thought it had something to do with her son who ran away, but he wasn't sure. He only knew she had gotten very upset the one time he'd asked her to deliver the order. That left Old Ted who didn't do deliveries and Lisa who didn't have her car today.

Mike motioned for Craig to come over to him. He put his hands on his hips and looked his nephew in the eye.

"Worried about Ms. Adler?" Mike asked.

Craig nodded.

Mike assured him she was harmless. He would be considered one of the bravest kids in town if he made the delivery.

"Yeah," Craig mumbled, glumly, "if I live to tell about it. When I left school today, I thought I would never have to see her again. I was pretty happy about that."

Mike laughed. "Don't worry, kiddo. You'll live. Besides, she usually tips ten dollars."

"Really?" Craig asked, perking up a little. He thought, *That would be cool especially if Jeremy plans on doing anything that costs money tonight.* He was broke thanks to his father.

"Really," Mike confirmed. "Help Dan finish the rotation and get those shelves stocked. It's going to be busy tonight since the day shift was so slow. I sent my cashier home early."

Craig gave his uncle a mock salute and returned to the can aisle. Dan was clicking away over some tuna fish. He nodded at Craig, but kept right on clicking. Dan was the stock boy. He got plenty of tagger practice. He could tag cans blindfolded if he wanted to. Craig was the gopher. The only job exclusively his was unloading the trucks when they came in. It was easy as long as the delivery was on pallets. Mike had an electric floor jack. Craig drove it like a pro and pulled the pallets off by himself. Sometimes the load was on the floor of the trailer though. The truck drivers usually helped him then. The items had to be stacked on pallets before Mike would accept them.

Craig was always in one corner of the store or another. He usually didn't have time to socialize with anyone for too long. He was glad he was working with Dan today. He felt good and he had to share it with somebody. He picked up the priced cans of tuna and stacked them on the shelf.

"So, Dan," Craig said, neatly arranging the cans. "What are you going to do tonight?"

"I don't know," Dan replied. "I might go to Candace Beals' graduation party. I have to talk to my dad about it when I get home, but he might not let me. After what happened last year with the accident, my mom's not too keen on grad parties. I'll probably watch cable, or something. Why? What are you going to do?"

Craig replied, "I'm going camping with Jeremy McKee."

Dan dropped the tagger. He turned as white as a sheet, his nose freckles darkening. Craig stooped over the cases and picked it up for him.

"Is Chris McKee going?" Dan asked.

"I'm not sure," Craig said. "Why?"

The night he camped out with Chris came back to Dan with such force, Craig seemed to fade away. Dan had never been so scared in his life. Panic overcame him. All he wanted to do was get out of that tent and forget he had ever heard Chris say the words, "I'm gay." He knew Chris was upset when he left, but Dan didn't care, not at the time anyway. He had to get out of the tent and away from him. It took him days to get over how skeeved he felt. He liked Chris, but Dan couldn't imagine associating with a queer. What would people think?

They would think I was one, too, Dan thought, an intolerable situation.

Dan wanted to talk to Chris about it after he had calmed down. The more the shock went away, the more he wanted to be his friend again, covertly at least. Chris was dodging his phone calls however which made Dan paranoid. He wasn't returning his messages either. Dan had even written him a note when Virginia came to the market to shop, but there had been no response. Chris was avoiding him at school, too, which wasn't hard considering Dan was a junior and Chris was a sophomore. They didn't share a single class.

He used to see Chris in the hallway a few times a day, but that was before the campout Dan had abandoned. Chris was nowhere to be found now. Today, Dan had come downstairs to the sophomore hall looking for him, but when he saw the army of bodyguards – it sure looked like that to him, especially with Dennis Copeland there glaring at everyone – accompanying Chris to his classes, Dan decided he probably wasn't welcome and went back upstairs. He didn't know what was going on.

Is Chris mad at me?

Dan didn't see how he could be. Chris had to know letting himself be gay would cause problems, especially since Dan was absolutely straight. How did he think Dan felt to find out the person he went camping with was a fruitcake? He hadn't honestly expected him to stay in the same tent once he knew the truth, did he? He couldn't! If Dan found out somebody was sleeping in the same tent with a known queer, he would know right away the guy was queer, too. Didn't Chris understand the risk? Dan thought he had to, unless he didn't care. Then the most incredibly scary thought came to him.

What if Chris is telling everyone in town he's gay?

Dan's paranoia exploded into panic again. He did not want the whole world to know about Chris – *No way!* – not after camping with him so many times. He could hear the rumors already and he couldn't handle it. The more he thought about it, the more he knew he was right. The more Chris dodged his calls, the more Dan realized he needed to do something. He had to make sure Chris intended to keep his gayness a secret, but when Chris wouldn't talk to him? Dan decided to go on the offensive before the whole town found out about him. He had to strike first, so Dan told everyone Chris had come out to him. He made sure they knew he had left the tent immediately after he did. Dan said his friendship with Chris was over. There was no way he was associating with a homo.

Derek's planning on going to the same campout Craig's talking about, Dan thought. *Forget that! I already warned him. He'd better be home when I get there.*

Derek wasn't going anywhere near Chris. Dan shuddered to think what would happen if Derek learned the truth. What if Chris told him what Dan was doing? What if Derek told their parents? If they learned Dan had been spreading rumors, he would be in big trouble. His mother wouldn't let him get his driver's license at the very least. Dan was overdue for that as it was. His parents already thought he wasn't responsible enough to drive. His dad and Thomas had been friends since childhood. His mother was friends with Virginia, too, which would only make things worse. They would ground him for eternity. Dan was determined not to let that happen. It was as simple as keeping Derek away from Chris. He hoped his brother understood how hard it would be to tell anyone anything if he were in traction.

"Why?" Craig repeated.

Dan shook his head and resumed clicking. Sandy Sturgess had convinced him to back off the other day when he punched him. Dan didn't care about that anymore though. The rumor was out there. It would do all the work for him.

"Is there a problem between you and Chris?" Craig asked.

"You could say that," Dan replied. "I wouldn't sleep in the same tent with him if I were you."

"Why not?" Craig asked, even more puzzled. "Haven't you camped out with him before?"

Jesus, even Dougan knows!? Grr!

"Oh, I camped out with him, all right."

Craig was sincerely confused. "So, if you camped out with Chris, what's the problem if I do?"

Dan motioned for Craig to come closer. He whispered in his ear that Chris told him he was gay, and said, "You should stay away from him. I already told Derek. He'd better not go there tonight, I swear."

Craig continued loading the cans. Their conversation was over. Dan didn't want to talk about it anymore. Craig had no idea what to think. He had never met a real live gay person before.

Does that mean Chris wears women's clothes? Does he want a sex change operation? Are his wrists weak? I don't think he has a lisp... does he?

Craig continued piling the cans on the shelf, his mind full of fascinated wonder.

*   *   *

Todd stepped into the barn and walked toward the ringing phone. It was on the wall across from Hiram's slaughter hook. The hook hung from a low ceiling beam between the silo and the manure pit. It was in the center of the room as if whatever Hiram was gutting needed to be on display. Todd thought that was gross.

There must be a more civil way to kill an animal.

The hook shined menacingly in complete contrast to its grubby surroundings. Hiram kept it spotless and razor sharp. Todd had watched him polishing it before. He stared at it like a long lost lover. He caressed it, spoke to it in hushed tones, and sometimes burst into hysterical laughter.

Todd thought, *We could easily rename the Milliken Farm as the Funny Farm.* He smirked. *Hiram's the prize lunatic.*

This area of the barn was cluttered and dirty. An old oak table stood against the wall with an assortment of antique furniture. There was a wingback chair with the gaudiest fabric pattern Todd had ever seen.

It looks like a pair of Michael Jackson's pajamas. They must be from the Victorian, unless Hiram's been raiding Antiques for the Colorblind. I wonder why they're in here. Isn't the rest of the Victorian's furniture in the attic? Hiram must hate this stuff for some reason. Why else would he keep it in the smelly old barn?

There was a pegboard on the wall nearby with an assortment of cutting implements dangling from it. They were clean and sharpened like the slaughter hook. The cutting tools resembled items from a medieval torture chamber. One of them looked like a clamp only in reverse. The hands moved outward when the crank was turned as if used for spreading something. Todd remembered seeing them all bloody and covered with gore once. When he asked Hiram about it, the farmer told him he'd butchered a calf that morning. They were spotless later as if they had been sterilized. It was the same for all of the implements.

Weird, Todd thought, looking at one of the tools. It resembled a hacksaw, but with a more jagged blade. *Is that for decapitating cows? Ick!*

Todd ignored the phone. The slaughter hook drew his gaze. The sun winked off it, blinding him. He squinted. It seemed to whisper, *How many lives have I taken? How many times have I killed without conscience? How many more will die before I'm through?* Todd reached out and gingerly touched the tip. He gasped as it sliced his index finger down the middle.

"Ow!" Todd cried, pulling his hand back.

He looked at his finger, his eyes filled with surprise. It was sliced wide open and bleeding. He shook it and angrily stuck it in his mouth.

My luck sucks today! Todd thought. *This is such crap! I barely touched the stupid thing!*

It wasn't enough that Dennis Copeland threw him around like a rag doll. Todd could live with that even if it made him want to chew nails. Dennis was a strong dude. There wasn't any shame in getting a beat down from him. No, it was the principal of the thing that annoyed him.

I got my butt kicked in favor of a queer? Todd thought. *Even Copeland's not that stupid!*

He would get Dennis back if it was the last thing he did. Todd wondered what he would say to a pound of sugar in the gas tank of his Mustang. How about a convertible top with a brand new moonroof cut in it? It was coming once Todd was high enough or drunk enough to muster the courage.

Let Chris think he's safe, Todd thought. *He has to come here sometime. When he does, I'm going to punch him right out of his dress. What's wrong with the world? Everywhere I look there's another queer this, transgender that. At least Hiram's normal.* He shook his head clearing the image of Hiram in an evening gown. *If he wasn't, he would be one nasty looking queer.*

Todd was going to mess McKee up. He knew Hiram would be mad at him for doing it, but that was his problem. The farmer seemed paranoid about Chris for some reason. It was always, "Leave Chris alone," whenever Todd complained about him. He couldn't resist. It wasn't like Chris was a lousy worker. He was pretty good as far as sissies went. There was just something about him that rubbed Todd the wrong way. Maybe it was the way he looked at Hiram with that glare of disgust. Chris wore an expression like Hiram was beneath him.

Who does he think he is? Todd thought. His finger throbbed. *Hiram's practically my surrogate father. McKee's got some nerve seeing as he's the one who's all screwed up. Him and Frank, the two biggest wussies I know.*

Despite being angry with him, Frank Garrison was Todd's closest friend. He was at Frank's house if he wasn't at the farm. Frank always had the best drugs. He told Todd what Dan Mellon had said while they were getting high before school this morning. It was just after Hiram had dropped him off. They went behind the gymnasium to smoke some weed. When Todd saw Chris in the bathroom afterward, he had to set things right. McKee was a queer, so he got a beat down. That's the way it was.

So why is Copeland sticking up for him? Todd wondered. *He should've helped me! Not that it matters. It'll even up soon enough. Frank's going to get his, too, for running out on me. We could've taken Dennis! All Frank had to do was bleed on him awhile as I jumped him from behind. He's going to wish he did. I'm going to pluck his peach fuzz mustache out one hair at a time as soon as I get my hands on him.*

It wouldn't be long now. Todd had weed and Frank didn't. Frank couldn't go for more than a couple of days without it and he didn't have any money to buy more. He didn't dare rip his parents off. He had done that once and paid a hefty price for it.

Addict, Todd thought.

He had come straight to the farm after the altercation with Dennis. He was so angry, he needed some space. If he had stayed in school, he would've gone off on someone else and got in trouble. Besides, after falling in the toilet, he smelled like piss. At least he had until September before facing the music about skipping the rest of his classes. They could go screw themselves in the meantime, and so could his father if the school called home to rat him out. Todd wasn't going home all summer anyway. There wasn't any reason to.

Charles O'Connor wouldn't notice. He was the night shift supervisor at Copeland Industries. Todd rarely saw him. He worked the graveyard shift and slept during the day. If Todd went home, his stepmother, Brandy, would kick him out like she had since he was eight years old, the age he first started hanging around Hiram. He spent nights with the farmer then, too. All he had to do was call Brandy and ask if he could stay at a friend's house overnight. She never inquired who the friend was before telling him he could. She seemed glad to be rid of him. Later, when he was eleven and she discovered that Hiram was his mysterious friend, she said nothing to him. She spoke with the farmer alone for a few minutes, but that was it.

Todd thought, *Has dad noticed I haven't spent a weekend at home since I was a little kid? Probably not.* He glared at the ringing phone. *Hold on a minute! I'm bleeding to death over here!*

Todd snatched up the receiver. "Hello!?" he barked.

"Todd?" a deep voice asked. It was Hiram. "What's wrong? What took so long to get to the phone?"

"Oh, nothing!" Todd replied. "I nearly cut my finger off on your slaughter hook, that's all!"

"Are you… bleeding?" Hiram gasped.

Todd wondered why he sounded out of breath. "Yes, I'm bleeding!"

"Do you need me… to come… look at it?"

"No thanks, nurse," Todd grumbled. "I'll be all right. What do you want?" His tone was a little sharp, but his finger hurt. *The old man's just going to have to deal with it.*

"As long as you're okay."

Todd said, "I'm fine. I have work to do. What do you want?"

Hiram cleared his throat. "You have a trainee coming in tonight. Do you know Teddy Bigelow?"

Todd felt a chill go down his spine. "The cop's kid?" *Oh, great! No getting high with him around!* "I know him."

"He's coming in this afternoon to do the night milking with you," Hiram said. "I need you to show him the ropes."

"Oh, joy."

"And he's doing the morning milking," Hiram continued. He cleared his throat again. It sounded like a half-laugh. "His father gave him permission to stay in the guest room."

"Gee, thanks, Hiram!" Todd cried. "I wanted to have a few beers tonight!" He shook his head. "What happened to Henry?"

"I don't want to talk about Henry!" Hiram snapped.

Todd was startled. "God, chill out, Hiram!"

"We don't discuss Henry, Todd," Hiram said, instantly calm again. "We had a conflict of interest."

"Whatever. Can I go back to my work now?"

"One more thing," Hiram said, suddenly rushed. "I left a pitcher of Kool-Aid in the refrigerator. It's for Teddy. Let him drink it, but no more than one glass, and not until after work. He can have water until then."

"Why only one?" Todd asked. He squeezed his finger in his tee shirt trying to stop the blood. "Did Kool-Aid suddenly become expensive?"

"Just do what I say, Todd!" Hiram raged again. After a few moments of stunned silence, he calmly added, "His dad said... he wets the bed. Don't say anything to him about it. I don't want you to embarrass him. Just make sure he drinks it. He goes to sleep early. Once he's out, you can have your beers."

"Fine," Todd replied. He thought, *Hiram's in a foul mood. He was a lot friendlier this morning when he dropped me off at school, and a lot bloodier, too. Who slaughters calves so early, anyhow? He didn't even bother to wash again. I swear, he's got some serious emotional problems. Who wants to walk around all day covered in dried blood? Gross!*

"I'm at the garage if you need me," Hiram said, and hung up.

Todd held the receiver out and stared at it. "Good-bye to you, too, jerk," he said, and slammed the phone down.

*   *   *

Craig paused his mountain bike where the market's driveway met Route 41. There were two plastic shopping bags tied to his handlebars on either end. He wiped his forehead with the back of his hand and checked for traffic. There wasn't any. He eased the bike across the street to Satchell Hill. It meant riding straight up all the way to Ms. Adler's house, but the only other route was Adler Road itself which was unfinished. Craig had elected to stay on the tar. The bags didn't weigh much. Despite his uncle's reassurances and the promise of money, he was afraid of his teacher.

Hang being brave, Craig thought. *The quicker I get up there and back, the better.*

The sun beat down on him. His gym shirt was soaked with sweat just crossing the parking lot. It was a humid summer day. Craig guessed the humidity was about one hundred and fifty percent. He couldn't believe how hot it had gotten in the short time he'd been at work. Wearing pants wasn't helping either. Thankfully this delivery was his last task for today. Mike said he could meet his friend as soon as he got back. The word *friend* felt good inside his mind. If this was the feeling he'd been missing all of these years, life really did suck.

Until today, Craig thought. He felt a twinge of self-pity, but he thrust it away. *It'll be a good day no matter what.* He wondered about his mood shifts. *Is this normal for a teenager? If it is, I seem able to control them better than most. I've seen kids at school get devastated over having a D. Maybe I get my strength from my grandfather. Grandma always said he was a pillar. I don't feel like a pillar, but I know I'm pretty strong. I have to be living with my dad.*

He jumped off his bike a quarter of the way up. He eased it to the side of the road beneath a row of weeping willow trees to escape the heat.

"God," Craig remarked, "I'm roasting!" The pungent scent of the yellow flowers assaulted his nostrils. He thought, *It must be a hundred degrees already and getting hotter by the second.*

It wouldn't level off until about four o'clock. Craig hoped to be at the pond by then. He needed time to clean up the mess his dad had made and get out of there in case Jack came home for something. That was a priority. He didn't know how his father would react to the campout. Craig decided he didn't care. If his father got angry, the beating would be worth making some friends. The bruises would go away. Hopefully, the friends wouldn't.

Craig marveled at the size and beauty of the houses surrounding him as he pushed his way up Satchell Hill. The people who lived here had to be rich beyond his wildest dreams. The first house he saw was an elegant ranch with light green siding. It belonged to Ronald Morris, the First Selectman. Lancaster wasn't big enough to warrant a Mayor. Craig had shaken his hand once after an anti-drug speech he'd given at the middle school. He thought Ronald was older than dirt. His glasses were an inch thick. He had a finely groomed lawn though. The cobblestone path leading to his front door was lined on either side with colorful flowers. They were vibrant in bloom and being whisked by a sprinkler sitting in the middle of the lawn.

Craig moaned. *I wish I could go stand in the spray for a minute.*

He admired other houses as he climbed. One of them had a large boat next to it. A few had backyard pools. He smiled when he reached a black mailbox with *McKee* stenciled on its side in large white letters. The maroon and black Colonial seemed like a castle. If this was Jeremy's house – he knew the road but not the address – everything he had heard about rich kids was way off base.

Except for Dabney. He's a stereotypical rich brat.

Jeremy was going to break Craig into the real world. Craig was overwhelmed with happiness. Still, he had an annoying feeling of dread that Jeremy wouldn't show up at his house. Craig crossed his fingers. From what he'd observed, Jeremy was an honest guy who never hurt anyone. That was reassuring. Craig nervously moved on when he realized he had been staring.

He walked his bike to the junction of Points of Light Road, the street where the Gardners and the Schwartz family lived. He felt like an idiot.

What if one of the McKees had come out while I was staring at their house? What would I say? It's a good thing no one saw...

"Hey, Dougan," Matt said, tapping him on the shoulder. "What brings you up to this neck of the woods?"

Craig jumped and his heart leaped into his throat. Matt was much taller than him. He looked down at him, smiling. He had a paper bag with food and a couple of pieces of clothing in it. There was a rolled up red summer sleeping bag under his arm. Craig tried to catch his breath.

Matt patted him on the shoulder. "Why so tense, Dougan?" he asked. "Too much caffeine?"

"You almost gave me a heart attack," Craig panted. He pointed to the sleeping bag. "Are you camping out tonight, too?"

Matt raised an eyebrow. He thought, *Word of the campout has spread so far Dougan knows about it? Are we in danger of being nabbed? That would be extremely bad.* He glanced around to see if his mother was nearby. The shining silver antennas protruding from her skull would be a dead giveaway.

"Yeah," Matt replied. "How did you know?"

"Max invited me, too," Craig answered, grinning.

Matt thought, *Dougan's coming? I wonder why nobody told me at school. Oh well, he's always seemed like a nice enough guy. Too bad his father's such a loser.* He wondered if that had been reason enough never to ask him to go anywhere before. He decided it hadn't.

"That's cool," Matt said. "Are you meeting us here right now?"

Craig replied, "I'm still working. Jeremy's meeting me at my house." He asked, "Who else is going?"

"Me, Chris, Jeremy, Ian, Sandy, Max, Ricardo, Derek Mellon..." Matt paused for a breath, "... and now you."

Craig thought, *Ian Sturgess is such a dick.* He had made up his mind he was going regardless. *No one's scaring me away, not even Ian. Derek's going, too? I wonder if he knows about Dan.*

"Derek's going?" he asked. "Are you sure?"

"Positive," Matt replied. "I talked to him this morning."

Craig nodded.

"Why?" Matt asked. He remembered Dan worked at Mike's Market. His expression darkened. "Did Dan say anything to you?"

"He told me not to sleep in the same tent as Chris," Craig said. He asked, "Is Chris gay?"

Matt replied, "I don't know, Craig, but I'll tell you something. Chris has been my friend for a long time. I've slept in the same bed with him let alone the same tent. Nothing's ever happened to me."

"It's not like I care, or anything," Craig said. "I like Chris."

"I like him, too," Matt agreed. "The McKees are the best friends anyone can have. As far as Derek is concerned? He's going whether Dan likes it or not. His father already told Dan to mind his own business."

"Cool," Craig said.

"You tell Dan if he doesn't like it, he can eat me."

"Well...," Craig replied. "Dan's a little bigger than me."

"Don't worry about Dan, Dougan," Matt said. "If Max invited you tonight, he must consider you a friend. Any friend of Max's is a friend of all of us."

Craig held his hand out. Matt shook it. There was that word again. *Friend.* He wanted to hug Matt in the middle of the street. He felt a sudden anger toward his father. How often had he wished Jack would just be nice to him and love him? How much pain had he endured over the years? Was it worth it? He didn't know anymore. All the times his Uncle Mike had begged him to move to his house came back to him. Craig felt a tear run down the side of his face.

Matt wiped it away. "Are you okay, Craig?" he asked. He bent down so they were face to face and put his hand on the back of Craig's neck.

Craig nodded. "I never had any friends before."

"Well, you do now!" Matt exclaimed.

Craig smiled.

"That's better."

"Thanks, Matt."

"No problem, dude," Matt replied. He pointed at the plastic bags on Craig's handlebars. He was confused. "Hey! If you're not meeting us now, what's with all the food?"

"I'm delivering these to Ms. Adler," Craig replied. He swallowed hard.

Matt shuddered. "You're going to her *house?"*

"Uh, huh."

"Jeeze, Dougan," Matt said. "You've got more guts than me." His expression was confused again. "How come you have to deliver them?"

Craig explained that Ms. Adler's food was delivered every Monday. Lisa Gibbons usually brought it to her.

Poor guy, Matt thought. *You wouldn't get me near that house on a bet!* His gaze became faraway as he remembered her words from class:

"You will all have the opportunity to bleed for me before this is over."

"Matt?" Craig asked.

"Sorry, Craig," Matt replied. He shook his head. "I was just creeped out for a second."

"It's okay," Craig said. "I have to get going. Ms. Adler wants her groceries."

"Yeah, I have to go, too. I'm meeting Jeremy and Chris here. I'll see you later though." He smiled. "I'm glad you're coming."

Craig hopped on his bike and rode again filled with renewed vigor. He waved to Matt who waved back as he crossed the McKees' front lawn.

Lucky him, Craig thought, changing gears. *I'd love to go inside their house. Maybe someday I will.*

Craig needed to finish this job so he could get home. He still had to go back to the store and punch out. Matt's words had filled him with such a good feeling he thought he could make the climb all the way to Ms. Adler's house without stopping.

He said he's glad I'm going! Craig thought. *Whoo hoo!*

The road became steeper past Points of Light. Craig peddled harder. The sheer happiness he felt gave him power and he advanced quickly. He grumbled as he neared Textile Road. The exertion and sweat caused him to develop a wedgie.

"Oh, hell!" Craig exclaimed, pulling over to the side of the road. *There's nothing in the world more uncomfortable than riding with a wedgie!*

He undid his pants and pulled them down over his thighs. He felt a slight breeze as he reached in and adjusted his underwear. He heard footsteps coming his way. He gasped trying desperately to get his pants back up before anyone saw him, but it was too late.

"So, Dougan," Dabney taunted. "Let me guess. Um… hemorrhoids? Small penis disorder? *Real* small penis disorder?"

"Shut up, Dabney."

Craig had never belted anybody before, but if Dabney didn't knock it off he was going to start today.

Dabney grinned. He was wearing blue Speedos, black Ray-Ban sunglasses, and a white fishnet shirt. His towel was draped over his freckled shoulders. He had a brand new pair of white Balenciaga Triple S sneakers on his feet with no socks.

They must've cost a fortune!

Dabney radiated superiority. Craig hated it. Dabney was the son of the wealthiest man in town while he was the son of the poorest. It was a fact Dabney rarely let him forget.

"Did your father find a job yet?"

Craig climbed on his mountain bike and said nothing. *Ignore him,* he thought. *It's too good of a day to ruin it messing around. Besides, I've got friends now. They may have ignored me, but nobody likes him.*

"I thought so," Dabney said. "Catch you later, pleb."

Craig rode away.

Dabney headed down Satchell Hill.

Craig wondered, *Is he going to the pool or the pond? If it's Lancaster Pond, what's going to happen when he runs into Max and everybody? Nothing good, I'm sure.* He rode the rest of the way up the hill without stopping. He was sweating when he reached the top, but his mind was clear. All his thoughts were about the campout.

Jeremy has a two-man tent? he thought. *What about the others?*

Craig had a tent, too, but it was a giant Army tent. His father had given it to him when he was ten. It was as big as a house. It had five poles, four for the corners and a longer one to hold up the middle. His father had called it a Command Tent.

Should I bring it? It's too heavy for me to carry. One person isn't going to help either. It would take four kids to carry the canvass plus two for the poles, the bag of ropes, and the pegs. I'll ask Jeremy. Unless they plan to sleep on the ground? No, that can't be it. Can it? What if it rains?

Craig looked up along Ms. Adler's driveway. It led to the right side of her house. He spotted her next. His mind went blank. She was on the porch in her rocking chair, her head slumped to one side. Craig thought she looked dead. He cursed himself for the relief that thought brought him. He pushed his bike slowly up the drive and set it against the house. He untied the bags and carried them around her ancient Mercedes-Benz. His eyes never left her. He was close enough to see she was breathing. Her breasts rose and fell with the even rhythm of sleep. Craig relaxed, sweat dripping from his hair onto his knee.

At least she isn't dead. No tip from a dead woman.

"Gross," Craig whispered.

He looked over his shoulder. The old house was sitting on a crest overlooking Lancaster. The driveway slanted downward at a horrendous angle, but the whole town spread out before him alive with green trees and magnificent houses. The view was breathtaking. It had an incredible sense of serenity. St. Peter's steeple thrust skyward in the distance. It looked like a finger pointing in God's direction.

Funny, Craig thought. *I wasn't sure I believed in God until today.*

After everything he had gone through, God had finally taken notice of him. He resisted the urge to yell, "It's about time!" at the top of his lungs.

Each step creaked as Craig climbed them. He heard Ms. Adler lightly snoring. It was a shame some of the items she'd ordered were perishable. Every instinct screamed for him to drop the bags and run. Ms. Adler looked worse than she usually did. Her hair was disheveled. Huge black bags hung beneath her eyes like rotten fruit. Craig scrunched up his nose as he got close to her. The scent of her body odor nearly made him vomit.

Doesn't she wear deodorant? he wondered, breathing through his mouth. *It doesn't smell like it.* He set the bags on top of the steps trying not to make any noise. *Not that it matters. I have to wake her up. Maybe I can go back to my bike and call to her.*

"Ooh," Ms. Adler moaned, turning her head toward him.

Crap! Craig thought. *My timing really blows!* "Ms. Adler?" he asked, not wanting to touch her.

She thrust out her hand and grabbed his arm. She'd moved so fast, he hadn't had time to dodge. Her eyes snapped open. They were blue, wild, and raging as she stared at him. She looked terrified.

Craig tried to pull away. He was about to scream.

"No! *Please*, Craig!" Ms. Adler begged, tears welling up in her eyes.

Craig's scream caught in his throat. He became lost in her frantic gaze. Her grip hurt him.

"Let go of me!" Craig whined.

"Please! *Listen!*" Ms. Adler cried, leaning toward him. "You have to help me! Help me warn them! Help me warn…!"

Ms. Adler stiffened, and then convulsed. Craig tried to get free, but she held him fast. He stared into her eyes, horrified. He couldn't believe what he was seeing. Her irises clouded. Her face distorted as if she was fighting some unseen enemy. She grimaced, straining. Craig watched terrified as her eyes changed color from blue to dark brown.

"… help me… *warn…*"

"Help you what?" Craig cried, almost in tears. "Warn who?"

"… *everyone…,*" Ms. Adler whispered, but then stopped. Her brown eyes widened. She glared at him. She looked surprised. "Help me… carry in the groceries, Master Dougan. I am an old woman." She scowled. "Where is the Gibbons girl who usually comes here? Have we not seen enough of each other this year?" She let go of his arm, forcing a calm. She rubbed her eyes. "You did well in my class. You passed with a *B.*"

Craig pulled his arm back and rubbed it. *I got a B in her class?* he thought. *That's good news. One less beating for me.* He swallowed and said, "Lisa's car… it's in the shop…"

"Quiet!" Ms. Adler commanded, peering into his eyes. It felt like she was reaching inside his brain with her gaze.

Craig wanted to turn around and run for his life. *Why are her eyes so shiny? Screw the bike and screw the tip! I just want to get the heck out…!*

"Relax, Master Dougan," she said, pinching the bridge of her nose. Her eyes returned to normal. "You have nothing to fear from me. If I had wanted to harm you, I would have simply flunked you and let your father do the dirty work." She grinned at the stunned look on his face. "I was… dreaming when you woke me. Now, *relax.*"

Craig felt the fear flow out of his body all at once and he *relaxed.* He suddenly had no idea what had scared him so much.

Her eyes! That was so freaky the way they…!

"So, Master Dougan," Ms. Adler said. "Can you carry my bags into the kitchen?"

"Sure, Ms. Adler," Craig replied, scooping the bags up by the handles. "Where do you want them?"

"On the counter is fine. Your tip is by the window."

128

Craig disappeared into the house. It was immaculately clean and orderly. He observed, *The furniture looks as old as she is, but in way better shape. She's borderline decrepit and old hag.*

"Have a care, Master Dougan!" Ms. Adler hissed.

Craig didn't hear her. There was a hint of disinfectant in the air. He scrunched up his nose. *It smells like a hospital in here,* he thought. He brought the bags into the kitchen.

"Sleeping out with the McKee boys tonight, Master Dougan?" she softly said. "Did you know you will be camping quite near Hiram's farm?" She smiled.

Craig set the bags on the counter next to the Hazardous Waste Container. He recognized it from class and looked at it, oddly.

What's that doing here?

It became a low priority when he spotted his tip. He supposed he shouldn't be surprised to see the container. Ms. Adler was not only their science teacher, but she was also a doctor. She had several PhDs hanging on her classroom wall and an MD in internal medicine. Some areas like Biochemistry and Genetic Engineering Craig knew, but he could barely read the names of some of the others. He never understood why someone who had spent a lifetime studying and gaining medical degrees would settle for being a ninth-grade science teacher. She had told her class not to refer to her as *Doctor* but as *Ms.* Adler since she wasn't working in a medical profession.

"Ms. Adler?" Craig asked, coming back onto the porch.

"Is something wrong?"

"Uh, well," Craig began. He held the tip out. "This is a twenty. Uncle Mike said you usually tip ten."

"Pshaw," she scolded. "Take the money. It is about time you had some for yourself."

Craig's eyes widened. He barely touched the steps as he fled to his bike. *Time to go!* he thought. *This is getting too weird!* "Thanks!" he called, but she was asleep again. He peddled for all he was worth. The farther he got away from her, the more his mind cleared. *Twenty dollars or no twenty dollars, I hope I never see that woman again. Her eyes! God that was so freaky! I don't care what anybody else thinks, Ms. Adler's a witch. That's all there is to it. How else could she know dad takes all my money? I never told anyone! How does she know so much?*

Craig didn't stop peddling until he was in the market's parking lot.

*   *   *

Ms. Adler waited until Craig disappeared over the crest of the hill before she stood up. She went inside the house, closed the door, and clenched her fists. Her lips curled up in a snarl.

"You fool!" she cried, her voice turning deep and throaty. "Do anything like that again and when this is over? I will not let you live as I had planned!"

She went to the kitchen and put her groceries away. She lifted the Hazardous Materials Container off the counter, went to the basement door, and vanished down the stairs.

"Computer?" she asked.

"Yes, doctor?" an electronic voice replied, in eerie monotone.

"Lights."

*   *   *

Craig nearly plowed Mike over as he burst into the market headed for the time clock.

Mike grabbed him by a belt loop and spun him around. "Whoa there, Flash!" he exclaimed. "Where's the fire?"

"No fire," Craig panted.

"Then what's the rush?" Mike asked. "How did it go with Ms. Adler?"

Craig debated telling Mike the whole story. He decided, *No, Uncle Mike is liable to think I'm nuts. I'm beginning to think I am!*

"Fine! She tipped me twenty bucks!"

"Don't tell Lisa. She'll have a spaz."

"I won't," Craig replied. "I ran into Matt Gardner on the way up."

"Oh?" Mike asked, wondering if there was a problem. He found the Gardner file in his mental customer index and relaxed. *Another good kid. Craig's on a roll.* "And?"

"He's going to the campout tonight, too. A lot of people are. Max, Chris McKee, even Derek Mellon."

Mike nodded. "Remember what I said about partying."

"I do," Craig nodded. "I'll be careful."

"Call me if you have any problems," Mike said. "Now, get going. You've got a lot to do at home before you can leave."

"Tell me about it," Craig sighed, rolling his eyes. He punched his timecard. He was gone before his uncle made it back to his office.

Be kind to him, God, Mike prayed. *Craig needs a break.*

He opened the office door, but paused. He felt someone watching him. He saw Dan on a milk crate behind the time clock in the middle of his break.

Mike gave him a half-wave and slipped into the office.

Dan glared back at him, but Mike didn't notice.

So, Dan thought, crushing his empty soda can in his fist. *Derek's going to the campout anyway? We'll see about that. We'll just see...*

*   *   *

"C'mon, mom!" Chris pleaded, leaning over the dining room table. "Will you give me a break?"

Virginia shook her head. She flipped over the grilled cheese sandwiches her sons were going to eat before they left whether they liked it or not. She suspected they would be drinking. They would have something in their stomachs besides the breakfast they had wolfed down before school.

"Sit," Virginia directed. She pointed to Chris' usual chair. "You're eating."

"We can eat at the campsite!" Chris groaned, checking the clock.

Virginia gave him *The Look*.

Chris sighed loudly with a growl. He sat at the table. He set his chin in his palms. Jeremy knew *The Look* as well as his brother. He slipped into the chair across from Chris and shrugged. Chris rolled his eyes.

Matt stood in the doorway not sure what to do.

"Excuse me, Mr. Gardner?" Virginia asked. "Have you eaten yet?"

"Uh... no, ma'am," Matt replied. He looked at Chris and Jeremy for guidance. They shook their heads.

"Then sit!"

Matt was in a chair before the last syllable faded into silence. "I was hungry anyway," he whispered to Jeremy, who smiled.

"Good!"

Matt blushed.

"She hears everything," Jeremy said. Matt blushed deeper. "She's got Bionic ears, or something."

"That's Susan Sturgess," Chris corrected. "Our mom has radar."

"My mom's got antennas," Matt said. "I've seen them pop out of her head before."

"Me, too," Chris said. *I'm going to have to eat to get out of here. It means being a little late getting to the pond, but Max will wait. He's good like that.*

"Now, boys," Virginia said. "It's not nice to talk about Linda that way even if it is true." She cleared her throat. "They're silver, I think, like old fashioned TV antennas."

The boys laughed. Chris knocked his baseball cap off when he went to wipe his eyes. His long bangs fell into his face. His hairstyle was the best, but sometimes it was a royal pain. Without the hat, he was blind as a bat. He slipped under the table, retrieved it, and slapped it onto his head backward.

"Are you ready for the game, Jeremy?" Matt asked, watching Virginia out of the corner of his eye. He quickly looked away when she turned toward him, sensing his gaze. *Yup. Radar.*

"Oh, crap!" Jeremy exclaimed.

"What's wrong?" Chris asked. "Need a smaller cup?"

"Eat me, donkey dick," Jeremy replied.

Virginia sighed, "My sons, the eloquent ones."

"Seriously," Matt said, grinning. He could imagine the look on his mother's face if she'd heard any of this. "Is something wrong?"

Jeremy got up from the table. "I forgot to talk to my dad about it. He promised to come to a game and this is the last one of the season."

"Not if we win," Matt corrected.

"But what if we don't?" Jeremy asked.

Matt assured him that as long as he was pitching there was no way they could lose. Jeremy shrugged and went to his father's study. Matt was curious why it meant so much to him to have his father there, but he decided not to ask. Cynthia Mellon was the nosy one, not him. Chris knew why and his heart went out to his brother.

Virginia's did, too. *Jeremy loves him so much,* she thought.

Thomas was his dad, but it was always more than the bond between father and son between them. They were mirror images of each other. Jeremy felt alone each time his father disappeared to save another small part of the world. Virginia could see him in her memory. He was eight years old standing in the yard wearing his baseball cap and holding his glove. Leaves were falling all around him as he waved goodbye to Thomas, the black Porsche easing out of the drive. Jeremy wore his forced smile until the car turned the corner. It would fade as loneliness blanketed his face in a shroud of desperate longing.

Jeremy would wait for hours refusing invitations from friends to go play. He wanted his father to see him there when he came home, a loyal knight at the castle walls, standing watch, awaiting the return of a wandering King. When Jeremy heard the low growl of the Porsche approaching, the sunlight would return to his eyes. His sadness would wash away as he ran into his father's arms laughing, holding on to him as if that might keep him from going away again. All would be well until the next time, and then the boy with the baseball cap and glove would wait all over again.

Virginia thought, *My shining silver knight, alone in his diligence, waiting for the King he loves more than anything else in the world.*

"What's wrong, mom?" Chris asked, watching her wipe away a tear.

"Hmm?" Virginia asked. She smiled. "I was just thinking about how much I love you guys."

"Oh," Chris nodded. "Cool."

Matt looked at him expectantly.

"What?" Chris asked.

"Don't you love your mom, too?" Matt asked.

"She knows that. It's not like I have to say it, or anything."

Virginia smiled. *Indeed, my love.*

Down the hall, Jeremy knocked on the doorjamb of his father's study. He watched Thomas dutifully typing instructions into the law firm's case files. It was part of his responsibilities as a partner in the firm even on his day off. Jeremy was proud. His father was a brilliant lawyer, but it took up a lot of his time, even on the weekends. Chris was okay with that because he spent most of his time with their mom. Jeremy needed his father. Every game he pitched was for him, all of the hard work he put into his grades was to make him proud. How many times over the years had he taken a back seat to his father's career?

Too many, Jeremy thought. *Just once, I'd like to be first.*

Virginia was always there for him when it came to activities like baseball. She went to every game. Chris was there when he needed someone to talk to, but part of Jeremy was always missing whenever his father was gone. The joy of triumph was paler, the agony of being beaten unbearable. Everything a kid could want in a lifetime surrounded him. Thomas had sacrificed a lot to be who he was and to give his family the best. Jeremy knew he was one of those sacrifices and that hurt sometimes. It hurt a lot.

"Dad?" Jeremy asked.

"Hmm?" Thomas replied, distracted. He had a pencil between his teeth. He stared at his monitor. He didn't look up. *No, Batchelder, you bonehead!* he thought, typing those words into the file. *Do not accept a plea bargain! You can win this case!*

Jeremy was about to walk away. His father was engrossed in his work. He didn't want to disturb him. *It's no big deal,* he rationalized. *There's always next year.*

As he turned, his father spoke.

"What's up, Remy?" Thomas asked. He set the pencil down and moved on to the next file. *Finally,* he thought. *An out of court settlement, piece of cake.*

"I was just wondering if you had a minute," Jeremy replied. *Remy. Nobody else calls me that except dad.*

"Sure, buddy," Thomas said. *Settle!* he typed and moved to another file.

Even though there were only twelve junior lawyers at Connecticut Legal Associates, there were over a hundred pending cases. It was Thomas' job to keep them flowing smoothly as he did with the probate and estate matters. The income from those alone paid for their house in four years.

Jeremy cleared his throat and crossed his fingers. "I was hoping you could come to my game on Friday. It's the..."

"Friday?" Thomas asked, looking over the next file. *Good girl,* he thought. He typed, *Push for a mistrial, Brenda-Lee. See me in my office Wednesday at noon.* "No can do, sport," he continued. "Big Probate matter I've got to handle. Mrs. Alberdeen, *The Hand Soap Queen?* Very old money. Maybe next time, okay?"

"Sure," Jeremy mumbled, and shuffled away.

He didn't even get the chance to tell him this might be the last game of the season. Jeremy knew his father loved him, but there were times it hurt to see how easily he was passed over. He returned to the dining room and sat down. His mother laid out sandwiches and a bowl of soup for each of them. He painted on his best smile. The boys didn't notice he was upset, but Virginia did. She could read him like a book. Once their food was in front of them with milk and a Twinkie, she slipped down the hall toward the den.

Time for a wake-up call for the attorney, Virginia thought.

"Oh!" Matt exclaimed, swallowing a piece of grilled cheese. "Guess who I ran into coming down here?"

Jeremy and Chris looked at each other and shrugged. They asked, "Who?" in unison.

"Craig Dougan."

"Really? What was he doing up here?" Jeremy asked. He wondered if there was a problem with Craig camping out tonight. He hoped not. Jeremy was glad he was going. He couldn't figure out why Craig never returned his gestures of friendship. Maybe he was just shy, or something. It could also be because his father was so mean. There was something about Craig that Jeremy liked.

"Yeah," Chris agreed. "Doesn't he live on the other side of town?"

"Gator Road," Jeremy said, "near Ramirezes' house."

Chris nodded stuffing the rest of his sandwich into his mouth.

"He was delivering groceries to Ms. Adler," Matt replied.

Chris choked on his sandwich.

Jeremy jumped up and patted him on the back.

Chris was okay after a hard swallow, but a little out of breath. It was a good thing, too. Jeremy was about to Heimlich his brother something severe.

"Is he crazy!?" Chris coughed, his face flushed. "She's a psycho!" He remembered her class well. All that stuff about genetics and how hard she pushed them to learn it? His head started spinning just thinking about it.

"I agree," Matt replied, "but that's not even the good part. Guess what he told me?"

Chris and Jeremy looked at each other again and shrugged. They chorused, "What?"

"Would you guys cut that out?" Matt whined. "That's so weird."

"You know what they're saying about McKees these days," Jeremy said.

"We're all messed up," Chris concluded.

They laughed.

Matt thought, *At least they're taking this rumor thing well. I don't know how I would handle it if I were in Chris' shoes. I would probably move to Alaska and get as far away from Lancaster as I could.*

"Max invited him to the campout."

"Really?" Chris asked.

Jeremy nodded, munching his sandwich.

"Seriously," Matt said.

"It's okay, you guys," Jeremy said. "Craig's cool. He's going to tent with me. It isn't his fault his father's such a bastard. I think it's about time someone asked him to do something."

"Exactly," Chris and Matt said at the same time.

They laughed again.

"You guys are infecting me," Matt said.

Jeremy said, "I'm meeting Craig at his house."

They nodded. Chris didn't know Craig. His reputation at school was non-existent except for the stories about how his father beat him up. He wondered if they were true. If they were, he hoped Craig wasn't all messed up in the head. Matt agreed with Jeremy. There was a lot about Craig to like even if he slipped beneath their attention sometimes. He knew a lot of people ignored him, but he didn't know anyone who disliked him.

Whoops! Matt thought. *Scratch that. Dabney's mean to Craig whenever he gets the chance.*

Matt was curious why no one had ever gone to Craig's defense before. He decided he would help him from now on if Dabney bothered him.

Virginia slipped into the study and sat down on the sofa. Thomas was so focused inputting data he hadn't noticed she'd come in. She cleared her throat. Thomas turned to his wife and saw *The Look*. He shut the monitor off and gave her his undivided attention. When she got *The Look,* he knew it was something important.

"Jeremy spoke to you a little while ago?" Virginia asked.

Thomas tried to remember what his son had just said to him. "Something about a Little League game?"

Virginia's eyebrows shot up. She rose and shut the door. She thought, *I knew it! I'll bet money he never even turned away from that computer screen long enough to look Jeremy in the eye!*

Virginia knelt on the floor between his legs. He saw the concern in her eyes. "Not just any game," she scolded. "The last game! If they win, they play in the tournament. If they lose, that's it for the year. How many times did you promise to go to a game, and how many times have you let him down?"

"Call him in here," Thomas said.

Virginia called Jeremy. She slipped her arm across his shoulders when he appeared looking bewildered.

Thomas cleared his throat. "I'm sorry, Remy. I messed up a few minutes ago. I'll reschedule with Clair so I can come to your game."

"Yes!" Jeremy cried, pumping his fist. He crossed the room in a bound and hugged his dad.

Virginia faded into the hallway. She left Jeremy alone with him, confident Thomas no longer needed coaching on the finer points of parenthood. She could tell by the way Jeremy was hugging him.

Thomas thought, *How much have I missed over the years? Jeremy will be off to college before I know it.*

"I love you, dad," Jeremy said.

"I love you, too, Remy," he said. "Did I ever tell you how proud of you I am?"

Jeremy shrugged. "Sometimes."

"I am, you know," Thomas said. "You're the most important thing in the world to me. I'm sorry for not being there like I should, and I'm sorry for what happened today."

"Jeremy!" Chris called from the hall. "Let's go, bro!"

"It's okay, dad," Jeremy said. "I guess I just need to hear that sometimes."

"You will, I promise. Will you do me a favor while I'm thinking about it?"

"Sure," Jeremy replied.

"Don't get too drunk tonight."

Jeremy looked at his father in stunned silence. He turned and walked out to meet his brother.

Thomas frowned. *Screw you, McKee,* he thought, *if you ever make your son feel like that again.*

Chris and Matt were waiting by the front door holding the gear. Jeremy took what was his and they stepped outside. Virginia kissed each of them on the cheek. She told them to be careful. They promised they would. They walked across the lawn in single file momentarily distracted by their thoughts. Chris was thinking about his upcoming conversation with Ricardo. Matt reflected on his anger toward Dan Mellon.

Jeremy asked, "Are we drinking tonight?"

Chris and Matt looked at each other. They exchanged knowing glances.

"Why?" Chris asked.

"Do you know what dad just said to me?"

"Nope," Chris replied, adjusting his backpack. "What did he say?"

"Don't get too drunk tonight," Jeremy replied.

Chris and Matt stopped. They weren't sure if their hearts were beating. They looked at each other. *Should we be worried?* they wondered.

Jeremy kept walking.

Chris shrugged at Matt who was holding his chest. They moved quickly to catch up.

"You know," Matt said, "my dad said the same thing to me before he left for work."

"Really?" Chris asked.

Matt nodded.

Jeremy felt like he was walking on air. "Dads are cool, huh?"

Chris agreed. He thought, *No need to worry. Dad would've said something if there was a problem. It's funny. Sometimes I forget how smart my parents are.*

Matt thought about it and decided Jeremy was right. He said, "Yeah, I guess dads *are* cool."

✳   ✳   ✳

Craig left the market and headed up Route 41. He peddled as if Max was chasing him again. He grinned at how that made him feel. It was the greatest feeling in the world, but not destined to last. As he reached Top Road, his back tire blew out with a loud pop. Craig hopped off his bike. There was a jagged piece of glass embedded in the rubber. The tire was slashed along the rim and beyond patching.

Why me? Craig thought.

He shook his head and started to push the bike home. He didn't get far before his grandmother drove up. She stopped on the side of the road and called him over to her red Ford Tempo.

"What is it, lad?" Nancy asked, kissing her grandson's cheek. "Your face is so long it's almost touchin' th' blacktop." She thought, *It hadn't better be that no good father o' his, or by God...*

"I got a flat, grandma," Craig replied. He pointed at the tire.

Nancy nodded. "Well," she said, trying to cheer him up, "a fine, working boy such as yourself should have no problem buyin' a new one, isn't that right?"

Craig shrugged. He lowered his gaze.

"Have ye no money lad?" Nancy asked.

Craig slowly shook his head. "Just the tip I got from Ms. Adler today, but it's not enough for a tire."

Nancy opened her mouth to ask him where his pay was, but she stopped. *Why put th' boy on th' spot?* she thought. *Ye know exactly where th' money's goin', into Jack's pocket, into th' bloody bar. Lord, I wish I had th' strength t' do somethin' about that.*

Nancy's guilt wouldn't allow it. Jack had given up years of his income for the family. If he required the same from his son, she couldn't say anything about it.

Wade didn't drink it away! she thought.

"C'mon, Craig, me love," she said, unclipping the trunk key from her key ring. "Load th' bike in th' back. I'll take ye t' th' bike shop in Stafford t' have it fixed."

"But grandma!" Craig exclaimed. "I'm meeting my friends at three o'clock to go camping!"

"Well then," Nancy replied, checking her watch, "we best be movin' along then, hmm? I'll have ye back in time t' meet your mates."

Craig threw the bike into the trunk. He tied the lid down with some twine she kept in a bucket in the back. His grin was worth Fort Knox to her. Nancy waited for him to buckle his seatbelt before she made a U-turn and headed toward Stafford.

They arrived at *Lester's Bike Shop* on Main Street in five minutes flat. Nancy claimed she obeyed the speed limit, but Craig knew better. She hardly looked at the speedometer. Luckily the bike shop didn't have any customers. Craig talked non-stop about the campout and the boys who were going with him while Lester changed his tire.

Nancy said she was happy he had made some friends. She thought, *Craig needs t' spend time with his peers. Jack lost his childhood to Hiram...* She forced her mind to change the subject.

A voice in her thoughts wouldn't let her. It whispered, *Guilt is it?*

Nancy swore it sounded like Wade. *He would speak through me guilt.* She scowled.

A mother knows, lass... ye knew.

She shook her head. *Afghanistan took pieces o' Jack as well! He didn't have th' heart for murder!*

It was Hiram, too... ye know it was. Ye made th' wrong choice... sacrificed him in vain.

Damn ye, no!

Nancy blocked out the voice. She said, "Ye mind yourself, lad. Treat others how ye want them t' treat ye and ye'll have friends for life."

Craig assured her he would.

The tire took longer than anticipated. Craig got into one conversation or another with the young man who owned the business, Lester Cross. Not only did he sell mountain bikes and Rollerblades, but he also raced Motocross. His trophies lined the shelves above his workbench. Craig listened as Lester described how he had won them. The largest one he got when he was only twelve.

"Wow!" Craig exclaimed, while Nancy patiently waited for him. "You mean I'm old enough to race?"

"I don't know," Les replied. "How old are you?"

Craig rolled his eyes and thought, *The curse of the eleven-year-old physique.* "I'm almost fifteen."

Les said, "You sure could."

Craig noticed the time and told his grandmother they should go.

Nancy paid for the tire with her *Discover Card* and they left. This time the conversation was filled with motorcycles and Motocross. Nancy prayed for strength. Such a sport would give her even more gray hairs.

Craig got home with little time to spare. He locked his bike up and ran back to kiss his grandmother goodbye. He slipped into the house to get the mess cleaned up and his camping gear ready. Jeremy should be there shortly. Craig closed the door, turned around, and his heart shattered. His panic rose at the sight that greeted him. A trail of blood on the living room floor led from the broken glass in the hallway to the kitchen table. Smeared footprints outlined the path.

Craig knelt down near them. Dread enclosed his heart. The worst thing that could possibly happen had happened. Jack had woken up, forgot about the glass, and stepped on it. It was a severe cut judging by the amount of blood. Bandages lay on the table. A dry pool of maroon rested beneath one of the chairs. Craig started to cry. He went out to the back porch and sat down with his face in his hands. Tears ran down his wrists.

Nothing matters now, Craig thought, sobbing with force. *I am one hundred percent dead meat.*

*   *   *

Lancaster Pond

Max and Ricardo stepped off the trail from Gibbons' Garage onto the hot parking lot at Lancaster Pond and knew it was going to be a long day. Nearly every square inch of the beach had a body on it. Ricardo observed they were mostly women and children. He pulled Max over to the sand.

"¡Ay Dios mío!" Max exclaimed. "Look at them all!"

A crowd was surrounding the lifeguard chatting with him. His name was Andre Lee. He was Andrea's older brother. He was going to be a senior in the fall. Max envied his physique. Andre was only five-foot-seven – all of the Lee kids were small – but he was ripped. He and his siblings were blackbelts in Taekwondo.

Their mom, Hope Cromwell-Lee, was a retired U.S. Army Intelligence officer. She had served her entire twenty years in South Korea where she'd met and married Chae-Ku, and where her children were born. She brought her family home to Lancaster when she retired. Chae-Ku owned the Lancaster White Tiger Dojang in the same strip mall where Linda Gardner and Dr. Stone had their offices. The dojang was on the right side. Tina's Salon was on the left. All the kids in town went to Tina to get their hair cut. She was wicked cool. Lancaster Pharmacy, Gardner's Insurance, and Dr. Stone were in the middle.

Max saw the Lees do a demo once at career day when he was in eighth grade at Lancaster Middle School. Andrea and her youngest brother, Andy, did a routine with their dad that included weapons. Andrea used Kamas. Andy used Nunchucks. Max thought it was the most amazing thing he'd ever seen. Andy whipped those things around so fast they were a blur. He would be a freshman next year. He was the same age as Derek. Although all of the Lee kids had Asian facial features, Andy looked the most Korean. He was a cheerful kid from what Max knew of him. He smiled a lot, was obsessively polite, and had a goal to earn every merit badge that Scouts had to offer. Max was positive Andy would still be a Scout when he reached retirement age.

The Ramirez bothers wondered, *How can there be so many people here?*

They didn't think there were these many people in the entire town. The swimming pool at Legion Field had crowds like this. The farmer, Hiram Milliken, donated the land and money to build it on the condition children from Lancaster swam for free. Adults paid a fee each season to help maintain the facility. It was the reason the Ramirez brothers and their friends liked coming here better. Lancaster Pond was usually vacant.

A diving raft floated in the middle of the dark water. It was held in place by four thick chains each attached to a fifty-pound block of cement embedded in the silt. It was alive with Lancaster High School kids. The Ramirez brothers recognized them. Colin Skinner stuck out more than any of the others. Ricardo thought Colin had given up on water after that day in the boys' room.

Ricardo smiled and thought, *It's a good thing Jeremy was there to save fat boy's bacon.*

Most of the kids were diving off the raft or cannonballing into the water. A few were hanging out on the platform in the bright sunshine trying to look cool. There were little kids on the sand near the edge of the water. Some were building sand castles while others dug holes. China was closer than people thought and they intended to prove it.

"¡Ay Chihuahua!" Ricardo cried, as a group of four Annie Potts Elementary fourth grade kids almost knocked him over. They were chasing a fifth grade boy who had shoved his little sister into their sandcastle trying to push her into the water.

"Get him!" they cried.

They tackled him, picked him up by his arms and legs, and threw him into the pond. He came up sputtering and sobbing. They walked back slapping their hands off.

"Serves him right."

"Yeah, the goober."

"Castle-wrecker."

Ricardo watched them pass with his mouth hanging open. He looked at Max who reached over and shut it for him.

"No lo sé, mi hermano," Max said. "Where did they all come from?"

"No clue," Ricardo replied. He scanned the crowd. "It looks like the whole town is here, man. Look over there."

Ricardo pointed toward the woodline. Max followed his brother's finger. His eyes found Dabney on the beach with a group of girls from school. He was wearing blue Speedos and black Ray-Ban sunglasses. He could see his barrage of shoulder freckles from here.

"Dabney Copeland," Max said. "Just what we need."

"No, Max," Ricardo replied. He wasn't pointing at Dabney. "Over by the woods."

Max strained his eyes until he saw what Ricardo meant. Sandy, Ian, and Derek were at the spot where the pond's lawn ended and the woods began. They were standing in the shade next to their gear. Sandy spotted the Ramirez brothers and waved to them. Ricardo waved back. They made their way across beach. The girls in Dabney's group stared at them as they passed.

Heidi Siemczyk smiled at Ricardo. He smiled back.

Dabney scowled at him.

Max took the gear from Ricardo and set it down with the rest. Ian was sitting on a stump next to his stuff. He had his chin in his hands and a scowl on his face. Max backhanded him on the shoulder. Ian gave a weak smile. Huge dimples appeared on his cheeks among his multitude of freckles. His blonde hair was clean, shining, and feathered back so perfectly it looked like he had just walked out of Tina's Salon.

Max stooped over and asked, "Who pissed in your Wheaties, Ian?"

"Sandy's being a jerk," Ian grumbled.

"Shut up, you wuss," Sandy said.

Max shrugged his shoulders and walked back to the group. Ian was moody. The Sturgess brothers were always bickering about something.

"Where did all of these people come from?" Max asked, stepping over to Sandy. "Shouldn't they be at the pool?"

Sandy replied, "It's closed today. The lifeguard quit." His tone was sharp.

Max thought, *Something's bothering him. At least I know why there are so many people here.*

Derek Mellon was about as tall as Max's chest. He walked over barefoot through the grass. Max thought he could get lost in the depth of his green eyes. His shoulders were already pink with sunburn. It gave some validity to his nickname, *the Lobster Boy.*

Max reached down and rubbed his soft red hair. "You should put a shirt on, Derek," he warned.

"I know, I know," Derek replied, rolling his eyes. "I'm going to look like a lobster."

"What's up with you?" Max asked, elbowing Sandy.

"Danielle," Sandy replied. "She wanted to come to the campout."

"You said no," Max said.

"Of course I did. This is guys only. She's acting like a total bitch about it."

Max understood. He had dated her in sixth grade. He felt a sudden chill.

Sandy said, "I can hear her now." He raised his voice to a whiny falsetto. *"Don't you think you've had enough, Sanford? Why don't you come over here and sit with me, Sanford? Can we take a walk alone, Sanford? You're not paying any attention to me, Sanford! Don't you love me, Sanford?"* He cleared his throat. "Screw that, dude. I want to party!"

"What's Ian's problem?" Max asked, thumbing toward the pouting member of their group.

"Omg, Max!" Sandy cried. "He's been a punk to Derek ever since he showed up at our house."

"I have not!" Ian exclaimed.

Ricardo thought, *Oh, God. Here we go already.*

"You have too!" Derek shot back, moving in-between Sandy and Max. Sandy put his hand on Derek's shoulder. He winced, but not at the sunburn. Sandy's hand was cold!

"Shut up, Lobster Boy!"

"You shut up," Derek replied. He looked up at Sandy. "All the Indians know him as *Pits in His Cheeks."*

Ricardo burst out laughing. Ian got up and walked toward Derek with his fists clenched. Sandy stood between them and warned his brother to back off. He wasn't in the mood for his crap today. Derek moved to the other side of Max.

"Chill out, Ian," Max said.

Ian went back and slumped down onto the stump. He thought, *Nobody remembers how much flak I take from Sandy, like it's okay for me to get teased! Whenever I say anything to anybody else they act like I'm a punk, or something. What's the big deal about ragging on Derek anyway? He's a wimp!*

The more Ian thought about it, the more he wanted to go home.

Forget these guys. I could always go hang out with Dan. At least he's cool, not like Derek-the-wuss. Is Dan on the level about Chris, or is he full of it? I might never know with everyone so mad at him. Sandy's on Chris' side. I couldn't believe it when he socked Dan at the grocery store! Even though I like Dan more than Derek, I had to point at him and laugh when he grabbed his guts, gasping. That was hilarious! He scowled at Derek. *It's bad enough having Lobster Boy in the same classes every day. All the girls ever talk about is how cute he is.* Ian rolled his eyes. *Still, I like Chris, but I don't like gays. I can't imagine a guy touching me. God, that would be so skeevy! Will I stop hanging around with him if he really is a flamer? You bet I will.*

Ian glared at Derek opening and closing his fist.

"Where's Matt?" Max asked. "I need to make sure he knows I invited Craig Dougan. It's his party after all. He paid for everything."

"I know," Matt said, coming up behind him. He put his arms around Max in a bear hug. "I saw him up on Satchell Hill. I swear to God, Max, Craig's so psyched his feet aren't touching the ground!"

"Hey!" Max exclaimed, easily flexing out of Matt's arms.

He spotted Chris and Jeremy a few feet away. They were a little behind since Matt had run up to grab Max.

"It's about time, you guys!"

Chris and Jeremy filed into the group and explained about having to eat. Ian got up, his frustration fading away at the sight of Matt and the McKees. They laughed and shoved at each other relishing a moment of teenage male bonding. Derek was immediately Chris' grinning shadow. Jeremy was still angry with Ricardo and walked up to him, scowling.

"Before you say anything," Ricardo said, leading Jeremy away from the group. "I'm sorry, okay? I was out of line last night, dude. I was a dick in school today, too."

"Yes, you were," Jeremy replied, showing no sympathy. "Chris wants to talk to you."

"I know," Ricardo said. "Max told me. I want to talk to him, too."

"Ricardo," Jeremy said. "I know you've got a thing about gay people..."

"I hate them."

Jeremy nodded. *This is going to be tough.* "You might not like what Chris has to say then," he continued, studying Ricardo's face, "but hear him out, okay?"

"But Chris is still... *gay,* right?"

"Talk to him, Ricardo," Jeremy replied. "You need to. We're friends, but I'm not a moron. You've always liked Chris better. Promise me you'll listen to him? He's my brother, man. I love him."

Ricardo lowered his head. *Should I say it? I have to.* "I know, Jeremy," he softly said. "I love him, too. I'm just angry, that's all."

The rest of the guys were talking about Craig. They passed around stories of some of the things they'd heard about him. Max told them what Lyle had said, but kept what he saw this morning confidential. They agreed Craig was a good kid and no one – except Ian who thought Craig was a geek – had any objections to Max inviting him. They shared the same opinion. It was about time somebody asked him to do something. Max was considered the leader when they were together. Whatever was okay with him was usually okay with everyone.

"Must be pretty lonely for the guy," Derek said.

"No kidding," Sandy agreed.

Matt walked away to check on his stash seeing as the pond was so crowded. He wanted to make sure everything was still there. Jeremy said he was heading over toward Craig's house to see if he was home yet. Chris asked Jeremy to call Sam Stone. He might want to come down, too. Chris hadn't seen him at school today and was wondering where he was. Sam didn't hang out with them much, but he was Chris' friend. Chris had a lot to say at the campout and figured it would be easier if all of his friends were together to hear it.

"Why?" Jeremy asked. "You know he doesn't party."

"I know," Chris replied. "He doesn't have to party to hang out." Another name came to his mind. "Have you seen Keith Keroack lately?"

"Sure," Jeremy replied. "He's in *B* group. I'm in *A*. He's in my gym class. He always asks about you. Every time I turn around, he brings up Scouts. I think he still goes, him and Andy Lee. I told him to call you. Did he?"

"Nope," Chris replied. "Call him, too."

"Why don't you call them? You have your iPhone with you."

Chris nodded toward Ricardo.

"Oh," Jeremy said. He held out his hand. "Give me a dollar then. I'm not your secretary."

"Oh, all right," Chris replied, digging into his pocket. "Here. Ask them to meet us if they can."

Jeremy said he would. He walked away toward the trail that led to the garage. Craig should be home by now. Maybe they'll hit it off. Jeremy hoped so. Craig seemed sad like he needed someone. Jeremy felt the same way a lot of the time. Friends surrounded him, but he didn't connect with anyone. The day seemed brighter as he crossed the parking lot and disappeared into the woods.

"Hey, Chris," Ian said, poking him in the side. "We don't have to set the tents up yet, do we?"

Chris looked at Max who shook his head. Chris agreed. There was plenty of time for that. Besides, there were too many people around and a lot of them were from school. No need to lead the whole town to their campsite. Their booze supply wasn't unlimited.

"Good," Ian smiled. His dimples split his cheeks in two. "I want to go swimming."

"Me, too," Derek agreed.

Ian said, "C'mon then, Lobster Boy."

Chris pulled Sandy aside and thanked him for sticking up for him with Dan. He was glad for friends like him. Sandy didn't even ask if it was true or not.

"You don't have to thank me, Chris," Sandy replied, patting him on the back. "I couldn't care less if you're gay. You're my friend."

"I'm glad, Sanford. I feel the same way."

"Besides," Sandy grinned, "what happens if Danielle isn't around come Prom time? I'm going to need a date." He held his chin and looked Chris over. He nodded. "You'd look pretty good in a gown. I could do worse than you, McKee."

"C'mon, Sandy," Max called, from the edge of the pond. "Let's hit the water!"

Chris silently thanked Max. He knew what he was doing. Sandy shuffled away leaving Chris alone with Ricardo. They stood in the shade facing each other. They were both worried about this moment. Chris didn't want to lose one of his closest friends over his natural sexual preference, but no real friend would walk away because of something like that. Ricardo felt torn between his memories and what he felt for Chris. He feared this conversation. He knew it would be the deciding factor over which of the two was stronger.

"I'd like to talk to you, Ricardo," Chris said, placing a hand on his shoulder.

Ricardo backed away from his touch. "Fine," he replied. "Not here. Let's take a walk somewhere."

Matt returned from checking on the cooler. It was still there. He didn't know what time Phil had dropped it off, but he was smart enough to camouflage it beneath some bushy pine tree limbs. Matt felt a flash of panic when he couldn't find it at first, but after a few moments of poking around he spotted its edge. Phil stuffed the red and white monstrosity with cans of Budweiser and a quart bottle of blackberry brandy packed in ice.

Matt winced feeling a slight pain in his wallet. He would probably have to ask someone to help him pay for everything when it came time to reimburse Phil. Chris would, he was sure, and so would Max and Ricardo. The only other person with a job right now was Craig, but Matt decided not to ask him. This was his first time hanging out with them. It wasn't much, but it was a kind gesture. A few of those might make him feel at home.

Well, not at home, Matt thought. He snapped his tongue. *You know what I mean.*

He was about to call out to Chris and Ricardo who were walking out into the woods when Max put his cold, wet hand on his shoulder. Matt jumped a little and spun around smiling. Max waved *no-no* with his forefinger.

Matt cocked his head, puzzled.

"Let them go, Matt," Max said. "Mi hermano's got a problem with gay people. Hopefully, Chris can… er… *straighten* him out."

"Oh, right," Matt replied, embarrassed. "Where's my head?"

Max said, "Ven, mi amigo, métete al agua."

"Huh?" Matt asked, having flunked Spanish One.

Max got behind him and pushed him toward the pond. Matt tried to dig in his heels, but it was too late. He was off-balance.

"Get in the water!"

Ian, Derek, and Sandy were on the shore laughing as Matt pin-wheeled into the pond. Matt wore a happy look of shock as he went under the water. He swam over to the diving platform. Max followed him. Sandy walked to the edge intending to join them, Derek and Ian right behind him. Matt and Max cleared a group of middle school kids off the platform.

It's amazing how fast Colin Skinner vanished, Sandy thought.

Before he could jump into the pond, someone called his name. Sandy cringed. The tone was like fingernails on a blackboard to him.

"Sturgess!" Dabney called again.

It sounded more like a command. Sandy walked over to him. Ian and Derek shrugged at each other and followed.

"What's your problem, Copeland?" Sandy asked.

Heidi winked at him. Sandy nodded. She was friends with Danielle.

She'll be on her cell calling Danielle as soon as I turn around, Sandy thought, grinding his teeth. *That's not going to end well. I deliberately didn't tell Danielle where we were camping to avoid any drama. Heidi's always at the pool, not here. This sucks!*

Brenda Pinkwell and Andrea Lee were sitting with her. What they saw in Copeland was beyond him. Sandy thought he was a little creep.

Dabney grinned. He took off his sunglasses and pointed toward the woodline with them. "I see Chris is talking a walk in the woods with Ricardo Ramirez."

Sandy clenched a fist. He saw where this conversation was going. "What about it, Dabney?" he asked, through his teeth.

Dabney shrugged. "Just curious. People are talking, you know? Are they a couple? Is Ramirez a homo, too? We know McKee is."

Grr!

"Is it true, Sandy?" Heidi gasped, holding her hand over her massive breasts.

"Shut up, Dabney!" Derek cried, before Sandy could say anything. "Chris ain't no homo!"

Dabney stood up and got in Derek's face. Derek stood his ground, but Sandy took charge shoving Dabney away with one hand. Dabney stumbled back, planted his feet, and stormed up to Sandy.

"Touch me again, Sturgess," Dabney said, his finger in Sandy's face, "and you'll wish you were never born."

"What're you going to do about it, wimp?" Sandy growled, snatching the finger in his fist. "Sue me?"

Max was about to do a flip off the diving platform when Matt grabbed his arm. He pointed toward the shore. Sandy had Dabney's finger and was twisting it back. Dabney was almost on his knees. Max looked at Matt and they dove into the water, swimming toward shore.

Sandy let go of his finger with a jerk.

Dabney exploded, "You screwed up big time, *Sturgess!* Nobody touches me!"

"Then don't talk about Chris like that, Dabney!" Derek yelled.

Dabney looked at him like he was crazy. "Screw you, Mellon! Your brother's the one telling everybody Chris is gay! What's the matter, *Lobster Boy?* Doesn't anyone in your retarded-ass family tell you anything, or are you really just as dumb as you look? Dye the hair, too, Bozo the Clown wannabe."

Derek's face turned scarlet. His green eyes narrowed to slits. "What are you talking about?"

"I'm talking about what Dan told me," Dabney replied, his grin returning. "Chris told him he was gay. It makes me wonder how many more of you losers are." He gestured at Derek with his chin. "You look like a little fag to be honest. What about it, Mellon? Are you McKee's little ginger butt buddy?"

Matt and Max came out of the water near the shore. Max swished his flattop out with his hands. Matt shook his long blonde hair like a dog. They were worried Sandy might be having a problem with Dabney. Their vision cleared. They looked over toward the guys in time to see Derek, his eyes blazing, draw back his fist and punch Dabney in the face.

*   *   *

Chris and Ricardo walked side by side in silence. They had left the trails and headed deep into woods. Every time Chris tried to get close to his friend, Ricardo moved out of arm's reach. Gray squirrels hopped from tree to tree nearby in the shade. They chattered warnings of the passing humans. Ordinarily, Chris loved it out here. The scent of pine and cedar mingled together. It smelled clean and pungent at the same time. He was in the wild, no pressure, one with nature, fully aware of the world around him. Today it seemed pale, muted, expecting. There was such a potential for pain in the air.

Ricardo sat down on a moss-covered log.

Chris maintained the distance between them and sat, too. He thought, *This is my fault. How many times did we poke fun at gay people? How many times did I initiate it? The subject aggravated Ricardo so much, I thought it was fun pushing his buttons. Now I know, all that time, I was laughing at myself.*

When Chris realized he was gay, he'd kept silent about his sexual preference for fear of this conversation more than any other. He had suspected Ricardo's dislike of gay people was rooted deep inside him. It was so intense it frightened Chris. Now he saw it as a time bomb wound down to the last dreadful seconds.

"Is it true, Chris?" Ricardo asked, staring at his feet. "Are you gay?"

Chris steeled himself. *Here we go.* "Yes, Ricardo. I'm…"

Ricardo jumped up. "I knew it!" He pointed an accusing finger at Chris. "How could you let yourself become a queer?"

"I didn't let myself become anything," Chris replied. "It's just natural for me. I think I've always known. I was born this way. Dan had no right telling everybody."

"I know that!" Ricardo snapped. "You're still *gay,* right?"

Chris stared at him.

Ricardo glared back.

Why is he so angry? Chris wondered. *This can't only be about me. Nothing ever happened between us to foster this kind of hostility.*

"Ricardo, we've been friends for a long time."

"Yeah, sure Chris," Ricardo said. "Probably so you could get me one day, right? Isn't that why you've wanted me around?"

"That's not true!"

"No?"

"I swear it's not!"

"You know, I trusted you, Chris," Ricardo said. "We've slept in the same tent, we've slept in the same bed, and do you know what? You were my best friend." Ricardo's tears fell as his anger gave way to despair. "But now I feel used. I can't stop thinking you only wanted to be near me because you like being near other guys." He wiped his eyes with the back of his hands. "Now that you know you can't get me, who are you going after next? Derek? Dougan?"

Chris raised an eyebrow. "I'm not a pedophile, Ricardo."

"There's no difference!"

Chris was about to argue the point when a look in Ricardo's eyes betrayed him. Chris felt his heart skip a beat. He thought, *Oh, my God, can that be right? It explains so much!*

"Jesus, Ricardo... were you molested?"

Ricardo recoiled as if struck.

"Talk to me, man," Chris insisted. "That's it, isn't it? Dude, you know you can trust me with anything."

"But you... *you're...!*"

"I'm your friend, man," Chris said. "You know that's the God's honest truth. Tell me what happened. We'll get through it together, I promise."

Ricardo shook his head.

"You need to, Ricardo," Chris said. "It's tearing you apart inside. I can see it!" He swallowed, but his throat was dry. He lowered his voice. "I know what you're going through, man, seriously."

Ricardo's face fell. "How could you?" he asked. Dread enclosed his heart. "Did it... happen to you, too?"

Chris didn't reply. He only nodded, then he frowned.

"God, Chris... what happened?"

Chris shook his head. "You first. I'm your friend and I'm here for you. You can be here for me after."

"Dude, I don't... know if I can."

"You have to. We both do. No secret is worth our friendship."

Ricardo slowly sat on the log. Emotions long suppressed rushed to the surface. He tried to shove them down, but they pushed through with the knowledge, *Someone molested Chris, too?* Ricardo had been alone in his agony for so long, and yet all this time Chris carried the same burden? *Is that why we've been such good friends? Because someone hurt us?* It made sense. Ricardo always felt bonded to Chris by something. He never dreamed it was his greatest pain and shame. He took a deep shuddering breath, lowered his head, and started to cry.

Chris moved next to him and put his arm across his friend's shoulders. Ricardo didn't pull away. A dam had burst inside his mind and for the first time in his life he told the story of the Big E. He described what the pedophile had done to him in frightening detail. Ricardo never knew how much he wanted to talk about what had happened to him until he started. He kept the story of the man at the fair locked deep inside. The secret ate away at his soul like cancer. Chris understood how Ricardo felt, how helpless and dirty. He mustered his courage, and when his friend had finished, Chris told Ricardo about Hiram Milliken.

It was the first time Chris had worked a Friday night alone, two weeks after he got hired at the farm. Todd had the night off and was spending it with Frank Garrison. Hiram was out somewhere playing poker. Arrangements had been made for Chris to stay in the guest room after he agreed to work for Todd the next morning. Chris' parents had no misgivings about him sleeping over. Thomas was a Lancaster native who grew up with a lot of Hiram's ex-employees. He'd known Arthur Kelly since he was eleven and Thomas was a senior in high school. Hiram used to bring him to watch Thomas play baseball at E.O. Smith. He felt if anything had been wrong with Hiram, he would've heard about it long before now. From what Thomas understood, Arthur practically lived over there through high school. He never said anything negative about the man. Virginia met with the farmer and he seemed fine to her. They were certain Chris would be safe.

Chris trudged over to the trailer after milking the cows and cleaning the milking parlor. He threw his clothes into the washer and jumped into the shower. He sat on the couch afterward wrapped in a towel. He watched TV while waiting for the dryer, a half a bottle of wine in his hand. Hiram had given it to him before he left. He said he always let his workers drink when they stayed over as long as they didn't squeal. Chris thought that was cool, kind of like Phil. He unscrewed the top and took the red wine into his mouth, but he didn't swallow it. He dashed to the sink and spat it out.

Jeeze! Chris thought, looking strangely at the bottle. *It tastes like medicine!*

Chris poured the wine down the sink and left the bottle on the counter. Whatever was wrong with it, he wasn't drinking it. When the dryer buzzed, he shut off the TV, retrieved his dry clothes, slipped his underwear on, and then headed to the guest room. He closed the door behind him. The bed was a little soft, but Chris was so tired he could've slept in the barn. He lay on his stomach on top of the covers and was asleep in minutes.

"What's so bad about that?" Ricardo asked.

"It's what happened after I went to sleep," Chris replied. He clenched his fist and closed his eyes. "I woke up and he was on the bed with me, you know? Doing things to me, like what happened to you? I was terrified, dude. I just laid there, paralyzed, pretending I was asleep, and trying not to scream. When it was over, he went to his room and closed the door. I went to the bathroom when I heard him snoring. I showered until the water ran cold and

I still didn't feel clean." He sucked in a lungful of air and let out a whoosh of breath. "I never cried so much in my life." He hugged his knees.

"Did you tell anyone what happened?"

Chris frowned. "I wanted to, dude, sincerely. My whole brain was screaming that I should, but I couldn't for some reason. I couldn't even say Hiram's name at first, and there was this fuzzy feeling in my head, you know? It felt like fingers were poking around in there."

"That sucks."

A tear slid down Chris' cheek. He wiped it away. "I couldn't believe what Milliken had done to me, man. I still feel dirty and used."

"I know what you mean," Ricardo said. "I felt the same way." He frowned. "You should've told somebody."

"You didn't, Ricardo!" Chris snapped. He checked himself and said, "Sorry."

"It's okay. How come you still work there?"

"I couldn't tell my parents," Chris sighed, "which is stupid because I knew they would support me, but anyway, I confronted Hiram the next day."

"You did?" Ricardo asked.

"I told him if he ever touched me again, I would tell somebody, and if I ever saw another kid sleeping over there, I would definitely tell somebody. It's been a year. I still haven't seen any kids there except Dabney, but he's such a jerk I don't think Hiram would dare."

"What about O'Connor?"

"Todd?" Chris replied. He scowled remembering what happened in the boys' room. "I asked him if Hiram had ever touched him. Todd said he would kill the old man if he even tried. I believed him. Hiram said he only did it because he was drunk. It sounded like bull to me."

"I'm sorry, Chris," Ricardo said. "Seriously, for everything."

"If you can accept me for who I am, I accept," Chris said.

"Deal."

They shook hands.

Ricardo asked, "Should we tell someone?"

Chris replied, "It's weird. Sometimes I'm overwhelmed with the need to tell someone. It's like, I'm shocked that I didn't run home and tell my mom and dad that first night. Then I get this feeling in my brain and everything goes wonky. I doubt everything. I think no one will believe me and I can't say Hiram's name for hours." He frowned. "It's strange. It's like someone else is thinking for me."

"We should say something, Chris," Ricardo said. "What if he's hurting other kids? What if he's molesting Dabney?"

"Copeland?" Chris asked. He thought, *Would Hiram dare? Dabney can be a real bastard. Is that why I feel something for him? When our eyes met on the bus this morning, something passed between us. Was that it? Is it more?*

"It could be why Dabney's such a dick."

"I don't know, Ricardo," Chris said. "Dabney doesn't strike me as someone who would tolerate Hiram for a second." He mumbled, "He's cute though."

"What did you say?" Ricardo cried, his eyes bulging.

Chris shook his head. "Never mind, smartass," he said. "We are not talking about who I think is cute, okay?"

"But... *Dabney?*" Ricardo whispered.

"I didn't say I liked him."

Ricardo pointed at him. "You so like him!"

"Pleading the Fifth," Chris muttered.

Ricardo couldn't stop laughing for five minutes.

They sat against the log for a bit before heading back to the pond. They walked slowly, their arms across each other's shoulders. They concluded they should tell someone and swore they would when they got home from camping, but by the time they got back to their gear neither thought anyone would believe them. They didn't feel like talking about it anymore either. Their friendship was saved. That was more important than anything that had happened to them what felt like a hundred years ago.

Derek was sitting with the guys holding a towel against his bloody mouth. Ricardo and Chris looked at each other. Max sighed with relief to see everything was okay between them now. Derek waved and smiled. He winced at the pain from a split lip.

Matt walked up to them. "Boy," he said, half-laughing, "have I got a story to tell you guys!"

*   *   *

Ms. Adler leaned forward, her elbows on her desk. She had her face in her hands and she was rubbing her eyes. They were burning, bloodshot, and would stay that way for the rest of the day. She needed to take better care. She was immensely fatigued after her exertions. She could sleep for a week, and sleep was her enemy. It was the only time her guard was down long enough for...

"But we have taken care of that now, have we not, my darling?" Ms. Adler asked, in her secret basement laboratory. She cocked her head listening for an answer. There wasn't one. "Ah, blessed silence." She sat back and crossed her arms. "It will not last long, but it is good enough for now." Her expression darkened. "Soon, it will be forever."

Ms. Adler felt her fatigue like a looming catastrophe. After securing her personal drama – which Craig had witnessed when he delivered her groceries – it took a great deal of effort for her to adjust Chris McKee and Ricardo Ramirez's thoughts from this distance, but she needed to. Their emotions were so intense, Chris nearly overwhelmed the psychic suggestions she established in him that kept him from revealing Hiram's assault. He was on the verge of calling his mother and telling her everything, but it wasn't time for that yet. She still needed the farmer. There were boys to kill and samples to gather. Her work was infinitely more important than Hiram diddling some teenagers.

Hundreds of boys had paid much higher prices to advance her experiments than being molested by a psychopath. The day would come when she would release all of Hiram's victims from her influence and they could tell their stories to Fox News for the rest of eternity. Destroying the farmer utterly had always been part of the plan once she'd achieved success. Until that day came, Ms. Adler couldn't care less if Hiram molested Chris McKee a hundred times. She would protect him from exposure.

The Hazardous Waste Container was on top of the table behind her. It was empty. The blood sample sticks were on her desk. She looked at her computer monitor. The words: **Compiling data, please wait...** flashed in three-second intervals. An hour had passed since she processed the boys' blood samples, but it seemed like an eternity. She needed the results. If they all failed, she would start preparing for the next school year. Principal Hogan had provided her with a list of upcoming freshmen which included Ian Sturgess.

I will be damned if I use that dimpled moron, Ms. Adler thought. *He is 'Black,' indeed.*

It was irrelevant. Ian's temper made him an impossible choice for a subject, just like his brother. Sandy's compatibility was high, too, which irritated her, but she couldn't give in to the temptation. Emotional control was a necessary factor. Sandy had the patience of a pit bull. The only one she had wanted more was Chris McKee. He was perfect for her needs except that Chris possessed the gene for homosexuality. Choosing him was impossible. There was no way she would risk his gay gene cross-contaminating her experiments. Chris had a part to play in the endgame if she found a pattern match, but that was all.

Ms. Adler turned to the lab table behind her. There was a white rat inside an empty ten-gallon fish tank running aimlessly inside a wheel. Behind it was a labyrinth of glass tubes and beakers from one end of the table to the other. Above them, on a reinforced shelf, large jars contained the brains of a select few of Hiram's victims. They were suspended in formaldehyde with an air pump blowing bubbles to keep the chemical circulating. She could have thrown them away. They were from her preliminary studies and those studies were complete. She wondered why she hadn't.

The sample she had collected from Sam Stone this morning hung upside-down below the shelf. It was inside a small bottle labeled with his name and age. It sat beside ten other bottles just like it. There were tubes in the center of each with valves in the lines that ran down to a large empty beaker. When the time was right, she would open those valves, and the future would be born. She only needed four more samples for fifteen total and she would be ready. Ms. Adler knew she couldn't rush things. At this stage, she needed her subject before she could go any further. The world had never seen such power as she was about to create.

The monitor's flickering light was giving her a headache. Her fatigue and impatience was growing. She needed to know if her search was over. It frustrated her. Too much time had passed already. Finally, the computer beeped. The words on the monitor disappeared. Ms. Adler grabbed her glasses from the corner of the desk and slipped them on. She stared anxiously at the screen as the words **Compilation Complete** appeared.

Ms. Adler smiled. "At last!" she cried, reaching for her clipboard and marker. "Computer? Results."

"Specify order."

"Random."

The synthesized computer voice echoed throughout the basement. **"Yes, Dr. Adler,"** it said, scratchy and electronic. **"Baseline data assimilated. Comparative analysis complete. Close research file: Dr. Carolyn Meyer-Brandis, The Agency. Close connection: Covert Ops, The Agency. Delete access logs. Begin. Sample thirteen, Subject: Jason Ryan Carlander: 77% match."**

Ms. Adler scratched seventy-seven percent on the clipboard next to Jason Carlander's name.

"Details," she said, shaking her head.

"Subject: Jason Ryan Carlander is an asthmatic. He possesses the genetic potential for age-related macular degeneration (AMD) and Alzheimer's disease."

Ms. Adler nodded. "Next."

"Sample two, Subject: Craig Scott Dougan," the computer continued. **"87% match."**

Ms. Adler smiled. "That's a high figure. Details."

The computer stated that Craig possessed the genetic potential for alcoholism. Ms. Adler shook her head. She jotted the figure down next to his name and told the computer to continue. Sample three was Dabney Shawn Copeland.

"Skip," she ordered. *Arrogant ass.*

"As you wish, doctor. He would not have suited your needs anyway."

"Genetically?"

"Yes, doctor, for the same reason as his brother."

"Lancaster seems to have more than its fair share of homosexuals," Ms. Adler sighed. "Next."

Sample eight, William Warren Wilde, was a mere sixty-two percent. He had a multitude of genetic personality disorders. Ms. Adler's patience waned. She told the computer to give her continuous results. The computer acknowledged.

"**Sample twelve, Subject: Matthew Randall Gardner, 78% match. Sample…**"

"Pause," Ms. Adler said. "Explain Matthew Gardner's percentage."

The computer replied that Matt had a high percentage risk for various cancers to include prostate and colon. He also possessed a gene for Muscular Dystrophy that could be passed to his offspring. She nodded, disappointed. She had hoped Matt would be a closer match. Physically, he was a perfect specimen.

"Continue."

"**Yes, Dr. Adler,**" the computer responded. "**Sample seventeen, Subject: Ricardo Juan Ramirez, 82% match.**"

Ms. Adler snorted. *A mongrel? Not likely. He is donor material.*

"**Sample twenty, Subject: Colin Andrew Skinner, 42% match. Sample one, Subject: Jeremy Alistair McKee, 97% match…**"

"Wait!" Ms. Adler cried, jumping up from her chair. She leaned forward against the desk. Her expression reflected intensity. "Details!"

"**Subject: Jeremy Alistair McKee…,**" the computer began, but then paused. After a moment, it continued, "**No genetic defects found.**"

Ms. Adler was puzzled. "No genetic defects? Explain percentage."

If there were no genetic defects, the computer was programmed to give a ninety-nine percent match. She didn't believe anything was perfect.

Why is the figure only ninety-seven percent? Ms. Adler wondered, as the computer relayed its findings.

"**Retrieving personality profile,**" it said. "**Stand by.**"

Ms. Adler searched her memory for the data regarding Jeremy. It was the main reason she had elected to become a teacher rather than work as a scientist. She could do that here in her laboratory. It was as complete as the most modern research facility which was simple to accomplish. The companies that supplied her with technology and machinery didn't remember delivering or installing any of the equipment to include a handful of government agencies and representatives. Ms. Adler had access to Top Secret research data, too, especially that belonging to Dr. Carolyn Meyer-Brandis, the world's foremost authority on genetics.

Dr. Meyer-Brandis was in the employ of the Agency, a branch of the intelligence community. With her research, Ms. Adler was able to map the entire DNA strand. Her experiments advanced Ms. Adler's work by decades and no one was the wiser. Her telepathy made it that way. It was well within her power and necessary to her work. Being a teacher allowed her the opportunity to observe any potential subject for an entire school year. She could determine a psychological match long before she concerned herself with their genetic potential. In the end, the personality of the subject was as equally as important as their genetic profile.

The computer beeped. **"According to available data, the initiation of trauma to Subject: Jeremy Alistair McKee has an eighty-five percent chance of inducing catatonia."**

Of course, Ms. Adler thought.

She noted that about Jeremy. He seemed so dependent upon the support and approval of those around him. He lacked the inner confidence and faith that his brother radiated with blinding force.

Oh, how I wanted Christopher, but then...

"Computer?" Ms. Adler asked, her brow furrowing. "Give the odds of finding another match in Lancaster."

"Time frame?"

"Two years."

"Stand by."

This was the first time any subject had been a perfect genetic match for her needs. Ms. Adler shook her head in disbelief. *Jeremy McKee?* She had never given him much thought. He wasn't blonde which she preferred, and he didn't seem perfect, although physically he was an excellent specimen. There was something about his sickeningly good nature that caused her not to give him serious consideration. How many times had she walked through his mind and found his thoughts simple and unassuming?

And his concerns? His lack of confidence, his lateness in reaching puberty, and his fear of being alone? Rubbish! Life did not depend on connections to others! What a waste of energy!

"Computation complete," the computer interrupted. **"Odds in the established time frame: 37%."**

Ms. Adler threw the clipboard across the lab. It crashed into a shelf of empty beakers shattering them. The glass rained down onto the black and white tiled floor.

No! Ms. Adler thought, her eyes glowing. The furniture in the room vibrated. *This cannot be! Another two years?*

She slammed her fist down on her desk. Her eyes dimmed. It was more than she could endure.

There has to be a way!

If Jeremy went catatonic at the onset of the trauma needed to complete her work, it would be disastrous. How could she give him the self-assurance and inner strength he lacked, the strength Craig Dougan possessed, for example? Craig had remarkable mental fortitude after years of abuse. He had to come up with a reason to keep living each time his father beat him. If only...

Ms. Adler paused, her face going blank. A wide grin spread across her features. *Craig Dougan!* she thought. *Of course!*

How many times had she sensed Jeremy's desire to befriend Craig? Was he aware it was Craig's inner strength that attracted him almost as much as his sympathy for the troubled boy? Each boy possessed the missing pieces the other needed to be whole. Together they would be powerful indeed.

Oh, this is delicious! And it has already begun!

Ms. Adler had seen it in Craig's mind when she calmed him earlier. He was so excited about being in Jeremy's company tonight at their campout. That was the answer!

"Computer?" Ms. Adler said. "Open file *Bremen One*. Begin preparation for the synthesis of the primary mixture."

"Yes, Dr. Adler," the computer voice replied. **"Estimated time of completion: 78.52 hours. Warning! Missing components must be available within 26.60 hours."**

"Begin."

Her hand shook with anticipation. She crossed the laboratory passing the shelving unit with the sealed glass containers on it. She paused to look at the brains floating inside. One was labeled: *Bobby Jones, Age 11.*

"Your mother still dreams about you, Bobby," Ms. Adler whispered, and then laughed. She tapped on the white rat's tank. "Your time is very near, Mr. Rat. I need to acquire a few things first, and then it will be your turn."

The white rat spun in its wheel oblivious to her. Ms. Adler separated Jeremy's blood sample stick from the others. She placed his next to the large beaker in the middle of the lab table. She threw the other sticks into the trash. She reached out and grabbed her car keys off her desk.

"The endgame begins," Ms. Adler said.

She left the lab headed for her Mercedes.

*　　*　　*

The Bigelow Family

Teddy Bigelow grinned at his mother in triumph, flashing his silver braces as he called the farm. His blue eyes twinkled. His brown hair shined. He didn't look like a boy who worked on a farm. He looked like someone destined to be a doctor or a lawyer, a professional man. That's what Anna wanted for her son. She intended to mold him to fit that future whether he liked it or not.

Is that so much to ask? Anna thought, glaring back at him.

She looked away pushing her shoulder-length blonde hair back. She sighed, adjusting her wide hips on the chair. She didn't want to deal with this job thing with Teddy anymore. She didn't like it and she didn't like the farmer either. She smelled a rat.

Hiram Milliken is a pervert, Anna thought. *He has all the signs. He's never been married. He's never social except with Lyle Gibbons, that flaming homosexual Arthur Kelly, or the impressionable young boys who often spend the night in his trailer. Why can't anyone see this? It's obvious to me! The farmer has his sights trained on my son. Doesn't Teddy understand how messed up his life will be if my suspicions prove true?* The thought sent chills down her spine. *Why is he so insistent Teddy spend the night with him? If anything happens to Theodore in Hiram's company, or while he's working at that dreadful farm, it's Robert's fault!*

Teddy patiently waited for someone to answer.

"God, what *now!?*" Todd hollered, into the phone. "I'm never going to get any work done if you keep bugging me!"

"Um… it's Teddy," he said. "I'm the new guy. Is everything okay?"

"Oh, hey," Todd said, annoyed. He let out a whoosh of breath. He reached into his pocket for his cigarettes. "I thought you were the old man."

"Nope," Teddy replied. His voice was froggy like the way Rod Stewart sang. "I turned fourteen in April."

Todd rolled his eyes. "What do you need, Ted? I'm kind of busy." He looked at the bandage on his finger. Blood was seeping through. The bleeding was slower, but it hadn't stopped. He hoped he didn't need stitches. *Ooo! That would piss me off!*

"I just wanted to know what time to come in," Teddy said, sounding anxious. He wanted to get started before his mom could find a way to change his father's mind. "Should I bring extra clothes since I'm spending the night?"

Anna cringed. The more she thought about it, the more her mind worked. *If I can find one good reason to stop him from going…*

"No need," Todd replied. "What you wear here is enough. Make sure they're old clothes. We can wash them after we get done with the milking. Just bring some clean underwear. You'll need something to wear while they're drying, unless you want to walk around in a towel like Dabney does. Either way, you don't want to ruin any good stuff. Things get pretty messy around here."

"No problem, dude."

"Don't you go to Lancaster Middle School?" Todd asked.

"Not anymore," Teddy corrected. "We graduated today. I'm going into ninth." He asked again, "What time should I come in?"

Todd thought, *New freshman? Heh, heh, heh.* He said, "Come in when you like. I'm here already."

"Cool. I almost didn't get to take the job. That's why I want to get started."

"Your parents don't want you to work?"

"Not my dad," Teddy said. "He was the one who let me take it. My mom's the one who said I couldn't."

"I still don't like it."

Teddy ignored her.

"Well? What happened?"

"Actually," Teddy whispered, going around the hall corner out of his mother's earshot. "My brother Tad fixed things." He smiled. "He always does."

The job argument started a year ago this past April. It was right after Teddy had turned thirteen. Tad heard raised voices coming from the living room. His pale blue eyes grew sad. His fair skin lightened. His thin brown hair lost more of its weak life. Teddy called Tad's hair *dead hair* since it hung so lifelessly from his scalp. He moaned at the yelling that had so lately been commonplace.

Tad thought, *This is damaging my fragile youthful psyche. Why doesn't mom just let Teddy do what he wants?*

There was no other reason for them to be arguing. It happened every time his older brother wanted to do something and their mother said no. Teddy had turned thirteen, so it would be that way from now on. He had a weapon to fight back with that he didn't have when he was twelve.

Tad blamed his mom. *It's her fault. How many times over the years did she tell Teddy:*

"You want to do what? Theodore, my parents never let me do anything until I was a teenager and I turned out okay. Talk to me when you're thirteen."

She asked for it, Tad thought.

Teddy turned thirteen and had a list of demands he'd waited a long time to spring on his mother. First, he wanted his own room. Anna didn't like the idea because it meant the attic or the family room. There were only two bedrooms on the upper floor of their raised ranch. Robert agreed with Teddy. He was old enough for some privacy. They would build him a room out of half of the family room. Teddy would pay for it with his savings. The great battle for the iPhone was next.

"Why do you need a cell phone when we have a perfectly good phone right here?" Anna asked. She held up the wireless handset for the landline.

"That isn't the point," Teddy replied.

"Well then," Anna said, "what's the point?"

"The point, mom, is simple," Teddy said. "I'd like to carry on a conversation with one of my friends without you listening in on it. I get so aggravated every time you pick up the other extension."

Anna's face flushed. *How does he know about that?* It was true, but she had always taken such care to make sure Teddy didn't hear her. *What's the big deal if he doesn't have anything to hide?*

Robert had warned his son about the eavesdropping. Anna wouldn't budge when he told her it was intrusive, so in a sense he had gone over her head. Teddy and his mother argued back and forth. Teddy had the upper hand throwing her off guard like that. It wasn't long before Anna hit him with a zinger that even Robert couldn't dispute.

"We can't afford it," Anna said. It was her ace card.

Teddy looked at his father hoping for a last minute save.

Robert shrugged. "Your mom's right, Teddy," he said. "Money's tight right now."

"What if I pay for it myself?" Teddy asked.

Robert supported the idea, but Anna didn't like it. Her victory evaporated. Teddy called Colin Skinner. He knew Colin had wanted to give up his paper route. A few moments later, Teddy was the new Hartford Courant paperboy. He got his phone with a loan from his dad – which he promptly paid back – and did the papers for a year. He gave up the route to Tad after that. He had enough money in the bank, especially after Christmas tips, to keep the phone on until he found something better. Teddy's wants were growing with him, and so were the prices.

Tad came home from school yesterday and heard them fighting again. It was worse than the room and phone battle. Mom and Teddy were screaming at each other. From what Tad gathered, Teddy had seen an ad on the bulletin board at the middle school and responded to it. Hiram Milliken wanted a part-time farmhand. Anna insisted he was too young for that kind of work and that was final.

Teddy wasn't giving up that easily. Tad knew why, too, but he was sworn to secrecy. Teddy didn't want to tip his hand to his mother before he was ready. He thought it was best to have all of his ammunition loaded before he took on Anna the *Queen of Zingerville*. Teddy's plans for the future required cash. He was fourteen. He would be old enough to drive in two years. He had to have the money for a car, the registration, and the insurance before he turned sixteen so his mother couldn't hit him with the old low finances tactic to keep him from driving.

Tad thought, *Teddy would make a great general. He has a strategy for everything.*

Tad slipped into his room and went to the window. He leaned on the sill watching his father gliding around the backyard on his John Deere, mowing the grass. It was weird Teddy had gotten into this discussion while his dad was outside. He usually waited until Robert was in the room since dad was the softy. He would give in as soon as Teddy started to pout or cry. Mom didn't argue once dad put his foot down.

No one with any brains did, Tad thought. *Dad may be soft toward us, but cross his path and watch out!*

Tad heard the phone ring. He picked up the receiver in the hall at the same time Teddy answered the one in the kitchen. He said nothing. He listened to the conversation his brother had with the farmer. Hiram sounded like a nice guy. He encouraged Teddy to take the job. He promised him it would be a lot of fun. Teddy explained he didn't have an answer yet, but promised to call soon. He hung up and went back to arguing with his mother.

Tad slipped past the combatants to the back door. He stepped onto the deck and made his way down the stairs to the freshly cut grass. It felt cool under his bare feet. He paused and wriggled his toes in it. He took a deep breath and walked over to his father.

Teddy needs help. At the rate the two of them are fighting, Teddy's going to say the wrong thing and dad will close the conversation indefinitely. He believes a discussion that sinks to disrespect has an unworthy subject.

"What's up, kid?" Robert asked his ten-going-on-eleven-year-old, lowering the mower's idle.

Tad shrugged. It was his best sympathetic maneuver. "Nothing, I guess," he pouted.

Robert shut the motor off and heard the raised voices. "Are they at it again?" he asked, picking his son up and putting him on his lap.

Tad nodded not looking his father in the eye.

"Hey pal," Robert said. "Don't get bent out of shape. Tell me what's going on and I'll handle it."

Tad started at the beginning. He told his father how Teddy wanted to work at the farm to save money for his car. Robert thought Tad sounded like a defense attorney. He was undoubtedly lawyer material. Anyone who could sway the opinion of a state trooper had potential. Robert didn't like the idea of Teddy working at the farm though. It was too early in the morning and too late at night, especially once school resumed in the fall, but he couldn't deny Teddy's reasoning. He was right. If he didn't have money, there was no way he could get a car. Robert wasn't a millionaire. Besides, he had to buy his own when he was a kid. It taught him to respect and value it more than his friends whose parents gave them cars. Robert supposed Teddy had gotten the idea from him.

After listening to Tad argue his brother's case, Robert made up his mind to let Teddy take the job. He didn't know Milliken well, but several of his old school friends did, like Mike Dougan. He had never said anything bad about the man. Robert tried to maintain an open mind about things since working as a cop made him cynical. Seeing the world from the bottom most of the time made that easy. It was something he constantly fought against. He tried to find at least one good thing about the world each day. He was hard pressed sometimes.

Once again, it's time to rescue my son from the clawing clutches of his overprotective mother, Robert thought, *just as long as Teddy agrees to the conditions. In a maneuver like this, conditions are a must.*

"C'mon, buddy," Robert said, setting Tad on the ground. "Let's go save your brother."

The moment Robert opened the back door, his son and his wife railed at him at the same time. Robert was six-four with a crew cut and steel blue eyes. He held up his hand and waited for silence. Tad walked over and poked Teddy in the back. It was their signal that everything was okay. His brother visibly relaxed. Robert told Teddy he could take the job under certain conditions. He was not allowed to work on Sundays and that was final. Going to church was a priority. His responsibilities as an Altar boy took precedence. He needed to maintain his grade point average when school started again or the job was history. Lastly, unless it was an emergency, he couldn't work past ten o'clock on a school night.

"You're going to have to do your own laundry, too," Robert continued, as Anna sighed away. He looked at her sympathetically, but ignored her otherwise. "Get undressed on the porch."

"Can I sleep over there?" Teddy asked, the one point his mother refused to bend on. "What if I have to work the night and then work in the morning?"

"Absolutely...!" Anna began.

"... fine," Robert said, cutting her off. "Don't make a habit of it, you hear?"

"Robert!" Anna exclaimed. "We don't even know Milliken! What if he's a pervert?"

Robert scratched his head. "Honey, Teddy's not a baby, for God's sake. He knows how to protect himself." He looked at his son. "Are you going to let anyone molest you?"

"No way!"

"See?" Robert asked. "Besides, only a lunatic would touch the son of a state cop. Hiram's been here all of his life and so have I. A lot of my friends worked for him growing up. Trust me, if there was anything wrong with the guy, I would've heard about it by now."

Anna relented, but she told Robert if anything happened it was on his head. Robert took the responsibility. He was confident in his son's ability to do the right thing. He went back to mowing the lawn. Tad returned to his room, but not before Teddy thanked him.

"You're a good brother, Thaddeus."

Tad grinned.

Teddy smiled at the memory. "I have a cool dad, huh?" he bragged.

"Sure," Todd replied. He thought, *For a stinking cop. You'd better not nark on me, boy. When I want to get high, I'm getting high.*

They said goodbye. Todd shook his head.

Something isn't right. Hiram said he wanted a part-time employee to help him in the afternoon, but we don't milk in the afternoon, so what's up with this? Is Teddy taking Henry's place? Is he working full-time then? It doesn't sound like it. Why risk having Teddy stay overnight? State and cop are two huge words. Robert Bigelow's pretty huge, too. Hiram bends the law a lot when it comes to drinking and stuff. Is he trying to get busted? If Teddy's in the guest room, where am I sleeping? The couch? Omg, that burns me! Hiram does the same crap to me whenever Frank sleeps over!

Todd kicked open the barn door and headed for the trailer.

*　　*　　*

Jack sat at the end of the bar staring down at his Jack Daniel's on the rocks. Jack drank *Jack* when Jack drank. It was an old joke. The look in his eye made Melissa Couture stick to the opposite side of the room. She was trying to look busy polishing the brass work. She didn't go near him for any reason other than to refill his glass when it was empty. She owned Misty's Café. Jack had been a regular since his tours in Afghanistan ended. She had seen him upset many times over the years. She even called the state police on him when he got out of control. Misty had only seen him this angry once before. It was the day Carol Sinclair told him she was pregnant.

Misty sighed stubbing out a Virginia Slim. She carried the bottle of bourbon down to Jack. She dropped a couple of fresh ice cubes into his glass and filled it to the top. She slipped his money from beneath the ashtray and took it to the register. He was her only customer. That frightened her. There was a lot about Jack to fear. She walked as if on thin ice when he was around. Jack had come through the door today fuming. He stormed past Misty without a word.

Misty thought, *Screw the thin ice. Today's the day to be walking on air.*

"Usual," Jack barked, as he sat down. He dropped forty dollars of his son's money onto the bar and slapped the ashtray on top of it. "Keep them coming."

That was Jack's key phrase. *Keep them coming* meant Misty had better fill his glass each time he set it down empty. He was angry and didn't want to keep asking for another drink. Jack's anger was familiar. Misty hated it, but running a bar was a business. Money was the bottom line. Jack wasn't a liability even if some customers refused to come in when he was there. The money he spent more than made up for them.

Misty knew Jack by the look in his eyes. Today she saw a look she hadn't seen in sixteen years. It frightened her. She slipped the bottle back into its slot on the shelf and returned to her stool. The dayshift mill workers would be out soon. The bar would fill up. Copeland Industries was right across the street. Misty thanked God. She said a quick prayer that they would stay out of Jack's way. At fifty-six, she had no desire to be dodging chairs and beer mugs in a free-for-all bar brawl.

It was odd his look reminded her of Carol. Misty had known her for almost two years before she disappeared. They had become friends. The way she left without saying goodbye bothered her.

She could've called me, Misty thought. She cautiously observed Jack's glass. *Whatever happened to make her leave without Craig must've been severe. She loved that kid.*

Carol Sinclair walked into Misty's Café the first time on a snowy November night. She was wrapped up like a Christmas package. She looked like a Playboy centerfold. Golden blonde hair flowed out of her knit cap and down the back of her suede coat. It perfectly highlighted her round face. Her cheekbones were high and perfect. Her eyes were a lovely hazel. They fairly burned in the bar's low light. Misty stared at her as she slipped off her coat and hung it on one of the hooks to the left of the door. She stuffed her cap and matching mittens into the pockets. Misty couldn't believe she intended to stay.

Carol crossed the room with every eye in the place, except Jack's, glued to her long legs, her perfect heart-shaped buttocks. Jack was sitting on his usual stool in the corner of the bar, his lunch pail deliberately placed on the seat next to him. It was a clue to the wary to leave him alone. Carol walked right up to him and poked him in the shoulder. The bar crowd held their breath.

"Is that pail yours?" Carol asked, her voice like a choir of Angels.

Jack didn't look up from his newspaper. "Yes," he replied, sipping his drink.

Carol put her hand on her hip. Her sweet mouth curved down in an elegant frown. "Then move it out of my way, *Jack!"*

Jack turned to her, his eyes bulging. Misty grabbed the edge of the bar. Jack glared at Carol. She held her ground and glared right back. Jack snatched up his lunch pail and slammed it onto the bar. Carol climbed onto the seat. A rush of air exited every pair of lungs in the bar. Donald Barry – the owner of the liquor store next door to Mike's Market – downed his gin and tonic in one gulp. Misty walked over holding her chest. Jack was staring at Carol like he'd never seen a woman before.

"Are you lost, honey?" Misty asked. She thought, *Nobody this good-looking comes in here on purpose. Not alone anyway.*

"Nope," Carol replied, holding out her hand. "I'm not lost. I'm Carol."

Misty shook it. "Misty. This is my place."

Carol gazed around the café. The bar stretched toward the door she had come through. There were tables with four chairs each spread throughout the room. Tired and overworked men filled the seats. Most were in dire need of a shave. All of them needed a drink. A few girls sat at the smaller tables, the ones with two chairs, along the wall to her left. They were beneath the tiny windows that made the café look like somebody's basement. They were overdressed and wore way too much make-up. Carol thought the best of them looked like a whore. Behind her, the men who had frozen when she walked in resumed playing pool. Behind them were the bathrooms, the door to the basement cooler, the back exit, and Misty's office.

"Nice place," Carol said. "Rough. I like it rough."

"You do?" Misty asked. She thought, *She's a Barbie doll, for God's sake!*

"Who's *Mr. Green Eyes* over here?" Carol asked, thumbing toward Jack.

"Lady, I'd better warn you...," Misty began.

Jack held his hand out to Carol. "Jack Dougan."

Carol took it and gave it a shake. She laughed. "So, I was right! Nice to meet you, *Jack*. Are you man enough to buy a lady a drink, or should I buy one for you?"

Jack pointed to his cash without taking his eyes off her.

Misty thought she was going to have a coronary. "I.D. please," she said, praying Carol was of age.

Carol dug her license out of her back pocket and flashed it. She was twenty-two.

"What'll it be?"

"Jack and coke, no ice."

"I don't know if I'll fit in the glass, sweetheart," Jack smiled.

Carol giggled.

He's flirting with her! Misty thought.

When Jack returned from Afghanistan after serving four tours, he'd sat on that same stool every single night. Misty welcomed him home. He was a soldier and she supported the military. Jack kept to himself. It wasn't long before people began to realize that he wanted it that way. A handful of ugly confrontations had seen to that. It was better to leave him alone than to risk his ire. Not once had he ever even bothered with any of the women who patronized the bar, not until Carol. It was like he had no interest in sex at all.

Too bad, Misty thought. *His green eyes are to die for.* She put the drink down between them.

Carol said she was a nursing student. She was trying to get her RN certificate before her parents moved out to California. She wanted a decent job and a place of her own even though they wanted her to go with them. Her father, Stanley, was in computers. He was taking her mother, Caroline, and her baby brother, Bentley – barely a month old! She had no idea how her parents managed that at their age! – to Hollywood to seek his fortune in special effects.

Jack and Carol closed the place. They left together that night and many nights after. She met Jack daily and moved in with him when he bought his house two months later. Misty never considered Jack a happy man, but when Carol came into his life he was a different person. He laughed. He talked about Afghanistan, too, a previously forbidden subject. Jack dug into his wallet and bought drinks for the house. They were like Bonnie and Clyde.

Jack stormed into the bar on their ten-month anniversary. Misty thought she was having a flashback. He was alone and looked ready to boil over. Misty brought him a drink and asked him where Carol was.

"My mother's," Jack replied, through his teeth.

Misty thought, *They're fighting. It was bound to happen.*

Jack slammed the drink down.

Misty poured him another. "What's wrong, Jack?" she asked, wearing her concerned bartender face.

"Carol's pregnant!" Jack raged, and slammed another drink.

Misty kept pouring. "Hey!" she exclaimed. "Congratulations!"

Jack glared at her.

"What's wrong, Jack? You and Carol are perfect for each other!"

"That's right," Jack snapped, "Carol and me. I don't want kids, Misty. This world's too messed up of a place to be a kid! Do you know the kind of hell kids go through every day?" Down went another drink.

Jack got loaded that night like never before. She hoped when he woke up in his cell at Troop C in Tolland he would get his act together, but it didn't happen. Carol went back to him, but he treated her like crap now. It stayed that way all through her pregnancy. Carol disappeared after Craig was born. A rumor suggested Jack had murdered her in a drunken rage until he received papers from a California court awarding him full custody. Misty was shocked.

Carol had told her how much she wanted her baby. She believed Jack would come around. Despite the constant bickering, she still loved him. The last time Misty saw her was the night her water broke in the bar. She went to the hospital in an ambulance when Jack refused to drive her. His mother, Nancy, stormed in a few hours later to inform him he had a son. Misty couldn't believe this short, stout woman had the guts to speak to Jack the way she did.

"Offa th' stool, bucko!" Nancy commanded, poking Jack in the side.

"I'm not going anywhere," Jack said.

"You're *goin'* t' th' *hospital* an' greet your *boy* into this *world,* Jack Wade Dougan!" Nancy spat. "If'n I have *t' drag* ye, I will!"

Jack went. Misty was glad. She almost asked Nancy for her phone number. Bouncers were hard to find. Nancy could handle any disturbance whatsoever if she could control Jack.

Misty smiled as she filled his glass again. She would *keep them coming* and hopefully Jack would pass out on the bar before anything bad happened.

Misty shook her head. *Give me strength.*

Jack was oblivious to everything around him. All of the day's frustrations had combined into a gargantuan rage that blinded him. He was trying to think, but the bourbon was feeding the fire. Jack wanted to forget he had ever gotten up, forget the throbbing in his cut foot, and that stupid woman in the unemployment office. He knew who was to blame for all of this.

Craig! Jack thought. *Everything is Craig's fault!*

The woman at unemployment set the wheel in motion when she said Jack couldn't file for a benefits extension. He gripped his glass as he remembered what he had said to her.

"What are you talking about?" Jack asked, going very red. "Are you stupid, or something?"

James Christopher

"I'm sorry, sir," the woman replied. Jack reeked of alcohol and was obviously unstable. She wasn't getting hurt over her crummy job. "I don't make the rules."

"Rules!?" Jack cried. "I was told I could extend my benefits at the end of this claim! What kind of crap is this?"

"It's the President's crap, sir. He discontinued that program."

Jack got nowhere even after screaming at three different supervisors. By the time he left – under the threat of having the police called on him – his head was pounding and his throat hurt from yelling, which in turn made his voice hoarse. He needed a drink.

These idiots have no idea what they've just done to me!

The only options they could give him were to try for welfare or call the President. Jack pushed his way out of the unemployment office. He knocked over an Armed Forces display before kicking the door open. He retreated to his maroon Monte Carlo. There was only a half a shot of bourbon left in his emergency bottle.

Oh, my God, Jack thought, swallowing it. *I'm going to kill somebody.*

He hit the key, started the motor, and floored the pedal. The 305 roared to life, a cloud of black smoke covering the parking lot. He laid two neat strips of rubber on the blacktop.

What else could go wrong? Jack thought.

He pulled up to the light. He had intended to take a left and go to the liquor store, but when he hit the brakes he heard a grinding noise from the front discs. Jack screamed. He turned right instead, straight into traffic. Cars were backed up along East Center Street to I-384 from road construction on Main Street. He ground his teeth as they inched along. Unbidden and unwelcome, memories of Carol flooded his thoughts.

She had to screw things up, right? Jack thought. *She had to go back on our agreement!*

When Carol had come along, life was good for Jack for the first time since he was a kid. Jack fell in love with her the first night they spent together. The next morning they sat in the kitchen having coffee. Jack was brooding. Carol lovingly drew him out and encouraged him to talk about what was bothering him. Jack said he was afraid she might get pregnant since they hadn't used protection. Carol laughed. She was on the pill. A child was the farthest thing from her mind. She needed to finish school and start her career. There would be time for children later.

"I don't want children, Carol," Jack said. "Ever. You have to understand that right now."

Carol slipped her arms around his neck and kissed him on the cheek. "Whatever you say, baby."

Yeah, right! Jack thought, reaching the entrance to the highway. *You liar!*

He hit the accelerator and shot out across three lanes to the fast lane. The Monte Carlo's engine roared. Red lights flashed behind him on the highway.

Jack had forgotten about the Connecticut State Trooper's relentless pursuit of the criminal speeder. He checked the speedometer and groaned. He was doing eighty-five. Carol's words of betrayal from the morning of their ten-month anniversary filled his mind as he pulled over. The state trooper got out of his car.

"I'm pregnant," she whispered, into his ear. She was nibbling on his earlobe.

Jack jumped up from the table enraged and ordered her to have an abortion. Carol tearfully refused. He advanced on her. She ran out the front door and flew down the steps into Mike's arms.

"Hey, now!" Mike exclaimed. "What's going on here?"

Carol burst into tears.

"Stay out of this, Mike!" Jack snarled. He reached for Carol.

Mike was like a Mack Truck by this time. He caught Jack's hand and twisted it back. "Are you crazy?" he asked.

Jack glared at him. "Let her go!"

"Carol," Mike said. "Get in the car, honey."

She moved. Jack lunged for her. Mike shoved him back.

Jack's mind filled with memories of Hiram Milliken. *No!* his thoughts exploded. *No more little Jack Dougans! No more babies to be used and thrown away, slaughtered like sheep in some foreign country! No more pain, damn it! No more pain!*

Jack fell to his knees sobbing. Mike almost reached out to him, but steeled himself. He drove Carol to Nancy's house. They got the call from the police later that night asking if they would pick up Jack at the station.

"No," Mike said, to the duty sergeant. "Keep him there."

Jack thought about that as he stared at the speeding ticket the state trooper gave him. His hands were shaking. It was a three hundred and fifty dollar fine and a notice to appear in court in Manchester. The Trooper tore up the pay-by-mail ticket when Jack became obnoxious and replaced it with a summons. He threatened to take Jack in if he didn't shut his mouth. The cop finally pulled away. Jack pounded on the steering wheel until he heard a loud snap. The adjustable column broke loose and fell into his lap. Jack held the column up with his knees as he drove, lost in the caverns of his psychosis.

Two weeks after Mike took Carol to Nancy's she came back. Jack refused to touch her. Their sex life was history. The baby was the last straw. He wasn't going to take any more.

She got pregnant on purpose! Jack thought. *She didn't hear a word I said! She got caught up in some stupid fantasy about raising a family with me and ignored what I told her!*

"You want another, Jack?" Misty asked, interrupting his train of thought. She pointed at the bar. "The money's gone."

Jack laid down another twenty. *No job,* he thought. *One last unemployment check... screw it. Just screw it all.*

Craig would have to work more. Jack did when he was a boy. He sacrificed more than anyone could imagine for his family. Craig could do the same.

The lazy little bastard.

Jack wondered at his motivations the night Carol tried to leave with Craig. *Why didn't I just let her take the kid and be gone?*

He swallowed the whiskey. It burned a path of fire straight to his gut. He knew exactly why he had stopped her from taking Craig. It was the only way left to hurt her the way she had hurt him.

Jack swaggered home from the bar that night on foot. Carol had taken the Monte Carlo earlier to run some errands since her car was in the shop. As he approached the house, he spotted Carol through the front window dressing the baby. It only took him a moment to figure out what she was doing. The suitcases on the porch confirmed his suspicions. Carol was leaving him. Jack opened the Monte Carlo, reached under the driver's seat, and grabbed his father's .45 caliber Colt. It felt good in his hand. The weight drove the anger away and replaced it with the knowledge that he was going to this time.

There were two plane tickets to California on the dashboard. He took the one with Craig's name on it, tore it up, and made his way to the porch. Jack knew how to move with stealth. The desert had taught him that. Carol was in the kitchen. The baby was on a blanket by the door. Jack slipped silently in and lifted Craig. He sat on the couch with the baby in his lap, the gun resting across his tiny stomach. Carol turned around, gasped when she saw him, and dropped the bottles of formula she had prepared onto the floor.

"You know what, honey?" Jack asked, his smile wide, his eyes insane. "I've been thinking."

"Oh… God…," Carol whispered, sinking to her knees.

Jack pointed the gun at her. He pulled the hammer slowly back until it clicked. "Do you know how many people I've killed?" he asked, rising to his feet. Craig dangled under his arm, cooing in blissful ignorance.

Carol's tears fell digging valleys through her make-up.

Jack leaned forward and pressed the barrel to her forehead. "Dozens, Carol. Up close. Like this."

Carol's bladder let go. The front of her jeans turned dark with urine. "Please … Jack, *please…"*

"No, babe," Jack replied. "Not this time."

Carol closed her eyes and sobbed waiting for the bang.

"Listen carefully," Jack said. He backed up and sat down on the couch.

Carol opened her stunned eyes.

"I'm only going to tell you this once. I should kill you now, but I won't. Not yet."

"Jack… let us go," Carol pleaded. "Please…"

"No," Jack replied. "You go. Craig's staying right here."

"No!" Carol screamed, lunging for the baby.

The .45 went off like a cannon. It split the floor beneath her ripping a hole through the carpet. Carol fell into a fetal position, screaming and sobbing.

The baby, startled by the loud noise, screamed with her.

Jack leaned back and said, "Look at me, Carol."

She shook her head.

"Look at me, you stupid bitch!"

Carol looked up, her vision blurred with tears. The baby was in Jack's lap with the gun pointed at his temple. Carol moaned.

"Take your plane ticket and leave," Jack said. "Go to California, see if I care. If you call the cops, I'll blow his brains out. If you call my family or anybody we know, I'll blow his brains out. If I don't get full custody within six months, I'll blow his brains out. If I ever see your lying face again, Carol, I'll blow his brains out. Then I'll kill you. Don't even test me."

Carol ran out the door convulsing and scared out of her mind. She took her bags off the porch, her plane ticket from the car, and disappeared into the darkness. It was the last time she was ever seen in Lancaster. It was a good thing, too. Jack guessed she had seen it in his eyes. He would've killed her if she hadn't left. Then he would've shot the baby, and then himself, one bullet in the head for each.

Jack sat up all night with Craig in his lap waiting for the cops to come. If they did, it was going to be bloody. He called the airport in the morning. Carol had boarded her plane and was gone. Jack called Nancy next and asked her to come over and help him with his screaming brat. He told her Carol had left him. That was all Nancy ever learned. She thought Jack might have killed her like a lot of people did. When the papers came from California, Jack made a point of reading them in public at every opportunity. The rumblings ended. Their hatred shifted from him to her.

How could a mother abandon her child to the likes of Jack Dougan?

Jack thought, *They're ignorant.*

The mill workers filed into Misty's Café through the front door. Jack felt a blackout on the horizon. He accepted it. He had one desire left. It ate at him like cancer. He would finish his drinks, get in the car, and drive home. He would wait for his son to return from work.

When I get my hands on Craig, I'm going to...

A loud voice interrupted Jack's thoughts.

"Well," Jerry Copeland sneered. He nodded at Jack. "If it isn't the town lush. Tell me, Dougan, have you beaten your kid lately?"

*   *   *

Jeremy thought, *I really need to get out more. All the other kids in town know which trails go where, but I wasn't on them five minutes and I got lost. I didn't even realize when I crossed Grady Lane that I was going in the opposite freakin' direction! It's a good thing my iPhone has GPS, or I might've come out by Ms. Adler's house. Eew!*

According to the map, the nearest road was Wickett Avenue by Kelly Hardware. He cut through the woods to get there, and then asked Siri for directions to Jack Dougan's house. She found them. He followed the AI's verbal cues.

"Turn left onto Wickett Avenue," Siri said.

Jeremy stood on the sidewalk. He dialed Sam Stone's house. He thought, *This is a waste of time. Sam's an exercise fiend. He won't be interested in going to a party. Still, I told Chris I would call, so here I am.*

"Hello?" a voice answered. It was Stephanie, Sam's little sister.

"Hi, Steph," Jeremy said. "Is Sam home?"

"Nope," Stephanie replied, sounding bored.

Jeremy heard an afternoon talk show in the background and wanted to yak. *They're so lame,* he thought. *Mom says they provide synthetic emotions for people not strong enough to have feelings of their own.* He agreed with her. *Is all of that violence and drama necessary? At least I learned what co-dependency is.* He pictured the Sturgess brothers on a show. *Sandy and Ian could fill a whole episode.*

"Sam went to camp," Stephanie said. "He won't be back until July."

"What?" Jeremy asked. "Since when does Sam go to camp?"

"I don't know. He left this morning. That's what my dad said."

"No kidding? Well, at least I know why he wasn't in school today. Tell him to call my brother when he gets back, okay?"

"Okay. I have to go. My soap is coming on."

Man, Jeremy thought. *They corrupt them young.* He ended the call. *Oh, well. It's not like we hang around Sam that much anyway. His jogging and health consciousness crap wears pretty thin after a while. This is my first time partying, too. I don't want Sam lecturing me about drinking and my health all night. I want to have a good time. Chris, Matt, and everybody else enjoys it, so why shouldn't I?*

Jeremy dialed Keith Keroack's house next. He picked up on the first ring.

"Hello?" Keith whispered.

Even with his hushed tones, Jeremy recognized his high voice. It was funny it hadn't changed yet.

"Keith? It's Jeremy."

"McKee?" Keith whispered. "Dude! Wassup? How's Chris?"

"He's fine," Jeremy replied, rolling his eyes. *See what I mean? Grr.* He said, "He asked me to call you. Why are you whispering?"

"He asked you to call me?" Keith replied, sounding surprised. He shushed himself. "Jeeze, I have to whisper. My parents are insanely pissed at me! If they catch me on my phone, I'm dead!"

"Why? What's going on?"

"They got my phone bill!"

Jeremy shrugged. "So?"

"I used a ton of data!" Keith whispered. "I went way over my allotment and they grounded me to death! I'm stuck here 'til I pay them!"

"How much?"

"Two hundred bucks!" Keith whined. He shushed himself again, and whispered, "But forget that. Chris asked you to call? Why didn't he call me?"

Jeremy told Keith about the party. He explained that Chris was at the pond getting everything organized. Keith seemed close to tears that he couldn't go, but that was Keith. He was easily upset. Jeremy remembered him crying in the hall last year because he couldn't find his pencil for math class.

"This sucks!" Keith moaned. "Chris wanted me to come?"

"You bet."

"Well, tell him why I can't, okay?" Keith asked. "And tell him to message me on social media. Make sure he understands, I'd come if I could, but my parents are stupid. Do you think he'll message me?"

"God, Keroack!" Jeremy cried. "Marry him already. He'll message you, don't worry."

"*Keith Richards Keroack!*" a woman's voice hollered. *"Get off that phone!"*

"Got to go!" Keith cried. "Tell him, okay? Bye!" He hung up.

Jeremy thought, *Holy hyperactivity, Batman!* He sighed. *Another kid who should be my friend who likes Chris better. What is it anyway? I use Scope! I wear deodorant!*

He remembered how well Chris and Keith got along during Boy Scouts. Jeremy should've known it was only a matter of time before he resurfaced. Chris had his picture on his Mr. Hot Shit bulletin board along with the rest of his friends.

Hard to believe Keith is such a pothead.

"Jeremy!" Arthur Kelly called. He waved from the entrance to his store, but continued walking toward his Lexus.

"Hi, Mr. Kelly," Jeremy called back.

Arthur was a friend of his father's. Thomas had been the star pitcher for E.O. Smith High School's baseball team when he was a senior and Arthur was eleven, before Lancaster had their own high school. Thomas joked that he thought Arthur had a crush on him back then because he came to every game, even the away ones, and followed him around like a lost puppy. He got permission to ride on the team bus by volunteering to be the water boy. It lasted until Thomas graduated and left for Harvard.

Four years later, he came home with Jeremy's mother who was two months pregnant with Chris when they tied the knot. Thomas and Arthur chatted up a storm every time the McKees came into the hardware store. Jeremy thought Arthur fawned over his dad, but Thomas said he was just being friendly. Now, knowing Chris was gay and understanding a bit better what gay people were like – and watching Arthur glide through the parking lot – he was sure the guy still carried a torch for his dad.

Jeremy rolled his eyes. He thought, *The two of them would have matching frilly aprons.* Arthur always tried to get his dad to go play poker at Gibbons' Garage, too, but Thomas declined. He wasn't much of a gambler. *That would be my mom. Dad swears she can count cards.*

"Where are you going?" Arthur asked. He sashayed as he walked.

Jeremy pointed toward the garage. He thought, *God? Please don't let Chris become this bad of a flamer, okay? Please?*

Arthur told him to wait a second. He was going that way and would give him a ride.

Good fortune smiles on the weary, Jeremy thought. He crossed Wickett Avenue to Arthur's Lexus. "Poker night?" he asked, climbing in the front.

"You bet," Arthur replied, starting the car. He backed up and then pulled out onto Wickett Avenue. "How are things at home?"

"Good. Chris is working a lot though."

"With Hiram?" Arthur asked. He was fidgety all of a sudden.

Jeremy nodded.

"Where are you off to?" Arthur asked, changing the subject.

"We're camping out tonight with the guys," Jeremy replied. He noticed Hiram's pickup truck parked at the garage. "I'm meeting Craig Dougan."

Arthur pulled into a parking spot on the Gator Road side of the garage and shut off the motor. He offered to buy Jeremy a soda from Lyle's machine, but Jeremy declined. He had the dollar from Chris, but he was saving it. Jeremy didn't have a job, so he had to scrounge cash wherever he could. He wasn't thirsty anyway. He thanked Arthur for the ride. He was about to continue to Craig's house when Hiram appeared.

"Have fun camping out," Arthur said.

"Camping?" Hiram asked, his heart skipping a beat.

"Jeremy and his friends are camping out tonight," Arthur said.

Hiram's palms began to sweat.

"Later," Jeremy said, nodding to the farmer as he walked away.

Hiram stared at him, hungrily. *So worthy,* he thought.

Arthur said, "Jeremy told me his brother works a lot of hours for you."

"Shut your mouth, Art!" Hiram exploded. His face flushed with anger.

"Calm down!" Arthur gasped, laying his hand on his chest. "I only wanted to ask if you knew…"

"I don't know anything about Chris McKee," Hiram said. "Drop the subject."

Arthur shook his head. "I don't understand you," he said, snapping his tongue. "Not two weeks ago, your lawyer… what's his name?"

"Chase Umbridge," Hiram said, crossing his arms. "He's a royal pain in the ass."

"Right," Arthur nodded. "Chase was here so you could sign your Will. If you have such a problem with Chris, why did you leave him your farm and everything else?"

Hiram's eyes burst into flame. "That's temporary, Art! I don't have an heir, get it? If I don't leave my estate to someone, the town gets it thanks to a clause in my father's Will. Umbridge wouldn't leave me alone until I gave him a name."

Arthur said, "You could've left it to Todd."

"Todd? Sure, Art. I'll leave it to Todd so he can liquidate my assets and keep himself in pot for the rest of his life." His gaze became faraway. "Or worse, he might keep it."

"And?" Arthur asked.

"No chance," Hiram replied. He poked Arthur in the chest, and said, "That's my farm. No one else is going to run it except me."

"Then why leave it to Chris?"

"You don't think McKee would keep the farm, do you?" he asked. "He'll bulldoze it and sell off the land."

"And if he doesn't?" Arthur asked.

"Arthur," Hiram said, "I don't want to talk about this anymore. It's only temporary. One day I'll have an heir. I don't plan on dying before that happens, so this discussion is pointless. Chris McKee will never get my land and that's the end of that."

He stormed away toward the garage.

Arthur shook his head. He thought, *Grouchy old pedophile. I was only going to ask if he knew Chris McKee was gay. Everyone in town is talking about it.*

Arthur sashayed into the garage.

*　　*　　*

Jeremy walked down Gator Road glad to be in the shade. Large full elm trees lined the street on the right side. The shade was thick and cool. The fence for Lyle's scrapyard was on his left. It was a chain link fence covered with green plastic so no one could see through it. Jeremy was sure it had something to do with beautifying Lancaster, or whatever.

Nobody wants to see a bunch of old cars and wrecks, especially if the accidents that brought them here were bloody. Ick!

The fence went down to the circular cul-de-sac across from Craig's house. He pocketed his iPhone and made a beeline for it. As he drew nearer, he heard someone crying.

"Craig?" Jeremy asked. He thought, *It's coming from around back!*

He ran around the house. Craig was on the back steps, his head hanging down, his arms wrapped around his knees. He was sobbing so hard he could barely breathe.

"Craig?" Jeremy asked. "Are you okay?"

Craig looked up at him, tears running down his face. He tried to speak, but no words came out. He shook his head. Jeremy sat down and put his arm around him. Craig leaned into him and wept with greater force. Once he was able to speak, he told Jeremy the story about this morning. He just let it out without a second thought about what he was saying. Jeremy listened horrified about the flying dishes and the terror of waking up to a possible beating. When Craig got to the blood on the floor and deduced the cut his father had sustained, Jeremy could see why he was so upset.

I'd be crying, too, in his situation!

"I never told anybody about my dad before," Craig hoarsely whispered, wiping his face with his shirttail. "I never trusted anybody."

"You can trust me, Craig," Jeremy sadly said. "I think everybody knows already though. People have seen things."

"I wish people would just mind their own business!" Craig cried, tears threatening again.

Jeremy squeezed him. "Take it easy, Spaz-Dougan! Some of us like you, that's all. Nobody wants to see you get hurt."

Craig looked stunned. "Really?" he asked, looking at Jeremy. There was disbelief in his tone. "You like me?"

"Of course I like you, Doubting Thomas-Dougan. I always have. I've tried to be your friend lots of times."

"I didn't think you were serious," Craig said. He lowered his eyes. "I didn't think anyone would want to be friends with Jack Dougan's kid."

"Well," Jeremy replied, "you were wrong."

"I guess I was," Craig said. "Are we friends now?"

"What's wrong with your ears, Helen Keller-Dougan?" Jeremy asked. "Of course we're friends."

Craig hugged Jeremy and began to cry again. Jeremy didn't know what to do. No one had ever gotten so emotional over being his friend before. He put his arms around Craig and hugged him back.

Wow, Jeremy thought. *He's really hurting.*

Craig regained his composure and let go. Jeremy kept his arm across his shoulders. Craig seemed so fragile all of a sudden.

He talked about his father, but is there more he wants to say? Jeremy thought. He hoped so, but not all at once.

Craig's life confused him. It would be better if they walked through it rather than diving right in. Jeremy could see they had something in common though. They were both lonely.

"So?" Jeremy asked. "Do we watch the sunset, sweetheart, or do we get moving? I think we have a mess to clean up, don't you?"

"Let's do it," Craig said.

The boys made their way into the house. Jeremy looked at the pool of blood on the green and yellow checkered tile. He cringed.

I can see why Craig was so freaked. It's a bad cut. I didn't think there would be this much blood. It looks like a dried-up red pond under the kitchen chair. Jack must be incredibly angry. Still, Craig has to know…

"This isn't your fault," Jeremy said. "You didn't smash all these dishes. Your father did."

"He won't see it that way," Craig sighed, handing Jeremy an old straw broom and a dustpan. He picked up the coffee table leg from the hallway while Jeremy swept. "He'll say the dishes wouldn't have gotten broken if I had put them away. Then he'll say I should've cleaned up the mess before I went to school this morning. I lose either way." He grabbed the Elmer's Glue from under the sink. He glued the leg back on and set the coffee table upright. It would dry fine without a clamp as long as no one touched it.

"Why didn't you just put the dishes away?" Jeremy asked, trying to sweep the glass from around the blood. "Wouldn't that have been easier?"

"It would've been, I guess," Craig nodded, spraying the bloodstains with *Fantastik.* "I just forgot, that's all. Besides, he would only complain about something else. Believe me, when he's… you know? He can make up some ridiculous crap."

"When he's what?" Jeremy asked, gathering the dish shards into a pile. He thought, *Duh!* "Drunk, you mean?"

Craig nodded looking away. *Can Jeremy stay friends with the son of the town drunk?* he wondered. *What are his parents going to think?* His heart sank. *They'll probably tell him to stay away from me. It's hopeless. Jeremy's from a different world than me. His father drives a Porsche, for God's sake. I'm not jealous or anything, I just feel like a mongrel at a purebred dog show. Jeremy's headed to college. He'll be successful. Where am I going? The mill probably.*

It took a few minutes to clean up the blood and the dishes. Craig didn't know what to do about the front window, but they picked up the glass inside and out. He found the cast iron pot-missile his father had heaved through it laying in the yard. He put it in the sink. Jeremy tossed the glass in the trash with the broken dishes. The floor was as good as new after a quick mopping.

Jeremy looked around. Dougans' decor looked like a late 1950's sitcom. It struck him that the house wouldn't look that different in black and white, right down to the rabbit ears on the television. There were no pictures anywhere, no colorful wallpaper. It was just plain. He said as much. Craig told him the furniture came from his grandmother's basement. His father never bought anything except alcohol. His grandmother bought the food.

"Bummer," Jeremy said. He thought, *It'll take a while to get used to how Craig lives. I must seem like a millionaire to him. I would find the whole thing pretty intimidating if I were him. Is that why Craig's so quiet?* Jeremy set the broom and the dustpan against the hallway wall and led Craig to the sofa. *A few things need straightening out right away. If I'm wrong, I can blame it on conceit, but if I'm right?*

"How come you're so quiet, Craig?" Jeremy asked. He took Craig by the sides of his head and turned his face back when he tried to look away. "Don't you like me?"

"Of course I like you," Craig replied. "Everybody likes you."

"Is that a shot?"

Craig shook his head. "No, it's not a shot."

"Then why are you so quiet?"

Craig shrugged. "You're just… really popular, you know?"

Jeremy laughed.

Craig looked at him oddly. "What's so funny?" he asked.

"Is that what's bothering you?" Jeremy asked.

Craig nodded looking away. It was starting to seem like a habit.

Jeremy turned his head back again.

"Everybody wants to hang around with you," Craig said, squirming. "With all those people and all your friends, why would you want to hang around with me? We're not rich, you know. I'm nobody at school… no, it's not that, it's… oh, screw it. I don't know what it is."

"Yes, you do," Jeremy insisted. He thought, *You're not getting off that easily, Dougan. You're going to spell it out for me.*

"I do?" Craig asked, blushing and staring at the floor.

Jeremy didn't answer.

Craig looked up. Jeremy's expression was stern. His eyes were so open like he could see into his mind. He was right too. Craig knew exactly what it was.

"How can you hang around with me? Everybody's going to think your nuts. What happens when they see us together and they rag on you? What happens to me then? I don't know if I fit into their world, you know? What if they don't like me? What if your parents don't want you around me?"

"Hold it right there, Dougan," Jeremy said. "You need to realize something. First off, my parents don't pick my friends. They don't judge people by their parents either."

"They don't?"

"No," Jeremy replied. "Neither do I. Nobody picks my friends, either. Do you know how many people I know?"

"Tons," Craig replied, dejectedly.

"That's right, tons," Jeremy agreed, "but do you know how many people are close to me? None. Not any who are only my friends. I don't have any friends of my own."

"That's bull."

"No, it isn't!" Jeremy cried. "Chris has all the friends! All my friendships are pale compared to his! The whole group is like that. Sure, they like me, but I'm not an idiot. I know they like Chris better."

"They do?"

176

"Sure they do!" Jeremy exclaimed, brushing his thick black hair back. "Do you think I ever talk to them? I mean, really deep personal stuff? It's just token conversation. Even the guys that hang around me in school. They want to use me to try and be popular. All they ever talk about is what everybody else is doing. Nobody wants to just hang out with me and the girls only want to mess around. Well, I'm not ready for that, okay? I feel like a step stool to Chris or Max. They're the popular ones. I'm just the nice guy."

"What's wrong with that?"

Jeremy slumped back on the couch. "It makes me convenient a lot of the time," he replied. "I don't like it, but I still do it. Jeremy McKee, the peacemaker. Max, Chris, Ricardo, Matt… they're my friends, but to each other they're best friends. I don't have a best friend. Who do I talk to about how I feel? True, I have Chris, and don't get me wrong, I love my brother, but he has answers for everything! I can't stand it. When it comes to the real personal stuff, where do I go? It's hard to talk to someone who solves all your problems without even trying."

Craig nodded. "I know the feeling. I can always talk to my uncle, but if I tell him anything that happens with my dad, they end up fighting. I get it later for opening my mouth."

"Dude, I don't know how you put up with…"

"I love him," Craig interrupted. "He's my dad."

"I love my dad, too," Jeremy said, "even though he's hardly ever around. He never seems to have time for me. Only once in a while."

"What about your mom?"

"My mom?" Jeremy asked. He shrugged. "She's great. She always has time, but it's not the same. She's so much like Chris. He's her son and I'm my dad's although she'll never admit it. They're overflowing with confidence, too. I'm a wuss."

"You're not a wuss."

"I'm a wuss!" Jeremy insisted. "I spend most of my time at home because my friends are all Chris' best friends. I try to make other friends, but they're all phony and full of themselves. That's why I came here. I want to be your friend. I figured you'd know what it's like to be, you know, alone."

"I do," Craig replied. "I always wanted to be your friend, too. I just figured I wasn't good enough."

"Well, you figured wrong," Jeremy said, holding his hand out. "I'm looking for a best friend, Craig. Do you know anybody who might be interested?"

"I know this French and Irish kid," Craig smiled. He took Jeremy's outstretched hand. "He has a tough time in school though."

"We can fix that," Jeremy smiled back. "I'm pretty good at helping people with their homework. I'm French and Irish too."

"Best friends?" Craig asked.

"Best friends," Jeremy replied. "Now, read your yearbook. You didn't peek, did you?"

Craig shook his head. He'd honestly forgotten all about it. His backpack was inside the door. He took his yearbook out, opened it, and read what Jeremy had written. It said:

Dear Craig,

I may be the only person who writes in here, but who cares? By the time you read this, we're going to be best friends. Who else do you need anyway?

Jeremy A. McKee

Craig set the yearbook on the table and walked back into the living room. He sat on the couch, sighed, and then hugged Jeremy again.

Jeremy laughed, "Man, Dougan, you sure hug a lot! Just don't kiss me!" He hugged him back. "You'd be making friends with the wrong McKee brother!"

Craig let go and asked, "Is Chris really gay?"

"Yes. Does it matter?"

"Nope," Craig replied. "I never met a gay guy before, that's all."

Jeremy muttered, "Me neither."

Craig got up and motioned for Jeremy to follow him. He went to the hall and pulled on the string hanging from the ceiling. He lowered and unfolded the attic stairs. Craig started up the steps. They were rickety. Jeremy held them for him. He followed Craig, snickering at his tight pants.

"Nice pants, Craig. Show off your crack much?"

Craig grumbled unsnapping them. He kicked off his sneakers and socks when he got into his room. He took the pants off facing Jeremy. Talking about his beatings was one thing, but showing the bruises was something else entirely. He tossed the pants into the trashcan on top of his ripped underwear.

Later for them, Craig thought, glad to be rid of them.

"Hey!" Jeremy laughed. "I didn't mean for you to throw them away!"

Craig frowned. "They give me wedgies when I ride. I hate wedgies."

"Not much to your room, huh?" Jeremy asked, strategically changing the subject. He thought, *Oh, God, did you just ask for it!*

"It beats the couch," Craig said. "I'm a wide-open target down there."

Craig fished around in his laundry basket for something to wear. He found a pair of black jeans that were only one day dirty. Jeremy suggested he wear shorts instead. Craig said he didn't have any that were clean. Jeremy said it was going to be hot.

"It'll cool off when the sun goes down," Craig said.

He grabbed a fresh pair of briefs and a blue sleeveless shirt out of his dresser. He found a pair of socks in the bottom drawer. He bent way over to get them, his bruises hidden in the attic's shadows, and that's when Jeremy struck. He reached over, grabbed the back of Craig's underwear, and hiked them – Craig swore – all the way up to his shoulders.

Craig pushed back and knocked Jeremy off balance. They tumbled onto the bed. Craig landed on top of him. Jeremy's explosion of laughter was immediately followed by a loud ripping sound. Craig gasped as the entire waistband tore off over his head. Jeremy scrambled away, but Craig tackled him. He grabbed Jeremy's underwear and returned the favor.

"No! *No!*" Jeremy cried.

"Oh, *yes!*" Craig exclaimed, yanking the underwear up with all of his might.

Jeremy laughed, *"Stop! I give, I give!"*

Craig gave one last good tug before shoving Jeremy onto the floor. He knelt on the bed, his backside facing out the window. He was trying very hard to look angry, but he laughed instead.

"I hate wedgies!"

Jeremy lay on the floor in a heap. Craig collapsed on the bed. They laughed long and hard. In the distance, mingling with their laughter, they heard the high whine of two state police sirens. Craig's smile slowly faded. He turned and watched them fly past Gibbons' Garage heading toward Misty's Café.

Craig's expression was concerned. "They're after my dad," he said.

"Are you sure?" Jeremy asked, grabbing the socks that had fallen on the floor. He tossed them to Craig. "It could be anybody, you know."

Craig shook his head stripping off the ripped underwear. He tossed them into the trashcan, too. He said nothing as he dressed. His underlying fear of his father coming home disappeared.

"The only time the cops ever go to Misty's is to arrest my dad."

Jack wouldn't be around for a few days now. Craig's uncle and grandmother would leave him in jail. He knew Jeremy was trying to make him feel better by telling him it could be someone else, but he knew it wasn't. Jack was probably on a short fuse after cutting his foot. Craig wondered what had lit that fuse this time.

Not much, I'm sure.

Craig set it aside. His Uncle Mike knew he was camping tonight. He would see his uncle at work tomorrow. Craig would probably spend the next couple of days with him and Sandra.

Jeremy wandered around the attic picking out his wedgie while Craig dressed. He thought the attic was unremarkable. There weren't a lot of items in here, not like his house. There were some boxes of storage and an old dressing dummy. They weren't taped up or in any order like the ones at home. Jeremy's mother considered the storage her domain. Virginia was an organized person.

O.C.D. more like, Jeremy thought.

James Christopher

A box marked *DO NOT TOUCH!* drew his attention. It took him to the far side of the room to the right-hand corner.

Jeremy squatted down and peeked inside the flaps. A neatly folded desert camouflage Army shirt was on top with PFC stripes sewn into the collar.

"Those are my dad's old uniforms from Afghanistan," Craig said, moving behind Jeremy. He rested his forearms on his shoulders. "He's got a lot of stuff he brought back from the war."

Jeremy nodded. "What's that?" he asked, pointing at a folded pile of tan canvass. There were five wooden poles with it. It was against the seam of the roof behind the boxes.

"It's a tent," Craig smiled. He almost forgot about it. "My dad gave it to me when I was a kid."

"Really?" Jeremy replied. "It must be huge!"

"It is!" Craig exclaimed. He grabbed a hold of a corner of the canvas. "It's heavy, too. Give me a hand pulling it out."

Jeremy took the corner on the other side. Together they tugged at the dry canvas. They pulled it free with a groan and extreme effort. A floorboard came up with it as they fell back onto their butts. They looked at the ceiling when they landed. Nails from the shingles were sticking through the roof looking sharp and threatening. They shivered. The pointed tips were inches from their heads.

Jeremy looked at Craig, his eyes wide. "We have to be careful."

Craig shook his head. "We should be glad we didn't get any butt slivers."

Jeremy reached beneath him and checked. He sighed relief when he didn't find any. "Dude," he said, kneeling by the canvas. "We could fit everybody in this thing!"

"Do you think they would want to?" Craig asked.

"Absolutely!" Jeremy exclaimed. He lifted the tent at the fold. "Look at it. It's totally cool!"

"I've never even moved it before," Craig remarked, stroking it with his finger. "Not since my father had me help him put it over there. I was going to put it under my bed when I moved up here, to try and straighten up a bit? He went through the ceiling and told me if I wanted to take it outside he would help, but if not to leave it where it was."

"Would he mind if we took it?" Jeremy asked, thinking how nice it would be to be to stretch out rather than being crowded all night.

Craig shrugged. "I don't think so. He gave it to me. We'll need some help though. It's pretty heavy."

"Brilliant deduction, Sherlock-Dougan," Jeremy said. "I'll text Chris."

"We'll need four or five of us all together," Craig remarked. "The bag with the pegs and stuff is over there."

Craig pointed at a laundry bag that was the same color as the tent. It had *U.S. Army* stenciled on its side.

Jeremy nodded. "The canvas is too heavy for us, but we could at least get the other stuff downstairs."

"Okay," Craig agreed. "Let's do it."

Jeremy crawled over the canvas careful not to hit his head on the protruding nails. He grabbed the loose floorboard and was about to put it back when he spotted something else. His eyes opened so wide they almost fell out of his head.

"Oh, my God!" Jeremy cried, his head snapping back toward Craig. "Freaking check this out!"

Craig crawled over next to him. He looked into the hole in the floor where his friend had pointed. His heart began to beat like a trip hammer. Tucked inside, neatly arranged, was an M4A1 Carbine assault rifle, eight hand grenades, and a bunch of boxes of ammunition. Craig grabbed the floorboard from Jeremy and quickly replaced it, sweat pouring down his forehead. He turned around and sat, holding his chest and panting. His face was as white as a sheet.

"What's wrong?" Jeremy asked, rubbing his shoulder. "Take it easy, Dougan!"

Craig shook his head, "If my dad finds out I know that stuff is up here, he'll kill me."

"Don't worry about it, Craig," Jeremy said. "I won't tell anybody. Can we look at it though?"

Craig thought about it. As long as they didn't touch the grenades, it should be okay. If they were leftovers from the war, there was no telling how safe they were. Jeremy agreed to his conditions and removed the floorboard again. The M4 carbine was dusty. Jeremy lifted it out of the hole and suggested they not clean it off. Craig stared at it. Jeremy handed it to him. The weight felt strangely good in his hands as he looked it over. Jeremy took the rifle back, held it up, and aimed it out the window toward the house next door.

Craig slapped it down and scowled. "Are you nuts?" he scolded. "Mrs. Turner's practically ninety! Are you trying to give her a heart attack?"

"Chill out, Spaz-Dougan!" Jeremy cried, laughing a little. He held the rifle toward Craig. "Do you want to hold it again?"

Craig shook his head. His stomach was full of butterflies. "My dad killed people with that thing."

Jeremy stared a moment longer. He slipped it back into the hole, careful to make sure he put it in the same spot.

"We'd better get going," Jeremy said, fishing his iPhone out of his pocket. "I'll text Chris now."

Craig replaced the floorboard and led the way back to the living room. *Dad killed people with that thing,* his thoughts repeated.

The chill he felt went all the way down his spine to his feet.

*   *   *

Officer Robert Bigelow had been writing a speeding ticket to a teenager who thought he could do a hundred and ten down Route 32 and get away with it when the call came in. He had the teen in the front seat of his cruiser sweating him a little while he made out the summons. Brandon Reilly was sixteen and in his mother's Honda CRX. There were two passengers in the car with him, little boys, both eleven. Robert's son Tad was ten-going-on-eleven which angered him more than anything else. Not only was the kid trying to commit suicide, but he was afraid to go alone. According to the DMV, Brandon had just got his license, too. Legally he had the right to arrest the kid and impound his car. Robert hoped he could scare him into driving like a sane person.

He wished they would raise the driving age to eighteen. They should've done that instead of pushing the drinking age to twenty-one. Irresponsible children had no business behind the wheel of a machine that killed people. Robert believed that more firmly every time he saw another mangled kid in a wreck.

"Unit six," the dispatcher called over the radio.

"This is unit six," Robert replied, into the handset. He set the ticket book down in-between him and his passenger. Brandon was close to tears. Robert couldn't have cared less. *Be glad you're not in handcuffs.* "What do you need, Tom?"

"I'll make it easy for you, Bob," Tom the dispatcher replied. "Misty's Café. Jack Dougan."

Robert acknowledged the call. It took him all of ten seconds to finish the ticket. He laid a whopping seven hundred dollar fine and a court appearance on Brandon before shoving him out of the car. Robert spun around his lights flashing and his siren blaring. Kate Pierce, a ten-year veteran officer with a humongous chip on her shoulder, radioed that she would answer the call as well. Robert was glad. Kate was a bodybuilder. She was a pretty strong woman. They might need some muscle. They met at the mouth of Wickett Avenue where Robert took the lead – his town, his bust, that's the way it worked.

Jack Dougan, Robert thought. *We haven't arrested him in a while. I'd hoped the guy had gotten his life together. Wishful thinking, right?*

They approached Misty's parking lot. A crowd of people were standing outside. Kate pulled in behind Robert. She jumped out of her car next to a thin man lying on the ground. His nose was broken and bleeding. She reached into her car, grabbed the handset, and radioed for an ambulance. Kate counted six more men on the ground moaning from an apparent beating. Jerry Copeland was one of them. He struggled to his feet and walked toward the crowd with a baseball bat in his hand. Blood was running from his left nostril. Kate told the millionaire to drop the bat and get up against the car.

"Do you know who I am, you *stupid* Black bitch!?" Jerry bellowed, his mouth full of blood.

Kate grabbed him by the arm, knocked the bat free, and slammed him face first on the hood of her car.

"Sure I do," she calmly replied, into his ear. She twisted his arm and put him in handcuffs. "You're a bigot. You're also under arrest."

"But…!" Jerry cried. "Dougan started it!"

"Tell it to Judge Thompson," Kate said. "She's a Black bitch, too."

Robert shoved his way through the crowd of mill workers who were surrounding Jack. He was growling and appeared drunk. A large man with a mustache saw the police officers and lunged for Jack intending to hold him down. Jack reacted like lightning. He caught the big man by the throat, punched him in the solar plexus three times, and then smashed his face into his knee. The man flipped over backward onto the dirt parking lot. Two more men dove. Robert caught one by the back of his shirt and threw him to the ground. Jack kicked the other guy in the balls.

"Back off!" Robert ordered. "If I have to, I'll bust every one of you morons!"

He meant business. They backed off. Robert didn't care that most of these men were his neighbors. He couldn't stand mobs no matter the reason. He knew Jack well enough to know the man may be a drunk, but he wasn't apt to pick a fight with thirty guys. The whole town knew enough to give Jack a lot of room. They were stupid to corner somebody like him. He was a wild animal especially when loaded and angry. Kate lined the combatants against her car. They were beaten and bleeding.

Robert thought, *They should thank God they're still breathing. Misty will fill me in on what caused the ruckus, but I'm sure Copeland has a part in it. I have to defuse the situation first.*

Jack stood in front of him, fists clenched, breathing through gritted teeth. His green eyes were wide and psychotic. Robert decided they were all coming down to the station if he had to call for a paddy wagon. He took a deep breath hoping to make this as easy as possible. The last time he had seen Jack this bad, it took five officers to subdue him, and two weeks for his black eye to heal.

"Jack," Robert said, holding his hand out. "It's Officer Bigelow."

Jack said nothing. Spittle came out of his mouth. His breaths were quick and shallow. He glared at Jerry Copeland.

Robert nodded. *I knew it.* "C'mon, Jack," he continued, inching closer. "You know the routine. Get up against the wall."

"No!" Jack raged, his fists opening and closing. *"I want Copeland!"*

"You're too late, Jack," Robert replied, three feet away and holding his ground. "Copeland's mine."

"The hell I am!" Jerry cried. "I'll have your badge, Bigelow!"

"I doubt that, Mr. Copeland," Sandra Dougan said, climbing out of her black Honda Accord.

She was wearing her press pass and television station ID. She was a news writer for Fox TV in Hartford. She had been on her way home when she spotted the fight. She stopped to see if there was a story here, but then saw her brother-in-law in the midst of the altercation. She'd stuck around in the car until the police arrived. Sandra was the one who had called them on her cell phone.

"Not unless you want to be on the news tonight," Sandra continued. "I can see the title already – *Millionaire Industrialist in Drunken Bar Brawl*. Wouldn't that look good on your résumé for the Senate seat you're vying for?"

Jerry glared at her, his eyes full of humiliated anger. Sandra ignored him and walked over to Robert. He motioned for her to stay back. She shook her head and moved in front of him. If there was one thing Nancy had taught her, there was no one better to handle family than family. She was frightened though.

Who wouldn't be seeing Jack like this? Sandra thought. *He looks like a raving lunatic. Is this what my nephew sees each time Jack flies off the handle?* She hoped not, but she knew that it was.

Sandra realized something as she made eye contact with Jack. *He looks like a little boy whose toys had been taken away by some punks on the playground, pathetic and picked on. Is this why Craig loves him so much despite the abuse? Jack looks so in need of sympathy. Somehow, even though I hate him for what he's done to Craig, I pity him.*

"You heard the officer, Jack," Sandra said. She painted her face with Nancy's no-nonsense look. "Do what he says before there's serious trouble."

Misty stood in the doorway nodding her head. Jack's enraged expression gave way to indecision. He muttered a string of curses, slapped his hands against the wall, and assumed the position.

Sandra looked at Misty relieved.

Misty mouthed the words, "Thank you. It wasn't Jack's fault." She pointed discreetly at Jerry.

Sandra nodded and walked away. Home could wait for now. She wanted her husband. She wanted to be the one who told him Craig would be with them for the next couple of days. She got into her car. Four more cruisers pulled into the parking lot. An image of Dabney Copeland greeting her at Hiram's door came into her mind followed by the hurt little boy look in Jack's eyes. Sandra glanced back as one of the newly arrived officers placed Jack in the back seat of his cruiser. A cold chill went down her spine. She drove away headed for the market. She decided it was time she and Mike had a little talk about Hiram Milliken.

*   *   *

Derek sat on the stump next to their gear staring intently at the dried blood on his knuckles. He felt like he could take on the whole world. He experienced a rush like never before when his fist connected with Dabney's nose. It exploded spraying blood and snot all over the place. The more Derek hit him, the better it felt. Dabney had managed to tag him once. He split Derek's lip and made it bleed, but that was it. The fight belonged to him from the very first punch.

Dabney collected his things after Derek finished beating the crap out of him. Andre Lee and a few of the parents had separated them. Tears streamed down his freckled face mixing with his bloody nose. He cursed and screamed at Derek in total humiliation. He promised his father would make life miserable for the Mellon family until the end of time. The guys laughed at him as he stormed away. So did the girls who were talking to Max and Matt now, wading in the shallow water. The remaining kids were on the diving platform. Derek had done what Chris told him. Once he was calm and his leg stopped shaking, he could head into the water.

It's Dabney's fault anyway, Derek thought. *He never should've said those things about Chris.*

When Dabney tried to drag Dan into it, Derek couldn't take it anymore. Besides, nobody got away with calling him *Bozo the Clown,* whoever that was, or *butt buddy.* His *butt* was certainly not *buddies* with anyone, and even if it was, it would be none of Dabney's business. He gazed out at the diving platform. Chris somersaulted into the water followed by Ricardo. Ian laughed and told them they were out of their minds. They were going to crack their skulls open when they hit the side of the platform.

Derek looked down at the blood-covered towel between his bare feet. He hoped somebody had a clean one he could borrow. He hated leaving the water without being able to wrap up. He decided the first thing he would do when he got home tomorrow was find his father and tell him what Dabney had said about Dan. If it was true and Dan was spreading lies about Chris, Kevin would deal with him harshly. Derek's father hated liars. In his house, if you did something wrong and you got caught, the punishment was worse if you lied about it or tried to cover it up.

"Face the music," Kevin said. "You're responsible for your actions."

Derek agreed even when it was his turn on the hot seat. It was usually for slugging Douggie who was a royal pain in his *butt buddy* ginger behind. One of these days, Derek was going to put a beat down on his little brother like he had on Dabney. He picked up the bloody towel and wet a clean corner of it on his tongue. He wiped the blood off his knuckles as Sandy came over dripping wet. He bent over searching in his bag for his own towel.

Derek liked Sandy a lot better than Ian, but he liked Chris the best. Chris was unhappy with Derek about the fight with Dabney, but he hadn't said much. He asked if it had been necessary to sink to violence. Derek assured him it was. Chris seemed sad about that like he felt sorry for Dabney. Derek decided he misread the reaction. No one had sympathy for Dabney. Chris didn't say anything else on the matter. He didn't treat Derek any differently either.

No matter where they went or who was there, Chris always treated him like one of the guys. Not like Dan who insisted he was an annoyance, or especially Ian. Derek felt like Chris was more his brother than Dan was. It didn't matter how many questions he asked or how many times he called, Chris was always nice to him. He was Derek's hero. Dan and Douggie were a lot alike. They got along better with each other than they did with him. His dad was gone most of the time at the airport. He was an air traffic controller. His mother had her hands full with Doug. Who did Derek have? Chris, that's who. As long as he could pick up the phone and call him, he never felt alone.

Derek got up and headed for the water. He jogged the last few feet and dove in. Max and Matt waved goodbye to Heidi, Brenda, and Andrea. They were leaving with Andre in his red VW Beetle. Matt couldn't keep his eyes off Heidi the entire time they talked. Max noticed the way Andrea kept looking at Matt. It was no secret she liked him. Max didn't think he even noticed. Matt only had eyes for Heidi's breasts.

Later for that though, Max thought. *It's good ammunition for the campout.*

The beach emptied as the minutes passed by except for some college students. They were having a party of their own and took to dominating the diving raft. Ricardo was standing next to Chris watching the people go. He had his arm around his friend and whoever looked at them with questioning glances got a wicked glare in return. Dan's rumor had spread everywhere. Ricardo was making a statement. He felt guilty for how he'd treated Chris. Standing on the front lines with him was his way of making up for it.

Chris smiled almost reading his thoughts. His eyes seemed to say, *"Don't worry about it."*

Sandy came up behind them and hugged them both around their necks. "Hey, you two!" he exclaimed, a wide smile on his face. "Glad to see you buried the hatchet!"

"We are too," Ricardo replied.

Chris agreed.

"When can we crack a brew?" Ian asked.

"Later," Max replied. "We have to set up camp first."

"Jeremy's not back with Dougan yet either," Matt added.

"Do you think anything happened?" Derek asked.

"No," Chris said. "Jeremy can handle himself."

"Maybe I should go over and check," Max reflected.

"I'll go, too," Derek said.

Ricardo shushed everybody. He heard something buzzing. "Is that your phone, Chris?" he asked.

"Sounds like it," Chris replied. He retrieved it from his bag. He pushed his long bangs back and read the text message. "Jeremy needs help," he informed them.

"What!?" they cried.

Chris put his hands up. "Take it easy!"

"Dude, is something wrong at Dougan's house?" Ricardo asked. "We heard sirens before."

"No," Chris replied. *God, they're paranoid.* "He needs some of us to help him."

"Help him what?" Matt asked, swallowing his heart. For a second, he was scared to death. Jack Dougan could give a person nightmares.

"Craig has a huge Army tent, or something," Chris said. "They need help carrying it."

"Oh, please," Ian groaned. "Just what we need! I suppose we have to go all the way to Craig's house now? This sucks!"

"Shut up, Ian!" Sandy, Max, Chris, Ricardo, and Derek all said at the same time.

Ian glared only at Derek who grinned back at him. He growled and went back to the stump to brood.

"How big is this tent?" Matt asked.

"I don't know," Chris replied. He texted the question to his brother. "Jeremy says he needs three more guys to carry all the stuff for it." He looked at Matt.

"I guess we could use it," Matt said.

They discussed it. Derek, Chris, and Max would help Jeremy and Craig with the tent. The rest of the guys would carry the gear and the cooler to the campsite and start gathering firewood. Sandy needed to go to his house for the fire extinguisher since he had forgotten it. It was a camping necessity per his father. Ian walked ahead of the group going to the campsite, kicking plants into the air in frustration. He didn't know how much more of this he was going to take. If anybody else got in his face today, no matter the reason, he was going to go home.

*   *   *

Dan was still in the canned foods aisle rearranging the stock and pricing the new inventory. He was so furious his hands shook.

That little…!

The more he thought about it the more he knew, when he got his hands on Derek? He was going to dropkick him right off the *freaking* planet!

What's wrong with that kid? Dan thought. *Doesn't he understand English? I told him not to go to the campout and that was final!*

His father confirmed what Craig had said when Dan called home. Derek had gone to the campout anyway. Dan slammed a can down on the floor in frustration. He nervously looked around to make sure no one had seen or heard him. They hadn't and his rage built anew.

After Craig left, Mike walked out of the office to key Bea's register from a bounced check alert. Dan's first reaction was to call home and see if Derek was still there. His brother needed to understand his life was on the line. He slipped into Mike's office and hit *Mom & Dad* on his Droid's speed dial. Dan was angry, but when his father told him Derek had already left to meet Sandy and Ian, he exploded.

"Why did you let him go!?" Dan yelled, into his phone. He cringed before his father even spoke.

"I beg your pardon?" Kevin angrily asked. "I'll tell you two things, mister. One: Don't talk to me like that if you want to see the light of day again other than through your bedroom window. Two: Whatever problem you're having with Chris has nothing to do with Derek. Maybe if you were nicer to him, he wouldn't want to hang around the older kids so much. In the meantime, it makes him happy. You keep your nose out of it and leave him alone."

Kevin hung up. Dan threw his phone across the office and knocked over Mike's penholder. The pens and pencils scattered all over the floor. His anger grew in his helplessness. He couldn't call his brother since Derek didn't have a cell phone. His parents thought high school was the time for that so he wouldn't get one until September. He dialed Sturgesses' home number hoping to catch Derek there. Susan informed him that he'd just missed them. They were on their way to the pond. Dan thanked her as cordially as he could manage, but then slammed his phone down on Mike's desk. This time Mike was in the doorway, his arms crossed. He scowled.

"Mind telling me why you're trying to bust my desk, Mellon?" Mike asked.

Dan sighed, his head down. *I'm in for it now.* "Family problem," he replied, hoping that excuse would placate Mike and he wouldn't pry. No dice.

"What kind of family problem would make you go into my office without asking?" Mike asked. He wasn't even trying to hold in his anger.

Dan stared at the floor.

"Pick up my pens."

Dan gathered them and returned the holder to the desk. It was cracked down the side and split open. The pens and pencils rolled onto the floor again.

"Get out of my office, Mellon," Mike growled.

Dan walked out, but then turned and apologized.

"Look, Dan," Mike said. "I don't have to tell you how much this bothers me."

"I know," Dan replied, trying to keep the edge out of his voice. "I'm having a problem with my brother, that's all."

"Leave that at home," Mike said, sliding into his chair. He bent over to gather his pens and pencils. "There's too much work to do today to mess around. Crap is something I don't need from one of my best employees."

"Is there a chance I could go home early?" Dan asked, hoping to head Derek off before he found out what he had done to Chris.

It was the last thing he needed. The guys at the campout would surely be talking about it. If his father and mother found out – and Derek would tell them, no question about it – the interrogation would go on forever. He could see it already. His mother would call Mr. and Mrs. McKee over to their house for a meeting. They would bring Chris.

Christ! Dan thought. *There goes my license again! He's just got to let me go!*

"No way, Dan," Mike stated firmly. "I already told you, there's too much work to do. It's only going to take longer the more you stand there flapping your lips."

In the canned food's aisle, Dan's frustration was boiling over. He wasn't far from losing it altogether when he felt the soft grip of a girl's hands on his shoulders. Dan nearly jumped out of his shorts.

"What's wrong, Dan?" Lisa asked, leaning by his ear.

Her long blonde hair fell in front of his face. The scent of strawberry was inviting. She kneaded his shoulders.

Dan looked up at her sadly. "Nothing's wrong, okay?"

"You're not a very good liar," Lisa remarked, placing her hands on her hips. She moved in front of him.

Dan said nothing. He kept clicking.

"Well," Lisa sighed, walking toward the Ladies' Room. She acted offended. "You know where to find me if you want to talk."

"Lisa?" Dan called, as she neared the end of the aisle.

Lisa paused, her back to him. She grinned. *Boys... they're just too easy.* She replaced her grin with a look of annoyance and spun around. She had one hand on her hip, smacking a piece of gum.

Dan cringed at her expression. "I'm sorry, okay? I just don't want to talk about it here, that's all."

Lisa nodded fighting back her grin. "Are you busy tonight?" she asked, her tone sharp on purpose. "I have a little time I can spare before the first grad party I'm checking out."

"I...," Dan began, trying to think up an excuse.

He had to get to Derek. When he saw Lisa's face darken, he changed his mind. It was going to be too late anyway.

"No, I'm not busy."

"Well, if you want, you can come out with me for a little while after work. We can talk, or something."

"I'd like that," Dan replied. "I have a lot on my mind. I could use someone to talk to."

"Good," Lisa nodded, turning away. "Don't leave when you're finished. José is supposed to drop my car off. I'll drive us somewhere private."

Lisa disappeared around the corner.

Dan grabbed the tagger and went back to work with renewed vigor. He had seen an intriguing look in Lisa's eyes even though she was trying to hide it.

Is she interested in me? Dan wondered, his heartbeat quickening.

Every worry he had about Chris vanished as Lisa paraded back and forth inside his mind.

*　　*　　*

Mike sat in his office satisfied he had won the battle with his anger once again. Jack wasn't the only Dougan with a bad temper. Mike endeavored to keep his in check, but when he saw Dan in the office – which was off limits to employees especially without permission – with his pens and pencils all over the floor, Mike saw red in a multitude of shades and textures. Then Dan slammed his cell phone down like he was trying to drive it through the desk and into the floor. Mike's blood began to boil. His first thought was to snatch him up by the back of his shirt and boot him out the back door. *Sayonara sucker! I'll mail your check!* Mike took pride in his ability to keep his anger in check and only scolded him. Dan was a good worker, but the next time Mike caught him in the office? *Bang! Zoom! To the moon!*

"Honey?" Sandra asked.

She noticed the hard look on her husband's face. It melted quickly at the sound of her voice. She knew he was having a rough day when he got up, took her into his arms, and planted a sloppy kiss on her lips.

No doubt about it, Sandra thought, kissing him back. *He's always romantic when the day's tough.*

Mike pulled her into the office and closed the door. "This is a welcome surprise," he said, smiling. He switched to his best Irish accent. "T' what do I owe th' pleasure o' this wee visit, lassie? Wait… I know that look. Something's wrong."

Sandra took a deep breath as they sat. She gave Mike the details of his brother's encounter with Jerry Copeland and the mill workers at Misty's Café. She was amazed at how easily Jack had taken down so many men. She believed he could have hurt them worse than he did. Mike felt a headache forming between his eyes. He held the bridge of his nose as she spoke. He didn't want to believe his brother was at it again. He'd hoped the brawling days were over. Sandra said she didn't think it was Jack's fault.

Mike was confused. "What do you mean by that?" he asked, a slight edge in his voice. "Nothing happens to Jack by accident, Sandra. He gets what he asks for."

"I know, honey," Sandra agreed, patting his hand. "There was something in his eyes though. I don't think I've ever seen it before."

"Like what?" Mike asked, leaning back in his chair and crossing his arms. *No matter what she says, there's no way I'm bailing Jack out. Hell would have to be selling ski lift tickets first.*

Sandra told Mike about the look in Jack's eyes, how he appeared like a hurt little boy. She reminded him of the day they had gone to Hiram's to inquire about land and Dabney Copeland was there.

"I remember," Mike replied. "Hiram said he worked there, right?"

"Exactly."

Sandra said it seemed strange at the time that Dabney would be wearing the clothes he had on to do farm work. She also thought it was odd that they were clean. Mike suggested he had changed before he left to go home. She said that was possible, but why was he so physically clean then? Did he shower before they got there? If so, why wasn't his hair wet? Sandra said she had noticed Hiram's teenage employees at the farm a lot since they moved into their house, Todd O'Connor in particular, but never one adult, not to mention any women. Hiram didn't go out on dates either. He never went out at all unless it was to Gibbons' Garage to play poker, but his farmhands came and went at all hours of the day and night. Some even spent the night there. They couldn't be working all those times, and why would they need to sleep at the farm?

"What are you saying, Sandra?" Mike asked. "Do you think Hiram's a pervert?"

"I don't know what I'm saying, Mike," Sandra replied, holding her hand up. "It's just, when I looked into Jack's eyes, some pieces fell into place."

"What pieces?"

"Wasn't Jack a completely different person before he started working at the farm?"

Mike said Jack was, but the work was such a strain on him, he became cold and arrogant. There was no way he could quit because the family needed the money.

Sandra nodded. "Wasn't Jack furious any time you went near the farm? Didn't he stay over there for days, sometimes weeks, on end? Didn't he seem angrier every time he came home? Wasn't he furious when he found out we were building our house on Hiram's land? What was the first thing Jack said about it?" She was getting more excited by the minute.

"He called me a *nogoodsonofa...*"

"Not that, you bonehead!"

"Oh," Mike said, trying to remember. "Oh! He said Craig was never coming to our house."

"Right!"

"Jack never said anything about Hiram being a pedophile," Mike replied.

"What was he going to tell Wade, Mike?" Sandra asked. *"'Dad, Hiram's molesting me?'* How would that have gone over with your dad's heart condition?"

Mike considered. Those pieces she mentioned were falling into place for him, too.

"I don't want to believe it," Sandra said, biting her lower lip. "It would explain so much."

Mike grew silent. *Could that be it? Did Hiram molest Jack?* He said, "There's no way to know for sure. It was too long ago."

"Do you know anyone else who used to work with Hiram?" Sandra asked.

"Hugh Kreeger did," Mike replied. "Hugh's a salesman now. He travels a lot. His son, Joey, came in the store looking for work a little while ago. Mike filed through his mental employee index. "He was too young. Eighth grade, I think." He continued, "Arthur Kelly... a couple of guys who moved away a long time ago, Jack of course. Jesus, guys I went to school with like Donald Barry."

"The Liquor Store owner?" Sandra asked.

Mike nodded. He reminded her she wasn't in New Jersey anymore. In Connecticut, it was called a *Package Store*. He continued before she could dispute him.

"It's funny. There are a lot of guys who worked for Hiram over the years. Roland Underwood, he owns the pharmacy now. Peter Rollins, I think, but I'm not sure. He was there before Jack, when Hiram's father was still alive, or just after. Something like that."

"What happened to him?"

"Caleb Milliken? My mother told me he drowned in the manure pit one day while Hiram was at school."

"That's horrible!" Sandra exclaimed.

"Agreed," Mike said. "My father died right in front of me. It wasn't a pretty sight. George Skinner worked there, too, for a summer."

"We could talk to them, see if anything strange ever happened."

"Oh, right," Mike replied, rolling his eyes. "We'll walk up to them and say, *'Hi, guys. How's life? By the way, did Hiram molest you a hundred years ago?'* I don't see that happening, Sandra."

"We could talk to Jack," Sandra suggested. "If Hiram is still molesting boys, we have to do something."

"What if you're wrong, honey?" Mike asked, searching her face. "What if Hiram isn't? An accusation like that could destroy a man regardless whether it's true or not."

"I know," Sandra replied. "I see it a lot working at the station. It's nauseatingly fashionable. Boys reporting their coaches when they get cut from sports teams, wives reporting their husbands during divorce proceedings… I'm surprised anyone even bothers with kids. It's a hard accusation to disprove."

"Disproving it shouldn't be what it's about," Mike said.

They sat in heavy silence.

Sandra reached over and opened the door. "What should we do, Mike?" she asked. "We should at least try to find out. We should choose to err on the side of caution if the kids are at risk."

Mike shrugged. "I don't know, babe. I could talk to Arthur. I know some of the kids that work for Hiram now. I could have a word with them. Chris McKee is one. Henry Schwartz used to. He applied here not too long ago, but he didn't want me to call Hiram for a reference."

"Oh?" Sandra asked.

"That's not uncommon for teenagers, honey," Mike replied. "They quit jobs on a moment's notice, or get fired for stupid things. It happens a lot."

"I'd talk to him, Mike," Sandra said, looking at her watch. "You never know. I should get Craig. Jack won't be home for few days."

"Don't bother," Mike said. He smiled. "He's camping out tonight with some friends. We can tell him tomorrow. Why ruin the kid's night?"

"Craig's out with friends?" Sandra asked, mirroring her husband's smile. "That's the best news I've heard all day. Anyone I know?"

"The Ramirez brothers, the McKee boys, the Sturgesses, Derek Mellon…"

"Sounds like a party to me," Sandra said.

Mike laughed as he picked up the phone. He dialed Robert Bigelow's cell phone.

"I spoke to Craig this afternoon. He'll be all right."

Sandra nodded, but an annoying fear settled in her breast. She shook it off as just nerves. Craig was too smart to get in trouble especially with alcohol. She mouthed a quick prayer there wouldn't be any drugs.

That reminds me, Sandra thought. *After the day I've had, the first thing I'm doing when I get home is rolling a nice fatty and sitting on the back porch with a glass of wine.*

Mike smiled as his old friend answered. "Bigelow!"

"Hi, Mike," Robert said, trying to sound light. "Guess you heard, huh?"

"Yeah, Bobby," Mike replied. "Sandra's here now. How's Jack?"

Robert told him his brother had gone quietly thanks to his wife. Mike looked at Sandra and told Robert she must have left that part out.

Sandra blushed.

"Jack's in a cell passed out," Robert said. "Copeland's lawyer will have Jerry and the mill workers bailed out as soon as we're finished booking them. All reports indicate Jerry started the brawl by deliberately antagonizing Jack."

Mike said, "I'm glad, but that's no excuse."

"Not ordinarily," Robert agreed, "but Jerry went way too far. He gave one of the arresting officers a hard time, too."

"Oh, yeah?" Mike asked.

Robert said, "Jack will be in court in the morning. He'll need to make bail. Copeland's lawyer insisted on pressing charges. Jack doesn't have the greatest record, but I'm going to encourage him to file counter charges when he wakes up. Jerry's also facing resisting arrest, so I think in the end all the charges will be dropped." He lowered his voice confidentially. "Jerry's campaign manager is on the way. Don't be surprised if he tries to contact Sandra. He knows she works for Fox. Jerry's leading the Senate race by a thread. He'll make any deal to keep this out of the news."

Mike told Robert he would let his mother know about the bail. Nancy was the one who decided those things. Robert thanked him. Mike hung up shaking his head. He had a sudden vision of the devil wearing a snowsuit.

*　　*　　*

Lyle Gibbons set up the poker table in the empty repair bay. José had *Lisa's Baby* in the other one finishing her tune-up. Once the new spark plugs were in, he needed to take her for a quick test drive, and then drop her off at the market. It was the last bit of in-house work for the day. Lyle would pick him up and bring him back to the garage.

"You've taken enough of my money, Art," Lyle said, unfolding the chairs and arranging them around the table. "Tonight, I'm taking it back."

"You say that every week," Hiram said.

Arthur continued filing his manicured nails. He blew on them. "I'll be happy to lighten your wallet some more, Lyle," he said. He looked over his glasses. "You have enough weight back there already."

Lyle narrowed his eyes. "You lookin' at my butt, Kelly?" he asked.

Arthur snapped his tongue and rolled his eyes. "You wish," he replied, throwing his leg over the other and bouncing his foot.

"Seriously, I don't," Lyle scoffed.

Hiram opened his mouth to insert a comment, but froze. He felt a familiar sensation like fingers reaching into his brain. He exited the garage and went around the side of the building near Arthur's car. His heartbeat quickened.

Hiram thought, *It's her! I hope it's good news.* "Hello?" he whispered. He felt her words projected directly into his brain.

"It is time again, Hiram," Ms. Adler said, her mind-voice as clear as day. *"Meet me at the middle school tonight. You will know when it is time."*

"I'll be there," Hiram replied.

The probing sensation of fingers left his mind. Hiram went back into the garage. He grabbed one of the folding chairs and sat by the bay door. He looked up at the Korean War Memorial on Tower Road. It was the second highest point in town after Margaret Adler's house. His gaze went faraway.

Lyle nodded, noticing the farmer's expression. *A lot of people get that way when they look at the tower.*

It was a hundred-foot-tall octagonal tower built from fist-sized stones with a sloping red slate roof. It had been open to the public once. There was a cast iron spiral staircase inside that led to an observation platform near the top. Large open windows faced the four points of the compass. Lyle remembered picnicking there with his parents before his mother died.

The kids used to party in it, Lyle thought.

The town welded the iron doors shut after Harold Kingsley's daughter, Candance, leapt out of one of the top windows trying to commit suicide. She had been a drug addict who got pregnant at seventeen. In her eighth month, she injected an overdose of heroin and took her chances with God. She succeeded, just not right away. She cracked her head open on the cobblestone path and died on the table giving birth to a baby boy.

Lyle had gone up to the tower that day after all the commotion had ended. The amount of blood on the cobblestones made him feel like he was back in Afghanistan. No one knew what happened to the baby, but there was a rumor he was living somewhere in California with his father, Lonnie Maccarello. Harold hated Lonnie for taking the baby from the hospital and disappearing with him before the Kingsleys could sue him for custody. He was within his rights as the boy's father, but Harold didn't care. Lonnie was a drug addict who had gotten Candace hooked. He was an unfit parent. Harold blamed him for his daughter's death.

Lyle thought, *I'll have to ask him about the boy some time. He'd be around Ricardo's age.*

Harold was the second shift supervisor at the battery mill. He came in to fill his car up every Friday like clockwork.

There was a small refrigerator beneath a shelf of brand new air filters. Lyle looked inside it and saw that Arthur's cognac was nearly empty.

"You're almost out of booze, Art," he said, not that he cared. He didn't drink.

"Oh, I knew I forgot something," Arthur whined.

Hiram said, "Don't worry about it. I'll get your liquor." He seemed a million miles away.

"Ask Donnie to put it on my tab," Arthur said.

Hiram rose to go to his pickup truck.

Arthur added, "I won't have any spare cash until after tonight's game."

"That's what you think, swish-bait," Lyle said.

Hiram couldn't hear them. He was feeling primed for the hunt and the kill. He climbed into the cab of his white Ford F-150 pickup truck and hit the key. His mind filled with images of dead boys dancing in his pasture. They made him long for the feel of their blood. It was all he could do not to drool. The need to kill was upon him again. His whole body felt charged with electricity. It was murder and Hiram knew that, but he'd done it before. His father, Caleb Milliken, was the first person Hiram dispatched to the other side. It was a most liberating experience.

Hiram had grown up slaughtering cows and hogs. He learned how to gut them at ten years old. It was necessary. Death equaled life on the farm. They depended on death for sustenance. It was the only pleasurable part of farm life. Hiram didn't know if he would've ever killed a human being were it not for his father, but Caleb had stuck his nose in where it didn't belong at exactly the wrong time. Hiram had only witnessed people die before then, twice. The memory filled him with ecstasy.

Hiram was nine years old the first time he saw someone die. From the age of two, Horace Milliken, his grandfather, had come into Hiram's bedroom every night after his parents had gone to sleep. He scooped Hiram into his arms and carried him across the hall to his room. Hiram spent his nights in his grandfather's bed. Horace did things to him in the dark, unspeakable things, agonizing things. If he cried, his grandfather hurt him worse. Hiram felt things he didn't understand, but he knew the crack of his grandfather's whip. The penalty for transgressions in the Milliken household was swift and merciless.

Horace was the lord and master of his domain. Crossing him meant a trip to the woodshed. It meant bleeding. Hiram had seen his father dragged out there for being a smart mouth, and Caleb was an adult at the time. Hiram understood terror. He learned how to hate. It was a black evil hatred that felt best when his grandfather hurt him the most.

Hiram woke up one morning when was nine and found his grandfather gasping for breath. He died a few minutes later his eyes wide open. Hiram stayed next to his cooling corpse not entirely sure what had happened. There was such peace in his grandfather's expression. The room was filled with a sense of finality. Hiram lay there until noon staring into his grandfather's sightless eyes. He touched his cold skin and listened to the silence in his chest. He put on his bedclothes and summoned his parents once he was sure his grandfather was never coming back.

Hiram developed a fascination with death. He imagined he was his grandfather hurting other boys the same way Horace had hurt him. The thought thrilled him, but death fascinated him even more. Killing things was easy. Hiram did it whenever he had the opportunity. It didn't matter what it was. The killing itself held the thrill. He beat squirrels and woodchucks with a board and mutilated them with his pocketknife, dissecting them with a pathologist's care. He was fascinated by their inner workings. He put fish on land and watched them flop and thrash about. He tortured rabbits and cats. No dog was safe if it wandered onto their property. Then something happened that opened a door in Hiram's mind. Time had stood still as God showed him the other side of His face. Evil, it seemed, was rooted in the fabric of everything good like a cancer.

Hiram's mother, Tonya, had been milking a sick and particularly stubborn cow by hand one evening when he was twelve. The uncooperative beast lifted its hind leg and kicked her, knocking her down. The cow bucked and stepped on Tonya's head with a sickening crunch. The impact caved in the front of her skull killing her instantly. Hiram watched as his mother's body jerked and spasmed. He felt no sorrow only an incredible fascination as he knelt next to her. A stream of warm blood passed over his trembling hands. His father found him there an hour later. Caleb thought Hiram was in shock as he dragged him away kicking and screaming. He thought Hiram was wailing for the loss of his mother, but it was because he wasn't finished playing with her corpse.

Hiram was handling school and the daily work on the farm alone by age eighteen. His father had been useless since Tonya died. He ambled around the farm, his eyes cloaked in despair. Hiram insisted his father allow him to hire some help – a boy, someone local – to assist with the daily workload. Caleb agreed not caring if the farm continued or not. Nothing meant anything without his wife. Hiram put an ad in the paper. Peter Rollins responded. He was a handsome twelve-year-old with dark eyes and brown hair. Hiram hired him instantly. Peter's soul belonged to the twisted teenager before the end of his first day.

Hiram attacked Peter in the milking parlor after they finished the morning work. It was the first time his unspoken fantasies had become a reality. He was thankful to his grandfather for showing him the way. Hiram understood him now. When it was over, he threatened Peter's life if he ever said anything. He told him to be on time for work the next day, too, or he would come and find him. Peter ran away with tears streaming down his face. Hiram closed the barn door laughing. When he turned around, his shocked father was standing behind him.

"What kind of monster are you!?" Caleb cried. He raised his hand to slap Hiram across the face.

Hiram caught it and bent it painfully down. "Don't even think about hitting me, old man," he said, forcing his father back. "Who are you to judge me, you useless waste of life?"

Caleb struggled to get free, but he couldn't. Hiram was stronger than him. He saw something in his son's eyes as they approached the manure pit at the end of the barn. It resembled the glee he exuded whenever they were working in the butcher shack. His rage melted away with the realization his son was about to kill him.

"You need help," Caleb gasped, struggling to keep his balance. "You're sick… it isn't your fault."

"On the contrary," Hiram smiled, pushing his father to the edge of the pit. "I've never felt better. You were watching me, is that it?" He laughed. "You know, grandpa did the same to me when I was two years old."

"Liar!" Caleb cried, glancing over his shoulder. The pit was dark and gooey. The stench was rank.

"Oh, no," Hiram said. "It's true. Don't tell me you and mom never heard me screaming. All those nights? All those years? And now, when it's finally my turn, you would ruin it for me? I'm sorry, pop. I can't let you do that."

Hiram shoved his father into the pit. Caleb quickly sank beneath the liquefied manure. Each time he reached the surface gasping for air, Hiram pushed him back under with his boot. Finally, his father floated face down on top of the reeking pool. Covering up the murder would be child's play. His father was old. His faculties were lacking. Everybody knew it. They felt sorry for Hiram and how hard he had to work. He would have no problem convincing the police this was a horrible accident.

Suddenly, Hiram felt a strange sensation like fingers probing inside his skull. A female voice invaded his mind.

"A splendid plan, Hiram!"

Hiram spun around, panicked. Margaret Adler stood in the doorway. He recognized her. Colonel Adler had adopted her and brought her home from Germany after the war. He thought her eyes were blue, but in the bright morning sun he could see that they were brown. Margaret clapped her hands, staring at him. Her eyes never blinked. Hiram froze in indecision. She'd caught him red-handed. The only thing left for him now was life in prison.

Howling, Hiram ran toward her with his hands outstretched, his fingers reaching for her throat. Margaret's eyes exploded with midnight blue light. She waved her hand. Hiram froze at attention, spun around, and slammed face first onto the floor. He strained to get up, but it was no use. He felt like he was encased in a block of concrete.

"You're from hell!" Hiram cried.

Margaret laughed, her eyes glowing brightly. *"No, Hiram,"* she thought-whispered, kneeling next to him. *"This world is hell. I am your Engel der Barmherzigkeit, your Angel of Mercy."*

"What do you want?" Hiram whined. The more he struggled, the stronger the grip became.

"I want you, Hiram," Margaret replied, standing up straight. *"You are going to help me. You are going to kill for me."*

Margaret convinced Hiram that attacking her again would be foolhardy. She dangled him in the air several feet above the floor with her telekinesis while she spoke. She said she would release him if he behaved. Hiram promised he would. She set him down feet first. He almost fell over when she released him from her hold. He stood in front of her near his father's floating body. He listened to her with growing fascination. Margaret asked him if he had enjoyed killing his father. She knew his answer before he said it. Something compelled him to speak the truth.

"Yes, I enjoyed it more than anything I've ever known.

"Would you like to kill again?" Margaret asked, the glow in her eyes dissipating.

"I… yes," Hiram replied, "but boys… I want to kill boys."

"Is that so?" Margaret asked. "Then you shall, Hiram, and I will make sure no one discovers you. I need boys for my research. Provide me with what I want and you will never need to worry about exposure again." She also assured him that when he came home from school this afternoon everything would be in order.

The police were at the farm after school. They said a passing officer had sensed something was amiss, stopped to investigate, and discovered his father. They assured him it was a horrible accident. Hiram pretended to cry, but inside his head he heard Margaret's laughter echoing. Hiram killed for her after that. Margaret appeared after each death either for the boy's brain or what she called the serum sample, sometimes both. Hiram was impressed with her skill when it came to dissecting a victim's head. She had a surgeon's careful touch. He wondered where she gleaned her knowledge. He knew she had studied in college, but this was beyond classwork. Eventually, she told him. When some of the local boys started calling her the Hill Witch, Hiram had to laugh. They didn't have a clue.

Hiram hungered to kill again. He was the shadow of death. He was in Lyle's parking lot, but he was also hovering over the boys camping in the woods. He wanted to hide in the bushes close enough to smell their innocence. When someone drifted away from the pack for a midnight leak, Hiram would take him. If no one came out, only then would he risk going in after them. It was like hunting sheep. He intended to kill and keep killing, tonight, forever. That was all there was to it.

"Did you fall asleep, old man?" Lyle bellowed, from the garage bay.

Hiram was startled. He drove up, signaled right, and pulled onto Wickett Avenue. He floored the pedal for a few seconds feeling the truck lurch forward. He rammed it into third gear. As he approached the town offices on the left side of the street before Lancaster Hill Road, he cried, "Wait!" and slammed on his brakes. Standing next to a Mayflower moving van in the parking lot was a boy more worthy of the *Gift* than Hiram had ever seen in his life. He signaled quickly and pulled in. A woman with auburn hair came around the side of the van and tapped the boy on the shoulder. She spoke to him in sign language. Hiram's lust for murder went into overdrive.

"Graham?" the woman signed, as she spoke. "Daddy will be out in a minute. Are you still hungry?"

Graham signed, "Yes, I'm starving!"

"I'm not sure where we can eat, honey," she signed. "Can you wait until we get home?"

Graham's only answer was to pout.

Hiram pulled into a parking space nearby and watched through the passenger's window. The boy had the same auburn hair as his mother only his was thick and wavy. Her hair was straight. He stood about five-foot-one with tiny dimples in the corners of his mouth. He wore Lee jeans with a red bandanna hanging out of the back pocket. He was shirtless. Judging by his tan, he didn't often wear one in the summer. He glanced over at Hiram when he noticed the man staring at him. He waved tentatively and smiled when Hiram waved back.

"Are they moving into town?" Hiram wondered out loud. He thought, *Those damned dimples have to go. I hate dimples.*

Graham nodded to him in big up-down motions.

"You heard me?" Hiram asked.

Graham laughed. His voice was sweet, but off-key. His soft brown eyes shined.

"My son's adept at reading lips," the woman replied, turning around and smiling. She signed to Graham asking him what the man said. Graham told her. "I see," she nodded. She walked over to the pickup and stuck her hand in. Graham followed her. "I'm Constance Shooter," she said. Hiram shook her hand. "To answer your question, we're moving in today."

"Well!" Hiram exclaimed, turning her hand and kissing it. "Welcome to Lancaster, my dear. I'm Hiram Milliken. I own the farm on the other side of town."

"Nice to meet you, Mr. Milliken."

"Hiram, please."

Connie smiled. *God, people really are friendly in the country. I guess Calvin was telling me the truth.*

"This is my youngest son, Graham."

"Nice to meet you, Graham," Hiram said, speaking very slowly.

Graham shook his hand. He signed something to his mother.

She nodded. "Graham says you don't have to speak so slowly," she said, leaning against the truck. "He can read your lips just fine."

"Amazing," Hiram said. "Has he been deaf all of his life?"

"Since I was born," Graham replied.

He spoke! His voice was similarly off-key as when he laughed, but easily understandable.

"Good Lord!" Hiram gasped. "That's incredible!"

"Graham's worked hard on his speech," Connie smiled, patting him on the head. "We're hoping he gets better at it now that he's here."

"Oh? Will he be going to the deaf school?"

"In West Hartford? The American School for the Deaf?" She shook her head. "Not right away, and maybe not at all. There's a woman here in town, Susan Sturgess?"

"She teaches special education," Hiram nodded. "She's a good lady."

Connie said, "I agree. She's going to tutor Graham in the high school a few days a week. He wants to give public school a shot now that he reads lips so well. The middle school doesn't have the facilities, but the high school does. We've made special arrangements."

"That might be tough," Hiram remarked, forcing his eyes to look at Connie and not her son.

"I can handle it," Graham signed.

Connie translated.

"I'm sure you can," Hiram said. He reached over and patted Graham on the head. His hair felt like silk. "If you ever want a job, you come and see me."

Graham's eyes lit up. "I can work in Connecticut?" he signed.

"I'm not sure," Connie shrugged. "How old do you have to be to work on a farm?"

"Fourteen," Hiram replied, discreetly crossing his fingers.

"Sorry, buddy," Connie said, signing to Graham. "You'll have to wait until January."

Graham's expression of disappointment was nothing compared to Hiram's.

"I take it you're not from Connecticut?" Hiram asked, painting a smile on his face. *Should I offer to pay him under the table? I did for Dabney.*

Graham winked at him and pointed toward a boy sitting on the curb smoking a cigarette. His brother since they bore a resemblance in the face. He had to be in high school though. His hair was dirty blonde and disheveled. Hiram watched as Graham walked over and tried to grab the smoke from him.

"Get away, you pain in my life!" the older boy snapped.

"Coco!" Connie exclaimed. "Give it a rest, huh?"

"Then tell dead ears to go away!"

She sighed. "Teenagers. No, Hiram, we're from Worcester. We just bought a house down here on Mary Circle."

"Mary Circle?" Hiram asked. "One of my best employees lives there, Todd O'Connor. He looks about your older son's age."

"Coco's sixteen going on ten."

"Todd's almost seventeen," Hiram said. He held his chin and examined Coco carefully. *Emotional trouble, family trouble, obviously a hardcase.* He noted the sadness reflected in his soft brown eyes. They were his mother's eyes, just like Graham's. He had to search for that sadness, but he found it behind his arrogant bravado. *That's a boy who needs some Kool-Aid and a friend.* Hiram smiled. "Your older son could certainly work."

"It's all we can do to get him to go to school," Connie sighed. She nodded, trying to be cordial. "I'm afraid a job right now is the last thing Coco needs." Thinking about the problems they'd had with their oldest made her stomach churn. "My husband's a homicide detective at Troop C in Tolland," she said, changing the subject. "He just transferred here from Troop D in Danielson."

Oh, my God! Hiram thought, with sudden rage. *It figures!* "Isn't that nice?" he asked, his smile more like a grimace. "Well, I have to go now, but please, call me if you need anything. I'm in the book. I don't have a cell phone. I could never get the knack of them." He thought, *Having GPS follow me everywhere is a non-starter anyway. That's the main reason I don't own a new truck.* He added, "Tell Coco to call me when he's ready. Graham can call me in January."

"I'm sure he will," Connie nodded. "New Year's Day. He'll be fourteen on the holiday. I grew up in Dudley. There are a lot of farms up there. My father's a retired Sheriff though not a farmer, but I've milked a few cows in my time. I'll bet Graham could do it. Would you like to meet my husband? He's inside the clerk's office applying for a building permit. He wants to enlarge the garage. There's only room for one car right now. We have two."

"I wish I had time," Hiram frowned, glancing at his watch. "Another day, perhaps?"

"I look forward to it."

Hiram told her to call him as soon as their phone was on. Connie pulled a pen out of her purse. She wrote her cell number down along with their home phone since it was already on. Hiram promised to call her soon. He suggested she take Graham to Mike's Market if he was hungry.

"You can get grinders at the deli counter."

She waved at Graham. He jogged over, bored with his brother and his stupid cigarette. If he wanted to smoke and die of lung cancer let him. It wasn't the worst thing Coco smoked anyway. Graham came up to his mother. She told him what Hiram had said about the grinders. His eyes grew wide with surprise. He jumped up on the truck, planted a light kiss on Hiram's cheek, and ran away laughing. Hiram's face felt like it was on fire.

"Graham Romeo Shooter!" Connie cried, but he just laughed, dodging her grasp as she reached for him. "Oh, Hiram! I'm sorry! It's just, well, Graham's very affectionate."

"Think nothing of it," Hiram replied. He smiled so wide he thought his face was going to crack. "He's a sweet kid."

Connie waved goodbye as Hiram backed out of the parking space. She thought, *Thank God!* She was sure they wouldn't find acceptance in the community with Graham being deaf and Coco a juvenile delinquent. She expected a lot of small-town prejudice. She had doubts about public school, too, but her husband had been right. They needed to get Coco out of the city. Between the gangs and the drugs, one or the other was going to kill him. Graham came up to her and begged her to get him a sandwich. She promised they would just as soon as his father finished inside.

"Hiram's a nice man," Graham signed. "Can I go down to his farm sometime? I can't wait until January!"

"As long as it's okay with him, honey," Connie shrugged. "I'll ask him when he calls us. I think you're right. He seems like a very nice man."

*　　*　　*

Donald Barry's heart sank when Hiram pulled into the liquor store's parking lot. He reached under the counter and took out a pint bottle of Seagram's Gin. He twisted the cap off and drank almost half of it in one gulp. He wiped his lips on his shirtsleeve and dropped the gin into an empty cardboard box at his feet. As the farmer neared the door, Donald's mind flashed with memories that almost made him vomit. He could still feel the shame of Hiram's abuse.

I was a fourteen-year-old boy! Donald thought. *Why did you have to hurt me? All I wanted was a job!*

Donald got a lifetime of regret and burning shame instead that only disappeared when he was too drunk to remember. The bell on the door sang out as it opened. Hiram entered without a word. He walked around the store thinking about Graham Shooter as he collected what he needed.

Graham will be an excellent addition to the Ledger, Hiram thought. *It would have to be slow though, not like Sam Stone.*

Hiram laid a bottle of Hennessey on the counter along with a six-pack of Schaefer. Donald rang it up, his hands shaking. Hiram scowled at him. Donald smelled as if he hadn't bathed in weeks.

Hiram thought, *I could have saved him from this.* He took the liquor and walked toward his pickup truck. *Forget Arthur's tab, too. He can fork up the dough later.*

Hiram headed toward Wickett Avenue and the garage. His thoughts turned to Todd who must be training Teddy by now.

Teddy better drink that Kool-Aid or the Hill Witch gets another sample, Hiram thought. *No more stupid mistakes like Chris McKee. I wish she would let me kill him. Why does she want him alive? She didn't show that much concern for the others, like Terry Greer, did she?*

Terry was a young blonde boy hitchhiking back to Connecticut after skipping a day of summer school to go to the beach. Hiram had picked up the grateful youth in Rhode Island and offered him a ride home. He said his name was Terry Greer. He was from Putnam. His voice cracked with apparent puberty even though he was only eleven years old. They were Terry's last words. Hiram offered him some drugged wine which Terry drank hungrily from the bottle trying to look cool. He met a gruesome end in the Victorian's living room.

The Hill Witch appeared after the kill. She knelt by Terry's head oblivious to the pool of blood surrounding them. She withdrew a syringe from the large pocket in the front of her brown skirt and removed the cap. Hiram stared at her as she inserted the needle into Terry's temple and pulled back the plunger. The clear tube filled with a pinkish colored liquid. She pulled the needle out when the liquid turned to blood. She squeezed the blood out and replaced the cap.

She stood up grinning, her eyes glowing. *"The presence of God in man, Hiram,"* she said, holding up the syringe.

The memory disappeared as Hiram pulled into the garage. *The clock is ticking,* he thought, and shut down the motor. *Tonight there will be blood and death.*

*   *   *

Dabney kicked open the left side of double doors of his family's estate. He charged through and headed straight for the grand marble staircase to his front. He was going to his room and private bath before anyone could stop him. Once he had his door locked – come hell or high water – he wasn't coming out again *ever!* Tears of frustration filled his eyes as he stomped up the steps. The smooth freckled skin of his round face burned with anger and humiliation. Dabney could still hear their laughter burning in his shame as he screamed empty threats at Derek, spitting sand and blood out of his mouth. The only thing that hurt worse than his nose was his pride.

There were plenty of people in Lancaster who didn't like Dabney. They would've given anything to punch him in the face. Dabney knew this and played on their fear of his father for protection. The threat of a lawsuit that could bankrupt their family was powerful. It allowed him to say and do whatever he wanted without fear of reprisal. No one had ever crossed that line before. He didn't think anyone would. His hubris backfired today in the form of a stupid ginger eighth-grader. Dabney never even saw the first punch coming.

PAIN!

That was all Dabney knew as he stumbled backward, shock invading his body. The high titter of female laughter was the only sound in the entire world. His body screamed, *Fight back!* in desperation each time Derek's small fist connected with his face. *Hold your hands up! Block the punches! Do something, you pussy! He's kicking your ass!*

Dabney couldn't. Cold panic swept over him as he realized he didn't know how. He'd never fought before. The punches were coming so quick, over and over, that Dabney couldn't find the time to think let alone figure out how to defend himself. He swung once getting a shot in, but that was it. One of the mothers grabbed him under his arms and pulled him away. When his vision cleared, he saw Andre Lee and another parent holding Derek. The fight had only lasted only a few seconds, but it seemed like forever.

Dabney trembled as relief washed over him, but then he felt the pain in his face. He reached up, touched his tender nose, and drew back a hand covered with blood. His tears began to fall. He felt so ashamed. He saw boys and girls alike pointing at him and laughing. Derek was thrashing trying to get loose. Outrage replaced Dabney's shame. *Didn't you do enough already!?* He grabbed his belongings, let loose a mile-long stream of threats and obscenities, and stormed away from the beach. Dabney cried hysterically at the end of Pond Road. He ran then and didn't stop running until he'd made it home.

Tammy McFarland jumped up from her sewing when she heard the front door bang against the inside wall. She thought it was Denise returning from Troop C – *Lord all hell was going to break loose!* – with Jerry. She rushed out of the nanny's quarters next to the greenhouse enclosed pool. She side-stepped through the doorway and lumbered down the hall toward the front doors.

She recognized Dabney's Balenciaga sneakers beneath the banister as he stomped up the staircase. It was only a quick glimpse, but that was all she needed. Denise had ordered them special for him. She always bought Dabney expensive designer clothes. Tammy thought she enjoyed playing dress-up with her son. She didn't think Dabney noticed. She doubted he would spend a thousand dollars of his own money on a pair of sneakers. She was sure Jerry would never allow it if he'd known her fashion ideas for her middle son had come from Out Magazine.

Tammy breathed a sigh of relief. She was content to let him go, convinced this was just another attempt by Dabney to enlist the attention of the entire household. *That child!* She had worked as the nanny for the Copeland family since Dennis was born. Dabney was the worst one of all three kids and the only one she couldn't tolerate. He was rude and obnoxious, a pushy carbon copy of a spoiled rich brat. He'd been that way for as long as she could remember. She loved the other Copeland children. Dennis and Diana even called her mom when Denise wasn't around, but she earned her money with this one. If it were up to her, she would tan his behind. She noticed a trail of blood leading across the floor and up the stairs. She snapped her head toward Dabney. His Balenciaga sneakers were covered with it.

"Oh, my God!" Tammy cried, sticking her hands into her dark hair. *"Freeze mister!"*

Dabney whirled around at the top of the steps. He opened his mouth to scream back and tell her to mind her own business, but all that came out was a broken sob. He watched through tear-blurry eyes as Tammy wobbled up to him. His fear returned at the look on her face. Her expression was rife with concern. He collapsed into her arms smearing blood all over the front of her pink sweatshirt.

"Good Lord!" Tammy exclaimed. "What on Earth happened to you!?"

Dabney sobbed something into her cleavage. She couldn't understand what it was. *Another boy's name maybe? A fistfight? Well, it's about time.*

"Never mind," Tammy said, trying to remain calm. "This was bound to happen sooner or later. Let's get you cleaned up."

She led him down the hallway to the left into the wing Dabney shared with his sister. Their rooms were across from each other. Dennis – Jerry's pride and joy – had the entire right wing to himself. Dabney continued to sob pitifully, his head resting against her side. His arms tried to encircle her waist, but they wouldn't reach. Sympathy rose in her which surprised her. Dabney hardly deserved any. Of course, *Mr. Stone Face* hadn't cried since he was in diapers. He was always angry. It canceled out any other emotion. Tammy wondered if it was just a front. Was he finally coming around? Did it take a beating to make Dabney realize the world didn't revolve around him?

They crossed through his immaculately clean room past his king size bed. He had a wallpaper mural of the famous Earthrise photograph from the Apollo 8 mission. It was more like a small apartment than a bedroom. It had a full bath, a walk-in closet, and a large room with windows from floor to ceiling along the northeast wall. It doubled as a living room and bedroom. They went into the bathroom.

Dabney shoved her away and sat down on the toilet cover. He avoided looking in the mirror. "You can go now," he said, wiping his face with the backs of his hands.

Tammy sighed. She thought, *So much for learning a lesson.* "I'll go when I'm good and ready, Dabney," she replied, opening the medicine cabinet. She pulled out the first aid kit. "Certainly not until I've fixed you up."

"I don't want your help!" Dabney spat, standing up.

Tammy grabbed him by the collar and sat him back down. "I didn't ask you what you wanted." She filled the sink up with hot soapy water and dropped a white face cloth in it. "It's my job to take care of you whether you like it or not. You don't sign my paychecks, your father does. Now, hold still."

Dabney opened his mouth to say something. Tammy put her finger over it. They stared at each other until he finally relented. His will to fight was gone. His nose – his whole face – hurt. He supposed he wanted her help, not that he cared much for her, but he was afraid to look at himself right then. His face felt ruined.

"Is my nose broken?" Dabney asked, sounding defeated.

"I don't think so," Tammy replied. She used the face cloth to wipe the blood off his cheeks, lips, and chin. His nose didn't look broken. It was red, a little swollen, and still bleeding though. He was destined for two black eyes. Tammy told him to pinch his nose with the face cloth and lean forward until the bleeding stopped.

"Aren't you supposed to lean backward?" Dabney asked. He sounded comical with his nose pinched.

"Just do what I tell you, okay?" Tammy asked. "Do you want to swallow more blood than you already have?"

Dabney shook his head.

"I didn't think so. I'm going to get some ice for your eyes. Don't go anywhere. If your father sees you like this, after the day he's had? There's no telling what it will cost you."

Cost? Dabney thought, glumly. He leaned forward. *That's what it's all about, isn't it?*

He cried more then. His warm tears touched the edge of his hand. He had never felt despair like he did now. Anger was his friend. Hate was his protector. When those emotions filled his mind, nothing bothered him, and no one could hurt him, especially his father. Dabney felt like a throwaway kid. He was born with all the attributes his father hated about himself, including his freckles. Dennis didn't have freckles. He was everything Jerry wished he was. They never let him forget that.

Dabney fought back his tears and thought about things that made him angry. He was safe there. Dennis and his father would have to look elsewhere for their petty satisfaction. A recent memory intruded. It brought the anger he so desperately wanted.

Dabney had been in his father's home office. Jerry was glaring at him. It was always like that. Dabney was used to it. He was furious about Dennis' brand-new Mustang. The Mustang he already had from his sweet sixteen party was only two years old. It was outrageous. Dabney felt, since his brother had gotten the car, that he deserved something, too. His grades were good and he wasn't in trouble for anything, so he gathered his nerve and asked for a dirt bike like Joey Kreeger's.

"Don't bother me with your nonsense," Jerry said. "Your grades are pale in comparison to your brother's accomplishments. Save some of the money you earn working for the farmer and buy your own dirt bike."

"But...," Dabney began.

"Don't answer me back, Dabney," Jerry interrupted. He lit a Marlboro. "I house you, I feed you, I clothe you, and when the time comes, I'll put you through college. The buck stops there. Now, get out."

Talking to Dennis about it only made things worse.

"You wouldn't have such a problem with dad if your attitude didn't suck so bad, Dabs," Dennis said, polishing his Mustang's bright green hood.

Dabney wanted to take a knife, stab it into the white convertible, and rip it all the way down the middle.

"It's Dabney, not *Dabs.*"

"See?" Dennis asked, pointing at his brother. "No wonder dad doesn't like you. Do what he said. Save your money."

Somewhere in the world it had to be legal to murder a sibling.

Save some of the money I get working for Hiram? Dabney thought. *Sure. I'll get the bike in a year or two. I made enough in the last three years, but I spent most of it. It's why I wanted a job in the first place.*

Dennis got a TV? No problem. Dennis got a stereo? No problem. At least what Dabney owned he bought with his own money. It was a small consolation considering the true cost.

207

Only my soul, Dabney thought, with a heavy sigh. Despair overwhelmed him. Thoughts of Hiram Milliken flooded his mind. *I'm trapped. I'm so scared. I should've told somebody! Why can't I tell anybody!?*

It was the same question over and over. Every time Hiram touched him, Dabney felt worse. He felt vile, dirty, and whenever he thought about it, he wanted to puke. That shame was a hundred times greater than anything he had felt at the pond today.

I can't get away. Somebody help me... please?

Dabney wiped his eyes and fought back his tears. As the pain in his face numbed, something snapped inside him. All he could think about was Chris and Jeremy McKee. He felt different somehow, deflated. It was as if he were a stranger in his own body. There was something about Chris he couldn't put into words, some understanding that had passed between them when their eyes met this morning. With Jeremy, it was different. There was a possibility of friendship, but he didn't dare even think the word. He knew if he was mistaken he would be devastated. These emotions were alien to him. He felt confused down to his core. Dabney wondered who he was. Is this what lay beneath his anger, all these confused feelings he never allowed himself to feel? He didn't know.

He sat up straight when Tammy returned with the ice pack. She checked his nose and informed him it was no longer bleeding. She touched the spot next to his left eye where she wanted him to put the ice pack. He stood up and looked in the bathroom mirror. When he did, he almost fainted. Both of his eyes were bloodshot and circled in a deep shade of purple. He had a large shiner next to the left one.

Dabney looked at Tammy, his face turning white. "Jeeze," he whispered, his voice full of honest sadness. "He really hurt me." His breath shuddered. He looked into the mirror again. "Who *are* you?" he asked his reflection. It stared dumbly back at him. He turned again. He was breaking down. "God, Tammy... why did I do it?" he asked, his tears renewed. "Why did I make everyone hate me so much?"

Dabney fell into her outstretched arms and wept.

Tammy held him and vowed to mark this day on the calendar. *Welcome to the real world, Dabney,* she thought. *What are you going to do now that you're here?*

*　　*　　*

"Do you like *Star Trek?*" Craig asked.

Jeremy flashed a wide grin. "Best show ever!"

They were sitting on Craig's front porch waiting for the guys. Craig was on the top step, his hands across his knees. Jeremy was almost lying on the walk. His head was resting on the bottom step, his feet crossed at the ankles.

Craig asked, "New or old?"

"Both," Jeremy replied, although he liked the old ones better. He was a noncommittal equal opportunity Trekker – not *Trekkie*. "The movies were great, too."

"Data's coolest on *Next Generation,*" Craig nodded.

"Riker's coolest," Jeremy corrected, shaking his head.

"Data."

"Get out of here, Borg-Dougan!" Jeremy exclaimed.

"Well," Craig grinned. *Borg-Dougan?* "I guess there's only one guy you can call coolest."

They looked at each other for a moment, and then said, *"Captain James T. Kirk!"* at the same time.

"Moment of silence, please!" Jeremy cried. They bowed their heads.

Chris, Max, and Derek sauntered up.

Max stared at them shaking his head.

Jeremy looked at him with a raised eyebrow.

Max smiled. "I figured you two would get along great," he said, satisfied he was all-knowing. "Where's the tent, Craig?"

Craig shyly led them through the house. Max noted it was a lot cleaner than he thought it would be, although the broken front window was odd. Derek commented on how plain it was. Max elbowed him and looked at him sternly. Derek gasped at his thoughtlessness and apologized. Craig told them a lot of his better things were at his relatives' houses. He had a bedroom at both his grandmother's and his uncle's. Everyone nodded. They didn't need to ask why. Jeremy wanted to tell them about the munitions they had found upstairs, but he had given his word not to.

Jeremy asked Derek, "What happened to your lip?"

"He beat up Copeland," Max replied.

"Dennis?" Jeremy asked.

Everyone looked at him.

Jeremy frowned. "Oh, Dabney," he said, with a hint of regret in his voice. "That sucks."

Derek's face fell. "Chris was like that, too," he said. "I didn't know you guys would be this upset about it."

Jeremy patted his shoulder. "It's okay, Mellon-head," he said. "Dabney's had it coming for a long time. He's just been acting different lately, that's all."

"Sincerely," Chris agreed. He thought, *I hope he's okay,* crossing his fingers. *I'm really worried about him.* He snapped his tongue. *How come it's so easy to forget he was passing around the rumor about me when Derek slugged him? I just… want him to be okay, that's all.*

"I thought he might be coming around," Jeremy said. "I hope this doesn't set him back."

"He was talking smack about Chris!" Derek exclaimed.

"A lot of people are going to, Derek," Chris said. "I hope you don't plan on fighting them all." He smirked. "Todd O'Connor was, too. If you come to the farm with me one day, you can have a go at him."

Derek's eyes widened.

Jeremy turned to Chris. "Sam wasn't home," he said.

"Oh?" Chris asked. *Sam's always home.*

Jeremy shrugged. "Steph said he went to some camp."

"Since when does Sam go to camp?"

Jeremy shrugged again. "And Keith is grounded."

Chris asked, "What else is new?"

"He said for you to message him."

They climbed the stairs to the attic. Craig slipped and almost fell, but Jeremy grabbed him by the butt and saved him. Craig looked over his shoulder, raised his eyebrows, and then smiled.

Jeremy goosed him. "In your dreams, Dougan!"

They formed a chain. Chris climbed back down and set the tent pieces in the living room. It was easy until they got to the canvas. It weighed a lot more than they had thought. Max went down and helped Chris take it from the bottom. Craig strained to lower it from the top. Derek sat on the bed flipping through a comic book he had found in a box underneath. Jeremy cuffed him and asked what he was doing.

"X-Men," Derek replied. "Dougan's got some cool issues."

"Maybe you can come over with me sometime and check them out," Jeremy said, looking over at Craig. He nodded. "In the meantime, Mellon-head, we've got work to do."

Max set the canvas down and climbed back up the steps to see what all the talking was about.

"Yeah, yeah," Derek said, slipping the comic back into the box. "I'm coming."

Everyone went downstairs. They moved the pieces of the tent outside. Max looked at the poles, the bag of pegs, and the canvas. He frowned. It was too heavy to carry all the way to the campsite. The guys let out a chorus of moans and stood there staring at it. The sun shined on them through the trees. Jeremy shaded Derek who had his shirt off. Derek looked up at him.

"Just looking out for the Lobster Boy," Jeremy said.

Derek tried looking over his shoulder at his back. "Why?" he asked, in a whine. "Do I have a sunburn? Please, tell me I don't."

"You don't," Craig said.

Derek smiled at him, relieved.

"You have a million freckles though."

Derek rolled his eyes. "You should see my brother, Doug. He's looks like he got hit with a nuclear explosion of freckles!"

"That's no lie," Jeremy agreed.

Derek leaned into Craig confidentially. "He even has butt freckles."

Craig bust out laughing.

"I've got an idea," Max said. "Chris, come with me."

Chris nodded.

They jogged toward the garage. Jeremy called to them and asked where they were going.

Max turned back and said, "We're checking on a ride!"

Jeremy nodded. Craig asked if anybody wanted lemonade. Derek was the first one through the door and into the kitchen. Jeremy and Craig looked at each other, shrugged, and then followed him.

Max and Chris raced to Gibbons' Garage. They tore around the corner where Chris collided with Lyle. It felt like hitting a brick wall. He fell to the ground, landing on his backside.

Lyle exploded with laughter. "Twice in one friggin' day! Is there a teenage contract out on me, or what?"

Chris blushed so severely that Max figured to start calling him Lobster Boy instead of Derek. José slammed Lisa's hood shut. Hiram and Arthur were seated at the card table. Hiram glared at Chris until they made eye contact. His expression melted quickly. Chris nodded at him and looked away.

That's right, Hiram thought, gripping the arms of his chair. *You're in control, McKee, for now.*

Lyle lifted Chris off the ground as if he weighed no more than Raggedy Andy. "What's up, McKee?" he asked. "You weren't trying to kick my butt, were you?"

"No way!" Chris exclaimed.

"I was worried," Lyle said. He leaned over so they were eye to eye. "I heard you came out of the closet," he said. He lowered his eyebrows. "That true, kid?"

Chris was surprised and a little shaken. *What do I do now?* he thought. *Lie?* He swallowed hard, lowered his head, and after a short pause he nodded.

Lyle stood straight and patted him on the shoulder. "You got cast iron nuts, Chris," he remarked, with a bit of sympathy. "Lancaster ain't the safest place in the world to be gay."

Chris replied, "So I found out. Two guys tried to jump me in school today."

"What!?" Max asked. "Who!?"

"Todd O'Connor and Frank Garrison," Chris said.

"You didn't say O'Connor tried to jump you!"

"Well, he did. You'll never believe who saved me."

Lyle crossed his tree trunk arms. "Someone with bigger nuts than you, if that's possible."

"Dennis Copeland," Chris replied. He grinned. "He threw Todd around like a rag doll."

"Cool!" Max exclaimed. "Now I know why he was around all day at school."

Lyle grunted. "Denny's a good kid. You're lucky you got him for an ally."

"No fooling," Chris whispered. He looked at Lyle. "Do you hate me now?" he asked, but wished he hadn't. It made him sound like a wuss.

"Nope," Lyle replied, walking away. He stopped within earshot of Hiram and Arthur. "Kelly's been my friend for years and he puts the flame in flamer."

Arthur raised his hand and snapped loudly.

Chris smiled.

"I tell you what, McKee. Anyone messes with you come and get me. I'll watch your back."

Max said, "Dude, Lyle doesn't watch anyone's back. You da man!"

"Nope," Chris said. "I'm da queer."

Max cracked him on the back of the head.

"Ow! Lyle!"

They laughed.

Hiram glared at Chris again. He thought, *You'd better not cross me, Chris. You better not even dream about it.*

Lyle walked over to Max and plucked him behind the ear. "You must want something," he said. "What is it? Money?"

"Nope," Max snorted, rubbing his stinging ear. "Your mama gives me enough of that." He dodged a slap and hid behind his father.

"Don't hide behind me!" José cried, shoving Max back into the lot. "We got your life insurance. We'll get by."

Max feigned hurt. "Oh. Great. Thanks."

Chris said, "We need some help with an Army tent. It's too big to carry down to the pond."

"Is that all you want, Max?" Lyle barked. He wasn't going to chase him. Not this time. "A ride?"

"Sí," Max nodded. *I don't believe it! I got away with dissing Lyle's mother!*

"English, you brat," Lyle said. "It's bad enough Lisa does that crap to me all the time."

"Lisa's a good Puerto Rican," Max replied.

José burst out laughing. Lyle tried to grab Max who easily dodged and slipped back over by Chris.

"Are you sure it's an Army tent?" Lyle asked, tilting his head and closing an eye.

Both boys nodded.

Lyle said, "I'll take you. I want to get a look at this thing." He shook his head. "I wonder if Dougan kept one from Afghanistan."

"I can take them in my pickup," Hiram volunteered.

Chris thought his smile looked phony.

"Forget it, old man," Lyle said. "I hate when kids ride in the back of a pickup truck. It's too dangerous."

"What about the Chevelle?" José asked, his accent slightly thicker than it was in the morning.

Max thought, *Dad's tired. It must have been a long day.*

"I'll take the kids over while you bring it to Lisa," Lyle said. "I'll pick you up at the market."

Max tapped Chris on the shoulder and pointed at the candy apple red Mustang convertible.

"We're riding in that, amigo!"

Chris' eyes lit up.

Jeremy, Craig, and Derek were back in the yard sipping lemonade when they heard the Mustang roar to life. They watched in awe as it whipped out of the lot speeding toward them. The rear end fishtailed and the tires smoked. It screeched to a halt in front of them. They saw Chris and Max inside and cheered. Ninety percent was for the car. Ten percent was for not having to carry the tent themselves. Derek was all over the Mustang when it stopped. He came around to the driver's side in front of Lyle who climbed out.

"Hi, Mr. Gibbons," Derek said, holding out his hand and looking up at him.

Chris watched from the other side of the car as Derek's whole arm disappeared in Lyle's grip. He snickered and pointed. Lyle seemed to shake Derek's entire body. The guys circled the big man as he looked down at the Army tent.

"Well, I'll be," Lyle said, squatting down for a closer look. He kneaded the long wiry hair on his chin. "How did your father get his hands on a Command Tent, Dougan?"

Craig blushed and shrugged.

Jeremy slipped his arm across his shoulders. "It's cool, huh?" he asked.

Lyle nodded, his mind drifting back to Afghanistan. The tent brought a lot of memories to the surface. He looked at Craig and realized how lucky his daughter Lisa was. He could've been exactly like Jack. Afghanistan often motivated him to get blind drunk when he returned to the States. He spent a good deal of time on the stool next to Jack down at Misty's Café. Jack used to save his seat by putting his lunchbox on it.

Lyle had given up drinking the day Lisa was born, when Marjorie died in childbirth. Lyle left the hospital, went to Misty's, and ordered a drink. He held the glass of bourbon in his shaking hand. Marjorie was gone. It felt like someone had blown a hole in his chest. He held the glass up and stared at it. The image of his crying baby girl came into his mind. He crushed the glass in his fist cutting the hell out of his hand. He stormed out of the bar and never went back. He glanced at the scar in his right palm. There were twelve stitch marks.

Lyle looked at each of the guys in turn. "You boys take care of this, you hear?"

Max couldn't remember ever hearing Lyle's voice that low.

"A lot of brave men slept under tents like her and died before they saw her again."

Everybody nodded soberly.

Derek put his hand on Lyle's shoulder. "Were you ever in a war, Mr. Gibbons?" he asked.

Lyle stood up. "You bet I was. Afghanistan. I ate Taliban for breakfast and crapped black turbans for days."

"Eew!" the boys cried.

Lyle moved to open the trunk. It took them two minutes to cram the tent in there. Chris wished he had remembered his boom box. Lyle told him they could stop at his place if he wanted. Max suggested it might be a good idea as Lyle put the top down. Chris sat in the front with Derek on his lap. The rest of the boys sat in the back with the poles lined up in the middle, sticking out of the rear. Lyle hit the key. The engine roared to life. They tore down to the dead end and spun around. The boys howled. Lyle smiled sheepishly at Mrs. Turner as they passed. She stopped sweeping her walk and shook her finger at him.

They made a quick stop at Chris' house for the boom box. Lyle chatted with Virginia while Chris and Derek ran inside. She was glad the boys were in good company. She wondered if Lyle could be the one buying the alcohol, but decided that was impossible. Lyle wouldn't do that. She noticed Craig Dougan in the car. That was more probable, but Virginia didn't think the kids were brave enough to even talk to Jack let alone ask him to buy for them. She caught a worried look from Craig and walked over. She leaned down and smiled at him.

"You're a pretty handsome young man, Craig," Virginia said, touching his soft cheek. "What a beautiful shade of hazel your eyes are."

Craig blushed, insanely.

Virginia ruffled Jeremy's hair. "Having fun, kiddo?"

"The hair!" Jeremy cried, covering it up with his hands.

"Oops!" Virginia gasped. "I'm sorry! It's just... well, it's so soft. I can't help it."

"I'll bet!" Jeremy scowled, giving her the evil eye.

Virginia looked at Craig again. He seemed terrified. She wondered why.

"I didn't know you were friends with Craig," Virginia said, to Jeremy. Her smile never left.

Craig cringed. *Oh, no! Here it comes. She's going to hate me and she's going to tell Jeremy he can't hang around with me. I knew it, I just...!*

"Not friends, mom," Jeremy corrected.

Craig's heart stopped.

"Best friends."

Craig let out a whoosh of breath as his heart restarted.

Virginia was delighted. Jeremy looked incredibly happy.

"That's wonderful!" she said, ruffling Craig's hair now. "You boys take care of each other, okay? Best friends are something very special."

"You bet," Jeremy agreed, elbowing Craig.

"You're not... mad, or anything?" Craig asked, lowering his head.

Virginia picked it back up. "Why would you think that, sweetheart? I don't pick Jeremy's friends. If he likes you, that's good enough for me."

"Told you," Jeremy said.

Craig flushed with happiness. "Thanks, Mrs. McKee."

"Call me Virginia," she said, and shook his hand. It was soft on the outside, but rough with calluses on the inside. They were working man's hands. She felt sympathy for him at once. "You make sure you stop in over here, too. You're welcome any time."

"Really?" Craig asked.

Virginia nodded. "Really." She leaned in and kissed Jeremy on the cheek. She returned to Lyle.

Craig snickered.

Jeremy crossed his arms. "My mother loves me."

Craig shook his head. "I don't have one."

"Where is your mom anyway?"

Craig said, "Hollywood. She left when I was a baby. I think it was because of my dad."

Jeremy agreed. *That had to be it.*

"Take care of my kids, Gibbons," Virginia said.

"Yeah, yeah," Lyle muttered. His eyes lit up. "Hey! Since your old man won't come down and play poker, why don't you?"

Virginia crossed her arms. "How bad do you want to lose?"

"Oh, ho-ho!" Lyle sang. "You think you got what it takes?"

"Next week," Virginia smiled, grabbing Chris as he attempted to fly by with his iPhone boom box. She kissed him on the forehead.

Chris squirmed. *"Mom!"* he whined.

Virginia ignored him and looked at Lyle. "You're mine, Gibbons."

"Huh?" Chris asked, his eyes as wide as saucers.

"Get in the car, Chris," Lyle said. "Your mom's just blowing smoke."

"We'll see," Virginia replied.

Chris escaped her grasp and got in the car. Derek came out of the house with a Twinkie in his mouth. He stopped short when he noticed that everyone was staring at him.

"What?" Derek asked, his voice muffled by the snack cake. He looked to see if his fly was down. It wasn't. "What did I do?"

"Where's *my* Twinkie?" Max yelled.

"Yeah!" Chris agreed.

"Yeah!" Jeremy and Craig chorused.

"Yeah!" Lyle bellowed. Everybody jumped, and then laughed.

"Okay, *okay,*" Derek whined, stomping back into the house. "Sheesh! What's a guy gotta do?"

"Get the Twinkies!" everyone yelled.

Derek stuck his head back out. "I'm getting them." He took a big bite off his own. *"Mm-mmm!"*

"Get the damn Twinkies!" Lyle hollered.

Derek ran to get them.

Once everyone was back in the car with the whole box of Twinkies, Lyle drove them to Pond Road. He parked the car by the woodline. The pond was empty. Lyle helped them carry the tent down to the swimming hole where their campsite was.

Oh, no! Max thought. *I didn't know he was coming down with us!*

Matt saw Lyle and tried to hide the cooler.

"Just bring the beer over here, Gardner," Lyle called. He saw what Matt was trying to do.

Everyone gasped.

Lyle looked at them like they were stupid. "Give me a break, will ya? Don't you think I know what you're doing down here? José's been yapping about it all morning."

"He has?" Ricardo asked.

Matt brought the cooler over.

Max looked stunned.

"C'mon, Ricardo," Lyle said, his hands on his hips. "Do you think your dad's blind?"

"But he let us go!" Max cried.

"Hey," Matt said, slipping in-between them. "My dad knows about it, too. It freaked me out."

Jeremy said, "So does mine. Do you know what he said?"

Matt nodded.

Lyle said, "Something like *'Don't get too drunk tonight?'"*

Jeremy asked, "How did you know that?"

"Oh, please," Lyle said, rolling his eyes. "José's been moaning the same crap all day. *'Jesus, Lyle, I hope they don't get too drunk tonight. I should've told them not to get too drunk tonight. Do you think they'll get too drunk tonight?'"* Lyle glared at them. They shrank back. He waved his hand. "Screw it, boys. Get drunk."

Everyone laughed, hysterically.

Lyle chuckled all the way back to his Mustang.

*　　*　　*

The Willimantic River flowed through the swamps behind Misty's Café and along the southwest side of town. It split behind Lancaster High School. The southeasterly branch became Lancaster Stream. It fed the pond and continued through the woods toward Stafford. About two hundred yards from the pond, the stream pooled up creating a small swimming hole. The guys went there when they wanted privacy.

Sandy – who had been gone the whole time the boys were with Lyle – finally rejoined his friends. He stepped off the trail that led from his house and marveled at the size of Craig's tent. He thought, *With that much sleeping space, we could've invited the entire ninth and tenth grades!*

"Holy cow!" Sandy exclaimed, dropping the fire extinguisher next to the woodpile. "This thing is huge!"

"Sandy!" Matt cried. He was sitting on a log draped over the swimming hole, dangling his feet in the water. He waved a beer at him. "It's about time, dude!"

"Yeah, man," Max echoed, walking over with Chris. "What took so long?"

"We were starting to worry," Chris said.

"Danielle," Sandy groaned. Derek handed him a beer. "She's history."

"Really?" Ian asked, his eyes widening. "You've been dating her forever, bro."

"Not after today," Sandy growled. "I helped Matt carry the cooler here, and then I left to get the fire extinguisher. She was on the trails heading toward the pond, and…"

Sandy told them what had happened. When he spotted Danielle, he couldn't believe it. *Her girlfriends finally let her know where they saw me,* he thought.

Apparently, Danielle decided "No, you can't come to the campout!" wasn't plain enough English for her. She paused in the middle of the trail and crossed her arms. Sandy walked past her without saying a word. Her smug satisfaction melted.

Danielle grabbed his arm. "What's wrong, Sandy?" she whined.

Sandy glared at her hand.

Danielle's long brown hair was crimped the way he liked it. She wore the perfume he liked the best, Obsession. She had her best-looking jeans on, a sleeveless white halter top, and make-up put on with patient care.

Sandy was livid. "Let go of my arm," he snapped, yanking it away from her. He continued toward his house. He hoped she would get the message and go away. She didn't, of freakin' course.

"Why are you being like this?" Danielle cried, trying to fake a sob.

Sandy stopped, looked up at the sky, and then turned to her. *Fine,* he thought. *You want to play games? Let's play.*

"Don't give me that crap, Danielle," Sandy said. "You were looking for the campsite after I told you no."

"So?" Danielle asked. "Can't I spend some time with my boyfriend?"

"You spend all of your time with me!" Sandy replied. "We've been through this before. Can't you give me some space?"

"I don't understand what the big deal is, Sandy," Danielle said. "What are you doing there that you don't want me to see?"

Oh, that's it! Sandy thought. He threw his hands up in the air and stormed away. *This conversation is over!* Whenever he wanted to spend time with his friends, she started this garbage. It was a never-ending tirade of jealousy, like he was her property, and he hated it. *Enough is enough!* he thought, kicking an acorn out of the road. He figured it landed on the moon somewhere.

Danielle followed him home. Sandy slipped his key into the garage door. It was on the left side of the house beneath his bedroom window. He opened it, ignoring her as he searched for the fire extinguisher.

"You didn't answer my question, Sandy," Danielle said. "Why don't you want me to go down there?"

"I'm not in the mood for this, Danielle," Sandy replied, as he crawled under the tool table. "You know why."

"Maybe you should tell me anyway," Danielle said. "You're my boyfriend. I have a right to know what you're up to."

Sandy went to stand and hit his head with a *whack. "Ow!"* he cried, rubbing it.

Danielle reached out to help him up, but he moved away from her.

"Don't touch me!" Sandy cried. "I'm sick of this! Every time I want to do something with the guys, it's like this! You can't go because the rest of the guys don't want you there. We want to have fun, but you're so possessive, it's impossible to do that when you're around."

"Why don't we go down and ask them?" Danielle asked. "It's not like I want to stay all night. I would if you asked me though."

"No," Sandy replied. He spotted the extinguisher on the floor next to his father's Craftsman tool cabinet.

"Are you afraid I'll find out you're lying?" Danielle asked. "You're the one who doesn't want me there, right?"

Sandy slipped upstairs to get his glasses. He had left them on the kitchen counter when he went to the pond. They were gold-rimmed John Lennon-style spectacles with transition lenses that got dark in the light. His mother wouldn't let him wear them to the pond since he had to take them off to swim. She didn't want them to get lost or broken. They were too expensive. Sandy slipped them on and hooked the rings over his ears. He took a deep breath before he went back downstairs.

They argued in the driveway for the next half an hour. Danielle accused Sandy of having something up his sleeve he didn't want her to discover. Another girl maybe? Were they using drugs along with the alcohol? Sandy angrily denied her accusations and continued to tell her to leave. His mother was due home from Annie Potts Elementary any minute. If she found them fighting, an hour-long counseling session at the dining room table would follow.

Sandy thought, *God, do I hate that!*

Danielle wasn't thinking about that. She believed she could push him until he finally gave in and let her go. It was a woman's prerogative to manipulate. That's what her mom said. Once she was there, she could ask if the guys cared whether she stayed the night or not. She was positive nobody did except Sandy. If he didn't act like it was some big secret, it wouldn't matter so much.

Sandy knew what things would be like if he brought her to the campsite. He was about to tell her to get lost when she finally crossed the line.

"It's Chris McKee, isn't it?" Danielle asked.

"What are you talking about?" Sandy asked, pushing his thick straight blonde hair out of his eyes. The question had thrown him off guard.

Danielle thought he looked guilty. She pushed the point. "I got a call from Heidi before I came here," she replied. "She said Dabney Copeland got into a fight with Derek at the pond because Chris is gay. It's all over school, you know."

Sandy rolled his eyes. "So?"

"Well, if Chris is gay and he's your friend," Danielle said, walking around him, "maybe that's why you don't want me there."

"What do you mean?"

"Are you gay for Chris?" Danielle asked, hoping an assault on his manhood would make him bring her to the campsite just to prove her wrong. Her mother said it was the most powerful weapon in a woman's arsenal next to the children. "Is that why you want to be alone with him?"

"What?" Sandy asked. "We're all together down there!"

"So?" Danielle said. "That doesn't mean you can't slip away somewhere private. Everybody knows Chris is gay and you're his closest friend. I can't think of any other reason why you don't want me to…"

"That does it!" Sandy exploded. "Get out of my driveway! We're history!"

Danielle's mouth fell open.

Sandy grabbed the fire extinguisher, slammed the garage shut, and stormed away.

"Sandy?" Danielle asked, tears starting to fall.

"Drop dead!"

"No! Please, Sandy!"

"Get lost!"

"Fine!" Danielle screamed back. "I'm going to tell everyone it's true, you faggot!"

Sandy opened his beer. He guzzled half, belched, and said to Chris, "I'm sorry, dude."

Chris shrugged. "I guess I won't have far to go for a Prom date."

Everyone laughed, except Ian. He was glaring at his brother.

Max patted him on the shoulder and took his beer to the log. Derek went with Chris to the iPhone boom box. He wanted Chris to play a song for him. Ricardo was in the water. Ian turned to go in. Ricardo splashed him.

"Quit it!" Ian whined.

Ricardo laughed and splashed him again.

Jeremy sat with Craig by the cooler. They were engrossed in such a serious conversation, Sandy didn't think they'd even noticed he was there. Everyone had a beer, but Craig hadn't opened his yet. Chris smiled as Sandy chugged the rest of his.

Jeremy said, "I don't think having a few beers is going to turn you into your father, Craig."

Craig shrugged. He stared at the unopened can. *Should I take the chance?*

Jeremy squeezed his shoulder, took the can away from him, and dropped it in the cooler. He took his beer and poured it out.

Craig looked up at him and smiled.

"I didn't want one now anyway," Jeremy said.

"Later maybe?"

"I will if you will."

An hour later, Derek's speech had slurred so badly it made him hard to understand. When he stripped to go skinny dipping, everyone laughed and joined him. Craig strategically positioned himself so no one could see his bruises. He was the only one not in puberty, too. Jeremy smiled as Max and Ricardo picked Ian up and chucked him in the water for teasing him.

Jeremy told Craig not to feel bad. "Puberty isn't all it's cracked up to be. The acne, the itching, especially in class, and especially in Ms. Adler's class. I swear, every time I reached down to scratch my nuts, she looked up at me. It was torture!"

Craig went to the cooler and retrieved two beers. He handed one to Jeremy and winked.

"Are you sure?" Jeremy asked.

Craig opened his and drank some. "I'm glad I came tonight."

"So am I," Jeremy agreed. He held up his can. "Best friends?"

"Best friends," Craig replied, and touched his can to Jeremy's.

*   *   *

Lyle stared intently from Arthur – who just shrugged – to Hiram whose turn it was. The farmer was a million miles away. A thick, foul-smelling cigar protruded from the corner of Lyle's mouth. The ash was about an inch long. The smoke formed a gray circle above their heads. Lyle only indulged in smoking when they played cards. Arthur wished he would go back to choking down cigarettes. At least they didn't smell like a burning piece of rope mixed with cat hair and irritate his sinuses.

I'm surprised the stupid thing didn't meow in outrage when he lit it, Arthur thought. He sighed. *The cigar is only half as annoying as Hiram tonight.*

The farmer kept getting lost in his thoughts and they had to remind him to play a card. Arthur was sick of it. His Hennessy was gone and he was tired. Lyle was on the verge of going from annoyed to downright pissed off.

"You wanna play a card, Hiram?" Lyle asked, his eyes narrowing.

The game was Seven Card No-Peek. Arthur opened with a pair of twos and bet two. Lyle beat them with a couple of queens on his fourth card and then rose.

"What?" Hiram asked, as if coming out of a dream. He reached for his Schaefer and took a long draw off the can.

Arthur moaned.

"Hiram!" Lyle bellowed, blowing out a cloud of blue-gray smoke. "What's your problem, old man?"

"My turn?" Hiram asked, glancing at the cards that were turned up and the money in the pot. "How much to me?"

"Five!" Lyle snapped. "Will you get your head in the game? We don't have all night!"

"Really, Hiram," Arthur agreed, straightening his glasses. "You've been a pain all evening."

Hiram snorted and tossed a five into the pot. Arthur was ahead as usual by a lot. Lyle and Hiram didn't have more than twenty dollars left of the hundred they had brought. Years of hiding his sexuality from the rest of the world had given Arthur a fantastic poker face. He would never have gambled with another gay man. It was too bad Hiram and Lyle never figured that out.

Too bad for them, Arthur thought.

It only took Hiram three cards to take the lead in this hand, a six of clubs followed by both black aces. He smiled and rose by ten. Lyle puffed vigorously on his cigar. He wished they could've passed over him. As Arthur reached for his cards, Hiram dropped his beer. It fell on the table and spilled soaking everyone's cards and money.

"Oh, for the love of Jesus Christ!" Lyle cried. He jumped up in time to keep from getting wet. He glared at Hiram, and then threw his cigar on the floor. "I can't stand it!"

Arthur shook his head. "Guess we should call it a night," he sighed, collecting his wet winnings.

"I guess so!"

"I'm sorry," Hiram offered, grabbing a towel from the rack next to him. "My mind isn't on the game tonight."

"No kidding!" Lyle snapped. He stormed out of the garage and slammed the office door.

Arthur took his money and followed him. It wasn't his mess.

Hiram waited until they were gone before smiling. The beer falling was no accident. It had been ripped out of his hand by an unseen force.

It's her, Hiram thought, his hand twitching with anticipation. *It's time for someone to die!*

*　　*　　*

Bea Jones carried her cash drawer back to Mike's office. She looked as tired and worn out as she felt. Her feet hurt, too, but she was glad she had worn sneakers today rather than the pumps she'd laid out last night. They would've made her feet feel worse than Christ's. Bea thought she was getting too old for these long hours, but she was glad the day was over. She swore the whole town had come in to do their shopping tonight. She set the drawer on the desk on top of Lisa's. Mike slid the two of them into his safe to count in the morning. He smiled at Bea and went back to the Adler delivery receipt, subtracting the appropriate amount from her account.

Bea glanced down, saw Adler's name, and her heart began to pound. Sadness crept into her breast as she remembered the argument she'd had with her son a few years back. Bobby was eleven years old. He wanted to attend an all-night skate session at the roller rink in Vernon. Bea had said no. He was too young. Bobby got angry. He said if she didn't let him go with his friends, he was going to run away. Did she try to comfort him then? *No.* Did she try to explain her reasons to him? *No.* Did she even bother to listen to what he was saying to her?

No, I didn't, Bea sadly thought.

Instead, she opened the front door and told Bobby to run away if that's what he wanted. She figured he would come home when he got hungry and had time to cool off, but she never saw him again.

How could I have been so callous? So hateful?

Bea thought that… maybe she went looking for him? There was something in her memory, a shadow. She reached for it. It was just beyond her thoughts where she could almost touch it. She was walking down Grady Lane with a flashlight near the farmer's field. *"Bobby!"* she called, for the hundredth time. She froze hearing muffled laughter. Slowly, she turned the light toward the field. A man in a ski mask was holding Bobby's remains.

His head was gone. He lifted Bobby's limp arm and jiggled it up and down, waving at her.

"I'm right here, mommy!" the man laughed, in a creepy falsetto.

He made his voice crack just like Bobby's did whenever he got emotional. He hated that. He hated puberty more than any boy ever had. Bea sucked in a lungful of cool night air and was about to scream bloody murder when she realized the man wasn't alone. There was a woman with him standing in the shadows. Her eyes exploded with midnight blue brilliance. Bea felt something, like fingers were reaching into her brain. She tried to scream, but she couldn't move. She was frozen in place like a statue. Only her eyes were free. They darted around, panicked, but then focused in on the woman's hand. The woman was carrying…

"No…," Bea whispered.

… Bobby's head…

"No!" Bea cried, in the doorway to Mike's office. She swooned and nearly fainted.

Mike jumped up and caught her. He shook her gently, "Bea!" and her eyes snapped open. Her face distorted and she fell against Mike's chest, sobbing. Dan had been mopping the floor in the vegetable aisle. He appeared, a worried look on his face. Lisa fell in behind him. Mike waved them away. Old Ted took their place. His face was stern. His body language conveyed his anger. He volunteered to walk Bea outside for some air. He slipped his wrinkled dry hand across her shoulders. She leaned against him. He led her away.

Mike scratched his head. He wondered, *What got into her?* He looked at the Adler receipt on his desk and picked it up. *I've never seen her this bad before. It must be a full moon. Craig seems to be the only one having a good day. At least, he was…*

Jack would be in jail for the rest of the week. Nancy ordered Mike not to bail him out regardless of the circumstances of the fight or how Sandra felt about it.

"A moment o' sympathy doesn't erase what your brother's done in th' past, Michael," Nancy said, when he called her. "A few days in th' pen might open his eyes t' what he's doin' t' himself and his son."

Mike didn't disagree. *At least Craig has a breather,* he thought. He hoped his nephew was having a good time. *He deserves it.*

Sandra's suspicions about Hiram made little red flags pop up in his mind. He bit his tongue and didn't tell Nancy what they suspected. Mike didn't want to upset his mother any more than she already was. Besides, Hiram was innocent until he dug up some proof of wrongdoing. He made a call to Arthur Kelly, but he wasn't at the hardware store. Mike left a message on his cell phone's voicemail. Hopefully, Arthur would call him tonight or maybe tomorrow.

"Can I go now?" Dan asked, reappearing in the doorway.

His voice completely cleared Mike's thoughts.

"Are the floors done?" Mike asked. He was still a little mad about the office business from before.

"Spotless," Dan replied, smiling a peace offering at his boss.

"All right, Mellon," he said. "Get out of here before I remember how mad at you I was for trying to murder my desk with your phone."

"I'm sorry about that, Mike," Dan said. "I…"

"Out!"

Dan ran out the front door.

Mike smiled and returned to his work.

In the parking lot, Lisa watched Dan barrel out the front door. She thought there might be a problem, but then she noticed his grin. She opened the passenger door. Dan smiled as the Chevelle roared to life. Lisa slipped it into gear, dumped the clutch, and tore out of the market's parking lot. She laughed when Dan grabbed the dashboard, his eyes bulging.

Oh, yeah! Lisa thought. *José has my baby running just fine!*

Lisa recalled the story of how her father had met José a few months before she was born. Lyle had been in Willimantic one day driving Marjorie's blue Oldsmobile Cutlass Cruiser wagon. He was heading back to Lancaster on Route 32 after visiting Windham Tech. He wanted to hire an auto student. Marjorie was a few months pregnant with Lisa and a lot of his time was being taken up caring for her. The pregnancy was difficult. Marjorie was sick most of the time. He needed help at the garage.

Lyle drove under the Route 6 overpass near the Mansfield town line and the station wagon stalled. He saw José walking back toward town after a fruitless job interview at a used auto parts operation. He stopped and asked if he could help. Lyle restarted the engine and waved him off. The wagon rolled a few feet and stalled again. Lyle got out and popped the hood.

"Are you sure I can't help you, señor?" José asked, peering into the engine compartment. "It sounds like a bearing to me. Do you have low oil pressure?"

Lyle glared at him. "Who are you? I was under cars when your mama was still wiping your backside. It's not a bearing. The oil pressure sending unit is bad. It keeps shutting the engine down, that's all. I can bypass it."

"I'd check the oil pressure before I did that," José warned. "You don't want to spin a bearing and throw a rod, man."

Lyle took the plug off the sending unit and bypassed it with a piece of wire from his shirt pocket. He slammed the hood shut and told José to get lost. He climbed back in, turned the key, and the engine started right up. He let it idle for a moment before he slipped it into gear and was on his way. He barely had time to flash a grin of satisfaction at the Puerto Rican before the whole car lurched to one side, a loud banging sound coming from under the hood.

Lyle rested his head on the steering wheel.

José walked up to the window. "You threw a rod, man," he said, shaking his head.

"Do you want a job?" Lyle asked.

Lisa chuckled as she pulled the Chevelle into the Lancaster Sporting Complex parking lot by Legion Field. Her mother had to drive Lyle's Mustang to Willimantic and pick them up. Lyle drove the wrecker back for the wagon. José said he had come from Puerto Rico by way of New York City looking for work as a mechanic. He lived in a rat-infested motel in downtown Willimantic. Lyle told him if he could put a new engine in the wagon in less than three days, he had a job. He did it in a day. Lyle hired José and gave him a room in his house, the one that was Max and Ricardo's room now.

Lyle lent José the money to fly Marianna up from the island and was promptly paid back. Marianna took care of Marjorie throughout the rest of her pregnancy. It was as much a glorious day as a heartbreaking one when Lisa was born and Marjorie died. Lyle sold the house to José shortly after. He moved into a new one over on Top Road. He couldn't stay in the old house. Everywhere he looked, he saw Marjorie's face.

"Why are we here?" Dan asked. He was confused. He thought, *Legion Field isn't that far from my house. Bog Dancer Drive's just down the street and around the corner.*

Dan had never called his parents to ask if he could go out after the way he'd angered his father before. He looked around hoping he didn't get caught.

"It's private here," Lisa replied, shutting off the lights and the motor. "We can take a walk and talk about whatever your problem is."

Dan locked his door and followed Lisa across the parking lot. There was a large aluminum street lamp glowing in the middle. They walked over the grass and around the fenced-in pool area. Lisa sat down behind the building away from the road on the dimly lit lawn. She patted the ground and invited Dan to sit with her.

"So," Lisa said, leaning back, and thrusting her chest forward. "What's up with you, Dan? Why were you so upset today?"

"Chris McKee, that's what," Dan said, to her breasts. He looked away, blushing.

Lisa smiled. "Isn't he gay?"

"He's gay all right," Dan replied.

"You sound pretty sure," she sighed. She knew Chris, but only through Max and Ricardo.

"We camped out together," Dan said. "He said he was gay and I went home. I don't want people getting the wrong idea just because I camped out with him a few times."

"So, you're not gay?" Lisa asked. She reached into her pocket, pulled out a condom, and handed it to him.

Dan's eyes grew wide.

"Show me."

They made love on the grass in the warm summer evening. Dan was awkward and inexperienced, but Lisa showed him how to please her. He learned quickly, giving himself to her. Her body spoke to him, her subtle curves drawing his caress, his exploration. His insecurity faded with her whispered coaxing. Each kiss validated him. He felt powerful. She was gentle, drawing him close, taking him entirely until they were lost in each other. When it was over, they lay together for what seemed an eternity. Dan stroked her shoulder, staring at the stars. She rested her head on his chest and listened to his heart. They dressed in silence. Dan wondered if he had done himself proud. Her smile was his answer.

"I can give you a ride home if you want," Lisa said, appearing relaxed and satisfied. She shook her head. "That was great."

"Really?" Dan asked.

"You're not gay, that's for sure."

Dan silently cheered. *Guess what, Chris? It doesn't matter what you say now!*

He passed on the ride home. His house wasn't too far. Besides, he had to sneak in. If he could make it to his room before his mom and dad saw him, he could claim he was home when he was supposed to be. She kissed him on the cheek. She sped away waving goodbye. Dan whistled as he walked across the parking lot. He didn't have a problem in the world. Once the guys heard about Lisa – and he was going to tell everyone in Lancaster High School – their jealousy would wipe out his betrayal. Chris would hate him. So would Max and the others, but Dan didn't care. He could make new friends. Chris had most likely told everyone at the campout by now including his brother, but it didn't matter anymore.

Let mom and dad ground me, Dan thought, feeling strong and untouchable. *It's Chris' fault anyway. I didn't tell him to be gay.*

Dan reached the edge of the parking lot near Lancaster Middle School, but paused sensing something. He had an odd feeling, a nagging itch on the back of his neck. He caught movement out of the corner of his eye and turned toward it. He strained to see what it was. It was too far away to distinguish from the shadows cast by the trees. Dan walked toward it, squinting in the darkness. It was a man in a ski mask.

In the summer? Dan thought. *How stupid is that?*

Then he caught the glint of something shiny in the man's right hand. It was the biggest hunting knife Dan had ever seen. The man charged toward him, knife first.

"Holy crap!"

Dan turned and ran. He raced through the parking lot and leaped over the embankment by the basketball court.

Jesus! What the hell is going on!? I have to get away!

He ran down the hill into the schoolyard. He flew around the right side of the building picking up speed. He felt like his heart was going to leap out of his chest. He tripped over a rock and screamed as he fell, swearing the man had caught him by the ankle. He hit the ground hard, the wind rushing out of him. He felt something crack and heard a pop. He thought it was a rib. His heart slammed as he gasped for breath. Panic moved him. He rolled to his knees, clenching his fists.

I'm going to punch him in the face if he even tries touching me! Dan thought, terrified.

He looked wildly around, scanning the road, the hill, the schoolyard, but there was nothing there. The world was silent. Dan caught his breath, his rib aching, his mind racing. *Am I seeing things?* Fear enclosed his heart. He leaned against a lower classroom window and closed his eyes. His breaths came quick and shallow. He felt pain in his knee and rubbed it. The denim was torn open. It felt wet and sticky.

Dan sobbed, "I'm bleeding!"

He opened his eyes and peered into the classroom. The lights in the room came on with a blinding radiance, the fluorescent bulbs on the ceiling flashing to life. His vision filled with colors and then cleared. His fear turned to terror as Chris McKee slammed against the window, groping for him.

Dan jumped back. He gasped.

"You're gay, too, aren't you, Dan?" Chris laughed, clawing at the glass. "That's why you're scared of me!"

"No!" Dan cried, and ran away, zigzagging across the lawn. *Oh, God, please! This can't be real!* His feet hit the pavement. He ran down Legion Avenue wailing. Terror kept his eyes wide. Panic gave him speed. *This is a nightmare!*

At the junction of Route 41, Dan ran into the street without looking or stopping. He charged across the road headed for the trails that led up to the cliffs. He didn't know why he ran in the opposite direction from his house. He only knew he had to. He raced like lightning straight up the hill. The man in the ski mask stepped from behind a tree directly into his path. He raised his knife.

Oh, my God! Dan thought. *How did he get ahead of me!?*

He tried to stop, digging in his heels, but he had too much forward momentum. The man neatly side-stepped and clotheslined Dan, slamming him into the dirt. Dan landed with a crunch, a stone driving into his left kidney. There was so much adrenaline pumping through his bloodstream that the maneuver barely slowed him down. He ignored the pain and rolled to his feet, glaring.

Dan screamed, "Back off!" and shoved him. When he pushed, he hooked the eyehole of the ski mask and tore it free. Dan's eyes widened when he saw Hiram's surprised face.

"Holy...! *The farmer!?*"

227

"You little bastard!" Hiram raged, planting his feet before he fell over. "You're going to pay for that!"

Dan opened his mouth to scream at the old man, but when he did, Hiram raised his knife. Dan ran away along the cliffs. He heard the farmer hulking after him. He barreled along the edge, farther away from Hiram with every step. Dan didn't know where the farmer had come from, but what he was doing was obvious. He knew if Hiram caught him he was dead meat.

Dan stumbled, losing his balance. His fingertips danced along the edge of the cliffs as he fought to keep from going over the side. He succeeded in regaining his balance and paused to see how far back the farmer was. Dan laughed nervously as the old man struggled along the trail.

There's no way he can catch me! he thought, relaxing slightly. *I could outrun him with two broken legs!*

"*Oh?*" Ms. Adler asked.

Dan whirled around at the sound of her voice. He had heard it through his ears and inside his head simultaneously. She was floating in the air in front of him, her eyes glowing. He screamed.

Ms. Adler cried, "*Let us test that theory!*"

She thrust her hand out. Dan felt his thighs lock in an invisible vise. She squeezed her hand into a fist. Both of Dan's femurs snapped. His vision went white with agony. He crumpled sideways, lurched over the edge of the cliff, and started to fall.

Ms. Adler screamed, "*No!*" her voice higher all of a sudden, more feminine.

Dan felt the invisible vise grip again only this time it was on his shoulders. It yanked him back from the edge, pulling him with such force he flew into a large oak tree. He crumpled to the ground, his shattered legs folding over to the side in either direction. He wailed at the pain. Hiram shot past him toward Ms. Adler. She knelt down holding her head. She was in agony. Dan whimpered, dragging himself away.

Hiram huffed, "Are you... alright?"

Ms. Adler's head snapped in his direction, her glowing eyes filled with hate. "*She stopped me again!*" she cried, in outrage. "*She will not let me kill him!*"

"Really?" Hiram panted. "You mean like this?"

Hiram stormed over to Dan, drew back his boot, and kicked him in the side. Dan felt two more ribs crack as he rolled toward the cliff. Hiram kicked him again. Dan pleaded for the reason they were doing this. Each time he looked up with his terrified expression, the farmer kicked him even harder. Hiram stopped at the edge of the cliff. He stood over Dan with a wide grin.

"Why?" Dan gasped, a sob catching in his throat.

He tried to speak, but he didn't have any words left. He never knew life had such a limited vocabulary. Did he use up his supply? Is that why he was about to die? He wanted to say that he wasn't a bad kid, not really. He tried to tell Hiram that he had plans. He wanted to go to college. He wanted to be someone better than the Mellon men before him. He tried to beg, to plead for mercy, but he couldn't. His ribs and his broken legs were so painful, they were preventing him from doing anything other than whimpering.

"Why?" Hiram asked, kneeling so they were face to face. His answer heralded the end of Dan's life. "Because I can."

Hiram stood up and kicked him one last time. Dan screamed as he rolled over the cliff finding his voice a moment too late. He was two hundred feet up in freefall. His arms desperately waved as he tried to grab on to something that might stop his plunge. He hit an outcropping of rock and heard a dull crack. His body twisted and his spine broke. There was no pain then. He went numb all over and continued to plummet. His eyes went dark. His heart stopped beating. Dan died a moment before his body hit Route 41 with a smack.

Ms. Adler stumbled next to Hiram. She looked over the cliff and nodded satisfaction. She reached into the front pocket of her skirt.

"Well, that was too easy, too," Hiram said, sounding disappointed. "This is starting to make me mad."

Ms. Adler ignored him. She withdrew a syringe and removed the bright orange cap. She held the needle up to Hiram's face. He stared at it, nodded, and she let it go. It hovered in the air like an angry wasp. Hiram followed its motion as it flew over the cliffs. The needle lodged itself into Dan's temple. The plunger pulled back filling the reservoir with the familiar pinkish liquid. The syringe popped out and flew back up to them. It paused in the air before gently lowering into her hand. She slipped the cap back on.

"Neat trick," Hiram remarked. "Another piece of God?"

"Oh, yes," Ms. Adler replied. Her eyes dimmed to brown. "Trauma is the key, Hiram. You serve me well."

"I owe you. You've protected me all these years."

Ms. Adler smiled.

A state police cruiser was approaching from Milliken Road. It was Robert Bigelow on his way home from work. He turned left onto Route 41, his headlights cascading over Dan's body.

"Time to go."

"We're not finished?" Hiram asked, his frustrated expression turning hopeful.

"Not yet," Ms. Adler replied, walking toward the trail that led down to Route 41. "A group of boys camping out in the woods? Honestly, Hiram. Do you think we can ignore such easy prey?"

"Wait!" Hiram exclaimed, thumbing toward Robert. He was out of his car, kneeling next to Dan. His police lights were flashing. "What about him?"

Ms. Adler replied, "Come now, Hiram. You know he can only see us if I let him."

Hiram followed her closely, his hands sweating. There was something in her eyes he'd never seen before, something that mirrored his own desire to kill. Whatever research it was that involved the murder of so many boys had to be something incredible.

Is she a witch?

Hiram couldn't care less. As long as he could molest who he wanted and kill when he wanted? She could be the devil herself.

*   *   *

"... and that's all there is to it," Chris said, wiping his face with his forearm. "You're either my friends or you're not."

The low flames from the campfire danced over the logs. The flickering light illuminated the faces of the boys encircling it. Most bore expressions of concern. Derek's was one of disbelief. Chris sighed as Matt and Max, on either side of him, placed their arms across his shoulders. They gave him a quick hug. Officially coming out to his friends seemed so easy earlier, but it ended up harder than he imagined. The more he spoke, the more emotional he got. He hadn't known how angry the whole situation made him until then. Drinking had a lot to do with it. The alcohol released his pent-up feelings. The silence now was deafening. Chris was more frightened than ever.

Still, it needed to be done. Chris had slipped into a funk after his first beer. His disappointment in Dabney spreading Dan's rumor grew into a deeper sadness that he'd gotten beat up over it. He didn't blame Derek. He loved Derek, sincerely. He just wished the situation hadn't deteriorated until Dabney wasn't only beat up but humiliated in the bargain. Chris couldn't help thinking, *Was I wrong about him? Did I see anything real in him at all, or was it just raging hormones?* The thought made him sadder still. Chris was pretty good at sensing when someone was on the level. Dabney's gaze had spoken volumes to him on the bus. *Could I really have been that off base?* It was worse because, regardless of where the day had taken him, Dabney had been right there in his thoughts. On its face, it was absurd. Ricardo was right to laugh at him. Dabney had done nothing to show he was anything other than what he had always been, a conceited rich brat who didn't care about anyone and only knew how to hurt people. Was this his real face?

Chris hoped not. Although he wasn't acting or feeling like the fangirl he had been this morning, there was still something inside of him drawn to Dabney Copeland. Chris wanted to get to know him, to talk to him the way Jeremy and Craig had been talking all night. Their feelings for each other were obvious. Their friendship was growing right in front of them all. That's what Chris wanted to experience with Dabney. He wanted to hold hands with him, walk with him, and just talk. His feelings were growing, but was it only his imagination? Was this whole thing just puppy love teenage drama? In the end, would it have Dabney laughing in his face and calling him a queer in Lancaster High School's hallway in the fall? Chris dreaded that. Spreading Dan's rumor was one thing, but hurting him deliberately to his face would crush him. Chris knew what he felt for Dabney was real and that those feelings were growing. If they were rejected so painfully, so publicly and deliberately hurtful, he knew it would break his heart. The campout wasn't everything he'd wanted it to be either. Hurt was the theme of the evening. Everyone sensed it, too. It wasn't long before it erupted in all of their faces.

It started with Ian who was drunk. He was going out of his way to needle the other guys after dinner. He teased Matt about being hairy, Jeremy about his new friend, Dougan the geek – which brought Craig close to tears – but mostly Ian focused on Chris. The rumor about him was like nuclear ammunition and the alcohol had made him brave. Even Max's warnings that he was near a beatdown didn't make him shut his mouth. Chris had heard enough. Everything Ian had touched on was so personal. He was bringing the entire group down. They were supposed to be there to have fun, but Ian had turned it into his own private put-down session.

Chris didn't care what Ian said about him. *Let him talk,* he thought. *He won't be the last person to give me crap.*

It was the hurt look in Craig's eyes and the gentle way Jeremy was consoling him that had spurred him to speak. His brother had never gotten along with anyone so well. If Craig and Jeremy's were friends now, he wasn't going to let Ian tear that down.

"You know, Ian," Chris said, sharply. "Why don't you shut up? You've been talking smack about everybody all night. I'm tired of it."

"What about it, McKee?" Ian asked, chugging the rest of his beer. He tossed the can in the fire. "Maybe I don't like Dougan or his drunk-ass father. Maybe I need to know if you're going to be sleeping next to me tonight."

"What's that supposed to mean?" Ricardo angrily asked, standing up.

Chris moved over next to him and shook his head.

"What?" Ricardo asked.

"Let him talk," Chris said. "I don't have anything to hide. Not from him."

Jeremy stood, too, glaring at Ian. He said, "You're a punk, you know that?"

"Hey, screw you, Jeremy!" Ian hollered, clenching a fist. "You started this by bringing Craig *the loser* Dougan here in the first place!"

"Hey!" Craig cried. "I didn't do anything to you, Ian!"

"You're the loser, Ian," Jeremy replied, raising his voice. His eyes narrowed. "Drop that fist, too, you wuss, before you make me mad. I'll beat your scrawny ass."

"Oh! I'm scared!" Ian sang. "The *fag's* brother's going to beat me up!"

Jeremy lunged toward Ian catching his shirt at the shoulder. He yanked him over, but Chris broke them up shoving Ian out of the way. He flew at Sandy who pushed him back.

Ian stumbled, but then planted his feet. "Don't touch me, Sanford!"

"Then shut your stupid mouth, Ian!" Sandy spat.

"This is too much," Max sighed. "This has to stop. You guys are bringing me down. Ian, man, you're going way too far."

"Yeah, Ian," Derek said, his face flushed with anger. "You sound just like Dabney Copeland."

"Well, don't think you're going to kick *my* ass, Mellon!" Ian exclaimed. "I'll waste you!"

"You're not going to waste anybody," Matt said, standing in front of Derek.

Derek peeked out from behind him and stuck out his tongue.

"I'm about sick of you, too," Matt said.

Ian shuffled back and forth in indecision. He felt cornered and very lightheaded. Chris' iPhone boom box was playing Motley Crue's *Dr. Feelgood* in the background. He wanted to slug Mellon right now. He knew the fight with Dabney had made Derek think he was Superman. His confusion made him angrier.

Why are they turning on me?

"I don't get you guys," he grumbled, backing down. "Why are you ganging up on me?"

"Because you keep talking smack!" Ricardo cried.

"Oh, sure, Ramirez!" Ian cried. "Like you've never said anything about gays before!"

"You're going a lot farther with this than mi hermano ever did, amigo," Max replied.

Everyone mumbled their agreement.

Ian stared at them in disbelief. "Maybe I want the truth!" he cried. "Maybe I want to know what's going on before I get in the tent and take my chances! How do I know I'm not going to get grabbed?"

"Who would want to grab you, *Pits in His Cheeks?*" Derek asked.

"Shut up, Lobster Boy!" Ian yelled, growing more hysterical.

"All right, Ian," Chris said, reaching out to him. "Enough is enough."

Ian slapped his hand away. "Don't touch me, McKee!" he exclaimed. "Answer the question!"

"You didn't ask a question," Craig responded.

"I did, too!"

"No, you didn't!" Matt, Max, Jeremy, Craig, Derek, and Ricardo all yelled back at once. They looked at each other and grinned.

"I don't get it," Ian whispered. He slumped against a tree by the tent and pouted. He slapped a mosquito that was stinging his arm and flattened it. He flicked the tiny corpse away. "Doesn't anybody besides me want to know the truth?"

"What do you want to know, Ian?" Chris asked.

Ian pushed him about Dan.

Chris told him the truth which opened the door to everything else he was feeling. He cried some, pounded on the ground a few times in anger, but there were no interruptions as he spoke. Ricardo glared at anybody who even breathed wrong. The hardest part was over now. Chris had laid his cards on the table. Derek was the first to pick up his jaw and stumble over to him. Chris was afraid Derek was going to slug him this time, but he didn't. He leaned over and hugged him. His green eyes, a shade deeper than his own, were brimming with tears.

"I'm your friend, Chris," Derek whispered. "Dan's a jerk."

"No, man," Chris said, hugging him back. "I think he was just scared of me, that's all."

"That's not much of an excuse," Matt remarked.

"Maybe not," Chris said. "Maybe if I'd talked to him when he called..." He shook his head.

They sat in silence for several minutes. Matt handed out the last of the beers, but Craig declined. He didn't want it. Jeremy smiled, resting against his shoulder. Today had been a good day. He felt remarkably comfortable in Craig's company. He didn't know how he'd gotten along without it. He felt like he'd known Craig all of his life. He understood the closeness his brother felt toward his friends. Chris smiled at him. Jeremy nodded, an understanding passing between them. Max turned up the music. Sandy grabbed a flashlight and motioned for Chris to follow him. They went down the trail away from the camp. Derek wobbled into the tent.

The beers and the brandy were gone. The last swig disappeared down Matt's throat. He followed it with a loud belch. They filed into the tent. Max left the fire burning for Chris and Sandy. He figured they had some talking to do about Chris' revelation, or Danielle, or both. The sleeping bags were spread out inside. Jeremy was against the far wall. Craig was next to him, and then Derek. There was a spot for Max, Sandy, Matt, a spot for Ian, Ricardo, and a spot for Chris against the other wall. Chris' iPhone boom box was next to Matt's head playing softly. Derek was the first to fall asleep, lightly snoring. Craig followed him. Jeremy rested his hand on Craig's shoulder and fell asleep that way, neither boy feeling alone anymore.

"Where's Ian?" Matt whispered to Ricardo, noticing he was missing.

"Don't ask me, man," Ricardo yawned. "He's probably out puking somewhere."

Matt nodded, but he had a weird feeling in his stomach. *I hope Ian doesn't do anything stupid,* he thought, closing his eyes. He was asleep a moment later.

*　　*　　*

Sandy and Chris walked along the trail in silence following Sandy's flashlight. Chris asked what was up, but Sandy told him to wait and just follow. Once they were sufficiently away from the campsite, Sandy shined his flashlight on a sturdy outcropping of moss. He asked Chris to take a seat. Sandy figured it was a good idea to talk about Danielle's intentions.

Sandy said, "So, Danielle thinks you and I have something going on."

Chris replied, "We don't though."

"I know, but that's what she said," Sandy replied. "She promised to tell the whole town, too."

Oh, great! Chris angrily thought. *Is this how it's going to be? How long before the world thinks I have the hots for all of my friends? I finally come out and the ones who aren't gay carry the burden? This sucks!*

"Look, Sandy," Chris said. "I'm…"

"Sorry?" Sandy asked. "Don't be. I don't care that you're gay and I don't care what Danielle says either. I've been thinking about it. I think I have the perfect solution."

"What's that?" Chris asked, hoping it was a good one. *Sandy doesn't deserve having his reputation tarnished because of me.*

"Danielle thinks we've got the hots for each other?" Sandy asked, grinning. "Let's tell everyone we do!"

"What?" Chris asked.

"Seriously!" Sandy nodded, adjusting his glasses. "What do I care what people think? Gay, straight, what's the difference? Besides, Danielle will go nuts. I can't think of a better way to get her back for the way she's trying to hurt us."

"You're crazy!" Chris exclaimed.

"Yeah," Sandy said. "Wait until the rumor gets to my mom. That's going to be hilarious!"

In the bushes five feet away, Ian's stomach lurched and he almost vomited. His brother and Chris were laughing in the light of Sandy's flashlight as Ian angrily backed away. He slipped up the trail, tears filling his eyes.

I knew it! Ian thought. *I knew something messed up was going on!*

Ian ran trying not to scream. He stopped suddenly, bent over forward, and puked. His stomach contents blasted out of his mouth onto his sneakers, soaking his socks. The scent hit his nostrils and he vomited again. Bile came out of his nose, burning his sinuses as he threw up again. Then a fourth time.

That's it! Ian thought. *I'm going home. I don't care if I get caught drunk! I don't care if everyone else gets caught either! I don't care about anything anymore!*

He trudged into the woods away from the trail heading north. The stars in the clear night sky were the only source of light, but drunk or not, Ian had grown up in these woods. He wasn't worried about getting lost. Crickets chirped and insects buzzed around his ears, but Ian kept walking. He lifted his feet high over the blown down branches, his mind on fire.

It's bad enough Dougan came tonight! Ian thought. *Jeremy had to go and make it worse by picking a fight with me! Then Chris tells everybody he's gay and nobody cares! They act like it's perfectly normal which it isn't! Now, my brother's in the woods planning to tell the entire town he's getting it on with the queer of the century? I can't stand it! Sandy's going to destroy my reputation, too! Those guys are messed up! They can hang around Chris all they want. I'm going to find Dan Mellon tomorrow and hook up with him. At least he doesn't like gays either! I've had it with all the...!*

"No!" Ian cried, as something caught hold of his foot. He fell face first landing with an *"Oof!"*

Ian lay there with his forehead on the ground, grumbling his frustration. He figured his foot had gotten caught on a stupid branch or something which was just typical. He wriggled his toes. The insides of his sneakers felt sticky and gross. He was glad he was going home now. He was sure he smelled disgusting. He looked up and groaned realizing he was about twenty yards from the farmer's field and nowhere near where he'd intended. The smell of cow manure hit his nostrils. He was going to puke again. He leaned up onto his elbows. The darkness seemed to close in on him. He tried to wrench his foot free. Terror seized him as the grip on his sneaker tightened.

Oh, my God! Ian thought, terrified. *Somebody's holding me!*

Ian turned his head back in time to watch a grinning man in a ski mask slice his Achilles tendon in half with a huge knife. His ankle felt like it was on fire. Ian gasped as warm blood poured into his sneaker. His foot felt like it was dangling by a thread. Ian screamed, but no sound came out. The man was on him in an instant. His weight was enormous. He ground his knees into Ian's shoulders pinning him to the ground. Ian tried to thrash and worm away, but his left foot was useless. He couldn't get any leverage. The man grabbed him by the hair, yanked his head back, and slit his throat. The last thing Ian heard before his life slipped away was the man's breathless words:

"You are... worthy... of the *Gift!*"

＊　　＊　　＊

Ms. Adler stood by the campfire, her eyes glowing. She glared in Sandy and Chris' direction, a scowl on her face. They were still in the woods plotting their deception.

Sanford Sturgess has no idea what he is doing, Ms. Adler thought. *Does he not realize that the love they share in friendship will become a romantic love for Christopher and ultimately this ruse will break his heart? Master Sturgess might be able to play the part of a gay or bisexual even to the extent of a physical expression of that circumstance, but he will never fall 'in' love with another male. He is thoroughly heterosexual.*

She frowned, turning away. *Will their friendship survive such a deception? His only consideration is to hurt Miss Wolicki. He does not see how this will hurt Christopher as well. As much as it grieves me, Christopher would be better off pursuing a relationship with Copeland, the obnoxious arrogant miscreant. Christopher's instincts about him are spot on. If he were ever to get through Copeland's arrogance, the two of them would know love like few ever do.* Her frown grew into a scowl. *Copeland does not deserve it.*

Ms. Adler looked toward the Army tent. *I need finish here, collect my next sample, and modify the memories of the Sturgess family. Ian is dead. Hiram has unspeakable plans for his corpse.*

She telepathically scanned the tent to make sure the boys were asleep, touching each of their minds. She telekinetically raised the door flap and slipped inside. She looked down at their sleeping faces. The light from her eyes banished the darkness.

How innocent they look lying together, and how filthy, like a pack of mongrels.

Ms. Adler bent over Jeremy and Craig. She reached out and touched their foreheads with her index fingers. Sparks of light emerged from each contact point. They rose into the air, leapt onto the opposite forehead, alighted for a moment, and then sank into their skulls.

"Two pieces of the same person," Ms. Adler whispered. *"Two sides of the same coin."*

She slipped out of the tent. She glanced at the fading fire and the rising crescent moon. She reflected a moment before disappearing in Hiram's direction to collect her latest serum sample.

*   *   *

Todd closed the barn door and slid the lock arm down. He was exhausted, his feet were killing him, and he wanted a beer. Teddy was standing next to him covered in manure. He was more embarrassed than upset. They had been shoveling out the hallway where the cows enter the milking parlor, the last job of the night. Teddy stepped in a large cow pie. He lifted his foot, cried, "Oh, gross!" slipped, and fell into the watery dung. Todd flashed a grin remembering the stream of expletives that had come out of Teddy's mouth.

"You've got some vocabulary for a cop's kid," Todd remarked.

Teddy grumbled, "I can't believe I fell in cow poo. This is so nasty."

Todd shrugged. "It happens. The only one who hasn't fallen in any is Dabney."

"I can't believe he works here," Teddy said.

Todd walked toward the trailer. "Believe it or not, he's pretty good."

"What about Chris McKee?"

Todd shuddered. *I forgot about that punk.* Engrossed in training Teddy, he hadn't had time to think about him.

"Him, too."

Todd led Teddy to the top of the trailer's steps. They took off their shoes and left them outside. Todd told him he had done pretty well for his first night. He meant it. Teddy didn't seem to have a problem getting dirty. Todd liked that. There was nothing worse than working with a sissy. Henry Schwartz was a good example. He tiptoed around the barn like a ballerina. Todd was glad he was gone.

They stepped into the trailer. Todd showed him the washer and dryer in-between the guest room and the bathroom. They stripped to their underwear and threw in their clothes. Todd measured the detergent and started the wash.

"You shower first," Todd offered. He wanted a beer and he needed a cigarette. "You need it more than I do."

Teddy asked, "Can I get a drink first? I'm dying of thirst."

Todd thought, *I almost forgot.* "Uh, sure... there's Kool-Aid for you. Hiram made it before he left."

"Sweet!" Teddy exclaimed.

Teddy found a glass in the strainer by the sink. He blew the dust off it and opened the refrigerator. There was a brown plastic pitcher inside surrounded by a phenomenal amount of beer.

I'd rather have one of those, Teddy thought.

He poured the Kool-Aid and drank the glass in one gulp. The taste hit the back of his throat and he retched.

"Oh, yuck!" Teddy spat. He set the pitcher back and ran to the sink. He stuck his head under the water and rinsed his mouth out.

Todd looked at him, oddly. "What's wrong with you?"

"That was nasty," Teddy complained, spitting into the sink. "It tastes like medicine."

Todd knew what he meant. "It's funny like that. It's been that way as long as I can remember and I've been coming here since I was eight."

Teddy sniffed at the running water. "It's not the water."

"No," Todd agreed. "Hiram buys generic Kool-Aid, or something. It won't kill you. It never killed me."

Teddy thought, *Cheap or not, I'm not drinking any more of that stuff.*

He shut the water off and walked to the bathroom. He paused in the hallway and looked into the guest room. He felt a sudden dread. He heard a small voice from far away that insisted, *"Don't go in that room!"* It sounded like Sam Stone. He went into the bathroom and slammed the door shut. He tried to lock it, but the lock was missing.

"Hey!" Todd cried, opening a beer. "Easy on the door, Bigelow!"

Teddy ignored him. He stared in the mirror. A clammy sweat beaded around his nose and on his forehead. His heart raced. His head swam. His vision doubled and returned to normal. He felt puffy like he was filled up with helium. He sighed, started the shower, and dropped his underwear to the floor. He climbed in and stood under the water struggling to keep his balance. He barely finished washing up before his vision went black and Teddy dropped to the floor of the tub with a smack.

Todd heard the noise and ran into the bathroom. He found Teddy unconscious. He shut the water off, yanked Teddy out of the tub, and shook him.

"Wake up!" Todd cried.

Teddy stirred, "… hurt me… he's… going to *hurt*... me…"

"Jesus, dude!" Todd hissed, clutching Teddy's ragdoll body. "Are you high?" He shook him again. "I want some!"

Teddy slumped backward unconscious again.

Todd tried to wake him, but he was gone.

Oh, great! Todd thought, trying not to fall over while holding Teddy up at the same time. *What am I supposed to do now?* He considered calling an ambulance, but then thrust that thought away. *If Teddy's on drugs and dies, it's not my fault!* He grabbed a towel and dried him as best as he could. Teddy flopped around completely dead weight. Todd snatched his underwear off the floor and slipped it back on him. There was a clean pair in his bag but that was his problem. *I can't believe I'm doing this! When he wakes up, he's giving me some of whatever he took! He's so zonked, a nuke wouldn't wake him!*

Todd carried him to the guest room and set him on the bed. He paused to make sure he was breathing before he went back to the living room. He swallowed his entire beer. He glanced at the refrigerator. He walked over to it. He took out the brown pitcher and pulled off the cover. He sniffed the Kool-Aid and made a sour face at the smell.

Same smell as always, Todd thought. *Is this what made Teddy pass out?* His brow furrowed. *I drink this stuff all the time though! I don't remember passing out. Have I ever?*

Todd put the pitcher back. He closed the door and went over to the couch with another beer. He opened it and took a large swallow.

Something weird is going on, he thought.

The cold he felt inside was accompanied by a gnawing need to get the bottom of this. His mind raced with a hundred memories that had never mattered until now. His eyes narrowed, his thoughts falling into a disturbing pattern.

When Hiram walks through the door, Todd thought, *he'd better have some answers, or I'm going to kick the living crap out of him.*

*　　*　　*

Jeremy lay in a field of soft grass, his eyes closed, his mind in a state of bliss. He felt warm and peaceful until a cool breeze blew over his skin. It whispered to him, but the words were faint and far away. A hint of despair clawed at his heart. It told him he should be crying. He was in trouble, in serious danger. It sounded like Ian, but he couldn't be sure. Jeremy felt the breeze dance across his face, its invisible fingers running through his hair and tickling his eyelashes. It blew over his body. As it did, Jeremy realized he was nude. He opened his eyes and stared into the crystal blue sky.

I'm dreaming. It can't be this pretty anywhere in the real world.

Jeremy looked lazily to his side. He grasped at the tiny blades of grass and ran his fingers through them. They felt cool and as soft as silk. He sat up and looked curiously around. The view was spectacular. He was on a sloping hillside. Fields stretched out in an endless landscape of bright green and beautiful flowers. Their colors were clean and vibrant, like rainbows, reaching toward an imagined sun. Despite the light illuminating everything, there was no star glowing in the heavens. The warmth was coming from all around him rather than from the sky. It radiated a loving innocence. Jeremy breathed in the clean air until his lungs were full. He held it, smiling. If he could, he would never leave this place.

He heard a muffled giggle. Someone was behind him. The sound played like music. It fed the world with more light, more peace, and the foreboding wind-voice vanished. Jeremy turned and saw Craig sitting on his mountain bike, smiling. The breeze came up and ruffled through his dirty blonde hair. Jeremy suddenly knew the innocence he felt was his. This land belonged to him.

"Nice place," Jeremy said.

Craig blushed. "No one's ever come here before," he replied, helping Jeremy stand. "Not my friends anyway." His face clouded. "You're my friend, aren't you, Jeremy?"

The landscape faded. Jeremy felt longing, desperation, and loneliness. It reflected in Craig's eyes as he watched Jeremy intently, his heart braced for rejection. Jeremy felt many things for Craig, but more than anything he felt like he couldn't survive without him.

"No, Craig," Jeremy said. "You're my friend. My best friend."

The landscape returned to its vigorous state with Craig's growing smile. He giggled once more, the tones tickling the inside of Jeremy's heart.

"I've never had a best friend before," Craig said.

Jeremy reached out, touched his hand, and then gripped it. "You have one now."

Craig nodded. "You, too." Again, he giggled.

Jeremy was puzzled. "What's so funny?"

Craig burst out laughing and pointed at him. Jeremy followed his finger and laughed, too. He'd forgotten he was nude.

"It's nice to see you, Jeremy," Craig said, "but I never expected to see so much of you!"

Jeremy held his arms out and whirled around. He felt so natural and pure. He was Adam in the Garden of Eden before *The Fall.* Craig closed his eyes and concentrated. In a flash of light, his mountain bike vanished, and clothes appeared on Jeremy.

Jeremy gasped, amazed. "How did you do that?"

"C'mon!" Craig cried, motioning for Jeremy to follow. "We can do anything we want in here!"

They ran through the fields laughing. They played with the toys Craig made out of thin air. A kickball, a Frisbee, each appearing in a flash of light. Jeremy discovered he could do the same. He made a pair of baseball gloves. Craig made the hardball. They tossed it back and forth. Jeremy vowed they would be friends forever.

"Do you mean that?" Craig asked.

Jeremy dropped his glove on the ground and walked up to him. He looked deep into his soft hazel eyes.

"Always. I mean it. I promise."

A tear ran down Craig's cheek. "It's been lonely here."

"I know," Jeremy said, wiping it away, "but it won't be anymore. I'm here now, and…"

Suddenly, the temperature dropped and a freezing wind began to blow, interrupting him.

Jeremy held Craig by the shoulders, his heart beating faster. "What is it?" he hollered, over the wind. "What's happening?"

From the far horizon, a deep inky black, the color of used motor oil, seeped through the fields. It drowned every color in foul-smelling darkness. The sky became metallic gray.

"Daddy's home," Craig softly replied. All of the emotion drained from his face and he walked away.

Jeremy called for him to wait, but he didn't. He ran to catch up, but he was thrown to the ground by a massive tremor. It shook the world with such force, he couldn't get his balance. Jeremy watched, wide-eyed and fearful. Craig stood a few feet away, his hands politely behind his back, staring at his feet.

A house tore out of the ground ripping through the oily grass. It rose through the fresh black earth sending dirt and dust everywhere. Despair gripped Jeremy as he stared at the one-story peeling monstrosity. The number 5 hung loosely on the wall by the front door.

Jeremy thought, *It's Jack's house!* The sight of it filled him with dread.

The screen door whipped open, snapping off the lower hinge. Jack stood in the doorway, dirty and sweaty. He was wearing a day's growth of reddish-brown beard on his face and had a huge bottle of Jack Daniel's in his left hand. He glared at Craig. His right hand opened and closed around the buckle of a thick black leather belt.

"Get over here," Jack slurred.

His voice was so malignant, Jeremy nearly wet his pants. He cried out as Craig shuffled toward him, begging him to stop, but he didn't. Craig inched forward like a sinner about to incur judgment. He paused at the bottom of the stairs. The sky was as black as the grass now. Gray clouds jetted by, the wind blowing fiercely. It uprooted flowers, slimy and dead, from all over the fields.

Jack lumbered down the stairs and dropped his bottle. It fell in slow motion and shattered on the porch. The bourbon splashed onto the house, sizzling and burning the paint like acid. Wisps of white smoke and flame rose up from the spots. Jack reached out and grabbed Craig by the hair. He twisted it in his fist as he pulled his son to him.

"I told you to come here, you little bastard!" He pointed at the broken bottle. "Look what you made me do!"

Craig cried, "I'm sorry, daddy, I'm sorry!"

Jack threw him to the ground. Craig's face hit the dirt hard. He looked up, frightened, his mouth bloody and filled with soil.

"No!" Jeremy cried, but they ignored him. He tried to move, but could only lay there paralyzed on the greasy grass.

Jack leaned down near Craig's face. "I hate you! You no good son of a whore! You ruined my life! I never wanted you! *Never!*"

Jack yanked Craig's pants down and held the belt up to the sky. It lashed the back of Craig's legs and buttocks. His smooth skin split open. Blood spattered into the air.

Jeremy's face contorted as he struggled to move. His outrage grew each time the strap fell. He could feel the pain on his own body as if Jack was whipping him instead.

Craig cried hysterically, begging his father to stop. "Please, daddy, I love you!"

"I hate you! It's all your fault! I have nothing because of you!"

Jack went into a frenzy. Welts raised on Craig's buttocks, back, and legs. Craig tried to crawl away. Jack caught him by the ankle.

Jeremy felt something like electricity flow through his body. His rage exploded. The pain he was receiving from Craig, the fear, the terror that he was about to die tore through him with a furious desire to save his friend.

This isn't a dream! Jeremy realized. *It's a memory! This really happened!*

Jeremy's eyes blazed with midnight blue light as a strange power filled him. He strained against the force keeping him on the ground. When Jack yanked Craig toward him and punched him in the face, Jeremy made a supreme effort of will and the barrier holding him burst. It fell around him like shattered glass and disappeared.

Jeremy ran straight for Jack intending to dive on top of him. Jack whirled around and effortlessly flipped him over his shoulder. Jeremy smacked onto the ground next to his weeping friend. He put his arms around Craig and tried to drag him away. Jack reached out and caught his son by the ankle.

"Leave him alone!" Jeremy cried.

"He's mine!" Jack maniacally smiled.

"Please… *please!*" Craig sobbed, burying his face in Jeremy's chest. "Don't… let him *kill* me…!"

Jack raised the belt. Jeremy felt the power surging within him. He lashed out with his mind, his thoughts merging with the energy. The force charged through his body as Jack's arm began its descent.

Jeremy cried, ***"Die!"***

The power lashed out from his forehead and Jack exploded in a gush of guts and blood.

*   *   *

Jeremy bolted upright in the tent, his eyes wide with fear. Sweat poured down the front of his face, his breaths coming quick and shallow.

Jesus! he thought. *Oh, my God! What was that!?*

Craig was asleep beside him. Jeremy saw tears on his face. He shook him, whispering his name. Craig was startled awake. He reached up and locked his arms around Jeremy's neck. His whole body shook as he wept.

Jeremy pulled him close, holding him, protectively. *Oh, wow! Is that true? Is that what it's like for him?*

Jeremy's tears fell. He could still feel Craig's pain from the dream. He heard the crack of the belt as he rocked Craig back and forth.

Sandy and Chris entered the tent and shined the flashlight on them.

Jeremy hissed at Sandy to "… shut that stupid thing off!" and snatched the flashlight out of his hand. He muffled the light in his pillow.

Chris looked at his brother worried.

Jeremy shook his head choking back a sob.

Chris patted him on the shoulder. "I'm here if you need me." He feared Jeremy might be hurt, but saw that it was Craig doing most of the crying.

In the time it took Jeremy and Craig to calm down, Sandy and Chris were snoring.

Jeremy thought, *Thank God the others didn't wake up.* He lay back. Craig went with him. Jeremy held on to him. "I had a nightmare," he said.

Craig shuddered, remembering his own nightmare. It hadn't started out that way. It had been a beautiful dream, so warm and peaceful. His special place always was. He felt silly that he dreamed Jeremy was…

"We were in a field and I was naked," Jeremy said, wiping his eyes.

242

Craig stiffened. "We were playing," he choked. "I made my bike disappear."

Jeremy slowly sat up. He stared at Craig feeling very afraid.

"It got cold."

Craig said, "The ground started shaking."

"I fell."

"And my house came up."

"Your father was there," Jeremy said, fearfully. "He was beating you."

"You saved me."

"Oh, my God!" Jeremy cried. "We had the same dream!"

Craig shook his head. "You were in my dream," he said. "I have it a lot."

Sadness filled Jeremy's his heart as he remembered, "That beating really happened, didn't it?"

Craig didn't answer. He rolled on to his side away from Jeremy. He unsnapped his pants and pulled them down in the back. Jeremy shined the flashlight on him. Craig pointed to a pair of jagged scars on his left buttock. Jeremy gingerly touched them. The skin was rough and thick. There were fresh bruises, too, purple and black. Jeremy traced them with his finger. He tried not to count them as his heart sank. He lifted Craig's shirt and followed the bruises up his back. He choked back a sob feeling helpless and very afraid. The dream came back to him more vividly – the strap coming down, splitting Craig's skin, the blood spattering. Craig didn't shrink from his touch. Jeremy examined every wound as if bearing witness to them might heal them and make them go away.

"Good... *Lord...,*" Jeremy whispered.

"They don't hurt anymore."

"God, Dougan," Jeremy said, as Craig pulled his underwear up. "Dude, I'm sorry."

"For what?" Craig asked. He buttoned his jeans. "You didn't hurt me. You're saving me."

Jeremy shut off the flashlight. He looked into the darkness. His eyes narrowed. "This ends now, Craig," he said, swallowing hard. "He's never hurting you again. I swear to God."

"I know," Craig sighed. "I knew it the moment you got to my house today. I knew when Max caught me this morning that everything would be different."

"Are you scared?"

Craig nodded.

"Me, too."

"We have to figure out how you got into my dream," Craig whispered, deliberately changing the subject. He felt amazed, but not frightened. "It's weird."

"Maybe you pulled me in?" Jeremy suggested.

Craig shook his head. "Not possible."

"Oh?" Jeremy asked. "What makes you so sure, Albert Ein-Dougan?"

Craig scowled. "Because you were naked. If I pulled you in, you would've had clothes on."

"Oh, now that's funny!"

"Maybe you're psychic?"

"Will you give me a break!?" Jeremy cried. He shushed himself as Derek stirred. He glared at Craig.

"Do you have any other ideas?"

Jeremy scowled.

"Uh, huh," Craig said. "You can't think of anything else, can you? Look at all the cool stuff you did in there. You blew up my dad!"

This is absurd! Jeremy thought. *There has to be another explanation. I have no idea what caused it, but one thing's for sure.*

"I'm not a bloody psychic," Jeremy whispered, and lay down.

The dream came into his thoughts again. He reached out for Craig and held him, the echo of his pain still fresh in his mind. Craig rested his head on Jeremy's shoulder feeling safe, protected.

"I meant what I said in the dream, you know," Jeremy said.

"Friends forever?" Craig asked, holding his hand up.

Jeremy gripped it with his free hand. "Forever."

They held hands as they breathed in perfect time with one another. Craig heard Jeremy's heartbeat clearly through the side of his chest. The even rhythm cleared his thoughts. The powerful sound lulled him back to sleep. Jeremy joined him a few seconds later.

*   *   *

The farm was dark when Hiram got there. The only light was coming from the TV flickering in the living room of the trailer. He parked the truck next to the barn and shut the motor off. He got out, jogged across the barnyard, and saw Todd through the front window. He was asleep, his head back, his mouth open, snoring. Hiram stole back to the truck and reached into the bed. He grabbed Ian's corpse, lifted it into his arms, and went inside the barn. He set it down on some hay and pulled up a floorboard. There was a hole in the dirt underneath big enough to hide the body. Hiram rolled Ian into it and replaced the board. He wasn't done with him yet. The Hill Witch had taken her sample, but the rest was his.

Hiram left the barn, crossed the yard, and walked up the metal stairs to the front door. He peered through the small window in the center. Todd was on the sofa. He didn't see Teddy. Hiram opened the door and went inside. He noticed an empty glass in the sink that smelled like the Kool-Aid. He smiled. He paused by Todd and rested his hand on his chest. Hiram observed his breathing. It was even. There was a clammy sweat on his forehead.

He's asleep, Hiram thought.

244

He could see that the door to the guest room was ajar. He pushed it the rest of the way open and entered. Teddy was passed out on top of the covers. Hiram knelt and sniffed his breath. He detected the scent of the Kool-Aid laced with the sleeping pills the Hill Witch had prescribed him. He climbed onto the bed. He didn't see Todd swaggering from side to side in the doorway, his hands over his mouth, his horrified eyes wide, watching him as he reached for Teddy.

DAY TWO
Tuesday

Virginia was sitting in the living room, her arm resting across the top of the sofa. Her eyelids were heavy, her eyes bloodshot from crying. It was all she could do to keep them open. Her tears threatened, but she fought them back. She stared through the front window into the night. It was black and her boys were out there. She feared the darkness would smother them while she waited for Robert Bigelow to arrive.

Ten minutes ago, her and Thomas sat straight up in bed after the first ring of the telephone. They looked at each other in the alarm clock's glow wide awake. They knew something was wrong. There was no other reason the phone ever rang at three in the morning. Virginia silently prayed as she reached for the receiver. She didn't know what she would do if anything happened to the boys. Thomas saw her hand trembling. He took her by the wrist.

"It's probably for me, honey."

Virginia shook her head. "I have a feeling I'm not going to like answering this call."

Thomas released her. "I'm here, babe," he whispered, kissing her cheek. He started praying.

Virginia held her hand on the phone waiting for the next ring. Part of her hoped it wouldn't come, but she knew it would. Every hair on the back of her neck stood rigid.

This isn't anything good, Virginia thought. *It couldn't be Danielle again, could it? God, I almost hope it is.*

The crickets sang to her through the open window. An odd sense of peace carried in their hum. It was humid outside. The scent of evergreen and cedar filled the air from the trees in their yard. Virginia cleared her throat, took a deep breath, and picked up the receiver.

"Hello?" she asked, forcing her voice to stay steady. *Please, God... please?*

"Virginia?" Cynthia Mellon asked. Her voice was irritated.

Virginia's heart sank. She could hear someone crying in the background. "Cynthia?" she asked. "Is that you?"

"It's me," Cynthia said. "I need a favor, okay? Robert Bigelow's in my living room. He's trying to tell me Danny's dead. Can you believe it?"

"Oh, my God!" Virginia cried.

"What?" Thomas asked, his heart skipping a beat. "Is it the boys? Jesus, Virginia! Did something happen to the boys?"

Virginia shook her head and covered the mouthpiece. "Robert Bigelow's at the Mellons'. Danny... he's..."

Thomas felt the blood drain out of his face.

"Virginia? Are you there?"

"Oh, Cynthia," Virginia whispered, her heart breaking. "I'm so sorry."

"For what?" Cynthia asked. "This has to be a mistake. Danny's not dead, for Christ's sake! Granted, he's not home, but he probably went camping with the rest of the boys."

"Cynthia, I..." *don't think so,* Virginia started to say. She had noticed the tension between Dan and Chris. *Something happened between them that's making Chris keep his distance. What about the message I brought home that he didn't even read?*

"Anyway," Cynthia continued, "I have to go to the hospital. Robert says I have to make a positive I.D. I'm already positive. It's not him. If we drop Douggie off, will you keep him overnight?"

"Of course we will."

"Great," she said. "Here, talk to Robert. I have to kick my husband in the backside. He's crying like he believes this crap. He's got Douggie all bent out of shape, too. I'll talk to you in the morning."

Virginia opened her mouth to say something more, but it was too late. Cynthia told Robert to pick up the phone.

Danny's dead? Virginia thought. *Jesus!*

It wasn't sinking in. The world was spinning. Virginia was glad she was lying down. If she'd been standing, she would've fainted.

Thomas asked her what happened.

Virginia only shrugged.

Robert got on the line. "Virginia?"

"Jesus Christ, Robert!" Virginia exclaimed. "Is it true?"

Robert paused before he spoke getting out of the Mellons' earshot. "I'm afraid so," he sighed.

"But Cynthia said..."

"She's in denial, Virginia," Robert whispered. "Christ," he added choking a little. "I hate this part of the job."

"What's happening?" Thomas asked, shaking her arm.

"How did it happen?" Virginia asked, leaning against him. She needed an anchor right now.

"He fell off the cliffs," Robert said. "I don't know what he was doing up there at this time of the night, but sit tight, okay? I'll be right there. You're going to have your hands full. Doug's pretty upset."

"I'll be waiting," Virginia assured him, and hung up.

She burst into tears the moment the receiver was in its cradle. Thomas held her until she was ready to go downstairs. She moved like a zombie. She felt empty. Nothing like this was ever supposed to happen to them or their friends. They were good people.

Why do the best always suffer the most?

Thomas brought her a cup of coffee from the kitchen, his face drawn up and sad. He thought, *How devastated Kevin must be. Cynthia isn't going to*

believe it until she sees Dan's body. Should I go with them? I want to be there
for Kev. We've been friends since we were kids.

Thomas decided against it. He had never lost anyone close to him. Losing one of his sons would crush him. He shared an unspoken belief in the immortality of all their kids. It was a belief suddenly shaken to the core.

Virginia took the cup and mouthed a weak, "Thank you."

Robert's car pulled into the driveway as she swallowed her first sip.

The McKees opened the front door together trying to hide their emotions. Cynthia and Kevin were in the back seat of Robert's patrol car. Cynthia was holding her husband's face to her chest. Her expression was stone, her eyes angry. Kevin was sobbing. Thomas looked at his pajama bottoms and wished he had grabbed a robe. Robert led weeping Douggie by the hand from the front seat. He was barefoot wearing plaid pajama bottoms and a white tee shirt. He broke loose halfway to the door and ran to Virginia. He leapt into her arms, his body shaking with powerful sobs. She held him, tears falling once more. She slipped inside and sat down on the couch. She drew him to her and gently stroked his hair. It was as soft and thin as a baby's. She rocked him back and forth shushing him.

"God, he's heartbroken," Thomas remarked, shaking his head.

"Who wouldn't be?" Robert asked. "Cynthia didn't help matters when she smacked him."

Thomas' eyes widened.

Robert shook his head. "She's losing it, Tom. She told him his brother wasn't dead. I saw him, man, and it was bad. Talk to him, okay? I have to get them over to Johnson Memorial Hospital."

"We will," Thomas said, shaking Robert's hand. "Let her know Douggie can stay with us as long as she needs. We'll collect Derek, too, if necessary. He's camping out with my boys."

"I will," Robert replied.

Thomas closed the door. He fought back his tears. Douggie's sobs were filled with despair. They broke his heart. The patrol car pulled out of the drive and disappeared down Satchell Hill. Thomas shut off the outside light. His wife kissed Douggie's freckled cheek. She was trying to help him hold his world together. Douggie and Danny were two peas in a pod. Thomas could only imagine how alone he felt right now.

Douggie looked up at Virginia, his blue eyes searching her face. They pleaded with her to lie to him like his mother had. Virginia couldn't speak. She slowly shook her head. Douggie fell against her, his tears staining the front of her powder blue robe. Thomas slipped in next to them and pulled Douggie's legs over his lap. He gripped his small foot and wrapped his arm around both of them.

"We're here, Douggie," Thomas whispered, patting his back. "We're here."

*   *   *

Hiram lifted the butcher shack's blackout curtain. He looked out the window and saw that the bathroom light was on in the trailer.

Good, Hiram thought. *The boys are up. I don't have to wake them.*

He had come out to the barn last night and got Ian's body once he was finished with Teddy. He slept with it in the hay, cradling the corpse in his arms. He woke up a half an hour ago and moved to the butcher shack where he performed unspeakable acts of depravity on the dead boy. He would document everything in his *Ledger.* He chained Ian's body to the ceiling afterward and mutilated it. He would have preferred his slaughter hook for this part, but he couldn't lock the barn, he wasn't alone, and the cows needed milking.

Hiram turned from the window and smiled. Ian twisted slowly back and forth, his cloudy eyes blank and staring. His fingers were locked together in front of him holding his heart. There was one dimple left to gouge out and he would be perfect.

Dimples, Hiram thought. *I hate dimples.*

He slid the knife into Ian's cheek.

*   *   *

Susan Sturgess stood on the back deck watching the sunrise. She held her robe tight against the cool morning. She needed to find the boys. She thought they might be out back since they camped there sometimes, but they weren't. She knew they had planned to party thanks to Randy Gardner. He always knew when they got alcohol although he wouldn't say how. It was enough he let them know. They only kept Cynthia, Virginia, Marianna, and Linda in the dark.

Susan planned to tell Virginia even though Thomas wanted to keep it secret. He wasn't sure how his wife would react. Susan couldn't believe how dense the man was.

Virginia surely suspects what's up, Susan thought. *She isn't blind, for Christ's sake. I don't know about Chris and Jeremy, by my sons are as transparent as a window pane. Ian couldn't keep a secret if his life depended on it.*

"Oh, right!" Ian's voice cried. It was hollow and far away. *"Thanks a lot, mom!"*

Susan shook her head.

They agreed the boys should be allowed some controlled rule-breaking fun. A little drinking never hurt anyone and she should know. She attended many parties in her youth. Still, she had to find them and fast. Linda would call soon to talk to Matt about what had happened to Dan. Susan didn't want any crap after what she'd gone through for Matt to be able to go in the first place. She couldn't stand the thought of Linda being one up on her. She turned and went inside. She had spoken to Virginia a short time ago when she called looking for the boys. She updated Susan about Cynthia.

Susan thought, *She popped her cork when she saw Dan's body in the morgue. They admitted her to the hospital. Kevin's with her now. If one of my kids got killed, would I be any better off?*

She decided not to think about it. She was angry enough she'd forgot about Ian leaving this morning. One of the camp counselors picked him up. She couldn't remember who that was, but she knew it was right. It was a good thing he had come back last night to remind her. She would have to reschedule his physical. It was supposed to be Wednesday and he wouldn't be back...

"Forever," Ian said.

... until...

"Never," Ian said again.

Susan violently shook her head. *What the hell was that?*

Ian would be glad about missing the physical at least. He got incensed every time Dr. Stone touched his testicles. Ian thought the doctor had some superlative nerve going there. There was the ballgame, too. She hoped Kevin and Randy wouldn't be too upset that Ian wouldn't be there. Something bothered her though. When it came to the family calendar, she was usually on top of things. It annoyed her to no end that camp had slipped her mind.

"Mommy?" Sean sleepily asked, from the hallway.

"Don't stand around in your underwear, Sean," Susan scolded. "Put some clothes on before some pervert spots you. Do you want to end up on a milk carton? What are you doing up?"

Sean frowned. "I had a bad dream. Is everything okay?"

Susan squatted down and hugged him. His soft skin was as warm as toast. "I'm not sure, honey," she said. "Get dressed. I'll get you some cereal. Mommy has to call Virginia."

Sean nodded and ambled away. He paused at the door to his room and peeked inside, his eyes wide and searching. He didn't see anything and let out his breath in a whoosh. He slipped in and opened his shades filling the room with light.

Nope, Sean thought, relieved. *No bloody, icky, scowling Ian anymore. Whew! That's good. It was the worst nightmare ever!*

Susan called the McKees. Virginia answered in the first half of a ring.

"Hi, Virginia," Susan said. "It's me."

"Any luck?" Virginia whispered. She was still on the couch. Douggie was asleep in her lap. Thomas was in the shower.

"Is Douggie still sleeping?"

"Yes. He looks peaceful."

"Too bad it won't stay that way," Susan sighed. "To answer your question, no. They have a dozen different campsites. They weren't out back. Linda's sure to be calling soon. We have to find them."

"Hang on," Virginia said. "I'll call Lyle. He gave them a ride to wherever they went."

She clicked Susan on to hold and dialed Gibbons' number. She clicked Susan back when it started to ring. Susan wondered if now was a good time to bring up the phone call she had gotten from Danielle Wolicki last night. She decided against it. Enough had happened without telling Virginia their sons were dating. Susan had always wondered about Chris, but Sandy? She never dreamed he would…

"It's a good thing I'm up," Lyle said. "Only a lunatic calls me this early in the morning."

"Oh, shut up, Gibbons," Susan said.

"It would have to be a woman."

"How about two for the price of one?" Virginia asked.

Douggie stirred in her lap and started weeping as soon as his eyes opened. She stroked his cheek and frowned.

"Who's bawling?" Lyle asked, sitting at the kitchen table with his coffee.

Lisa picked up the line upstairs in her bedroom. "Hello?"

"Douggie Mellon," Virginia said. "Robert Bigelow dropped him off here on the way to the morgue last night."

"Morgue?" Lisa asked, her heart sinking. "Daddy? What's going on?"

"Oh, Jesus," Lyle whispered. "Come on down here, baby. There's bad news."

"You know already?" Susan asked.

"I heard it on the scanner," Lyle said. Lisa hung up. He heard her footfalls as she made her way to the stairs. "I called the police barracks and asked a buddy of mine. How're the Mellons?"

"They had to sedate Cynthia," Virginia replied. "Kevin's with her, but he's coming back to tell Derek. We need to find the boys."

"Yeah, Gibbons," Susan said. "Where did you put our kids?"

Lyle sighed, pulling Lisa onto his lap. "Meet me here in an hour," he said. "I'll lead you down there. I have to talk to Lisa right now."

Susan offered to call Linda. Virginia said she would take care of Kevin and José.

"What about Craig Dougan?" Susan asked. "Should we call Jack?"

"Don't bother," Lyle said. "Call Mike. Lisa told me Jack got busted again yesterday. He's in the can. He beat up Jerry Copeland. It's probably the only good thing he's done in years."

Lyle hung up.

Lisa stared at him with fear in her eyes. She had heard the words *Douggie Mellon* and *morgue*. Her tears began to fall the moment her father opened his mouth.

*   *   *

Craig yawned as he stretched waking from the best night's sleep he'd ever had. He looked up at the ceiling of the tent and smiled. The sunrise illuminated the roof. He debated rolling over and going back to sleep, but he decided against it. Once he was up, he was up. He would only lay there like an idiot. He eased onto his elbows trying not to wake Derek whose head was against his hip. He smiled. Derek had the tip of his thumb in his mouth. Jeremy lay on his side facing him. Everyone was still asleep, a tangled jigsaw puzzle of bodies. Sandy was snoring, his head tilted back, his mouth hanging open.

Craig moved to get up. Derek snuggled closer to him. He eased Derek off and rolled him over toward Max. Craig froze when the Puerto Rican stirred, but then sighed relief. Max slipped an arm around Derek, patted him gingerly, and fell back to sleep. Craig snuck out before anyone else woke up. He noticed Ian wasn't there. He scanned the site thinking he might be outside.

Craig frowned. *No Ian, but there's a ton of beer cans and garbage. Maybe Ian went home?*

Not that he cared. He had enough of Ian to last him a lifetime. Wherever he was, he was glad the little rodent was gone.

"Hey, screw you, Dougan!"

Craig froze. "Hello?" he asked, straining to listen. He shook his head. "Hearing things."

Craig walked over to the stream, unsnapping his pants. He urinated into the water, but gazed around behind him. The site was a mess. He figured he would show his appreciation for the invite by straightening up a bit. It was the least he could do. His Iron Man watch said it was five a.m. He had plenty of time before he needed to be at work. It was nice to clean because he wanted to not because he had to. He also planned to chip in some of his tip money to help Matt pay for everything. He thought that was fair since Matt allowed him to come in the first place.

Craig dumped the water out of the cooler into the stream. He placed the leftover food inside and set it against a tree out of the way. He carried armfuls of cans about ten yards into the woods and deposited them in a rotted out tree stump. It wasn't until he'd set the brandy bottle inside that it dawned on him someone might want the returnables. They were worth a nickel apiece. Craig started pulling them back out, but then stopped.

The heck with the cans, he thought. *If anyone wants them, I can get them later.*

Craig went back to the site. He was pounding out the ashes from the fire when his heart jumped into his throat. In the distance, he heard Lyle Gibbons bellowing at Matt's father.

"Would you get a move on, Gardner?" Lyle barked. "I've got a business to run this morning. I ain't got all day."

From the sound of it, they were at the edge of the clearing. Craig strained his ears. He heard several more voices making their way up the trail. He panicked and charged into the tent. He tripped over one of Matt's feet and fell flat on top of Ricardo. Ricardo opened his eyes and looked at Craig with death in his gaze.

"I swear to God, Dougan," he said, through his teeth. "I know you're not trying to get queer with me."

"Get up!" Craig cried, shaking Jeremy, Derek, and Max. "There's trouble!"

"What?" Matt asked, sitting up. "What's wrong?"

"Parents!" Craig exclaimed. "They're coming down the trail!"

The boys stumbled over each other as they fought to get outside. Matt dove through everyone hoping he could dispose of any incriminating evidence before his mother got there. He didn't have to, to his incredible relief. The site was spotless. They looked at Craig with expressions of surprise and profound gratitude.

Craig shrugged. "I cleaned," he said, and smiled.

Matt lifted him off the ground in a bear hug and then dropped him. "Dougan?" he asked. "Anything you want, it's yours!"

Max leaned over to Craig and whispered, "Tell him you want a handy."

Craig gasped.

"Hey!" Matt exclaimed, looking around. "Where's Ian?"

Everyone froze.

Jeremy looked into the tent and turned back, shaking his head.

"I'll bet he narked on us," Ricardo said.

"Don't worry about it," Sandy said. "There's no evidence thanks to Craig. If Ian narked on us, I'll kick the crap out of him. I'm leaving his stuff here, too."

"You didn't save the cans, did you?" Matt asked, elbowing Craig.

"I hid them."

Matt nodded. *Good, I need the returnables to help pay Phil back.*

Lyle came off the trail first and nodded at the boys. *Good,* he thought. *No sign of a party.*

Craig mouthed, "Thank you," at him for being so loud.

Lyle discreetly nodded. He had planned it that way with Randy. Linda slipped around him and headed straight for Phil's cooler. Matt froze. Craig touched his arm and shook his head, grinning slyly. Matt sighed relief.

Linda flipped open the lid intending to yell, "Ah, ha!" She was sure the boys were up to something when she learned they had camped out behind the pond. *Phil's cooler, too?* There was nothing inside but leftover food. She stepped back, scratching her head.

"Good morning to you, too, mom," Matt said, trying to look offended. It was obvious this was a surprise inspection. "Looking for something?"

"Uh... Matt?" Jeremy asked, tapping on his shoulder. "Look at Coach Mellon."

Everyone turned toward the adults. There were more people there than they'd noticed. Aside from Lyle and Linda, there was Nancy, Mike, and Sandra Dougan, Thomas and Virginia, José and Marianna, Randy, Susan, Douggie, and in the midst of all of them, Kevin. Their jaws dropped at his expression. The circles under his eyes were huge. His face was streaked with tears. He looked ragged and tired. His eyes were bloodshot. Derek walked over to him, worry filling his heart. Kevin knelt down and whispered something into his ear. He reached out for his son, but Derek stepped back. He turned toward his friends and walked to them, his eyes locked on Chris. Derek cracked a little bit with each step. He stopped in front of Chris, his eyes filling with tears.

"Dan fell off the cliffs last night," Derek said. "He's dead."

He fell into Chris' arms, sobbing. Chris held him, shocked, while the rest of the boys hurried to their respective parents. Craig sat right where he was and wept. He decided he would miss Dan even if they didn't talk that often. Jeremy sat with him putting an arm across his shoulders. Nancy came over to them. Jeremy was about to move, but she held out her hand.

"Stay there, laddie," she whispered, patting him on the head. "Craig'll go t' who he wants. Seems t' me he's picked ye."

"He's my friend," Jeremy choked. He felt so sad, but he didn't know why. He didn't know Dan all that well and dead or not, he was still mad at him for what he tried to do to his brother.

"Aye, that he is, an' he needs one, t' boot."

The boys bombarded their parents with questions as they dressed. *Was it true? Could it be? Where did it happen? How did it happen?* They split into groups. Matt had a bone to pick with his mom. She did, after all, go straight for the cooler.

Thomas put his hand on Kevin's shoulder. He was embarrassed that Derek walked away from him and went to Chris. He apologized for that.

Kevin sighed, "It's okay, Tom," holding Douggie against his leg. "I can't blame him. Derek usually gets lost in the shuffle, you know? Cynthia can't be a hundred places at once. Douggie's hyperactive... well, it's just difficult. I work a lot of hours, too."

Thomas glanced at Jeremy. "I know the feeling."

"I'm glad Chris makes time for Derek," Kevin continued. "They're on the phone together constantly. I'd hate to think where he would be right now if he didn't have Chris."

Thomas watched how tenderly Chris comforted Derek. *He's a good kid my number one son. As soon as we get home, I'm going to tell him so.*

"I'm taking Douggie to his grandmother's house over in Willington," Kevin said, sadly. "Cynthia… won't be coming home right away. Can you keep Derek for a few days?"

"From the look of it," Virginia remarked, thumbing toward Chris, "you'd need a crowbar to get them apart. You know you don't have to ask, Kevin. We're happy to have him."

Kevin nodded and said he would call Derek later. She could tell he was about to break down again as he walked away. He stood six-foot-two, but looked five-eight the way he was hunched over. His red hair seemed pale like it was losing its color. His blue eyes appeared darker.

Matt gathered his things and gave his mother a piece of his mind as they hauled the cooler away from the campsite.

Virginia thought, *It's about time.*

Sandy was by the water looking at his mother like she was out of her mind. Virginia couldn't hear what they were saying, but whatever it was he was having a hard time believing it. Thomas led her to the Dougans who were consoling Jeremy and Craig. José said something to his sons in Spanish. Lyle was next to him rolling his eyes.

"What do you mean Ian's at camp?" Sandy asked. "Since when?"

"He left this morning," Susan replied. "I guess I forgot to tell you. I don't want to talk about that though. He'll be back… whenever. I want to talk about something else."

"Like what?" Sandy asked. He thought, *Camp? That's bull! How come I didn't get to go? Oh, well, the heck with him anyway. He's a pain and I need a vacation…*

"Forever."

"Ian?" Sandy asked, looking around. He felt a sudden pang of loss. He swore he'd heard his brother's voice.

"I'm sorry, Sanford… so sorry."

"No, not Ian," Susan said, regaining Sandy's attention. He felt strange all of a sudden. "Danielle called me last night. She said you broke up with her."

"I did," Sandy said.

"She also said you and Chris were… together."

Sandy searched her expression. "What of it?" he asked.

Susan replied, "Well, I'm surprised, that's for sure. I didn't think you went that way. Chris I wondered about, but you?"

Sandy shook his head. "We're thinking about officially dating."

"Sandy!" Susan gasped. "I'm not sure Lancaster's ready for that!"

"Why not?" Sandy asked, crossing his arms. "There are plenty of teens who date. Girls dating girls, guys dating guys, guys and girls dating each other. This isn't 1950, you know. It's the twenty-first century. If we decide to do it, they can just deal with it."

Susan scowled. "Your father's going to have a heart attack."

Sandy smiled. "Wait until Virginia hears about it."

Oh, God, Susan thought. *Give me strength!*

Mike squatted by Craig. "Are you okay?" he asked, searching his nephew's face. "You're taking the day off today."

"Dad's in jail, isn't he?" Craig asked, not moving his head from Jeremy's shoulder. "I heard the cops go by yesterday."

"Aye, lad," Nancy replied. "He is. I'm goin' t' see him this mornin'."

"You can stay with us if you want, handsome," Sandra offered, wiping his face with a hanky. "He'll be gone for a couple of days, I'm sure."

"Thanks, Aunt Sandra," Craig sighed, but he looked up at Jeremy. "Can I stay with you instead? Would that be okay?"

Jeremy replied, "I hope so."

He looked up for his mom, the authority in this matter, but Nancy was leading Virginia out of everyone's earshot. The Ramirez brothers, Sandy, Mike, and Lyle packed up everyone's stuff, rolled up the sleeping bags, and took the tent down.

So much for camping tonight, Chris thought, squeezing Derek.

Ricardo handed them their bags from inside the tent. Alex took Ian's backpack. Ricardo lifted Derek up and wiped his eyes with his thumbs.

"Put some clothes on, okay?" Ricardo whispered. "It'll be all right, Derek. I promise."

"Yeah, buddy," Chris added. "You're going to stay with me for a couple of days."

"Really?" Derek asked, taking his bag. He looked around, confused. "Where's my dad?"

"Gone to take Douggie to your grandmother's," Thomas said.

"Can I sleep in your room?" Derek asked Chris, a sob catching in his throat.

"Anything you want, Derek," Chris replied. "You know I'm here for you."

"You always are," Derek sighed, reaching into his bag for his clothes. He felt completely drained of every feeling. He was a walking void of nothingness.

Nancy led Virginia by the water where the Sturgesses had been. She waited to ensure Craig wasn't listening before she spoke. Virginia knew Nancy more by reputation than anything else. She could only guess at what she wanted to say to her. Before she began, Virginia motioned for Thomas to come over. Whatever Nancy needed, she suspected it involved the whole family.

"Ye have a fine son there," Nancy began, nodding at Jeremy. She slipped her glasses off and cleaned them.

"Craig seems like a nice boy, too," Thomas replied. "He wants to stay with us while his father's... gone."

"He does?" Virginia asked.

"Aye, lass," Nancy nodded. "Your boy's th' first friend he's been able t' make, I'm afraid."

"That seems so unreal," Virginia said. "Is it because of his father? We've heard stories..."

"... and they're all true," Nancy interrupted. "'Tis what I wanted t' speak t' ye about."

"We're listening," Thomas said.

"Craig's not had it easy, t' be sure," Nancy started. "I'm goin' t' give his father an ultimatum today. He either gets help, or I'll find a way t' take th' boy away from him."

Thomas and Virginia stood motionless while Nancy told them about the abuse Craig had suffered. They had heard the rumors, but never thought they could be true. How could anyone hurt their child so badly? She thought Craig's resistance to help was because he was so alone.

"He's made a friend now," Nancy remarked. "It might be th' chance we've been waiting for."

Virginia said, "I don't think I've ever seen Jeremy this close to anyone before."

"No," Thomas added. "Me neither."

"This might be what we need t' draw him out o' his shell," she continued. "Jackie's me boy and I love him dearly, but I'll be damned if'n I watch him hurt Craig any longer."

"He can stay with us if you think it will help," Virginia said. "I'm not sure if we can do anything else."

"Lass," Nancy said, "if'n ye open your heart t' him, ye'll be doin' wonders. He refuses t' talk about his father t' us, but to ye? And maybe Jeremy? If he opens up, we might be able t' help him."

Thomas shrugged, "I'll talk to Jeremy. If what you're saying is true and Jack is abusing Craig... well, I'm a lawyer. I could help you file some papers, or something."

"If'n it comes t' that," Nancy said, "ye can be sure we'll be payin' ye for your services."

Nancy said she would call and tell them how her meeting with Jack went. Thomas walked over to the boys and helped them gather their things. Craig raised his shirt to wipe his face. When he did, Thomas spotted the bruises on his back. He felt a chill go down his spine. He had never raised a hand to his sons and couldn't imagine doing so.

If Craig asks me, Thomas thought, *I'll give the boy all the legal assistance I can. The Dougans can keep their money.*

"Where should we put the tent?" Lyle asked, scratching his beard.

"Do you want to bring it to my house?" Jeremy asked.

Craig nodded. "If it's all right. I don't want to go home if I don't have to."

"You'll need clothes, won't you?" Mike asked.

"I guess," Craig replied. "Most of the clothes that fit me are at your house though."

"I need clothes, too," Derek mumbled.

"I'll take you to your house later," Virginia said. She turned to Sandra and asked, "Can you put a bag together for Craig? I'll pick it up."

"Sure," Sandra replied. "Thanks for letting him come to your house. He needs some friends."

"Dougan doesn't need friends," Ricardo corrected, catching him in a headlock. "He's got us, right guys?"

"Bet," Max agreed.

"Damn straight," Sandy echoed.

"I'm your friend, too, Craig," Derek whispered, walking up to him. Ricardo let Craig go. "I guess we… all need somebody today."

"I'll miss Dan, too," Craig said.

Jeremy slipped his arms around both of them. "C'mon, guys," he said, leading them toward the path. "Let's go home."

"Hey!" Lyle bellowed, his hands on his hips. "Somebody want to help carry the friggin' tent?"

"Let them go, big guy," Mike said. "We'll help, won't we guys?"

Sandy, Max, Ricardo, and Chris nodded.

Lyle leaned over to José. "Ask your old lady to go see Lisa," he whispered. "She's taking the Mellon kid's death hard."

José nodded. He thought, *It's a sad thing, the death of a child.* He took his wife by the hand and told her, all the while praying it would never happen to them.

*   *   *

Tammy heard Denise trying to calm Jerry down all the way upstairs, but she was failing. It wasn't a surprise. When he had come in yesterday after being bailed out of jail, he stormed into his office and slammed the door. Tammy tried to tell Denise about Dabney out of Jerry's earshot, but Denise didn't want to hear it. She had a headache. The trip to the police station was dreadful. She lay in bed the rest of the day alone with her Xanax. Jerry brooded in his office all night until he exploded this morning.

Tammy walked down the grand staircase. She knew she couldn't wait much longer to tell them about Dabney. If the Mellon family called to speak to them about the fight, it would look like she had concealed it. She could see Jerry pacing back and forth from mid-way down the steps. His hands waved as he ranted. Tammy picked up pieces of his comments. Something about, "… buy the TV station and fire that bitch!" and "Bigelow hasn't heard the last of me!" and "Judge Thompson? I'll buy her four times over! I'll have all their badges, you hear? All of them!"

Tammy stood in the doorway and motioned to Denise. She shrugged sadly and discreetly pointed at her husband. Jerry caught the action out of the corner of his eye as he poured a drink. He demanded to know why Tammy was tiptoeing around.

Tammy thought, *If the answer to that isn't the most obvious thing in history, I don't know what is.* "I just need Denise, sir," she said. "It'll only take a moment."

Jerry swallowed his drink in one gulp and poured another. "Whatever you have to say, you can say it right here."

"No, sir, really," Tammy said, backing away. *Jerry's angry enough as it is. Dabney can wait until later.* "It'll keep until…"

"I said now!" Jerry cried, slamming the bottle down onto the sterling silver tray. "Are you deaf? Don't forget who signs your paychecks!"

Tammy shrank back, stung by his ferocity. "If you say so, sir," she sighed, with a hurt expression.

"I say so," Jerry said, downing his drink. "I don't stutter."

"What is it, Tammy?" Denise asked, moving in-between them. She was a petite woman, bleach blonde, with cherub cheeks and round innocent eyes. Jerry towered over her. She appeared quite delicate in his looming presence. "Is something wrong?"

Tammy took a deep breath and told her how Dabney was when he came home from the pond yesterday including the bloody nose and the black eyes. Jerry hit the ceiling halfway through her story. A tirade of profanity came out of his mouth. Tammy felt her heart skip a beat as he shoved past her and charged up the stairs toward Dabney's room. Tammy and Denise followed. They slowed down by the top of the steps as Jerry pounded on the door.

"Go away," Dabney said. His voice was small and sad.

Tammy cringed. *Oh, boy. This isn't going to end well.*

"Open this door before I kick it in!" Jerry hollered.

Tammy and Denise inched in behind him.

Dabney unlocked the handle and slowly opened the door. Jerry took one look at his damaged features, raised his hand, and slapped Dabney across his face with such force he stumbled backward, his arms pinwheeling. He hit the edge of his bed and fell on the floor, blood flowing from his nose again. Dabney burst into tears, his face creased with hurt and shock as he held his cheek.

"Oh, my God, Jerry!" Denise exclaimed, holding her hand up to her ample breasts.

Tammy stared at him in disbelief.

"Get out!" Jerry yelled at them.

Denise backed away. Tammy moved with her. They slipped into the hallway. Denise dumbly shook her head. They both jumped at the sound of another slap. They cringed as Dabney began to wail louder.

"Who were you fighting with?" Jerry demanded.

Dabney was crying so hard he couldn't speak. Jerry hit him again.

"D... erek...," Dabney sobbed, forcing the words out. He held his hands up by his head to defend himself. *"M... m...,"* he choked, *"m... Mellon... Derek Mellon!"*

"You stupid...!" Jerry raged. He hit Dabney repeatedly, accenting his words. "Are you trying – *slap* – to ruin me? – *slap, slap* – Derek *Mellon?* – *slap* – How many times – *slap* – have I told you – *slap* – to avoid fighting at all costs – *slap* – with these blue-collar nobodies? – *SLAP* – How many?"

"It wasn't my fault, *okay!?"* Dabney cried, blocking as best he could.

Tammy peered around the doorjamb in time to see Jerry kick Dabney in the shins. Dabney howled in pain, rolling on the floor, holding his leg.

"The court doesn't care whose fault it is!" Jerry exclaimed, balling up his fists. "Don't you know they can sue me now? My father spent a lifetime building the company. I've worked my ass off to become who I am, and you? You want to tear it down in one day!?"

"I'm sorry, *all right!?"* Dabney sobbed. Tears rolled down his cheeks mixing with the blood from his nose.

"No, it's not all right!" Jerry spat. "It's never all right with you! You're a selfish, self-serving little nobody, a thorn in my side since the day you were born! Don't you realize how many losers become rich at the stroke of a judge's pen over something like this? I swear, as God is my witness, if the Mellons file papers because of you, I'll kill you with my bare hands!"

Jerry stormed out brushing past Tammy and Denise. Denise ran after him. Tammy moved toward the room to try and comfort Dabney, but it was too late. He jumped up, slammed the door, and locked it. She knocked, crossing her fingers.

"Go away!" Dabney sobbed.

Tammy heard him crying in earnest as she turned. When she did, she also heard a crash from the other side of the door as something smashed against the wall. There was another crash... and then another...

*　　*　　*

Nancy stood outside Jack's cell with her arms crossed. It took some effort seeing him like this, shaking and pleading, but she swallowed her sympathy and denied his request to bail him out. Whatever happened all those years ago was no excuse for what he was doing to Craig or himself. Jack glared at her with flaming eyes. She never knew they could hold such hatred.

"What do you mean you won't bail me out?" Jack asked, leaning against the bars. His hands were shaking. He was sweating profusely. "I'm going out of my mind in here!"

"I'll get ye out on one condition, bucko," Nancy said, standing her ground. "Ye have to go t' alcohol treatment."

"Rehab!?" Jack cried. "Are you crazy? I don't need rehab! I need to get out of this hole!"

Nancy shook her head. "That's th' deal. If'n ye don't, I'm warnin' ye, I'll be takin' th' lad away from ye."

"Craig!?" Jack raged. He's mine, you hear? Mine!"

"For what?" Nancy asked. "T' beat up when th' mood hits ye? T' treat like a dog? T' take his money an' drink it all away?"

Jack exploded, *"Don't you dare talk to me about money!* You don't know what I went through for *my* family! I was paying the bills when I was *twelve,* remember!?"

"Why don't ye tell me what ye went through, Jackie?" Nancy asked, lowering her voice. "Tell me an' we'll help ye, lad. Ye need help. I'm givin' ye a chance here."

Jack stepped back from the bars. His whole body was convulsing from D.T.'s and rage. *Doesn't she know I'm going crazy? Can't she see how badly I need a drink? It's all I can do not to hang myself with the goddamned sheet!* Every cell in his body was crying out for alcohol. His head swam. His chest felt like an enormous vacuum. *God, is there no mercy? They're trying to kill me!*

Jack's arm shot through the bars reaching for his mother.

Nancy stepped back.

"No!" Jack raged. His eyes were green atomic mushroom clouds. "Come closer! Let me get my hands around your neck! You try and take my kid and I'll kill you! Do you hear me!?"

Nancy turned away. "Good-bye, Jackie," she said, waving to the guard to let her out. "Ye think about what I've said."

Jack screamed at her some more, but the words pouring out of his mouth made little sense. He felt such hatred and betrayal. If he could've squeezed through the bars, he would've killed her, and then everything would be okay. The outer door slammed shut and she was gone. Only a wisp of her perfume remained to remind him she had ever been there at all. Jack broke down, tears of rage running down his face as he fell onto his cot.

Alone... I'm all alone!

At least, he thought he was.

A rank scent filled his nostrils. It was the foul stench of his nightmare. Jack looked up and his heart stopped in his chest. There was a dead man sitting on his bunk, his vacant eyes glaring at him.

"Well, Dougan," Lt. Sweetwater said. *"You've finally hit bottom, soldier. How does it feel to be lower than snake shit?"*

Jack felt Sweetwater's death breath on his skin. He stared wide-eyed into the green face of his decomposing platoon leader. Sweetwater leaned over him, the bones of his skull visible through his tightly drawn skin. Jack spastically shoved backward against the wall. He held up his hands trying to ward off the apparition. He cried out to the security camera begging for someone to save him.

The officer on duty at the monitor shook his head. Drunks he knew. Ten years behind a desk taught him well the stuff they pulled to get attention. He would watch in case Dougan tried to commit suicide. It wasn't happening on his shift. Too much paperwork.

"Get a grip, soldier!" Lt. Sweetwater yelled. His black greasy tongue lolled inside of his mouth. *"This isn't a social call, Dougan!"*

"Go away!" Jack cried, swinging wildly with his fist.

Sweetwater caught it in his left hand. He grabbed Jack by the neck with his right and squeezed. Jack gasped for breath.

"Don't mess around, Jack," Sweetwater said, his lips curling into a snarl. *"Not many people get a second chance. You have a lot to atone for, boy. You'd better be ready."* He let go.

Jack panted, his hands over his face, struggling to breathe. "What… do you… want from me, man?" he asked. Silence was his only answer.

Jack peered over his fingertips. He was alone again. The apparition was gone although Sweetwater's foul reek remained. It mixed with Nancy's perfume. Jack burst out with nervous laughter. His body resumed shaking as the convulsions returned. He got up and stumbled to the sink. He took handfuls of cold water and splashed it onto his face. He held the last splash to his cheeks letting his hands slip slowly down.

Sweetwater, Jack thought. *He would be tough enough to come back, wouldn't he? I must be going out of my…*

His gaze fell on his neck. Five neat bruises were forming where Lt. Sweetwater had grabbed him. Jack stumbled back holding his chest. His eyes rolled into his head and he fainted.

*   *   *

Thomas and Virginia sat on the den sofa on either side of Chris. His face was against his father's rib cage as he sobbed. Virginia nodded at her husband, a silent message passing between them. Thomas winked back. She was right. It had taken some serious willpower to hold in all these emotions until he'd gotten them someplace private. Thomas held the shaved side of Chris' head lightly patting it.

"It's okay, kiddo. Let it out."

When they got home, Jeremy led Derek and Craig upstairs while Chris helped the men with the tent. They stuffed the canvas into the garage next to Thomas' golf clubs and leaned the poles & pegs against the wall. Mike commented on the cleanliness of everything. Lyle remarked something about a real man's garage needing a little dirt.

Chris said, "My dad does with the law what you do with motors, Mr. Gibbons."

"Lyle," Lyle said, with a hand on his shoulder.

"Lyle," Chris said, a half-smile breaking the gloom on his face.

"Your dad should be proud to have a son like you, Chris," Lyle said, giving his shoulder a squeeze. "If I had a son, I'd want him to be just like you."

"Gay?" Chris asked.

"If my son consoled his friends in their time of need the way you did Derek Mellon?" Lyle replied. "He could be a flaming Arthur Kelly drag queen." He ruffled Chris' hair.

Chris took a breath and hugged him.

Lyle was surprised, but after a moment hugged him, too, patting his back.

Mike leaned into Lyle. "You old softie," he said.

Lyle rubbed Chris' back and let him go. "Ignore him, Chris," he said, with a snort. "He just wants someone to hug him."

Chris shrugged and hugged Mike, too.

Mike smiled and gave him a squeeze. He asked, "What is it with McKees anyway?"

Chris let go of him. He said, "We love our friends, Mr. Dougan."

"Mike," Mike said.

"Mike."

"Did your dad ever tell you he declined an offer to pitch for the Red Sox?" Lyle asked.

Chris stared at him.

Lyle leaned in, confidentially. "When I came back from Afghanistan, my father couldn't stop talking about him. He was a huge baseball and football fan. He went to every game at E.O. Smith even after I graduated and enlisted. Your dad was a junior when I shipped out. My father was so amazed at your dad's arm, he used to drive to Harvard to watch him pitch." He leaned back. "When he graduated the university, the Red Sox put an offer on the table. Your dad told them he loved the law more than the game and came home with your mom. My father, who was a huge Red Sox fan, called it a cryin' shame."

"Are you serious?" Chris gasped. "My dad could've played for the Red Sox?"

Lyle pointed toward the doorway to the kitchen.

Thomas was standing there leaning against the jamb, his arms crossed, smirking.

"Dad!?" Chris cried.

Thomas lowered his head and nodded. He cleared his throat. "Carl Gibbons was in Hartford Superior Court one day for a probate issue."

Lyle said, "My Uncle Billy had passed away. It was six months before my father died."

"That's right," Thomas said, pointing at him. He touched his chin, reflectively. "He was leaving when he spotted me in one of the courtrooms. He sat down while I was cross examined a businessman who had accused my client of embezzlement."

Lyle slapped Chris' arm with the back of his hand. "They railroaded the guy. He was fresh out of college, broke, and expecting to go to prison. The suits took the damn money. Your dad was a public defender. They thought they had it in the bag."

"Carl told you about that?" Thomas asked.

Lyle rolled his eyes. "Tom, my father said...," He cleared his throat and did a perfect imitation of Carl Gibbons' gruff manner of speaking. "... *'Son, it was the most friggin' amazing thing I ever saw. Tommy McKee...*"

"Tommy?" Chris interrupted.

Thomas nodded. "Carl called everyone Tommy, or Bobby, or Jimmy. It was just who he was."

"Anyway," Lyle continued, *"'Tommy McKee lit into this suit all grinnin' and preenin' like a Hollywood fairy...*" He leaned over to Chris. "No offense, Chris. Believe me, my father was no homophobe. That was just how he talked."

"None taken," Chris assured him.

"He says '*... like a Hollywood fairy and Tommy McKee took him apart! I'm tellin' ya, Lyle, it was the most amazin' thing I ever saw next to your one-hundred-thirty-yard rushin' game. McKee ate this creep on toast and got the kid acquitted. It was son-of-a-bitchin' in-friggin'-credible!'*"

Thomas smiled. "He came up to me after the verdict and shook my hand. He had the biggest hands I ever saw."

"You ain't lying," Lyle snorted. "Try having your ass tanned with 'em." He rubbed his left buttock.

"Did he say anything, dad?" Chris asked.

Thomas replied, "He said I did the right thing walking away from the Red Sox. He said the law was my true calling." He gestured at Lyle with his chin. He also did his best Carl Gibbons voice. "He said, *'Tommy? I ain't seen a natural like you 'cept my boy Lyle. What you can do in a friggin' courtroom, he can do with a motor. Best friggin' mechanic I ever saw.*"

Lyle nodded, his eyes tearing.

Sandra offered him a tissue from her purse.

"Will you get outta here with that?" Lyle cried, wiping his eyes roughly with his hands. "It's all the damned cologne in this house!"

Thomas shook his head and went back inside.

Chris thanked them for their help and brought Sandra and Mike into the den. They were going to discuss Craig while they waited for Nancy's call. He walked Lyle to his car and told him to give his best to Lisa. Lyle said he would and drove down Satchell Hill toward Route 41. Chris let the good feelings Lyle's story brought him fill his heart. They kept his sadness at bay for a time, but it didn't last. His emotions almost floored him in the hallway, but he clamped down on them real tight. He wasn't going to cry in front of anyone except his parents. He grabbed four cokes out of the refrigerator and brought them to his brother's room where the boys were. Craig stared at Jeremy's computer in awe. Jeremy told him he had mowed a lot of lawns to pay for it.

Chris handed out the sodas and cracked his open on the way to the shower. He had woken this morning scared at Dougan's panic, but feeling on top of the world at the same time. Now, after hearing about Dan, he felt like he was under it. He decided a shower might help clear his head. He was angry with Dan, but he never hated him. He wished he'd answered his messages. He might've been camping with them last night rather than walking on the cliffs. It was a regret he would carry for the rest of his life.

Jeremy heard the shower and cursed. He wished he'd thought of that. He hated waking without an available shower. No matter what, he was next. Derek and Dougan would have to wait. Craig was surfing the Internet trying not to think about Dan. He was glad he had the day off. He was on an emotional rollercoaster. A feeling of loss tugged at his heartstrings, but it kept fading. He felt anger toward Dan then. He had no idea why. They didn't feel like his feelings at all. It kept cycling like that, up and down, sad and angry. He didn't understand it.

Derek leaned against the window staring out into the backyard.

Jeremy reached over and touched his shoulder.

"I'm okay," Derek said. He sighed a shuddering breath. "I'm just sad, that's all."

"You have a right to be," Jeremy said. He pulled him over to the bed and sat him down. He seemed so small just then. "It's okay to cry you know."

"I know," Derek replied. "I will, I'm sure. I don't feel like it now though. I feel numb I guess."

Craig joined them on the bed.

Derek saw the sad look in his eyes, and then his tears fell. *Danny's gone?* he thought.

"I'm right here, you stupid little..."

They were still brothers despite his anger.

"He can't hear you, Mellon, you wuss."

"Shut up, Ian!"

Derek felt crushed. Dan was always so strong, invincible. *I'll never see him again? Ever?* Anxiety filled him. He drowned in a desperate longing to have his brother back. *It's not real, is it? Danny can't be gone forever!* Derek didn't think he would feel good about anything ever again.

Jeremy didn't know how long they had been sitting there before Chris came in wrapped in a towel, his long bangs wet and dripping. He scooped

Derek up into his arms and carried him away without a word. He patted the back of his head as Derek attached himself to Chris like a redheaded tick. Craig leaned against Jeremy. He wanted to cry, too.

Jeremy sat him up. "What about you, Craig?" he asked, looking into his eyes. "How do you feel?"

"About what?" Craig asked. "Dan? My dad?"

"All of it," Jeremy replied. "You're not alone anymore, you know. You can talk to me."

"I know," Craig whispered. "I just don't know. With Dan, one minute I feel angry with him for being a jerk to Chris and the next I want to bawl. It's weird."

"I feel the same way," Jeremy nodded. "You're right. It is weird."

"And my dad? The more I think about him, the angrier I get."

"Why?" Jeremy asked. "I mean, besides the obvious."

"I had fun last night," Craig replied, "for the first time in my life. Is this what I've been missing? Remember when the guys said I was their friend? Do you know how that made me feel? Almost as good as when you called me your best friend."

"You are my best friend, Craig."

"It makes me hate my dad something fierce!" he cried, falling back. "Now that I know what I've been missing, I don't ever want to go back."

"Maybe you won't have to," Jeremy said.

"What do you mean?" Craig asked, coming up on his elbows.

"My dad's a pretty good lawyer. Maybe he can help you."

"Help me what? Hurt my father?"

"Would you rather he hurt you?" Jeremy asked. He patted Craig on the arm. "Sorry, Dougan. That was out of line. I get angry thinking about anyone hurting you."

"It's okay," Craig said. "I know, it's stupid. I love him."

"Maybe you could get something temporary," Jeremy suggested. "It might force him to get some help."

Jeremy felt a wave of emotion pass over him. Craig was crying. It almost made him cry, too.

"I *love* him," Craig sobbed, "but I can't let him *hit* me anymore! *I can't stand it!*"

Jeremy said, "When you're ready, we can talk to my dad. Is that okay?"

Craig nodded, but he cried for a long time. Then he talked, and Jeremy listened.

In the other room, Chris was sitting on his bed with Derek until he had sobbed himself to sleep. He got up carefully, dropped the towel on the floor, and threw on some clothes.

Let him sleep, Chris thought. *That's what he needs.*

The office phone rang downstairs. He hoped it was Nancy. He needed to talk to his parents. After last night with the guys and the news about Dan, there were things he needed to say. He'd made up his mind he was coming out to them. It was the only way he could face himself in a mirror. He took a seat at the top of the stairs, his head on his forearms. He wasn't trying to eavesdrop, but he heard every word Craig was saying to Jeremy.

Jeeze, the poor kid. He's been living in hell.

Jeremy wanted Craig to talk to their dad about helping him. Chris hoped he would. The more he was around Dougan, the more he felt for him. He didn't like the idea of someone hurting him. His thoughts drifted to Dan and to happier times. Despair overcame him. Chris felt a tear go down his cheek. His mother brought Mike and Sandra to the front door. She said something about seeing what they could do before she let them out. Virginia spotted Chris at the top of the stairs when she turned.

"Do you want to talk?" she asked.

Chris nodded and walked down to her. She led him into the den. Thomas picked up another phone call. Chris slumped onto the sofa. Virginia sat next to him brushing his bangs out of his face. They watched Thomas rub the bridge of his nose. He had a headache. It had taken some fast talking when he called Thurman to get another day off, but he was owed and his boss knew it. The lack of a good night's sleep was taking its toll. Thomas wanted to rest, but with the new phone call it wasn't going to happen. He mumbled something into the receiver and hung up.

"That was Kevin," Thomas said. "We're going to Dan's funeral. He'll call later with the day and time."

"How's Cynthia?" Virginia asked.

Thomas glanced at Chris who nodded for him to continue. "They sedated her again," he replied.

Chris nodded once more, but he didn't press.

Thomas was glad. Kevin had informed him of the debacle in the morgue after the attendant pulled out the drawer with Dan's body in it for Cynthia's identification. Cynthia went off the deep end when she saw how messed up he was. Kevin vomited into a trash can. His wife required sedation after trying to drag Danny's corpse out of the drawer and force him to get up. She railed at the attendant that this was the sickest joke anyone had ever pulled on her. The damage to Dan's body made Kevin feel every moment of pain his son had endured.

Thomas changed the subject by asking about Chris' formal wear. Did his suit still fit him? His son snorted, indignantly. He hadn't worn his suit since his brother's First Communion, Jeremy either. Virginia suggested they go to the tailor. Thomas frowned, flipping through his schedule book. He was only clear today. There were Derek, Douggie, and Craig to consider, too. Thomas told her Kevin had asked if she could pick up Derek and Douggie's suits while they were at the house and take them to the cleaners. They had relatively new ones.

When it was his turn to speak, Chris laid everything on the table. He told them he was gay and that all of his friends knew including Jeremy. He was surprised his parents had suspected the truth, but never brought it up. Thomas assured him the guilt he was feeling about Dan was unfounded. His anger was justified. No one should make him feel guilty about his sexual preference. Virginia said Dan must have felt bad with his persistent attempts to contact Chris. It was the only regret they couldn't help him with.

Chris cried a lot. It was a day of mourning for everyone. Thomas suggested they hold each other up. No matter how bad it was for them, it was worse for Derek. Virginia waited for Chris to calm down before she brought up the subject of Danielle Wolicki. Chris rolled his eyes at the mention of her name.

"Danielle called here last night, crying," Virginia said. "She wanted to thank you for stealing her boyfriend."

Chris shook his head. "She's a bitch," he said, wiping his cheeks with his shirt.

"Then it's true?" Virginia asked. She looked at her husband.

Thomas only shrugged. He had no idea what to say.

"About Sandy and me?" Chris asked. "I love Sandy."

"Yes, but how intimate is this relationship?" Virginia asked.

Thomas held his hand up. "Hang on," he interjected. "Chris, you don't have to answer that if you don't want to."

Virginia agreed. "No, you don't. If I'm prying, you can tell me to mind my own business."

"No matter what, Chris," Thomas said, "your mother and I love you. We'll stand by you, I promise."

"I love you, too," Chris said. He hugged them both. "I know Sandy's straight. We can't have the kind of relationship either of us needs. I think we both know it would be more about getting back at Danielle."

"Are you sure you want to do that?" Virginia asked.

"It seems petty, Chris," Thomas said.

Chris smirked. "I'll try to let Sandy down easy."

"Smart kid," Thomas said, to his wife.

Virginia smiled.

Chris went to the half bathroom to wash his face. Virginia went upstairs to inquire about Craig's suit. Her youngest son had just finished informing Craig about the McKee sexcapades by the time she had reached the top step.

Zero tact, Virginia thought, clearing her throat in his doorway.

Craig smiled sweetly at her.

Nancy's call told them Jack had refused to get any help for his drinking. Mike and Sandra were adamant about keeping Craig away from him. Virginia felt Sandra wanted to talk about something else, too, but Mike's stern gaze had convinced her not to. Virginia wondered what it could be. One thing was for sure, Craig's father was abusing him. Mike feared for his nephew's life. It seemed excessive, but you never knew. Virginia looked at Craig. He had to want it. Pushing him risked alienating him, a mistake that could cost him his life.

"Two things, boys," Virginia began, giving Jeremy *The Look.*

"See!" Jeremy exclaimed, elbowing Craig. "That's *The Look!"*

"Man," Craig said. "No kidding."

"Thing one," Virginia said, crossing her arms. "We have a cot in the basement. Do you need to bring it up here?"

"No," they replied in unison. They looked at each other, curiously.

"Where's Craig going to sleep?"

Jeremy shrugged. "He can sleep with me. There's plenty of room."

Virginia raised an eyebrow. "Chris just told us he was gay. Do I have another son to worry about?"

"No," they replied in unison once again.

"Will you stop that?" Jeremy whined.

"Me? You stop it!"

"All right," Virginia said, "for the time being. If something happens and Craig has to stay longer, he'll need his own bed."

"Okay," they said.

"You'd better not snore," Craig insisted. "My dad does. I can hear him through the floor."

"Wait until you get an earful of what comes through my wall!" Jeremy cried.

"Thing two," Virginia interjected once again. "We have a funeral to go to."

"Eew..." they replied.

"Okay, cut that out!" she snapped, giving them *The Look* once more. "You act like you're sharing a brain."

"Sorry," they said, and then shuddered. The dream came into their minds at the same time.

"Craig? Do you have a suit to wear?"

Craig frowned and shook his head, looking away. "My dad doesn't buy me clothes."

"Fine, we'll get you one," Virginia replied. She turned to Jeremy. "Your father is taking you to the tailor's today. Make sure you have..."

"... clean underwear on," Jeremy sighed. "I want to take a shower."

"Me, too," Craig echoed. "You know, my grandma would probably give you the money for my suit. My dad won't like it if you buy me one."

"Uh, oh," Jeremy cringed.

"What?" Craig asked. "What did I say?"

"Mr. Dougan," Virginia scowled. "If we want to buy you a suit, we're buying you a suit, understand?"

"Yes, ma'am," Craig whispered.

"Do I look like I give a rat's ass what your father thinks?" She put her hands on her hips and locked *The Look* on him.

Craig grinned. "No, ma'am."

"Good!" Virginia exclaimed. "Make sure you have clean underwear on, too. Borrow a pair of Jeremy's if you have to. I'm not sure if we'll be back with your clothes before you have to leave."

"My underwear won't fit Craig," Jeremy smirked.

"Oh?" Virginia asked. "Who are you? Long Dong Silver?"

Craig laughed, pointing at him. Jeremy screwed up his face.

Virginia walked to Chris' room. Jeremy threw a minor fit when Craig beat him to the shower. She shushed him in the hall when she saw Derek sleeping. She decided not to wake him. The trip to his house and Sandra's could wait. Chris flashed a wan smile as he walked by to retrieve his sneakers.

Virginia sighed. *A gay son?* she thought.

She went downstairs to make the boys something to eat.

* * *

Max walked out of the garage bay and sat in a metal folding chair next to his brother. They looked at each other, shrugged, and then shook their heads. José was standing behind them flushing a radiator. He knew how they felt. Hiram and Lyle were bickering. They'd started trading shots with each other the moment Hiram arrived. It was an old argument that started, as usual, with Lyle commenting about Jack Dougan. Hiram jumped to Jack's defense. Max and Ricardo wanted to say something, but they didn't dare. José wouldn't tolerate them sticking their noses into adults' conversations. Hiram was so wrong though! Didn't he realize that?

"You're nuts, old man!" Lyle cried, slamming a wrench down.

"Lyle," Hiram said. "He was your friend once."

"Yeah?" Lyle barked. "That was a long time ago!"

"It was the war," Hiram said. He leaned against the rear of the car José was servicing. "Jack wasn't like that before Afghanistan."

"That's a crock!" Lyle exclaimed. "I was there. I don't beat my kid like that! Jack's a sick bastard and you know it!"

"The hell I do."

"Really?" Lyle replied. "How many times have we heard the kid screaming?"

"That's beside the point."

Max motioned for Ricardo to follow him. Ricardo was glad. He'd heard enough. The discussion had no end. At least Craig was safe at the McKees. If he ever went home again, things were going to be different. Max and Ricardo had already informed their parents they weren't ignoring the screaming anymore. Every time Jack laid a hand on Craig, they were calling the cops. Max crossed Wickett Avenue and jogged into their front yard. He sat down on the steps scrunching over so Ricardo could sit next to him. José looked up from the car and saw that the boys were gone. They waved to him.

Gracias, guys, José thought. *Leave me alone with these two, why don't you?*

"I couldn't listen to that loser any longer, man," Max said. "Too much went down today already."

"Seriously," Ricardo nodded. "Any idea what to do now?"

"I know what not to do," Max said, leaning back. "I'm not answering my phone again."

Ricardo agreed. "I shut mine off already." Of the three thousand high school kids in Lancaster, half of them had called today.

"Did you hear? Dan Mellon's dead! Did you know Chris McKee was gay? Why do you guys hang around with him? Did you know he hooked up with Sandy Sturgess? It's true, Danielle said so! Brenda Pinkwell says she saw them kissing once. Eew!"

"I know what you mean," Ricardo said. "There will be a lot of crap once school starts again."

"You're right," Max said, "but I'll mess up anyone who lays a hand on Chris."

"Me, too," Ricardo said. He asked, "What should we do? I'm bored stiff."

"We could invite somebody over," Max suggested. "I mean, Chris and Jeremy have Derek and Craig. They seemed pretty upset about Dan, but I don't care."

"I don't think Jeremy does either," Ricardo said. "Chris was trying to hide it, but I think he's taking it hard."

Max smiled.

Ricardo scowled. "You know what I mean!" he cried, shoving his brother. "All right, so Chris is gay. Do we have to talk about it anymore?"

Max shook his head.

"Good," Ricardo replied, and changed the subject. "Who can we invite over? What are we going to do if we do?"

"How about Matt? We could always call Dabney."

"Copeland!?"

"Why not?" Max asked. "I'd love to see how messed up he is. I could use something funny right about now."

Ricardo smirked. "You know, Chris has a crush on Dabney."

Max's mouth dropped open.

Ricardo laughed. "He admitted it when we were talking at the campout.

"Why didn't you tell me?" Max cried. "Omg, dude! I would've had his ass!"

Ricardo's eyes bulged. He grew a wide smile.

Max shoved him. "You know what I mean!"

Ricardo shook his head. "I can't believe you want to do this.

"Call Copeland?" Max asked. "More than anything now!"

Ricardo gave in. It was impossible to change Max's mind once it was made up. If he intended to call Dabney, he would. They went inside where Max called Matt first. Marianna set sandwiches down in front of them and told them to eat. Max bent down and kissed her on the cheek. He paced the kitchen waiting for Matt to answer his cell. Marianna told them to try on some of their father's suits so she could alter them in time for the funeral.

"When is it?" Ricardo asked Max. He shrugged and asked his mother.

"No sé," Marianna replied, pouring milk for them. "Soon."

"Hello…," Matt's voice said.

"Hey, dude, what's…?"

"… this is Matt. Apparently I went too far with my mom today, so she took my phone. Leave a message at the tone. I'll call you tomorrow when I'm not grounded anymore… but I was right! She went straight for the cooler before telling me about Dan! I have witnesses!"

Max chuckled and waited for the beep. "Yeah, Matt," he said, half-laughing. "It's Max. Call me in the morning, okay?"

"Voicemail?" Ricardo smiled. "What did he do this time?"

"Being a wiseass to the…"

"Max!" Marianna exclaimed.

"Oops!" Max cried. "¡Disculpa, mamá!"

Marianna reached over and cuffed him. Ricardo pointed at him and laughed. She cuffed him, too. Ricardo dodged too late and slipped off his chair. He landed on the linoleum with a thump and burst out laughing. Max set his cell phone on the table and ran an Internet search on it for the Copelands' phone number.

Marianna shook her head. She stepped into the parlor, eased into the recliner, and put her feet up. There was laundry to do, dinner to consider, but she was worn out. Lisa had been so sad when she went to see her. It broke her heart. Marianna raised her. Lisa was the daughter she'd never had. If only she had talked about why she was so upset. She worked with the Mellon boy, but the way she carried on?

¡Dios mío!

Lisa felt guilty for not driving Dan home. She blamed herself for his accident. Marianna said his death wasn't her fault. Why would he refuse a ride home, and then go to the cliffs unless he'd planned to all along? What was he thinking going somewhere so dangerous in the dark? She hoped none of her children were that estúpido. Marianna glanced at Ricardo, thought a silent prayer, and then closed her eyes.

"No number for Copeland," Max said, helping his brother up. "It must be unlisted."

Ricardo peered around the corner before he sat down. *Safe!*

Max asked, "Want to take a walk?"

"May as well," Ricardo replied. His eyes lit up. "We can go to the cliffs! Maybe we can find where Dan fell!"

"Cool!" Max morbidly agreed. "Let's do it!"

They kissed their mother – Ricardo rather quickly – and headed out for the cliffs.

*   *   *

Dabney climbed out of his bedroom window and went down the emergency ladder. It had been a long time since he'd done this, but he needed to get out of the estate. He needed to walk and think. He didn't want to be anywhere near his father and this was the only way to get out unseen. Dabney didn't know what he was feeling anymore. His emotions were a jumbled mess. He needed some air and some distance, but most of all Dabney needed a friend. He just didn't have any. He stepped onto the edge of the greenhouse. Experience had taught him it was strong enough to hold his weight.

What's the worst thing that can happen? Dabney wondered. *I fall and go splat? Big deal. Like anyone would miss me?*

He shook his head. He wasn't like this. He wasn't someone who felt sorry for himself. Still, he felt defeated. Nothing made sense anymore. He knew what it was like to be in pain. People had hurt him all of his life.

They're just lining up to do it now, Dabney thought. *Is this how broken feels? If it is, then I'm broke. I'm busted. I'm... so sick and tired of my father's crap!*

He moved across the top of the greenhouse and slid down the drainpipe. He glared at Dennis who was doing laps in the pool, but then ran away before his brother spotted him.

He can go to hell, Dabney thought. He ran toward the woodline and the trail that led to the cliffs. *I don't want him to see me all messed up like this. I don't need him laughing at me. Not today. I couldn't take it!*

Dabney made it to the woodline and stepped behind an ironwood tree. He looked back. He felt a rush of adrenaline as he scanned the estate. The lawn was bright green and perfectly groomed. Precious seconds passed. He tried to control his breathing. Dabney didn't run often. In gym class, he was only average at physical activities. It brought him some flak since Dennis was good at everything. Some felt he should be, too, since they were brothers. He let it roll off his back. It wasn't like he cared what people thought.

Dabney lowered his head. *No one's coming. Why would they? I could die tomorrow and nobody in Lancaster would care, not even my family.* He thought, *Tammy might, but it's not like she doesn't get paid for it.* Money wasn't a stranger to him. He knew how it motivated people. *Would Tammy care about me if it wasn't her job?*

Dabney doubted it. No one cared about him. Everybody treated him like an unwanted dog. He couldn't remember when, but at some point they had broken his heart one time too many. He got angry then. Hating felt terrible, but sorrow was even worse. Everyone who got close to him was the next person in line to hurt him. Dabney wasn't going to let that happen. He shoved them all away. It was a test. Were they willing to fight him for his friendship? Did he mean enough to them to come back even when he treated them like he felt?

Like garbage, Dabney thought, turning to the cliffs.

"There's always Chris and Jeremy."

Dabney whirled around. *Who said that?* he thought.

He heard the voice as clear as day. He thought it was Ian Sturgess. He looked wildly around. A light breeze blew through the trees. There were squirrels everywhere. Birds chirped and the air was fresh with the scent of Lady Slippers, but no Ian.

Dabney scratched his head. *Weird,* he thought. *I swear I heard Ian's voice.* He wondered, *Chris and Jeremy? They're the exception to the rule... maybe.*

Dabney turned toward the cliffs and looked up at the rock face. A sign on a nearby tree announced in large black letters:

You Are TRESSPASSING On COPELAND Property. We Will PROSECUTE Violators To The Fullest Extent Of The LAW!

"Prosecute me," Dabney scowled.

He started to climb, clinging to the rock face as he ascended. It was dangerous. There was no margin for error. It was twenty-five feet from the ground to the top of the cliffs. He could've taken the trails. It was safer, but Dabney wasn't looking for safe. He wanted peril. He almost hoped he would fall. The pain wouldn't be worse than what he was feeling inside. He pulled up, gripping the rough black rock with all of his might. He tried to build up his anger. He needed his hatred, but he couldn't find it.

Why can't I get mad? Dabney thought, looking down. He was ten feet up. *Eew. Better keep climbing.*

He dragged himself over the rocks at the top where he scraped his thigh. He looked at it and decided soccer shorts weren't the best for rock climbing. He rolled over and sat on some moss. It was thick, cushiony, and felt cool against the back of his legs. He put his hands on his knees and looked out over Lancaster. The view was spectacular from up here. Dabney noticed something he had never seen before. From this point, he could see into the McKees' backyard. There was no mistaking the maroon and black Colonial.

Dabney thought, *What is it about the McKees? What did I see in Chris' eyes? It made butterflies go crazy in my stomach. Making fun of him at the pond was so stupid. And Jeremy? Why is he so perfect?*

He wasn't jealous. Dabney found hating people easy. Chris and Jeremy were different. They had something others lacked.

"Sincerity."

That's what it was. They were sincere. They might be the only people in Lancaster who didn't hate Dabney.

Is that why I made fun of Chris? I don't want Chris to hate me. That was never my intention. Did I try to earn his hatred because of what I saw in his eyes?

If that was true, he was sure it didn't work, unless his fight with Derek changed things? Dabney doubted it. Chris wasn't that shallow. He wouldn't confront Dabney in anger. He would ask what he had done to make Dabney treat him so badly.

Dabney touched his sore nose. He thought, *I wish his friends were that patient.*

He was struggling with his feelings for Chris. They confused him. Thinking about him made Dabney feel warm inside. Chris was feeling it, too, he was sure. Dabney didn't understand why he'd said those things at the pond. Was it his arrogance? His need for attention? It seemed so petty and hurtful.

Dabney frowned. *Did I ruin things with Chris? I didn't, did I?* He sighed. *God, I hope not.*

"It's not possible, dude."

One thing's for sure, Dabney decided, setting his jaw. *I'm going to apologize to Chris the next time I see him. I was an ass. I want him to know… I want him to see… Christ, what is it?*

"You're changing."

I'm changing, Dabney concluded. That was it. He was changing. It was important to him Chris knew that.

Jeremy was different. He had given Jeremy his cell phone number. It was an invitation. He'd opened the door a crack. Something told him he needed to. Would Jeremy get the clue?

He will, Dabney thought, hugging his knees. *He's smart. What will I do if Jeremy calls?*

Yesterday, he knew the answer to that. He would treat him like crap, and then see if he came back. Today, he wasn't sure. He checked his iPhone, but there were no calls or messages. He put his face in his hands. His body was sore and his spirit ached. He felt so utterly alone… until the very next moment.

Dabney heard another voice. This time there was no doubt. She was right behind him. He nearly jumped out of his soccer shorts.

"May I ask what you are doing on my property, Master Copeland?" Ms. Adler asked, crossing her arms.

Dabney gasped. *Oh, no!* he thought, startled.

He was scared to death of Ms. Adler. She always leered at him like she wanted him dead. He tried to move, but he couldn't. Something had him paralyzed.

Legs! Move legs! Holy Jesus, move!

"*Come with me,*" Ms. Adler commanded. Her eyes glowed in the sunlight. Her voice was a booming echo that filled the whole world. "*We will discuss this.*"

Dabney was horrified as his body obeyed her words against his will. It stood on its own accord. He opened his mouth to scream, but only a whimper escaped. He struggled to run, but all it did was make his movements jerky, zombie-like. Dabney followed her down the path through a row of cedar trees and into her backyard. They crossed the overgrown lawn and walked through her garden. It had tomatoes, beans, and some herbs he didn't recognize. The dirt was fresh and black. The rows were neat and without a single weed. Dabney tried to look down at his feet, but his head wouldn't move. He saw the back of her long black skirt and a sob escaped.

She's not leaving any footprints in the garden! Dabney thought-screamed. *She's walking on air! Oh, God, she's going to kill me!*

Ms. Adler turned, her expression angry. "*Oh, stop that!*" she snapped. "*If I were going to hurt you, I would have tossed you off the cliffs. Would that not have been special? A Dan Mellon swan dive.*"

Dabney was shaking all over. *Dan Mellon? What about him? Her eyes! It's a trick of the light! They aren't glowing! This is crazy!*

She continued toward her back door.

Dabney lumbered along behind her, his heart slamming in his chest. He followed her into her house.

The stories are true! She's a witch! She killed someone, right? Her father? No! He died of a stroke, didn't he? What's she doing to me? I was on her property? Big deal! Why can't I run? Oh, please, God! Get me out of here! I'll go home! I'll be good!

"*Sit down, Master Copeland,*" Ms. Adler said, gesturing at the kitchen table. "*There is no God. There is only me. Now, keep quiet.*"

Quiet? Dabney thought, desperately. *But I haven't said anything!*

"*Silence!*" she ordered, facing him. She grabbed his chin, examining his bruises. "*My, Derek Mellon did a number on you. Sobering to find out you are not invincible, is it not? You arrogant little bastard.*"

Dabney cringed. *Her eyes are glowing!* A wave of nausea came over him. He felt something like... *Fingers! It feels like fingers!*

They reached into his skull. His whole life flashed before his eyes. He became lost in her gaze, locked in a perpetual state of déjà vu.

She's in my mind! She sees my secrets! My father, the farmer, all of it! No! Get out of my head! Get out, get out, GET OUT!

Ms. Adler stumbled back, wincing and holding her forehead. Dabney jumped up, free from her mental grip. He made a dash for the back door, but then something grabbed him. The force covered him like a wet blanket. He tried to scream, but there wasn't any air. He was yanked back into the chair. He hit his head against the wall with a crack. He was stunned, but he opened his eyes.

Ms. Adler was in his face. *"You are strong, Master Copeland,"* she hissed. Her eyes were pulsating with power. Dabney could feel it. *"So, you were not spying on me? That is good. You can go. You will not discuss our encounter with anyone. You cannot speak or write my name, or anything about me. Now, get out."*

Dabney bolted out the back door. He tripped over her watering can and sprawled onto the lawn. He snapped his head back and glared wide-eyed at her.

"Boo!" she cried, from the doorway and burst out laughing.

Dabney scrambled to his feet and charged through her garden, whimpering as he picked up speed. He leapt over the side of the cliffs and slid down the incline on his backside. The sharp rocks cut into his flesh and scraped his legs, but he ignored the pain. He barreled away down the trails, racing past the Copeland property line. His mind was swimming as it tried to make sense of what had just happened.

It's true! There are witches! Jesus, there really is a devil!

Dabney ran without a backward glance along the trail. He was on the opposite side of Owen Road behind the McKees' house. No matter what, he wanted…

Somebody! Anybody! Help me!

Dabney burst forth from the woodline and charged into Route 41 right into Max's arms.

"Copeland!" Max bellowed, yanking him out of the way of an oncoming car. Its horn exploded at them. "Are you trying to get yourself killed!?"

"Yeah, man," Ricardo said. "What's your problem?"

Dabney grabbed hold of Max's arms, his eyes wild with terror. They shifted from one brother to the other as he tried to speak. *I have to tell them what I saw! I have to tell them what she is!* He struggled to say her name, but only guttural sounds came out. *No words! I have no words! What did she do to me!?*

Ricardo spun him around and shook him. "Dabney!" he cried. "Snap out of it, man!"

Dabney felt lightheaded. The world was spinning. He stiffened and his eyes rolled back into his head. He collapsed into Ricardo's arms and fainted.

*   *   *

Ashton Tailors in Hartford echoed with Craig's giggles each time Mr. Ashton attempted to measure his inseam. Craig was standing on a step stool in the back room of the shop wearing a formal white shirt and a pair of Jeremy's Calvin Klein underwear from last year. Suits and shirts of all kinds were hanging around them. Chris and Jeremy looked at each other. Mr. Ashton's employees were altering their suits already, as well as Craig's jacket, but it seemed they were never getting him into a pair of pants. Mr.

Ashton tried again. Craig stooped over, laughing hysterically. Jeremy snorted trying to hold in his own laughter. There wasn't anything funny about this at all, but every time the tailor touched the inside of Craig's thigh, Jeremy felt a tickling sensation on his own. It was driving him crazy.

"C'mon, Dougan!" Jeremy whined, adjusting his seat, trying not to laugh.

"I can't help it!" Craig giggled. "It tickles!"

"It's not like there's much there to tickle, Craig," Chris grumbled, crossing his legs.

"You are the expert!" Craig replied.

It was funny how easy that remark came to him. Craig had never considered himself particularly quick-witted, but Jeremy? He was the wit master. Mr. Ashton took advantage of the momentary distraction. He ran the measuring tape from Craig's groin to his ankle. He stood up and shifted his weight to one side. He placed a hand on his hip as he checked the measurement. He snapped his fingers and sashayed out of the back room toward the sewing machines.

Jeremy looked at his brother and smiled.

"If you say one word," Chris warned, "I'll brain you!"

"Walks like a lady," Jeremy sang, and burst out laughing.

Craig joined him while he tried to get into the jeans Jeremy had lent him. It was a good thing there was meat in his buttocks to hold them up since Jeremy didn't have a spare belt to give him and the Levi's were a little big on him. Chris offered him a bandanna to tie around his waist, but Craig declined. The only ones he had were pastel. Craig hated pastels. At least, today he did. That was funny, too. He didn't remember hating them yesterday. Jeremy grabbed a piece of string off Mr. Ashton's desk and tied two of Craig's belt loops together. Craig smiled at him.

Jeremy mocked a frown. "I'm tired of looking at your crack, Craig," he said. "You want to be a plumber?"

Craig patted him on the head like a good doggy and smiled at the way Jeremy's hair felt. It was thick like wire, but soft, not kinky like a Brillo pad. He stepped off the stool and bent over for his sneakers. When he did, Jeremy grabbed his underwear.

"How would you like the world's biggest wedgie?"

"How about if I fart?" Craig asked, pretending to strain.

Jeremy whipped his hand away.

Mr. Ashton stood in the doorway shaking his head. "Boys," he sighed.

Jeremy and Craig blushed, scurrying for a seat. They hid their faces in their hands. Chris laughed and pointed at them.

"No touchy-feely back here, okay?" Mr. Ashton lisped.

Dean Ashton was five-foot-eight with curly balding orange hair and a beard. He was as thin as a rail and moved like he had ball bearings in his hips. He ended his sentence with two snaps up and grabbed a box of sewing needles.

Chris practically fell off his chair. Jeremy shoved him to help him on his way. He landed on the floor, but grabbed his brother's ankle trying to pull him down, too. Craig took hold of Jeremy in a McKee tug of war. Chris pulled up, threw his weight back, and yanked them both on top of him. Thomas had been out front paying for the suits with his American Express Gold Card. He appeared in the doorway. He cleared his throat and the boys froze. Chris was on the bottom with Craig's butt in his face. Jeremy was lying across his midsection holding his leg. They looked up and smiled.

"Hi, dad," Jeremy said. "Chris was showing us some of his *moves!*"

"In your dreams!" Chris cried. He grabbed Craig by the belt loops and tossed him aside. *Whoa!* he thought. *He's heavy!* He pushed up with his leg. Jeremy fell on his stomach in front of his father.

Thomas shook his head. He thought, *At least they're handling this Dan thing well.* "Will you get off the floor, please?" he sighed. "You're going to give Queen Ashton a coronary."

"I'll have you know, Thomas," Mr. Ashton said, sashaying past him, "that I am not a Queen today. That's Saturdays." He held out his hand and helped Jeremy up. He brushed him off and continued, "Even though Jeremy's gorgeous blue eyes set my tiny little heart aflutter, he's much too young for me."

Jeremy flushed again.

Mr. Ashton turned to Thomas. "You on the other hand... well, you know how I feel."

"You rarely let me forget."

"Hey!" Chris cried. "There's only one gay guy in this family!"

"It's you," Mr. Ashton nodded. He held his hand to his chin. "I saw that a mile away. You set my gaydar off with a resounding *ding-ding-ding. Ooo!* I love green eyes, too!"

Chris smirked.

Mr. Ashton shook his head. "Thomas? Would you take your suits and get this raging bag of hormones out of my shop?"

Thomas asked, "Is this what I have to look forward to having a gay son?"

"Honey," Mr. Ashton replied, "just wait until you see his Prom date."

Thomas grabbed the suits off the table behind him. The black pinstriped one was for Chris, the straight black for Jeremy, and the Navy was for Craig. Jeremy and Craig followed him shaking their heads. Chris pulled Mr. Ashton inside for a second and hugged him. His first time being openly gay in public and Mr. Ashton had made it very cool. He smiled and gave Chris a business card.

"My cell is on the back," he said. He seemed to lose a bit of his femininity. "It's not an easy road, you know. If you need to talk, you can call me."

Chris nodded. "I appreciate that."

Mr. Ashton fanned his face with his hand. Chris walked out the front door, climbed into the Porsche, and Thomas drove them away.

*   *   *

Virginia waited in the car while Derek got out and went up to Sandra. She was standing in the doorway with an overnight bag in her hands. The logo for the television station she worked at was on its side. Derek approached her, tentatively. He seemed disoriented. He glanced around as if looking for something to hold him up. He didn't have any skin, that's what it was. He was raw and bleeding, but trying his best to keep it hidden. How was he supposed to stand when his foundation had been torn out from under him?

"Here you go, sweetheart," Sandra said, forcing a smile. "These are all of Craig's clothes plus some money in case he needs anything."

Derek nodded. "Thank you," he said, his voice scratchy.

"Would you like to come in for a minute?" Sandra asked. "Have something to drink maybe?"

"No thanks," Derek sighed. "Virginia's taking me out for food. We have to stop at the cleaners and drop off our suits for the... for his..." He struggled to hold back his tears. He took a deep shaky breath. "The funeral."

Sandra leaned over and kissed his forehead. "I'm sorry, honey," she whispered. "This must hurt pretty bad, huh?"

Derek lowered his eyes and nodded. Sandra hugged him and sent him on his way. It was apparent he didn't want to get into it. She waved to Virginia who rolled her window down.

"I'll call you," Virginia said.

Sandra nodded. She almost said something more, but begrudgingly decided against it. Derek climbed into the front seat. They pulled out of the driveway and drove up Grady Lane. Sandra watched them until they were gone. She hoped Derek wasn't stuffing his emotions. The fog in his eyes reflected such pain. He had to let it out. She closed the door and turned around. Mike was standing behind her shaking his head.

Sandra nodded. "I know, Mike," she said. "I shouldn't have invited him in. I'm sure he has enough on his mind."

"That's not it," Mike replied. "You know what the problem is."

"You're right," Sandra moaned, falling into his arms. "I think we should tell her, you know? Her son works for Hiram..."

"... and has for the past year," Mike interjected. "We can't say anything without some facts. It doesn't matter what we think, only what we can prove."

"Err on the side of caution, remember?"

"That's not an err, baby!" Mike cried. "That's a nuclear blast."

"Have you called anyone yet?" Sandra asked, walking over to the window. She stared at the road for a moment. *Where was Sam this morning?* she wondered. She didn't remember seeing him. *Did he go by and I missed him? I was up at the usual time when I called out sick. Maybe when we were at the campsite? Did he run that late? Earlier maybe?*

"I'm right here!"

Sandra shook her head. Her ears were ringing. "Will they come over and talk about it?" she continued, clearing her throat.

"I spoke to Hugh Kreeger," Mike replied. "He's leaving for California on a business trip. He was planning to stay there until Saturday, but with the funeral he's cutting his trip short. The whole town's going it seems. He said he would drop by though. He sounded miffed that I was being so evasive, but I didn't want to blurt it out. I was pushy about him coming over, too. I left a message for Arthur Kelly to stop by the store, but I didn't say what for."

Sandra nodded and sat on the couch. She felt dizzy. "And the others?"

"Right now I have to go to work," Mike said. "Bea's running the front alone. Lisa took the morning off because of Dan. I think they were together last night, if you know what I mean."

"Oh?" Sandra asked.

"She's kicking herself for not driving him home."

Sandra shook her head. "That's a tough one. Tell her to call me if she needs somebody." She went back to staring at the road.

"Good morning, Mrs. Dougan!"

Sandra smiled. She could almost hear Sam's voice.

"I will," Mike promised. *But first,* he thought, walking out the door, *I need to find that application from Henry Schwartz.*

* * *

Virginia pulled into the Mellons' driveway. Derek asked if he had time for a quick shower. She said that was fine since she wanted coffee. They followed the walk to the front door of the Mellons' brown raised ranch. Derek opened it with a key from under the flowerpot on the steps. It had a single dead marigold in it. He stepped inside, stripped on his way up the stairs, and dropped his clothes in the laundry chute next to the bathroom. Virginia was surprised at his lack of modesty and said so.

"You should see me at the Resort," Derek said.

"Resort?" Virginia asked. She thought, *Cynthia belongs to a resort? Which one? Prudes R Us?* She chuckled.

"Sure," Derek nodded, stepping into the bathroom. His voice echoed as he spoke into the shower stall. "My mom and dad have a membership at a nudist camp in Woodstock. We go there a lot in the warm weather. Douggie, too. Nobody's shy about that around here."

Virginia raised an eyebrow. *As I live and breathe!* she thought, with a wry smile. *Cynthia? A nudist? I can't believe it!*

Derek streaked past her into the living room. Virginia got the impression the Mellons walked around nude at home a lot, too. Derek wasn't even trying to cover up. He pulled a photo album from under the coffee table, handed it to her, and returned to the shower. Virginia set the album on the kitchen table while she made coffee. She called Susan on her cell phone. There was no answer, so she called the Sturgesses' landline. Sandy picked up sounding tired. She asked for his mother. He said she had a meeting at the high school with a new special-ed student who had just moved into town.

"Graham Shooter, I think," Sandy said. "He's going into high school. Mom's going to help him because he's deaf."

"Deaf?" Virginia asked, stirring in some Coffee-Mate. "He's going to public school?"

"Mom said he reads lips," Sandy replied. "She thinks he can do it."

Virginia opened the photo album as she sipped her coffee. She gasped and choked. There was an 8 x 10 glossy color photo on the first page of the Mellon family waving at the camera. They were completely naked. Virginia slammed the cover closed and stood up, coughing.

Sandy asked, "What's wrong?" When she didn't answer, he got nervous. "Virginia!" he cried. "Sean! Get off me! *Virginia!?*"

"Sean get - *cough* - off me?" Virginia coughed, catching her breath.

"Don't scare me like that!" Sandy gasped. He said, "Yeah, Sean was on my lap. I don't know what's gotten into him today, but he's awful clingy. He's pouting now. All right, rug rat. Hop on up."

"That's sweet, Sandy," Virginia smiled, clearing her throat. She took a quick peek at the picture again.

My God! she thought. *She's numbered the pages!*

"Sean's not that bad," Sandy said. "Ian gives him a lot of crap though."

"I didn't see him this morning," Virginia remarked, gathering the strength to turn the page. The entire album was Resort photos. She thought, *There are more naked people inside than at the Playboy Mansion. No wonder Derek isn't shy about being undressed.*

"He went to camp," Sandy said.

"No, he didn't," Sean insisted. "He told me…"

"Will you clam up?" Sandy interrupted. "I heard about your nightmare already."

"Sean had a nightmare?" Virginia asked, pausing at a picture of a rather buff man. He was facing away, but flexing for the camera. *Ooo! Nice butt!*

"Yeah, about Ian," Sandy informed her. "He said he saw Ian dead, or something, but he was talking to him. He was all gross and bloody, you know? Too many horror movies?"

"Vir… *ginia?*" Derek asked, his voice filled with sadness.

Virginia turned, smiling, but her smile faded instantly. Derek was standing in the hall dripping wet. All of the color had drained from his face. He was holding a monogrammed towel in his outstretched hands that said **DANNY** in big black letters.

Virginia quickly said goodbye to Sandy, dropped her cell phone, and caught Derek in her arms as his knees buckled. They sat on the floor against the kitchen doorjamb, half on the linoleum and half on the hall carpet. Derek was sobbing and wracked with grief. Virginia held him, gently rocking him the same way she had with Douggie.

I knew this was coming, she thought. "It's okay, baby," she whispered. "Let it out."

Derek cried long and hard, holding on to her for dear life. An hour passed before he'd calmed down enough to get up and get dressed. Derek robotically put on faded jeans with holes in the knees and a white sleeveless shirt. He spiked and gelled his hair in the bathroom. He washed his face and put on a pair of Adidas sneakers. Virginia helped him put some clothes in a bag. She grabbed his suit from his closet and Douggie's from his room. She reminded him they were going out for dinner. Derek's eyes lit up a little. He asked for pizza. She promised him anything he wanted. He put the photo album back on their way out.

"Did you get to page twenty-six?" Derek asked. He closed the door and locked it. He put the key back under the flowerpot.

"No," Virginia replied. She put her arm across his shoulders and led him toward the Camaro. "Why?"

"A guy's standing with my mom in that one," Derek said. "He's got the biggest dong I ever…"

"Derek!" Virginia gasped.

"… saw in my life," he finished. He frowned. "I don't understand how they can get so big. I saw this horse once and his was hanging…"

"Would you stop!?" Virginia scolded, trying not to laugh. "Jesus, Derek! Where's your mind?"

Halfway to the pizza parlor, Virginia looked at him. Derek was staring out the window, his mind a million miles away. His expression suggested he wasn't thinking about Dan. She wondered why he had such a preoccupation with sexual organs. She asked if his parents ever talked to him about human development.

"Well, it's weird," Derek replied. "Whenever I ask my dad anything, he says to ask my mom. If I ask her, she says to ask him. I never learn anything! Like with Chris and Jeremy. They're not circumcised, neither are the Ramirez brothers."

"Nope," Virginia said. "I don't know about Max and Ricardo's parents, but we considered it unnecessary surgery."

"Right," Derek said. "Well, I saw them once when we were camping, so I asked my mom about it. She said I had to ask Chris if I wanted to know something about him. How embarrassing is that?"

"Chris told you?" Virginia asked.

"He did," Derek replied. He rolled his eyes. "Talk about awkward. I thought they were deformed, or something."

"You never saw an uncircumcised person at the Resort?" Virginia asked.

Derek shook his head. "No, and I asked Chris about that, too. He said it was probably because everyone there's a Born Again Christian."

"You told Chris about the Resort?"

"Sure," Derek replied. "He said he would talk to you about going sometime. He said you probably would since you breastfed him and Jeremy in public all the time."

"Oh, well, that's a little different, Derek," Virginia said.

"How so?"

"I covered myself with a baby blanket. I didn't just flop them out there for everyone to gawk at."

"Do you think you'll come?" Derek asked. "Chris and Jeremy will, for sure. We go skinny dipping all the time when we camp at the swimming hole."

"Sure, I guess." *Skinny dipping?* She rolled her eyes. "Can we talk about something else?" she asked. She continued, "If there's anything about human development I can answer for you, I'll try my best help."

"Well, there is something I've always wondered about," Derek said.

"What's that?"

Derek's brow furrowed. He asked, "What's a clitoris?" looking up at her.

Virginia muttered, "Ask your mother."

It was late afternoon before all the McKees had made it home. Virginia and Derek beat the others by a half an hour. She had taken extra time after eating and bought Derek some shoes. He was under the impression he was wearing sneakers to the funeral. *Wrong!* They dropped the suits off at the cleaners on their way back. They would be ready by tomorrow afternoon. Thomas had to stop and get shoes for Craig, too. Chris insisted on buying a new pair on his own. Jeremy gave in after some prodding and picked out a pair for himself. He didn't see the point. He would probably never wear them again after the funeral was over.

They ate dinner at a steakhouse, then raced back to Lancaster. They stopped at Jack's house to get Craig's bicycle. A repairman had just finished replacing the front window. Craig found out his grandmother had paid for it. Thomas put the bike on the rack behind the Porsche. He had bought it for Chris' bike for when he had to pick him up from work. Craig was thrilled by the ride. He had never gone so fast in a car before. The Porsche felt glued to the ground. He'd never seen so much food in his life as there was in that restaurant either. He couldn't figure out how Chris, who was so skinny, could eat so much. He just kept shoveling it in.

"Fairies have a fast metabolism, man," Jeremy said, when Craig asked.

Craig burst out laughing. Thomas rolled his eyes. Chris paused to flip his brother the bird in the middle of munching another carrot stick.

No sooner were they upstairs and in their respective rooms when Chris' iPhone rang. It was Hiram calling to tell Chris he didn't have to work the morning shift. He had the night shift instead. Kevin called on the house phone and told Derek he would be at the hospital with his mother if he needed to talk. Derek asked to speak to her, but Kevin said she was sleeping. In truth, they'd sedated her yet again. Cynthia woke up screaming. She said she saw Danny's bloody ghost sitting on the end of her bed. He was weeping.

Kevin didn't tell Derek that. They spoke briefly. Derek was keeping his father at arm's length. Chris wondered why. He had never noticed the distance between them before. It was a chasm. Sandra spoke with Craig who raved about his new suit. Jeremy was sprawled out on the bed rolling his eyes and yawning. He didn't want Craig to think it was a big deal. When Max called – standing in the stairwell at his house, laughing hysterically – things got interesting.

"What's so funny, Max?" Chris asked. He called Jeremy and put Max on speakerphone.

"Hello?" Jeremy asked, walking into Chris' room with Craig.

Derek shrugged at them. "No idea," he said.

"What's... so *funny!?*" Max struggled. He exploded with laughter.

In the background, they heard Ricardo angrily exclaim, *"... tell them anything and I'll kill you, Max!"*

Max got as much of a grip as he could and proceeded to risk death at his brother's hands. He thought, *This is way too good to keep secret!*

Dabney's slide down the cliffs had caused him to get several slivers of slate rock in his buttocks and legs. Since Ricardo had achieved a First Aid Merit Badge in Scouts, his mother elected him to pull them out with tweezers and treat the wounds with antibiotic cream. Dabney lay on his stomach on Ricardo's bed with his soccer shorts and underwear pulled down to his knees. Max was watching them from the doorway, but kept walking away because he couldn't stand it. He thought he was going to die laughing.

Ricardo wasn't handling it well at all. He plucked the slivers out as professionally as possible, one by one. An hour into it and he still wasn't finished. Dabney had refused to go to the doctor. Doing so meant Jerry would need to be there since the insurance was in his name. He decided his father could drop dead. Ricardo would've told Dabney to drop dead, too, if Marianna hadn't looked on him with genuine sympathy.

Like he deserves any, Ricardo angrily thought, *even if he is all battered and bruised!*

Dabney was quick to object. He didn't like the idea any more than Ricardo. Marianna asked him if he'd ever had an infection in that location. What would he do if it spread to his more sensitive areas? Dabney was so shocked at her frankness, he ran up to the bedroom. Ricardo decided if word ever got around about this? He would end up in prison for murder.

"Ow!" Dabney cried, as a large sliver came out of his right buttock.

Ricardo scowled. "I mean it, Copeland!" he warned, leaning down to his ear. "One word about this to anyone and they'll never find your body!"

"Don't worry, Ramirez," Dabney sighed, turning away. "Like I want this on the evening news?" He chuckled. "This is absurd. I only thought McKee went here."

Ricardo's eyes became flaming orbs of death.

"It feels a lot better though," Dabney continued. He smiled, sensing Ricardo's biblical anger.

Grrr! Grrr! Grrr!

"Although you might want to ask Max what he plans to do with the picture he took with his phone. Does he have Instagram, or something? Snapchat? Not sure I want my ass on the Internet with your handprints all over it."

"MAX!"

Once Chris finished showing everyone the picture Max texted to him and laughing his head off, he expressed surprise that Dabney was in the same room as Max and Ricardo let alone at their house.

Max didn't understand it either. "He's acting weird, Chris," he said. He told him about the incident on Route 41. They practically carried Dabney to their house when he refused to go home. He had blood running down his legs. "He's acting almost nice. He doesn't seem like the same Copeland I've always known, that's for sure."

"Did he hit his head?" Chris asked. *Dabney's acting different? God, please, let it be the beginning of something, okay?*

"No," Max whispered, "but Derek did! You should see him, man. He's all messed up."

"Maybe that's what he needed," Jeremy said. He remembered the phone number in his yearbook and decided to use it. "Ask him if I can call him. He gave me his number and told me I could, but you never know with Dabney."

"We should," Craig said.

"You have his number?" Chris asked.

"You jelly?" Jeremy asked.

"No!" Chris cried.

Craig snapped his tongue. "You are so jelly."

Max walked into the bedroom. Dabney was spreading antiseptic cream on his backside. Ricardo had finished with the slivers, but stormed out refusing to do any more.

Dabney pulled up his underwear and shorts. He sat on the bed. "That hurt," he said. He snickered. "I'm never going to live this down." He remembered Ms. Adler and shuddered. He still couldn't say what he'd seen no matter how hard he tried. He believed she'd done something to him, a spell or whatever.

"Jeremy wants to know if he can call you," Max said.

"I gave him my number, didn't I?" Dabney snorted. He caught himself. "I'm sorry, okay? I didn't mean that."

"God, Copeland," Max said. "What's gotten into you, man? You almost seem human."

Dabney shrugged, looking defeated. "I don't know, Ramirez. My life seems so messed up today. Yes, Jeremy can call me. I'd like that." He swallowed. "Is Chris there? I want to tell him I'm sorry about what I said at the pond."

Max was stunned. He stared at Dabney with his mouth open. "Do you want to talk to him?"

Dabney held his hand up. "Not on the phone. What I said was really low and stupid. I want to apologize to him in person if I can."

"Did you hear?" Max asked, putting the phone back to his ear.

"I heard," Jeremy replied. "I don't believe it, but I heard it."

"Me neither," Chris added. "Something weird is going on. Tell him we can talk whenever he wants. I'm not mad about the pond. It was stupid on everybody's part."

Max said he would tell him. They were going to walk Dabney home. Chris and Jeremy said goodbye. Chris hung up.

Jeremy noticed an odd expression on Chris' face. It was something like confused happiness. He smiled. "Really, Chris?" he asked. His smile grew wider. He pointed at his brother. "You like him!"

Chris bit his lower lip.

"Oh, my God!" Jeremy cried.

Chris grumbled, "Oh, be quiet."

Derek received a ton of phone calls on the house phone from newly graduated eighth-grade well-wishers. He took them graciously, but by bedtime he felt drained. When the *"Is Chris really gay?"* calls started coming in, Virginia intercepted them and said that Derek was asleep.

Jeremy and Craig were watching *Star Trek - The Undiscovered Country* on DVD. Craig got up to hang his suit in the closet. He didn't want to leave his on the doorknob like Jeremy. He was afraid it might get knocked onto the floor. It was the best ensemble of clothes he'd ever owned. His eyes were focused on the TV rather than on what he was doing. There was a pin left in the jacket. It jabbed him in the finger. Craig cried out in pain…

… and so did Jeremy.

They stared at each other. They were rubbing the same fingers. Jeremy wasn't bleeding like Craig, but it still hurt. Craig walked over, laid backward, and put his head on Jeremy's side. Jeremy's head was against the headboard.

"You felt that?" Craig whispered.

"Uh, huh," Jeremy whispered back. He swallowed hard. "Holy Vulcan Mind-Meld, Spock-Dougan." He felt Craig's fear, too, and he said so.

"I can feel you, too," Craig said. "I didn't notice it until now. You're not scared?"

Jeremy thought about it before he answered. He had a hard time distinguishing between his feelings and Craig's. He shrugged.

Craig nodded. "I'm scared," he said, staring at the ceiling.

Jeremy said, "I know you are."

"What's happening to us?" Craig choked, almost sobbing. "First the dream and now this? I don't understand. What's going on?"

"I don't know, man," Jeremy replied. "I'm just glad it's happening with you. If it were anybody else, I'd be going nuts."

Craig nodded. That made him feel better, but only a little. "We should tell somebody about it. Your parents maybe."

"Are you crazy?" Jeremy asked. The pain in his finger was almost gone. "Hey dude, my parents may be Liberal, but psychic phenomena? They'll think we're losing our marbles."

"Maybe we are," Craig replied.

He felt Jeremy's annoyance and regretted his fear. Jeremy felt Craig's regret and tapped on the top of his head.

"Sorry, Craig. I guess I'm a little scared, too. It's kind of neat in a way, you know? I can feel whatever you feel."

"It's like we're mutants," Craig said, feeding into Jeremy's growing fascination.

"Yeah!" he exclaimed. "Like X-Men!"

"Yeah!" Craig agreed, sitting up.

They stayed awake most of the night rifling through Jeremy's comic book collection. It was the only place to find answers since Chris and Jeremy weren't allowed on their computers or cell phones this late. They were starting to get the hang of their predicament, but it was a slow process. They were linked somehow. They were feeling each other's emotional and physical states, but they had trouble distinguishing between the feelings. Jeremy got up to pee only to realize he didn't have to go, Craig did. Craig went downstairs to get a drink, but he wasn't thirsty, Jeremy was. He gladly relieved Craig of the soda he had acquired. The comic books they always enjoyed kept them open-minded. They accepted what was happening with a sense of awe rather than panic. It was a freak occurrence. It would disappear, they were sure. It was sunspots, a full moon.

"It's a crescent moon," Craig corrected. He pointed at it through the window.

James Christopher

Jeremy scowled at him.

Craig shrugged and they laughed.

They crawled into bed around four in the morning and fell asleep.

DAY THREE
Wednesday

Hiram looked cautiously around before he stepped out of the butcher shack. The morning air was clean and fresh, but Ian was not. His remains were in a black plastic Glad bag. Hiram threw him into the bucket of the backhoe. It was time for his burial. It was the reason he'd told Chris not to come in this morning. Ian was purple and reeking. He had to get rid of him before the scent carried on the wind across town. Hiram opened the garbage bag and peered in at Ian's destroyed face. The stench was like roses to him. Ian was potpourri after a day in the wretched June heat.

He tied the bag closed and hopped onto the seat. He started the engine and drove toward the middle of the pasture. Hiram's field stretched from Milliken Road to the edge of the Sturgesses' property on Ribbon Road. The southwestern side of the expanse was specifically for grazing. The cows ate joyfully above the bodies of Hiram's children. He paused by an appropriate spot between two of the larger hills hidden from the road.

Hiram climbed out, retrieved the bag, and tossed it to the side. It hit the pasture with a wet squish. He got back onto the backhoe and dragged the bucket across the ground, tearing up the grass in a large patch. It was easier that way. He could replace it over the dirt like covering a bare spot on the carpet with a throw rug. He dug a four-foot deep hole with the backhoe's claw pouring the excess dirt at the top of the grave. A small skeletal hand and forearm hung from the last scoop.

Hiram glared at it. He thought, *It might be time to expand my burial ground if I'm burying them on top of one another.*

He climbed down, grabbed it, and gave it a quick once-over. Judging by its size, it could've only belonged to one of his victims.

"Giuseppe Luciano," Hiram said.

A cold breeze blew over him. He shivered, glancing around.

There's no one in sight.

Hiram looked into the hole and dropped the arm on top of the skeleton. He tossed in the bag.

"Poor little Giuseppe," Hiram said. "Can't find your mommy? Let nice Farmer Hiram help you. Hop into the pickup." He laughed, and thought, *It took forever to clean out the cab.*

He filled in the grave, packed the dirt in with the claw, replaced the grass covering, and drove back to the barnyard. Ian Sturgess was fertilizer. In a day, no one would be able to tell he'd been digging out there at all. Cows ambled from the holding area where they ate after milking. They mooed at him as he passed. He parked the backhoe and watched as they ambled toward the new grave. He scowled hoping they didn't disturb the grass. They stopped short of the spot, shifted directions, and walked away.

They smell him, Hiram thought.

He shut down the backhoe with a broad smile on his face.

＊   ＊   ＊

Jeremy woke as Craig climbed out of bed headed for the shower. He looked over sleepily and groaned at his computer's alarm clock app.

Why did we stay up so late when I knew Craig had to work today? he thought.

Jeremy wanted to roll over and not open his eyes again until the sun went down. It was too bad that wasn't possible. He was up now and he couldn't go back to sleep. It was another thing they had in common. What did they stay up for anyway? *Mind-link indeed!* It seemed like such crap. He was glad Craig hadn't mention it. It was a delusion or something, that's all.

Jeremy went to the kitchen for breakfast. He paused in the hall when he heard the shower come on. He remembered Craig's snoring comment.

If anyone should talk, it should be me! How many times did I elbow Craig during the night? He wasn't snoring loud, but it was enough to keep waking me up!

Chris and Derek were at the dining room table eating breakfast. Jeremy poured a cup of coffee and sat down. Chris told him their mother had gone to the store for milk and their dad was on his way to the office. Jeremy wasn't too happy about black coffee, but the cereal mongers had cleaned them out of moo juice. Derek appeared to be feeling better. The color had returned to his cheeks, the light to his eyes. Jeremy thought that was cool as he reached for the sugar, but then he froze. He felt something like an itch or… no, that wasn't it. It was… *a hand!* It was touching his sides, rubbing them.

Jeremy whirled around to confront whoever it was who had the nerve to tickle him, only no one was there. He was puzzled. He felt it again like someone was scrubbing him with a bar of soap. It was on his chest, his sides, his… *whoa!* Jeremy wiggled as the invisible hand moved all over his body. He spilled his coffee down the front of his boxers and laughed through the pain of being burned. He stumbled to the side feeling off balance. It was as if he'd lifted one of his feet up. He glared down at them. They were still on the floor. Then the feeling reached underneath them by his toes. Jeremy laughed hysterically, slapping them.

"Stop it!" he cried, dragging his feet on the floor. He knew what it was. He reached inside his shirt and gave himself a hard tit twister.

"Ow!" Craig cried, from the shower.

"What's wrong with you?" Derek asked. He glanced over at Chris who only shrugged.

"You little creep!" Jeremy hollered, jumping as if someone had goosed him. He glared at Chris and Derek, growled, and then ran back up to his room.

292

Chris and Derek looked at each other.

"Jeremy's weird sometimes," Chris remarked, chomping on his corn flakes.

"Yeah," Derek agreed. He smirked. "It must run in the family, you know? Like having a crush on Dabney Copeland?"

Chris raised his chin. "Dabney would make a great Prom date for Junior Prom next year. That's one guy who knows how to dress."

Derek's eyes bulged.

Jeremy slammed his door. *No!* he thought. *The mind-link isn't real!* He pulled off his coffee stained boxers and wrapped up in a towel. Craig walked into the room a few minutes later similarly wrapped in a towel and whistling. He found Jeremy with a deep scowl on his face and a fiery look of anger in his eyes. Craig could feel his aggravation.

"Tell me something, Dougan," Jeremy growled. "Do you always wash so much?"

Craig glared at him, accusingly. "You gave me a tit twister."

"The next time you tickle my feet," Jeremy snapped, "so help me God, Craig, I'll strangle you!"

Craig looked into Jeremy's deep blue eyes. He felt his embarrassment and his anger. He did the only thing he could think of doing at that moment. He started laughing.

Jeremy glared at him. "You think that's funny, Dougan?" he asked, tackling his hysterical friend onto the bed. "Just wait! I'll show you something really funny!"

Craig laughed as they wrestled. Jeremy joined him. If the mind-link was going to be around for a while, he would pay Craig back in spades!

Let's see how he likes the same thing done to him while he's at work, or better yet, a tit twister in church! Jeremy thought. *Oh, Dougan! You are so in for it!*

Craig squirmed and got on top. The door opened. They looked at each other, looked down, and panicked. Their towels were half off. They grabbed the sheets and scrambled to cover up. Chris stood in the doorway next to Derek whose mouth was hanging open. Chris was smiling so wide it looked like his face was going to split. Craig blushed violently. Jeremy buried his face in his pillow.

Oh, great! Jeremy thought. *Just what I need!*

Chris cleared his throat. "Um… sorry to interrupt," he said, the grin never leaving.

"Holy cow!" Derek cried, his heart pounding. "What were you guys doing!?"

"Well…," Chris replied, and burst out laughing.

Jeremy whipped his pillow at him and caught him square in the face. Chris winged it back.

"Out," Jeremy commanded. He held his hand up and pointed.

"Mom's home," Chris snickered. "She wants… *wants…*"

"Out!" he cried again.

"… to know if you're hungry! *I'll tell her you're already eating!"*

"Out!" Jeremy and Craig cried together.

Chris closed the door.

Craig got up and grabbed a pair of his underwear from his overnight bag. "Well," he said, slipping them on, "I suppose it could be worse."

"Really?" Jeremy groaned. "We're lying on top of each other on my bed with no clothes on! How could it be any worse than that?"

"We weren't doing anything."

"Everybody's going to hear about this, you watch."

"Chris would do that?" Craig asked, his eyes widening.

Jeremy grabbed his towel. "I'm going to get crap for this all day."

"You can come to work with me if you want," Craig suggested, buttoning his pants.

"Will your uncle be mad?"

"Nope," Craig replied. "He's cool."

Jeremy stepped into the hallway and headed for the bathroom. *Spend the day at the market?* he thought. *Why not?*

Besides, something inside told him he would feel depressed when Craig left. Spending the day with him would be cool. They were best friends, after all. Jeremy smiled. He liked the way that sounded. Just before he closed the bathroom door, he heard Chris on his iPhone.

"I'm telling you, Matt! They were buck naked!"

Jeremy shut the door and rested his head against it. He thought, *Oh, God… here we go…*

*   *   *

40 Annie Potts Road was an immaculate two-bedroom red raised ranch. The piggy bank mailbox bore the name *Garrison.* It had six-foot-high bushes around the backyard with an opening in the center where a small metal gate led to the trails. The house was stone-faced by the front door with an attached two-car garage on the left side. The music of The Grateful Dead blared into the neighborhood from the back bedroom. Frank was in there humming along with *Sugar Magnolia* and packing his water bong with weed.

Todd doesn't know what he's missing, he grinned. *'Course, he doesn't know I have this. Why smoke mine when we can smoke his? He works. He can afford it.*

Frank's pot was in a plastic sandwich bag. He rolled it up, licked the flap to seal it, and slipped it into his bedside drawer. That's where he always kept it. Francis and Vicki Garrison knew it was there, but they never bothered it. Vicki had told him it was an excellent place to keep it, right next to his head. They kept their stash in the same place in their room. The owners of *Garrison*

Limited, a clothing store in the Buckland Mall in Manchester, were fierce potheads. So was their son.

The house was Frank's today. His mother and father had gone to a seminar in Boston and weren't coming home until Saturday night. Jean Terry, the lesbian assistant manager, was running the store for them. It was the perfect time to get high. Frank liked getting high. His mother had turned him on to it when he was eleven, the same age she'd started using it. The whole town knew he smoked pot. They assumed he did so behind his parents' backs. That was because his dad beat him once when he'd gotten caught getting high at school with Todd. The beating wasn't for getting caught or even toking at school. The pot he'd shared that day belonged to his parents. He had broken one of the cardinal rules they established when they gave him permission to toke: *No dealing and no stealing.* He was expected to work to buy his pot or the deal was off.

Everyone he knew was getting ready for Dan Mellon's funeral tomorrow, even Todd and Hiram, but Frank wasn't into dead people. Todd said he could stay with him at the farmer's tonight if he wanted even though he was still pissed about the McKee-Copeland thing, but Frank passed until next week. He invited him to come here instead. Frank had something planned that was no good for Hiram's place, although he'd stayed at the farm a lot. He'd been going there with Todd since he was ten. Hiram was a grumpy old dude, but he let Frank get high right in his living room. Plus, he always let Frank have the guestroom. Hiram made Todd sleep on the couch. Was that cool, or what?

"I wish he'd get some better Kool-Aid," Frank mumbled. "That generic stuff is nasty."

Frank stoked up his water bong sucking hard on the mouthpiece. The fetid smelling liquid bubbled as the smoke filtered through it. He held it in and lit an opium-scented incense. He let it whoosh out and he grinned. Getting stoned was the best way to start the day, but now it was time for the next phase of his planned activities. He took four small camouflage-colored paper squares out of a tin container he kept on his dresser leaving six for another day. He popped the LSD squares into his mouth and slipped them under his tongue.

Larry Singleton, the E.M.T., sold them to him. He was the local drug connection for Lancaster. Frank liked LSD even more than pot. He sat on the edge of his bed. He hung his head forward and let his long brown hair fall into his face. He closed his eyes. The acid would take effect shortly and he could trip all day. He ought to be pretty level by the time Todd arrived, the trips down to a minimum, but he wasn't sure. This type of LSD was new to him. He'd never dropped it before, but Larry said it was great. He had to trip now since Todd didn't do acid. Frank didn't like tripping around people who weren't tripping with him. It always brought him down. He felt the drug beginning to take effect and he laughed a little.

This is going to be great! he thought.

The music from his Bose SoundDock III suddenly stopped playing. Frank lifted his head and opened his eyes to check on his iPhone. His heart leapt into his throat when he saw Sam Stone's ghost sitting on the edge of the bed staring at him.

"Hi, Frank," Sam said. His breath smelled like rotten meat.

Sam's hair, clothes, and New Balance running shoes were filthy and wet with blood. There was a large bruise in the middle of his chest shaped like a fist. His torso was riddled with stab wounds.

"Holy crap!" Frank cried, jumping back on the bed and against the wall. His heart hammered behind his ribcage. "Bad trip!"

A chorus of hollow laughter arose. Frank glared around his room in disbelief as the drug blazed to its full effect in his mind. The air swam with liquid unreality. He felt as though he were underwater, yet the water was thick like mucus. Sam wasn't alone. He had brought an entourage of dead boys with him. Frank counted them as they distorted out of view and focused again. There were seventeen ghosts spread throughout his bedroom. They were different ages, but they were all young. Frank's worry faded. Their sudden appearance had startled him, but he knew how to handle things when he was tripping. He quickly calmed down. A few of them looked familiar. He knew if he relaxed he would mellow out. When he saw Dan Mellon, he almost jumped out of his skin.

"What's the matter, Frank?" Dan asked. Fresh blood stained his mangled body. *"Never seen a ghost before?"*

"No way!" Frank exclaimed. He grabbed the tin with the paper squares in it and dumped them into the trashcan. He spit out the ones in his mouth. "This is crazy! You're dead, Mellon! The whole town's getting ready for your funeral!"

"We know," Dan replied. *"Right guys?"*

They nodded, never taking their eyes off Frank.

Frank thought he was going out of his mind, but then something dawned on him. *Duh! Where's my brain? I'm tripping!*

He had seen freaky things before when he was on acid. This was no big deal. He just needed to chill and let it ride. He could handle it. The more he thought about it, the more ridiculous it seemed. Of course Dan was here. Frank had been thinking about him a minute ago. He didn't know many of the others, but he knew Sam. There was a kid in the corner by the door that looked like Bobby Jones. The top of his head was missing. His brain cavity was empty. He'd run away or something. Frank ought to recognize him. His mother had put pictures of him all over town. Ian Sturgess he knew, the punk-ass little bitch.

"Hey, screw you, Garrison!" Ian cried, his angry voice hollow.

Frank felt nauseous. Ian looked awful. His neck was a tangled mess of torn veins and tendons. There was blood all over the front of his shirt and in his hair. His dimples were gone as if someone had cut them out, and he smelled like vomit.

"Wait!" Frank exclaimed. "You heard me?"

Ian shook his head while the other boys laughed.

"He's a genius," the redheaded twin by the Bose SoundDock III said.

"Einstein," his brother echoed.

Their voices were empty. Whatever kind of acid he'd dropped, this was wild. Frank burst out laughing. The boys grew cold and angry when he did, except for the little one. He sat on the edge of the bed on the opposite side. He had curly black hair and a sweet face, but his color was all wrong. He was pale white like Elmer's glue. Smelly black dirt covered him. His neck was raggedly cut open like Ian's.

Frank stopped laughing and looked at him, intently. He felt sad suddenly. "Are you okay, little dude?" he asked, reaching out to him. His arm looked like it was a mile long.

The boy shrank from his touch, but nodded, shyly.

"What's your name, man?" Frank pressed. He was sure he didn't know this kid from anywhere. *What's he doing in my trip?*

"Giuseppe Luciano," the boy whispered. *"I'm eight."*

Frank stared at him. *Giuseppe? The name doesn't ring a bell. It sounds like spaghetti sauce to me. What's going on here?*

"About time," Terry Greer said. *"He thinks we're part of an acid trip."*

"It's why he can see us," Ian said, his throat wagging as he spoke. *"He's a burnout. What did you expect?"*

Frank noticed they were all messed up in one way or another. Some of their throats were torn open. The twins, whoever they were...

"David Leech."

"Donald Leech."

... were missing large patches of red hair from their scalps. The blonde sitting on the floor...

"Kyle MacGuire."

... had a hole in his chest where his heart should've been. Frank could see he was holding it in his hand. It was black and crusty. Frank's stomach heaved and he almost threw up. Realization came with a sense of dread. His palms felt clammy and he started to sweat.

"All right!" Frank demanded, fear making him angry. "What's going on here? This is more than a lousy trip! This is real!"

"Yeah, Frank," Sam said. *"It's real."*

"But how can that be?" Frank asked. He leaned over to touch Sam, but his hand went right through him. He drew it back and cried out. It felt like he had dipped it in ice water.

"You can't touch a ghost unless he wants you to, dummy," Bobby said. He voice cracked when he spoke. He shifted from side to side.

"Shut up, Jones!" Frank snapped. "You guys can't all be dead! Mellon yes, but Sturgess? Stone? How can you be dead and no one knows about it?"

"You'll see," Terry said.

"Guys?" Ian asked. He tilted his head up as if listening to something. *"She's close."*

The dead boys looked west. They nodded.

"It's time," Terry said. They all stood.

"Time for what?" Frank asked. He pinched his arm trying to wake up.

"We're going to stop this," Ian said. *"We're putting an end to the murder."*

"We need you to help us, Frank," Sam said. *"I'm sorry it has to be this way."*

"What are you talking about?" Frank asked. He whimpered. "Dudes… please… what's going on here?"

"Hell, Frank," Ian said.

"Yeah," Donald agreed.

"You're the key to helping us fix it," David added.

"We need you, Frank," Sam whispered. *"We need you to die so nobody else has to."*

"Die?" Frank cried. "Sam! *Ian!* No! *Please!*"

"I'm sorry, Frank," Sam said. *"There's no other way to stop the monster."*

Frank gasped as Sam stepped forward and walked into his body. He cried out as the frigid spirit sank through his skin, invading his mind and soul. He witnessed Sam's death, felt Sam's pain, saw Hiram's face, and cried out in horror.

"When you're dead, she'll come," Terry whispered. *"She can't resist."*

Terry dove into Frank next. Four more spirits followed him. Frank convulsed and writhed as the pain and memory of each of their deaths became one with him.

"When she takes your sample, she'll take us, too," Bobby said, *"but it'll be worth more power than she bargained for."*

"N… no…!" Frank struggled. He ran from his bed, but fell to his knees. *"Please!"*

"It's too late, Frank," Bobby said. *"I'm sorry… we all are."*

Bobby sank into him. The remaining boys rushed Frank like a foul-smelling hurricane. They tore into him without mercy, invading his body. Frank experienced all of their pain and deaths at the same time. He held the sides of his head, his scream continuous. Frank's sanity crumbled. He leaped onto his bed and dove out the window trying to escape. The pane shattered. Shards of glass sliced into his body. He landed face first on the grass. A jagged sliver entered his head through his left eye and it popped. He sank down on it, his body jerking, his hands clawing the grass until he was still.

Ms. Adler screeched to a halt on Wickett Avenue. She made a U-turn to Route 41 and pulled onto Annie Potts Road. She parked in front of the Garrisons' house and stepped out of her Mercedes. She walked to the backyard and stood next to Frank's body with her hands on her hips. She stared at him, confused. She had felt his death as she drove by, but she couldn't believe it. She reached into her skirt pocket for a syringe. She inserted the needle into Frank's temple and withdrew the pinkish liquid from his brain.

"Mein Gott!" Ms. Adler cried. She thought, *It filled the syringe to the top! It is ten times the amount I have ever collected!* She wondered what trauma had caused him to commit suicide. *Did it affect the production of the fluid?* She sniffed near his mouth. *Marijuana. Did that cause the chemical to surge? If everyone had this much, I would have only needed half the boys Hiram killed!* She capped the syringe and slipped it into her skirt. She removed another. She stabbed it into his wounded eye and filled it with blood. *I will run a drug screen and see if marijuana was all he was using. This bears further study.*

She walked around the side of the house, but paused, listening. *Children laughing? I sense no one near.* She shook her head. She climbed into her Mercedes and sped away.

Giuseppe Luciano walked out of the closet he'd hid in when his fellow spirits attacked Frank. He had slipped through the door to get away and cowered in the darkness. They were doing bad things! They were breaking the rules! Giuseppe wanted no part of it. He sat on the edge of Frank's bed again and wept. He had been asleep somewhere in the cool black ground waiting for something, for someone, but he'd woken up scared and all alone. The others made him go with them.

They're angry! Giuseppe thought. *Why couldn't they leave me alone? Why did I have to wake up at all?*

Giuseppe sensed the presence of another spirit. He jumped up intending to run away. A firm hand grabbed him by the shirt and spun him gently around. Giuseppe gasped, but then relaxed sensing the goodness in the ghost before him.

"*You scared me!*" Giuseppe whispered. "*I thought you were one of them!*"

"*I didn't mean t' do that, lad,*" Wade Dougan smiled. "*After all, I need ye t' help me. It wouldn't do t' have ye scared o' me, now would it?*"

Giuseppe shook his head.

Wade took Giuseppe's hand and led him away through the Garrisons' back wall.

*   *   *

"So, what's this meeting about, Mike?" Arthur asked, setting his groceries on the conveyor belt.

Lisa ran them over the scanner. Mike looked at her with concern. She forced a weak smile.

Arthur continued, "It's not like we know each other all that well."

Mike held his breath and counted to ten. He was in a perpetual state of counting to ten in Arthur's presence. He wanted to reach out and grab him by the throat. Thank God he'd gotten a hold of George Skinner before Arthur came in to do his shopping. Mike would've blown the whole deal if he hadn't.

Son-of-a...! Mike thought. He squeezed the edge of Arthur's cart. *How was I supposed to know? Arthur's loyal to Hiram? Jesus! It's unreal!*

George was adamant about it. It was all Mike could do to protect his hearing once the fat man started yelling.

"Colin!" George bellowed, when Mike finished relaying his suspicions about Hiram.

Mike winced, pulling the phone away from his ear.

"What?" a small voice asked from the other room.

"Get outside and walk the dog!"

"I did already," Colin replied.

"Then walk her again!" George cried. "I've got a private call here! I don't need you eavesdropping! Now scoot!"

"Sheesh!" Colin cried. "What a grouch! C'mon, Sassy."

George waited for the door to slam before opening up on Mike. "Are you crazy, Dougan!?" he spat. "You called Kelly before anyone else?"

"Not exactly," Mike replied. "I called Hugh first. He's coming."

"Good!" George exclaimed. He pulled a chair out from the kitchen table and sat. He held his chest and checked his pulse. His heart was racing. He was an obese man with thin black hair, bushy eyebrows, and a mustache. His blue eyes were wide with his fear. "I'm going to have a heart attack. I hope you didn't give Kelly any details. If you did, you could bet the farmer already knows."

"What makes you say that?" Mike asked. He turned toward Craig's knock on the rear door and hit the lock buzzer. He wasn't alone. "Hang on, George. My nephew's here. He's got a friend with him."

"Good God, Mike! Don't say anything in front of the kids, okay? They go to school with my son!"

"I won't," Mike replied. He pressed the phone to his chest.

Mike kissed Craig on the cheek and held his hand out for Jeremy to shake. The kid had a good grip. Jeremy nodded, politely. Craig went into a long-winded explanation of why Jeremy was there. Each time Mike opened his mouth to speak, Craig cut him off. By the time he finished, Mike had a year's worth of reasons why he should let Jeremy stay and help during his shift. It was a waste of words. Mike intended to keep McKee around and for two good reasons. One: He wanted to talk to him about Hiram. His brother worked at the farm. Two: He wanted to ask if he would help them convince Craig to be firm with his father. Nancy told him Jack had gone over the edge in a big way. He feared for his nephew's safety.

Mike reached out and put his hand over Craig's mouth. "All right, motor mouth!" he cried. "Jeremy can stay."

"Yes!" they exclaimed, at the same time.

"Under certain conditions," Mike added, sternly.

"Anything!" they replied together.

Mike looked at them, oddly. "Are you two okay?" he asked. "You're acting strange."

"It runs in the McKee family," Craig replied.

"We're okay," Jeremy said. "It was just a rough morning, that's all."

"You can say that again," Craig said.

"It was just a rough morning."

Craig scowled.

"Oh?" Mike asked, shaking his head. "How so?"

Jeremy rolled his eyes.

"His brother was in rare form this morning," Craig said, thumbing toward his friend.

He wasn't lying. From the moment they stepped downstairs, Derek and Chris were on them about what they had seen. It didn't matter how many times they said they were only wrestling, Chris kept asking, "In the nude?" At least he had the decency not to say anything in front of their mother. When Virginia asked what was so funny, Jeremy and Craig scampered out of the house and left Chris to do the explaining. They hoped they wasn't a mistake.

"He's a wiseass," Jeremy offered, excluding Craig's watchful uncle from the details.

"But good to me, right?" Craig interjected. He didn't want Mike to get the wrong idea.

Jeremy nodded.

"Okay," Mike continued. "This is the deal…"

He told them that by law neither one of them were old enough to work in the store because he sold liquor. There was some leeway with Craig since they were related, but Jeremy needed to keep a low profile. There were too many busybodies in Lancaster. It wouldn't take half the day before the entire town thought he worked at the market. It was a hassle Mike didn't need. He also informed them that with Dan gone and Craig off yesterday they were way behind stocking the shelves and doing the inventory.

"You need to finish it today," Mike said, holding the phone with his chin. He grabbed both boys by their collars. "There's too much going on this week to screw around. Do we understand each other?"

301

"Yes, sir!" the boys proclaimed.

Jeremy stared at Mike's forearms. They resembled the Incredible Hulk's.

"And you, McKee," Mike continued. He let go of Craig and pulled Jeremy to him nose to nose.

Jeremy smiled. *His breath smells like Scope.*

"As soon as I'm off the phone, I want to talk to you."

"Sure, Mr. Dougan."

"Mike."

Jeremy nodded. "Sure, Mike."

The boys left the office.

Mike heard Jeremy ask Craig, "What does he want to talk to me about?"

"I don't know," Craig replied, punching his time card. "Maybe my dad."

They opened the door for Bea. She was working a double today. It was the dayshift cashier's day off. Mike usually handled the register since it was historically slow on Wednesday, but there was too much to do this morning. When Bea called him earlier, she was shocked and dismayed over what she had heard through the grapevine. She needed to know, was it true? Was Dan dead? Mike sadly confirmed the bad news and mentioned something about being swamped with work. Bea was feeling better after her emotional display last night and volunteered to help. Mike was glad. Until then, he had no idea how he was going to make it to closing with his sanity intact.

Old Ted came in with his arm around Lisa. She looked like she hadn't slept much. It was true. Every time she turned the light off, she felt like she wasn't alone. It drove her up the wall until she finally left the light on. She was glad to see Marianna yesterday. Her Puerto Rican mother convinced her she wasn't responsible for Dan's death. Lisa hadn't given her much detail other than her guilt over not driving him home. Marianna comforted her, but it didn't make the feeling of loss go away. She hoped she could make it through the day without crying.

Mike nodded at Old Ted. Lisa kissed him on the cheek, clocked in, and then walked away with Jeremy and Craig under each of her arms.

"Rough week around hee-ya," Old Ted said to Mike. "I ain't seen so many long faces since Tim died."

"That's right," Mike said. "You knew Timothy Adler, didn't you? Were you at Margaret's graduation party the day he died? You and the Colonel were friends?"

"Boy," Old Ted said, "don't you know nuthin' 'bout Lancaster's history? I grew up with Tim. I served with him in WW Two. I was an Engineer. 'Course, there wasn't much choice for coloreds back then, but I served all the same." He brought his hand to his chin. "Tim was in Patton's 3rd Army. My unit was attached to 'em. He liberated one of them death camps, killed a Nazi doctor, too. Bremen was his name. He was experimentin' on kids, torturin' them. Tim caught him in the act an' shot him dead. They pinned a medal on his chest." He looked at Mike. "Tim was my best friend," he said. His gaze became faraway and sad. "He died in my arms the day of that party."

"Really?" Mike asked. He lifted the phone. "Hang on, George," he said, and covered it with his hand. "There are a lot of rumors about what happened that day. Some say Margaret killed…"

"If you're askin' me 'bout things that're none of your concern," Old Ted snapped, "I wouldn't. I don't gossip. Ma… *Mar…*" He paused, his expression frustrated. "She never laid a hand on her father." He motioned to the boys who were up in front with Bea and Lisa. "You there! Youngins! I got to hack up some pork chops this morning. Care to watch? I got the whole pig."

"Eew!" they exclaimed.

Jeremy and Craig made it inside the butcher shop before Old Ted.

Mike grunted. *Just what they need to start off their day. I hope neither one of them has a weak stomach.*

"Mike?" George cried. "Did you forget about me?"

"Oh," Mike replied, feeling foolish. He put the phone to his ear. "Sorry about that, George. I was distracted. Let's see, where were we? Oh, yeah. No, I didn't give Arthur any details about Hiram. I just left a message for him to call me."

"Colin? Go in the other room."

"Jeeze!" Colin whined. "Can't I eat anything around here?"

"My foot with your buttocks if you don't get moving!" George exclaimed. There was a pause. "Well, thank God for that," he continued, his voice lower. "Kelly was involved with the farmer longer than anyone. Take my advice, unless you want Hiram to know what you're doing, don't tell Arthur anything!"

"Are you saying my suspicions are true?" Mike asked, rubbing his forehead. *I'm getting a headache.* "Why didn't you guys…?"

"You can stop right there, Mike," George said. "I'll be at your house Friday. I'll bring Peter Rollins, Roland Underwood, and Don Barry with me. If you can get Kelly to come, more power to you, but you and I are not going to talk about why we did or didn't come forward, understand? You haven't got the foggiest idea of what Hiram Milliken did to us. Until you do, don't even presume to pass judgment!"

Mike winced at the memory. George slammed the phone down in his ear. Arthur stared at him oddly while simultaneously handing Lisa a fifty-dollar bill. He cleared his throat. Mike frantically searched for an indisputable reason why Arthur needed to be at his house for the meeting. He opened his mouth, but he paused when someone tugged on his sleeve. He looked down into Jeremy's shining blue eyes. Mike glanced at Arthur whose attention was now focused entirely on the kid.

Is Arthur as sick as Hiram? Mike thought. His mood went ebony.

"Jeremy!" Arthur cried. "What are you doing here?"

"Hi, Mr. Kelly," Jeremy replied. "I'm just visiting my friend. You know Craig, right?"

Arthur nodded, taking his change. The light faded from his eyes. "Yes, I know him," he said. *I know the boy's screams better.* He thrust that thought away. He perked up some and forced a grin. "You were headed to his house when I gave you the ride, remember?"

"Right," Jeremy said.

"Well, you're a good boy, Jeremy," Arthur said. "I'm sure Craig could use a real friend."

"So can I," Jeremy mumbled. He turned to Mike.

Arthur's eyebrow went up.

"Craig told me to tell you there are customers at the deli counter."

Thank you, God! Mike thought, placing a hand on Jeremy's shoulder. "I've got to go," he said to Arthur. "About Friday? It's just a social thing, you know? Bring something to drink if you don't like beer."

Arthur's eyes were fixed on Jeremy. "I'll be there," he said, no longer concerned with Mike's reasons for inviting him. He didn't care now. He turned on his heel, grabbed his bags, and sashayed away.

Mike kept his hand on Jeremy's shoulder as they walked toward the back. He thought, *Jeremy's the best thing that's ever happened to Craig. I'll do everything I can to ensure he feels welcome around here.*

Craig was waiting at the end of the bread aisle holding two clipboards.

Mike looked at him, confused.

"We're doing the inventory," Craig said.

"How can you both be doing the inventory?" Mike asked, reaching for the clipboards. "It took me weeks to get you to fill the forms out right. Jeremy couldn't possibly learn how to do them in such a short time."

"See for yourself," Craig replied.

Mike examined the forms. *They're perfect so far. Come to think of it, the boys worked together all morning and everything they've done is perfect. I expected Craig to have to go over Jeremy's work.* He eyed them, curiously. They watched him, expectantly. *It's the oddest thing. It's like Jeremy's worked here as long as Craig.*

Mike let the clipboards go with an approving nod. They walked away resuming their inventory. Craig didn't have to repeat a single instruction. It was the same when they stocked the shelves and crushed the cardboard in the compactor. Jeremy was the fastest learner Mike had ever met. He slipped behind the deli counter and sliced some olive loaf for Mona Keroack. Keith snuck over to Jeremy and Craig. He glanced back at his mother.

"Did you give Chris my message?" Keith asked, pulling them into the aisle.

They looked at each other and smiled. Keith had brown eyes, shaggy blonde hair, and a pug nose. His expression was perpetually pouty, but when he smiled, it was wide and revealed perfect teeth. He was emotional and easily upset. He was two inches shorter than Craig who nodded at Jeremy They were thinking the same thing.

It's nice not to have to look up at someone for a change.

Not all of the Keroacks were short. Keith had an older brother, JT. He was as tall at Matt with the same brown eyes and pug nose as his brother, but JT was a strawberry blonde, his shaggy hair down to his shoulders. It encircled his face, unlike Keith's which was more like a shaggy bowl cut. JT had dimples in his cheeks, not as bad as Ian's, wore glasses when he didn't have his contacts in, and had braces. He was a really friendly guy like Keith, smoked just as much pot, but was nowhere near as sensitive. He was turning seventeen July fourth. Keith would be fifteen on August eighth. JT would be a senior in the fall with Lisa Gibbons although his baby face made him look younger.

"Would you relax, Keroack?" Jeremy asked. He half-laughed. "Of course I told him. Why don't you just call him?"

"Are you kidding?" Keith cried, checking on his mother. "I got royally reamed when you called me! If she caught me calling out, I'd get killed!"

"It's your fault, man," Jeremy replied.

"Really," Craig agreed.

"I know," Keith nodded, rubbing his buttocks. "My dad tanned my hide."

Jeremy felt a chill go down his spine. He looked over at Craig and discovered it wasn't his chill. It was Craig's. He knew by the faraway look on his face. This was the second time today he'd felt that same chill. The first time was when Mike called Jeremy into the office and closed the door. Craig knew whatever his uncle wanted to talk about involved his father. He was right, but that was only part of it.

Jeremy was very open with Mike when they discussed Craig's feelings about his father. He understood well how Craig felt. Mike assumed the boys had done some heavy duty talking in the short time they'd been friends. They did, but they didn't have to talk about emotions. It was the mind-link. Jeremy knew Craig's feelings as well as his own. He told Mike that convincing Craig to turn on his father wouldn't be easy. He loved Jack, pure and simple. Mike explained Jack's condition when Nancy visited him. Jeremy agreed with his assumptions and felt angry. Mike was right. Jack would go too far. Craig might end up badly hurt or even worse. Were they willing to let that happen?

No, Jeremy thought. *We're not. He's hurt Craig enough. It's time to end it.*

Jeremy promised to do his best to convince Craig his life might depend on Jack getting help.

"There's something else before you go," Mike said, leaning back in his chair.

Jeremy nodded, shifting in his seat. He felt Craig's anxiety. They'd been in the office for a long time. Jeremy tried something. He focused on his feelings that everything was all right. He projected them to his friend. Craig stuck his head out from around the corner and smiled. Jeremy left the contact open. Their feelings entwined. It was a warm sensation that spread through both of them.

"Your brother works at the farm?" Mike asked, spotting Craig. He waved him away.

Craig ducked back behind the wall.

"Since last year," Jeremy said. He scratched below his left eye. Around the corner, Craig did the same thing.

"Has he ever complained about anything? The working conditions, or...?"

"Nah," Jeremy replied. "Chris likes the job, I guess. I don't know how he could though. He's such a woman about his looks." He cocked his head and asked, "Why are you asking me this?"

"Well... uh, with Dan gone there's a position open here," Mike lied. He slipped his left hand into his pocket and crossed his fingers. "I thought he might be interested."

"I doubt it," Jeremy said. "Hiram gives him a lot of hours. He could get more, but he doesn't like sleeping over there."

"Oh?" Mike asked, a rush of adrenaline flowing through his heart. "Did he ever say why?"

"Chris stayed over there once last year. He said the bed in the guest room hurt his back. He refuses to stay over there now."

"Is that so?"

"Yeah," Jeremy confirmed. "He lets Todd O'Connor or Dabney Copeland do the overnights. Todd practically lives there."

Mike instantly filed that in his mind. He saw Todd a couple of times a week when he stopped in for sandwiches. His heart sank, but he held in his anger – now a strong desire to commit murder – and continued.

"What about Dabney Copeland?" he asked, and mumbled, "the little snot."

Jeremy smiled, "Hard to believe he works there, huh? He's been acting weird ever since Derek Mellon beat him up. He's almost human."

Mike looked surprised.

Jeremy shook his head. "Believe me," he said. "Dabney can be a real bastard. He can be as mean as Jack."

Mike felt a dagger of ice stab into his spine. *I'm going to put my hands around Hiram's neck and squeeze his head off!* he thought. *Chris, Dabney, Jack, George... how many kids has he done this to?*

Mike asked if Jeremy could have Chris call him and to keep him posted about Craig. Jeremy said he would. Mike sat in the office for a long time after he left, his mind filled with thoughts of his brother. Sandra's instincts had opened a can of worms he never even knew existed. He felt like a fool. His anger toward Jack blinded him to what was so obvious.

What about mom? Mike wondered. *She never lets a thing escape her notice. How could Hiram hurt Jack right under her nose? Under all of our noses?*

There was an answer in there. Mike wasn't sure he wanted to hear it.

Jeremy and Craig escorted Keith back to his mother. Mike was slicing Swiss cheese for her. They waited until he finished. Mona led her errant son away into the dairy aisle.

Poor Keith, Jeremy thought. *His summer's history except for Scouts, I guess. Who gets grounded from that? Go to your room, son! You can't be a better citizen today! The old geezers will have to take their chances in traffic!* He smirked.

He promised to relay a message to Chris. Keith would be at Dan's funeral and hoped to see him. His breath smelled like pot. He was stoned, but insistent. Keith wanted to touch base.

Mike glanced down at them. His steady gaze interrupted Jeremy's train of thought.

"We're hungry," they said together.

"Jesus, Craig!" Jeremy whined, elbowing his friend. "Would you get a brain of your own?"

"Look who's talking!" Craig retorted, elbowing him back.

"I'll make you guys some sandwiches," Mike offered. *These two are too much.* "What do you want?"

"Ham and cheese," they replied in unison.

Jeremy reached around and pinched his left buttock. Craig jumped and glared at him, rubbing his own.

"Ham?" Mike asked Craig, puzzled. "You hate ham."

*　　*　　*

Jack woke with a start. His body was shaking with convulsions. He felt panic as he realized, *I'm not breathing!* He sat up, gulping for air. Every nerve in his body burned with pain. His stomach knotted and heaved. He dug his fingernails into his palms and clenched his teeth. He groaned, forcing a calm. His breathing slowed. The reality of his circumstance sank in as the shaking subsided.

God, how did this happen to me? Jack thought. His answer came in the image of a man at the edge of his consciousness. *Jerry Copeland. What I wouldn't give to put a bullet in that bastard's brain. I showed them though, didn't I? The lot of them couldn't even get me off my feet. I could've killed them easily.*

"No, you couldn't, Mr. Dougan," a small voice said. *"You're not a murderer. You may be lots of stuff, but that's not one of them."*

"Who said that?" Jack cried, jumping to his feet and whirling around. He balled up his fists, holding them at the ready. "Show yourself! Sweetwater?

307

Is that you? Where are you, you gross-looking son-of-a-bitch?" He heard a child's muffled giggling. A chill settled in the pit of his stomach. "Who's here?" he cried, his eyes wide as he glared around his cell. "Answer me, you...!"

Jack gasped as the answer appeared on the edge of his cot. The boy became visible a little at a time. He was sitting with his ankles neatly crossed, his hands folded in his lap. He flowed out of the shadows, his face unnaturally white. There was a gaping wound in his neck as wide as his smile.

"You're funny, Mr. Dougan!" the boy giggled, holding his small hand over his mouth. His neck wound wagged as he laughed.

"Who are *you!?"* Jack demanded, moving over to the bars. He gripped them from behind his back, holding tight to keep steady. The world started spinning.

"Giuseppe Luciano," Giuseppe whispered.

"Oh, Jesus, this is insane!" Jack cried, pressing against the bars. "Sweetwater, I can understand, but I don't even know you! What are you doing in my hallucination?"

"You're not hallushi... hannucin...," Giuseppe struggled. He groaned. *"You're not seeing things, Mr. Dougan. I'm really here."*

"That's not possible!" Jack snapped, his eyes blazing. "I don't even know you!"

Giuseppe sighed. He breathed in and out through the gash in his neck. It was an imitation of respiration. He didn't need air anymore.

"Nobody knows me, Mr. Dougan," he replied. *"I'm dead."*

"No... God, no..." Jack sobbed, sinking to his knees. His hands shook. *This is too damned much...*

"Please don't cry, Mr. Dougan," Giuseppe said. His legs swung back and forth in a child's display of anxiety. *"I'm not here to make you unhappy. I don't like seeing people sad."*

"God, what do you want from me?" Jack pleaded. "Why are you doing this to me?"

Giuseppe replied, *"I'm supposed to help make you feel better."*

Jack wiped his eyes, choking back his sobs. He stood, glaring at his spectral intruder. "What for?" he asked. "Don't you know who I am? I'm a dangerous man. I'm good for nothing. I've killed kids your age."

"I know," Giuseppe whispered, his dark eyes sympathetic, *"but in the war, not because you're a murderer."*

Jack fell into his eyes. They were so open, like pools of black water.

"I've been there," Giuseppe said. *"I saw what you did. It was self-defense. You were a soldier. Killing was your job, but you're not a murderer."*

Jack felt his words like a physical blow. They smashed through his anger and tore him wide open. He fell forward and grabbed Giuseppe's sneakers.

He pressed his face against them and started to cry. He touched the boy's cold flesh above his filthy dirt-covered socks. He smelled the fresh soil covering his clothes and hair. He climbed Giuseppe's body as he wept and drew the horribly injured child to him. He hugged him, sobbing into his shoulder. Giuseppe laid his head sideways and hugged him, too, gently patting his back.

No one's ever said that to me before, Jack thought, through his sorrow. *No one ever knew.*

Jack never shared the real source of his agony, even greater than what Hiram had done to him. He locked it away so deep he didn't even think about it anymore. It made all of his other pains more severe. His mind filled with images of dead children lying in pieces all around him. He could smell their bodies burning.

I couldn't cry! Jack thought, feeling his heart break. *I didn't have any tears left! Hiram took them all away!* He didn't want to do the things he did in Afghanistan, but Giuseppe was right. It was his job. *But it was wrong! I was wrong!*

Jack had gone to Afghanistan for redemption. He wanted to do something honorable, but it wasn't possible. There was no glory. There was no vindication. There was no justice in a land littered with the bodies of so many babies. Jack drew the line at killing kids. Some of the Taliban fighters were barely tweens. No matter what the daily exposure to murder and destruction turned him into, he refused to sink to that depth. War was hell though, and even the best intentions soured.

"Yes," Giuseppe whispered. *"You need to remember."*

Jack's squad was patrolling the mountains around the Baylough Bowl in the Dey Chopan district. The merciless sun beat down on them in ever increasing waves. They moved behind some rocks when snipers opened up on them from two different positions. While Lt. Sweetwater called for support, Jack caught movement out of the corner of his eye. It was a child running toward them. He couldn't have been more than ten years old. Jack thought he might be fleeing the fighting until he saw the bomb vest.

"Allahu akbar!" the boy screamed, charging at Jack's squad.

Jack spun around and fired his weapon on fully automatic. He emptied an entire clip into him. The boy shook and convulsed like a macabre marionette as the bullets cut him to ribbons. Everyone saw what was happening and dove for cover. The entire world thrust into slow motion as the bomb vest exploded. The boy was blown apart. Guts and blood rained down on them. At the same time, a hail of artillery took out both sniper positions. Something landed in front of Jack. It hit the dirt with a wet thud.

As the smoke cleared, his mind scanned his body for any sign of injury. He was okay. He'd saved everyone. When he looked up, he saw a gruesome horror. The boy's decapitated head lay in front of him. It glared with accusation. Its lips slowly mouthed, *"Allahu akbar...!"* and went still. Dale

Kerrigan laughed. Jack looked over his shoulder. His buddy was swinging around a small severed arm. Dale opened his mouth and cried...

"Good kill, Jack," Giuseppe whispered, holding him tighter. *"That's what he said, right?"*

"Oh, *Jesus* Christ!" Jack sobbed, his body trembling. The memory, and the pieces of that kid...

Jack had gathered them all and buried the boy. He wanted to weep. He wanted to cry until he had drowned Afghanistan in an ocean of his tears. He drank afterward trying to get the boy's head and staring eyes out of his mind. It was always sitting on the bar next to him, glaring at him.

Those angry accusing eyes...

"Oh, God!" Jack wept. "Why did you make me remember that? *Why?"*

Giuseppe patted Jack on top of his head. *"Because you have to, Mr. Dougan,"* he replied. *"Even children go to war. You need to remember because it's the only way you'll get better. I want you to get better."*

"But why?" Jack sobbed. He looked into Giuseppe's eyes. "I'm not worth it. Why can't I just die?"

Giuseppe touched Jack's face. His icy fingers ran through the growth of beard on his cheeks. Jack held his hand in a vain attempt to warm him.

"Your chance is coming, Mr. Dougan," he said, with a nod. *"Don't be sad, okay? Things will be fine if you're ready when it's time."*

"Ready?" Jack whimpered. "Ready for what? Please tell me. Please?"

"I can't," Giuseppe said. He wiped Jack's tears away with his small fingers. *"It's against the rules. You're not a bad person, Mr. Dougan. Don't forget that."* He paused and added, *"Craig loves you."*

Jack's hands slipped through Giuseppe's midsection as the boy began to fade away. Jack groped at him, desperately, begging him not to leave him alone.

Giuseppe shook his head. *"I have to,"* he whispered. *"Just remember, okay?"* And he was gone.

Jack sank to the floor. His tears fell onto the cold concrete. The rich black earth on his hands... it was so familiar.

If only he could remember from where.

*　　*　　*

Jeremy was sitting on the front windowsill of Mike's Market finishing his sandwich. Craig was cleaning the windows with a squeegee having wolfed his down already. He was sweating in the blistering heat. Jeremy swallowed the last of his lunch and scrunched over to give Craig room to work. He saw a poster hanging on the inside of the window. It said: *Come to the Carnival!*

"There's a carnival?" Jeremy asked.

Craig ran the squeegee down the window. "Sure," he said. "It's at Johnson Memorial Hospital."

Jeremy said, "I didn't know they had a carnival there."

"They don't usually," Craig replied.

"How do you know?" Jeremy asked. *Oh, he just thinks he knows everything!*

Craig frowned. *Like I know everything?* "My uncle supplied some of the concessions stuff. It's a fundraising thing, or whatever."

Jeremy grunted. He asked, "Want to go?"

"To the carnival?"

"No, Craig," Jeremy replied. "To the gynecologist."

"That would be your brother."

They laughed.

Craig stopped washing and sat down next to him. "Sure, I'll go," he decided. He had a great reason why he should.

"It might take your mind off Dan," Jeremy said, suggesting Craig's reason.

"I think so. Who's going to take us?"

"My mom will," Jeremy replied. He looked across the parking lot. Todd O'Connor was riding by on his bicycle headed toward Milliken Road.

You'd better leave my brother alone, Jeremy thought, since Chris was working tonight.

"I have some money," Craig said, feeling his right pocket. "I'm giving some to Matt. It's my tip from Ms. Adler."

"Yeah," Jeremy smiled. "She left twenty bucks on her dresser for you."

Craig retched. "That's disgusting!"

Jeremy agreed. He thought, *Who would even touch her? Gross.*

"Who would even touch her?" Craig asked. "Gross."

Jeremy looked at him.

"Do you want to ask anyone else to go?"

"I don't care," Jeremy said. An idea struck him. "We could call Dabney."

"Copeland?" Craig asked. "I know he's been acting weird lately, but he hates me. I don't think that's changed."

Jeremy shook his head. "He hates Max and Ricardo, too, and he was at their house yesterday."

"What if Derek wants to go?"

"Good question," Jeremy replied. He honestly didn't know. His curiosity was getting the better of him though. "Chris works tonight, so he won't go. Dabney said I could call. Do you think I should ignore him?"

Craig replied, "Nope. You can't do that to anybody. I just hope you know what you're getting us into." He went back to cleaning the windows.

Jeremy stared off into space. *What's going on with Dabney anyway?* he wondered. *What about Chris? He's got a crush on Dabs, for real. I know Dabney's sorry for what happened at the pond, but what happens when he finds out how Chris feels? He won't get all homophobic, will he? God, I hope not.*

Then there was the matter of the taste of salami in his mouth. It was like that all the way through his ham and cheese sandwich. He swore he could still taste it every time he belched.

Yuck! I don't understand how Craig can eat that stuff!

Jeremy belched as if on cue and then retched. He thought he was going to puke all over the sidewalk. Craig looked at him, curiously. He didn't know what Jeremy's problem was, but he knew if he didn't get the taste of ham out of his mouth soon, he was going to puke all over the sidewalk.

*   *   *

An hour after Jeremy and Craig returned home from the market, Chris left for the farm on his bicycle. He made it there in record time. He pulled into the barnyard and skidded to a halt in front of the entrance to the milking parlor. He set the bike against the barn and locked the rear wheel with his chain. Even Lancaster wasn't immune to the occasional bicycle thief. He stood, hearing something, and turned toward the sound. Hiram came out of the Victorian. He closed the door, locked it, and slipped the keys into his pocket. They saw each other, but said nothing. Chris went in the barn to prepare for the milking.

This was the first day Chris could remember wanting to call out sick. Just being in Hiram's company was making his flesh crawl. Tomorrow wouldn't be so bad. At least when he worked in the morning, the old man rarely got out of bed. Chris sat down on the bench in the narrow coatroom and took off his sneakers. He fished around underneath for his waterproof boots. He found them and yawned. He was tired after staying up with Derek most of the night. It had been a busy day around the house, too, especially after Matt showed up. Chris shook his head remembering what happened when his friend arrived. Matt was such a bonehead sometimes. He'd managed to say the exact wrong thing at the exact wrong time. The whole day was filled with drama that started first thing in the morning.

Jeremy and Craig had just left for the market narrowly escaping Virginia's ever-vigilant inquiries. It was up to Chris to explain why they were laughing so much. Derek was no help. Each time Virginia glanced in his direction, he burst out in renewed giggles. It wasn't long before he was rolling around on the kitchen floor, gasping for breath, his face the color of a tomato. Chris bent over, picked him up, and slung him over his shoulder like a sack of wheat.

"C'mon, Lobster Boy," Chris sighed, trying to keep a straight face. "Time to take a shower."

"I suppose no one's going to tell me what's so funny?" Virginia asked.

312

Derek laughed even harder. Chris said nothing as he climbed the stairs, choosing *the best answer is not to answer* option. Derek was laughing so hard he couldn't answer.

"Guess not," Virginia said, walking to the coffee pot. "I have a strange household."

Chris deposited Derek on his feet in the hallway and gave him a moment to compose himself. He almost had a coronary when Derek slipped his underwear off and tossed them into his room. He went into the bathroom and closed the door. A few seconds later, the shower came on.

Chris grabbed Derek's underwear off the floor and tossed them into the laundry basket in his closet.

That's another thing! Chris thought, aggravated. *I know how Derek keeps his room at home, a lot like Jeremy's. If he thinks he's going to turn my room into trash central, he's out of his redheaded skull. If it's the last thing I do, I'm teaching that little ginger how to be neat!*

Chris grabbed a pair of cutoffs out of Derek's bag and tossed them on his bed. He found a concert shirt from the rock group *RATT* in his closet that used to be his dad's. He decided Derek could wear it for the day. Chris kept the *Megadeth* one for himself. He was fishing in the bag for clean underwear when Matt walked in.

"Dude, I am so glad to be out of that house," Matt moaned, lying back on the waterbed.

"I'll bet," Chris said. He found Derek's clean underwear and put them with his shorts.

"I hate my mom," Matt said. "Trade?" He smiled, hopefully.

Chris shook his head. "Not in a million years, thanks."

"That's it," Matt said, rubbing his eyes. "I'm trapped."

"Better you than me."

Derek walked into the room dripping wet. He was carrying the towel he had found in the bathroom closet. Chris shot him an irritated glare.

Derek made a sheepish, "Oops!" and closed the door.

Matt's mouth hung open. Chris reached over and shut it for him. He insisted Matt tell the tale about why he had gotten grounded. At the same time, he pointed at Derek and scowled.

"What?" Derek asked, innocently.

"Put some clothes on, Lobster Boy!" Matt cried. "Who wants to look at your bare ass?"

Derek snorted, "Besides you?"

Matt opened his mouth to protest, but Chris interrupted. If he got Derek going, there would be no end to this. He had such a need to be shocking. If they raised the ante, he would go right along with it. It wouldn't be long before he was standing in the middle of the front yard, a naked pubescent ginger lawn ornament with freckles.

"So?" Chris asked. "What happened yesterday?"

Matt smiled. The battle between him and his mom started the moment they got into his father's car. Her antennas shot up out of her head and she began firing questions at him.

"I thought you were camping out in Sturgesses' yard. Who permitted you to move the campsite? Why didn't you call me and let me know? Did you have something to hide? Where did you get Phil's cooler? How come I didn't see you leave with it? Why was there a faint aroma of beer in the air?"

Nag, nag, nag.

In the short drive home, his head was spinning. Matt fielded every question with such practiced precision, however, that he had to pat himself on the back.

"I don't get it," Derek said, tying his sneakers.

"Why doesn't that surprise me?" Matt asked.

"Seriously," Derek said, wrapping his arms around his knees. "How did you get grounded if you answered all of her questions?"

"I won the argument," Matt replied.

"Huh?" Chris asked.

"She didn't catch me doing anything wrong," Matt said. He stretched out his long hairy legs. "It was the first time, too, so I couldn't resist getting in the last shot."

"Last shot?" Derek asked.

"The cooler," Chris said.

"The cooler," Matt confirmed. "She walked right up to it and opened it before saying a word to me about Dan being road pizza..."

Matt stopped right there. He never realized how easily his size ten foot fit into his mouth. All of the color drained from his face even as Derek's flushed. Matt would never have said anything like that on purpose. The hurt in Derek's eyes shattered his heart. He struggled to say something, anything, but the words weren't there. He reached out, but Derek angrily slapped his hand away and ran out of the room in tears.

Chris sighed, shaking his head. "I don't have to tell you how dumb that was, do I?"

"No," Matt whispered, but it was too late.

Chris was gone, chasing Derek down the stairs. They were out the back door and in the yard before Chris caught him.

The memory faded as Chris turned on the compressor for the milking machine and let the first ten cows into the parlor. They ambled through the gate and lined up five on each side. He washed their utters vigorously with a hot water hose. He got the first cow hooked up to the milking machine, and then something dawned on him. He had been distracted and forgot to punch in.

Chris jumped out of the valley and went to the time clock. He grabbed his card and punched it making a mental note to pencil in his actual time. He slipped his card into its slot. He was about to turn away when he saw his card, Todd's card, Dabney's card, and one other. Chris looked at it, carefully. The extra card belonged to Teddy Bigelow.

I forgot about him.

Chris went back to the milking parlor with a black cloud hanging over his head. He was almost as mad as Derek had been.

That took some talking, Chris thought.

Derek eventually came back into the house. Matt was in the bedroom feeling like a complete ass. Derek's anger melted away when he saw how upset he was. He slapped his shoulder and told him it was okay. He knew Matt would never be cruel to him on purpose. They listened intently to Derek as he talked about the good times he'd had with his brother. There seemed to be a lot for all the fighting they did. It was clear that he would miss Dan. Matt and Chris could clearly see Derek had already selected his brother's replacement in Chris.

Virginia stopped in the doorway. She asked Derek to come up into the attic so she could use him as a model for some of her sons' old clothes. She told him they were for Craig. It would be easier this way since the two of them were about the same size. She wanted to have them washed and dried by the time he got back from work. Derek nodded and followed her.

"I'm sorry I snapped at you, Matt," Chris said. "I didn't sleep much last night. I'm kind of tired."

"It's okay," Matt said. "I deserved it. I didn't even get the chance to tell him I'm going to be one of the pallbearers at Dan's funeral."

"You are?" Chris asked. "How come?"

"I'm tall," Matt replied, lying back on the waterbed once more with his hands behind his head. He stared at the ceiling.

Chris went to the shower. His iPhone rang. Matt picked it up. It was Sandy checking up on Derek. Matt told him he was okay, but there was a strange message on his voicemail from Danielle. It said something about Sandy and Chris being lovers, or whatever.

Matt gasped when Sandy said, "So?"

They spent the rest of the afternoon close to home. Matt ran back to his house and got his baseball glove. He figured it was a good idea to throw a ball around since there weren't any team practices scheduled for this week. Randy couldn't host them because of a backlog of work. Kevin was supposed to, but Dan's death had shot that down. He played pepper with Derek and Steven Stone who wandered over with nothing better to do. The summer was boring for him without Sam.

Chris helped his mom with the laundry. He was surprised there were so many clothes that would fit Craig. He hoped he liked them and didn't feel funny about accepting them. Derek was so incredibly sad that Chris had to work, but he perked up when Jeremy and Craig arrived. They were going to go to the carnival. Derek wanted to go, too. Jeremy and Craig were worried about that since they had planned to invite Dabney to go and to spend the night. Chris' heart skipped a beat when they mentioned Dabney's name. His face came into his mind, his chocolate brown eyes, the splash of freckles on his face and shoulders.

Chris smiled. *He wants to talk to me about the pond and apologize. I wish I didn't have to work tonight and tomorrow morning. I'm not sure we'll have a chance.* He shook his head. *Could he really become friends with us? What would these feelings I have mean then? I'm attracted to Dabney, I know that. Ricardo called me out on it when we were camping. Jeremy saw it all over my face when we were on the phone with Max. I saw something in Dabney's eyes. Is he feeling it, too?* He snapped his tongue. *Will you listen to me? There's only one way to get to the bottom of this. We have to talk, but where can I find the time? I'll be sleeping when they get back from the carnival since I have to get up and go back to work, and tomorrow's the funeral, too.*

Chris didn't know. The only thing he knew for sure was that they would talk. He just didn't know when.

Jeremy and Craig's voices grew louder. Chris' attention was drawn to them. They were arguing about something that didn't make sense. Chris heard Craig say something about tasting ham every time he bit into his salami sandwich. Jeremy had a similar complaint only the opposite. They were blaming each other. Chris mounted his bike and rode away wondering about the two of them.

Now, in the milking parlor, Chris' thoughts were focused on Teddy. His mind was filled with the terrifying memory of Hiram's abuse, only Chris wasn't the one being hurt this time, it was Teddy. Chris ground his teeth, holding back his anger. He prayed his forgetfulness regarding the altar boy hadn't led Teddy into the same nightmare.

Chris thought, *Could I ever forgive myself?*

He resumed milking. His suspicions and anger were growing.

*　　*　　*

"Dabney?" Tammy called, tapping on his bedroom door. "I have your dinner out here."

"Just leave it there," Dabney called from inside.

His tone was different than its usual arrogance. Tammy wondered why. She decided it warranted investigation. She set the tray down in front of the door, hid beside the doorjamb, and waited. She crossed her fingers. When she heard his door handle click, she made her move. She swung around, pushed the door open, and barged into his room.

Dabney moved to the side at the last second to avoid getting knocked over. "Get out of my room," he ordered, pointing into the hallway. He was in his underwear.

No explosion? Tammy wondered. *Mr. Perfect not dressed for the day? Okay, what's going on?*

She sniffed the air for marijuana. There wasn't any. She examined Dabney closely. The swelling in his face was gone and the bruises faded. There was still a deep purple streak above his right cheekbone. He would carry that for some time. He was healing nicely though. She wondered where he'd gotten the scrapes on the backs of his legs. They seemed to go all the way up his buttocks to the small of his back. They were fresh, too. Tammy ignored his order and sat down on the end of his bed. She crossed her arms and legs, shaking her head.

"Fine," Dabney said, stooping to pick up his tray. He kicked the door closed. "Stay here. See if I care."

Dabney dropped the tray on his desk and ate. Tammy smiled, a victory won. She looked him over some more. She saw by his hair and the dirt on his legs – *Dirt? How did he get dirty in his room?* – that he hadn't showered in days. His underwear was the only clean thing on him. His room was a disaster area. It was very unlike him. He had clothes strewn everywhere and his cologne bottles were knocked off the dresser. There were posters ripped down and half of Dabney's video game discs lay on the floor near the door, their cases broken. At least she knew what he'd been smashing after his father stormed out. Tammy felt sorry for Dabney. Jerry had been a little hard on him, more than usual.

He was a lot hard on him, Tammy thought. *I would comfort him if he'd let me.*

Tammy decided Dabney must be in pain after what happened. He needed to talk to someone. His eighth-grade yearbook lay open on the bed. Tammy picked it up to see the picture next to the name *Derek C. Mellon* had been neatly cut out of the seventh graders' section.

"What happened to this picture?" Tammy asked, holding it up.

"Isn't it obvious?" Dabney snorted, his mouth full. "Fool."

"Hey! That wasn't called for, Dabney!" Tammy exclaimed, acting hurt. "I was just trying to start a conversation."

"For what?" Dabney asked. "You've never talked to me before."

"Maybe I would have if you were nice to me sometimes," Tammy replied.

"Oh, well," Dabney whispered, stuffing the last of his steak into his mouth. "Life sucks, doesn't it?"

Tammy never understood how a boy with such a sweet face could be so sour. She had an idea after what Jerry said to him. She wondered why she'd never noticed that before.

Probably because Dabney's so irritating, she thought.

Tammy was about to leave. Her curiosity over Dabney's condition was satisfied. She would settle for that. He wasn't going to talk…

"I cut it out," Dabney said.

Tammy looked at him, surprised. *Will miracles never cease?* "You might regret that one day," she said.

"Doubt it," Dabney grinned, visibly appearing to relax. There was a light in his eyes. He seemed happy.

"I suppose you threw darts at it?" Tammy asked.

"You bet," Dabney replied, pointing at his dart board. Derek's picture was covering the bulls-eye. He picked up his plate and licked it clean.

"I hope it made you feel better," she said. She started to pick up some of the mess. "Maybe you can put it behind you now."

Dabney said, "I can't seem to hate him right now. His brother got killed. That has to suck."

"You sound like you feel bad for him."

Dabney shrugged. "I guess I do. Weird, isn't it?" He saw his comments had caught her off guard. *Now they squirm when I'm nice? Sheesh, life is seriously absurd.*

Dabney flipped on his clock radio as he rose to help her. He sang along with every song. It was another thing Tammy had never known about him. Dabney could carry a tune. She disappeared to secure the vacuum cleaner, a rag, and some spray cleaner. The room was spotless a half an hour later. It made him feel a lot better. Being at Ramirezes' house felt good, too, even if he was still embarrassed. He wondered about that. Would he have been so kind to Ricardo? Dabney didn't think so and that bothered him. It wouldn't have a week ago. That bothered him, too. Something was different inside of him, and although he wasn't afraid, he was curious.

Dabney thought, *There might even be something good about Tammy, too, but I'm not telling her that. Not yet.*

Tammy wondered why Dabney seemed so innocent all of a sudden. She didn't want to spoil the mood by asking him. She heard the rest of the family gathering for dinner. It was time to leave before Jerry came looking for her. Heaven forbid he had to prepare his own plate.

"I'd better go," Tammy said, ruffling his hair. Dabney didn't duck away. "If you want to talk later, I'm here."

"You'd talk to me?" Dabney asked. "After all the things I've said to you over the years?"

She smiled before she kissed his soft cheek. "I suppose you have to dump on somebody, Dabney. Everybody dumps on you."

Dabney considered her words. Before she closed his door, he said, "I might just do that."

"You know where to find me," she said.

Dabney jumped when his iPhone rang. Dread enclosed his heart. *Jesus, not Hiram!* he thought.

He prayed the farmer wasn't calling him to work. He wasn't due at the farm until Sunday. He didn't want to go there before then. The next time the farmer touched him, he was going to snap like a toothpick. He'd had enough. He waited for the caller ID to tell him who it was. The answer pleased him.

He really called me, Dabney thought. "Hello?"

Jeremy said, "Hey. Are you busy?"

Dabney snorted, "Wait, let me check my calendar." He paused to see if Jeremy got the joke. Jeremy patiently waited for him to check. He sighed, "No, I'm not busy."

"Do you want to go to the carnival at Johnson Memorial?" Jeremy asked. He was glad Dabney's calendar was open.

Dabney lay back on his bed. *An invitation? Hmm...* "I don't know. Who else is going?"

Jeremy paused. He appeared to be moving to another room. "Well, me and Craig," he began. He took a breath and said, "Max, Ricardo, Sandy, and Derek Mellon."

Dabney sat up. "Derek?" His nose twinged a little.

"I knew you wouldn't be too keen on that," Jeremy said. "Just so you know, I talked to him already. He doesn't want to fight with you anymore. Did you hear about Dan?"

Dabney nodded to the phone. "I heard. Too bad about that." He added, "I don't want to fight either." He meant it. "Chris is working, huh?"

"He is, yeah, but I know he wants to talk to you," Jeremy replied. He bit his tongue. He didn't want to let Chris' feelings for Dabney slip.

"I want to talk to him, too," Dabney said. "I was a total dick at the pond. I want to apologize to him personally."

"Seriously, Dabs?"

"I'm serious. It was a dick move and Chris didn't deserve it. You were right about what you said at the bus stop. It was common and low."

"Is that the only reason you want to apologize?" Jeremy asked.

Dabney was taken aback. "No, actually," he replied. "To be honest, it's bothering me that I might have hurt Chris."

Jeremy's mouth dropped open.

"I want him to know that wasn't my intention. I was being an ass. It's not going to happen again."

"I'm sure Chris will forgive you," Jeremy said. He held his hand on his chest. *Good God! Am I hearing this right?*

"I hope so," Dabney said. "There's something... sincere about Chris. I hope I didn't screw things up with him."

"Dude, that's not possible with my brother."

Dabney asked, "Where's the carnival again?"

"It's at the hospital. We're going, and then everyone's crashing here. You can spend the night, too, if you want."

Dabney thought about that. *Spend the night at McKee's? I never spent the night at anyone's house before except Hiram's. Is that wise? What's*

James Christopher

going to happen? Sandy Sturgess doesn't like me. Still, I don't want them to think I'm afraid. Maybe Chris and I could talk? That would be cool.

"I guess," Dabney said. "Where will I sleep?"

"My room. Max, Ricardo, and Sandy can crash with Chris. He's working in the morning, too, so he'll probably be asleep by the time we get back."

Dabney frowned. *No chance to talk tonight then.* "So… it's me, you, Craig, and Derek?"

"Yeah, if that's all right."

Dabney looked around his room. It seemed empty all of a sudden. *Am I ready for this?* he wondered.

He'd spent a long time treating people like trash. They seemed awfully willing to open up to him without a whole lot of effort on his part. Did they notice something different about him, too? When Dabney opened the door and his father knocked him across the room, was it the final nail in the coffin of who he used to be? He thought maybe everything had changed in that split second. He didn't want them to think he was afraid, but Dabney was scared to death.

Am I making friends with these guys?

"It's all right," Dabney finally said. He asked, "You know what, McKee?"

"What?" Jeremy asked.

"I never would've done the same for you." He regretted saying that the moment the words were out of his mouth, but he felt compelled. "I never would've been nice to you."

Jeremy laughed. "Yeah, I know," he replied. "Can you really be an ass forever? Don't answer that. Things change, dude. We'll be by in about twenty minutes."

"I'll be ready," he said, and hung up.

Dabney stared at the phone for a while. Walking out the door was the beginning of something new. It was strange, but not as strange as Ms. Adler. He still couldn't say her name no matter how hard he tried. She wouldn't let him. Dabney was scared over what happened there. Is that what was changing him? Fear? He had never been afraid of so many things at once. He was never fearful at all except when he was at the farm, only then it was more like terror.

Dabney showered. He dressed in jeans, a white Tommy Hilfiger shirt, and his Balenciaga sneakers that Tammy had washed the blood out of. He packed an overnight bag with probably too much stuff. He stopped when he went to put a roll of toilet paper in there. He assumed the McKees had that part covered. He felt stupid. He had zero experience in the *spend the night with friends* department. He shut off his lights and stepped into the hallway with his bag on his shoulder. There was no turning back now. He wondered if they planned on dragging him outside and kicking the crap out of him. He hoped not. He'd been slapped around enough this week. Dabney turned. His father was standing in the hallway waiting for him.

"I heard you on the phone," Jerry scowled, crossing his arms. "Where do you think you're going?"

"I'm spending the night with my friends," Dabney replied. *Friends? I don't think I've ever said that word before.*

"Who might that be?" Jerry asked.

Dabney's iPhone rarely rang. When it did and he was near, Jerry always eavesdropped. He'd hoped it was the farmer.

Jerry thought, *Dabney should spend some more time there. Anywhere but here would be nice...*

"Jeremy McKee," Dabney replied.

... except there!

Jerry seemed uncomfortable. "Not tonight you're not," he said. He grabbed Dabney by the arm. "You're going back to your room."

Dabney yanked his arm away. They stood in the hall, glaring at each other.

"If you think you can cause trouble for me with McKee's father, think again," Jerry said. He thought about Sandra Dougan and he cringed. *Millionaire Industrialist Beats His Son!* "You try to screw with me, and I'll leave you out in the cold."

"You know what?" Dabney asked, pulling his overnight bag tighter to his shoulder. "I've been out in the cold all of my life." He headed toward the stairs. "It's actually warming up a little."

Dabney took the stairs down two at a time.

*　　*　　*

Ms. Adler looked up from her desk. She'd been examining data printouts when she detected something odd from the minds nearby. At close proximity, thoughts were impossible to block. She had heard the Copelands without even trying for decades. It was torture. They didn't have issues, they had subscriptions – to codependency, depression, arrogance. She endured it because her plans were delicate. They needed to be nurtured and protected. If anything was amiss, any suspicions about her or Hiram, the Copelands would know about it first. She spent too many years preparing for what was finally reaching fruition. Nothing could be allowed to stand in her way, yet these thoughts she sensed concerned her. Something had changed. A previously disregarded factor was in play. It was an unknown. Ms. Adler didn't like unknowns. Dabney Copeland was an unknown.

"Computer?" she asked, leaning back in her chair.

Behind her, the valves were open and the liquid she had collected was slowly dripping into a large beaker containing a slimy black ooze. The ooze moved and twitched as if it were alive. Chemicals bubbled and flowed mixing with it. Its color deepened with each drop, becoming blacker. It glowed with a faint midnight blue light. Coincidentally, the white rat was gone.

"Status report."

"Yes, Dr. Adler," the computer replied. **"Serum *Bremen One* formation: On schedule. Analysis of primary mixture complete. 110% potency. All systems..."**

"Pause," Ms. Adler said, looking at the mixture. *It is only a quarter of the way finished. How could it...?* "Explain percentage? Should it not be 25%?"

"Working... standby." The computer flashed an analysis routine on the monitor. It beeped upon completion. **"Explanation unknown. Data suggests sample: Frank Kyle Garrison is the cause."**

"Explain."

"Unknown," the computer replied. **"Potency of sample exceeds established parameters."**

"Indeed?" Ms. Adler remarked. She eyed Frank's sample with suspicion. *Could it be his drug use?* She grew nervous. *His blood screening revealed a plethora of chemical substances – THC, Ecstasy, LSD.* "Is there a chance it could contaminate the mixture?"

"Unknown. Insufficient data."

"Theorize," she commanded. "I need an answer."

"Searching theoretical..."

There cannot be a problem when I am so close! If I must help Hiram murder every child in this town, this ends! I swear, this...!

"Complete," the computer said. **"Indications suggest an increase of psionic potential to the fourth power."**

"You must be joking!" Ms. Adler cried. She leaned forward and examined the data. Her mind raced as she double checked every calculation the computer had made. "Lieber Gott!"

The fourth power? This is incredible! Her mouth watered in anticipation. *This is more power than the world has seen since Creation!*

Ms. Adler stood up and grabbed her keys. "Continue the process," she commanded and headed upstairs. "Log into the computer system at Aldujara Trucking in Hinesville, Georgia. Alter the Mike's Market delivery time to 8:00 a.m. Friday."

"Confirmed."

Ms. Adler's thoughts returned to Dabney. *He is involving himself with Jeremy and Craig. This needs to be watched. Dabney must not detract their attention from one another. He might require removal from the equation. No one can be allowed to interfere at this stage.* Her eyes narrowed. *No one.*

*　　*　　*

Dabney's mouth fell open when Virginia's Camaro pulled into the estate's circle driveway. She drove to where he was waiting on the porch. He had no idea how she managed to get so many people into her car, but it was packed.

Dabney wasn't sure how to proceed. *Where am I going to sit?* he wondered. *Do they call being crowded like that fun?*

Sandy glared at him from the front seat.

Dabney sighed. *If looks could kill, I'd be flat on the ground holding a lily.*

Sandy looked suspicious. Dabney didn't blame him. He would've felt the same way. How could Sturgess know how he felt? He had no idea where his life was taking him. He had been swept up in the tide. It was all he could do to keep from drowning.

Jeremy elbowed Derek who was next to him in the back seat. He suggested he climb into the hatchback with Ricardo. Derek nodded and slipped over the seat. Ricardo groaned, but made room. Max squeezed over by the passenger window. Craig moved in next to him.

Jeremy tugged on his mother's seat. "Let me out," he said, pushing on the door.

Virginia opened it. "Is everything okay?" she asked. She looked at Dabney, concerned. *He looks like a deer in headlights. Derek did a number on him, the poor kid.*

"I think he's scared," Jeremy whispered, climbing out.

"Good," Sandy said.

"Sandy!" Virginia gasped. She looked at him with disapproval.

"I'm sorry, Virginia," Sandy said, shaking his head. "You don't know him like I do."

"I know Jeremy," Virginia replied. "If he thinks Dabney's redeemable, I'm not going to argue."

"It'll be cool," Max insisted, but he crossed his fingers. "I don't know what's up with him, but whatever freaked him out yesterday did something to his head. He even let Ricardo…"

"Max!" Ricardo cried, reaching over from the back and covering his brother's mouth. "Don't do it. I swear, brother or no brother, I'll strangle you!"

Max smiled. *I'm going to tell the whole world before this is over. I have to. It's just too funny! I have the picture to prove it!*

Jeremy held his hand out and took Dabney's bag. "Are you okay?" he asked.

Dabney shook his head. He looked at Sandy, nervously. "Sturgess looks mad."

Jeremy smiled. "He is."

Dabney eyed him, strangely. "That doesn't bother you?" he asked.

"Why should it?" Jeremy replied. "Sandy doesn't need a reason to be mad. He's always mad about something."

"You're willing to risk alienating your friends for me?" Dabney asked. "You're something else."

"Everyone gets a chance, Dabney," Jeremy said. "Even you." He shifted his weight. Dabney's bag was heavy. "Why are you so different?"

Dabney shrugged. "I don't know," he said. "Maybe I'm tired of all the conflict."

"Fair enough," Jeremy said. "For now. Let's go, huh? Everybody's waiting."

Dabney followed Jeremy strategically staying out of Sandy's line of sight. He felt nervous enough without Sturgess making it worse. Jeremy opened the car door and handed his mother the bag. Virginia took it and said, "Oof!" as she lifted it over her legs. She put it between her and Sandy. Sandy looked at the bag, puzzled. He grabbed the handle and tested the weight.

"Jeeze, Copeland," Sandy said. "Moving in?"

Dabney took it in stride. "I might." He looked at Virginia and asked, "Can you cook?"

She smiled. "If God needed one, he would call me, sweetheart."

"You've got yourself another kid."

Virginia pulled him over and kissed his cheek. She did her best to ignore his bruises. "You're sweet."

Dabney blushed. He couldn't believe it, but he did.

"Like a rattlesnake," Sandy frowned.

Jeremy climbed into the back. He reached over and cuffed Sandy. "Lay off him, Sanford," he said. "He hasn't done anything to you."

"Yet," Sandy said. He ducked under another swipe.

Dabney got in next to the driver's side window. Four people in the back seat of the Camaro made for a tight fit. He felt tense. He didn't want anyone touching him. He thought if he got too comfortable, he might seem needy, or something. Jeremy rested his leg against Dabney's and put his arm across his shoulder. Dabney shook his head, but let him.

"This is going to be great!" Jeremy exclaimed. He smiled at Dabney.

Dabney chuckled.

"What's so funny?" Craig asked. He wanted to be let in on the joke.

"This is so different than riding with my family," Dabney said. "You don't touch the person next to you. We're practically sitting on top of each other."

Derek flipped over the seat from the hatchback. He landed laying across them with his head in Dabney's lap. He looked up.

"This is sitting on top of someone," Derek said. He grinned.

Dabney looked at him like he was crazy. "You know something, Mellon?" he asked, feigning anger.

"What?" Derek asked. He cringed. *I hope I didn't make him mad. I promised Jeremy no confrontations.*

"You have a killer right cross," Dabney replied, rubbing his nose. "My face is killing me."

Everyone laughed, including Dabney. Derek looked closely at Dabney's face and frowned. He felt guilty. He touched Dabney's bruised cheek and winced like it hurt him.

"I'm sorry, Dabney. I feel bad about hitting you."

Dabney raised an eyebrow. He nodded. "It's okay, Derek," he said. "I asked for it. It was a wakeup call." He sighed. "I'm sorry about Dan."

Derek held his hand up. "Friends?" he asked.

Dabney gripped it. "You're number two."

"Two?"

"Two friends," Dabney said. "First Jeremy and now you. I'm on a roll."

"Hey!" Max interjected. "What am I? Chopped liver?"

"What about me?" Craig asked, leaning over Jeremy. "Can we be friends, too?"

"God, Dougan," Dabney said, rolling his eyes. "I've treated you like crap forever. Why would you want to be my friend?"

Craig shrugged. "I have no idea."

Dabney smiled and held out his hand. "Fair enough."

Ricardo's hand appeared above him. Dabney looked back and shook it. When he let go, all eyes were on Sandy who deliberately looked away.

"Sandy?" Virginia asked.

Sandy looked at Dabney. He shook his head and motioned for him to come closer. Dabney was apprehensive, but leaned over Derek. Sandy grabbed his face a planted a sloppy kiss right on his lips.

Dabney cried, "Oh, *yuck!*" and fell back into his seat. He wiped his lips with the backs of his hands. "Sturgess germs!"

The boys laughed hard. Derek climbed back into the hatch beet red.

Sandy looked at Virginia and motioned at the road. "Let's go before I realize what I'm doing."

"You don't fool me," Virginia whispered. "You were testing him."

"I don't trust him... yet."

Virginia tore out of the drive. She turned up the music and headed toward Milliken Road. She was bringing them to Johnson Memorial Hospital. Susan was picking them up. They had agreed the carnival was a good idea. Dan was dead. There was nothing they could do to change that. The boys needed something to take their minds off of how much everyone was hurting.

Susan was out of sorts when Virginia talked to her about the carnival. She said Ian would want to go, too. Virginia had to remind her that Ian was at camp. It was the oddest thing. Susan nearly started crying. It was barely noticeable except to Virginia. Nothing escaped her, like with Jeremy and Craig. She wasn't sure what was going on, but they were fidgety. They kept finishing each other's sentences, scratching at the same time, wanting the same food. It was strange. Virginia glanced up to see if it was a full moon.

Dabney caught her motion in the side view mirror. "It's not a full moon," he smirked. "I already checked."

No one paid any attention to the black Mercedes-Benz following them.

* * *

The Downing Carnival

It didn't take long to get to the carnival. Milliken Road led right into Stafford. They arrived there in minutes. Craig was glad. He didn't mind togetherness, but he felt squished. Max was very particular about how much room he was going to have. That left one seat for him, Jeremy, and Dabney to share. Their three butts together were a bit bigger than that. Virginia pulled over near the ticket booth. She put the Camaro in park and asked if anyone needed any money.

Dabney was startled. He felt his back pocket for his wallet. *Oh, I don't believe this!* he thought. He looked at Virginia with big doe eyes.

"A little short?" she asked. She dug into her purse, pulled out a twenty, and handed it to him. "You can pay me back later."

Sandy smiled, widely.

Dabney scowled. "Oh, be quiet, Sturgess."

"Who me?" Sandy asked. "What did I say?" He smiled again.

Dabney thanked Virginia and climbed out of the car. Sandy, Max, Ricardo, and Derek headed straight for the rides. Jeremy, Craig, and Dabney stood by the entrance waving goodbye. Dabney marveled at the number of people present. He looked at the games of chance. The rides seemed fun, but he wasn't ready to stand in a line. Craig leaned over and whispered something into Jeremy's ear.

Jeremy smiled. "Craig doesn't think you've ever been to a carnival before."

Craig snickered.

Dabney rolled his eyes. "That's absurd, Dougan. I watch *Wheel of Fortune* all the time." He walked toward the games of chance. They followed him laughing.

Jeremy and Craig let Dabney take the lead. They got a kick out of watching him. He moved from booth to booth, evaluating the players, carefully. He stopped at the wheel and spotted a large werewolf stuffed animal. His eyes grew three times their normal size.

"I want that!" Dabney smiled, looking at Jeremy and Craig.

Craig gestured toward the number board. "Pick a number."

Dabney seemed puzzled. He held out his twenty and waved it around over the board. He looked at Jeremy, looked at the board, looked at Craig, looked at the board... and finally threw his hands up.

"What number do I pick?" Dabney asked.

"Fourteen," Jeremy and Craig replied. They looked at each other.

Dabney nodded, "Okay, fourteen it is." He slapped down the twenty.

Jeremy zipped over and picked it up. He looked at the burly man behind the counter and said, "My friend wants change."

The burly man scowled and broke the twenty.

Jeremy handed the money to Dabney. "One dollar, Dabs," he said. "You want to lose it all in one shot?"

Dabney shook his head. The money disappeared into his pocket.

"Any more bets?" the burly man asked, looking into the crowd. He was about to spin the wheel when a small albino boy with platinum blonde hair walked in front of Dabney. He cleared his throat.

"Seventeen, please," the boy smiled, placing a dollar on the number. His eyes were crystal blue.

The burly man leaned over and scowled at him. "Mickey," he said, "why do you have to pick on my booth?"

Mickey smiled. "Yours is the easiest."

Jeremy, Craig, and Dabney observed the boy as he put his hands behind his back and patiently waited. His skin was so white, Jeremy thought it looked see-through. The blue-green veins in his arms were clearly defined.

Ms. Adler was three yards behind them. She watched with growing interest. She attempted to probe Mickey's mind, but gasped when she failed. Her anger rose. No one ever resisted her mind reading ability before.

What makes this child so special? she wondered.

The crowd cheered as the number seventeen came up. Mickey selected the werewolf and handed it to Dabney.

Ms. Adler scowled.

"Here," Mickey said. "You can have it."

Dabney was shocked. "Why *thank you!*" he exclaimed, examining the werewolf. He looked down at Mickey and asked, "Why would you do that for me?"

Mickey replied, "You looked like you needed someone to do something nice for you."

Dabney didn't know what to say. *Is everybody like this?*

Craig held his hand out. "Craig Dougan."

Mickey shook it once hard. He grinned. It was a perfectly innocent expression.

Craig thought, *He should have a halo, or something.*

"Mickey Downing," Mickey replied. He met Dabney and Jeremy in that order. "I work here."

"At the hospital?" Jeremy asked.

Craig and Dabney looked at him.

Dabney checked his forehead for a fever.

"What?" Jeremy asked.

Craig leaned over to Dabney and whispered, "Has your father thought about mining rights to Jeremy's head?"

Dabney chuckled.

"No, not the hospital," Mickey replied. "The carnival. My parents own it. My grandmother's the fortune teller."

"Really?" all three boys asked.

"Sure. Want to see?"

The boys looked at each other.

"Lead the way," Jeremy said.

Mickey walked toward the hospital.

Ms. Adler weaved through the crowd behind them. *It is not supposed to be this way!* she thought. *Dabney is more of a distraction than he is worth! Jeremy and Craig need to stay focused on each other, but instead they are worried about making him happy!*

They cut through the concessions area. The fried dough vendor hypnotized the boys. They bought four pieces. Jeremy handed one to Mickey who blushed.

"You're nice," he said, taking a bite.

Mickey continued toward a row of tents set back from the rest of the carnival. One of them had the world's smallest horse in it. Craig tried to peek, but a very short woman with a mean look stopped him. She told him he needed to pay his dollar like everyone else. Craig did and went inside to look. The boys waited for him. When he came out, he shook his head.

"That was weird," Craig said. "It's so tiny."

Mickey said, "You should see it when it gets loose. They have a heck of a time catching it. It's fast!"

They passed the next tent which was full of leather belts, buckles, and drug paraphernalia. Dabney turned his nose up and kept walking. He despised drugs. They were the ultimate weakness. Jeremy and Craig agreed with him. The last tent in the row had hay spread all over the pavement. There was a woman bent over feeding a small goat. Mickey jumped over the rope and pulled on her skirt. The boys stood next to a sign that read:

Madame Ezmerelda — Advice, Past Lives, and Future.

"Yes, darling?" she smiled, kissing Mickey's cheek.

Mickey gestured with his head toward the boys. "They're here," he whispered.

Ezmerelda looked over Mickey's shoulder. Her expression was concerned, but it melted quickly. A broad smile replaced it. She wore a colorful flowing gown. She had a scarf tied around her head and looked like a Gypsy. She had two-dozen bracelets on her wrists at least. Jeremy looked at Mickey. He guessed he was maybe eleven. Mickey informed him he was ten. Ezmerelda looked eighty if she was a day.

"Are you a real Gypsy?" Jeremy asked.

Ezmerelda replied, "I am, yes." She sounded sad. "The Nazi's weren't fond of the Romani. Did you know that?" They sensed her hatred for the Nazis. They also heard her accent.

"Are you from Germany?" Craig asked.

"Once," Ezmerelda replied, "but that was a long time ago."

Mickey went into the tent and came out with three folding chairs. The boys each took one and sat down. Dabney put his werewolf on his lap. He looked around, confused. Ezmerelda asked him if something was wrong.

"I was looking for your crystal ball," Dabney sheepishly replied.

Ezmerelda laughed, "I don't have one anymore, Dabney. Too bothersome to travel with."

"Oh," Dabney nodded. He gasped, *"Wait!* How do you know my name?"

She smiled. "I'm the fortune teller, aren't I?" She looked at the boys and asked, "Who wants to go first?"

Dabney and Jeremy pointed at Craig.

"Gee, thanks!" Craig cried, crossing his arms. "She's probably going to tell me I'll be bald, or something."

Ezmerelda shook her head. "No, Craig. You won't be bald." She looked at Jeremy. He touched his hair, self-consciously. "Jeremy's brother will be, like his father."

Whew! Jeremy thought. *Sucks to be you, Chris!*

Ezmerelda walked around them, observing. She moved past Jeremy to Craig. She stood over him and put her hands on his shoulders. She closed her eyes and lowered her head. After a moment, she leaned down by his ear.

"Your father won't beat you for very much longer," Ezmerelda whispered. Craig stiffened. He tried to turn, but she held him fast. "Not yet, Craig. You have an important part to play in this little drama. You have to be strong. Can you remember that? *You must be strong. Jeremy needs your strength."*

She moved to Jeremy next. He was suddenly very nervous. She squeezed his shoulders.

"You are the chosen one," Ezmerelda whispered, into his ear.

Dabney strained to hear her, but couldn't over the din of the carnival.

"You must not despair. You must fight even when you can't find a reason to anymore. Craig. *Remember Craig. He is your salvation. The alternative is damnation."*

Dabney was last. He could tell by the haunted looks from Jeremy and Craig that he wasn't going to like this. She took his shoulders. Her hands were like ice through his shirt. He clutched his werewolf.

"You represent chaos in a planned order of events," Ezmerelda whispered. "There is love in your future, a powerful love like you have never known, but you must take care. The sins of the farmer are greater than you imagine. *Stay with the McKees and Craig. You are in grave danger if you get separated.*"

Dabney's mouth dropped open.

Ezmerelda walked away without saying another word. She rubbed her temples as if in pain. Mickey came up to the boys and shook his head. His expression was concerned.

"She's never wrong," Mickey said. He gave them a little wave. "Be seeing you."

Mickey followed his grandmother into the tent. Jeremy, Craig, and Dabney walked away feeling disoriented. They convinced themselves it was a trick. Craig suggested they ride some rides. Dabney was all for that. His shoulders were still frozen where she'd touched him.

In the fortune teller's tent, Mickey brought his grandmother some tea.

Ezmerelda smiled, weakly.

"I wish we could do more," Mickey said.

Ezmerelda shook her head. "You cannot tamper with fate. My mother did that once and paid the ultimate price." She patted his cheek. "When the time comes, my love. When the time comes."

Mickey scowled, looking through the door flap. "She's here," he said.

Ezmerelda nodded. "I know. I can feel her."

Mickey peered outside.

Ms. Adler was standing beyond their tent area, glaring at him. *"Who are you?"* her mind-voice asked, probing him. She winced in pain as her words were reflected back at her. Her eyes filled with surprise, and then outrage. *Be careful, child! You have no idea what you are fooling with!*

"Don't I?" Mickey asked. He pulled the flap open.

Ezmerelda's eyes glowed with a deep midnight blue light.

Ms. Adler took a step back.

"Go away," Mickey said. "You can't hurt me."

"This is not possible!" Ms. Adler cried.

Ezmerelda grimaced. *"Did you think you would never see me again, Herr Doktor?"* She stepped boldly forward. *"Let us end this right now!"*

Ms. Adler gasped, *"You!"* She stumbled backward. She felt the beginning of a psychic assault claw into her mind. The power was on par with her own. *No!* she desperately thought. *Not when I am so close!* She turned away and fled toward the parking lot. "This is not over!" she cried. "You cannot stop me!"

Ms. Adler disappeared into the crowd.

"No, it isn't over," Ezmerelda whispered, her eyes dimming. "Heaven help us all." She fell into her chair breathing heavily.

"Nice bluff, grandma," Mickey whispered, his forehead creased with worry. "You should've held back. You're weak from using the sight."

"We… can't risk…," Ezmerelda struggled. She swallowed hard. "I'm nowhere near strong enough… I can't… stop…"

"Rest, grandma," Mickey said. "Sometimes all we can do is sit back and watch no matter how much it hurts."

"I taught… you that," Ezmerelda said, and she fell asleep.

Mickey held her hand to his face and closed his eyes. "Yes, you did," he whispered. "That, and a whole lot more."

*　　*　　*

By the time Chris finished the last group of cows, he was livid. He washed the milking parlor trying to calm down.

If Hiram did anything to Teddy, I'll never forgive myself for not turning him in.

Chris threw the hose onto the floor and stormed over to the time clock. He clocked out, grabbed Teddy's time card, and brought it with him to the trailer. He could see Hiram through the window watching TV. Chris threw the door open. He didn't notice Todd's bike parked next to the propane tanks.

"Teddy's working here?" Chris asked. His eyes searched Hiram's face. He waved Teddy's time card in front of him.

"He was part-time help, but now he's taking Henry's place," Hiram replied. "Henry quit without notice. I needed a replacement."

Chris shook his head. He never talked to Henry about Hiram. He was older. Chris figured he could handle the farmer. He hoped that wasn't a mistake. And Teddy?

Something fishy is going on. Hiram has to know Teddy's dad is a cop. He isn't that stupid, is he?

"Just remember what I told you a year ago, old man," Chris warned, dropping the time card on the floor. "You molested me. If you touch another kid, you're history." He walked away before Hiram could answer. If that wasn't clear enough, Chris didn't know what was.

Hiram watched through the window as Chris closed up the barn and rode away on his bike. There was no doubt in the farmer's mind that his death would bring him more pleasure than any other. The thought made his hands shake. It wouldn't happen quickly either. Chris McKee would be the template for pain by the time Hiram was through.

Todd was lying in the guest room staring up at the ceiling. *Jesus, Chris, too?* he wondered. He felt nauseous. *How many kids has Hiram done this to?*

He shut his eyes when Hiram came down the hall. He peered inside the room. Todd's sleeping performance was worthy of an Academy Award.

*   *   *

It was after midnight when Susan dropped the boys off at the McKees'. Dabney was talking up a storm about what a great time he'd had. No one could get a word in edgewise for the first ten minutes of the ride home. He even admitted he had never been to a carnival before. The rides were sweet! Jeremy said if he liked that one, he would love the Brooklyn Fair. It was in August. They had a lot of cool stuff and live bands, too. Dabney thought that was a fantastic idea. He asked if he could go. Jeremy said he could go with them anywhere he wanted. Dabney realized it was an open invitation and grinned. He told them he never knew having fun could be so much... well, *fun!* He held his werewolf close. He felt it signified his new beginning. This was exactly what it was, too. He knew that without question, just like he knew he had to clear the air with Chris. Dabney was going to do that the moment he saw him.

They said hello to Thomas and Virginia who had waited up for them. Virginia had been nervous the second she left the carnival because of Dan. It was a passing thing and she knew that, but she couldn't help it. Thomas needed to see Dabney Copeland hanging around with his son. It was no secret he intimidated Jerry. The Copeland's lawyer was a friend of his. They played golf together a lot and had told him so. Thomas also wanted to see Dabney's face. He didn't believe Derek could do the damage Virginia described. Thomas' eyebrows shot up when he saw how wrong he was. Dabney looked terrible. Thomas shook his hand in the front hall. He had a good grip.

Chris had to work in the morning, so he was already asleep as expected. Dabney was disappointed. He hoped to talk to Chris tonight. Max got on Chris' computer. Ricardo and Sandy watched as he cruised the world looking for girls to chat with. Virginia allowed Jeremy to bring the PlayStation upstairs so she and Thomas could have the living room to themselves. They were watching James Cameron's *Titanic.*

Derek was sitting cross-legged on the floor in his underwear playing House of the Dead Overkill. Dabney went to shower. The excitement of tonight had been so intense, he needed a few minutes to relax. He sat his werewolf in Jeremy's desk chair. Craig was lying on the bed next to Jeremy brooding that Derek was in puberty already and yet he was younger. It didn't seem fair, although his orange pubic hair made Craig snicker.

Carrot top is carrot crotch, too! That's hilarious! But seriously, it's so unfair. Am I going to be a little kid forever? Derek's a year younger than me!

"Big deal," Jeremy's voice said, appearing inside Craig's head.

Craig jumped. He stared at Jeremy, wide-eyed. He heard his friend talking, but his lips weren't moving!

Then he heard, *"Haven't I said puberty isn't all it's cracked up to be? Besides the zits and the itchy pubes, there's that voice cracking crap. It's more annoying than anything else. Of course, it might help Craig with that little boy look he's got going on."*

"Oh, thanks, Jeremy!" Craig cried.

Jeremy looked at him, oddly. His eyes widened. "You heard me!?"

Derek paused the game and glanced back over his shoulder. He had a puzzled look on his face.

Craig and Jeremy looked at each other, and then at Derek. "Play the game!" they cried.

Derek said, "You guys are getting weird."

"Let's be careful," Jeremy thought, sternly.

Craig nodded. *"This is too much, Jeremy!"* he cried. *"We have to tell somebody!"*

"Like who, Craig?" Jeremy asked. He cringed.

"Smooth move, Ex-Lax!" Craig thought, crossing his arms. *"Why not just tell Derek everything?"*

"Fine!" Jeremy exclaimed, leaning over Craig. "Derek! What if I told you Craig and I can hear each other's thoughts?"

"I'd say you weren't really wrestling," Derek replied.

They groaned.

"See?" Jeremy thought. *"Nobody's going to think anything different than him."*

"All right," Craig thought, holding up his hand. *"I give. What are we going to do?"*

Jeremy shrugged. *"It's not like I can read your mind. I just hear what you're thinking."*

Craig nodded. *"Same here."*

"Well, it's obvious something's happened to us," Jeremy thought. *"We just have to figure out what that was."*

"How are we going to do that?" Craig asked, and covered his mouth.

Jeremy rolled his eyes.

"I'm tired," Derek yawned, flipping the game and the TV off. "Can we go to bed?"

"You can go to floor anytime you want," Jeremy said.

Derek ignored him and slapped Craig on the thigh. "Move over," he nodded.

Craig slid pushing Jeremy to the wall. Derek nestled in despite the protests for more room. He flipped off the lamp on the night table. Jeremy and Craig lay facing each other. They tried to fill themselves with outrage, but laughed instead. Derek was pressed against Craig. His skin felt warm and soft. Jeremy thought that was hilarious. Derek began to sob after a minute, and their hearts sank. Craig pulled him into the middle between them. They said nothing. For Derek, just being close to someone was enough. He fell asleep with his face against Craig's chest as his friends held him.

Jeremy said, "Looks like he's your baby tonight."

Craig pursed his lips.

Dabney came back from his shower wrapped in a towel. He sat on the edge of the bed and looked at the other boys. He shook his head.

"What?" Jeremy asked.

Dabney replied, "I was just thinking how crowded the bed's going to be." He dropped his towel and put on his underwear. He squeezed in-between Jeremy and the wall.

Jeremy looked at him like he was crazy.

"You don't think I'm sleeping on the floor, do you?" Dabney asked. He rolled over, leaned back against Jeremy, and shut his eyes. "Good thing this is a double bed, huh?" he yawned. He was asleep shortly after, snoring lightly.

Now it was Craig's turn to giggle. Dabney's skin was just as warm and soft as Derek's.

"Oh, shut up."

Jeremy and Craig lay there for a while before they drifted off. Their thoughts reached out and entwined as they got closer to sleep. Their minds flowed like Mercury, merging. They let it happen. They weren't afraid. They were together as if it was meant to be that way. Thinking words became unnecessary. They had hundreds of conversations in the space of a few minutes. They shared everything, their secrets, their dreams, hopes, and their fears. The good and the bad. They hid nothing. They were more than friends now. They were each other. They would never be lonely again. They matched like puzzle pieces, each filling the missing spaces in the other.

They slept apart in body, but in mind they were one person. Jeremy lived Craig's life from the beginning, every harsh word, every beating. Craig's agony and despair became one with him forever. Craig did the same. Opposed to Jeremy's sorrow, Craig knew only anger. He saw in Jeremy what his life should have been. He felt Jeremy's love. Jeremy felt his in return. They made a pact as they fell asleep. They promised no one would ever hurt them again.

No one. Ever.

*   *   *

A few hours later, Chris slipped down the hallway as quietly as he could leaving for work. He paused outside Jeremy's door and looked inside. He nodded at the four boys in Jeremy's bed and smiled. Dabney had made it through the night. He was glad about that. He had his doubts with Sanford going. He was about to leave when he noticed that Dabney was awake and looking at him. He raised his hand and gave him a half-wave.

Dabney returned it sitting up. His eyes bored into Chris' searching for what he had seen on the bus Monday. *It's still there,* he thought. He smiled.

Chris returned the smile and sat on the edge of the bed. Dabney offered his hand. Chris took it.

Dabney added his other hand, too, and squeezed. "I want to say how sorry I am for what happened at the pond." He frowned. "I was a total dick and I deserved to get a beat down from Derek."

Chris brought his free hand to Dabney's face. He was bruised beneath his freckled cheeks. He seemed so fragile just then. Chris had never seen Dabney like this, so unguarded and vulnerable. He thought he might want to hold him for a while and show him everything was okay. He wanted to tell him he wasn't alone anymore. He hadn't realized it, but every one of those thoughts was communicating perfectly through his expression.

Dabney held Chris' hand to his face. The Gypsy's words came back to him in a flash of realization.

"There is love in your future, a powerful love like you have never known..."

Dabney was startled. He suddenly understood exactly what he'd been seeing in Chris' eyes. *Oh, my God,* he thought, holding Chris' gaze. *Is this really happening?*

"Chris, I...," Dabney began.

Chris pulled him close until their foreheads touched.

Dabney closed his eyes. For the first time in his life, he dropped every one of his defenses, and allowed his feelings to flow free.

Chris whispered, "It's all right, Dabs. I forgive you. I promise."

He reached out and they embraced. It was a warm hug filled with what they were both feeling at that moment. It was the first time they had consciously realized and acknowledged what was happening. Their feelings were indeed mutual. They drew back, looked at one another, and smiled.

Chris was about to say something, but then he looked past Dabney. Dabney turned to see Jeremy, Craig, and Derek staring at them.

Chris and Dabney lowered their eyes and smiled.

Derek gasped, "Seriously!?"

Jeremy elbowed Craig. "You saw that, right?"

Craig nodded and lay back down. "True love," he muttered. He closed his eyes.

Derek rolled his and threw the covers over his head. "I didn't see anything!" he cried, his words muffled by the blanket.

Jeremy smiled and lay down, too. "You so saw it."

"Not listening!"

"Unbelievable," Dabney smirked, shaking his head. He said, "My entire life changed today, Chris. I mean every aspect of it."

Chris patted his shoulder. "We should talk."

Dabney nodded. "A lot. We should talk a lot."

"Are you coming back tonight?"

Dabney replied, "If that's okay?"

Chris said, "It is, I swear. You can stay with me this time if you want."

"I look forward to it."

Chris ruffled his chocolate brown hair and disappeared down the stairs. Dabney lay back. Jeremy snuggled into him as everyone got comfortable. Dabney did, too. He felt warm and safe, he felt accepted and wanted, and as Jeremy sleepily put his arm around him and gave him a light squeeze, he felt loved.

"This is really happening," Dabney whispered. He closed his eyes and drifted back to sleep. He was smiling.

DAY FOUR
Thursday

"Counselor?" Judge McDaniel asked.

He was a heavyset man with a round face and a thick salt & pepper beard. His receding hairline was something he and Thomas joked about regularly. They met for monthly golf games when the weather was warm and for luncheons when it was cold. Impending baldness brought both of them a few chuckles. He stared at Thomas over his glasses.

"Is the youth in question present in this courtroom?"

Thomas cleared his throat and nodded, adjusting his tie. "Yes, he is, your Honor," he replied. He turned toward the first row of benches and motioned for Craig to come forward.

Craig looked at Jeremy who sat to his right. A flash of understanding passed between them. Craig stood up. The confidence he had when he marched up to Thomas at the breakfast table this morning and asked for his help was almost gone. Jeremy was feeding him more right now. He was giving back what Craig had given him. Thomas jumped on the chance to assist Craig and called in a favor. He telephoned the witnesses. They were in a Rockville courtroom three hours later. Jack was temporarily losing custody of Craig. It was the consensus it was the right place to start.

Craig didn't think anyone outside of his family would come to the hearing, but there were a lot of people standing behind him. He knew he wouldn't have gone through with this if it hadn't been for Jeremy's presence in his mind, yet it wasn't Jeremy's strength he felt. He realized it was his. It was the confidence Jeremy had lacked until the mind-link. Craig lacked the presence of mind to understand his father wouldn't get better without help. It was a trade of missing pieces. There were many others. This was the hardest thing Craig had ever done. He was glad he wasn't asked to relate the stories personally.

Judge McDaniel cleared the courtroom except for the people who had come to testify on Craig's behalf. He inched past Virginia. She patted him on the shoulder. They all did until he was standing at the table next to Thomas. Mike and Sandra had answered the call this morning. So had Lyle, Max, and Ricardo. Lyle was sitting on the edge of the bench with his arms crossed looking mean. Nancy was next to him. Lyle was called first, and then Max. Mike gave an emotional account of how many times he had seen his nephew with bruises.

Judge McDaniel stopped the hearing before Nancy spoke. He claimed to have heard enough. "Counselor?" he asked, glancing over the paperwork on his bench. "You're seeking temporary guardianship to be granted to Nancy O'Dell Dougan?"

"We are, your Honor," Thomas replied, placing a hand on Craig's shoulder. "We also request an Order of Protection. We ask the court to order Jack Wade Dougan evaluated for PTSD while attending treatment for substance abuse."

Judge McDaniel signed his name to the petition. "So ordered. I will refer the case to DCF. The father is unavailable?"

"He's presently incarcerated, your Honor," Thomas offered.

"See the clerk for your paperwork," Judge McDaniel said, standing up. "The court will stand in recess until one o'clock."

Whack!

Craig tugged on Thomas' jacket sleeve. He furrowed his brow as the judge left the courtroom. "That's it?" he asked. "He didn't even ask me anything."

Thomas replied, "There will be other people to do that, Craig. This was the easy part. DCF will notify your grandmother when they want to see you. You'll have all the questions you can handle then, believe me."

"Jeremy?" Craig thought, looking over toward him.

"I'm here, man," Jeremy thought back. *"You did good."*

"I didn't do anything, you mean!"

"You were here," Jeremy said. *"That's enough for now. C'mon, mom says we can leave. We have to get ready for the funeral."*

Nancy and Thomas went to see the clerk. She paid a small fee and a sheriff was assigned to serve the orders to Jack in his cell. He received them later in the day, another nail driven into the coffin of his sanity.

*   *   *

The Funeral

It was as if the entire town had come out for Dan Mellon's funeral. St. Peter's Church was standing room only as Father Fraleigh sadly read the service. Teddy Bigelow was the only altar boy. He turned the pages each time the priest winked at him. The Mellons were sitting together in the first pew directly in front of the long black casket. Cynthia quietly sobbed on her mother, Celia Beasley's, shoulder. Kevin was beside her fearing that his wife was near a nervous breakdown. He couldn't blame her. It was all so senseless. He called out in his mind, searching for Danny, but only silence answered. He felt an unnerving sense of impending doom. This wasn't over yet. It engulfed his heart in a shroud of despair.

Friends filled the pews and the aisles in a somber living mass surrounding the Mellons. They flowed out the doors into the street, parents, practically the entire high school, and all of the middle school kids. Some were here without adult escorts, drawn to the death of one of their own, their core belief in their immortality irrevocably shaken. They were standing next to something inconceivable just days before. Death was for old people. A child's life wasn't fragile. The organ played and the people sang out. The church shook with emotion. The faithful hoped that God would grant Dan eternal life.

Jeremy squirmed, uncomfortably. The starch in his shirt was making him itch. Craig was next to him itching, too.

Dabney was absent. He didn't want his bruises on display. He offered Derek his sincere condolences this morning before he returned home with his werewolf. Jeremy asked if he was taking Chris up on his offer to come back and spend another night. Dabney said he was without a doubt. There was a lot he needed to talk to Chris about. He said nothing to his father when he walked into the estate. Jerry ignored his silence, but glared at him and his werewolf with suspicion. When Tammy asked if he was attending the funeral, he spouted a resounding, "No!" before vanishing into his room. Jerry was elated Dabney had spared him the embarrassment of his weakling son sitting next to him.

Craig raised his arm at the same time Jeremy did. He was scratching the same spot on his body as Jeremy. Chris was sitting on the other side of Virginia next to his father, directly behind Derek. He eyeballed both of them, curiously.

"Will you stop itching?" Craig thought at Jeremy. They mimicked each other's scratching again. The service seemed to go on forever. *"You're driving me crazy!"*

"I can't help it, Craig!" Jeremy thought back. *"It's this stupid shirt!"*

Craig rolled his eyes.

Jeremy pinched the back of his hand.

Craig jumped. He glared at him, his eyes wide. *"Just wait, McKee!"* he thought angrily. *"Yours is coming!"*

"Oh!" Jeremy thought-cried. *"I'm scared!"*

Everyone sang the final hymn. Sandy looked across the aisle to Chris as Dan's coffin passed. Chris met his gaze and nodded, gesturing at Matt.

Matt caught the look between them as he walked with the other pallbearers. *Thanks a lot, guys,* he thought. *I already feel like a total dweeb.*

The congregation filed out behind the casket. Kevin walked in front of them with Cynthia, nearly having to carry her. Jeremy's gaze met Dr. Stone's as he stepped into the line. The doctor looked nervously away. Jeremy wondered what his problem was. Craig thought it was probably hard for all the parents with kids Dan's age. Jeremy agreed. His mother was undoubtedly wigging.

Dr. Stone filed in a few people behind the McKees. He was having a hard time taking his eyes off Jeremy. Every time he looked at him, he remembered how odd this week had been. Each morning he had gotten up and went into Sam's room to wake him for his run. Each morning he stood in the doorway overcome by an incredible feeling of loss. In the words of his youngest boy,

Steven, Dr. Stone was *bugging out*. It got worse throughout the service. The way Jeremy McKee and Craig Dougan kept scratching themselves at the same time in the same places? They were mimicking each other's movements perfectly. Dr. Stone walked outside into the sunlight and felt a chill as he watched Jeremy and Craig scratching their left ears in unison.

Keith Keroack reached over and pulled Chris out of the line. His expression denoted concern. Chris looked at him, puzzled. Keith cupped his mouth to Chris' ear and whispered something to him. Chris drew back, his face filled with surprise. Keith's face reflected sincerity. Chris nodded, slowly. He put his hand on Keith's shoulder.

"Thanks, man, seriously," Chris said. "Call me when you're not grounded. We can get together, or something."

"Sure," Keith replied. "I'm glad I finally got to say that. I haven't been able to message you. Mom's watching me like a hawk."

"It's cool, Keith."

Mona yanked Keith away. Chris got back in line with his family.

Jeremy asked, "What was that all about?"

Chris replied, "He wanted me to know he's still my friend no matter how many rumors Danielle starts. He said he doesn't care what Dan said either, and that he'd share a tent with me camping anytime I liked."

"Oh," Jeremy nodded. "Cool."

The graveside services were behind the church in the cemetery. The boys from the campout stood together hand in hand on the opposite side of the casket from the adults which included Hiram and Todd O'Connor. Todd was looking at Chris not with his usual arrogance, but with honest fear. He closed his eyes and looked down. Everyone hung their heads in prayer – except Hiram – as Father Fraleigh read the twenty-third Psalm. Chris looked up sensing Hiram's stare. He answered it with a gaze filled with contempt. When Ricardo joined Chris with the same hatred in his eyes, Hiram knew Chris had broken his long-held silence. It didn't matter. The Hill Witch would help him. She had to. She needed him. He grinned at Chris as they lowered the casket into the ground. Chris nodded back, his expression superior and challenging.

The crowd broke apart. The Mellons' close friends were gathering together to go to a reception at their house. Teddy Bigelow paused to let Ms. Adler pass. She leaned over and whispered into his ear. Teddy froze. Her words engulfed him. He heard them and felt them at the same time. They were inside his mind. They had flowed into him so quickly, it felt like they had talked for an hour. Listening to her brought on a feeling of dread. There was a memory in his mind that he couldn't reach. It concerned the farm, the night he slept over. He strained to remember what it was even though the thought of it scared him out of his wits. *I've forgotten something! It's there, but what is it?* She told him to be patient. She was holding his memories at bay. They would come back to him when the time was right.

"Do as I say, Master Bigelow," Ms. Adler's voice said, into his brain. *"I will protect you from the trauma Hiram inflicted on you for now, but you will have it back when the time is right. Chris McKee is right there. Speak to him before you leave."*

"I will, Ms. Adler," Teddy said. "I promise."

He waited until Todd and Hiram had walked toward the parking lot. Hiram opened the pickup truck door for Todd, but Todd declined saying he would see the farmer later. He walked away in the direction of Annie Potts Road and Frank Garrison's house.

Teddy went over to Chris and his friends. Chris looked at him, curiously.

"Chris?" Teddy asked. "Have you got a minute?"

Chris nodded and led him away from the other boys. "What's wrong, Teddy?" he asked. He had a bad feeling what it could be.

"Can I sleep over your house tonight?" Teddy whispered, not looking up.

Chris frowned "Is there something you need to say?"

"Yeah," Teddy replied. His braces glinted in the sunlight as he spoke. "Not here, though. It can't be here."

"Does it have to do with Hiram?" Chris asked. He leaned over and looked into Teddy's blue eyes.

Teddy looked away. "I can't talk about it now," he insisted, waving to his mother. She motioned for him to come along. "Can you have more than one guest overnight?"

"Sure," Chris said. He wanted to press him about Hiram, but didn't for fear of scaring him away. "I could have a sleepover party if I wanted. I worked the morning milking. Todd's working tonight."

"I know," Teddy nodded, his mind drifting for a moment. "I'm working tomorrow night." He gestured toward the other boys. "Can you invite all them?"

"They'll be there."

"C'mon, Theodore!" Anna exclaimed, her hands on her hips. "You still have to change!"

Teddy nodded. "Okay!" he called, and turned back to Chris. "I have to go. I have to change out of my robes. I can come over at about eight. I'm bringing someone, too, okay? Thanks!"

Chris watched him jog away. The guys filed over with confused looks on their faces.

"What was that all about?" Ricardo asked.

"We're having a sleepover at my house tonight," Chris replied. "And you're all coming."

They nodded. The expression on Chris' face was deadly serious.

They turned toward Wickett Avenue just then as the sound of police sirens filled the air.

*   *   *

The Copelands were first in line out of St. Peter's parking lot riding in Jerry's green Cadillac Escalade. They had been heading toward Satchell Hill when they spotted the cops blocking off Annie Potts Road. Jerry was content to drive by, but his wife said he should ask what all the fuss was about. He was about to tell her not to be such a busybody when Dennis suggested it was a good idea to demonstrate his concern. The election was in November. Jerry gave in. Dennis possessed a keen business mind. He was going to be something special in the world of high finance one day unlike his other useless son.

Dennis shook his head almost reading his father's thoughts. Too bad that didn't work the other way around. Too bad for Jerry. Dennis didn't care about the elections. He wanted to know what was happening. He just knew the right buttons to push. Dabney had never learned that. Dennis had a doctorate in getting around their old man. He needed it. If Jerry ever found out about his visits to Provincetown or Greenwich Village? Dennis shuddered to think what he would do.

Jerry rolled the window down. He motioned for an officer to come over to him. His heart leaped into his throat. The woman approaching the car was the same Black cop that had arrested him the other day. Jerry silently groaned.

"Mr. Copeland," Officer Kate Pierce said. She scowled behind her mirrored sunglasses. "Can I help you?"

"We were concerned about the commotion," Jerry said. His eyes never broke contact with her lenses. "Is something wrong?"

"A boy's dead," Kate replied. She didn't like the expression on his face. She silently prayed for a reason to bust him again. "It looks like an accident, maybe suicide. The detectives are investigating."

"Good Lord!" Denise gasped. "Who is it?"

"Well, I really can't say…," Kate began.

Dennis interrupted her. "It looks like Frank Garrison's house, mom," he said.

Like father, like son, Kate thought.

Jerry watched a crowd gathering. People from the funeral were parking their cars and walking over to the barricade. He mumbled, "Thanks," to Officer Pierce and reluctantly pulled the Escalade onto the shoulder. Jerry wanted to go home not screw around here, but Dennis was right. He needed to demonstrate his concern for these idiots. Jerry climbed out and joined the other parents with Denise and the kids behind him.

Robert Bigelow fielded questions from the concerned group of Lancaster residents. A detective walked over with a tiny evidence bag filled with little square camouflage-colored pieces of paper. Virginia remarked, "LSD," to her husband. She said it loud enough for most of the group to hear her.

Thomas nodded. Jerry was next to them. He wondered how she knew that was LSD. He wouldn't be surprised if she was a drug addict, the stupid Liberal. Thomas was too good of a lawyer to screw around with, so Jerry kept his mouth shut.

An ambulance arrived, lights flashing, but its siren was silent. Larry Singleton looked nervously at the police. He had the supply of illegal drugs he was dealing stashed underneath the oxygen masks. They waved him through the barricade and directed him to the Garrisons' house. Larry cringed. Frank had been a regular customer for a long time. He hoped he wasn't implicated in his death. Robert and Kate ordered the crowd to go home. They didn't want anyone to catch a glimpse of Frank's corpse. It was a truly disgusting sight after a day exposed to the elements with insects crawling all over him. *Ick.*

Jerry was glad. He'd seen all he cared to see. He volunteered his vocal support to leave the officials to their duty and went back to his Escalade. He arrived at the estate in record time and followed his family inside. Denise made a beeline for her medicine cabinet and her Xanax. Diana found Tammy making lunch in the kitchen. Dennis jogged up the grand staircase to his suites. Jerry closed the door to his study and sighed. He walked over to his desk and slid into the big leather chair.

I hope that's the last funeral I have to attend in my life except my own, Jerry thought, rubbing his temples.

He wouldn't have gone in the first place, but after the altercation between Dabney and Derek – who seemed scrawny when Jerry saw him convincing him that Dabney was indeed the biggest pussy on the planet – he had to show up. The Mellons might not think twice about suing if he showed contempt for their loss. The fact they were so civic-minded only prodded him further. Jerry did not like mingling with the cattle. He wouldn't do it again if he could help it. He considered them beneath him.

"It is nice to see someone with a concept of superiority," a woman's voice said. "It must be your German blood speaking to you."

Jerry's gaze snapped toward the leather sofa under the window. Ms. Adler was sitting on it with her feet on the coffee table.

"Holy…!" Jerry exclaimed, standing. "How did you get in here!?"

"I walked in," Ms. Adler scowled. Her eyes started glowing. *"Sit down, Mr. Copeland. Now."*

Jerry sat in his chair. He struggled, but he couldn't move. "Oh, God!" he cried. "It's true. You're a witch! Just don't hurt me, all right? We can work it out whatever it is."

Ms. Adler shook her head. The light from her eyes dimmed a little. *"I did not come by to hurt you, Jerry. Can I call you Jerry?"*

Jerry whimpered.

Her eyes narrowed. *"You are a lot braver when you are mistreating your son,"* she remarked, coldly. *"There is something you are going to do for me, Jerry. Then I am going to do something for you."*

"What... do you...?" Jerry asked, fear bringing a lump to his throat. He swallowed hard. "What do you mean?"

She leaned back on the sofa. Her face became stern. Her eyes glowed with greater intensity. Jerry felt something strange in his head like fingers were touching his brain.

Ms. Adler told him, *"You will call your lawyer and drop the charges against Jack Dougan. I want him out of jail this afternoon. Is that understood?"*

"No way in...! I... *yes...,*" Jerry replied, his face clouding. His eyes rolled back into his head. "Yes, of course. Whatever you want."

"Good," Ms. Adler smiled, her fingernails digging into the leather. *"Now, I will do something for you."*

"What are you... going to... do for me?" he asked, his voice cracking.

"I am going to pull a thorn out of your side, Jerry," Ms. Adler said. *"Dabney is mine."*

Jerry's mind filled with images of his son's impending fate. He saw the killer, but not his face. He saw Dabney's murder, vicious and painful. Jerry had never seen anything so horrible in his life, yet he agreed with barely a moment's consideration.

Jerry asked, "Will they find his body? The insurance... well, you know."

Ms. Adler laughed. "Oh, yes," she replied, her eyes returning to normal. "I guarantee it."

"Fine," Jerry said. "It's a deal." He picked up the phone and dialed his lawyer.

Ms. Adler stared at him. *I did not even have to push him,* she thought. *How black-hearted. He should have been in the SS.*

Upstairs, Dabney had been preparing to go back to the McKees' house. He had a great time last night. He didn't know anything that felt as good as being with them made him feel. He liked it. He wanted more of it. The thought of staying with Chris this time made him so happy, his face beamed with perma-grin. He couldn't get away from the estate fast enough. He changed into white satin shorts, a navy-blue tank top, and a pair of blue Versace Nappa Leather Achilles sneakers. He was glad no one tried to force him to go to the funeral the way his bruises...

Dabney's mind went blank in the middle of that thought. He had another destination for today that filled him with a sense of urgency. Dabney slipped out of his room, went downstairs, walked outside, and climbed into the black Mercedes-Benz that was waiting for him in the driveway.

*   *   *

Jeremy thought the reception at the Mellon's house was boring with a capital B. Cynthia had center stage from the second she climbed out of her Subaru Outback. She'd cried so much her tears had washed her make-up away. Jeremy saw huge black bags under her eyes. She looked like she hadn't slept for days despite her repeated sedations. He didn't blame her or intend to take away from her grief, he just wasn't feeling sympathetic. Jeremy couldn't forgive Dan for starting the rumor about Chris. His brother had no defense now that he was gone. There were three thousand kids in the high school. Next year would be a trial. It was the legacy Dan had left them. Jeremy hoped they could handle it.

The parents had gathered in the living room for quiet reflection. The hot subject among the kids was Chris' intended sleepover. Matt was pleased his mother was in a bind. The other parents had given their quick approval. Linda opened her mouth to say no, but when she caught Susan Sturgess' suspicious eye, she immediately changed her stride. She left the decision up to Virginia.

Bad move, Jeremy thought. *When it comes to having friends stay the night, mom rarely says no. We still have to ask, but she's usually fine with it unless we have some kind of family thing going on.*

Craig heard his thoughts and agreed.

There wasn't a lot to discuss. Virginia requested the boys go home early in the morning to get ready for the ballgame.

"I'm taking Chris to the mall tomorrow," she said, much to Chris' surprise. "I don't have time for you guys to hog the shower all morning. Is that agreed?"

"Sure, mom," Chris replied. "I just wish you'd given me some notice about shopping. Can I bring somebody?"

"That's fine," Virginia nodded.

"You're not going to the game?" Susan asked, disappointed that her cheering section would be broken up. Cynthia wouldn't be much help if she went at all.

Virginia wasn't sure which mother made more noise at the games, her, Susan, or Cynthia. The three of them always sat together along with Linda in the center of the bleachers. Sometimes they got so loud Randy would come over with a warning from the umpire to keep the noise down. Virginia grinned. She remembered how embarrassed Linda got when Susan told Randy, "Tell the umpire to eat my clit." It kept Virginia in stitches for weeks. Garth McKee was a regular at his grandson's games, too. He rolled his eyes, but said nothing. Modern women were way out of his league.

"Thomas is taking Jeremy to the game," Virginia replied, winking at Susan.

Thomas blushed as they murmured, *"Oh,"* at the same time. It made him feel like crap. Everyone seemed to know how little time he spent with his youngest son.

Kevin leaned over. "I know how you feel, Tom," he whispered. "I feel the same way about Derek sometimes."

Thomas shook his head. "I'm such a loser," he whispered.

Jeremy heard him. He walked over and hugged his father. "I love you, dad."

Thomas' eyes watered.

Craig's did, too. He felt how strongly Jeremy loved his father. It was a familiar feeling. Craig missed his dad despite the beatings and the harsh words. Jeremy glanced over in his direction. He was about to think something at him, but Craig scowled.

"Don't say anything, okay?" Craig thought. *"He's still my dad."*

Jeremy left Thomas and put his arm across Craig's shoulders. He led him down the steps into the front yard. Craig started crying as soon as they hit the grass. Jeremy was overwhelmed by his sadness and cried, too. Thomas watched them from the window. They sat beneath the big elm by the mailbox. He wondered why the boys were crying. Jeremy didn't know Dan all that well and neither did Craig other than working with him. He gathered that from listening to them talk. Thomas saw the tears running down their faces. He politely excused himself. He nodded to Virginia who looked at him curiously, but he only shrugged. He walked out into the yard.

Kevin suggested the boys go outside and give the adults some time alone. Derek led them out back to his fort. Douggie stayed planted next to his mother refusing to leave her side. That was fine with Derek. Douggie might be the only brother he had left, but he still didn't like him very much. He had always taken Dan's side no matter what even when Dan was completely wrong. It didn't foster many good feelings.

The boys crowded into the small shack. It had a sign that read *Derek's Place* which Derek had made in woodshop in seventh grade. It hung loosely from a nail outside the door. The wooden walls were gray and water damaged. There was a vague scent of mildew. No one knew if it was coming from the walls or the ratty-old mattress inside. Max said he was going back for Jeremy and Craig, but Chris told him not to bother. They would probably be out front until it was time to leave once his father got talking.

"I hope that's soon," Ricardo whined, tugging on his collar. "This suit is driving me nuts."

"Mine, too," Sandy echoed, loosening his tie.

"What do you think is up with Teddy?" Matt asked.

Chris and Ricardo glanced at each other, and then looked away.

Max noticed the action and scowled. "Hey, man," he said, pointing at Ricardo. "If you know something, now would be the time to tell us." He turned to Chris. "You were pretty pushy about sleeping over tonight, too. I didn't ask about it at the cemetery because our parents were there, but come clean, Chris. What's going on with Teddy?"

Chris looked at Ricardo.

"They're going to find out anyway, Chris," he said, glumly.

Ricardo wasn't ready to talk about what happened to him at the Big E, but he didn't have a choice. He wasn't going to let Chris go out on a limb alone.

"Find out about what?" Derek asked.

"Yeah, what?" Matt echoed.

Chris sighed, took a deep breath, and told them all about the night in Hiram's trailer. They had to hold Max back to keep him from following the trails down to the farm and beating the crap out of the farmer. He kicked out the back wall of the fort in his rage. Sandy and Matt put it back up. They used a rock to pound the nails in. Ricardo calmed Max down before he started his own story. He softly gave everyone the reason he had hated gays so much. He told them he'd since learned he was wrong about them. Max listened to his brother intently. He hugged Ricardo as tightly as he could without breaking him in half.

"What are we going to do about this, Chris?" Sandy asked. His mind was raging with a desire to rip Hiram's arms off. "Do you think he touched Teddy?"

"I don't know, Sandy," Chris replied, feeling spent. "I suppose we'll find out tonight. If he did, I'll go to the cops, no question about it. I wish I knew who he was bringing."

"Why didn't Teddy tell his father?" Sandy asked. "He's a cop."

"Like I said," Chris replied, "I'm not even sure that's what Teddy wants. I just have a feeling."

"What about O'Connor?" Matt wondered.

"I doubt it," Chris said, shaking his head. "I talked to Todd about it once. He said if Hiram ever even tried to touch him, he'd kick his ass. I believe him."

"So do I," Ricardo agreed. "O'Connor may be a punk, but I don't think he's a pussy."

"If anybody but you had said that," Chris whispered, "I'd have taken it as a major insult."

Ricardo scowled. "I didn't mean it that way, dude. I'm sorry."

"I still say we should mess him up for what he did to Chris," Max growled.

The group murmured agreement.

"Let's wait for Teddy," Chris replied. "I wish I knew already. Wondering about it is driving me crazy."

In the front yard, Thomas sat down between Jeremy and Craig and put his arms around them both. Craig was upset because of the restraining order against his father. Thomas understood that. Nancy had made it clear that he loved Jack despite the abuse. He assured Craig the order was to try and force his father to go into treatment, not take him away forever. Craig calmed down after that. So did Jeremy. Thomas didn't know why he was crying. When he asked, Jeremy and Craig looked at each other for several seconds like they were having a silent conversation.

"I can feel whatever Craig feels," Jeremy said, and cringed.

Thomas nodded. "That happens a lot with friends, kiddo. You guys are getting pretty close, huh?"

"He doesn't get it," Craig said.

Jeremy frowned.

"I don't get what?" Thomas asked. He looked back and forth between the boys with a confused look on his face.

"Show him," Craig said.

Jeremy stood up. He held his hand out to his father. Thomas took it and rose. He followed Jeremy across the yard to the driveway. Jeremy told him to get in the Porsche and close the door. Thomas watched him walk around the car and get in on the other side. Thomas got in and started it. He turned on the air conditioner full blast.

"What's this all about, Remy?" Thomas asked, crossing his arms.

Jeremy stared at the floor. He said, "Tell me something I don't know that Craig couldn't possibly know."

"Look, Jeremy," Thomas said. "I don't think this is the time for games..."

"This isn't a game, *all right!?*" Jeremy cried, bursting into tears.

Thomas' mouth dropped open. *Christ!* he thought, his heart skipping a beat. *I don't remember ever seeing Jeremy this upset!* He rubbed his son's shoulder.

Jeremy put his hand on top of his. "Just do it, dad," he whispered, fighting for composure. "Please, okay? We're going out of our minds."

"Jeremy," Thomas said. He leaned over to look him in his eyes. "Tell me what it is. We'll work it out."

"I can't tell you, dad," Jeremy replied, wiping his face with the backs of his hands. "You won't believe me. I have to show you. Bear with me, okay? Just tell me something I don't know that Craig couldn't possibly know."

Thomas frowned. "All right. Let's see... Oh! Thurman's going on vacation the first week of September. I found out yesterday."

"Fine," Jeremy nodded. "Go see Craig."

Thomas climbed out of the car and asked if Jeremy was coming. Jeremy shook his head. He stared forward, his face etched with worry. Thomas left the Porsche running. He saw Virginia in the window. She looked down at him, questioningly. Thomas scratched his head and crossed the lawn. Virginia sat down confused. Craig patiently waited for Thomas. He opened his mouth to ask Craig what was going on, but Craig shushed him.

"Thurman's going on vacation the first week in September," he said, his hazel eyes fearful. "You found out yesterday."

Thomas stared at him in disbelief. He looked back toward the Porsche. Jeremy was still inside. He turned to Craig. Craig held up a finger motioning for him to wait.

"Watch this," he said. He whispered, "Jeremy, open the car door and get out."

Thomas watched in amazement as Jeremy got out of the car.

"Wave to us," Craig whispered, covering his mouth.

Jeremy waved.

"That's amazing!" Thomas laughed, clapping his hands. "How did you do that? Is it a magic trick?"

"He still doesn't get it, Jeremy," Craig whined, standing up.

Thomas frowned remembering Jeremy's explosion from a minute ago.

"What do you mean he doesn't get it!?" Jeremy called, jogging over. "Jeeze, dad! Do we have to spell it out for you? *Magic trick!?* Who put your brain in backward?" He threw his arms up to the sky. *"Buy a vowel!"*

"Good Lord," Thomas said, reaching for the tree. "Are you trying to say you guys can read each other's thoughts?"

"Bingo," they replied.

Thomas sat down. They told him about the night at the campsite when they had the same dream. They gave him a moment to absorb it all, and then told him the rest. Thomas stared at the boys. Jeremy had been right. If they'd tried to tell him, he never would have believed it.

Mind reading? he thought. *Empathy? What is this, a lost episode of the Outer Limits?*

Thomas gathered his wits. He could see that Jeremy and Craig were genuinely upset. He was, too.

"There has to be a logical explanation," he said, shaking his head. "I don't believe in goblins and witches guys."

Craig stiffened. So did Jeremy. Images flowed between them like a macabre filmstrip. *Ms. Adler!* The scene on her porch with Craig and her groceries. Jeremy could see it clearly as if they were his memories and not his friend's. Craig climbed the stairs. Ms. Adler grabbed his arm. Her eyes were a bright shade of blue. Then the pleading, *"Help me warn them! Help me warn...!"* and the terror he felt as her eyes... they... her eyes...

"Jesus!" Thomas cried. He shook them roughly by their arms. "Snap out of it!"

Thomas felt a flash of fear as both boys collapsed onto the grass on their knees. He knelt with them. He watched in horror as they alternated words from the same sentence.

"Her...," Jeremy said.

"... eyes...," Craig said.

"... changed..."

"… color…"

"Holy crap, dad!" Jeremy cried, his terrified face turning toward his father. "I saw it! Her eyes changed color!"

"Who, Remy?" Thomas cried. "Whose eyes?"

"The Hill Witch, Mr. McKee," Craig said, his hand on Thomas' forearm. "Margaret Adler."

*　　*　　*

"Hiram?"

Hiram looked up from his lunch with a puzzled expression.

"Yes?" he asked, keeping his voice low. He didn't know why. No one else was there and Todd wasn't due for another hour. He set his fork on the table.

Ms. Adler's mind-voice replied, *"I need you."*

"I'm here," Hiram smiled. *Another one so soon?* he thought, feeling his excitement grow. *God, I love this woman!*

"Come outside. I have something for you."

Hiram pushed back from the table. "Be right there," he replied.

He went into the kitchen, grabbed a large sharp knife, and stepped outside. His mouth dropped open. Ms. Adler was standing next to her Mercedes. Dabney was on his knees in front of her, sobbing. He was trying so hard to move, to run away, but he was frozen. She had him again as easily as at her house the other day.

Why? Dabney thought. *What does she want with me? Why is she doing this?*

Those questions rushed through his mind, but there were no answers. He wondered what she wanted with the farmer, too, until his eyes fell on the knife in Hiram's hand. Dabney cringed.

"Dabney?" Hiram asked, surprised. "I thought you didn't want him."

"I do not," Ms. Adler said. *"This is not business, Hiram. Dabney is interfering with my experiment."*

"I haven't done anything!" Dabney cried. "Hiram! Help me!"

Ms. Adler looked down at him. *"You have involved yourself with Jeremy and Craig,"* she projected into his mind. *"You are distracting them at a critical juncture in my work."*

"Hiram?" Dabney begged. "Make her let me go!"

Hiram ignored him. His hand started to twitch. "McKee told Ricardo Ramirez. It's only the beginning I think."

Ms. Adler nodded. *"Nothing happens in Lancaster without my knowledge. We will deal with McKee and his friends."*

"Hiram?" Dabney asked. He was terrified. *Oh, no!*

"What about him?" Hiram asked, walking over. He pointed at Dabney with the knife. The tip was inches from his nose.

Dabney whimpered.

Ms. Adler's expression darkened. *"I want to hear him scream."*

Hiram reached over and grabbed a handful of Dabney's hair. He yanked with all his might and a clump tore free from his scalp.

Dabney screamed.

"Like that?" Hiram smiled, shaking the hair off his fingers.

"Yes, Hiram," Ms. Adler replied. *"Just like that."*

"Oh, God!" Dabney cried. "Please, no! *Please!?"*

"Good-bye, Master Copeland," Ms. Adler said. *"I never liked you anyway."*

"Come on, Copeland," Hiram said. He grabbed Dabney by the hair again and dragged him toward the Victorian. "I've been dying to give you the *Gift* for a long time."

"No!" Dabney cried. Ms. Adler mentally released him. He kicked and thrashed as Hiram dragged him. "Hiram! *Please! No!"*

Hiram slammed Dabney's face into the Victorian's back steps. His nose exploded all over again. There was no doubt it had broken that time. He was dazed. Hiram dragged him up the stairs and unlocked the back door. He stepped inside pulling Dabney with him. There was another door in front of them next to a row of coat hooks. Hiram opened it and threw Dabney inside. It was the stairwell to the basement. Dabney sailed up and then down feeling his shoulder crack as he struck the thick wooden stairs. He rolled to the bottom onto the dirt floor below.

Basement, he thought, struggling to get his bearings. *I'm in a basement.*

Dabney's broken nose twitched at the stink. He retched. There was an awful smell down here mixed with the dank odor of old water. It was like nothing he had ever smelled before. It was a rotten smell like meat gone bad only it was worse, much worse. It was death, the reek of decay. It assaulted his nostrils. He felt the urge to throw up. There was a single window facing the front of the house. Pale light streamed through the dirty glass. His eyes adjusted. He gasped when he saw patches of dried blood all over the room.

Holy God! Dabney thought, terrified. *He's going to murder me! Oh, please! Don't let him do this! I'm not that bad! I'm changing, aren't I? I'm doing good! Please, I have friends! I've never had friends before! It can't be like this! It just can't! Oh, Lord! Please, save me! Please, help me! I don't want to die!*

Hiram lumbered down the steps. The knife glinted in the light. He grew a savage grin as he came closer, but paused and inhaled through his nose.

"Smell that?" Hiram asked. "I bring them down here sometimes when I can't use my slaughter hook. The hook's a lot more fun. You should be hanging there right now."

He lunged forward and kicked Dabney in the stomach. The wind rushed out of him. He doubled over, gasping for breath.

"This will do," Hiram said, raising the knife. "This will do just fine."

Ms. Adler waited in the barnyard listening to Dabney's thoughts. Hiram tore into him causing him more pain than he had ever known.

A voice cried out, *"You can't do this!"*

Ms. Adler scowled. The voice had come from her own mouth. "You have freed yourself once more?" she asked. "Easily rectified." She closed her eyes. *"I can do whatever I like."* A soft glow appeared under her lids. She clenched her teeth, focusing. *"He is a threat!"*

"Because he's lonely?" the voice asked. It was her voice only more feminine. *"Because they're teaching him what it's like to have friends?"*

"Because it is nearly time and I cannot afford his distraction!" Ms. Adler snapped. *"An old enemy has found me. She can make things difficult for me. I cannot fight this battle on three fronts, her, you, and my work. I must complete my work. Jeremy and Craig must be ready!"*

"I'll fight you!" the voice threatened.

"You... will... lose!"

"Eventually, but at least I'll be able to save him!"

Ms. Adler's eyes exploded with brilliance.

"You... do this...," Ms. Adler struggled. Her face contorted as she fought with all of her will to keep control. *"I swear... I will lock you in... so deep... No! Stop! No...!"*

"Yes!" Margaret Adler cried, victoriously. She opened her eyes, eyes that she controlled at last if only for a short while. They were bright blue. She set her jaw, stiffening up, and fearlessly vowed, "Hiram is not going to murder this boy!"

She stepped toward the Victorian, her blue eyes pulsating power. She went inside and down the basement stairs. Hiram had Dabney by the neck, beating him severely. His right eye was swollen shut. Blood ran from his lips and nose. Several of his ribs were cracked making each movement agony. He thought the farmer had hurt him before, but he never knew what pain was until now. Hiram jerked Dabney's face up and held it against his. He liked the feel of the blood against his skin. He licked Dabney grossly from his neck to his eyebrow.

"I've wanted to do this... for so long...," Hiram panted, into his ear. "You'll thank me someday when we meet on the other side. You'll see."

Dabney bit down as hard as he could on Hiram's cheek. He seized up and back ripping a chunk of flesh out of the farmer's face. Hiram cried out and let him go. He stumbled back holding the wound. Dabney fell to his knees. He looked up, his eyes blazing, and spat the chunk of flesh at the farmer.

Dabney screamed, *"You're never touching me again, do you hear me!? Never!"* He burst into fresh tears. *"I hope you burn, you bastard!"*

"Oh, I'm going to do more than just touch you, Dabney!" Hiram growled, holding up the knife. His cheek was bleeding. His eyes were wide with insanity. "I'm going to tear you apart inside and out!"

"I don't think so!" Margaret cried. She stood at the bottom of the stairs, her eyes alive with power.

Hiram whirled around. Her voice was higher than usual and there was no trace of her accent. It only took him a moment for him to realize what had happened.

"Margaret!" Hiram spat. He charged toward her, the knife flashing.

Margaret held up her hand. *"That's right you maniac. Margaret."*

An unseen force paralyzed him. The knife twisted out of his hand. It flew through the air and lodged into the railing next to her. She raised her arm. He lifted off the dirt floor. Hiram raged at her. She thrust her hand to the side. He sailed across the room and smashed head first into the rough stone wall. His keys flew out of his pocket landing in the dirt. Margaret rammed his face repeatedly into the foundation. She didn't stop until he was broken and unconscious. She dropped him on the floor. Hiram landed with a dull thud. Margaret rushed to Dabney's side, her eyes dimming. He scrambled away from her.

"Get *away* from me!" Dabney cried. "What *are* you!?"

Margaret lowered her head. "Trapped, Dabney. I'm trapped." She looked at him with grave concern. "I can only keep control for a short period. We don't have time to dawdle. We have to…" She paused, her expression changing from concern to surprise. It contorted in horror. "Oh, no!"

Dabney glared at her, weeping. She stood, her body shaking, her eyes shifting color from blue to brown and back to blue. She struggled, fighting something. Dabney limped toward the stairs, crying hard. He felt like he was breathing razor blades. He made it halfway up before her paralyzing force grabbed him again. He gasped, wrenched backward. He spun around in mid-air and floated over to her until he was face to face with the Hill Witch. Her eyes were glowing. Her expression was harder, deadlier.

"Going somewhere, Master Copeland?" she asked, her voice deep. The distinct accent had returned. *"Margaret may have saved you, but your ordeal is far from over."* Her eyes narrowed. *"You are coming with me."*

Dabney felt her power reach into his skull, and then everything went black.

*   *   *

Jeremy was lying against his headboard. Craig was sitting next to him. The room was crowded as the guys played Mortal Kombat 10 on the PlayStation. Sandy had been whipping everyone until now. Derek was his present opponent and had won the first round. Jeremy shook his head at the same time as Craig. Their entwined thoughts cleared. Max observed this, curiously.

Craig caught his expression. He thought to Jeremy, *"We need to be more careful."*

Jeremy agreed. He was glad none of the other guys had noticed. Thomas told them to keep everything a secret while he investigated. There was a logical explanation, he just didn't know what it was yet. The boys were sure the answer had something to do with Ms. Adler. Craig thought it was black magic. Jeremy believed him after seeing the memory of her eye color change.

Thomas was unsettled when they left the reception. He went to his study when they got home and surfed the Internet for answers. Jeremy and Craig hoped he would find something soon, but he wouldn't. Thomas was in the middle of reading a psychic website when he couldn't remember why he was there. He patched into his work file figuring if he did something else for a while it would come to him. It didn't.

"Yes!" Derek exclaimed. He jumped up and did a victory dance around Jeremy's room. It was the first time he had ever beaten Sandy.

Sandy shook his head. *I don't believe he beat me. I'm a pro at Mortal Kombat. The only person who ever whips me is Jeremy. This is bull!*

"You got lucky, that's all," he snorted.

Derek mooned him. Sandy made a lunging grab for him as the doorbell rang. Derek dodged and leapt onto the bed. Jeremy started to get up, but Chris told him he would get it. He hoped it was Teddy. He was going crazy for some answers.

On the front porch, Herman Schwartz looked up at his brother's scowling face. They held their overnight bags and waited for someone to answer the bell. The sun dipped beneath the horizon. The sky was a bright reddish orange. It reflected against Henry's angry cheeks. Herman sighed. He was the cause of his brother's irritation, but it wasn't his fault. Henry would realize that once he calmed down. Herman wasn't the one who promised to take Henry to the movies tonight. Henry had tried to back out after Teddy Bigelow called, but their father wouldn't let him. Henry either brought Herman with him, or he wasn't going. There was no choice. After Teddy's call, Henry had to go.

"It's Hiram Milliken, Henry," Teddy whispered. "You're not his only victim. You have to come."

How does he know about that? Henry wondered. *I never said anything to anybody! Is he guessing? Did Hiram do something to him, too? Why go to McKee's house? Did he get Chris as well? Oh, Lord!*

Virginia opened the door as that thought ended. Henry forced a smile. He didn't want her to see how flustered he was. She smiled back and invited them in. She didn't know Henry that well, but she recognized Herman. She was taken aback at how much the Schwartz brothers looked alike. They had light brown hair, hazel eyes, and wore the same style glasses with copper-colored frames. Henry had a more prominent Adam's apple and a deeper voice. Aside from the differences attributed to their ages, they were virtual twins.

"Hello, Herman," Virginia said, holding her hand out. Herman took it, blushing. "This is your brother, right?"

"Henry," Herman said. He let her hand go and shoved his into his pockets.

"Nice to meet you, Mrs. McKee," Henry said, also shaking her hand. He adjusted his yarmulke.

"It's Virginia," she replied. "I see you at the bus stop in the morning. I've seen you at the baseball field a few times, too."

Henry nodded. "Yes, but you're always in the bleachers. My parents like sitting in the shade by the left field foul line."

"That's right!"

"We still hear you though," Henry grinned.

Virginia laughed, embarrassed.

"I think the whole town hears my mom at Jeremy's games," Chris said, from the top of the stairs.

"It wouldn't hurt for you to come once in a while, young man," Virginia turned, feigning irritation. She placed her hands on her hips.

"She-yeah!" Chris cried. "Ex-squeeze me?"

"I'll squeeze you," Virginia said, waving her index finger. "How many kids are coming tonight? You've almost got an army here already."

"Just Teddy," Chris replied. "As far as I know."

"As far as you know?" Virginia asked. "What did you do? Pass out fliers? Just make sure they all know to be up and gone early. They're not taking ten showers here in the morning. Who's going to the mall with us?"

"Dabney, I hope," Chris replied. "He's not back yet. Sandy if Dabney can't go. Everyone else is going to the game except Craig. He has to work."

"All right," Virginia nodded. "Dabney, Sandy, and Craig can shower here, but I want everyone else out by nine o'clock. We're leaving then."

"C'mon up you guys," Chris said, motioning to Herman and Henry, "before she has a cow."

Herman giggled. Henry nodded. He followed his brother up the stairs. Chris stopped them in the hall and pointed Herman toward Jeremy's room. He heard soft music through the closed door. It was *Elton John's Greatest Hits* much to Sandy's chagrin. He was a headbanger like Matt. Jeremy liked Elton, so that was just too bad. Henry frowned as Chris led him the opposite way toward his room.

Herman entered. Jeremy, Craig, Derek, Matt, Max, Ricardo, and Sandy greeted him. They were crowded around the PlayStation. It was Jeremy's turn now. Derek was surprised he was beating him. They had played each other numerous times in the past and Jeremy always won. He would be winning now, too, if not for Craig. Craig kept thinking about what moves he would use. He was blowing Jeremy's concentration.

Chris noticed that Henry was keeping him at arm's length. He frowned wondering if the rest of his life would be like that. Henry was irritated and distant which convinced Chris whatever Teddy was up to involved Hiram, unless Henry was just a homophobe. He sat on the edge of his waterbed and placed his hands in his lap. Henry sat in the beanbag chair. He crossed his arms.

"I take it Teddy invited you here," Chris said, not hiding his annoyance at Henry's attitude.

"Invited isn't the word I'd use."

"Do you know why?" Chris asked.

"No, I don't, Chris," Henry replied. "Why don't you tell me?"

"I would," Chris sighed, "but I don't know either."

"Look, McKee," Henry said, standing. "I don't like this. You're messing with me. You know as well as I do this has to do with Hiram, and don't tell me it doesn't."

"All right," Chris replied, glaring at him. "I won't. I suspected that, but Teddy didn't say much. He said he wanted to sleep over, asked me to invite all the guys who are here, and said he was bringing a friend. I assume the friend he meant was you, although I don't know why Herman's here."

"My father wouldn't let me come without him," Henry said, sitting back down. He shook his head. "We need to talk you and me, and no nonsense. I'm not in the mood. After what happened with you and Dan Mellon, I already don't trust you."

"Fair enough," Chris scowled. "I'm going to tell you though, if you're half the dick you're acting like right now you may as well leave. I don't need any of your attitude and, for the record, I don't trust you very much either."

Just then, the Bigelows pulled into the driveway. Teddy kissed his father on the cheek and climbed out of the car. He had a clean change of clothes in a brown paper sack. He waved as Robert drove away headed back to work. Teddy stood at the McKees' front door waiting for the word.

"Proceed, Master Bigelow," Ms. Adler mind-voice said, inside Teddy's brain. *"I have arranged for Jeremy, Craig, and Herman to leave shortly. Use the time wisely. My enemies conspire against me and time is short."*

"I understand," Teddy said, and pushed the doorbell.

Chris told Henry to wait a minute while he slipped out to answer the bell. He zipped down the steps and cut Virginia off as she came out of the kitchen. He opened the door for Teddy. Teddy smiled at Chris, flashing his braces. There wasn't a hint there was anything amiss from his expression. Chris wondered if he was wrong about Hiram.

"Who's this handsome young man?" Virginia smiled, holding out her hand.

"Teddy Bigelow, ma'am," Teddy replied, his blue eyes shining.

"C'mon, mom!" Chris whined. "I told you Teddy was coming. You see him at Mass every Sunday."

Virginia replied, "I know that, silly! Teddy's never been here before. I was trying to be sociable."

"Gag me, okay?"

"Man, you're cool," Teddy said to Virginia. "My mom usually gives my friends the third degree the second they walk through the door."

"We don't do things like that around here, Teddy," Virginia said. "I trust my boys."

"Hey!" Teddy cried. "Want another kid?"

"Dude," Chris said, leading Teddy to the stairs, "if we did, you'd have to fight Matt Gardner and Dabney Copeland for the position."

Virginia stopped them. She asked Chris to find out what kind of pizza the guys wanted. She was about to order. Chris looked at her like she was crazy. Everybody in the world wanted pepperoni. How hard was that to figure out? He said as much. Virginia told him to make sure. After a quick stop in Jeremy's room, Chris threw his hands up. He went to get a pen and paper to write down the different combinations being thrown at him. Teddy drifted into the group of kids. They looked at him, expectantly. Teddy merely nodded. It wasn't time yet. She would tell him when it was.

Craig elbowed Jeremy. "Where's Dabney?"

Jeremy shrugged, reached for his iPhone, and called Dabney's number. It picked up on the fourth ring.

"This is Dabney Shawn Copeland. Whoever you are, I better want to talk to you or you might as well hang up."

Jeremy smiled. *Shawn?* he thought. "Voicemail," he informed Craig, as he waited for the beep. When it came, he said, "Yeah, Dabs. It's Jeremy. I thought you were coming back. What's going on? Call me, okay? 'Bye."

Craig shook his head. He heard the voicemail announcement through their mind-link. "I guess he hasn't changed that yet."

"Dabs will call," Jeremy insisted. "There's no way he could've faked his excitement about spending the night again."

Craig nodded, but his expression suddenly grew confused. He asked, "What were we talking about?"

Jeremy opened his mouth, but then closed it. His brow furrowed. "I'm not sure," he replied. He thought about it for a second, and shrugged. "Wait awhile. It'll come to me."

It didn't. It was the same for Chris. The moment he wondered where Dabney was, the thought was driven right out of his mind. A few minutes later Jeremy, Craig, and Herman left with Virginia to pick up their dinner and some soda. Henry joined the others in Jeremy's room. Teddy closed the door. Chris watched his expression change dramatically. The cool and collected Teddy was gone. A very nervous-looking frightened boy replaced him.

"Now, Teddy," Ms. Adler's mind-voice said. *"Just as we discussed, tell them what they need to hear. I am not going to hold your pain back much longer. Tell them what he did to you, but do not mention me."*

Teddy frowned. "The reason I asked all you guys to be here..."

"Don't you want to wait for the others to come back?" Matt interrupted. He was puzzled. "Jeremy's going to want to…"

"No!" Teddy cried, his eyes filling with tears. "If I don't do this right now, I never will."

"Then do it, man," Max said.

Teddy spoke. Their hearts pounded in horrified disgust as he told them in gruesome detail what Hiram had done to him the night he slept over at the farm.

*   *   *

Dabney's eyes fluttered as he struggled to regain consciousness. The pain wracking his body tried to force him to stay asleep. The blackness was like a cocoon insulating him from the agony. His face was on fire. His broken nose sang to him if he even twitched. His mind teetered precariously between despair and shock. Light attempted to pry his eyelids open. He kept them shut wanting to die. There was too much pain. Then he remembered Margaret Adler saving him from the farmer and his eyes snapped wide open.

The fluorescent lights hanging from the laboratory ceiling were impossibly bright. Dabney whimpered trying to force his vision to adjust. He heard something that sounded like water boiling, but that wasn't exactly it. It was a bubbling noise, a crackling. He turned his head weakly toward the sound. He pushed up from the black and white tiled floor and focused on a black Formica laboratory table in the center of the room. There was a refrigerator against the wall behind it at the foot of a stainless-steel examination table. There were thick leather restraints mounted at the wrists, feet, and neck.

Dabney gasped when he saw human brains floating inside glass containers on the lab table shelf. Small bottles hung upside-down underneath. Their pinkish liquid contents were flowing down tubes and dripping onto a black-green mass writhing inside a large beaker. It spasmed and twisted with each drop that fell. Tiny blue flames erupted where they landed filling the air with a carbon scent. Dabney could feel the ooze. He sensed it was alive. It felt like an ocean of blankness without form or thought. It simply hungered. It hungered for life.

"You are very perceptive, Master Copeland," Ms. Adler said. "It is difficult to believe there is some intelligence buried beneath all of your arrogance."

Dabney jumped when he heard her and spun his head toward her voice. She was sitting at a large metal desk watching her computer screen as figures flashed by at an incredible speed.

"What *are* you!?" Dabney whispered, fearfully.

Ms. Adler raised an eyebrow. "I am the Hill Witch, Master Copeland," she said. "I thought you knew that." She turned back to her computer.

Dabney's heart sank. He started to cry. His body shook all over as he emotionally broke. He wept with force, holding his knees to his chest, rocking back and forth. The arrogance that had burned in his heart for so long disintegrated entirely. He felt shattered into a billion aching pieces. There was no Dabney anymore. There was only despair. He clung to his sanity with both hands. He was dangerously close to slipping into a bottomless pit of madness. He felt a sudden rush of anxiety, a burning need to escape. He glanced up, scanning the room, but he didn't see a door. Confused, he fought back his tears and wondered where he was.

"We are in my laboratory," Ms. Adler said.

"Stop that!" Dabney cried. "Stay out of my mind! It's private property!"

She turned to him. "That would be impossible, Master Copeland," she replied. "My telepathy cannot simply be turned off." Her eyes flashed with power and returned to normal. "You are concerned I might learn your secrets." She shook her head. "Your gay brother? You know he is, do you not? That is why he is protecting Christopher McKee, a boy you have feelings for. Did you not confirm those feelings with Christopher in the presence of Jeremy, Craig, and Derek?"

"Oh, God…"

"You, Dennis, and Christopher share certain genes that make you impossible for my experiments, just as other potential subjects have, past and present. It is more common than many would believe." She frowned. "Or is it your molestation by the farmer you do not wish me to see? The humiliation of being bent over a hay bale? The pain? Your father saw that, you know. It is part of the reason he hates you so much. He witnessed Hiram assaulting you in the barn and thought you were enjoying it, the Schwein. Your father is truly an idiot. He will make an excellent politician." Her eyes narrowed. "There are no secrets in Lancaster, Master Copeland. Not from me."

Dabney attempted to stand. Ms. Adler's eyes flashed with midnight blue force. His legs were knocked out from under him. He hit the tiled floor flat on his back with a smack.

Dabney glared up at her. "Stop it! Let me up!"

"I cannot allow that," Ms. Adler said. She flipped off the computer monitor. "My work is at a critical phase. You cannot be allowed to interfere."

Dabney asked, "Why did you save me then? So you could torture me? You're no better than the farmer!"

Ms. Adler waved her hand, the energy returning to her eyes. Dabney rose off the ground encased in a smothering force of telekinesis and floated over to her. He stared into her glowing irises horrified as she held him immobile.

"I am nothing like Hiram Milliken," Ms. Adler said, through gritted teeth. *"I am much worse."* She dropped him.

Dabney landed on his buttocks. He scooted backward crab-walking away from her. "If you're going to kill me, why don't you just get it over with?" he cried.

"Because she will not let me kill you, Master Copeland," Ms. Adler said, her eyes glowing. Her words blasted into his skull. *"Although I could trick you into an accident, or will someone to run you over, I cannot directly act to take your life. She saved you, not I."*

"Who?" Dabney asked, reeling from the abhorrent sensation of fingers touching his brain. "Who are you talking about?"

Ms. Adler seemed surprised. Her eyes dimmed. "Why, Margaret, of course."

"You're Mar... *M...!"* Dabney struggled, trying to say her name. He still couldn't.

"So everyone believes."

Dabney scanned the lab looking for a way to escape. There had to be one unless Ms. Adler walked through walls. There was no evidence of a door or a window. The lab was a solid concrete room that resembled a bomb shelter. There were vents in the ceiling circulating air, but none of them were large enough for him to crawl through. Dabney felt trapped. He almost started crying again, but he fought it off. He wasn't giving her the satisfaction.

There were seven filing cabinets to Ms. Adler's right overflowing with file folders. She had a colored drawing of a DNA strand next to her desk. It was the same as the one in her classroom showing an additional branch sticking out from the helix. Her class on Genetics was grueling and detailed. He had never seen any DNA helix representation from any other sources that was the same as those.

"You would not have," Ms. Adler said. "That picture is a representation of my DNA."

"Why do you want me dead?" Dabney sadly asked. "What did I ever do to you?"

"You interfered with my experiment," she replied. "Your budding friendship with Jeremy and Craig was distracting them from each other."

"You were going to let Hiram kill me for that?" Dabney asked. He shrank back from her. "I don't understand." He started to cry again, ashamed at his lack of self-control. He struggled to rein in his emotions. "I'm just a kid."

"So were they," Ms. Adler said, pointing to the small bottles hanging under the shelf. "Look at them," she ordered. "Perhaps you will begin to understand."

Dabney didn't move at first. Her scowl deepened and she thrust her finger toward the bottles. He went to the lab table. He looked at the bottles confused.

"I don't understand," Dabney said, reading the labels. "Sam Stone... Ian Sturgess..." He swallowed hard. "What does it mean? What are these? Where did you get them?"

Ms. Adler crossed her arms. "The fluid is a chemical released into the brains of pubescent boys during times of extreme duress. The greater the duress, the greater the amount of fluid. It is a small slice of the power of God."

"Extreme duress?"

"Yes," Ms. Adler said. "Duress caused when Hiram murdered them."

Dabney's heart skipped a beat. "M… *mur…,* " he struggled. The color drained from his face. *"Murdered them?"*

"As he would have murdered you," she reminded him, "were it not for my daughter and her wretched interference."

"Your daughter?" Dabney asked. His head was spinning. *Sam's dead? Ian, too? Oh, God… oh, Jesus!* He swallowed hard. "You're not Timothy Adler!" he choked. "There's no way!"

"No, I am not," Ms. Adler said. She gazed at the small bottles. "These boys are the architects of the future, Master Copeland. Hiram would have killed them anyway, or others, but killing them in my service gave their deaths meaning. They died for the greater good."

"They were murdered!" Dabney snapped. "Where's the good in that?"

"The good of my continued existence!" Ms. Adler shot back. Her eyes exploded with power. *"Can you not see it? Can you feel my power inside your mind? Telepathy, telekinetics, they are merely the beginning. I can mentally access computer systems. I invaded the classified databases of universities, scientists, the government. I stole from the Agency, a branch of the intelligence community feared all over the world. I broke through their encrypted security as easily as breathing. They had a phenomenal storehouse of genetic research. Dr. Carolyn Meyer-Brandis, the world's leading authority in the field, is an Agent! Her research was leaps beyond even mine. I acquired their technology to build my computer system, a clone of their WolfBoyGod satellite. I buried it under the floor. No one remembers delivering the parts, assembling the system, or constructing my lab because I will not let them! My telepathy is absolute. I can read thoughts or project them, invade technology by a means I call techno-telepathy. I can cause hallucinations, rearrange memories, erase minds, plant suggestions… I am invincible!"*

She pointed at the green-black ooze.

"The new formula will bring me even greater power." She stabbed into his mind. *"I have labored a lifetime to achieve this level of perfection. You are not going to interfere with my work!"*

Dabney gripped the sides of his head as waves of pain shot through his skull. "I won't! *I won't!"*

Ms. Adler let him go.

Dabney fell to his knees, gasping for air.

"I have tolerated all of the interference I can stand from my daughter," Ms. Adler said. *"I control her body, but now and again she has disrupted that control. She tried to save Dan Mellon, but she failed. She managed to save you, but was weakened so badly she will never recover before I am*

finished. Still, her subconscious revulsion to taking human life renders me impotent. The power will not obey my commands to kill you."

"Hiram killed Dan, too?"

"And Bobby Jones," Ms. Adler replied, *"and many others. Margaret's damnable influence over me made Hiram a necessary evil to get the serum samples I needed."*

"You're the one who's evil!"

"Evil in that sense is irrelevant," Ms. Adler said. *"I am a scientist."*

"You're a murderer!"

"I have killed, Master Copeland," Ms. Adler said, *"to advance my work. You are upset over fifteen boys? At Buchenwald, I killed thousands. Is the concentration camp the clue you needed to discern my true identity? Are you well versed enough in Lancaster's history? Are you aware they hailed Timothy Adler for murdering me? They gave him a medal! I am alive inside the child he brought home with him, my daughter! She was the first success in my attempt to infuse a human being with godlike abilities."* She gestured at the bottles. *"What are their lives compared to that power?"* Her eyes narrowed. *"You should be thankful I did not complete my quest for power until the final minutes of the war. If it had been earlier, you would be speaking German right now."*

"B... Brem... *something...,"* Dabney struggled. *History... I suck at History!* Then it clicked. The name of the Nazi doctor Timothy Adler shot during the liberation of Buchenwald. He gasped and yelled, *"Bremen! Günter Bremen!"*

"That," Ms. Adler said, her eyes dimming, "would be me. Commissioned by der Führer to endow the soldiers of the Reich with artificial ESP."

"You're insane!" Dabney cried, struggling to his feet. He shifted back and forth.

"Hiram is insane," Ms. Adler corrected. "Of course, he will not be a problem much longer. He has outlived his usefulness. I have sown the seeds of his downfall. Christopher McKee will bring about his destruction. I am influencing him as I influenced all of Hiram's victims to remain silent. That is why you never told. I would not let you. It was a small reward for his loyal service. The abuse of some irrelevant boys was of no consequence." She sneered at him. "Like you, abused hundreds of times over these last years by a pedophile mass-murdering necrophiliac lunatic. Did you think you were Hiram's only victim? No, Master Copeland. There are many more, but now he is exposed. I am releasing his victims from my influence and fanning their desire for revenge. All of Lancaster will be in an uproar while I complete my work and be gone before anyone is the wiser."

"Then why kill me?" Dabney whined. "Haven't I suffered enough? You can erase my memory! You can...!"

"Master Copeland," Ms. Adler replied, "I want you dead simply because I despise you. I have listened to your petty, scheming, hateful thoughts for years. Having your family's estate in such close proximity has been torture. My telepathy hears everything. You disgust me. I will not deny myself the satisfaction of terminating your existence. You are a waste of the good German blood you inherited from your grandmother. Our heritage cries out for your removal from the bloodline. It is a favor I do for a man whose boots you are not fit to lick."

"Just let me go!" Dabney cried. "I can't even say your name! I've changed, damn it! I'm not that person anymore!"

Ms. Adler's eyes grew bright. *"I can read your thoughts. You are already trying to find a way to warn Jeremy and Craig. You would, too, if I released you."*

"They're my friends!"

"They would have been," Ms. Adler snorted. *"Friends like you have never had in your pathetic life, and in Christopher McKee? You would have found true love like few in the world ever know."*

Dabney gasped. *Chris? Oh, God!*

"Yes, Master Copeland. He is falling in love with you, too, a deep enduring love that would have sustained you both for a lifetime." She smirked. *"You are as perfect a pair as Jeremy and Craig. They, too, would have known a love as great as you and Christopher, if not greater. The mind-link I formed between them is so total, their feelings for each other will transcend any moral considerations or ridiculous sexual orientation, and do you know why?"* She leaned toward him.

Dabney whimpered.

"Because they will know honesty in their feelings for each other, because they can never deceive one another. Every emotion is shared. Their friendship will grow into love. Each will see that love in the other without reservation and they will return it with equal intensity. When they understand that love, they will realize they could never love anyone else with that depth of feeling and nothing else will matter anymore except each other." Ms. Adler smiled. *"That is what I take from them because they must die for my work to be complete. That is what I take from you because you do not deserve to be loved the way Christopher McKee would have loved you. You are not worthy."*

"No!" Dabney sobbed. "You can't do this!" His tears ran freely as his heart broke. "Please, I... *I...*"

Ms. Adler brought her hand to her chin. *"Go ahead, Master Copeland. Say it. It will be the most honest thing you have ever said in your life."*

"I love him, too," Dabney whispered. He lowered his eyes. He knew he was right. He had never known anything more clearly in his life. "Oh, God... I do love Chris... so much."

She nodded. *"Fitting those should be your last words. You give me great satisfaction knowing I am taking all that away from you."*

Ms. Adler's desk drawer opened at her mental command. A roll of duct tape sailed out. Dabney tried to move, but she held him fast. The tape whizzed around him, binding his wrists behind his back, and then his legs from his ankles to his groin. A small piece tore free from the roll and covered his mouth. Ms. Adler lifted him up with her telekinetics and set him gently on the floor. She released him from her hold and sent the tape back to her drawer. Dabney attempted to break free, but the tape was too strong.

Her eyes dimmed. "There you will remain until the end of the game," she said. "When I have completed my work, I will destroy this place and everything in it." She glared down at Dabney. "Including you."

Ms. Adler strutted over to the lab table and picked up Jeremy's blood test stick. She held it over the green-black ooze.

"It is time to bind the power to its future host," she said, lowering the sample into the beaker.

The ooze shot up and engulfed the stick hungrily. It sucked it down, flashed brightly, and then spat the stick into the air. Ms. Adler caught it in her hand and threw it into the trash.

She said, "The power is bound to Jeremy's genetic structure. The serum will form. Soon, I will be free!"

Ms. Adler turned to Dabney and flooded his mind with her memories of Buchenwald. *"You thought you knew horror? I will show you the meaning of the word."* When she was through, she held her hand up toward the far wall, her eyes glowing. The wall pulled away from the foundation swinging open like a bank vault. She rose off the floor and floated past the two-foot-thick concrete slab into the darkness of her basement.

"Computer?" she commanded. *"Lights off."*

"Lights off."

Dabney screamed into the tape covering his mouth as the lab went dark. Memories of murder, brains in jars, dead bodies lying in piles waiting to be cremated, the stink of death and burning flesh, the cries of boys beaten to death and executed ripped through his mind. *The horror! Tragedy! The children! Oh, God, hundreds of children!* The hidden door swung shut and engulfed him in pitch-black. The only source of illumination remaining came from the lab table. There was a flash of energy as a drop of fluid hit the green-black ooze. Then there was another… and another…

* * *

Teddy finished his story. He told them he had been torn out of his drug induced sleep by the pain of Hiram's assault just long enough to see Todd O'Connor standing in the doorway watching. Max filled Henry in on what Chris had told them in Derek's fort. Henry listened with his mouth agape at the hauntingly familiar tale. His experience wasn't much different. He didn't drink Hiram's Kool-Aid concoction either, but he wasn't too scared to move when Hiram made a move on him. Henry ran out of the trailer and never went back. Hiram mailed him his check. He was ashamed and humiliated. He thought no one would believe him since he wasn't a little kid.

Ricardo demanded they do something. He empathized with their experiences. He had an overwhelming desire to take out a lifetime of pain on Todd O'Connor for not doing anything to help Teddy. "He didn't stop him, man!"

Chris grabbed him by the shirt, got in his face, and yelled at him to shut his mouth. Ricardo was stunned and hurt. The look in Chris' eyes had the same effect on him as everyone else in the room. They froze and went silent. Chris' thoughts whirled. Guilt and sorrow clouded his mind as realization sank in. He was overwhelmed by the knowledge that this was his fault for not turning Hiram in. He burst into tears and reached for his iPhone.

Teddy cried out when he saw Chris hit *911*. "No!" Tears streamed down his face. He ripped the phone out of Chris' hands, canceled the call, and slammed it on Jeremy's desk. "You can't do that!"

"Why?" Chris cried. "We have to turn him in!"

"You didn't!"

"And look what happened!" Chris snapped. "What do we do? Wait for another kid to get molested?"

Teddy begged him. They couldn't call the cops. His father would kill Hiram. Robert's career would be over, their family ruined.

"We should mess their world up at least," Max said.

"Yeah," Derek added. "Kick the crap out of them."

Chris heard his mom's Camaro pull into the driveway. He told everyone to drop the subject. He brought Teddy to the bathroom so he could wash his face. Matt and Max went downstairs to get the pizza. Jeremy was the first to notice the depressed mood blanketing everyone. He asked what the problem was. Teddy made up a story about his grandfather dying. Jeremy said he was sorry.

Herman stayed in Jeremy's room with Jeremy and Craig. Everyone else filed into Chris' room. They set themselves on the floor except for Sandy and Derek. They shared the waterbed with Chris. They laid there in silence, but no one slept. They heard Thomas and Virginia turn in a short time later. The thoughts whirling around in Chris' mind finally stopped as his self-anger turned to Todd.

That bastard! Chris thought, grinding his teeth. *He's as much to blame for what happened to Teddy as I am!*

Chris sat up, climbed over Sandy, and grabbed his clothes. "Let's do it," he said.

"Yes!" Ricardo whispered, pumping his fist.

They dressed, slipped out the window, and climbed down a nearby tree. They went to the trails on the other side of Owen Road and walked in single file toward the farm. The stars and moon gave enough light to see by through the thick treetops. No one spoke until they neared the pasture. Chris agreed with Max's idea. They would pound the farmer until he confessed. It would keep Teddy's father from becoming a murderer. It was impossible to deny they were doing the right thing. It made too much sense. After Hiram was safely behind bars, they would turn their attention to Todd. The boys crossed the pasture, stepped into the barnyard, and froze as the light in the milking parlor went out.

*   *   *

Todd stormed out of the barn and flung the door closed. The latch failed to connect and the door swung open again, creaking loudly. Todd clenched his fist. He spun around, whipped the door shut, and kicked it several times before he punched it. The pain cleared his mind. He shook his hand, whimpering. He was so angry he couldn't see straight. The evening chores were finally finished. One of the airlines had broken in the middle of milking. It had taken him forever to fix it. Hiram could've done it in minutes. Todd struggled until he nearly set the machine on fire. Now, it was so late, he would barely get to nod before having to milk again.

Hiram! Todd thought, angry and sad at the same time. *I need you! Where are you?* He sank against the door seeking its support to hold him up when all he wanted to do was fall on his knees and cry. *Why, God? Why Frank? He was my bud! I don't have anyone else!*

Todd couldn't believe he was dead. Now he knew why Frank hadn't been home when he dropped by yesterday. He thought Frank had stood him up. The more he thought about it, the more it tore him up inside. He didn't understand why he didn't go around to the back of house and throw stones at Frank's window. He had dozens of times before, but this time he felt compelled to just walk away. The thought of Frank lying there dead the whole time was driving him crazy. Todd wanted to talk to Hiram when he got to the farm. He needed to speak to him about Frank and other things. He wanted Hiram to explain what he had witnessed the other night. He wanted to hear everything was all right and that he wasn't going mad. He wanted to know that the man he'd trusted since he was eight years old wasn't drugging him and using his body the way he had Teddy. He wanted to hear it from him. He wanted Hiram to tell him he wasn't a *sick twisted baby-raper and he wanted to know now!* His emotions raged with despair at the loss of his friend. They churned in outrage over his perverted surrogate father.

"Where are you, you bastard!?" Todd yelled.

The low mooing of the cows was his only answer. Todd felt like he was losing his mind. The floodgates opened when Frank died and now he was drowning. He fell to his knees at last, Frank's smiling face burning into his memory. He wept. Loss ripped a hole in his soul. An ocean of red poured over the mind-picture.

Blood. It's Frank's blood. His time was too short! Todd couldn't get it out of his mind. *It was suicide, wasn't it? Something happened and Frank gave up. Drugs they said. They found LSD in his room. What nightmare vision drove Frank over the edge and sent him flying out that window? When I die, will Frank be waiting for me?* He punched the dirt driveway. *I hate you, Hiram! The time I need you the most and you're not here? I hate your guts!*

Todd glanced up at the trailer, his tears blurring his vision. He laughed through the sorrow at what he had done inside. The living room was in shambles. He'd torn it apart with the fit of rage that exploded when he realized Hiram wasn't home. There was broken glass everywhere. He had overturned the entertainment center. The television screen imploded when it hit the edge of the coffee table. He smashed the living room phone against the rear wall. It lay in pieces around the old man's plants.

Hiram was probably out with Arthur Kelly since he hadn't taken his truck. Burning the trailer down would've been too easy and leaving even easier. Todd wanted Hiram to see the pain in his face while it was still fresh. He wasn't going until the old man came back. Todd would confront him when he did. Hiram would give him the answers he needed to keep his world from coming apart, or Todd would break every bone in his fat perverted pedophile body.

The pain in his fist subsided. Todd realized he had broken his knuckle on the door. He wiped his eyes and moved to stand up, but a firm grip fell on his shoulder forcing him back down.

"Don't get up, O'Connor," Henry said, his eyes burning with anger. His grin was more like a snarl. "If you do, I'll knock you back down again."

Todd clenched his fist and was about to swing. Connecting with flesh and bone would be a lot more satisfying than punching the door even with a broken knuckle. Todd looked up. His anger melted away to uncertainty. Henry wasn't alone. Ricardo looked down at him, scowling. Across the barnyard, Chris McKee led Max, Matt, and Sandy into the trailer. Todd saw them through the windows as they moved from room to room. Derek and Teddy lurked at the edge of the driveway.

Todd's heart raced. *Oh, God!* he thought. *They're looking for Hiram!*

Chris kicked the screen door open. He crossed the yard to Todd with the others right behind him. Ricardo was on his other shoulder, his nails digging into his collarbone.

"Where is he, you *son-of-a-bitch!?*" Chris cried, as he swung his fist. He punched Todd square in the face. A loud crack echoed in the barnyard.

Todd flew back landing on his rear end. His eyes grew wide. He jumped to his feet, his fists at the ready. His upper lip was split and bleeding.

"I don't know why you did that, McKee," Todd spat, his eyes narrow, "but if you think you're getting away with it because your pussy friends are here, think again!"

367

Ricardo jumped forward. He punched Todd twice in the stomach and once in the chin knocking him down again. Todd fell flat, but scrambled to his feet. He moved into the middle of the barnyard. Ricardo lunged again. Todd spun around and leg swept him, flipping him over backward. Ricardo hit the dirt hard knocking the wind out of him. Max glared at Todd, but did nothing. He bent over to help his brother up.

"What's going on, Chris?" Derek called, from the driveway. "Where's the farmer?"

"Gone!" Chris yelled. He pointed at Todd. "This scumbag's going to tell me where!"

"What do you… want Hiram for?" Todd asked, spitting blood as the boys circled him.

"Why don't you tell us?" Max asked. He shoved Todd into Sandy who clotheslined him. Todd smacked down onto the dirt on his back.

"Yeah, O'Connor," Sandy said, through his teeth. He leaned over so they were face to face. "You tell us. After what we heard tonight, you might walk away from this still breathing."

Todd glared at Teddy who looked nervously away. "What did you tell them?" he cried. "You liar!"

Max kicked Todd in the gut. The wind rushed out of him in a loud whoosh. He curled up, holding his stomach. Ricardo kicked him in the side of his face. The skin below his cheekbone tore. The boys dropped on him, pummeling him. Todd wheezed trying to crawl away. Ricardo wanted to kick him again, but Chris held him back. He wanted answers.

"How could you do it, Todd?" Chris demanded, shoving him with the tip of his sneaker.

Todd fell over onto his back. He groaned, "You're… dead," and spat a wad of blood-filled phlegm at Chris. It hit his pant leg. "You're all dead!"

"I'd worry about myself if I were you," Henry said, feeling an enormous sense of satisfaction. "Hiram's sick, but you just stood there and watched."

Todd looked over. His left eye was swollen shut. His lip felt like a slice of liver.

"Yeah, Todd," Chris replied. "How could you just stand there and watch what that maniac did to Teddy?" He grew angrier by the second. "You lied to me! I asked you if that bastard had ever touched you! He has, right? A *lot,* right!? So much and so many times that you're just like him! Is that why you just stood there and watched? Is that why you didn't help Teddy?"

"No!" Todd cried. "It's not true! I'm not like him!"

"Maybe you aren't," Matt said. "Not yet, but you're sick, man. You need help."

Max moved toward Todd. "He needs to be beat on some more!"

"No," Chris said, holding Max back. "We've done enough." He turned to Todd. "This isn't over. It's too bad it's come to this. You had a chance to come clean, man, like I did. We could've prevented this if we had turned Hiram in. You know that, don't you?"

Chris turned leading his friends away. He said, "Call the cops and tell, Todd. We're telling them tomorrow."

Todd watched them walk away. He thought, *They're right. It's my fault. Why didn't I stop him?* His mind went black, burning with vengeance. *I can still stop him.* He hit the ground with the side of his fist and started to cry. *He has to come home sometime!*

Chris and the others faded into the darkness.

DAY FIVE
Friday

Jack lay face down on his bedroom rug four feet from his bed. Consciousness slowly intruded into his hungover body. His head pounded. He smacked his lips His tongue tasted like he'd been licking the bottom of a cat box last night instead of slamming straight Jack Daniel's in Misty's Café until two in the morning. He didn't dare open his eyes for fear they would fall out of his head. His optic nerves were surely no more than pus-covered yarn. He groaned, his breathing shallow and quick as he tried to get some oxygen into his bloodstream. He was moments away from puking. He felt for the only salvation left to him. His fingers alighted on the neck of the bottle and slid down the twisted glass to the square body. He gripped it like a drowning man with the last life preserver.

Jack rolled onto his back. He slipped the cap off the bottle with his thumb, his forearm securely pressed over his eyes. He used his other hand to tilt the bottle to his lips. The whiskey poured onto his chin first. The cool liquid ran down his neck and soaked the collar of his tee shirt. It stank from a week's worth of body odor since no one in his wretched family had brought him a change of clothes and some Right Guard while he rotted in his cell. The opening found his lips. Jack drank deep waiting for the alcohol to take away the pain and give him a new lease on his living death.

Jack rotated between sleeping and pleading with the cops to slip him a bottle after the visit from Giuseppe Luciano. It was maddening. The shakes and the visions the delirium tremens brought to him were horrid. He considered suicide by hanging rather than enduring the sickness. He prayed to God for a drink, just a tumbler glass filled to the brim with bourbon. He would swallow it in one gulp. Later, he cursed the Lord for having no mercy on him whatsoever. The forgiving God? The loving God?

Yeah, sure! Jack thought.

Once the whiskey passed through to his brain, Jack felt better. The nausea faded and the pain in his head subsided to a dull ache. He sat up cracking an eye toward his alarm clock. The bright red numbers informed him it was 8:00 a.m. on what he hoped was Friday morning. He was confident he hadn't drunk enough to put him out for more than one evening. The silence of the house was deafening. He longed for the sound of the television, for Craig to be in the living room in his pajamas. He would be sitting in front of the screen quietly giggling at *Loony Toons* or whatever other cartoons drew his fancy. As quickly as the feeling of loss descended upon him, Jack slammed it back with another jolt from the bottle.

Screw that kid, just screw him! The backstabbing...! A restraining order!? A lawyer? He's dead meat when I get a hold of him! Take my kid, will you? I have news for Thomas McKee. This isn't over. It won't be long either! I'll get my hands on Craig. When I do, he'll regret the day he crossed me. Nobody crosses Jack Dougan. Nobody!

Jack downed the last of the bottle and threw it against the wall. He growled when it didn't break. It only dented the plaster and tumbled to the floor. He cracked open another bottle of bourbon in the kitchen. It was the second of four bottles he'd purchased shortly after his release. He had no idea why Copeland dropped the charges against him and he didn't care. He was at the package store in a flash shelling out the last of Craig's paycheck He walked the trails home, grabbed his final unemployment check from the mailbox, and made it to the bank in time to cash it. He went straight to Misty's glad to see the Monte Carlo was still there, bad brakes and broken steering column notwithstanding.

The crowd gave him a wide berth when he entered. He recognized a few of the men from the fight. They were still sporting bruises. They looked away when Jack made eye contact with them. He asked Misty if she knew why Copeland had cut him loose, but she sadly shook her head. Jack commanded her to *keep them coming* until he blacked out. He couldn't remember leaving the bar or getting home. At least he didn't wake up in that cell again. The worst hallucination of all had come to him the morning before they let him go. It was the worst since Jack believed the ghost of Giuseppe had been real, especially after waking up with his hands covered in that same black soil.

The smell of that dirt, he thought, a chill running down his spine. *It was so familiar.*

Jack felt okay when he woke. The shakes were finally gone. He shaved under supervision and cleaned up as best he could. Everything went nuts shortly after the guard left. Jack had been staring in the mirror at his ragged reflection when he saw something behind him. Someone was sitting on the edge of his cot waiting for him. He squeezed his eyes shut, holding on to the sink. He froze not daring to breathe.

"I guess ye never thought t' have t' face me, right, Jackie?" Wade said, his voice booming. *"Turn around, boy. I'll not be leavin' until ye hear what I've to say."*

"You're dead!" Jack cried, spinning around and glaring into his father's face. "This isn't happening! Who do you people think I am? *Ebenezer Scrooge!?"*

Wade sighed, *"Your manners leave a lot t' be desired."*

"My manners are fine, thank you!"

"In your eyes, it seems!" Wade retorted.

Jack took a step back, his hand over his mouth. "Good Lord," he whispered, his anger fading away. "Is it really you, dad?"

"Aye, lad," Wade nodded. *"'Tis me a'right."*

Jack threw his arms around his father's cold dead neck and wept again. He had cried more in the past week than in his entire life. He said how sorry he was. The years spent with Hiram came back to him all at once. He was so

372

ashamed at what had happened, so full of sorrow over who he was now. He felt the raging loss of the years he'd spent missing his father. He wanted desperately to tell him and to beg his forgiveness.

"Ah, Jackie," Wade whispered, patting his son on the back. *"I know everything now. Can ye ever forgive me for not savin' ye?"*

Jack pulled back, his eyes filled with tears. "Forgive you?" he sobbed. "I love you! God, dad, I've missed you… so much…"

"I've missed ye, too, lad," Wade replied, grabbing Jack by the back of his neck. *"I always loved ye, Jackie. Always. No matter what ye've done, you're still me son."*

Jack held his father's ghost for a long time. Wade's icy fingers stroked his hair. He had so much to say to him, so much he wanted to ask, but Wade only shushed him. He said to relish the moments they had together. He would be gone soon. Jack held him tighter. He begged him not to go. Everything seemed fine for the first time since he was twelve.

"Me time is short, Jackie," Wade said, sternly, holding his son away from him. *"It takes a lot o' effort t' allow ye t' see me as such. Ye need to hear what I've t' say afore I go."*

"Please," Jack begged, "tell me what's going on."

"As th' boy told ye," Wade sadly replied. *"I cannot. 'Tis against th' rules."*

Jack nodded and thought, *Somehow that makes sense.*

"Soon ye'll be given a chance," Wade continued, *"t' show what kinda man ye truly are. Make th' right choice, lad. Make me proud."*

"How could you be proud of me now?" Jack sighed, looking away.

"If'n it's Craig on your mind," Wade said, turning Jack's face to his, *"th' boy has more'n enough heart t' forgive ye for what ye've done. He'd walk through th' pit for ye if'n he had t'. How could I do less? He needs ye, lad. Ye've got t' help him. If'n ye don't, there'll be hell t' pay for a lot o' people."*

"But…," Jack began.

Wade held his hand up, fading away. *"Ye'll know, Jackie,"* he said, his voice going hollow as he disappeared. *"Make me proud."*

"No! Wait!"

"Wait for what?" the officer unlocking Jack's cell asked. "For hell to freeze over? Too late, Dougan. I think it already has. You're sprung. Let's move it, huh? I haven't got all day."

Jack poured a shot of bourbon into his black coffee chuckling at the memory. *Delirium tremens… God, they're weird!*

He vowed never to have a sober moment again in his life if that's what was in store for him. By the end of the night, after spending nearly all of his money at Misty's, everything that happened in that cell seemed like a dream. Even the bruises on his neck, the dirt on his palms…

… the smell of the soil, its black richness… so familiar…

The realization of where he knew that scent came to him in the bar.

It's the pasture! Hiram Milliken's pasture!

Jack shut it out completely.

He finished his coffee and walked onto the porch. He gripped the whiskey bottle in his hand and looked out into Lancaster's morning light. Jack didn't know what would happen to him, but he knew one thing. Regardless of what his hallucinations had said, and despite the restraining order, he was going to get his hands on his errant son. When he did, he would wring Craig's neck.

"You're coming home, Craig," Jack whispered. "Heaven help you, you're coming home."

A breeze came up. In what Jack swore was the sound of his father yelling at him was a woman's voice.

She was laughing.

*   *   *

Mike was about to leave the house for the market when the phone rang. Sandra was sitting on the couch watching out the front window with the oddest look on her face. She mumbled something about whether or not he wanted her to answer that. Mike reached out and tapped her on the shoulder. She dreamily looked up at him. He asked her if she was okay. Sandra frowned like she always did when something wasn't making any sense to her. He knew it was something important. Sandra told him she usually saw Dr. Stone's son, Sam, jog by their house in the morning, but she hadn't seen him since Monday.

"Did you call Dr. Stone?" Mike asked, ignoring the phone. It had eight rings until voicemail picked up.

Sandra nodded. "I called his house. I thought Sam might be sick, or something, you know?"

"And?" Mike asked.

"His sister… Stephanie I think her name was," Sandra replied, rubbing her temples, "answered. She said Sam was away at camp."

"So?" Mike asked, kissing her on the cheek. "What's wrong with that? Mystery solved."

"I suppose," she whispered.

"What's that supposed to mean?"

"Well," Sandra said, sitting up a little, "when I asked her what camp, Stephanie said she didn't know. She said she was surprised he even went since he hated camp."

"Really?" Mike asked. The voicemail picked up. He watched for the message icon.

"Yes, and not only that," Sandra continued, pushing her hair back, "I called the Connecticut Department of Energy & Environmental Protection from work the other day. They said there were no camps in session this week. It was too close to the end of the school year. Some schools weren't even out yet."

"Maybe he went to a camp out of state," Mike offered.

"It's possible," she said, glancing out the window again. She stared at the road. "But Sam told me he had no plans for the summer. There was something else, too, something Stephanie said when I called her back that didn't make any sense."

Mike gave a quick nod in a questioning gesture as the phone rang again.

"When I asked her if she could find out the name of the camp from her father," Sandra said, worry creasing her features, "Stephanie said she doubted he even remembered."

"That's odd," Mike agreed.

Sandra said, "Not as odd as when she said Dr. Stone kept going into Sam's room in the morning to wake him up for his run."

"That's really strange."

Sandra agreed. "She said she and her brother kept finding him sitting on Sam's bed. They had to remind him Sam was away at camp."

Mike shook his head and went over to the phone. He snatched up the receiver. He recognized the voice on the other end of the phone. It was Scott Wells from Aldujara Trucking in Hinesville, Georgia. It was the company that delivered some of his produce.

"Thank God I caught you, Mr. Dougan," Scott said, sounding nervous. His Southern drawl was thick.

"What's up, Scott?" Mike asked, rubbing his eyes. "I was just on my way out."

Scott said there had been a terrible error. His boss, Victor, was furious. Someone had gotten into the computer file and changed the time of Mike's delivery making it earlier. The driver was someone they'd had problems with before. He received notification of the time change en route.

"He's a real bastard, Mr. Dougan," Scott said. "I'm sorry."

"Don't worry about it," Mike said. "What time will he be here?"

"I hate to say this, but he already is."

"What?" Mike asked, looking at the kitchen clock.

"The driver called Victor at home," Scott said, "and boy is he mad! He said your store ain't open. Victor just got back from Mexico, too. Merle – that's the driver – woke him up. Believe me, Mr. Dougan, if Merle Wrightwood gives y'all any trouble, call the police. It ain't worth arguing with him. He's a thick-headed stubborn old redneck. Praise Jesus he don't drink no more. He was one mean and nasty drunk."

Mike hung up the phone. He hugged Sandra and told her he had to go. He said not to worry about Sam. She forced a smile to get him on his way, but it faded once the door was closed. Sandra had a sick feeling in her stomach. It had moved in Tuesday morning when she hadn't seen Sam.

It could also be nerves, Sandra thought, heading to the coffee pot. *The farmer's ex-employees are coming here today.*

She was anxious, but they would know the truth at last. She was glad Jack had forbidden Craig to go near the farm. She was glad they obeyed his wishes at least that time. She poured a cup of coffee, went back to the sofa, and returned to staring out the window.

Where are you, Sam? Sandra wondered. She closed her eyes and whispered a Hail Mary.

*   *   *

Mike made it to the market quickly. He pulled into the parking lot and knew right away there was going to be trouble. The truck driver, a burly old man, was pacing back and forth in front of his Mack, kicking at the dirt with his pointy-toe cowboy boots. He looked mean and ready for a confrontation. This wasn't what Mike needed to start off his day. He parked his tan Buick Regal figuring he could call the McKees and have Craig come down now rather than wait. His nephew would be happy since he had wanted to go to Jeremy's baseball game. Mike would have given him the day off, but Henry Schwartz was coming in to interview for Dan's position, and he didn't have time to handle the unloading. That all changed when Mike opened the car door.

"Are y'all the manager of this here shithole?" Merle snapped, hiking his belt up to his beer belly.

Mike glared at him for a moment, counted to five, and pointed to the marker in front of his parking spot.

"See that?" Mike asked, sharply. "It says *owner*. I *own* it. It's *my* shithole."

"Well, la-de-dah!" Merle snapped. "It's about time! Get on up there and get me unloaded. I've been in this pissant state long enough and I ain't going to wait one more minute!"

*   *   *

Virginia carefully opened the door to Jeremy's room. She was glad he had left it unlocked so she didn't have to knock. She slipped inside to wake up Craig. She had heard Jeremy's alarm go off from downstairs in the kitchen. As quickly as it began, it stopped. She shook her head and climbed the steps. She knew her sleepy-headed son had reached over and shut it off. Although Craig claimed to be a light sleeper when he first came to stay with them, Virginia discovered he slept like the dead. For the first time, he felt safe enough at night to drift into deeper periods of sleep than ever before.

She stood above the three sleeping boys in her youngest son's bed. They looked cozy. She was loath to wake Craig at all.

Herman was on top of the covers in his underwear. His head was down at the foot of the bed. Craig and Jeremy were lying face to face, their foreheads touching.

He's such a handsome boy, Virginia thought, tenderly touching the dirty blonde hair hanging in Craig's face. *Jeremy seems to honestly care for him.*

Craig was the first intimate friend her son had ever made. It was unrealistic how Jack could hurt him. What kind of man treated his son that way? Virginia was glad her husband had gone to bat for Craig and that Jeremy convinced him to let them help. She leaned over and kissed his cheek.

Craig's eyes fluttered as he woke. Virginia envied his long lashes. He smiled meekly up at her. She whispered it was time for him to get up and get ready for work. Today would be the first shift he worked without Jeremy. He promised to try and get done in time to see the last part of the game. There was a trailer due at eleven, the same time the game was scheduled to start, and Craig had to unload it.

A big job for such a little guy, she thought. As he slipped from under the sheets, she smiled.

Craig's body was tone. He was going to be gorgeous when he grew up. The girls would just die for the open warmth of his smile. She helped him stand. Craig tapped Herman on the back to get him to move out of the way. He stirred and rolled over.

Craig selected an outfit from some of the new clothes Virginia had given him. He wished he could wear them all. He thought they were incredible. She moved into the hallway and stopped by Chris' door where she heard Chris tell Sandy it was okay for him to shower first.

Virginia shook her head and smiled. *Chris will give anything for a few more minutes of sleep,* she thought.

She went downstairs to brew some coffee. Chris would want some and so would Matt. She wasn't sure about the rest of the boys, so she made a full pot. She set bowls on the table, a gallon of milk, spoons, and some boxes of cereal. The boys filed downstairs looking groggy. It served them right. She heard them sneak out last night. She said nothing as they crowded around the table and poured some breakfast.

"Can I have some coffee, Mrs. McKee?" Matt asked. He yawned and rubbed his shining blue eyes.

"Me, too?" Derek yawned.

"And me?" Teddy asked, shaking his head trying to clear the cobwebs. He felt woozy and detached. He couldn't hear Ms. Adler's voice in his head anymore. That scared him. *Hello?* he thought. *Hello!?*

"Okay," Virginia sighed. "How many of you guys want coffee? Raise your hands."

Every hand at the table went up.

She mumbled, "Oy vey."

Henry chuckled. "You'd make a good Jew, Mrs. McKee. My mother says that all the time."

"Our mother always says *¡Ay Dios mío!*" Ricardo yawned.

Max snickered.

"With my mom, it's always *'Lord, give me strength with this child!'*" Matt exclaimed.

They all laughed including Virginia. That one she'd heard.

Teddy nodded. "Mine always says, *'Shit on a stick!'*"

Matt laughed so hard he fell out of his chair onto the floor. Teddy blushed as the rest of the group joined him in whoops of laughter. Max reached out and helped Matt up.

"What does your mom say, Derek?" Herman asked, wiping his eyes.

Derek shook his head, *"'Jesus H. Christ!'* but I'm not sure what the *H* stands for."

"Henry," Henry said, as he polished his glasses with his tee shirt.

"Dream on!" Herman smiled. "It's Herman!"

"Herman?" Ricardo laughed. "I don't think the Lord would pick such a dweeb name, amigo!"

"Yeah, dude," Max agreed. "It has to be a Hispanic name like *Hernandez,* or something. We all know God is Puerto Rican."

Derek laughed so hard he thought he was going to wet his pants. "Jesus *Hernandez* Christ?" he howled.

"Oh, yeah?" Max grinned. "Derek *Carson* Mellon!"

Derek stood on his chair and mooned them.

"Derek!" Virginia cried, her hand to her chest.

"Oops!" Derek grinned. He quickly sat back down.

"God," Matt said. "You're never going to keep your pants up, are you, Mellon?"

"Not when you're around, big boy!" Derek lisped, bending his wrist.

Everybody laughed, but when they remembered Chris was in earshot they went silent. Derek covered his mouth. Ricardo lightly cuffed him. Virginia cringed. She hoped politeness was their motivation and not that Chris was insecure about his sexual preference. At least the boys knew about it. She wasn't keen on the idea of discussing it with the other parents, especially Cynthia or Linda. Susan was okay. She was a Liberal, too.

"I heard that, Derek!" Chris called, from the top of the stairs. The whole room groaned. "How could you cheat on me after all of the nights we spent together?"

Derek furiously blushed as he laughed. The group followed his lead. Virginia smiled with relief.

"God!" Ricardo cried. "Look at Lobster Boy!"

Derek's face looked like he was going to explode.

Chris snickered as he made his way back to his room. He had to say something when the weight of the mood fell firmly on his shoulders. They were his friends. They needed to know he wasn't offended by good-natured gay humor.

The Schwartz brothers left shortly after breakfast. The rest of the boys were in the living room waiting for their rides and listening to iRockRadio.com on Matt's phone. Matt had declined the Schwartz boys' invitation to walk with them even though they lived on the same street. He wanted to talk to Jeremy before he left. The guys had decided to get to the field a little early and toss the ball around. He figured maybe he would like to go. There was some confusion about Ian and whether or not he would be back from camp for the game. There were a few eighth-grade alternates on their team, so it wasn't a big deal. Matt thought he would miss Ian's big mouth though. It was still a team advantage.

Derek started singing Stone Temple Pilots' *Plush* a cappella. He knew every word. His dad played the song all the time. The room grew quiet. They listened, intrigued. Max was in the recliner with his feet up drinking his coffee. He was surprised at how well Derek sang. He had a great voice. Ricardo stood against the banister in the hall watching and shaking his head. Matt shrugged his shoulders and smiled, pointing at Derek. Matt thought he was pretty good, too. When he and Ricardo started laughing, Derek thought they were laughing at him. He sat down angrily and pouted. Max got up and pulled on one of his red spikes.

"Ow!" Derek whined. "Why are you pulling my hair, Max?"

"Because, mi amigo," Max replied, squatting down in front of him. "Don't assume anything, okay? They weren't laughing at you. In fact, I think you sing wicked good."

"Really?" Derek asked.

"Really!" they all said.

"I want to sing in the choir at church," Derek said. "My mom thinks it's a good idea."

They told him he should. So did Virginia calling from the kitchen. Matt climbed the stairs to Jeremy's room. He found Craig standing half-nude – he had a shirt on – in front of Jeremy's closet door mirror combing his hair. Jeremy was lying in bed watching him and grinning wryly. He could feel the comb going over his scalp as if he were the one using it. Craig sensed Matt's entry and quickly reached for a towel. Matt waved him off and closed the door.

Craig blushed. "I thought you were Mrs. McKee."

"Nah," Matt said. "She's got bigger boobs than me."

"Oh, my God!" Jeremy moaned. "Who in Creation notices that about somebody's mom? Gross!"

"Matt," Craig said, reaching for his clothes.

"Apparently," Jeremy scowled.

"We're going to the field a little early," Matt said. "I thought you might like to go."

"No, I...," Jeremy began. He paused when he felt a flash of jealousy from Craig. It was so strong, it plowed through everything else in his mind.

"You know we're going to talk about that, don't you?" Jeremy thought. Craig nodded pulling on his underwear. He grabbed his cutoffs.

Jeremy continued to Matt, "Dude, I never get to spend any time with my dad. He's taking me today. I want to wait as long as possible. Everybody's going to be gone soon, you know? It'll just be the two of us."

"Are you sure, man?" Matt asked, disappointed. *Maybe if I push a little? No, that wouldn't be cool even though Jeremy would probably cave.*

"I'm sure, Matt," Jeremy said, "but thanks for asking."

"No problem," Matt replied. "I'll see you there. Later, Craig."

"Later, Matt," Craig replied, sounding sad.

Matt paused at the door, but then continued, closing it behind him.

Craig glanced over at Jeremy who pointed at the edge of his bed. He mentally ordered him to *"Get over here!"* They said nothing as their eyes locked. They had an hour-long conversation in the space of a few seconds. Their thoughts flew back and forth between each other with incredible speed. Jeremy wanted to know the reason for Craig's flash of jealousy. Craig flooded his innermost thoughts and feelings to the surface where Jeremy could easily read them. Jeremy did the same for him. They decided they were best friends and would be for life. Jeremy felt a sting of sadness they wouldn't be together today at least for a little while.

Craig said, "I'll come to the field right after work."

"I'll be waiting," Jeremy said. "Get going before you're late. You know, you ought to think about playing ball."

"Baseball?" Craig asked, putting on his sneakers and tying them.

Jeremy scowled. "No, Craig," he snorted. "Golf."

"Very funny," Craig replied. "I'm no good at baseball. I want to play football though."

"Okay," Jeremy nodded. "In the fall. I'll play, too."

"Will your mom let you?" Craig asked.

"Are you kidding? Her name is Virginia, not Linda."

Craig walked out with a smile and headed for the stairs. He slipped down to say goodbye to Virginia. He was surprised to find her alone. She poured him a bowl of cereal. She told him he wasn't leaving before he ate something. His uncle could wait.

Craig smiled. *Is this a real family or what? I want to call her mom.*

"Oh, just do it!" Jeremy thought at him. *"She'll eat it up, cry for an hour, and then you can stay here forever!"*

Craig thought back, *"I might do that anyway."*

He ate quickly, gave Virginia a goodbye kiss, and went to the garage for his mountain bike. Jeremy called out to him and asked where he was. Craig said he was just leaving the driveway. Jeremy told him he wanted to see if their mind-link had a range limit like a CB radio. Craig concurred it was a good idea. They opened themselves to each other's thoughts as Craig rode down the hill. The link appeared stable, but when he crossed Route 41 and entered the market's parking lot, the link went fuzzy. Just before he was out of range completely, Craig said goodbye.

Jeremy smiled, but then frowned deeply. He felt such an incredible sense of loss. All week he'd felt Craig's thoughts and feelings mingling with his. They were part of him. He was beginning to get used to it, to desire it, when suddenly the feeling was gone. He felt empty and hollow. He wondered if it was the same for Craig and decided it had to be. He heard his mother call up the stairs to Chris. She said they were going in fifteen minutes. His smile returned. He was glad at last to have a day to spend alone with his father.

*   *   *

Craig stopped his bike at the corner of the market to catch his breath. His head swam and he felt faint. When the mind-link disappeared, Craig was so overwhelmed by a feeling of loneliness that he almost burst into tears. He wondered what was happening to them and where the mind-link had come from in the first place.

Does it have something to do with seeing Ms. Adler on Monday? Craig wondered. *Is one of us psychic and doesn't know it?*

If one of them were, it was Jeremy. Craig never had a psychic experience in his life except for knowing when someone was lying. That wasn't ESP, was it? Hopefully Thomas would find some answers. He was smart. If anyone could figure out what was happening to them, it was him.

Craig wondered why they hadn't asked him about that yet, but then his mind drifted to other things. He wasn't looking forward to meeting with any DCF representatives as was planned. He felt the restraining order had hurt his father in some way. At least, he liked to think it had. It wasn't a malicious feeling. It was regret that it had come to this. Craig understood it wasn't his fault. Everyone was right. His father had problems that needed to be dealt with, issues that caused his drinking and made him violent.

If he doesn't get help, one day he'll beat me to death.

That was the fear Jeremy had found in his thoughts, the one Craig barely knew was there.

Craig pushed his bike around the corner. His eyes opened wide when he saw a tractor-trailer parked in the dock already. He was afraid he had his shift time wrong, but no, that wasn't it.

Uncle Mike said the delivery wouldn't be here until later, he thought.

He locked up his bike, turned around, and headed toward the stairs to the back door. He glanced at the cab. It was an immaculately clean gray cab-over Mack with a sleeper. There was a mean-looking old man with white hair and a beard in the driver's seat glaring at him. He was wearing a white wicker cowboy hat and sucking on the nastiest smelling cigar ever to invade Craig's nose.

Craig looked away and jogged up the stairs where Mike was patiently waiting. He stopped short and looked at his uncle. Mike motioned him to come into the employee bathroom after propping the door open with the stopper. Craig went in first and stood between the two sinks. His uncle locked the door behind them.

"Jesus," Mike said, pacing back and forth in front of the two stalls. His patience melted away. "I am so glad you're here!"

"What's going on, Uncle Mike?" Craig asked.

Mike seemed angry and frightened all at the same time. "I think I'm going to commit bloody murder, that's what!" he growled, waving a fist at the ceiling.

"Are you having a problem with the driver?" Craig asked, thumbing toward the door.

"Am I ever!" Mike exclaimed. "I've never met anyone in my life I wanted to beat the snot out of more than my brother until today!"

Craig listened intently as his uncle told him what had happened. He smiled when Mike paused to catch his breath. "What time was that?" he asked, amused at his uncle's imitation of a Southern accent.

"Eight-fifteen," Mike said. "I was going to call you, but the guy made me mad. I decided he could wait until hell froze over, maybe longer."

"I can see why!"

"That wasn't the only thing," Mike sighed, placing a hand on his nephew's shoulder. "There's more bad news. The phone was ringing when I got here, too."

"Oh?" Craig asked. "Who was it? Did someone call out sick?"

"Nope," Mike replied, squatting down. "It was your father."

Craig's heart leaped into his throat. Mike said Jack demanded that Craig come straight home after work or there would be hell to pay. He reminded Jack about the restraining order, but Jack said he didn't care about any piece of paper. Craig had better not make him come and get him. Mike said he would call the police if he even tried. Jack told him to go right ahead.

Craig burst into tears. It was easy to be brave when his father was locked up with no way he could hurt him, but now? He'd never felt so close to death before. Somewhere inside him a voice said, *"If your father gets a hold of you, you're going to die."* Mike held his nephew. He said there was no way he would allow him to be hurt again.

"Promise?" Craig sniffled, wiping his eyes.

"I swear to God, Craig," Mike whispered. "If he comes anywhere near you, he's mine!"

"I hate him, Uncle Mike!" Craig blubbered. *"I hate him!"*

"I know, kiddo," Mike replied. "I hate him, too."

Mike held on to Craig for a few minutes more allowing him to regain his composure. He was content to hug his nephew all day long. He missed him terribly. Craig was at work most of the week, but he was reluctant to go anywhere without Jeremy. Mike wasn't petty. It was okay for his nephew to bring his friend to the store. He was glad they were getting along so well. God knew Craig needed a friend. Mike just felt bad he'd become accustomed to being his nephew's only confidant.

"What's goin' on?" Merle yelled, pounding on the bathroom door. "In two minutes, I'm going to drop this box, bobtail back home, and y'all can kiss my rebel ass!"

Mike clenched his fist and moved toward the door.

Craig stopped him, wiping his eyes. "It's not worth it, Uncle Mike."

Mike smiled as Craig unlocked the door. He walked past the truck driver and onto the loading dock

"Bring them into the walk-in refrigerator, Craig," Mike called, glaring at Merle.

"Jump," Merle challenged.

"Don't even tempt me, fat man," Mike snapped, poking him in the chest. "You're tap dancing on my last nerve."

Merle laughed moving to light his cigar. Mike told him to take that foul smelling piece of dogshit out of his store. Merle snorted and walked out the back door. He climbed into his cab to wait. He wasn't sure how much more he could take, but it wouldn't be a lot. Merle hated Connecticut. The state was full of New York clones, the freakin' Liberals. He wanted to be on his way back to good ol' Georgia. Another minute of delay and he was going to blow a gasket.

"We would not want that to happen," Ms. Adler said, appearing in Merle's passenger seat.

Merle jumped, crushing the top of his cowboy hat against the roof of the cab. "Sweet Jesus, woman!" he exclaimed, grabbing the steering wheel. "Where in tarnation did you come from?"

"I have been right here," Ms. Adler said, her eyes glowing. *"You could not see me until I let you. I have something for you, Merle."*

"What... do...?" Merle asked, his head swimming, "... you... have?"

"This," Ms. Adler replied. She handed Merle a fifth of Jim Beam.

"But... I don't... drink..."

"Sure you drink, Merle," she said, her eyes glowing brighter. *"You are a real man and all real men drink, do they not? Is that not what your father always said?"*

Merle looked hungrily at the bottle. He took it.

"Nothing like a drink when the day is making you angry," Ms. Adler said. *"Very angry indeed."*

* * *

Craig came out of the cooler after making sure there was enough room for the oranges and asked for the invoice to do the count. He inquired as to the driver's whereabouts. Mike smiled.

Craig frowned. "What did you do to him?" he asked, his eyes narrowing.

"Nothing," Mike replied.

"Okay, then," Craig said, crossing his arms, "What did you say to him?"

"Well…"

"Forget it," Craig interjected, holding his hand up. "I don't want to know."

Mike smiled. *That's my boy.*

They heard a quiet rapping on the front door. Mike turned to see Henry Schwartz waving at him through the glass. He had initially called Henry in for this interview yesterday, but his father said he was an overnight guest at the McKees' house. Mike told him he would call at nine o'clock this morning. Ira said that wasn't necessary. Henry would be back early. He would see his son got right over there.

Mike was glad to see he'd gotten the message. He had an ulterior motive for calling Henry. God knew he wasn't first on the list of kids who wanted to work at the market. Every employee was a teenager except Mary Seaver, his Monday through Friday dayshift cashier, Beatrice Jones, and Old Ted Collins. Bea and Lisa alternated working on Saturdays, and the market was closed Sundays when Mike and Sandra went to Mass. It drew other teens to apply like flies. He felt guilty about pushing Henry to the top of the list. He decided to do it when his suspicions regarding Hiram turned into a bonfire. It was worth more to know the truth than turning a blind eye to one of Lisa's friends who would become as proficient at sneaking beer out the back – paid for, of course – as she was.

Mike unlocked the front door, greeted Henry, and led him to the office. Craig waved to him. Henry returned it.

"I didn't know you were coming here today," Craig said, shaking his hand.

"Me, neither," Henry replied. He adjusted his glasses. "My father told me when I walked in the door."

"Well, cool," Craig said. "I have a trailer to unload right now, but I'll talk to you later, okay?"

"You bet," Henry said. He closed the office door and sat down in the interview chair.

"I guess you know my nephew?" Mike asked, pulling Henry's application from the file.

"Craig? Sure. Great kid."

"I'm glad you think so," Mike nodded. "You'll be working with him a lot at first."

"No kidding?" Henry asked, his eyes lighting up. "You're hiring me?"

"That depends on one thing, Henry," Mike replied.

"Anything!" Henry exclaimed.

"Your application says you worked for Hiram Milliken," Mike said. Henry's face clouded.

"I want you to tell me why you quit," Mike continued, leaning forward, "and I want the truth. I'm suspicious of that guy and I think you might have the answers I need. Just don't lie to me, Henry. I'm not that patient of a person."

Henry was still feeling the satisfaction of beating up Todd last night. He swallowed hard and hid it. He wasn't sure how to handle this. He never expected anyone to come right out and ask him about the farmer. Todd must be convinced to call the cops now, so what would it matter if he told the truth? The whole town would know soon enough.

Should I involve Craig's uncle in the whole thing? Henry wondered.

"If he's done something to you, Henry," Mike said, encouraging him to speak, "I need to know. I have a bad feeling he was involved with my brother years ago and maybe a lot of other kids since."

Henry nodded. "All right, Mr. Dougan. I'll tell you what you want to know, but I want you to understand something. It isn't only me, okay? Nothing leaves this office until I have a chance to talk to the other guys. If they say that they don't want you involved, you forget anything I'm about to tell you. Do you promise?"

Mike held up his hand. "I swear on my father's grave."

Outside, Merle sat in the Mack drinking deeply from the bottle. Ms. Adler's eyes glowed. She felt his rage as a white-hot angry thing. She fanned the flames pushing him harder. Merle's hand shook, his anger burning like never before.

*   *   *

Jeremy stood beneath the warm water of the shower. He leaned against the mirrored stall with his eyes closed, his head on his forearm. He was desperately trying to relax. His head was swimming in doubts and insecurities he'd forgot were there. They came upon him in a tidal wave shortly after Craig left his mind. He loathed the feelings and he struggled to find some confidence. He reached for the soap and began to wash. He tried to focus on the day ahead. It was off to a very slow start.

The effort to get out of bed when the mind-link dissolved was Herculean. Tripping over another comic book and falling on the floor didn't help either. He was glad Chris wasn't there to see it this time. It was an uncoordinated start to another day, but Jeremy wasn't going to let it stay that way. Today was the big game, the finals before the league championships. His clumsy entry into the morning wasn't getting the best of him. He needed his edge.

He needed to be at his best. Everyone was counting on him to pitch the best game of the season. He was determined not to let them down.

"I have to get it together," Jeremy said. "Today is my day. It's all or nothing."

He took his time in the shower enjoying the warm water. He washed with an obsessive care. He wanted everything to be perfect. He even took the time to condition his hair which he almost never did. He scrubbed his face for what seemed an eternity. He wasn't allowing a single zit to spoil the day. Jeremy religiously washed his face three times a day. It was a trick he'd learned from Chris. His brother rarely had acne. Jeremy wasn't taking any chances.

He observed his reflection in the mirrors as he rinsed. He didn't have an ounce of fat on him. Working out had given him a defined shape, broadening his shoulders just a little. He was proud of that. It gave him confidence, but not like the mind-link did. He felt invincible when Craig was with him. Craig was more confident and at ease, too. Jeremy couldn't remember feeling lonely or out of place all week. Craig was tougher than he knew. Was it rubbing off?

You bet it is, Jeremy thought. *We're canceling out each other's weaknesses with our strengths.*

Jeremy didn't have a clue how he knew that, but it seemed right. He shut the water off and reached for the towel laying over the sink. Hair filled the trap in the bottom of the tub. He felt sorry for his mom since she was the one who had to clean it out. He wasn't going to. They weren't all his seeing as some of them were orange. He dried off, picked up his jock, and suited up. He looked forward to driving past the market and thought-screaming, *"Hey, Dougan!"* at the top of his mental lungs. That would be so cool! Craig would have a heart attack!

The smell of cinnamon charged up his nose and put his saliva glands into overdrive. His stomach started to growl. He quickly tied off his cleats, bounded out of the bathroom, and charged down the stairs, his feet click-clacking on the wooden steps.

"Easy on the floors there, sport!" Thomas called, from the kitchen.

Jeremy froze and peered over the railing. His father was loading French toast into the frying pan. He smiled, but then rolled his eyes. Thomas was wearing his mom's white apron with the pink ruffles again. Jeremy entered the kitchen staring at his father oddly.

"What's wrong, sport?" Thomas asked, although he already knew.

Jeremy scowled "Now I know where Chris gets it from, dad. At least he's not into women's clothes. Not yet anyway."

"You're probably right," Thomas agreed. "They say sexual preference is in the genes. I figured I was pushing it when I put on the pants. The apron would look a lot better without them, don't you think?"

"Gross, dad."

He walked over to the table and sat down. Thomas loaded two plates with French toast. They ate in silence occasionally glancing up at one another. They smiled. Everything seemed relaxed and normal, but Thomas could see right through Jeremy's bravado. His son was shaking in his cleats. It was a crucial game. The playoffs were on the line and his father would be in the stands. His son must be climbing the walls with worry.

Thomas realized how much Jeremy was like him. Chris and Virginia were bursting with self-confidence. Thomas loved his wife's strength and her unfailing devotion to the family. Many women wouldn't put up with the long hours and little extras his career demanded. Virginia was understanding. The more he thought about her, the more he realized he missed her, too. He made a mental note to spend some extra time with her as well. Taking Chris shopping this morning had been a good start. He needed to pull Jeremy out of the back seat of his life.

"This is going to be cool!" Jeremy exclaimed, wiping his mouth. "It's going to be my best game ever!"

"Hey, slow down, sport," Thomas said. "It could be your worst game ever and I wouldn't care. The only thing important is you do your best."

"Oh, very *Leave It to Beaver* dad!" Jeremy replied. He added, "Thanks, though. I needed to hear that."

Thomas nodded. *I knew that.*

Jeremy noticed his father staring at him. It was the long hard kind of stare that signaled a father and son chat was on the horizon. He tried to remember if he had done anything wrong lately, but his mind drew a blank. He hoped it wasn't anything that would put a damper on the day. Jeremy had enough on his mind. He didn't need anymore. He wanted to ask his father about his research into psychic phenomena, but he couldn't get the words out.

Oh, well, later for that, Jeremy thought. *It's think positive day.*

He was positive his team, the Kelly Hardware Wildcats, were going to win big! Jeremy was determined to get his fifteen minutes of fame. Today was the day that would set him for the rest of his life.

"Take a picture, dad, it lasts longer."

Thomas shook his head and replied with the snappy comeback, "Huh?"

"Good comeback."

Thomas rubbed his eyes and laughed, "Sorry for staring."

"No hay problema, mi padre," Jeremy said. "I just figured you wanted to talk about something."

Thomas smiled and patted Jeremy on the head. He thought, *No, I don't want to talk about anything. Just the opposite. I have a lot of thinking to do.*

"I love you, kiddo," Thomas said. "You know that, right?"

"I know, dad," Jeremy replied. "I love you, too."

He's growing up without me. What have I been doing? I'm missing so much. Not today. Not ever again.

"What time is it?" Jeremy asked. He thought it must be close to time to leave. He was relieved there was no long conversation on the agenda. He was restless. He wanted to be at Legion Field with the guys.

"Ten," Thomas replied. He asked, "Is it time to go?"

"Yup," Jeremy said, downing his milk.

They got up at the same time and pointed at each other laughing.

Jeremy tossed his dishes into the sink feeling like he could take on the entire world.

*   *   *

Old Ted Collins gave Mike a half-wave as he punched his timecard. Mike remained motionless staring at the floor. Henry was on the dock helping Craig unload the last of the oranges. He was thrilled to have a job, but felt wary about what he'd told his new boss. He hoped he hadn't broken anyone's confidence. He was afraid he had since he'd told Mike everything. It made him feel better, but part of him was screaming, *You just made the biggest mistake of your life!* When he was through, Mike told him to make out a time card so he could punch in. Craig would show him where the lockers were. He needed to put his cell phone in one. After Dan tried to destroy his desk, stock workers weren't allowed to have them on shift anymore. They could check them on break. Henry complied seeing a very scary look in Mike's eyes. It said: *Murder.*

Merle watched the boys in his side view mirror. His could barely contain his rage. The strange woman was gone. He thanked her for the fifth although he didn't know why. He hadn't wanted it. The bottle was on the floor empty. Waiting for the boys to finish was torture. The more he thought about the time it had taken to pull off a few pallets, the more he wanted to break some heads. Merle watched as the larger boy stood back and the smaller boy lifted an empty pallet to turn it over. He lost his balance. The pallet flipped – or rather *flew* – over. It sailed off the dock and hit the trailer. A loose nail dug a deep groove down the aluminum side. Merle's mind snapped. He believed he was going to have to pay for that. It would cost him more than he'd made on this trip. He exploded out of the cab. He charged up the stairs onto the dock.

In the office, Mike's fingernails had broken through the skin on his arm. He hadn't realize he was squeezing so hard. What he was feeling was beyond description. Everything had fallen into place so grossly perfect. His emotions were a raging hurricane. He had been drowning in his hatred for his brother, the loss he felt when his father died in front of him, the beatings Craig endured, the tears Henry cried a few minutes ago, the strain on his mother's face when she went to work in his father's place, and the pain of the children assaulted by the farmer. They had formed a picture in his mind. His hatred had a face. That face belonged to Hiram Milliken.

Mike caught movement out of the corner of his eye and he looked up. He watched Merle Wrightwood shove Henry onto the concrete floor and reach for Craig. Mike stared at this with an odd expression on his face. Merle twisted Craig's arm up almost lifting him off the ground.

Craig cried out for help.

Mike's thoughts snapped into focus. *Good Lord! This is really happening!*

Mike jumped up practically foaming at the mouth. He kicked his office door off the hinges. He charged Merle, grabbed him by his hair, and delivered repeated punches into his *"... stinking, dirty, rotten, no good...!"* face. Merle's mouth was bleeding. His breath reeked of alcohol. He struggled to pull away. Mike launched him off the dock. He hit the pavement with a smack.

"You bastard!" Mike yelled. *"Touch my nephew!? I'll kill you!"*

"Dead...," Merle whispered, struggling to his feet. His hands were bleeding where he landed on them. His pants were split open at the knee. "You're *dead!"*

Merle stumbled to the cab. He climbed in and dove toward the sleeper. He reached under the pillow to where he kept his sawed-off shotgun.

Merle's eyes grew wide. He cried, "It ain't here!"

He slipped into his chair and started the motor, his vision doubling. He had money. He had a Visa card. They took his gun?

I'll get another one! Then I'm a-comin' back and they're all dead!

Ms. Adler watched from the side of the building, her eyes glowing. *"Timing is everything,"* she said. She clenched her fists.

*   *   *

Jeremy opened the passenger door of his father's Porsche and slipped into the seat. He reached for the seat belt.

"You do not need that."

He let go of it. It wound back up.

Thomas armed their home security system and made sure the front door was locked. It was a family ritual when no one was home.

"The hills... the beautiful hills."

Thomas looked up at the hills surrounding the town. They protected Lancaster from the bigger towns nearby and their bigger problems. The only time he had ever been away from here was Harvard Law School where he earned his degree and met Virginia. She was working as a waitress paying her way through Boston Technical College. It was love at first sight. When Thomas graduated, he brought his fiancé home with him. Virginia had graduated the year before with a degree in Architectural Drafting. She adored Garth and Amanda McKee, her future in-laws.

"Time to go."

Thomas smiled as he walked to the Porsche. He remembered how quickly his parents took to Virginia. Her parents were gone. Christopher Boudreaux died from a stroke when she was ten. Katherine died from cervical cancer while she was in college. Amanda treated Virginia like family. They planned every detail of the wedding. She fawned over the beautiful bride her shy and reserved son had managed to woo. They were married a month later in a small ceremony at St. Peter's. Garth stood as Thomas' Best Man. Amanda was the Maid of Honor. Thomas wouldn't allow any other man to stand up for him. Garth was a retired supervisor from Pratt & Whitney. He was a hard worker, a loving father, and Thomas' best friend. Chris was born seven months later.

"So many memories."

Thomas worked for the Public Defender's Office in Hartford early in his career. Thurman Millner had been the District Attorney. He was from the *old boys* network. He slid his conviction percentage up through plea bargaining. Thomas threw Thurman for a loop the first time he refused a plea agreement. The case was going to court. It remained like that until Thurman returned to his private practice. Thomas had whipped him every time.

"I'm leaving office, McKee," Thurman said, on the steps of Superior Court.

"Tired of getting your butt kicked, Thurman?" Thomas laughed.

"You'd better believe it," Thurman replied, puffing a thick cigar. "To make sure you don't go after my old job and I end up facing you as a prosecutor, I'll make it worth your while to come and work for me. How does a six-figure salary sound to you, Thomas? To start."

It sounded fine.

"Good career... good life."

Thomas climbed into the Porsche. He looked at their home and smiled. *I'm happy,* he thought. *So damned happy.*

Jeremy reached over and poked his father in the ribs. "Today, okay?" he said. "I don't want to be late. I have to warm up."

Thomas nodded and started the car. The seatbelt warning light flashed, but then it went out. He looked over his shoulder as he backed out of the driveway. Jeremy held his glove in his hands. They were sweating profusely as his anxiety grew once again. It was always like this before a game. His groin itched, his head swam, and all he could see were his teammates' faces. His grandfather would be there, too. He's the one who had taught Jeremy how to pitch. Today was so special, he wanted to do better than ever before, but he was scared.

Jeremy wondered, *Can I overcome it? God, help me, please?*

"Come, Thomas... faster!"

They reached the bottom of Satchell Hill quickly. Jeremy noticed people exiting their cars in the market parking lot.

"Go! You do not want your son to be late!"

Thomas reached over as they pulled onto Route 41 and gripped his son's shoulder. "Don't worry, sport," he said, looking at Jeremy as they entered the lane. "You'll do fine."

Jeremy nodded, but his attention was diverted from his father's voice to something of ahead of them. A tractor-trailer barreled out from behind the market, charging toward Route 41. Its back doors were open and swinging. At that instant, the mind-link reestablished itself.

Jeremy thought-spoke, *"Would you look at this idiot? He's going to cut right in front of us!"* Jeremy could feel Craig's fear, the pain in his arm, and he immediately became confused. *"Craig?"*

The tractor-trailer raced out in front of the Porsche and cut sharply left headed right for them. Thomas was looking at Jeremy. The last thing he saw was his son's eyes grow wide before the entire world went black.

✳   ✳   ✳

Craig was trying to calm his uncle down. He stopped talking in mid-sentence, frozen and staring. Mike and Henry looked at him. Mike's anger drained away as Craig's face contorted with agony. With a wrenching jerk, he flew backward through the air as if something had picked him up and thrown him. He slammed into the wall next to the water cooler and slid to the floor. Craig hit the ground, opened his eyes wide, and screamed.

✳   ✳   ✳

Bea Jones climbed out of her car admiring the sleek black Porsche and fantasized it was hers. What she wouldn't give to wrap her hands around its steering wheel and fly down the highway. She envied the McKees for an instant before she spotted the tractor-trailer. It came out of nowhere speeding into the same lane as the Porsche, but heading in the opposite direction. The world disappeared and she gasped. Suddenly, it was Bea, the truck, and the Porsche. There was nothing else in existence until the sound of crunching metal shattered the silence.

The two vehicles hit head-on with a loud bang. The lights of the Porsche exploded sending tiny glass shrapnel flying everywhere. The bumper of the tractor climbed the hood of the car, crushing it. It continued, tearing through the driver's side of the windshield with a dull rip. Bea knew that whoever was driving the car was dead. The truck driver flew through the tractor's windshield. He careened in the air, bounced off the roof of the Porsche, and slammed face first onto the market parking lot ten feet away from her. The driver's head split open down the middle exposing his brain. Blood spurted as he skidded to a halt. He leaned up, cried out, and fell dead.

Bea stared at him, horrified. *The tar burned his face off!* she thought.

"Oh, Christ Jesus... *help!*"

*   *   *

Craig sprang to his feet before his terrified uncle could get to him and ran toward the front doors. Henry and Mike followed him as he raced outside. He spotted Bea first standing in the parking lot with her hands over her mouth, screaming. The truck driver's body lay nearby. Henry yelled for someone to call 911. Mike ran back to his office. His cell phone was on his desk. Henry's was in his new locker.

Dread enclosed Craig's heart. He saw only black through the mind-link and felt incredible pain in his left arm. He ran toward the destroyed Porsche, fear racing down his spine. He passed the trucker's body and sidestepped his busted skull. He stared at the gruesome sight before turning away in disgust. Merle was twitching. His blood was everywhere.

Craig stopped a few feet from the Porsche, but close enough to see inside. He swallowed hard and gathered his courage. He eased slowly to the passenger window his mouth moving as he tried to cry out. Terror ripped down the middle of his soul. He eased up next to the car and stood there motionless. He felt the color drain from his face as the stone grip of shock entered his body.

Jeremy felt a sharp pain in his left arm as consciousness slowly returned to him. His father's hand was still groping his shoulder like it had been before he spotted the tractor-trailer. It reassured him that everything was going to be all right. He searched his mind. The last thing he remembered was colliding with the rig. The impact slammed his forehead into the dashboard, and then nothing. Darkness.

Jeremy sensed Craig close by and smiled weakly. He could feel his friend's worry, his anguish, and his terror. Craig was scared to death and near to breaking apart. Jeremy was about to project his thoughts at him that everything was okay when he realized something warm and wet was dripping onto his face. The groping on his shoulder hadn't stopped either. Jeremy opened his eyes. His head was tilted back facing the ceiling. He struggled to clear his vision and focus the double images tinted in deep red. He finally did. Once Jeremy could see, he desperately wished he'd been struck blind.

Jeremy tried to scream, but it caught in his throat. The blood spraying onto the crushed ceiling of the Porsche rained down into his mouth. The groping hand was still on his shoulder. Jeremy stared, wide-eyed and terrified, as sorrow sliced through his heart. The tractor's bumper was sticking inside the Porsche through the smashed windshield. Jeremy felt his world shatter in one agonizingly horrible vision.

Oh, Jesus, he thought, shocked. *Dad's head is gone.*

Jeremy knew where it was. He could feel its weight in his lap, but he couldn't turn to look down at it. His paralyzed gaze was locked on his father's convulsing body. A piece of his spinal column jutted up through the ragged mess of Thomas' neck. Blood was spraying out of the arteries as his heart continued beating. It doused the inside of the car soaking Jeremy's white baseball uniform. Both of Thomas's hands were opening and closing. His left leg was torn open by a jagged piece of metal sticking through the dashboard. It twitched, spastically.

Jeremy tried to close his eyes. His tears fell as he turned and looked into Craig's terrified face. Their eyes met in identical expressions of horror. They felt themselves falling into an abyss. Jeremy reached for him with his left hand. His broken arm dangled, sharp bones protruding through his skin. Blood was running out of him like a river.

"Help... *please...,*" Jeremy choked, with an expression of abject despair.

Craig grabbed the door handle. His movements were liquid, alien. He pulled it open, but it seemed so far away. Thomas' body convulsed violently twice and stopped moving. Craig pulled Jeremy toward him. Thomas' head fell out of Jeremy's lap and landed on the concrete with a crack. Its eyes were closed, its features frozen in an expression of surprise. Craig screamed and jumped back pulling Jeremy with him. He hit his behind painfully on the curb and landed on the grass. Jeremy fell on top of him, shaking and sobbing uncontrollably. Craig wrapped his arms around him staring at the severed head on the ground between Jeremy's feet.

"Mother Mary preserve us," Mike whispered.

Craig turned toward his uncle's voice. He felt Jeremy's right arm grip him and he began to cry.

*   *   *

Lisa turned onto Route 41 from Wickett Avenue. She had left the garage moments earlier after José filled her car up. She pulled over to the side to let a Connecticut State Trooper pass. His lights were on and his siren blaring. She sighed relief that he wasn't after her. She didn't need a ticket. This week had been messed up enough. She was about to re-enter the lane, but then slammed on her brakes as an ambulance flew by. Two more cops were following it with their sirens blaring, too.

"What the...?" Lisa asked, quickly tailing the last cop.

Her baby's motor roared as she hit the gas. She had a terrible sense of déjà vu. She came around the corner and saw the accident in front of the market.

"Oh, my God..."

Mike's heart broke as he looked into his nephew's terrified eyes. *This is it,* he thought. *Oh, God, I know it. After everything Craig's suffered, this will send him over the edge. It has to.*

The horrid sight was playing havoc with Mike's sanity, too. He couldn't imagine what it was doing to the kids.

Oh, God, sweet Jesus, poor Jeremy.

Mike watched them weeping. He didn't have a clue what to do. He saw Thomas' head between Jeremy's feet. He jumped down and kicked it under the truck.

The state troopers – Robert Bigelow, Kate Pierce, and a big rookie named Tyrone Johnston – blocked off Route 41 at Top Road and Legion Avenue, above and below the wreck, re-routing the traffic. A crowd of market customers had gathered in the parking lot. People ran over to the scene from Lead Sinker Road. Mike watched Lisa drive over the lawn in her Chevelle. She hit the parking lot, screeched to a stop, and parked sideways. Mike called to her as she ran toward him stopping her ten yards from the Porsche. He told her to take over the store. He was going to the hospital with Jeremy and Craig.

Lisa's face drew tight with panic. "Are they okay!?" she cried, choking back a sob. *Please, let them be okay!*

Mike nodded and replied, "Take care of Bea! She saw the whole thing! And call my wife! Tell her where I'll be!"

Lisa took a few clumsy steps backward. She ran over to Bea. Tears were rolling down her face. Lisa put her arm around her and led her toward the store. Mike turned to the boys. Larry Singleton was trying to separate them. Jeremy had his arms locked around Craig, even the broken one, and he wasn't letting go.

Mike looked at his expression and ordered Larry to *"Back off!"*

Jeremy's sobs were coming with such force, his chest was heaving. He was shaking all over.

"Christ!" Larry exclaimed, panicked. "Help me, Mike! The kid's going into shock!"

Mike knelt next to Craig. "Buddy," he whispered, "you've got to listen to me…"

His uncle's voice was steady, but it sounded far away. *Jeremy,* Craig's mind echoed. *I have to help Jeremy. My best friend needs me.*

Craig tried to stand. His knees shook and threatened to buckle. Jeremy locked on to him tighter, but Craig held him up and they stood together. Jeremy was hunched over, his arms around Craig's waist, his face buried in his side. His mangled arm bled down the back of Craig's cutoffs. Craig sobbed as he walked them to the ambulance, assisted by Mike, with Larry right behind them.

"Please…," Jeremy wept, "… don't *leave* me…"

"I won't," Craig said, tears streaming down his face. He didn't recognize his own voice. "I swear to God, I won't."

Mike and Larry sat the boys on a stretcher and lifted it into the ambulance. Mike went in backward. Larry motioned for him to come over as he quickly bandaged Jeremy's broken arm.

"Can you ride with them?" Larry asked. "We're short an E.M.T. so I have to fly them to the hospital as fast as I can. I need you to keep pressure on the kid's arm to slow the bleeding."

"Try and stop me," Mike replied.

*   *   *

Amanda McKee was working in the backyard of her Lancaster Hill Road home stuffing hedge trimmings into a Glad lawn bag when the phone started ringing. She glanced over. A light breeze caught the hair sticking out from her wicker gardening hat. There were still some blonde stands mixed in with her grays. Her pale skin glowed. Her green eyes lit up in the bright sunlight. She was a small woman, five-five in her bare feet. She set her hands on her hips.

She grumbled, "There's always an interruption whenever I'm trying to get some work done." She thought, *You should've listened to Thomas and let him get you that smarty phone for your birthday. He was right. It would've come in handy.*

The landline said, *"Ring -ring."*

"Oh, be quiet."

It was enough she had gotten up later than usual for a Friday, at eight instead of six, but she wanted to sleep in with her husband. Garth needed all of the energy he could get for Jeremy's game today. He planned to help out Virginia's shouting section since his daughter-in-law wouldn't be there. It was a matter of honor. His grandson was pitching.

Garth asked for pancakes. That's what was waiting for him when he tiptoed into the kitchen. He snuck up behind Amanda as she cooked. He put his arms around her thin waist and kissed her neck ferociously. Amanda spun around and almost belted him with a spatula.

"Garth McKee!" she snapped, holding her chest. "Are you trying to give an old woman a coronary?"

"Hah!" Garth exclaimed, grabbing her sides and tickling her. "If you were going to have a coronary, you would've had it last night in the bedroom!"

Amanda cracked her husband's knuckles with the spatula handle. He darted away rubbing his hand and snickering. *That man!* Thirty-eight years of marriage and he'd slowed down everywhere except in the bedroom. She didn't know how he still had it in him, the old goat. She was sure there was some Viagra hidden somewhere. Amanda blushed. Her thoughts were positively pornographic. Virginia would laugh at her and claim it was the sex-drive curse of the McKee men. She said Thomas was no slouch in the bedroom either.

Amanda counted the phone rings to five. *They're not hanging up. Maybe they'll leave a voicemail.* The rings stopped at six and the voicemail picked up. A few moments later the ringing began anew. She dropped her white gardening gloves on top of her electric hedge trimmers and walked toward the house.

She thought, *As if all those sirens from a little while ago weren't disturbing enough! You'd think the police would have the decency not to disturb everyone's peace on such a glorious day.*

Amanda smiled, tipping up the brim of her wicker summer hat. She looked into the bright blue sky. There wasn't a cloud in sight. Jeremy must be in his glory. Virginia told her Thomas had canceled an appointment to bring him to the game today.

The weatherman said rain for tonight, Amanda thought. *Horrible thundershowers. It hardly seems possible.*

Jeremy missed his father. They all knew it. Amanda silently applauded Virginia for taking Chris shopping today, although what they could buy this time was beyond her.

That boy!

Chris had more clothes than most women she knew except his mother. It was his money, she supposed, and she was proud of him. Farming was hard work. She would've bet Chris wouldn't last a week knowing how much her grandson hated to get dirty. Amazingly, he'd managed school, the high honor roll, saving money, and working at the same time. Amanda crossed herself. Their family was lucky to have done so well.

"I'm coming!" Amanda snapped.

She was in the back hall trying to get her sandals off so she wouldn't track dirt across the carpet. The phone was on its third ringing rotation. "Leave a message, for Heaven's sake. Give an old woman a break!"

Amanda dropped her hat on the kitchen counter as she passed. She wasn't exactly running, but she was walking very fast. The only phone in the house sat on the table next to Garth's recliner in the living room. She reached down to snap up the receiver, but stopped as the line went dead. She stared at it, blankly. A feeling of dread came over her. She didn't want it to ring again. She wanted to walk away and forget it had ever disturbed her landscaping. The ringing resumed. She picked up the receiver with a trembling hand. She instinctively sensed the world she knew was about to end.

*　　*　　*

Garth McKee was standing in the hot sun by the bleachers tapping his fingers on the infield fence. He was staring at the police officer over on Route 41 redirecting the traffic up Legion Avenue away from the main road. It was twenty minutes to eleven and still no sign of Thomas and Jeremy.

Garth's brow furrowed with concern. *There must be a logical explanation for the delay,* he thought. *The cops probably made them go around the long way. Game time is eleven. Thomas knows that. How could anyone forget after all the hoopla from Jeremy? They should've been here for warm-ups.* He silently prayed nothing was wrong.

Randy Gardner was on the mound pitching to Ricardo for batting practice. As the team's head coach, this was the way he liked to start things. He usually had Jeremy at his side though. Randy was concerned his star pitcher hadn't shown up yet. It was bad enough Ian Sturgess was still at camp. Gary Rollins was playing right field to free Herman to take Ian's base. Randy hoped Max was on the ball in center today. Gary wasn't the greatest player. He was just going into eighth grade in the fall and not very coordinated. Randy hoped no one hit anything in his direction. Gary would probably miss it and take one in the face again.

Everyone's anxiety level was up especially after the barrage of sirens. Randy saw a look of dread come over Kevin's face. He couldn't blame his assistant coach. If anything happened to Matt, Randy would never get over it.

Where's Jeremy? Randy thought, as Ricardo clipped one to third. Billy Wilde, his blonde curls bouncing, snagged it. His throw to Matt was right on target.

"Nice throw, Billy!" Randy called.

"Thanks, coach," Billy smiled.

Randy would have to give the starting line-up to the umpire soon. Joey Kreeger was his only other player since two eighth graders were on vacation and a ninth grader was sick. Joey was okay at third, but Billy sucked in the outfield. He supposed he could start Herman at pitcher and try Joey at second, but he didn't want to. Herman was good, but Jeremy was an ace.

God, can that kid throw! Randy thought.

The point was moot. If Jeremy didn't show up there wouldn't be a game. All of his other players besides Gary and Joey were either on vacation or ill. There were no extras. Herman couldn't pitch nine innings. Ian was the only other backup besides Roman Beauber and he was one of the kids on vacation.

"Dad?" Matt called, from first base.

"Yo!" Randy called back, trying to sound cool.

Matt shook his head. *My father is such a geek.*

He looked toward Derek at shortstop. Derek rolled his eyes. Matt held his glove up and flipped him the bird from behind it. Derek chose that precise moment to flip down his sunshades and quickly adjust his cup.

"Where's Jeremy?" Matt asked.

"I don't know," Randy replied.

"Jeremy's not here yet?" Max called to Herman.

Herman shrugged.

Ricardo hit a shot out toward right field.

Gary backed up, stumbling and cursing. "Oh, nuts… *idiot!*" he cried. "He's batting lefty!" He caught it, but just barely.

Randy scowled over at Kevin who yelled, "Gary! Watch out for lefty batters!"

"No duh," Gary mumbled.

"Wake up, Gary!" Max called. "You want another shot in the face like last year?" He chuckled and thought, *That was so funny! It was like* **whack!** *Lights out! Gary laid in the outfield like a sack of potatoes for ten minutes. His black eyes were even worse than Dabney's!*

Gary scowled and threw the ball at him. Max fielded it cleanly, whipped it over to Derek, who relayed it to Matt over at first.

"You're out, Rollins!" Matt exclaimed.

Gary growled.

"Get in here, Rollins!" Kevin called. "You're up!"

Max yawned. *Oh, well, break time for me,* he thought. *Gary couldn't hit a ball out of the infield with a tennis racket.*

Matt looked at his watch. It was quarter 'til. *C'mon, Jeremy!* he thought.

He knew he should have talked Jeremy into coming earlier like he'd wanted, but the way he complained about his father never being free? They were probably making up for lost time. Matt nearly fainted when he heard the sirens. Visions of Todd O'Connor popped into his head.

What we did last night was so stupid! Matt thought. *What if Todd has us all arrested for beating him up? It could happen!*

Matt didn't think he had ever been so angry as when Teddy finished talking. Now, he only felt drained. Did the other guys feel that way, too?

Kevin walked over to Garth and tapped him on the shoulder. The old man jumped, but then smiled, weakly. Kevin couldn't remember seeing him so nervous and he'd known the McKees since he was a kid. Garth was his baseball coach back when Thomas used to pitch. Thomas had a killer fastball, but was always a quiet kid. Garth reminded him of Billy Martin. He was a fierce competitor. Kevin handed him a team hat.

"Hey!" Garth exclaimed, his smile wide. "Thanks a lot, kid."

"No problem, coach," Kevin replied, patting Garth on the back.

Garth slipped on the cap. He was about to express his condolences for Kevin's loss when he glanced up and saw Amanda's light blue Oldsmobile Cutlass pulling into the park. He was glad to see she'd changed her mind about coming to the game. He noticed how fast she was driving and his heart skipped a beat. Amanda drove like a little old lady. She looked more like Kyle Busch right now. Something was wrong.

"Hey, coach," Randy called. He pointed at the Oldsmobile. "Isn't that your wife?"

Garth stood there as she charged toward them too busy praying to answer him.

*   *   *

The Emergency Room at Johnson Memorial Hospital was alive with activity the moment Jeremy and Craig were wheeled in on the stretcher. Dr. Henry Montclair, the physician on duty, ordered Larry to take them into the cubicle labeled Examination Room One. He ordered the nurse to type Jeremy's blood *STAT!* He was bleeding like a sieve through the temporary bandages. He ordered the patients from the waiting room to clear the area.

Craig was in a panic. He could feel Jeremy through their mind-link slowly slipping away. Jeremy was desperately trying to hang on. If he slipped into that comfortable darkness, he was terrified he might not come out again. He mentally cried out to Craig, his body going into Grand Mal seizures. He begged his best friend not to leave him alone. Craig repeatedly swore that he wouldn't.

Nurse Raymond closed the curtain and ordered Larry and Mike to get out. They made it to the flap, but stopped short of leaving. The nurse reached between the boys and tried to separate them. Mike watched shocked as both boys' faces contorted with outrage at the same time.

They screamed, *"No!"* and punched her in the face. Her nose broke, oozing blood. She ran out of the room. Dr. Montclair called for orderlies. Mike came over with them. They wrenched the thrashing boys apart.

"Craig? *Craig!"* Jeremy cried, struggling against the orderlies holding him down.

"Let me go!" Craig wailed.

He tried to bite the men holding him. One of them was his uncle. Craig looked like a wild animal. Mike thought his earlier guess had been right. His nephew was losing it.

"Should I sedate them, doctor?" Adele Weissenberg asked, reaching for a syringe.

"Severe trauma, loss of blood, shock?" Dr. Montclair asked. "I think not. Restrain them. Where's the blood for the boy with the broken arm?"

"He's O negative, doctor," Adele replied. "We're out. Somebody's calling Rockville."

"Wait!" Mike interjected. "My nephew! He's the same type!"

"Where are his parents?" Dr. Montclair asked. "Somebody will have to sign the release forms."

"I'll be doin' that, doctor," Nancy said. She appeared in the doorway with the court papers in her hand. "I have guardianship o'er me grandson."

"Nurse Weissenberg," Dr. Montclair called.

"Yes, doctor," Adele replied. "I'll get Nancy the paperwork. We go back many years."

"I didn't ask for a life story excerpt, nurse."

The orderlies holding Craig wheeled the bed he was on next to Jeremy. Mike stared as the boys perfectly clasped hands without looking.

Christ! What's going on here?

Jeremy and Craig stopped struggling once they were back in physical contact. The doctor unwrapped Jeremy's broken arm. Mike winced and he backed away. The bones were sticking out. Blood was pouring down his arm, pooling under the doctor's feet. Dr. Montclair grabbed above and below the break. With a quick snap and a loud crunch, he set Jeremy's arm.

Jeremy and Craig screamed.

Two nurses, the orderlies, the doctor, Mike, and Larry watched in horror as they wailed at the top of their lungs, and then fainted.

"Good Lord," Mike whispered.

"Are you positive about your nephew's blood type?" Dr. Montclair asked. He didn't have time to be stunned.

"It's barely reading, doctor," warned the nurse taking Jeremy's blood pressure. The other nurse applying direct pressure to his wound glanced over.

"Mike!" Larry cried.

Mike jumped. "Yes!" he replied, backing up. "It's O negative. They typed him at birth. It was my father's blood type, too, that's how I remember."

"Any history of illness?" the doctor asked. "H.I.V., hepatitis…?"

"None," Mike interrupted. "Craig's fit as a fiddle."

"All right," Dr. Montclair said. "Type him and test him anyway, nurse. If he comes out okay, bleed him. I want them in the operating room *STAT!* As soon as he's stitched up, get him down to X-ray for a complete skull series."

"Doctor?" the orderly asked. He was a big man struggling to separate Jeremy and Craig's hands. "I can't get their hands apart!"

"Then put them on the cart together," Dr. Montclair ordered. "Just get moving."

*   *   *

Virginia sat on a bench in the middle of the Buckland Mall in Manchester and rubbed her calves. She told the boys to go ahead without her. She needed to rest for a few minutes. They'd hit five stores in one hour. Four were, four in different corners of the mall and one in the middle. Her feet were killing her. An ounce of forethought would have told her to wear something with an arch support like her running shoes, but she had to be stylish and wear flats.

Sometimes, Virginia swore, *I have no brain.*

"C'mon, Sandy," Chris said. "Leave the old bat to her aches and pains." Sandy chuckled.

"In your ear, junior," Virginia groaned.

"Maybe we ought to wait, man," Sandy suggested. "Do you think we should leave her here alone?"

"Just because I'm gay," Chris replied, hands on his hips in a genuine feminine gesture, "doesn't mean I'm a nursemaid, okay?"

"Just go, Sandy," Virginia said. "Chris has PMS today. It's in his female hormones."

Sandy laughed. The boys moved on to the music store.

Virginia checked her cell phone. The baseball game should be underway. She would call Susan at noon and get the score. She crossed her fingers. Jeremy needed this day to be perfect. She frowned when she noticed she had no cell signal. She decided it was the mall's fault. She would recheck it outside. Chris and Sandy returned a few minutes later. Chris claimed the music store's prices were too high. He wanted to go to Vernon Circle where the prices were lower, or to Walmart.

Virginia smiled thinking, *My son, Mr. Thrifty.*

She suggested they have some lunch first. She didn't want fast food, but she thought Denny's might be nice. Sandy frowned. He didn't have any money. Now he understood how Dabney had felt at the carnival.

Virginia ruffled Sandy's thick blonde hair. "It's on me," she said.

"Cool!" the boys chorused.

The door closed tightly behind them as they left.

The PA system announced: *"Will Virginia McKee please come to security? We have an emergency phone call for Virginia McKee."*

*　　*　　*

Amanda drove like a wild woman straight across the parking lot. She went over the curb, raced to where Garth stood, and slammed on the brakes. The car dug two strips in the grass as the Oldsmobile skidded to a halt. She threw it into park, left the car running, and jumped out into her husband's arms. Tears streamed down her face as she wailed.

Garth's heart was beating a mile a minute. *Amanda never gets this upset!* He felt completely helpless. Amanda buried her face in his chest. Kevin motioned for Randy to come in from the mound as she rambled off details of the phone call. Randy dropped the baseball and told the boys to stay where they were. Colin Skinner, behind home plate, leaned against the backstop listening intently. His eyes grew wide.

"Should we stay here?" Ricardo called to Max from left field.

401

"Screw that!" Max replied. "Something's going on! That's Jeremy's grandmother!"

Matt hollered his agreement followed by Derek. The team jogged toward the pitcher's mound. They could see Garth McKee crying. Ricardo looked at Matt, his face drawn up with panic. Matt shook his head. Whatever was going on it was bad. They remembered the sirens at precisely the same time. Dread filled their hearts. Colin motioned for the team to come over by the dugout. Randy and Kevin frantically asked if Jeremy was all right.

"What about Jeremy?" Derek demanded, glaring at Colin.

Colin looked at him like he was crazy. The rest of the team circled them.

Max got into Colin's face. "Don't mess with me, fat boy!" he growled. "Answer the question! Where's Jeremy?"

"Those sirens from before?" Colin began, his voice quivering. His hands started to shake. "It was Jeremy. There was an accident. His father's dead."

Max lashed out so fast Colin didn't have time to breathe. He slammed the chubby boy against the side of the dugout and held him to the wall. The rest of the boys moved in with him.

"One more time," Max raged, "and I'll wreck you! Where is Jeremy?"

"He's in the hospital!" Colin sobbed. "Johnson Memorial in Stafford!"

Max dropped him. The team followed as he stormed over to the parents and kids gathered around the coaches.

Colin waited, breathing hard as he tried to compose himself. *Sometimes I hate Max Ramirez so bad!* he thought.

Kevin led the McKees to his car. He and Cynthia had volunteered to drive them to the hospital. Randy shut Amanda's car off and locked it. He turned to find the team standing behind him. He opened his mouth to tell them they had to go home, but then he saw the look in Max's eyes. He nodded instead.

"We're going," Max said.

"I'll get the parents together," Randy replied. He paused by Matt whose face looked like it was about to slide off.

"Are you okay?" Randy asked, placing a hand on his son's shoulder.

Matt didn't look at him. He shook his head. Derek began to cry. He'd lost enough this week. Ricardo slipped his arm across his shoulders fighting back his own tears. They were scared. Nobody knew if Jeremy was all right. They only knew his father was dead.

He must be devastated, Max thought. *I am, too.*

The umpire walked over from the opposing team's dugout looking stern and irritated. He had no idea what was going on. He only knew the team of boys that was supposed to be playing was leaving.

"Where are you going?" the umpire asked. "What about the game?"

Derek spun around. His cheeks were flushed and soaked with tears. He yelled, *"Screw the game!"*

"Yeah," Herman whispered. "Screw the game." He ran to his frightened parents to tell them he was going with the others.

*   *   *

Nancy slammed her cell phone down onto the Emergency Room counter with so much force the screen cracked. She glared at it fighting an urge to throw it across the room. She had called every mall in the state and still couldn't find Virginia. Amanda told her she'd gone shopping with her oldest boy and his friend when Nancy called her after receiving news of the accident from Sandra. Amanda had given her Virginia and Chris' cell phone numbers. Virginia's cell kept going straight to voicemail. Chris wasn't answering his.

Aren't teenagers supposed t' be glued t' the bloody things? Nancy thought.

Sandra was in the E.R. lobby trying to comfort Mike. Whatever had gone on behind the curtain while the doctor worked on the boys had shaken him to his foundations. Robert Bigelow was with them carefully asking Mike questions about the accident.

When Nancy called the senior McKees' house, Amanda tearfully told her she would get her husband from Legion Field. Nancy promised she would contact Virginia, but she had failed thus far. She couldn't locate her good-for-nothing son either. Craig was in a bad way. Jack was still – although she was loath to admit it – the boy's father regardless of the restraining order. If there was a lick of love in him anywhere, he had the right to know.

Damn that man! Nancy thought.

She drove to the hospital as soon as she was off the phone with Amanda. She made the twenty-minute trip from Copeland Industries in less than ten. Sandra assured her Craig had no injuries, but she described what he had witnessed. Nancy wouldn't let Craig face such horrors alone. He'd suffered enough. She blamed his cow of a mother for abandoning him to Jack.

Mike moved down the hall outside of X-ray. Sandra held his hand and leaned against his shoulder. Robert followed them. They watched through the window. Nancy was alone in the waiting room except for Margaret Adler. She was slumped in a chair, lightly snoring. Nancy was startled. She hadn't see Margaret there a moment ago.

Where did she bloody come from? Nancy wondered. *What in God's name is she doin' here?*

Nancy's heart skipped a beat as Ms. Adler's head snapped up. Her dark brown eyes burned into her brain. Nancy felt completely transparent.

"Oh, Miss Adler!" Nancy exclaimed, gasping and holding her chest. "I'll be beggin' your pardon!"

"Nonsense, dear lady," Ms. Adler said, her tone superior. "Your surprise does not offend me. I am well aware of what people think of me, but I can help you in your endeavors."

"My...?" Nancy began.

"You called Misty's Café looking for your son?"

"Aye," Nancy replied. "That I did. He wasn't there."

"He is in the men's bathroom passed out inside one of the stalls."

Nancy's mouth dropped open.

Ms. Adler walked away, but stopped in the doorway. Without looking back, she added, "And Virginia McKee? She is having lunch with the boys at Denny's in Vernon. Their cell phones are working now."

Nancy broke out in a cold sweat as Ms. Adler disappeared around the corner.

＊　　＊　　＊

Chris stood in front of the mirror on the back of the men's room door looking over his shoulder at his reflection. His new jeans fit perfectly.

He thought with a grin, *Sincerely, I have a nice...*

Sandy burst through the door.

Chris gasped, flushing red. He thought, *I wasn't looking at my ass! I swear!*

"It's your mom," Sandy said, his voice trembling. "Her cell phone rang. When she answered it, she just collapsed. Chris, she's crying!"

Chris pushed past him and ran out of the bathroom. He didn't care that the door banged loudly against the outer wall and dented the paneling. He nearly collided with a waitress. He stopped next to their table. Virginia was on her knees sobbing into her hands. Her cell phone lay on the floor next to her. A crowd had formed around them, their faces concerned.

Chris angrily snatched up the phone. "All right!" he demanded. "Who is this and what did you say to my mother?"

There was a moment of silence before a voice spoke.

"It's Nancy Dougan, lad," Nancy replied.

She spoke slowly, but with the deliberate frankness that was Nancy's way. Chris felt his world crash down all around him. Tears filled his eyes, but he fought them back.

Dad's dead? he thought. His heart cracked. *Oh, please... God? Don't let this be real, okay?*

Virginia desperately sobbed. Sandy tried to comfort her. Her mascara streaked down the sides of her face. Chris swallowed his emotions harder than he'd ever thought possible.

"Listen t' me carefully, lad," Nancy said. "Ye have t' be strong, do ye understand? You're th' man o' th' house now."

"Yes," Chris replied, weakly. His head was spinning. He thought he was going to faint. "I understand."

"Good lad," Nancy sighed. "Ye have t' help your mother, do ye hear? She has t' come t' Johnson Memorial Hospital. Your father's gone, son, and for that I'm truly sorry, but your brother is not. He needs ye, Chris. Ye have t' get here."

Chris hung up the phone, his mind numb, his movements forced. He knelt on the floor in front of his mother. He took her hands away from her face and held them in his.

"Mom?" Chris whispered.

Virginia shook her head.

"Mom?" he whispered again.

How could this be happening? Virginia's mind raced. *How? Lord, tell me it's a lie!*

Chris cried, *"Mom!"*

"Oh, *Chris...,"* Virginia sobbed, slowly looking up at him. "Dad's gone, baby. He's gone..."

"What?" Sandy gasped. "Holy... Jesus, Chris!"

"I know, mom," Chris replied, choking back a sob, "but Jeremy isn't. He's in the hospital and we have to get to him, okay? He needs us."

"Oh, God!" Virginia cried. "My baby! I have to get to my baby!"

She got up and pushed through the crowd toward the door. Sandy was right behind her. Chris dropped two twenties onto the counter near the waitress, and then grabbed his mother's purse and car keys from their booth.

*   *   *

Nancy understood why they called Margaret Adler the Hill Witch. There was a logical reason how the woman knew where to find Virginia and that her cell phone was working again, but she didn't know what that was.

Faith! Nancy thought. *She was even right about Jack!*

Misty apologized for missing him. She rambled something about never going into the men's room. That's why she paid a barback. Nancy only half-heard to her. She was watching what seemed like the entire little league passing through the Emergency Room doors. Their parents and Garth and Amanda McKee followed them.

"I found her," Nancy said to Amanda, covering her phone.

Amanda mouthed, "Thank you," but no sound came out.

Nancy watched the boys in the baseball uniforms fill the seats by the window. A small red-headed lad was sobbing. His brother had died recently. The younger son of the mechanic over at Gibbons' Garage was holding him in his lap. Nancy shook her head as she waited for Misty to return with Jack.

Damnation! she thought. *He would be loaded this early! Right back where he started a day after bein' let out o' jail!*

"Hi, um, Mrs. Dougan?" Misty asked, returning to the phone. "Jack refuses to get up."

"Did ye tell him his *mother's* on th' phone?" Nancy snapped.

Her voice brought every eye in the waiting room to her.

"Well... no, I...," Misty began.

"Ye listen to me, ye silly sow!" Nancy exploded. "Ye tell that drunken no good son-of-a-bitch that if'n he ain't down t' Johnson Memorial within th' hour, his mother's comin' t' get him! If'n I've got t' do that, he'll be beggin' for a new set o' balls!"

She ended the call and threw her phone. It hit the window frame and landed in a potted plant. Billy Wilde retrieved it. He handed it back to her, but kept a discreet distance.

"Thanks, lad," Nancy mumbled.

She was aware of the sudden silence in the Emergency Room. "I'll be beggin' your pardon," she said, adjusting her hairdo.

There was a chorus of "No problem." People shifted, uncomfortably. Nancy moved by the doors where Mike was speaking to Robert Bigelow again.

"Whew!" Matt remarked. "Remind me to stay on her good side!"

"No kidding," Max agreed.

Mike told Robert everything that had happened with the truck driver before the accident. He left out the conversation he had with Henry being true to his word, but was irritated for promising such a thing. It was worse than he'd ever dreamed. Bobby was one of his best friends. He felt like a heel for keeping this from him especially with Teddy involved. Teddy was Mike's godson. Mike intended to put Henry on the spot. He instructed him in no uncertain terms that he and his friends would be at his house tonight for the meeting. From the way Robert was acting, their plan to have Todd O'Connor expose the farmer had failed. Mike knew it when he asked Bobby how Teddy enjoyed working at the farm. Robert said with a smile that he loved it.

Mike was sure Chris wouldn't come now after losing his father. That was a shame. He finished the story of Merle fully accepting the blame for everything that had happened. He felt on the verge of tears. He held his hands out waiting to be arrested.

"Are you nuts, Mike?" Robert asked.

"Look, Bobby," Mike said, "I beat the guy up pretty badly. I probably caused the accident, too. I think you should take me in."

"All right, Mikey," Robert replied.

Nancy gasped.

"I'll take you in just as soon as Merle Wrightwood walks his dead ass up here from the morgue and files a complaint."

"That's not funny, Bobby!"

Robert put his hands on his shoulders. "Mikey, the guy was drunk as a skunk. His brains were leaking whiskey all over your parking lot, for Christ's sake. He assaulted your teenage nephew, killed Thomas McKee, and injured Jeremy DWI. Will you relax? No one's pointing a finger of blame at you. In fact, you're lucky to be alive. There was a sawed-off shotgun in his cab. We found it under the mattress. Now, how are the boys?"

"They're in a room," Mike said, a shiver running down his spine. In his mind, he could still hear Jeremy and Craig screaming.

They finally managed to separate their hands, Mike thought. *Jesus, it's all so strange.*

Sandra reappeared from the ladies' room and embraced Nancy. Mike pulled Robert to the side and insisted he come to his house tonight. He didn't say why. He only said it was a matter of life and death.

For Hiram Milliken, it was.

*　　*　　*

Jeremy woke with a start and bolted upright, gasping for breath. *My heart!* he thought. *It isn't beating!* Sweat poured from the top of his head and ran down his face. He wiped it away. He felt the weight of the cast on his left arm and had a small bump on his forehead.

Where am I? Jeremy thought, gazing around the room.

Craig was on the other bed lying on his side staring at him. Jeremy looked at the cast, curiously. Suddenly, he knew he was in the hospital. Fear filled his chest. He began to shake. The image of his father's headless body – *his hand groping his shoulder, blood spraying all over him* – ripped through his mind. He was falling into an abyss. Despair and loss, sorrow and heartbreak, attacked him all at once, and then the tears came. They fell over a face paralyzed with emotion. Jeremy felt Craig in his mind. He grabbed hold of that feeling in desperation. Craig jumped out of his bed and climbed onto his friend's. Jeremy was shaking all over. His tears fell, but no sound was coming out of his mouth. His lips moved, guttural noises came up from his throat, but he wasn't breathing. Craig grabbed Jeremy by the shoulders and shook him.

"Breathe!" Craig cried.

Jeremy's lips started to turn blue. Craig slapped him across the face. Jeremy's eyes widened.

"D... dd... y, d... add... eee, daaaaddddyyyyy!"

Jeremy screamed with such force, Craig thought the windows were going to blow out. He pulled Jeremy's head to his chest. Jeremy cried, hard crying, gasping for air crying. Craig felt his tears against his skin through his paper gown. They ran down his belly. Craig cried with him, holding him tight. The floor nurse rushed in and was about to ask what on Earth was going on when she saw Jeremy crying.

She thought, *Wailing is more like it.* The color drained from her face. She stood there, mouth agape.

"Get out!" Craig cried, his voice harsh and choked up.

The nurse glared at him. *Who does he think he's talking to?*

"Get out!" Craig screamed, his face twisting. *"Get out! Get out!"*

"I'll... get the doctor," she managed to say.

Craig was ferocious as he spat his words at her. She quickly dialed the Emergency Room and asked for Dr. Montclair *STAT!*

"Dr. Montclair."

"Yes, doctor. This is Nurse Templeton in Pediatrics. The McKee boy is awake, sir, and he's hysterical."

"I'm on my way," Dr. Montclair said. "Leave him alone as long as he isn't violent."

"Yes, doctor," she replied.

"Is the Dougan boy still with him?" he asked, scratching his head at the top of his receding hairline.

"Yes," Nurse Templeton replied. "He ordered me out of the room!"

"Then stay out, nurse," Dr. Montclair said.

The line went dead in her hand. She stared at the receiver.

Jeremy stopped shaking and was only crying now. Craig saw flashes of the accident through their mind-link and a mental picture of Jeremy that kept bursting into flames. Each time it did, Craig put it out. Jeremy held him tighter. Craig forced visions of his dreamscape into Jeremy's mind. Jeremy relaxed a little as he thought about the cool breezes, the lush green grasslands. Craig used this to fight off the darkness, the pit that wanted Jeremy to fall into it. He filled his mind with all the love he had for his friend and promised not to let him go.

Dr. Montclair entered the room. He closed the door on the nurse before she could walk in behind him. *If the boy wants her out, then out she stays,* he thought. He looked at Jeremy and Craig huddled together. He saw they were both crying. *Thank God. That's what they need.*

Dr. Montclair sat on the edge of the bed. Craig looked at him. The doctor had a kind face. Craig knew he was there to help.

"Are you all right?" Dr. Montclair asked, touching Craig's forearm above the bandage where they had taken his blood.

Craig shook his head. He cried with more force as he lay his face sideways on the top of Jeremy's head.

Dr. Montclair patted him on the arm and got up. "You stay with him, okay?" he said. He left the room to speak with the nurse.

"Stay with him?" Craig thought-spoke. Jeremy heard the words. *"You couldn't drag me away."*

Jeremy took Craig's hand and held it.

Dr. Montclair told the nurse they were not to be disturbed. He was to be advised immediately if anything else happened.

Jeremy and Craig stopped crying in time, but neither one of them moved. Every once in a while, Jeremy felt Craig hug him, so he hugged him back. The mind-link was all that was keeping him sane.

"My... dad's...," Jeremy whispered, tears threatening.

"I know," Craig said. "I'm here, okay? I'm here."

*　　*　　*

Ms. Adler sat on top of the Emergency Room nurses' station next to the sign that read: *In-Patient Processing*. She was in clear view of everyone, yet no one saw her. She wouldn't allow it. She was invisible as she had been before she fell asleep in the waiting room when Nancy was on the phone. It was a simple trick. A tiny suggestion radiated from her mind ordering everyone's eyes not to see her. Their imaginations filled in the space she took up. The security guards couldn't see her on their monitors either although the cameras could. She ignored them. With her ability to mentally access AI, she could erase any video at will.

She had used the same ability to block Virginia, Chris, and Sanford's cell phones. Using her techno-telepathy, she sent a tiny command through the cell tower blocking their calls until she released them. At the same time, she kept tabs on them through GPS. She had the end game choreographed to the final act. Everything would happen in stages. Her pawns were weaving the tapestry precisely as she'd intended. There was nothing to do except wait and avoid the Gypsy at all costs.

Damn her! Ms. Adler thought. *How did she find me? I have been so careful!* She remembered the albino boy with the platinum blonde hair. *Yes, he is the one. He found me, but how?*

The boy was a clear threat. His mental defenses were formidable. Every time she tried to scan him, he resisted her without effort. She wondered where he obtained such power. He hadn't demonstrated any abilities, but he must possess some in order to block hers. No ordinary person no matter how disciplined was immune to her telepathy.

Resistant to it, yes, but not invulnerable, Ms. Adler thought, *It is ordinarily a matter of whether or not it is worth my effort and expenditure of power and will to overcome them. It is often easier to engage more subtle manipulations with the strong.* She considered, frowning. *It is possible they might not interfere at all. Maybe they cannot? If they could, they would have, would they not? Why are they waiting?* She dismissed her concerns. *It does not matter. I know they are here now. I have come too far to fail.*

Ms. Adler caught a distant angry thought. Jack Dougan was almost at the hospital. Chris McKee and his mother weren't far behind him. Everything was on schedule. Jeremy would be hers. She scanned the surface thoughts around her. Adele Weissenberg, a Lancaster native and a long-time friend of Nancy, Garth, and Amanda opened the Doctor's Lounge for Amanda and Garth. They were grateful to be able to grieve in private.

Ms. Adler found Garth's weakness sickening. She gleaned worse thoughts from the children in the waiting room. Max Ramirez was the only genuinely honorable one of all of them. It was a shame he was a mongrel. He would have been a much better choice than Jeremy. Matt, a true Aryan, a demi-god in boy's clothing, would have been perfect, too, but for his genetic shortcomings.

Ms. Adler floated down from her perch. She walked silently through the crowd toward the elevators. She entered one when the doors opened and pressed the button for the top floor. She felt the large syringe in her skirt pocket. She recalled Dabney's terror as he watched her prepare the serum's final composition. She opened her mind to him completely and allowed him to witness all of the murders Hiram had committed, the legacy of her power. She added that to the horror of the Buchenwald memories he was already drowning in. Dabney was lying on the floor of the lab when she closed the concrete door for the last time. He was drooling, wide-eyed, and on the verge of insanity.

She then proceeded to write the last chapter of Thomas McKee's life, a work of telepathy equivalent to fine art. She could not openly kill Thomas, but utilizing distraction and influence, she set in motion a series of events her daughter's subconscious aversion to murder couldn't thwart. She intended to destroy her and then her house the moment she claimed the new power. It would require nothing more than a stray thought to blast it all to atoms, the lab and Dabney included.

Ms. Adler exited the elevator on the Pediatrics floor slipping past two confused nurses. They wondered why someone would send the elevator up with no occupant. They passed it off as a prank. Dancing clowns holding bunches of colored balloons grinned at her from the hallway wallpaper. Ms. Adler stuck her tongue out at them making a childish face before continuing. She pushed open the door to Jeremy and Craig's room with her telekinetics. They looked up, appearing drawn and weary.

Good, Ms. Adler thought, not allowing either boy to see her. *It is essential they stay that way.*

The door closed. The boys lay back down. They blamed the movement on the wind. Ms. Adler scanned them. She heard Craig's soothing words of comfort as he spoke to Jeremy through the mind-link. It had served its purpose well. It's what made Chris a more perfect choice for her needs than his brother, his strong will, his independent spirit. Jeremy was weak. If Chris had been the chosen one, he would have endured a similar accident but with his mother. It was necessary, to break the spirit and weaken the will. There was no better way to crush someone than by taking away a loved one.

Without the mind-link to draw on Craig's strength, the shock of the accident would have left Jeremy catatonic, trapping him inside of his mind. Chris didn't need a cushion. Craig wouldn't have needed one either if she had chosen him. His genetic imperfections and his maternal grandmother's Jewish heritage made that impossible.

Race contamination is so disgustingly common these days, Ms. Adler thought. *I can smell it in Craig. It is nauseating.*

Jeremy's lineage was pure, albeit not German, yet unspoiled by the sub-human mixtures that ruled out so many of the other children. Ms. Adler felt his love for Craig. It was stronger than she had hoped. It was an emotion impossible to force. It had to grow naturally. Friendship would have been enough, but love was better. She concentrated, her eyes busting midnight blue brilliance.

Sleep, children. The time has nearly come.

Their bodies obeyed and slipped into Craig's dreamscape. Ms. Adler locked them in there and levitated Craig back to his bed.

Your usefulness, Master Dougan, she thought, *is not yet over.*

She sat on the windowsill and waited. She sensed the tension rising in the waiting room downstairs. Another pawn in her grand play was taking center stage. She felt his raging presence.

Jack Dougan had arrived.

✳   ✳   ✳

Mike stood in front of his unsteady brother with his arms crossed over his chest. He had given every detail of the accident and how it involved Craig. It was hard seeing Jack like this, drunk and arrogant. It was impossible to dredge up any of the sympathy he had gained after learning the truth about Hiram. As he spoke, he remembered it wasn't Jack's fault. Jack was only to blame for not getting help as an adult.

The look in his eyes, Mike thought. *The way the kids are staring at him like they want to kill him.*

It drove Mike to squeeze and loosen his fist under his armpit.

"So, Craig's not hurt?" Jack asked, his words slurring.

"Physically he's fine," Mike replied, biting hard on his anger. "It's the shock we're worried about."

"Shock?" Jack asked. "From seeing a dead body?" He rolled his eyes. "Big deal! Do you have a clue how many dead bodies I've seen? Do you know how many of them I killed myself?"

"In the war, Jack," Mike said.

"That's right, in the goddamned war!"

"Excuse me, sir," Adele interjected. "You'll have to tone it down a bit."

"Will you mind your own business?" Jack snapped. "Stupid bitch."

"That's enough, Jack," Mike said.

"You're right, Mikey!" Jack cried. "It's more than enough! I want my kid out of this hospital right now!"

"What?"

Sandra grabbed Mike's arm. "Jack," she said, "you can't be serious. Craig's had a very traumatic experience."

Jack burst out laughing. "Traumatic? The only thing traumatic will be the bill this place sends me. Who's going to pay it, Mikey? You?"

411

The men in the waiting room along with Sandy, Matt, Max, and Ricardo gathered together. Everything they had ever heard about Jack was true. The second things got out of control they were jumping in. Nancy could see what they were planning to do. She held up her hand and told them to wait. Randy gritted his teeth. Kevin clenched a fist.

José moved in next to his sons. He whispered, "Don't wait for me, ¿entiendes?"

Max and Ricardo nodded.

Garth was standing in the Doctor's Lounge doorway. He'd come out when he heard Jack's voice. Garth had known Wade Dougan. He was a fine man. If Jack only knew how badly he was shaming his father's memory. He motioned for Amanda to stay put and filed into the group of men. He hated everything about Jack. How could a father care so little for his son? Garth would've given his life to have Thomas back. Max looked up at him. Garth nodded.

"You might not have Craig much longer, Jack!" Mike growled, his fists clenched and ready to strike.

"Did somebody forget to tell you McKee's dead?" Jack asked. "It's all over the news. You think you're going to pull another high-priced ambulance chaser out of a hat? I want Craig out of here now. He's coming home with me!"

"You're not taking Craig anywhere," Virginia said, from behind him.

Jack spun around.

Virginia was unaffected by his furious glare. "There are a lot of things I've been dying to say to you, little man," she snarled.

"Take your best shot, bitch," Jack said. "I've heard it all before."

Chris stepped forward, but Virginia stopped him with *The Look.*

Chris nodded and backed up. *Whoa, mom's tougher than I thought!*

Sandy put his hand on Chris' shoulder. *I'm ready if Jack crosses the line,* he thought, stepping in front of his friend. He looked toward his mother. Susan nodded to him, gripping her husband's hand. Sean held Alex's leg, biting his lower lip.

"You'd like that, wouldn't you, Jack?" Virginia said. "Create a scene, blow off some rage?"

"Don't stick your nose where it doesn't belong," Jack replied. "I'm a bad man to screw with."

"And I'm the nastiest *queen* bitch you've ever crossed swords with!" Virginia exploded, poking Jack in the chest. "Getting Craig away from you didn't die with my husband! I know more attorneys than you have pecker inches and they all owe my family favors! One way or another, I'm going to make sure you never get your stinking rotten hands on that kid again. So help me God, Jack, you've messed with the wrong broad!"

Jack shook with rage. *No one talks to me like that! No way!* He looked deep into her eyes. She glared back at him daring him to strike. Jack raised his fist. The whole room moved toward him.

Nancy got to him first. "Just what're ye plannin' t' do with that fist, boyo?" she asked.

Jack wavered in indecision.

"I thought ye had th' right t' see your boy, Jackie," she continued, "but I was wrong. Get out. Go back t' whatever hole ye crawled out of tonight. I don't ever want t' see your face again."

Jack hovered. He gazed at the faces glaring at him.

They think they can take me? That's a laugh! I could kill all of them with my bare hands!

Jack was about to hang everything, dive into the group of men, and start taking them apart when Giuseppe Luciano appeared in front of them. His weeping eyes were filled with betrayal and angry accusation.

Jack gasped and walked quickly out the door. *No more ghosts!* he thought. *No more!* He stumbled to the Monte Carlo. He was about to ram his key into the ignition when a woman's voice appeared inside his head. Jack relaxed just as she commanded. He nodded and listened. He smiled. He set his keys on the passenger's seat and waited.

Garth and Amanda went to their daughter-in-law. Virginia's bravado melted. They threw their arms around her and she began to cry. The adults gathered with them. Chris waded through the crowd to the waiting room. A tear ran down his cheek. Max came to him. Chris crumbled. Max reached out and drew Chris to him as he sobbed. Chris leaned into him, his body turning to rubber. He remained standing only because Max was holding him up.

"Let it out, Chris," Max said. "We're all here."

Amanda watched as Chris' friends surrounded him. She stayed with Virginia. She thought, *They're such good boys*.

Garth led her and Virginia to the Doctor's Lounge. Virginia wasn't ready to greet the neighborhood, not yet. Cynthia fell against her husband, her tears falling anew. Every wife's heart went out to Virginia.

Virginia grieved on the small leather sofa in the lounge. She was sitting between Garth and Amanda, her mind flooded with so many torturously happy memories. Adele looked in, nodded at Garth, and closed the door.

Chris cried in Max's arms for about two minutes. Max told him it was okay to keep crying, but Chris shook his head. He would cry later in private. He asked them if they would come to his house again tonight. He was sure his mother was going to stay at the hospital with Jeremy. He wanted to go home, not to his grandparent's house. Seeing them cry made Chris feel strange, out of control. He couldn't handle it. They said they would.

Linda Gardner put a damper on things. "Boys?" she asked. "I'm not sure tonight would be appropriate…"

"Shut up, Linda!" Cynthia exclaimed, her eyes brimming with tears. "Where's your mind, woman? Virginia's not leaving Jeremy! Don't you think Chris needs some support, too? He's reaching out! Derek can go with him! What do you think they're going to do? Throw a party!?"

"Oh, Lord, Chris," Linda gasped, her hand over her mouth. "I don't know what I was thinking. Please, I'm sorry! Matthew, of course, you can go and be with your friend."

"Y tú, Max y Ricardo," Marianna said. José translated for her. Cynthia was talking so fast, it sounded like Chinese to her.

"You don't even have to ask, Sanford," Susan said.

Max and Ricardo held Chris tightly. They told him they loved him. Chris nodded. He loved all of them more than ever. He needed them and they were there. It was all anyone could ask. Max led them over to the chairs and they sat down. He kept his arm around Chris. Sandy took his hand. Chris observed those who had come to support him and his family. It felt good to know there were people like this in the world.

His saw Derek next to his father. His eyes were pink and puffy from crying. Kevin came over to Chris. He squatted down in front of him and said they were there if he needed them. Chris only heard half of what he was saying. He nodded, appropriately. Kevin was a good guy. He was doing for Chris what Chris had done for Derek.

Kevin patted him on the thigh and went back to his wife. Cynthia had Douggie on her lap. He was watching TV with his thumb in his mouth. Alex and Susan were next to them with Sean. Chris noticed that Herman was sitting alone. They knew his mother hated hospitals, but they didn't know why. Matt slipped into the bathroom. He couldn't look at Chris. He knew it would make him cry, too. He thought if he had only convinced Jeremy to come to the field early, he could have prevented this. He sat on the toilet, his face in his hands, overwhelmed by guilt.

Derek ambled over to Chris, his head down, his fingers working. Chris waited for him to say something, but he just stood there, his lower lip quivering. Chris reached out and tilted his head up with his forefinger. Derek's green eyes were filled with tears.

"Chris... I hope... Jeremy, I *mean...,*" Derek struggled, holding in his emotions. "You know, huh? He's... well... *Chris?* Are you okay?"

Derek's tears fell. Chris let go of Sandy's hand and drew him into his lap. Derek figured everyone thought he was a crybaby, but he didn't care. Jeremy was in shock they said. He didn't understand what that meant, but he knew it wasn't good. Chris was his friend and his dad was dead. Derek knew how he felt after losing Dan.

"I'm worried, Chris!" Derek blubbered.

"Me, too," Chris sadly replied, "but you're here for me, and I'm here for you. We can both be here for Jeremy."

Chris held back his tears. José spoke to Marianna in Spanish, wiping her tears with his thumbs. Ricardo moved to the other side of his mother. He winked at Chris who tried too hard to smile. Adele led Mike, Sandra, and Nancy into the corridor. Chris assumed they were going up to see Craig. Colin was sitting on the floor in the corner picking his nose and eating it behind a copy of Newsweek. Billy Wilde stared at him with his mouth hanging open, thoroughly disgusted.

Adele paused at the nurses' station. "Dr. Montclair? I'm taking the Dougans to Pediatrics. The McKees want to see you when you're ready."

"Well, Nurse Weissenberg," Dr. Montclair replied. He took a deep breath. "Let's not keep them in the dark. Make sure the Dougans understand their visit needs to be brief. They can have all the time they like tomorrow, but tonight it's immediate family, mother or father, that's it."

Garth watched the young doctor enter the room and sit behind the desk. He thought, *He can't be older than thirty-two.*

"First off," Dr. Montclair began, slipping his nameplate onto the desk, "let me say that I'm sorry for your loss."

Virginia sadly thanked him. Amanda nodded.

"I'm Dr. Montclair," he said, pointing to the plate, "the Emergency Room attending physician for today."

"I'm Virginia McKee. These are my husband's parents, Garth and Amanda McKee."

She struggled through that, Dr. Montclair thought. *Best not to ask too many questions.* "Your son, Jeremy, is not in any physical danger."

They sighed with relief.

Virginia picked up on the keyword in the doctor's sentence. "Physical?" she asked.

Dr. Montclair spoke slowly and professionally. Virginia locked on to every phrase.

"Jeremy's suffered a severely traumatic experience. He's a strong young man and appears to be drawing a lot of support from Craig Dougan. From what I understand, Craig pulled him out of the wreckage. Are they friends?"

Virginia replied, fighting to level her voice, "While he's stayed with us, I've watched the two of them grow very close. Craig has been through some hard times with his father. Jeremy's helping him cope. They consider each other best friends."

"The reason I'm asking," Dr. Montclair said, "is because the boys became very agitated when we tried to separate them. Jeremy has quite a grip."

"He works out regularly," Garth hoarsely said.

"I'm sure he does," Dr. Montclair said. "The two of them broke a nurse's nose when she tried to pull them apart."

Virginia and her in-laws gasped.

Dr. Montclair continued, "She's all right. A hazard of the profession. They only calmed down after I set Jeremy's arm when they fainted. A short while ago, Jeremy woke, extremely agitated. Craig was with him and helped calm him down. I think Jeremy may be holding on to Craig like a buoy. The accident, as I understand it, was severe, and your husband's injuries... extensive."

Virginia inhaled sharply. *Oh, God!*

"I don't think it's wise to separate them at the moment," Dr. Montclair said. "Jeremy needs someone who understands. I believe that's Craig. I doubt we could separate them if we wanted."

Virginia felt her heart crack. *I should've been here! Jeremy's pain must be enormous!* Her anger rose. She cursed God for putting her family through this. *Oh, Jesus, I'm sorry!*

"There is no sign of a concussion," Dr. Montclair read from the chart with Jeremy's name on it, "no internal bleeding. However, Jeremy has suffered a severe fracture of his left arm. We were able to set it without having to put pins in it, but he has several stitches where the bones had pierced the skin. There will be a visible scar. As I said, I don't believe he's in any physical danger. How he copes with the trauma of the accident, time will tell. I recommend grief counseling for the whole family and for Craig. They've been through hell today. They'll need all the support they can get."

Virginia asked if she could see them. Dr. Montclair said they could, but they needed to promise not to wake the boys. As of the last report, they were sleeping. The McKees agreed. The doctor rose to leave.

Virginia stopped him for one more request. "Many of our friends are here," she began, looking at the floor.

"So I see."

"Could you give them the details? I have to see my son."

Dr. Montclair said he would and led them back to the waiting room. Chris got up when he saw his mother, gently setting Derek on his feet. He didn't like the expression on her face. He knew she was worried. He prayed there was nothing wrong with Jeremy. She motioned for him to come.

"We can go up now," Virginia said, her voice low and strained.

The doctor gathered the parents together as Adele led the McKees to the elevator. She hit the button for Pediatrics. Amanda slipped her arm around Virginia who placed her hand on Chris' shoulder. He leaned into her wanting very much to wake up from this nightmare, *now, okay!?* There was a stab of incredible loss. Chris could see his father's face inside his mind. He nearly doubled over from feelings that hurt like physical blows.

I'm never going to see my dad again? Chris despaired. *Ever? Forever?*

The elevator doors opened. A grinning wallpaper clown with big red shoes and a handful of balloons greeted Chris. He looked around the corner and saw that they were everywhere.

What's my brother doing on this floor? Chris wondered. *Do they think Jeremy's a baby? God, how lame!*

Each clown grinned differently. Each wore a bright baggy jumpsuit with a funky collar that looked like an aluminum cupcake wrapper.

"Gag me," Chris scowled.

Amanda and Adele walked together murmuring. Chris knew the nurse was reassuring his grandmother that everything would be okay. He was avoiding Amanda. He felt terrible about that, but it was too painful to see her upset. She was always bubbling over with confidence and strength. Chris supposed losing her son...

It hit him again like a ton of bricks.

Dad... man, this is real. He's gone.

Virginia walked into the room. Chris followed her closely. Jeremy was in the bed to their left with a massive cast on his arm. Virginia choked back a sob. He looked so helpless and fragile lying there. She thanked God He hadn't taken her baby as well as her husband.

The Dougans were sitting in white plastic chairs at the head of Craig's bed. Mike saw the look on Virginia's face and stood up. She was trying desperately to hold in her emotions. He asked if she needed a hug. She responded by hugging him. Chris went to Jeremy's bed. Nancy took hold of his hand.

"I love him, Mrs. Dougan," Chris said.

"I know ye do, lad," Nancy replied.

Virginia held on to Mike and stopped her tears once again. *Not yet,* she thought. *Once I begin, there's no way I'm going to stop.*

She overheard downstairs that Mike had been at the accident scene.

"You were there?" Virginia asked.

Mike nodded. She saw by his expression the story wasn't going to be pretty. Mike mentally edited what he planned to tell her. He would leave out the part about Thomas' head at the boys' feet, or how he had kicked it under the truck.

"I have to know, Mike," Virginia said. "Did Thomas...? Was he...?"

Mike shook his head. "It was instantaneous."

Virginia sighed relief. *Thank God for that.*

She asked Mike to give her the whole story and not to pull any punches. She needed to hear it. Chris listened, too, even though they were speaking in hushed voices. Tractor-trailer... head on collision... the more Mike revealed, the more his heart went out to his brother. Chris let go of Nancy's hand and touched the side of Jeremy's face. He looked so peaceful, but he knew that peace would be short-lived once his brother woke up. Mike told Virginia what happened between Jeremy and Craig. Craig pulled Jeremy out of the Porsche. They sat together crying. Jeremy refused to go anywhere without him. Craig promised not to leave him.

Chris walked over to Craig's bedside. His dirty blonde hair was wet with sweat, his face stained with tears. Every story of every mean thing Jack had ever done to him came into Chris' mind. He was glad his mother had put Jack in his place. The best part about it was he knew that she was serious. Virginia made a comment about how much they owed Craig. Chris silently agreed. She believed he had saved Jeremy by being there at the moment of trauma. That was the clincher for Chris. He leaned over and kissed Craig's forehead, and then his cheek. His tears were salty on his lips.

"I owe you," Chris whispered. "Come back to us, okay? I swear, Craig, we'll never let you go."

"You know," Sandra said, "Craig's a damn good kid."

"You don't have to sell him to me, Mrs. Dougan," Chris choked. "I swear to God, I'll never let anybody hurt him again. Not ever."

Virginia and Mike looked at Chris, nodding soberly.

Chris scowled. "What's wrong with you dweebs?" he asked.

Virginia kissed him on the cheek. Chris hugged her, kissed his brother, and left the room. Once his mother got over to Jeremy, her tears were going fall. Chris didn't want to watch. He couldn't take seeing her like that. He needed his friends.

Virginia sat on the edge of Jeremy's bed and wept. Mike went into more graphic detail about the accident once Chris had left the room. She was thankful for that. The images were horrifying. She was only beginning to understand what Jeremy had gone through. She was afraid. She looked down at her little angel, at the thick plaster encasing his left arm, and prayed for his mind.

I'll endure any torture, any pain, but please, God, spare him the agony he'll face when he wakes up.

Memories invaded her thoughts, times that had promised a bright future for their family – Thomas' graduation from law school, the offer of a prestigious position with Thurman Millner's firm, and a lifetime of security. She reached inside for that feeling, but it wasn't there. The winds of her despair had blown it away.

Oh, Thomas, my love, my life, Virginia desperately thought. *Tell me what I'm supposed to do now.* Her tears fell silent and warm down her cheeks.

Mike reached out to her, but Nancy held him back. She needed to grieve. She had the right to have her tears go unrelieved, her sorrow undiminished by a sympathetic touch.

Virginia remembered the child Knight in the front yard waiting for his wandering King to come home. Her heart broke when she realized that now the wait for the King would be forever. Time was moving on already. A big part of her boy, perhaps the biggest part of all, was gone. The thought brought her tears in force. Virginia lay her head on Jeremy's chest and cried.

Chris waited in the hall for his mother to come out. Garth left Amanda with Adele and moved over to his grandson. They walked together for a few doors, neither looking at the other, trying to decide what to say.

Chris broke the silence. "I miss him already, Gramps," he said. His words and the tone of his voice sounded hollow.

"I know, Chris," Garth whispered. "I do, too."

"Will you be there for my mom?" Chris asked, suddenly feeling his mother's loneliness.

Garth held his arm out and stopped him. "Of course I will."

Chris hugged his grandfather.

"I don't like seeing them cry," Chris said.

Garth sympathized. He didn't like it either, but he accepted it as part of the healing process. He put his hand on Chris' shoulder and led him to where his mother and grandmother were waiting. Amanda motioned for Garth to come with her into the room. She stepped aside long enough to allow the Dougans to pass and they entered.

The Dougans said goodbye and promised to be in tomorrow. Virginia said they would be here as well. Mike told Chris in the faintest whisper to call him at the market as soon as he was back in Lancaster. Chris was puzzled, but said nothing. He promised he would. He sat down with his mother outside the room in the chairs the floor nurse had provided. He told her they should talk. Virginia nodded, but said nothing. Her pain was deep and raw, but she knew she should say something.

"It's hard…," Virginia began. She sat with her head down.

Chris put his arm around her.

Virginia looked at him. She watched tears well up in his eyes. He was hurting as badly as she was, but he wouldn't show it.

"Chris," Virginia whispered. "The doctor said parents only tonight, but if you want, I'll see if he'll make an exception."

"It's okay, mom. I invited some friends to stay with me. I knew you wouldn't leave Jeremy."

So, Virginia thought, *he's reaching out on his own.*

She felt relieved. She needed some time alone and to be here for Jeremy. She needed to know everything was all right with her baby. She needed to talk to him and hug his pain away.

Virginia wondered, *Should I have Chris stay with me? No, he won't want to. Let him cry with his friends in a way he would never cry with me.*

"Chris?" Virginia asked, resting her palm on the side of his face. "Do you think I'm abandoning you?"

Chris held her hand to his cheek. "I understand, mom," he said. "I'm hurting, too." He laid his head against her chest and started to cry.

*   *   *

Everyone in the lobby waited for the McKees to return. They were hoping for some firsthand news about how the boys were doing. Mike remained downstairs long enough to give Randy the details of the accident, but then he left. He was heading for the market and the barrage of questions waiting for him there. He decided Chris calling might not be good enough especially after today. Another idea came to his mind. He would implement it once he was back at the store. He didn't know why, but having Chris at the meeting was suddenly an obsession. They needed to stop Hiram. Max, Ricardo, Sandy, Derek, and Matt were going with Chris to his house.

Susan was glad Virginia would be there if Jeremy and Craig woke up. She thought, *If my sons were in the same position, would I stay with them? God, I hope I never find out. If anything happened to my kids or to Alex? I would be at the funny farm making baskets out of wicker and paper flowers.*

Linda and Cynthia were the first to greet Virginia when the McKees stepped out of the elevator. They exchanged hugs. Linda asked if she knew Chris had invited the boys to stay over.

Virginia whispered, "I would appreciate it if they could. He needs his friends right now. Besides, I'm staying here with Jeremy."

Cynthia nodded. Linda volunteered to stay with the boys if Virginia wanted. Virginia said there was no need. She trusted them. The boys had never given her reason to be overly concerned. Besides, they were there to support Chris on the day his father died. It wasn't exactly an occasion for a party. Linda felt a touch of déjà vu.

They expressed their sympathies. Kevin and Cynthia told Virginia to call on them if she needed anything. It was a gesture she appreciated although she probably wouldn't take advantage of it. José and Marianna volunteered to drive the boys home, but Linda said they would since Matt was going and it was closer to their house. The boys told her they needed to stop and change clothes. Max, Ricardo, Derek, and Matt were still in their baseball uniforms. Sandy had no clean clothes at Chris' house. Randy said that wouldn't be a problem.

Colin Skinner's parents hadn't come to the game. They never did. He asked to ride with the Sturgesses since they were already taking Billy home. Susan said that was fine. Virginia and Chris thanked them all for their support. Susan told them that support had a price tag. She expected Virginia to lean on her and her family.

"In fact," Susan said, taking her hand, "I friggin' insist."

Virginia nodded, her eyes watering.

Chris gathered the guys together while Virginia went with Adele to sign the necessary paperwork. He hugged them all. Sandy held him tight, Max a little too tight. Ricardo held his hips away from him. Colin was a *quick hug, okay now let me go now* type. Billy patted his back awkwardly. Herman, who

Chris only knew from the bus stop, had a hug that was genuinely sweet. His intimacy was unreserved.

Chris whispered, "Thank you," in his ear.

Herman smiled.

Derek held on to Chris as if holding on for dear life. "I love you, Chris," he said.

"I love you, too, little buddy," Chris replied, and let him go.

Virginia stood in the parking lot and watched the Gardners' mini-van pull away. She waved at Chris in the back seat with Sandy and Max. He waved back and blew her a kiss. They were going to Max's house for clothes, and then Sandy's. They had two quick stops to make at Herman's house and the Gardners' before dropping the others off with Chris.

Images of the accident rushed into Virginia's mind. They were pale pictures related by Mike, but she understood something. Jeremy's world had ended. Craig caught the pieces. She thanked God there were pieces to catch.

*   *   *

Mickey Downing stood in the hospital parking lot looking up at Jeremy's window. The carnival carried on behind him. He was unnaturally calm. He had an inner peace that denied his youth. His gaze was even, his jaw set in a manner that suggested arrogance. Mickey didn't know the meaning of the word. His parents and grandmother had raised him with strict Christian values. They helped him sharpen his abilities for use in the service of God and humanity.

His grandmother had passed the potential for the power to her daughter, Mickey's mother, but Alberta was psychically impotent. They discovered after Mickey was born that the power had not only skipped a generation, it manifested itself in an entirely new way. Mickey was born with abilities even his grandmother didn't understand. He possessed an intuitive version of the sight that was useful with games of chance, but his real power involved the dead and dying. Mickey's domain was death and he used that power to find the evil one who haunted his grandmother's nightmares. Ezmerelda's premonitions had brought them to this moment. At long last, it was time for them to intervene.

Ezmerelda had warned him they were no match for Margaret Adler as they now knew their enemy. A direct confrontation would be futile. Ezmerelda's power had faded with age. Mickey, at the present moment, lacked any offensive abilities capable of doing battle with the Hill Witch. He possessed psychic defenses, but to overcome Adler he needed to be able to fight her. As his powers matured, Ezmerelda theorized he would develop them, or some type of psychic talents, and then he could destroy her, but they didn't have time to wait.

They had been lucky the other night. Their bluff caught the Hill Witch off guard. She couldn't attack them without the risk of exposure or defeat at Ezmerelda's hands. It was the only thing that had saved them, but they had to take the chance. They needed to make contact with the boys. From what Wade Dougan revealed to Mickey, Margaret was targeting them. They needed to know why. Ezmerelda was too weak to manage it from a distance and they didn't dare go to Lancaster. They had to stay out of range of Margaret Adler's telepathy, and yet lure the boys to the carnival. The poster at the market had been left by ordinary carnies and served that purpose well.

Ezmerelda had seen everything when she read the boys' fortunes. It chilled her to the bone. There wasn't a thing they could do to stop it. Fate was fickle. Attempting to alter destiny often did more harm than good. Ezmerelda knew this thanks to her mother and grandmother. She vowed over her mother's body never to make the same mistake. Ezmerelda's weakened abilities included glimpses of the future just as her grandmother's had. She knew Mickey had been born to help face the coming evils. He was one of *The Nine*. The Hill Witch was the first foe. They had to stop her. She could not be allowed to claim Jeremy McKee.

Mickey lowered his head, prayed for guidance, and then stepped into Johnson Memorial Hospital.

"Go with God, my sweet one," Ezmerelda whispered, from the doorway to her tent. "May He have mercy on our souls for our part in this."

* * *

Ms. Adler used her power to push Virginia and the chair she was sleeping in across the room to the far wall. She put her to sleep, deep and exhausted. She climbed off the windowsill and focused her telepathy on Craig. His eyes opened, blank and staring. He rose off the bed zombie-like and tore open the plastic bag with his bloody clothes in it. He dressed robotically, tied his sneakers, and left. The nurse was asleep at her desk. He took the stairwell at the end of the hall to the bottom floor. He exited the heavy steel door on the side of the building and went to where Jack was waiting for him.

The Monte Carlo's motor was running. The broken steering column rested on Jack's knees. He let the car roll forward and stopped in Craig's path. The sound of grinding brakes was horrid. Craig sat in the front seat and closed the door. Jack hit the gas. The tires screeched and they sped away.

Ms. Adler watched them from the window. The afternoon sun was blood-red in the sky. Storm clouds were gathering, plunging the world into darkness. She had to hurry. Her power attracted lightning better than a lightning rod. It took a tremendous amount of concentration to redirect the energy with her telekinesis if lightning struck her. If she didn't, the jolt could kill her. She was insulated in her lab, but not out here.

She closed the shade and made the light switch flip to the off position. She withdrew a large glass syringe from her skirt pocket. She unwrapped the duct tape surrounding it and revealed a glowing midnight blue liquid in the reservoir. She removed the cap and screwed on a long thread-thin needle. The light from the serum filled the room. She sat on the edge of Jeremy's bed, leaned over, and pressed the needle into the corner of his left eye by his nose. It pierced the thin bone of his eye socket and entered his cranial cavity. She squeezed the plunger, emptying the glowing liquid into his head.

She pulled out the needle, her eyes flashed, and the syringe disintegrated into powder. Jeremy went into convulsions. Gurgling sounds came up from his throat as if he were drowning. Ms. Adler watched, elated. Her telepathic laughter projected into every mind within a mile of the hospital.

* * *

"Isn't that Henry Schwartz?" Randy asked.

He pointed at the young man on the McKees' doorstep as they pulled into the driveway. He wasn't there a minute ago when they passed so Matt could go home and change his clothes. Randy hadn't seen him walking down Points of Light Road either. He wondered if someone had dropped him off.

Chris eyed him, curiously. *What's Henry doing here?*

The other boys looked at him, concerned. Each felt the weight of their actions from the night before. Thomas' death brought everything into a hazy focus. Regret stabbed through their hearts. Todd was one of Hiram's victims. It was the farmer they had wanted when they went there. They had a burning desire to watch him squirm and make him bleed. The rage they felt – so unlike Matt or even Max – seemed alien now. Not knowing where it had come from scared the crap out of them.

Chris decided Henry must be here to pay his respects. He said as much. Linda nodded. The Schwartz family had been their neighbors for years. She didn't give it much thought beyond that. She was distracted. Linda was an intensely focused individual. It caused her to come across as conceited all too often, but this was something different. She didn't know why she felt so uneasy about Matt being here tonight instead of at home. The word "No!" danced on the tip of her tongue. She bit down on it as Matt kissed her on the cheek and the boys climbed out.

Henry uncharacteristically threw his arms around Chris when he got to the front porch. Max and Derek waved to the Gardners as they drove away. Derek noticed Linda's worried stare, but he didn't say anything. Everyone knew she was paranoid. Chris thanked Henry in a whisper and told his friends to wait while he disarmed the security system.

Henry thought about Mike and the drawn look of concern on his face when he returned from the hospital. He was wrestling something and weighing his options carefully. He called Henry into the office. He was taking him to the McKees' house so Henry could bring Chris and the others to the meeting. Henry saw in his eyes that disturbing Chris today was the last thing he wanted to do. When he questioned Mike about it, Mike told him the real tragedy would be if Hiram got away. After what they did to Todd last night, time was short. He refused to let any more children get hurt. He hoped Chris would understand that. So did Henry. Mike had dropped him off seconds after the Gardners passed by the first time.

Chris disarmed the alarm. The boys filed into the living room. Derek came in last. He went to shut the door, but a pair of small hands stopped it.

"Wait!" Teddy cried, squeezing past. He stood in the hall, panting. He looked like he had run all the way around Lancaster to get here.

"Teddy?" Chris asked, moving in front of the others. "What's going on? What are you doing here?"

Teddy panted, "I'm not... sure. They're having... some kind of... meeting at Mike... Dougan's house. I'm supposed to go... with you."

"With us?" Max asked. "But we're not going anywhere."

"Oh, God," Henry said. "I think we'd better slow down, okay? I've got a few things to tell you."

"Look," Chris said, "I don't know what's going on, but I have to make a phone call..."

"... to Mike Dougan?" Henry asked.

Chris snapped, "Okay, how do you know that?"

"Hey, calm down, Chris," Henry replied. "He's the one who brought me here to tell you about the meeting."

Ricardo angrily asked, "What's all this crap about a meeting?"

"Mike Dougan," Henry said. "He's gathered together everyone in town who ever worked for Hiram Milliken. He knows about the old man, Chris. He said his brother Jack was one of his earliest victims."

"Holy...!" Sandy exclaimed.

"No kidding?" Matt asked.

"Yeah, I know," Henry continued. "He's hoping you'll be there. I'm sorry, Chris. He called me in for an interview to take Dan's old job and he cornered me. He asked all kinds of questions about why I quit working at the farm."

Sandy asked, "You didn't tell him about Chris, did you?"

"Or about last night with Todd?" Ricardo added.

"I'm sorry, okay?" Henry cried. "He cornered me! I didn't have a choice!"

"You stupid...!" Max began, stepping toward Henry.

Chris grabbed him by the arm. "Wait," he said. "It's all right, Max."

"Please, guys," Henry choked. "Mike wants to help. You have to believe me. He said Todd might even warn Hiram now. He might get away!"

"I believe you, Henry," Teddy said. "Mike's my godfather. My dad's going to that meeting, too. Maybe that's why we're all here." He turned to the rest of the guys and asked, "What do you say? I'm ready."

"Teddy, man," Ricardo said. "What about your father?"

Teddy shrugged. He couldn't remember why he didn't tell his father what Hiram had done to him in the first place. He said, "If he's there, he's going to find out anyway."

"It's settled," Chris said. He didn't want to go, but he knew he had to. "We're going."

"Yeah!" Sandy cried. "Let's burn that scumbag!"

The boys followed Teddy out of the house. Chris reset the alarm, but paused by the front door. There was a family portrait hanging next to the jamb. He reached out, touched his father's image, and choked back a sob.

"God, I need you, dad."

He stepped outside and locked the door.

* * *

Jeremy's dream began with an explosion of light and color. The skies of Craig's dreamscape filled with bright midnight blue ribbons of energy. They dove out of the air and wisped around him, caressing his skin as they passed. They lifted him off the ground, held him for a moment, and then set him back down. They rode on a warm welcoming breeze. Jeremy watched in awe at their striking beauty. He reached out to touch them. They were calling to him.

Craig had been talking to him a moment ago as they sat together lending each other support, but now he stood frozen in the field. His eyes were empty and soulless. Jeremy reached for him. He wanted to wake him up and show him the beautiful ribbons so he could enjoy them, too. He was startled as his hand slipped through Craig's body. He felt fear as his friend and the dreamscape he made so beautiful vanished. Jeremy was alone in a vast black emptiness that stretched into forever, except for the flying ribbons.

"Craig!" Jeremy cried. His voice echoed all around him.

The ribbons whizzed past him and lined up next to one another above him. They hovered motionlessly but for their rhythmic pulsations. Jeremy felt their power. He slid his hand through the air. Energy crackled around his fingers. The ribbons shot toward him moving so quickly he didn't have time to run.

Sweet Mother of Mercy! Jeremy thought. *They're after me!*

Jeremy screamed as the ribbons plunged into his eyes. Their power surged into his brain. It felt like the energy was ripping him apart atom by atom. He was knocked over in an explosion of midnight blue. He hit the ground painfully. Images filled his mind as the power grew inside him. He felt it race through his body like electricity. The glow expanded all around him and the blackness disappeared. The faces of people, millions of people, filled the sky, the horizon, and the ground beneath him. Jeremy cried out as their voices called to him all at once. The sound boomed inside his head. Thoughts not his own tried to overwhelm him, to touch him, to be him! Soon, every ribbon was inside of him as more and more faces filled the sky.

*   *   *

Craig slumped back in the front seat of his father's Monte Carlo. It felt like he was coming out of a dream. He felt detached, fuzzy, disoriented. He struggled to focus, to clear his mind as a cold dread filled his heart. At the same time, an evil thought whispered to him. It told him he wasn't in the hospital anymore. He resisted, thinking, *That isn't possible, is it?* The car came to an abrupt halt, the brakes grinding in outrage. The smell of the Monte Carlo's interior and the feel of the material against his skin was familiar. The motor shut down. Craig drifted off. Sleep opened its warm arms and engulfed him in a sensation that promised relief and rest. He should have known it was too good to be true.

Craig cried out feeling a sharp pain in his scalp. His eyes shot open into his father's drunk and enraged face. Jack dragged him out of the car by his hair.

"Let me go!" Craig cried, struggling against the pull. He felt some of the follicles rip out of his scalp. "You're not beating me again!"

Jack's expression went wild. He lifted Craig off the ground by his hair and slammed him onto the walkway. He let go and kicked his son in the face. Craig's lips split. Blood filled the inside of his mouth. Jack grabbed him by the collar and lifted him. His breath stank of liquor as he growled into Craig's face.

"If you try that again, I'll kill you right here, you backstabbing little bastard!"

"You... *won't...,*" Craig struggled, his head lolling backward. Blood flowed out of the corner of his mouth. *"... beat* me anymore... you won't..."

Jack threw him to the ground again. "Don't talk to me like that!" he raged, kicking Craig several times. *"You hear me!?"*

The world spun. Craig's consciousness waned as he lay on the walk. He couldn't move. He couldn't stop his father as he was dragged by his foot up the stairs. He reached out with his thoughts, broken and crying, hoping that by some miracle Jeremy was still with him. The last thing Craig heard before his head hit the top step and everything went black was the sound of his father kicking in the front door.

*   *   *

Jeremy stood at the center of a storm of light, energy, and knowledge. It whirled around him like a tornado. He screamed as it ripped his mind wide open. Everything there was, everything there ever could be, stood at the end of his fingertips. It was so simple, unfathomable, and perfect. He was everywhere and nowhere at the same time. History opened itself to him, all history, every history, and in a flash Jeremy knew more about humanity than all written words combined. He stood on the Earth, beneath her, and above her. He felt her terrible beauty as his mind touched every person, every thought, everywhere on the planet. He felt like an Angel, like a god.

He felt a thousand people die in a split second. Their lives passed over him like flowing water. Everything they had experienced, everything they'd ever felt – the heights of their glories to the rapture of their greatest pains, their deepest shames – became one with him for a fleeting moment before they vanished to somewhere else. He felt the rebirth. A thousand new lights came into being in the same second. Their minds were empty but for the most basic emotions and instincts, filled with the potential to shake the world. They could change all of humanity with a flex of their incredible will. They would never be closer to God again until death. Jeremy fought desperately not to get lost in the storm. He heard Craig calling to him from somewhere. He was in agony. He was terrified and crying.

He's dying! Jeremy thought, his heart breaking.

A pure white light shined all around him. Jeremy bathed in it. He opened his eyes. It was a power that was above power, beyond force. It was knowledge above understanding. It fostered knowing and it knew infinitely more than even he was aware of now. He reached out and wanted to touch its source. Instinctively, he knew what it was and why it was. It held a place for him where he would be safe forever. He would never know fear again, or anger, or hatred, or sorrow. Jeremy cried out to it and stretched toward it, but before he touched it the light flashed and vanished.

Jeremy fell to the ground, sobbing. He was overwhelmed by a terrible feeling of loss. The world returned to the vast emptiness it had been before the ribbons invaded him. There was a picture in his thoughts which only moments ago had been more vibrant, more alive, than any other, but now it fading like the faces in the sky and with them all he knew. It was knowledge not meant for a human being no matter their power. His tears ran free as it left him. The last image he saw before the awareness disappeared was the careworn face of an old man holding a white dove with glowing eyes. He was watching Jeremy with an expression of compassionate sympathy, and smiling.

"Confusing, isn't it?" Sam asked, helping Jeremy stand.

"It was the same for us, man," Ian said.

"Yeah," Bobby echoed, *"the light."*

"Sam?" Jeremy asked, confused. His voice seemed far away. "Ian? Oh, God... *please...* help me!"

"Oh, we'll help you, Jeremy," Sam assured him. *"Won't we, guys?"*

A murmured chorus of agreement erupted.

Jeremy looked at the boys surrounding him. They were immaculately groomed and dressed in black tuxedos with purple cummerbunds. Ian's blonde hair was feathered back effortlessly and shining. Jeremy gripped the sides of his head. His mind was on fire. In that instant with the fading of things no man should ever have learned, seen, felt, or been, Jeremy knew the truth. He felt their rage, their horror, and their pain like he did of those who had fallen before them. His brow furrowed. His experience with the light and the world were gone as quickly as they had come, replaced by the outrage of the murdered. Jeremy stared at them. They smiled.

"We need you," Ian said.

"What can I do?" Jeremy asked. "I'll miss you, Ian. You were my friend. I'm sorry you're dead."

Ian nodded coolly and reached out. He hugged Jeremy, sank into his flesh, and was gone. Jeremy embraced all of them until only one spirit remained. It was Frank Garrison. He was crouched low, his arms over his knees, his head resting on them as he wept.

"Frank?" Jeremy asked.

Frank looked up, his tears streaming. *"They used me!"* he sobbed. *"I didn't want this!"*

Jeremy held out his arms.

Frank hugged him, sobbing into his shoulder. *"I'm sorry, man,"* he choked. *"I'm so sorry."*

"Me, too, Frank," Jeremy whispered.

Frank disappeared inside of him. Jeremy was alone again. He knew what he had to do. He focused the power raging within him and reached out for Craig, his anchor, his lifeline, the other half of his soul. The echo of his friend's cries came into his mind. He hoped he was all right. He needed Craig right now more than ever. Jeremy's thoughts entwined with his, but what he saw, what he felt, didn't give him support, but instead sent him careening over the edge right into the abyss.

*　　*　　*

Ms. Adler gasped, her eyes wide. "What in the...? *Oh, no!"*

Virginia woke with a start at the same instant Jeremy sat up in his bed. Despair seized her heart. She stared at him, fearfully. Jeremy's face contorted and flushed with rage.

Virginia froze, her mind racing. She thought, *Oh, God!* desperately trying to move. *My baby!*

With all the strength she could muster, Virginia stood and took a step forward, but then gasped and stumbled back. She fell against the wall, her expression wide with horror. Jeremy floated off the bed, his eyes raging with eerie blue brilliance. It filled the room so bright it nearly blinded her. She felt its force penetrate her head, racing through her brain.

Jeremy screamed, *"CRAIG!"* as a pulse of energy burst forth from his body and the room exploded.

The walls and windows blew out into the night sky. The debris showered the cars below in an avalanche of glass, bricks, and plaster. People at the carnival looked up, crying out and pointing. Ms. Adler and Virginia were caught in the blast and thrown off their feet. Ms. Adler put up a telekinetic shield in time, but flew through the door into the hallway. Virginia crashed through the partition into the room next door. She hit the floor and slid into the far wall crushing the plaster.

She struggled to lift her head. Her body was broken and wracked with agony. Blood flowed from her nose, ears, and leg. It was twisted upside down at the knee. She watched in double vision as Jeremy's cast shattered, rained onto the floor, his stitches disintegrated, and his fracture was healed. He stretched out his arms. Telekinetic power radiated from him in waves. His eyes crackled with midnight blue energy that pulsated with his heartbeat. On his forehead, the symbol for Infinity formed. He looked like an Avenging Angel. Jeremy floated through the hole in the wall into the dark cloud-filled sky sailing toward Lancaster.

Virginia slumped backward and died.

Ms. Adler stumbled through the doorway, witnessed Jeremy's exit, and rushed out again headed for her car. She had no idea what was going on, but it was big trouble.

As soon as she was gone, Mickey emerged from the hall closet where he had been hiding. He stepped into Jeremy's room. It took all of his concentration to keep the Hill Witch from detecting him, but he succeeded just as his grandmother had predicted. He walked through the hole in the partition, knelt down next to Virginia, and took her hand.

"I'm ready," Mickey whispered, focusing. He prayed, "Lord, guide my hand." His irises vanished. They were replaced by a dim light that shined from his perfectly white eyes.

*　　*　　*

Roland Underwood, a thin man with bookkeeper's glasses and a bald head, was staring at Teddy with his mouth hanging open. His palms were sweating and his hands shook. He wished he had never answered the message George Skinner left him. He hadn't thought about Hiram Milliken in years. It hurt too much. Coffee splashed out of his cup and onto his legs. It burned his skin, but he didn't even flinch.

Donald Barry sucked on a fifth of gin. Peter Rollins dashed into Mike's bathroom and vomited into the sink. Robert Bigelow held his sobbing son in his arms, a look of horror in his eyes. George Skinner and Mike were holding Hugh Kreeger down on the couch. He was thrashing wildly as his son, Joey, pleaded with him to calm down.

Arthur shook his head. *Oh, Hiram,* he thought. *You stupid man.*

"Let me go!" Hugh hollered, his mind filled with pain and shame. He was a boy again. He was being violated again only this time he would fight back. "I'll kill that bastard! I swear to God I will!"

"Hugh," Mike said. "You've got to calm down."

"Dad, *please,*" Joey echoed. His pale gray eyes brimmed with tears. His strawberry blonde hair was all askew.

"No!" Hugh cried, his face flushed. "I'll…!"

Robert jumped up and pushed the others aside. He grabbed Hugh by the collar, twisting his shirt up in his fists. "You'll do what, you moron?" he snapped, shaking Hugh. "Commit murder? This is your fault, Hugh!" He glared around the room. "It's all your faults! You're all to blame!"

Hugh's eyes went insane as he looked into the men's faces. Then he saw the boys' frightened expressions, saw the fear in his son's eyes, and his rage crumbled. He reached out for Joey. Robert released him. Hugh held his son close and wept. Robert pulled Teddy over and pressed him against his thigh. Peter came back from the bathroom as white as a sheet.

"Robert's right," Roland whispered. "It's our fault."

"Well, you may think so," Arthur snapped, crossing his legs.

"You don't?" Sandra asked.

Everyone looked at Arthur. He sighed, "Mrs. Dougan," wiping his eyes. "I'm not ashamed of being gay. Hiram never took anything from me that I didn't freely give to him. Despite my age, I knew what I wanted."

"Impossible," Sandra disagreed. "No child can make such a choice. You've been brainwashed to believe that."

"What about the rest of us, you stupid queer?" Hugh yelled. He leaned forward and almost tossed Joey to the floor. "We didn't ask for what he did to us!"

"Hey!" Chris angrily interjected. "I don't like that word, all right?"

"Chris," Sandra said, leaning over the kitchen counter. "Are you trying to say that you're gay, too?"

"Not that it has anything to do with it," Chris snorted, "or that it's any of your business, but yes, I am."

"You probably liked it, too, just like Arthur," Hugh said.

"Don't say that!" Joey snapped, glaring at his father.

Hugh covered his face with his hands. "I'm sorry, Joey, okay? I'm sorry."

"We should've said something back then," Roland said.

George said, "It's my fault he got you in the first place, Roland. I brought you there."

"But I went."

"But we didn't know what he was!" Hugh cried. "Not at first!"

"You could've gone to the police after it happened!" Robert snapped. "You could've said something!"

"Oh, bullshit, Bigelow!" Donald exclaimed, his words slurring. "My father would've beaten me to death!"

Peter added, "It's these boys who are to blame for what happened to Teddy."

"Oh, that's rich!" Sandy exclaimed. "Just dump all your guilt on our doorstep."

"You could've stopped this years ago!" Matt added.

"Yeah, man," Ricardo said. "Who do you think you are?"

"You punk!" Peter snapped, reaching for Ricardo. "I'll kick your ass!"

"You and what army?" Max yelled, shoving Peter back.

Peter fell over a chair, his arms pinwheeling. He landed on the living room floor, but jumped to his feet, his fists clenched.

"Knock it off!" Mike raged, stepping between them. "You're in my house, get it? If anyone needs an ass-kicking, they'll get it from me! Now, sit down! All of you!"

Begrudgingly, they sat. Mike's hard stare convinced them. Sandra was proud he had taken charge without hitting anybody, but she felt like crap. She had never wanted her suspicions about the farmer to be true. She regretted gathering them together and putting them on the spot, but her and Mike couldn't think of any other way to confront them with their suspicions.

"Where's Todd O'Connor?" Robert asked, rubbing his temple with one hand and stroking Teddy's face with the other.

"We don't know," Chris replied. "We beat him up pretty badly last night."

"Good!" Hugh snapped.

"No," Robert said, shaking his head. "Not good."

"What do you mean by that?" Roland asked. "Look what that kid watched Milliken do to your own son, for Christ's sake!"

"You don't think I know that?" Robert shot back. "How stupid are you, Underwood?"

"How could you have any concern for him at all then, Bobby?" Peter asked.

"I don't," Robert replied. "If I weren't a cop, I'd break him in half."

Teddy thanked God his father was a lot smarter than he had thought, but then he'd always know that, right? Why hadn't he trusted him? It was... *it was...?* Teddy didn't know anymore. It was like his mind had been locked up and now it was free. Was it the same for the others?

"I don't understand, Mr. Bigelow," Derek said. "Why isn't it okay if Todd got beat up?"

"Yeah," Sandy added. "I'd like to do it again!"

"Me, too," Ricardo grumbled.

"It isn't a matter of whether or not it's okay," Robert said. "We need him to testify."

"What for?" George asked, wiping his forehead with a hanky.

"Really," Henry agreed. "You've got me, Teddy, and Chris, not to mention the adults."

"The D.A. can't charge Hiram with what he did to the adults, Henry," Robert said. "The Statute of Limitations has passed for those crimes."

"Well, hell," Mike said, "charge the punk. Why use him as a witness? He's as guilty as the old man."

Robert said he was probably a victim, too. If he stood against them in court and denied what happened, it might be difficult to convict Hiram since there isn't any physical evidence. If they could convince him to come forward, he might be able to lead them to other boys.

"Well, that's a bunch of crap!" Matt exclaimed.

"I know," Robert agreed.

"All right, guys," Sandra interrupted. "I think I've heard about all I want to hear about this. What are we going to do about it?"

Hugh nodded. "She's right. We've talked enough. Robert's got to go and arrest him."

"Agreed," George added.

"Well then," Peter said, "what are we waiting for?"

Robert pulled out his cell phone. As much as he wanted to, he couldn't arrest Hiram. He was too personally involved. He needed someone else to do it, someone he trusted. They could hold Hiram for seventy-two hours while they took statements and passed everything to the detectives. With this much evidence, he was sure the District Attorney would prosecute.

"Kate?" Robert asked, when she picked up the line. "I need a favor."

*　　*　　*

"Lord!" Dr. Montclair cried, as he looked around the destroyed room. He ran over and knelt by Virginia feeling for a pulse. *"Nurse! Code: Blue!"*

Nurse Jacobsen stared at the gaping wound that used to be the wall, paralyzed with fear. The massive hole opened into the black sky.

"Get a cart in here, now! She's in cardiac arrest!"

Nurse Jacobsen shook her head and, drawing on her professionalism, rushed to the intercom. Dr. Montclair began CPR on Virginia ignoring the mystery boy seated next to her, mewling. His was sweating, mumbling words that didn't make sense.

"Don't go, nice lady," Mickey whispered. His irises were gone and his eyes were completely white. *"Stay with me, okay? Stay away from the light."*

*　　　*　　　*

Jeremy sailed over the Dougans' house and landed on the front lawn. His eyes were pulsating with power. Ms. Adler pulled her Mercedes-Benz into Mrs. Turner's driveway. She'd used her telepathic abilities to track him as he levitated cross-country while she remained on the roads. She was livid. This was not part of her plan. Jeremy should have been hers already. He shouldn't have recovered from the infusion of power so quickly. He should be helpless in bed waiting for her to finish him.

What the hell is going on? Ms. Adler thought.

She scanned him. His thoughts burned with outrage and hatred. She hid from his telepathy, but she knew the effort would fail if he scanned for minds nearby. He was more powerful than her, but she was safe for the moment by the distraction of the Dougans and Jeremy's inexperience.

Jeremy scowled at the Dougans' front door. A breeze blew around him. His hospital gown opened from behind. Jeremy couldn't have cared less. He wasn't bothered by levitating here either. Floating above the trees in the dark was as easy as taking a stroll through the yard. He didn't know what had happened to him and he didn't give a damn. The mind-link was more powerful than ever before. Jeremy could feel Craig's pain. He sensed his broken body on the living room floor. He was slipping closer to death with each passing second. Jeremy sensed Jack's intense satisfaction. He sensed the PTSD in his damaged mind. He knew trauma from the war and Hiram had turned him into this monster. He was sitting on the couch, drinking his liquor, glaring at his bleeding son like an animal.

Jeremy's hatred turned to blind fury. He lashed out with the power coursing through his brain and the front door exploded. A million tiny splinters of wood and glass blasted into the house like shrapnel. Jack dove for cover. He rolled and came up on one knee, holding his bottle. He glared at the boy with the glowing eyes floating in his doorway.

"Holy Jesus Christ!" Jack exclaimed.

"Jesus, Jack!?" Jeremy raged. He lowered to the floor. The bottle in Jack's hand exploded. *"Even He can't help you now!"*

Jack scrambled to his feet, dropping the neck of the bottle. It was all that was left. He felt Jeremy's words reverberate around him and in his head at the same time. He ran through the kitchen toward the back door. He reached for the doorknob, but Jeremy snatched him with telekinetics. Jack spun around, frozen at attention, and then slammed face first onto the floor. He jumped up, his eyes crazy, his fists clenched. Jeremy focused and snapped Jack's tibias and fibulas in half with a thought. He crumpled to the floor, the world turning white with agony, and he screamed.

"That's right," Jeremy whispered, but his voice was an explosion of decibels. *"Scream, Jack. Scream real loud. It's all you've got left."*

Jeremy mentally scanned Craig's battered body. Craig was struggling to breathe through his broken ribs. Jeremy broke all of Jack's in return, one at a time. The skin on his chest jumped each time a rib snapped beneath the surface. Jack writhed, crying out for mercy, as some of the jagged bones pierced his flesh. Then they broke in a running wave like a line of falling dominoes. Blood gushed down his stomach.

"This is only the beginning, Jack!" Jeremy screamed, shaking his fist at him.

Jack's clothes tore away leaving him naked. Jeremy knelt next to Craig, cradling him in his arms. He probed his mind. He felt his pain as the strap was raised and repeatedly whipped across his body. Jeremy winced at the cracking sound echoing in his thoughts, the flesh splitting as it replayed in Craig's memory. Welts covered his buttocks, back, legs, and arms. Some of them were open and bleeding. Jeremy pulled Craig close, holding him in his lap as he began to cry.

"Craig?" Jeremy wept, tears streaming down his face.

Jack's belt flew up from the floor next to the couch. It twisted through the air like a snake, the buckle bobbing and weaving.

Jeremy glared at Jack. *"You bastard."*

"No…," Jack begged, coughing up blood. "Please… no more…"

"Isn't that what Craig said, you son-of-a-bitch!?" Jeremy roared.

Every window in the house blasted out as a wave of force exploded from his body. Ms. Adler watched from the yard in awe. She dove to the ground in time to avoid being decapitated by the flying glass. The entire house shook with Jeremy's rage. She rose and watched as the belt slashed across Jack's face splitting his cheek. He howled as it hit him on his back taking chunks of flesh out of his ass and cracking like a bullwhip. Jack held his hands up vainly trying to deflect the lashes as it whizzed around him continuing to strike.

"How do you like it, Jack? Huh? How do you like it!?"

Craig stirred, drifting between the light and the dark. His eyes were swollen shut. He reached up and gently wiped the tears streaming down his best friend's face. He sensed Jeremy's fury and his power through their mind-link. He was terrified. It was intense, and yet beneath his wrath was the love Jeremy felt for him. It blazed through Craig's agony straight to his heart.

"Craig?" Jeremy blubbered, his tears falling even faster. *"Please, man… don't go. Stay with me, okay? Please? I… need you… so bad."*

"Jer… my…," Craig managed. His fractured jaw ached. "No more… kay? Please? He's… m' *daddy*… he's m'…"

Craig slumped backward and died. The belt whipping Jack fell to the floor.

"Craig? Craig!" Jeremy cried, the mind-link dark and silent. *"No! Oh, God, no, please!"*

434

Jeremy felt his power rise. Blue light flowed from his fingertips into Craig's body. He was startled as the power responded to his feelings. It did the impossible because Jeremy wished it to. The mind-link roared to life as Jeremy willed Craig's injuries away and brought him back. He watched as the bruises clouded over. The welts and cuts closed up. His broken bones knitted together. The swelling around his hazel eyes vanished, and they opened.

Craig wrapped his arms around Jeremy's neck and hugged him as the light went away. Their thoughts entwined. They were one again. Craig saw the power, felt it, acknowledged it, conceived its continuously deepening depth, but he had no clue where it had originated. It didn't matter. There was something else that needed doing. Jeremy helped Craig to his feet. He heard Craig's thoughts and stared at him in disbelief.

"You can't be serious, Dougan!" Jeremy exclaimed. *"You want me to do what!? You just died, man!"*

"I know, Jeremy," Craig said. He looked at his bleeding sobbing father and nodded. "He's my dad. I don't know what's happened to you and I'm too scared to care right now, but you were in his mind. You may not be able to see it because you're angry, but I can. Somewhere under all of his rage, all his pain, the real Jack Dougan is still alive. You saw him. I see it in your thoughts. Help him, okay? I need you to do this for me as my friend."

Jeremy stared at Craig for several moments. He threw his hands in the air and stormed over to Jack. He glared at him, hatefully. He was glad he had the power to hurt him the same way he had hurt Craig.

"Help me…," Jack coughed.

"You suck, Jack," Jeremy said. *"If it weren't for Craig, I'd let you die, you scumbag."*

Jeremy reached out and touched Jack's forehead. His healing power rushed into his body. It was instinctive. He told the power what he wanted and it happened. He had no idea how it worked, it just did. He purged Jack of the alcohol and the disease of alcoholism, but he took his time. He wanted Jack to feel every moment of pain.

Ms. Adler gasped from the shattered front window. She thought, *This is incredible!*

She stared in fascination at her creation. Jeremy was all she had hoped for and more powerful than she ever was. Then her heart skipped a beat. She realized Jeremy had no idea how to control the abilities he possessed. He was acting on instinct. Telepathy was a subtle power. Jeremy was using his like a battering ram. He smashed through Jack's memories, his greatest pains, and secret shames.

"Oh, no!" Ms. Adler cried.

All hell broke loose inside the house. Dishes flew around the room. Craig dove under the kitchen table. The furniture jumped through the broken windows into the yard. Ms. Adler dove for cover again as silverware from the strainer sliced through the air toward her. The kitchen table launched through the back wall. It sailed into a large elm by the woodline and snapped in half. Craig stared through the gaping hole. Rain fell and lightning flashed, but the thunder was mute compared to Jeremy and Jack's screaming. Jeremy held Craig's father by his shoulders. Jack shook violently as energy coursed through him. Craig saw terror through the mind-link, wonder, and a reflection of his desire to heal his father. He ducked as the utility drawer tore out of the counter and smashed against the refrigerator. The utensils whirled around in the air.

The farther Jeremy dug into Jack, the more pain he found, the more wounds that needed healing. He peeled back the layers of his mind, digging, probing, diving through the rage, the self-hatred, and the despair. He lived each of Jack's nightmares, mentally reaching out to Craig for more strength, for an anchor to keep him from getting lost in Jack's black hole soul. The three of them were linked now sharing each other's memories, each other's pain. Jack felt Craig's lifelong agony, his thoughts, and feelings. He ran from them, cowering behind his shame.

Jeremy felt Jack losing hold of his sanity. His guilt was overwhelming. He knew if Jack didn't help them fight, none of them were going to make it out alive. He searched, probing deeper, repairing Jack's heart every time he found it broken. They heard a voice from outside of them then. It called to Jack. It was a child's voice. Craig pleaded for Jeremy to make the voice louder. Jeremy said he couldn't. He wasn't the one making it.

"Remember," Giuseppe whispered to Jack. *"Make the right choice."*

Choice? Jack despaired. *What choice is there?* He had seen enough. All he wanted to do was die.

"Make me proud, Jackie," Wade said. *"Don't run away, lad. Face what ye've done. Don't make th' same mistakes ye made before. Fight for your son!"*

Jeremy and Craig felt a burst of determination in Jack's mind. They cried out, their thoughts racing together. They relived the war, Wade's death, Hiram's assaults, the accident that killed Thomas, Dale Kerrigan blasted to pieces, Craig's beatings, Carol – all of that pain flowed through them into Jeremy. He drew it out, healing each of them. In the eye of the hurricane of that agony, Jeremy saw what Craig always had, the real Jack Dougan. Fear rose in him as he realized he could never completely heal Jack, unless…

A little poetic justice? Jeremy thought.

He concentrated, drawing strength from the souls hiding inside of him despite their wails of protest. They hated Jack. They blamed him for their deaths. Jeremy shut them out and took what he needed. Ian, Dan, Sam… the Leech twins… Terry… howled. Jeremy devoured them until only his imagination limited his power. Jack's feelings overwhelmed him. Jeremy flooded him with all of the healing power he could muster. He threw his head back and screamed. Pure oily black thought energy shot out of Jeremy's eyes.

It blasted through the ceiling, exploded through the roof into the stormy night sky. The black light expanded, and then imploded with a loud *whump!*

Craig and Jack flew away in opposite directions. Craig slammed against the kitchen cabinets, rolled off the counter, and landed on the floor. Jack crashed into the living room wall and smacked down onto a pile of pots & pans. Craig struggled to focus, but then everything went dark as he fell unconscious. Jeremy stumbled through the living room toward the front door, dizzy, but chuckling. The storm within him had ended and the flying items inside the house crashed to the floor.

"Take that, Jack," he whispered, exhausted. *"Let's see you hurt Craig now, you bastard."*

Jack got to his knees, stared at his hands, gasped, and then fainted.

Outside, the rain was pouring. Jeremy leaned against the doorjamb, his head swimming. Craig's conscious presence was missing from his mind. Without it, the power surged. He walked into the yard. The rain soaked his paper hospital gown. The water flowed down his back as he panted for breath. The power was replenishing already. He discovered a suggestion planted in his mind that forbade him to discuss the mind-link. He banished it from him and Craig. He wondered who had put it there. A chorus of voices filled his mind and he cried out. The spirits within him were trying to bend him to their will, taking advantage of his distraction. Jeremy fought them. He stumbled into the walkway, holding the sides of his head. They clawed their way through his mind trying to control him.

"No! I won't let you!"

"Jeremy?" Ms. Adler asked, from behind him. She trained her telepathy on him with all of her will.

Jeremy responded to her voice. It was impossibly inviting as his mind went blank. He turned toward her, the glow from his eyes matching hers.

"Now, my savior," Ms. Adler sneered, grabbing the sides of his head. *"The game is over, and you are...!"* but she stopped. Her expression was surprised. She cried, *"What!?"* as something blocked her attempt to reach into his mind.

Awesome telekinetic force struck her. She flew across the lawn, slid through the grass, and smacked into the side of her Mercedes. She glared at him, her dress soaked and covered with mud. Jeremy stood in the walkway, grinning. His glowing eyes were blank.

It is not possible! Ms. Adler thought. *The force that cast me aside was not of his doing! What is...?*

A sea of ephemeral faces appeared in the air around him. Their hate-filled eyes glared at her. Ms. Adler's heart raced. She knew every one of them. They were Hiram's victims.

"No!" she screamed, scrambling to stand. She ran toward Jeremy, her hands groping. *"He is mine!"*

The faces laughed at her. They shimmered and vanished. Jeremy's expression animated and he joined their laughter. He floated into the air, arms out to his sides, twirling away from her groping fingers. She watched as he drifted over the trees toward Hiram's farm. Ms. Adler raged a string of curses. Her power didn't replenish as fast as his. She couldn't risk draining hers by levitating after him.

Jeremy McKee is mine, damn you! Ms. Adler thought. *I have worked too hard, planned too long... you cannot have him!*

A bolt of lightning struck nearby. She felt it as electricity curved away from its original target and shot straight at her. She panicked, but managed to redirect the energy through her body into the ground with a loud boom. Her ears rang and the sky rumbled.

The storm! she despaired. *It's coming closer!*

Ms. Adler ran to her Mercedes. She started the engine, slammed it into gear, and tore out of Mrs. Turner's driveway chasing after Jeremy.

*　　*　　*

"Craig?" an unfamiliar voice called into the darkness. "Can you hear me?"

Craig moaned as he sat up holding his forehead. *Why would anyone want to wake me up? I was having the most beautiful dream.*

A hand reached under his arm and helped him stand. Slowly, hunched over, he opened his eyes. His vision focused on a pair of small feet. He looked at them, oddly.

Who...? he wondered, but then gasped.

Craig snapped his head up into the shining green eyes of a boy whose picture he had seen at his grandmother's house thousands of times. It was twelve-year-old Jack Dougan, his father, only instead of being in a frame on Bog Dancer Drive, he was standing next to him holding him up.

"Holy crap!" Craig exclaimed, stumbling back.

Jack grabbed him by the hand before he fell onto a pile of broken glass. "That was close, Craig!" he cried, holding his small chest. His voice was high. His long reddish-brown hair wisped in the wind coming through the hole in the wall. He pointed at the glass. "Maybe floor diving isn't such a hot idea right now, huh?"

Craig stared at him with his mouth hanging open.

Jack shook his head. "Aren't you going to say something?" he asked, twirling around. "Quite a difference, huh?"

Craig looked at his father's child-body. "Dad?" he whispered, reaching out. He poked the apparition in the arm. "Is that you?"

"Ow!" Jack whined, rubbing the spot. "Easy with the fingernails, Craig!"

"But..." Craig stuttered, "... you're a kid!"

Jack laughed. "Isn't it cool? Your friend did it!" He shook his head. "I can't believe I have to go through puberty again."

"Jeremy?" Craig asked, spinning around. His eyes searched. Panic filled his heart when he couldn't find him. "Oh, God! Jeremy!"

Craig moved, intending to run outside.

Jack grabbed him by the arm. "Wait, you bonehead!" he cried.

Craig glared at him. "Are you nuts? Do you know what they want to make him do?"

"I know," Jack replied. "I saw them in his mind, too. They were pretty mad he was helping me. We've got to get to him, kid, but not without putting on some clothes first!"

"Who are you calling kid?" Craig snapped. "By the looks of it, I'm older than you now!"

"You are!" Jack exclaimed. "I'm twelve again! Don't you get it? I'm Jack before Hiram, before the war! It's the only way Jeremy could completely heal me. He took it all away, but that's not important now. We need clothes and we need what I've got upstairs if we're going to stop them."

"The gun?" Craig asked, remembering the M4 carbine rifle that he and Jeremy had discovered. "The hand grenades?"

"I knew you had your nose in my stuff," Jack smiled. "So, the rifle and the grenades were all you found?"

"There's more?" Craig asked. His mind tried to absorb the insanity facing him.

Jack ran over to the attic's folding stairs and reached up for the string. He frowned. He was no longer tall enough to reach it. He put his hands on his hips and sighed.

"Could you get that?" Jack asked, pointing.

Craig reached up and grabbed the string. "Shorty."

Jack rolled his eyes and headed up the steps first, Craig right behind him. He told his son to get them some clothes. Craig whipped through his drawers trying to find something small enough for his father to wear and something clean for him. Jack grabbed the first floorboard. He figured trying to pull it up with his hands was in vain. He had hammered them in tight when he was a man, but he tried anyway. He fell on his backside tearing the board loose with ease. Jack dropped it and stared at his hands.

"Jesus," he muttered, opening and closing his fists. He felt the strength in his grip. "I'm... still strong?"

"What?" Craig asked, sizing up a pair of his old jeans.

Jack shook his head. "It's... nothing," he replied, nervously. He reached forward and yanked up the next floorboard. It came loose just as easily. "Get the clothes. We need to get moving."

Good God! Jack thought. *What the heck did that kid do to me?*

Craig threw the pants at his father. Jack reached back and snatched them out of the air without looking.

Craig managed a half-smile. "Good catch."

Jack pulled the jeans in front of his face. He stared at them, his eyes wide and his mouth hanging open.

*   *   *

The familiar stench of the Victorian's basement invaded Hiram's nose. He had killed a lot of boys down here. The thick walls were perfect for muffling their screams. The dirt floor made getting rid of any evidence a breeze. Near total darkness engulfed him. He groaned as he stood. His body ached. His face was sore and stung where Dabney had bitten him. His forehead felt worse. He reached up and touched where it hurt. He felt a large bump covered with dried blood.

Margaret! Hiram angrily thought, gently rubbing the tender spot. *I don't know how you got control of the body and I don't care. Letting me live was the biggest mistake of your unnatural life!*

He made his way to the stairwell. Lightning flashed and the room shone with white brilliance. He cried out, covering his eyes with his forearm. As he did, he whacked his left knee painfully against the railing.

"Ow!" Hiram cried, grabbing his knee with both hands. He lost his balance and fell into the rough stone wall. It scraped his back from his neck to his waist. *"Ow!* Son-of-a…!"

Hiram's eyes blazed. He charged up the stairs and pushed open the door to the kitchen walkway. The outer door to the barnyard was locked. He felt in his pockets for the keys, but they were missing. It was pouring rain outside. Thunder exploded in the sky. Hiram reared up and threw his shoulder into the door. The jamb splintered and tore free. The door flew open and crashed into the side of the house. Hiram charged down the stairs. He crossed the barnyard headed for his butcher shack and a really big knife.

As he approached the barn, Todd slammed into him sending him sprawling. Hiram fell back, twisting, and plowed into the barn doors. They flew open. He tumbled inside. His face hit the cement with a smack. He slid across the wet hay, scraping the side of his cheek. Todd was on him in an instant, his fists flailing. He punched Hiram repeatedly in the face. Words poured out of his mouth. They were garbled and unintelligible until Todd jumped to his feet.

"You bastard!"

He kicked Hiram in the ribs. Hiram grunted as Todd's steel-toed boot sank into his body. His mind whirled with confusion. He tried to speak. Todd leaned back and kicked him in the face. The pain focused Hiram's thoughts. When Todd went to kick him again, Hiram was ready. He rolled toward him and grabbed his leg at the last second. He twisted it over and wrenched Todd off his feet. Todd slapped onto the concrete. Hiram rolled on top of him and drew his fist back. He was about to punch him when lightning struck again. The illumination shone on Todd's bruised and battered features.

"Holy Christ!" Hiram gasped. "What happened to you?"

Todd cried, "You happened to me, you sick freak!" He wriggled away and got to his feet.

Hiram let him stand, confused and worried. "I don't understand, Todd," he said. "Who did this to you?"

Todd spat, "Chris McKee, that's who!"

Hiram was stunned. "Chris did all of that?" he asked, pointing at his ruined face.

"Yeah!" Todd sneered. "And Max Ramirez, and Henry! All of McKee's punk friends! They came here looking for you because of what you did to Teddy!"

"What are you talking about?" Hiram asked, feigning ignorance. *Uh, oh.* "I didn't…"

Todd angrily cut him off, "Don't lie to me, you pervert! *I saw you!*" He clenched his fists and his teeth. Hiram shadowed his movements. They circled one another. "You drugged that kid and you molested him! That's why they kicked the crap out of me because I stood there and watched and didn't do anything to stop you!" His eyes filled with hurt and betrayal. "How long have you been doing this? I remember the smell of that Kool-Aid! It was the same you used to give me! Did you molest me in my sleep, too? *Did you!?*"

"Actually," Hiram smiled. "I used to do it a lot."

Todd's expression fell. "You… did what?" *Oh, God… please, no…*

"C'mon, Todd," Hiram said. "Get with the program." He feigned a strike. Todd jumped back. "You should blame your parents, you know. It's their fault. They practically gave you to me."

"That's a lie!" Todd snapped.

"It's not a lie, you idiot," Hiram said. "Your moron stepmother put you out when you were eight years old and your father was too pussy whipped to do anything about it. You were mine from the very first night. You don't honestly believe they didn't know, do you? They're fools, but are they that stupid? Brandy suspected. She came to see me once and told me I'd better not *diddle* you since she was the one who allowed you to stay over here. She didn't want anything to come between her and your father, especially anything scandalous. Can you believe it? I mean really, *diddle?* I did a lot more to you than just *diddle* you."

"No!" Todd screamed, and lunged at him.

Hiram easily stepped to the side and dodged. "I don't see your problem, Todd. You were sleeping every time. What does it matter?"

"You bastard!" Todd cried. "I was only a little kid!"

Hiram chuckled, "I know. That was the best part. And then you brought me Frank. A little Kool-Aid and I had two boys for the price of one. You were never awake though, not like Dabney. I took him with his eyes wide open, again and again, and again."

"Oh, my God, you monster!"

"You're too old now, Todd. I haven't touched you in months, but Frank? He's still a boy under all that hair." He smiled. "Just like Henry."

Todd lunged at him again with his fists flashing. Hiram didn't move this time. He leaned into Todd's attack and shoved him back with all of his weight. Todd crashed into the wall. He hit his lip with his hand on the way to the floor and it opened again. Blood ran down his chin. Hiram stared at it. His hand started to twitch. Todd came up on his knees. He coughed twice and spat blood on the ground in front of him.

"You're through, you scumbag!" Todd sneered. He glared at Hiram. "I trusted you. You were like a father to me." He spat again, this time at Hiram. "All you are is a twisted baby-raper!" He turned toward the door, struggling to stand. "You're so busted, it isn't…!"

Todd never finished his sentence. He was so caught up in his anger, his feelings of betrayal, he didn't hear Hiram running toward him. Hiram snatched him by the back of his neck. Todd felt his grip and managed to turn around. Hiram held Todd's throat so hard he thought the old man was going to squeeze his head off. He struggled, fighting for breath.

"That's right," Hiram panted, his gaze locked on Todd's blood. He leaned into him and licked it away. "You have no idea how long I've wanted to do this."

Todd gagged. "Oh, disgusting! *You're sick!*"

Hiram lifted him off his feet. "And you're dead, Todd. Remember all those calves I told you I butchered?" He turned Todd toward the shining slaughter hook. "They weren't calves."

Hiram carried Todd through the barn, holding him in the air by his neck. Todd twisted to watch as Hiram moved faster toward the hook. It glinted at him. Todd felt a wave of terror wash over him.

"Oh, Christ!" Todd choked, struggling in earnest. His arms thrashed and his feet kicked. "No, Hiram… *please!*"

Hiram lifted him higher with both hands and threw him backward. Todd sank onto the slaughter hook with a wet sucking sound and a crunch. He screamed as the hook sliced through his back and punctured his heart. He looked down, his eyes wide. The bloody hook was sticking out of his shirt. He was hanging from it, squirming. His blood shot out of the wound like a macabre waterfall. Hiram stood under the spray spastically rubbing it all over. His expression filled with glee. Todd wriggled like a worm. He wasn't dead yet. He reached up and grabbed the hook. His face grimaced as it sliced open the palms of his hands.

Hiram snatched him by the ankles. He was drenched in blood. It stained his teeth. "Like I said, Todd… you're dead!"

Hiram yanked him down. Todd felt a flash of pain as his rib cage split, and everything went dark. His shocked eyes stared at his killer.

"Now that was worth the wait!"

Hiram went to the butcher shack. He shielded his face from the rain to keep it from washing off Todd's blood. He slipped inside for his knife. As soon as he had it safely in his grasp, he returned to the barn and the implements hanging on the wall. Hiram selected one and went to the grisly work of making Todd perfect.

*   *   *

Jeremy set down inside the Grady Lane fence in the far corner of Hiram's pasture. His semi-conscious mind was oblivious as the rain and wind destroyed his hospital gown. It fell to the ground leaving him with nothing. He walked forward, his feet swishing in the mud and runny cow pies. He was blank as he moved, no longer in control of his body. It was Ms. Adler's fault. She had interrupted his internal battle with Hiram's victims at a critical moment and they took over. He smiled not caring at all. They wouldn't let him. He thought he could hear Craig calling to him through the mind-link, warning him, but Jeremy wasn't sure. The rain drenched his wiry black hair. It hung down over his brightly glowing eyes.

Cows were scattered all over the pasture. They mooed as they ambled toward him. Their utters streamed milk onto the wet ground. They needed to be milked. They stopped as if sensing something amiss. They looked at Jeremy, but then ran away toward the barn.

Ms. Adler pulled her car off to the side of Grady Lane. She watched as her creation walked toward the center of the pasture. A feeling of dread came over her.

The existence of disembodied spirits is not logical! she thought. *There is no soul! There is only the energy of the mind, and yet they are here and they have possessed him, but to what end? Why come to the pasture?*

Ms. Adler felt their hatred through their connection to Jeremy. She sensed an overwhelming desire for revenge, but they were losing control of him. He was fighting them on a sub-conscious level much in the same way Margaret prevented her body from committing murder. They had invaded his mind. He was struggling to regain control. They had underestimated him. Jeremy was stronger than they thought he would be thanks to Craig.

Ms. Adler sensed approaching thoughts. She radiated a general suggestion making her and her car unseen. The Black woman cop sped by headed for Mike Dougan's house. Ms. Adler scanned the farm. Hiram was gleefully working on Todd in the barn. She hadn't planned on that, but it worked out well. Hiram's life was over. He just didn't know it yet.

She heard the patter of small feet splashing in the puddles up the road. She stepped out of her Mercedes-Benz beside Jack Dougan and his now older son Craig. They ran toward the pasture. Jack was carrying an assault rifle. Craig had a gym bag filled with other souvenirs from Afghanistan. He was toting it very carefully. Ms. Adler felt their fear. She tasted the power she intended to steal from Jeremy.

"Jeremy!" Craig called, running up to the barbed wire fence. He repeated the call through the mind-link. He was scared when Jeremy didn't answer.

"They're going to make him do it," Jack said. He wiped his long wet hair out of his face.

"Oh, God!" Craig cried. He felt his friend's power building. *"Jeremy! No!"*

Bright light burst from Jeremy's eyes. The Dougans shielded themselves from its brilliance. Ms. Adler watched as the spirits of the boys Hiram murdered walked out of Jeremy's body and hovered over their graves. One flew straight toward her and growled. She spat through Dan Mellon's ghostly face. He flew away for the cemetery behind St. Peter's Church. Another spirit flew in the opposite direction.

The morgue at Johnson Memorial, Ms. Adler thought. She smiled, wryly. *Frank Garrison will certainly raise some eyebrows there.*

The remaining spirits sank through the fresh black earth, mud bubbling around them. Jeremy's eyes glowed wildly, his face contorting with pain as he struggled against their control. He felt them enter their dead bodies using their energy and his power to link themselves solidly with their remains. Dan came alive in his grave. He clawed his way through the black casket reaching for the surface. Frank Garrison shoved open the drawer he was in at the morgue. The attendant watched him sit up and she fainted. Frank looked at her with tears in his one good eye. He left eye socked was dark and skeletal. He climbed out of the drawer and ran for the back exit.

Jeremy fell, the strain causing him to lose consciousness. His eyes pulsated power beneath his eyelids. The dead boys tore up from under the pasture, their hands reaching skyward. The stench of their decomposed bodies carried on the wind.

"We have to get to Mike's house!" Jack cried. He yanked on Craig's arm. "C'mon!"

"But Jeremy!" Craig whined pulling back. "We have to help him!"

"We have to help Mike!" Jack said. He pointed in the distance. They made out the cars parked near Mike's house. "Look! Arthur Kelly's car, Peter Rollins! They're all there!"

"What?" Craig asked. "What are they doing there?"

"I don't know!" Jack yelled, starting to run. He pulled Craig with him almost yanking him off his feet. "Jeremy's okay where he is. You know what's going to happen!"

"I know!" Craig replied. He picked up the pace and they sprinted at top speed. "They're going to kill everyone who knew about the farmer but didn't turn him in!"

They ran with all of their might. The images they had seen in Jeremy's mind were coming through vivid and terrifying. Jack pulled out ahead. His legs felt like they still belonged to someone six-foot-one. He didn't have time to think about that now. He knew it was his cowardice that allowed Hiram to kill so many boys. He was as much to blame as the men gathered at Mike's house. Did his brother know? It couldn't be a coincidence they were there. Jack swore as he approached Mike's lawn that if the dead boys didn't get Hiram? The joy of killing that bastard was going to be his.

*   *   *

"Come over here," Ian growled. He crooked a swollen rotting finger in Ms. Adler's direction. *"We know you're there. You can't hide from us."*

They glared at her as they dressed in their decayed clothing.

Ms. Adler walked toward the fence and levitated over it, shaking her head. She landed on the pasture, her eyes dimming to brown. "For all the good it will do you," she said, with a patronizing tone. "You cannot stop me. You must know that. I do not even believe in you."

"We don't care what you believe in!" Terry sneered. His jaw worked even though it had no skin or muscle, only white bone.

"We'll get you," Ian said, his voice distant and hollow.

"Right here...," Donald Leech began. The driving rain made a large patch of flesh fall from his head.

"... right now!" David Leech finished. He picked up his brother's scalp and handed it to him.

Ms. Adler threw her head back and laughed. When she did, the zombies swarmed her, moving faster than she had thought possible. Ian grabbed her hair and yanked her to the ground. Kyle and Sam punched her in the face and tore at her flesh. Ms. Adler screamed. Her power burst within her. She tossed them away in every direction with her telekinesis. She rose and floated toward Ian. Her groping hands reached for him as she scanned trying to pinpoint their locations. Kyle leapt up behind her with a rock in his hand. He bashed it into the back of her skull. Ms. Adler dropped to the ground. The zombies ambled toward her intending to rip her apart.

"Wait!" Terry exclaimed, his ragged neck flapping. They paused and looked at him. *"Can you feel it? He's here! They're all here!"*

"She dies first!" Ian cried.

"I... do not think... so," Ms. Adler whispered, levitating.

She lashed out at the dead boys with all the strength she could muster. She lifted them off the ground and threw them all over the pasture. She was dizzy, trying to focus. Her skull throbbed. She had to get away. There was no way to finish with Jeremy if she couldn't concentrate.

He can... wait... for now, Ms. Adler thought, struggling to stay awake. *He is... not going... anywhere.*

She had to clear her head and regain her strength. She glided to her car. She fell into it and drove away before the dead boys could stop her. She flew past the pond and turned left at the end of Grady Lane. She pulled into Gibbons' Garage and parked her car a moment before she fell unconscious.

José was inside his house watching the rain through the window. He saw the Mercedes' lights shining on him and he shook his head.

A service problem now?

José was on call tonight. He hoped he could find his raincoat.

*   *   *

"We'll get her later," Terry said to Ian.

Ian walked away from him. He went down through the pasture toward the barnyard. He kicked in Hiram's tool shed door and a few of the dead boys armed themselves with implements from inside. They moved toward the trailer sensing Hiram's presence.

"We're coming for you, old man," Terry said. *"It's time you got the Gift!"*

Hiram heard footfalls on his steps. He was finished with Todd and had gone inside for his shotgun. The cops were coming, he was sure, but they weren't taking him without a fight. He wondered where Dr. Bremen was. He decided the Nazi had either abandoned him or wasn't in control anymore. Either way, he was on his own. The fun was over. The dying time was about to begin.

Hiram gasped as the dead boys burst into his trailer. They pounced on him and shoved the business end of shotgun into the couch. He fired, but the shot went into the cushions, muffling it. His screams echoed through the barnyard as they dragged him into the storm. They ripped the rifle out of his hands and tossed it away. The zombies tried to cover him, but Hiram fought like a wild animal. He gouged out Terry's eyes. He bit Sam's bloated wrist. He felt no revulsion over the taste of dead flesh and decomposing body fluids. His savagery caught the dead boys off guard. Hiram took advantage of their confusion.

Do they honestly believe fear is a strong enough weapon against me? Hiram thought, fighting harder. *Or that children no matter their motivation, alive or dead, can take a grown man?*

Hiram barreled through them and ran into the pasture. "I killed you once!" he yelled, into the thunder. "By the devil, I'll kill you all again!"

He ran through the fields and fell over the barbed wire fence. He got up and charged into the woods.

"Bring him back alive!" David snapped at Kyle.

Kyle grinned. He grabbed two other boys and chased after the farmer.

* * *

Dabney swam in a state of semi-consciousness as images of wholesale slaughter ripped through his mind. He heard the screeching of metal against metal as trains towing cattle cars came to a halt. Hands were sticking out, desperately reaching for freedom. They beckoned to him, frightened and pleading. A horrible smell filled the air. It was the rancid stink of excrement, vomit, unwashed bodies, and burning flesh. A voice yelled at him from somewhere inside telling him to wake up, to hold on, but Dabney wasn't sure he could. Madness was in his mind ravaging whatever was left of him to rip and tear apart.

Dabney had seen evil today. He had fought it with all his might, but it crushed him. He was waiting for death to claim him. After everything he had gone through with his father, all he was forced to witness, and what that maniac farmer did him, Dabney decided death wasn't that bad at all. He heard a young boy's voice. It was close yet sounded far away. The duct tape binding him popped and fell apart. Its adhesive was no longer sticky, but an inert powder. He gulped for air as he stretched his arms and legs.

"It's not your time yet, Dabney," Giuseppe said.

Wade said, *"Ye need t' come back now, laddie. Death'll not be takin' ye t' day."*

"Lights!" Giuseppe exclaimed. He giggled as the laboratory's lights came up.

"Lights."

Dabney was momentarily blinded. "Who's there?" he asked, his voice raspy. He shook as he fought to find his center.

The boy giggled. Dabney's vision cleared. His eyes focused on Giuseppe. He was sitting on the lab table covered with black dirt. Dabney's mouth dropped open when he spotted the horrible gash in his throat.

"Don't be afraid, Dabney," Giuseppe said. *"I'm Giuseppe Luciano. I'm here to help you."*

Dabney was about to scream when another ghost appeared. He was an older man only not as visible as Giuseppe. He was almost see-through. He shook his head and smiled, cheerfully.

"Hop t' it, laddie," Wade said. *"Ye haven't much time. Ye'll be gettin' out o' here, don't ye fret. There be people needin' t' know what ye know about th' Hill Witch."*

"You're a ghost?" Dabney asked, a tremor in his voice.

"Of course," Giuseppe said, *"and we're also the only way you're getting out of here."*

"Oh?" Dabney snapped. "And how are you going to do that?" He glared at the huge concrete door. *"Open sesame* doesn't work! I tried!"

Giuseppe chuckled. *"Ghosts can make things move, too, dummy!"*

447

"It won't be easy," Wade said, *"but in th' meantime stand ready. Your friends need ye, lad. Somethin' horrible has happened an' ye've got t' help them."*

"Who are you?" Dabney demanded.

"Wade Dougan," Wade said. *"Craig's me grandson."*

Dabney's mouth fell open.

The two spirits closed their eyes. Giuseppe faded as they concentrated on the heavy door. Dabney was numb with shock. He stared at them in disbelief. Then he saw the door move an inch... and then another...

✱   ✱   ✱

"This is insane!" Mike hollered, pacing in his living room. He stopped and pointed at Jack. "You can't be here!"

"Mike," Sandra said, feeling lightheaded. "I don't understand what's going on either, but hear him out, okay?"

"Hear out what?" Mike cried, slamming his hand down on the coffee table.

Arthur Kelly jumped and put his hand over his chest.

"Uncle Mike, please!" Craig exclaimed. "They're coming!"

Mike ignored him and sank onto the sofa next to the window, his face in his hands. He remembered opening the door more than a little aggravated at the people pounding on it. He was punching somebody then. He'd had all the stress he could deal with for one day. Having to listen to part of Teddy's story again didn't help any. It was for the benefit of Kate Pierce. They were in the middle of that when the boys started banging. All Mike wanted to do was get his hands on Hiram. He wanted to take out a little of the pain the pervert had visited on Jack for all those years on his face!

Mike shuddered. *It's all too much...*

"Sandra?" Jack whispered, into his sister-in-law's ear. There was a terrified urgency in his tone. "Please! Call Lyle Gibbons. Tell him to get over here right away. Tell him we've got bad trouble coming our way."

Sandra examined the boy's face and she knew him. She knew his eyes. She recognized him from pictures. Somehow, impossibly, this was Jack. She fought it with all of her sense. She dealt in the news, in fact, and every fiber of her being told her this couldn't be happening. She reached out and touched his smooth arm. Jack smirked that same half a smile, that same sly grin she had seen here and again over the years. A cold chill ran down her spine. She walked away to the bedroom with her cell phone in her hand.

"Son?" Kate asked, tapping Jack on the shoulder. She held the loaded M4 carbine assault rifle out in front of her. "Would you mind telling me where you got this?"

Craig discreetly picked up the gym bag and slung it over his shoulder. He walked past the officer over to Chris.

448

"Chris?" Craig said. "You've got to believe me! They're going to be here any minute!"

Chris took Craig by the hand and led him into the kitchen. Joey, Max, and Sandy followed.

"I got it in Afghanistan, you stupid bitch!" Jack snapped, grabbing the rifle out of the officer's hand. "Keep your paws off it!"

Kate stepped forward. She intended to chastise him for his belligerence and his thoroughly preposterous story about being the same man she and Robert had arrested on Monday. Robert held her arm. She looked over her shoulder at him, her eyes questioning.

"You don't seriously…," Kate began.

Robert held up his hand. "I don't know what to believe," he replied, gently hugging Teddy who lay across his lap, "but I remember Jack Dougan as a kid. I've been friends with Mike for years. I'm telling you, if that isn't Jack, it's his ghost."

Kate snorted, "Well, it certainly sounds like him."

"Bobby?" Mike asked, choking back a sob. "Am I going crazy?"

Jack stepped up to him. Mike shied away. Jack grabbed him by the chin and turned Mike's face to his.

"I could go through all the memories two brothers share, Mikey," he said, "but we don't have time. We've got to get out of here. Trust me, okay? The Jack you've grown to hate all these years is gone. Don't ask me how, but I've got a second chance. Trust me, Mikey. I love you, okay?"

Mike pulled Jack into his arms and hugged him. This couldn't be his big brother, but right now he didn't care. Robert was right. If it wasn't Jack, it was his ghost. He could sense the truth of it, but in the logical world, the only sane it made was insane.

"I love you, too, Jackie," Mike choked, feeling the weight of the assault rifle against his thigh. "I always have."

Chris was in the kitchen shaking his head. He liked Craig a lot, but he couldn't believe a word of his story. "Look, Craig," he said, patting him on the shoulder. "You went through hell today, okay? With my… with the accident and everything. If you relax and think about this for a minute, you'll realize none of it can be true. Dead people don't walk around, man, and my brother isn't some mental mind-god, or whatever. I'd rather hear about how you got out of the hospital."

"Chris! Sandy!" Craig pleaded. "You have to believe me!"

Donald waddled into the kitchen past the whispering children. He stank of liquor and wished he was someplace else. He stared out the back window, remorsefully. George headed for the coffee pot. Arthur Kelly sat on the couch. He didn't want to hear any more about Hiram. He wanted to go home. They had exposed the old man's pedophilia. Arthur didn't intend to weather the scandal. He decided an extended vacation was in order.

Mexico, Arthur thought, discreetly examining Ricardo's behind. *Someplace with a cute cabana boy...*

"Look, guys," Peter said. "Let's bust the old man and get this over with, okay? Surely there's enough to charge him with sexual assault. I want to go home."

"Sexual assault!?" Jack cried. "Are you nuts, Rollins? Do you think that's all the bastard's done?"

"Is there more?" Kate asked.

Jack glared at her. "Honey," he said, "you don't know the half of it! Do you know what's out in Hiram's pastures?"

"We won't know until you tell us," Roland replied.

"Dead kids!" Jack exclaimed. "Craig and I have been trying to tell you that since we got here! They're coming for us!"

"Oh, that's it!" Arthur groaned, standing up. "Hiram may be a child molester, but he's not a murderer. I've had enough of this garbage. If anybody wants me, I'll be home having a glass of wine."

Arthur walked indignantly across the room to the front door. *Enough is enough. Dead kids? A twelve-year-old Jack Dougan? I'm not listening to any more of this insanity.* He grabbed the handle, flung open the door, and didn't even have time to scream as Ian plunged his bloated hand into Arthur's chest. He tore Arthur's heart out with a loud rip. Kyle smashed through the kitchen window, seized Donald Barry, and crushed his throat. Donald fell back, clutching his neck. Someone screamed. Chris thought it was Joey.

The rotten stench of decaying flesh rushed into the room. It made the already nauseous Peter Rollins gag. They turned toward the stink and watched in gut-wrenching horror as Arthur fell to the floor. Blood poured from the rip in his chest. Derek screamed and so did Sandra. George grabbed her. Derek dove over the kitchen counter into Chris' arms. The rest of the boys stood with their mouths hanging open staring down at Donald. George clutched his chest, a sudden pain shooting down his left arm.

"Hi, guys," Ian grinned. His voice was hollow, his eyes cloudy.

He was covered in black mud. It was smeared across his cheeks where his dimples used to be. He teetered from side to side, steam coming off his rain and blood soaked clothes, and from the heart in his hand. He crushed it in his fist and dropped it on the floor. When he spoke, his breath was putrid and stinking.

"Are you ready to party?"

"Party this," Kate said. She jammed her .44 Magnum against Ian's forehead and fired.

"No!" Sandy cried.

Ricardo grabbed him by the arm. Sandy watched his brother stumble back a few steps. Ian's brains splashed out of the back of his head all over the doorjamb. There was nickel-sized hole above his right eyebrow. His decaying flesh fell to the floor with a sickening squish. Everyone waited for

Ian to drop, but he only looked up with a smirk. He stuck his index finger into the bullet hole and ripped the flesh open exposing his skull.

"You can't kill what's already dead, homegirl!" Ian sneered, mocking her ethnicity with gangster rap gestures.

He grabbed Kate's hand. She reacted instantly. She recoiled from his ice-cold touch, snap kicked him in the testicles, and punched him in the face. Ian flew off the porch. He landed on his back in the middle of the walkway.

"Oh, my God!" Sandy cried. The boys joined him as he screamed, *"Ian!"*

"Kate!" Robert cried, drawing his weapon. "Are you all right?"

"I've always said the only good bigot was a dead bigot," Kate grumbled, spastically wiping her wrist. "I guess I shouldn't have said that so much."

Henry took a few steps back until he felt the wall behind him. He froze, his eyes wide, his hands flat against the paneled surface. His panicked breaths came quick and shallow. The wall beneath his left wrist burst. A skeletal hand reached in and yanked him into the paneling. Henry screamed as two more zombies punched inside and ripped him through the wall into the backyard.

Chris, Joey, and Ricardo stared out the kitchen window. Max hit the wall switches by the back door until he found the one for the backyard floodlights. The lights came up beaming into the gloom. The boys watched in horror as two of the zombies ripped Henry's arms off and tossed them into the woods. Henry fell face first into the muddy yard. The pouring rain washed his yarmulke off. It floated away in a river of blood.

"¡Madre de Dios!" Ricardo cried. "What's going on!?"

The front picture window shattered as the Leech twins jumped through it landing in the middle of the room. David rolled to his feet and jammed a pitchfork into Peter's heaving chest. Donald reached for Teddy who squealed. Jack leg-swept David and knocked him into his brother. The twins fell on the floor. Jack whirled around with the assault rifle and fired at them on fully automatic. Bullets sprayed into their dead flesh, riddling them with holes. David's cloudy right eye popped. It leaked pink and white pus down the front of his face. Donald's nose flew off and landed in Mike's coffee cup. Mike dashed over to Peter. He was flopping around on the floor with the pitchfork sticking out of his chest. He gasped with his back arched, but then he was gone.

"Everybody!" Mike cried. "Outside!"

Robert and Kate waved them through the door. They called to Jack to come on, but he was busy kicking David in the face. He raised the rifle and slammed the butt down on the side of Donald's head caving it in. More white pus squished out spraying his sneakers.

"You're dead, Dougan!" Donald wailed. *"Don't you get it? Dead! You're meat!"*

Jack dodged as David reached for him and got out the door. Robert opened up with his 9mm. He hit the zombie twice in the head. His face split down the middle, pus pouring out of the crack. The twins laughed. Robert scolded himself for believing it would be that simple. He covered his mouth to hold back a gag from the stench. He grabbed Kate by the arm and pulled her out of the house. Sandy was wrestling his brother at the bottom of the steps.

"Ian!" Sandy cried, grabbing his hair. "Snap out of it, man! This is crazy!"

Ian laughed in his face. Sandy choked at his brother's reeking breath. He yanked Ian's hair down intending to pull him to the walkway. Instead, a third of Ian's blonde blood-streaked scalp tore loose in his hand. Sandy held it out, looked at it dumbly, and dropped it on the grass. He spastically wiped his hand on his shirt. He glared at his brother with revulsion. His slimy red skull was exposed. Ian shrugged and grinned. His gums were greasy and black. His head dripped blood from where his scalp used to be.

"You don't snap out of being dead, bro!"

"But you're not dead!" Sandy cried, his eyes filling with tears. "You're at camp!"

"Yeah," Ian nodded, reaching for his brother's throat. *"Camp Milliken. Good-bye, Sandy."*

Ricardo drop kicked Ian from behind and sent him sprawling onto the lawn. Max grabbed Sandy by the arm and pulled him over to the other boys. They watched as more zombies approached from the road. Ian stood up. Teddy and Derek screamed. Ian had bitten his tongue in half when he fell. It was hanging out of the front of his mouth by a thin vein. Ian looked at it, rolled his eyes, and tore it off the rest of the way. He grinned and threw it at Derek. It stuck on his arm with a wet slap. Derek looked at the tongue and fainted. Chris caught him, peeled the severed tongue off, and threw it back at Ian.

"Nice toss, fag boy!" Ian laughed, mush-mouthed. He caught the tongue in his hand and reattached it. The flesh grew together instantly.

"Oh, shut up!" Kate spat, and shot Ian in the face.

He shrugged it off and stepped toward her. She fired again hitting him in the shoulder. He stumbled back.

"How many times do I have to tell you?" Ian asked, bebopping on the lawn. *"You can't kill what's already dead!"*

The zombies swarmed from every direction. The stench of death filled the night. The pouring rain did nothing to wash it away. George spotted Bobby Jones, saw his missing skull cap and empty cranial cavity, gasped, and fell over sideways, his heart stopping in his chest. Roland knelt down and checked him for a pulse. He was about to start CPR when he didn't find one, but Sam hurled a hatchet at him from the road. It whizzed past Sandra, nearly clipped Teddy, and embedded in the back of Roland's head with a *whack!* He jerked up, his eyes wide, and fell forward on top of George.

Hugh grabbed Joey by the arm and frantically dragged him toward their car. Joey pulled against him. He said they had to stick together. They couldn't abandon the others. Hugh screamed at his son to stop fighting him and get moving. Joey hit the ground as David Leech slide tackled him. Matt plowed into the dead boy as he jumped up reaching for Joey and knocked him into the side of Hugh's car. Matt pulled Joey back as Sam and Ian dove on Hugh. They plunged their hands into his neck, wrenched with all their might, and tore off his head.

Joey screamed as his father's blood sprayed out like a geyser. The zombies laughed. They took the head, Hugh's mouth moving, his eyes shifting, and threw it at Joey. He dodged and screamed again as it splattered against Mike's chimney. Robert moved toward his car trying to get to the radio. Donald Leech stepped in front of him blocking his path. Robert leveled his pistol, but didn't see Sam running toward him. He slapped the gun out of Robert's hand and stood with the zombies. They grinned as they inched closer to everyone who was still alive.

"Leave us alone!" Teddy cried, grabbing his father by the leg.

"No chance!" David spat. *"You're all dead meat!"*

"Run, boys!" Robert yelled. He shoved Teddy at Max. "Get out of here!"

Everyone froze hearing the roar of Lisa's Chevelle coming down Grady Lane. Lyle's Mustang followed it closely. They came to a screeching halt at the edge of Mike's driveway. Their headlights blared on the group of people in the yard and the bodies on the ground. Father and daughter stared not believing their eyes. When Sandra called rambling something about, *"Need you now… bad trouble… Jack's twelve… help us, please!"* Lyle told Lisa to get ready. He figured Jack was after Mike. Lisa wanted to see him get his just rewards for hurting Craig. Lyle thought now was as good a time as any, but from what he was seeing, he had it all wrong.

Robert opened his mouth to warn them, but it was too late. Bobby Jones tore off his own head and threw it at Lisa's Baby. She screamed as it smashed through her windshield showering her with glass. It landed in her lap. She looked down in horror at the hanging veins, ripped tendons, and empty skull cavity. She screamed again when it moved, its mouth working, its eyes rolling around. It sank its teeth into the smooth flesh of her inner thigh. It bit through her jeans and drew blood. Lyle leaped out of his car, ran over to her, and glared in through the window. She looked up at him, terrified. Lyle froze.

Jack reached into the gym bag Craig was holding. He grabbed a grenade and ran over to them. He squeezed past Lyle who stared at him, stunned. Jack grabbed Bobby's head by the hair and yanked it free. It came out of the car with a chunk of Lisa's thigh between its teeth. He pulled the pin on the incendiary grenade, stuffed it inside the head, and threw it back at Bobby. He caught it the moment the grenade went off. Bobby burst into flames. He writhed, his head screaming, and fell on the ground burning.

Dan Mellon stepped out of the woods and lashed out with a broken branch hitting Kate in the face. Lisa scrambled out of the car through the passenger's side door right into Terry Greer. He grinned at her. She kneed him in the genitals. He raised his arm. The flesh around his elbow was green with decay and dangling. He brought it down to hit her in the face, but Lyle grabbed it before it made contact. He wrenched upward, snapped it in half, and ripped it off. Terry recoiled. Robert put a bullet between where his eyes used to be. He was thrown back, landed on the ground, and burst out laughing.

Dan reached for Derek, but Chris yanked him away. He slapped Derek in the face and woke him up. Matt and Ricardo dove together. They tackled Dan and drove him to the ground. Jack and Robert fired at the others. Max grabbed Dan's tree branch and tossed it to Sandra. She spun around and hit Sam in the face with it sending him reeling. She looked down, saw the branch was covered with stinking goo, gagged, and threw it into the road.

Terry caught Teddy by the hair and tried to drag him away. Joey was kneeling over his father's headless body crying. He caught Terry by the leg and flipped his feet out from under him. He dove on top of him his fists flashing. He punched Terry in the face repeatedly. Sandra drew Teddy into her arms and set him down behind her. Terry rammed his skeletal finger into Joey's right eye, gouging it out, and stabbing into his brain. Dan grabbed Chris by the ankle.

"You killed me, McKee!" Dan wailed, struggling against Matt and Ricardo.

Derek reached down and snatched the .44 Magnum out of Kate's hand. She was fighting to stay conscious, but was losing. Derek convulsed all over. His head jerked to the side as he held the pistol out in front of him. He walked over to Dan and pressed it against his brother's forehead.

"Do us all a favor, Dan, okay?" Derek whispered in a sob, cocking the hammer back. "Stay dead this time."

Derek pulled the trigger. The gun went off with a loud bang. It blew Dan's head apart and at the same time broke Derek's wrist. He cried out and dropped the gun. Matt and Ricardo jumped up gagging at the sight of Dan's pus-filled brains splattered all over the ground. His body thrashed. Jack pulled the pin off another incendiary and dropped it into the running goo. Dan burst into flame. Chris spun around and pulled his foot free. Robert grabbed Jack by the shoulders and ordered him to get the kids out of there.

"Not without Sandy!" Chris cried.

Sandy was in the driveway wrestling with his brother. Ian bit his left middle finger off. Sandy screamed. Lyle, Mike, Sandra, and Robert ran over by Mike's car. Jack leveled his assault rifle, but cursed when he couldn't get a clear shot. Sandy rolled off Ian and stood with his legs apart. His left hand was bleeding like crazy. Craig called out to him and tossed him a hand grenade. Sandy caught it with his good hand and gripped it, tightly. Ian chewed Sandy's severed finger wildly before spitting it out.

"Screw you, Sanford!"

"I love you, Ian," Sandy whispered, pulling the pin. "Please, man. Let me help you!"

"Help me? You killed me, you idiot!" Ian cried, weaving back and forth. He was ready to pounce.

"Me?" Sandy asked.

"Don't listen to him, Sandy!" Chris called.

Sandy shushed him. "What are you talking about, Ian?" he asked, the two brothers circling one another. "How did I kill you? You're supposed to be at camp!"

"It was a lie!" Ian spat. *"That psycho Hill Witch brainwashed mom and dad just like Dr. Stone, just like Mrs. Jones! Like all of you!"*

"I don't understand, man!" Sandy cried. "What happened the night of the campout?"

"You were talking about letting everyone think you're queer," Ian sneered. *"I heard you! I couldn't take it anymore. I was running home when the farmer got me. He was out in the woods!"*

"Oh, Jesus."

"He murdered me, Sanford!" Ian cried, tilting his head back.

Sandy looked at the hanging tendons and veins that used to be his brother's neck. He felt his gorge rise.

"He cut my throat like I was a pig!"

"I'm sorry, Ian," Sandy whispered. He held up the grenade. "Let me help you... please, just let me help you..."

"You can help me by dropping dead!"

Ian knocked Sandy off his feet and landed on top of him. Sandy had the grenade clutched to his chest between them. Sorrow filled his mind. He stared up at this dead thing that was his brother, the brother he fought with, the brother he picked on, but most of all the brother Sandy loved but never realized it. He didn't know what to do, how to help, and Jesus, was it really his fault? Ian glared at him. The rain ran down his face carrying away pieces of gore. Sandy closed his eyes and started to cry. Ian grabbed his finger and twisted it painfully back. The grenade's safety catch sprang off landing by Chris' feet.

Ian cried, *"Gotcha!"*

"No!" The boys screamed.

"Holy Christ!" Jack hollered. *"Grenade!"*

The grenade went off with a boom blowing Sandy and Ian apart. Sandy's head ricocheted off Mike's chimney, hit the siding, and slid down to the ground. Ian's head landed on the walkway. Their blood flew into the air and rained all over everyone. A piece of shrapnel pierced Mike's gas tank. His car exploded and sent a fireball into the sky. The boys dove for cover. Lyle,

Sandra, Lisa, Mike, Kate, and Robert were flung through the air by the force of the blast. They hit the ground riddled with shrapnel, bleeding, and unconscious.

"*Sandy!*" Chris cried, holding the sides of his head.

"Holy crap!" Max cried. "Run, you guys! *Run!*"

"*Don't you listen?*" Sam snapped. The zombies encircled the boys. "*You're not running anywhere!*"

Craig reached into the gym bag and showed Jack the item he had withdrawn. Jack nodded, encouragingly. Craig pointed the flare gun at Sam and pulled the trigger. Sam screamed as it struck him in the chest. He stumbled back, sparks flying, opening a hole in their circle.

"Eat that!" Craig cried.

He reloaded the flare gun and fired again. This time he caught Donald Leech in the face. It set his broken head ablaze. Donald fell dead once again. Chris grabbed Derek and led the way through the opening. Max, Matt, and Ricardo followed with Teddy between them. Craig went next, and then Jack slipping through just in time. They dove through the woods headed for the trails. The zombies regrouped in the road. Ian was gone, so were Dan, Donald, and Bobby Jones. Sam had a hole in his chest where the flare had burned through. David glared at the others insisting that Craig was his.

Terry growled, his jaw hanging loosely from his face. "*You can have him,*" he replied. "*There are others. It's time to split up. Here's what we're going to do...*"

*   *   *

Nancy woke suddenly, sat up in her bed, and glared around the room. Her heart was beating a mile a minute. She was sweating profusely. Something had disturbed her usual sound sleep. She assumed it was a dream. She scowled. She despised being woken up. It would take her forever to get back to sleep. It was bad enough today's stress had led her to retire early. She shifted her heavy short legs over the side of her bed. She decided on a hot tea with a shot of whiskey to set her straight. She felt around on the floor with her feet searching for the slippers Craig had given her for Christmas last year.

That boy's so thoughtful, Nancy thought. *Always remembers me birthday, never missed a holiday from th' time he was old enough t' know what a holiday was.*

She smiled when the tip of her toe met one of them. They were fuzzy and pink. The other one was next to it. She slipped them on, reached out, and switched on her bedside lamp. Light filled her upstairs bedroom. Nancy squinted and smacked her lips. Her ears reached out and searched her house for any sounds out of the ordinary. It was a practice she had followed religiously since the first night she lived alone.

Nancy rubbed her eyes and yawned. She detected the low hum of the water pump in the cellar. It kept running due to a leak in the bathroom toilet tank. It drained into the bowl causing it to continuously fill. Nancy was reminded for the umpteenth time to have Michael take a look at it. She'd forgotten about it more times than she could count. She looked lovingly yet sadly at the picture of her deceased husband on the nightstand. He looked so proud in that shot with his head was held high, his jaw set firm. His gaze was steady and unwavering. He had lost none of his character in the black and white print. Nancy remembered the day they took that picture. It was the day she found out she was pregnant with Jack.

Wade was pleased and proud as he led her around the Brooklyn Fairgrounds. He beamed, determined to try every game of chance to win a teddy bear for their new baby. He paused long enough to pose for a man selling snapshots. Nancy had the photo enlarged years later. It had been sitting on her nightstand ever since. She looked at Wade's face. Suddenly, her heart leaped in her chest when she noticed Wade was glaring right at her.

"Ye've much t' answer for, Nancy O'Dell!" Wade snapped.

Nancy screamed and jumped back. She tumbled off the bed and fell onto the floor. She scrambled to her feet, her pulse rushing through the arteries in her neck. She backed up to the windows, her chest heaving as she struggled for breath. Her eyes were wide with terror. Panic made her hands shake.

Wade sneered, *"There's blood on your hands, woman. Would ye like t' meet th' boys ye helped murder by protecting Hiram Milliken? Ye knew what he did to our boy! Ye turned a blind eye! They want t' meet ye. Should I show ye what Milliken did t' th' wee lads? Trust me, it'll kill ye!"*

Nancy opened her mouth to scream. Something inside told her if she did, and loud enough, this terrible apparition would go away. She heard the unmistakable sound of a gunshot. She spun around and gazed terrified through the blinds. She heard another shot, and then a whole series of shots coming from Michael's house. A loud explosion ripped through the darkness shaking the windowpanes. A fireball launched into the sky directly above her son's house. Lightning shot across the clouds and the wind picked up. The rain drove against her window.

Nancy cried, "Heavens above! *Michael!*"

Wade's picture fell silent. It was frozen again in his proud stance as she grabbed the telephone. His eyes no longer glared at her with hatred. She dialed *911*. The line was busy. Nancy was enraged and on the verge of a nervous breakdown. She smashed the phone down and immediately picked it up again. She prepared to dial once more, but the monotone busy signal was still there. Her eyes bulged. Nancy crushed her finger down on the carriage. She angrily counted to three before releasing it. The line clicked free and she dialed. She repeated nearly the same actions three times in a row before the phone rang. Nancy's anger and fear grew well beyond her ability to hold it in.

The dispatcher answered, "State police, can you please hold?"

"Not for one damned second!" she hollered, her voice cracking.

It echoed through the house. She heard other lines ringing in the police barracks in the background. She ignored them, certain no one else's business was more important than hers.

Wade? Oh, Lord, Wade! I did it for ye!

"There's been an explosion, ye buffoon! An' gunfire! *Are ye out o' your mind!?* Hold indeed! It's comin' from…!"

"Milliken Road, ma'am?" the dispatcher sighed.

Nancy's mouth dropped open. "Why… *yes…!* but…?" she managed before the dispatcher cut her off.

"We're on it, ma'am," he patiently replied. "The read-out says you're at 57 Bog Dancer Drive, is that correct?"

"Aye, lad," Nancy panted. She held the side of her night table to keep from falling over. "I'm…"

"… Nancy O'Dell Dougan," the dispatcher finished for her. There was a cocky smile in his voice. "You're entire neighborhood is calling, ma'am. We're on our way, okay? Just stay inside your house and try to remain calm. Everything is under control."

"But…," Nancy started. The line went dead in her hand. She dialed Michael's house next. It was busy. Both his and Sandra's cell phones went straight to voicemail.

She moved to her closet. It took forever to get dressed. The panic inside demanded she get to her son's house regardless of what the dispatcher said.

Stay home and remain calm, me pasty-green Irish ass! Nancy thought.

She ran to the kitchen and frantically tried to tie her boots while holding her purse in her teeth.

Michael! I've got t' get t' Michael!

She wasn't going to lose another son for lack of action. She stood, wiped the tears from her cheeks, and barreled through the door to the garage right into David Leech's frigid arms.

*　　*　　*

The boys stopped running at Derek's fort. They doubled over gasping for breath. The rain fell in buckets cooling their burning bodies. Matt and Derek held Chris who was crying hysterically. The others gathered around them lending their support. Jack rolled his eyes and stepped away with the gym bag. He sat against the wall of the fort, rain pouring on him as he reloaded his clip. The danger wasn't over, didn't they realize that? They had to get to Jeremy. Jack sighed wishing Jeremy purged his memories entirely. He didn't feel the pain of the war anymore or the effects of PTSD, but he still saw it in his mind. He guessed it was his punishment, but there wasn't time to grieve. If they didn't get their acts together…

"More people are going to die, you know," Jack said. He slapped the clip into the M4. "We don't have time for this."

"Shut up, Dougan!" Max snapped. "Would you get a clue? We just lost our friend!"

Jack dropped the rifle, jumped up, and got in Max's face. "You idiot!" he yelled, lightning reflecting in his fiery green eyes. "Don't you get it!? If McKee doesn't cut the shit, we're all going to die!"

"Who died and made you king, Jack?" Matt asked.

"Yeah, man!" Ricardo echoed, balling up his fist. "You're not so big anymore!"

Jack sneered. "You think that makes a difference?" He stepped into the middle of the trail beckoning them. "C'mon then! We can wait for the goddamned zombies while I stomp your asses all over the trails!"

Ricardo considered that an open invitation. So did Max. If this little squirt who was smaller than Derek really was Jack Dougan, he had it coming. They came from either side and tried to grab him. To Jack, they looked like they were moving in slow motion. Matt moved to join them, balling up his fists.

Craig grabbed his arm. He shook his head and said, "You can't. He's right. They're wrong."

Matt angrily thought, *That doesn't mean I have to like it!*

Jack ducked down and punched Ricardo in the testicles. Ricardo dropped, holding his crotch. He didn't know it was possible to be hit that hard by someone so small. It felt like Jack the man had belted him. Waves of pain rifled through his body. Jack pivoted on his heel and elbowed Max in the solar plexus. Max's thoughts were similar to his brother's as the wind rushed out of him. He fell to the ground next to Ricardo. Jack stormed over to Chris and shoved Derek out of the way.

Derek thought, *Jeez, throw me off the world why don't you!*

Jack drew back his hand and swung, intending to slap Chris across the face. Chris grabbed his wrist as it came down and gripped it hard. He felt the strength in Jack's arm.

"Don't," Chris said. He stifled his emotions. "You're right. I'm sorry."

Jack nodded, his anger fading as his eyes teared. "It's okay," he replied, choking on his emotions. "I just don't want to see anybody else get killed."

Matt helped Max and Ricardo stand, the wind taken out of their sails. They were soaking wet. Matt shook his head.

Max grumbled, "Don't even think about saying what you were going to say."

"Who me?" Matt asked.

"Man, he's strong," Ricardo wheezed, tenderly rubbing his testicles.

"No doubt," Max agreed, holding his sore chest. He nodded at Jack and asked, "What's up with that, Dougan? How can you be so small and still be so strong?"

"I don't know," Jack shrugged. "Ask your buddy, Jeremy. He did this to me."

"Strong?" Craig asked. "What are they talking about, dad?"

Jack reached out and grabbed his hand. He squeezed it.

"Ow!" Craig cried. "That hurts!"

Jack let him go and looked at his small fingers. "Strange," he muttered. "I'm a kid, but I feel as strong as a man."

"You are," Ricardo grimaced. "Trust me."

Max nodded.

Jack shook his head, "I'm starting to feel pretty freaky about this now."

Chris patted him on the shoulder. "Now you know how we feel."

They walked over to the fort and went inside to seek shelter from the storm. Derek winced as he pulled the door closed. His wrist was blowing up like a balloon. Jack instructed Matt to cover the front window. Matt looked back with irritation, but did as he said.

This is nuts, Matt thought. *Absolutely insane.*

Craig told them everything he knew as quickly as possible about the mind-link, the beating, Jeremy healing Jack, what they saw in his mind, raising the dead… their heads were spinning by the time he had finished.

"I know it's hard to believe…," Craig began.

"Dougan?" Ricardo asked, his voice hard and filled with anger. "The corpse of our friend just murdered our friend, okay? What's not to believe?"

"I've got to get to my brother," Chris said, standing up.

Jack put his hand on his chest and eased him back down. "Soon," he nodded. "First things first."

Derek began to shake uncontrollably.

Jack grabbed him by his broken wrist. "No!" he cried, squeezing it.

Derek yanked his arm away from the excruciating pain. His face flushed with anger. *"That hurt, asshole!"*

"Keep yourself together!" Jack shot back. "We can't afford to have anyone losing it!"

"All right!" Derek sobbed. "I'm sorry, *okay?* I'm *scared, okay!?"*

"We're all scared, Derek," Max said.

He felt it like the others. It was on the horizon of each of their minds. Hysteria. It would be so easy just to let go.

"What are we going to do?" Teddy whined, his leg shaking. He grabbed it when Jack glared at him. "My dad's still back there!"

"Your dad will be fine," Craig assured him. He walked over to the mattress and sat down with him.

"What makes you so sure?" Matt asked, but he didn't turn away from the window.

Jack told Ricardo to take Matt's place. While they switched, Jack opened the gym bag and took the munitions out.

"They're after specific people," he told Matt, handing him a hand grenade. "The people who knew what Hiram was and never turned him in, me included."

"And me," Chris said.

Ricardo patted him on the back.

Jack shot him an angry glare.

Ricardo looked back out the window. "Sorry," he mumbled.

Jack said, "Sorry is toilet paper. You can wipe your ass with it. In combat, sorry is dead."

"Hey, man," Max said. "This isn't a war, you know."

"People are getting killed, Max," Craig replied. "It sounds like war to me."

"Me, too," Chris agreed.

"What's this for?" Max asked, holding up the grenade Jack handed him.

"Besides killing people?" Jack replied. He sighed, "I'm sorry, kid. I guess there's still some of the old Jack in me. More than I want."

"The ass-kicking part maybe," Max remarked, rubbing his chest. "I know what you're doing. We're going to split up, right?"

"We have to," Jack nodded. "They're coming after McKee and me, maybe even Bigelow. We have to get away from you guys. They're going to try to kill us and anyone who gets in their way."

"Where are you going?" Craig asked, placing his hand on his father's shoulder. It was a gesture filled with concern.

Jack felt his eyes tearing once again. *God, I don't deserve it.*

"We're going hunting," Jack said, wiping his eyes and nodding at Chris. Chris nodded back. "Let's do it."

"We have to…," Jack began, but then froze, cocking his head.

Derek asked what was wrong in a whisper. Jack shushed him and pulled a bayonet out of the gym bag. He removed it from the scabbard. They strained to listen, every ear searching for what had alerted him. They didn't hear anything except thunder and the rain pinging off the aluminum roof. Jack eased over to the door. After a few torturous moments, they heard it, too, footsteps running down the trail heading toward them. Teddy whimpered. Matt slapped his hand over his mouth feeling his braces. He yanked him away from Craig and into his lap. Teddy grabbed Matt's thighs and held on. Chris hugged Derek as the sound grew.

They were sure it was one set of feet, but the rhythm was uneven. Ricardo saw headless Bobby Jones stumbling along in his mind. He cringed and shook the image away. They held their collective breath as the footsteps neared the fort. Jack put his hand up to them. He waited until the exact moment and flung the door open. The runner slammed into it with a loud smack and a painful:

"Ow!"

461

Jack was on top of him in a split second. He held the bayonet up to his left eye.

"Oh… damn it…," Dabney sighed, at the knife.

"Dabney!" the boys cried, rushing out of the fort and into the rain again.

Jack recognized him as a Copeland, but judging by the other's reactions he was a friendly. *If that's possible for a Copeland,* he thought. He got off him and helped him up.

Dabney winced as he stood. He was all beat up and looked like hell.

"Where have you been!?" Chris demanded. He threw his arms around him and held him, kissing his cheek.

"Pleading the Fifth, my ass," Ricardo muttered.

Dabney gripped Chris' shoulders, smiled weakly, and then his knees buckled. Chris held him up. Lightning flashed, lighting up the trails. The boys stared wide-eyed at Dabney's appearance. Chris looked down at him and grabbed him by the cheeks.

"You're hurt!" he cried, brushing his soaking hair back.

"No time… to be," Dabney gasped. "Need… help…"

"Bring him in the fort!" Jack barked, clearing a path.

Ricardo scooped him up and carried him in. He laid Dabney down on the mattress. Chris sat on the bed next to him, holding his hand.

Dabney squeezed. "I have to get… to Jeremy."

"That's it!" Craig exclaimed. "Jeremy!"

"Bingo," Jack nodded, glad to see his son finally got it. "They used him to come back. He's got to be able to stop them."

"Yes…," Dabney managed to say before he passed out.

Chris felt his heart sink. *Oh, Jesus, not Dabney, too!*

Jack caught his expression of worry. He took Chris' hand and placed it on Dabney's chest to show him there was still a heartbeat. He tilted his head down by Dabney's mouth and nose. He asked Chris to do the same. He nodded, weakly, feeling Dabney's breath.

Jack turned to the others, gave grenades to the rest of the older kids, and then quickly explained how they worked. There was a three to five second time delay once the safety catch was sprung. There was no margin for error. He divided them into teams. They listened respectfully. Jack's commanding manner convinced them he knew his stuff. He, Chris, and Teddy were heading toward the other side of town. They would be safer in a denser population.

"Derek and Dabney need a doctor," Jack said, pointing to Derek's swollen wrist. "So do the people at Mike's house."

"We'll take them there," Matt said. He sheepishly asked, "Can we have some more grenades? Dabney worked for Hiram, you know. He might be a victim who never told, too."

"Man," Ricardo said. "Do you think?"

"It would explain why he was so nasty all of the time," Max said.

Matt shook his head, "Dabney's always been like that... at least until recently anyway."

"He's our friend now," Chris said, "and he needs our help."

"Maybe more than a friend?" Ricardo said, elbowing Chris.

Chris bit his lower lip. He looked at Dabney. He whispered, "Way more."

"How about those grenades?" Matt asked again.

Jack nodded. There were eight standards left, four incendiaries, six flares, and about four hundred rounds of ammo for the assault rifle. He gave the flare gun to Craig and asked if the mind-link was still active.

Craig nodded. "I feel him."

"Yes, but can you find him?" Chris asked.

"He's still in the pasture," Craig replied.

"I'm going with you," Max said, pointing at Craig. "You may need back up if there's trouble."

"Go now then," Jack barked, opening the fort door. "We've wasted enough time."

Ricardo lifted Dabney into a fireman's carry and walked out behind them.

Chris touched his wrist. "Take care of him, Ricardo, okay?" he asked, holding Dabney's cheek. "Please?"

Ricardo nodded.

Chris brushed Dabney's hair out of his face. He kissed his forehead. "It's important to me that he's okay."

Max and Craig moved toward the pasture. Matt and Derek went with Ricardo toward Mike's. Chris and Teddy followed Jack a few minutes later. They cut through the Mellons' backyard and nodded at each other when they heard sirens heading toward Milliken Road. Jack stopped at the edge of the Mellons' front lawn. He glanced tentatively at his mother's house.

What's she going to think of the new me? Jack wondered.

He felt a stab of regret over the way things had been between them. He vowed he would make it better. The monster he was laid dead inside him, but his sins were still apparent and unforgiven. Chris patted his head as they stood there. Jack nodded, shyly. Chris was showing him affection like any other kid. It felt good.

I am a kid now, aren't I? Jack thought. He decided he could grow to like Chris McKee.

They turned to cut across Nancy's lawn, but froze when they heard a loud crash. They watched as David Leech flew out of Nancy's house right through the garage screen door.

*   *   *

"*Je*-sus Christ!" Detective Shooter cried, as he climbed out of his gray Crown Victoria.

He had parked across the road from Mike's burning car. He was a tall man, six-foot-four, with raging brown eyes and dark blonde hair. His face was thin and drawn. He had a nose like a vulture. He angrily glared at the two officers standing over Robert Bigelow.

Shooter asked, "Will somebody get the firemen down here already? What are you waiting for, Ricci? McMahon? Christmas?"

Officers Ricci and McMahon were rookies in their first year on the force despite not being old enough to purchase alcohol in Connecticut. They glared at their superior, fear and anger momentarily clouding their more professional judgment.

"We've got officers down, Calvin!" Ricci cried. He pointed at Robert and Kate.

"Yeah!" McMahon echoed. "What gives, Shooter?"

Shooter strutted over with a Marlboro clenched between his teeth. His pea-green tie wagged back and forth like a dead tongue.

"That's *Detective* Shooter to you, officer," Shooter snapped. Smoke curled up into his face. *Twenty years on the force and this pup wants to play games with me? I don't think so!* He took a long drag off his cigarette trying to keep it dry from the rain. He turned to Ricci. "Now, do what I told you to do before I get angry. Get those other cars away from the Buick before the heat blows them up, too. I don't care if you have to check the pockets of every corpse for keys, got it?"

McMahon and Ricci headed toward their squad cars.

Shooter glared around the horrid scene. He thought, *Remind me that we moved to Lancaster to get away from the rising crime in Worcester. Well, Coco had a lot to do with it. God, we've had problems with that kid. It isn't easy having a cop for a father, I get it, but Coco acts like he wants to be on America's Most Wanted before he turns seventeen.*

Shooter took another long drag off his cigarette and inhaled deeply. He shook his head as he held the smoke in his lungs. *Honestly, I can't blame the young officers for being unsettled. I've been a homicide detective for twelve years, a patrolman for eight before that, and I've never seen anything like this before. The Buick Regal is toast.*

Black smoke billowed into the stormy sky as bright orange flames licked at the interior. The steering wheel was slag. It dripped down to where the carpet used to be. Rain hissed and evaporated as it hit the roof.

Shooter looked around the yard. There were body parts everywhere. Some looked like they had been dead for quite a while. There was a headless corpse burning in the middle of the yard. There were two others in pieces nearby. One looked fresh. Shooter was sure a hand grenade caused his demise.

Who has hand grenades in a little town like this? Shooter wondered, chewing on his smoke's filter.

There was a group of injured people scattered around like leaves in need of the ambulances he heard in the distance. A decapitated head sat in the walkway. Ian's surprised eyes stared at him.

Man, Shooter thought. His stomach churned. *He's just a kid.*

The whole scene was horror central. Shooter was glad his wife hadn't let their thirteen-year-old come with him. Graham had gone to crime scenes with him before, but he always waited in the car and watched from there. He was fascinated by the complexity of his father's job. There was a morbid excitement in being so close to a real murder. Still, the crime scenes were never hot ones like this. Connie objected to the reports of gunfire. She was right. It was too dangerous. She was completely wrong about not wanting to move away from Worcester however.

Shooter was the one who drew the line then. They needed to get Coco away from the gangs and the drugs. That's what they did even though Connie was adamant about making a go of it there. She was never very streetwise. They bought the house on Mary Circle before the one in Worcester had sold. Looking around, Shooter had to wonder if violent crime really was everywhere and even the boonies weren't safe anymore.

What's this world coming to, anyway?

Shooter walked over by the front door of the house. His gaze followed a river of blood flowing down the front steps onto the walkway. It came from a body lying just inside the doorway missing its heart.

Ugh, Shooter thought. He spotted the crushed muscle in a pool of blood near Arthur Kelly's feet.

He tiptoed over the corpses inside. He saw into the backyard through a hole in the wall. The floodlights were shining on the armless remains of another kid about Coco's age. Shooter felt ill now. The stench of death was all around him.

Whatever happened here, it was bad, Shooter thought.

He was going to get some answers starting with the kids by the ambulance. Three of them seem around Coco's age. The other two were closer to Graham's age, if not younger. The blonde walked over to the side of the house by the chimney. There was a blood smear running down the wall that led to another severed head.

Jesus! Shooter thought, twitching his nose as he moved toward him. *The stink!*

This was no place for Graham. Being deaf enhanced his remaining senses. The smell would have been a lot worse for him. Shooter reached out for Matt as he came up to him, but Matt pulled away. He cradled Sandy's head to his chest as he wept. There was blood all over his arms and down the front of his shirt.

Shooter thought, *Guess he knows who the fresh corpse in the front yard is. That makes things easier.*

He left Matt and went to the boys over by the ambulance. He tossed his smoke into a pool of blood by the roadside. Shooter looked back. Matt sat on the lawn in the rain with Sandy's head in his lap.

If the kid wants to sit there holding a severed head, let him, Shooter thought. *The uniforms can deal with it.*

He heard more sirens in the distance – fire trucks, ambulances, and officers for the roadblocks Shooter had ordered.

No one is leaving this town tonight and reporters are staying far away from my crime scene.

Shooter stepped up to the boys, and asked, "Would one of you guys mind telling me what happened here tonight?"

The kids looked like they had been involved in a nasty scrape. He wouldn't be surprised if they were behind this whole mess with the way things were today. He made a point to forget they were kids. The blood and gore on their clothing helped that. They were his only suspects.

If they want to play in the big time, I'm going to give them a class.

"Don't all of you talk at once," Shooter barked, his patience wearing thin. "We can do this downtown if you'd rather. How about you, red? You seem kind of upset."

"Suck me!" Derek spat, and burst into tears.

When they spotted the cops, Ricardo told Derek they shouldn't say anything. There was no way he was going to. Besides, he was scared, his wrist hurt, and he was in no mood for this crap.

Shooter shook his head. *Okay, a hard ass. Great.*

"You wouldn't believe us if we told you," Ricardo said.

"I might believe you," Shooter said. "Make it good though. I'm not in the mood to be jerked off right now."

They looked at each other, their eyes narrowing.

"You asked for it," Ricardo replied, and told the detective everything.

*   *   *

Hiram barreled out of the woods by Lancaster Pond, his eyes barely open, his arms swinging powerfully up and down. He was a man running for his life. The rain strafed him like bullets drowning out all of the sound around him except for the thunder. He crossed the beach's grassy section with images of *Steve Austin* in his head…

… better, stronger, faster! Hiram thought. *Oh, yes, have to move faster!*

Hiram hit the wet sand, lost his balance, and his feet slid out from under him. He hit the ground with a thud. His chest heaved as he fought for breath.

Christ, they're fast!

He glared around the pond. Nobody in town knew the woods or the trails better than he did. Years of hunting made him a virtual living GPS. Still, every time Hiram thought he had lost those sick-looking little bastards, one of them would pop out of nowhere. He charged full bore down the trails along the southeastern section of town. He made it to the trail that led to the pond only to find they were already there. It was as if they had known where he was going. Three zombies were right in front of him in the middle of the path.

They cut cross-country, Hiram thought, *right through the woods!*

He caught them off guard when he lowered his head and plowed through them. They assumed he would run away. Not likely. Hiram had the advantage in the open. He concluded the good thing about being chased by someone dead was that he could smell them at a thousand paces.

Hiram rolled to his knees and scanned the woodline. He wasn't running anymore. He had taken on the lot of them in the barnyard and lived. There were only three of them after him now. He would take them down right here on the beach. The sirens he'd heard a short time ago must be the fire department. Something had blown up over at Dougan's house.

It has to be Margaret! Hiram thought. *That black magic bitch raised the dead and sent them after me! Well, it will take more than that!*

Lightning crashed nearby and he jumped. Thunder followed right along with it. The storm was overhead now. Hiram was glad. There were no streetlights down here. It was as black as pitch. He only saw clearly when the lightning flashed. It wasn't as clear as he wanted, but it was enough. He wondered exactly where those dead freaks were and...

What about their buddies? Hiram wondered, his breath about caught. *Why are only three of them after me?* He decided, *Let's not question good fortune!*

Hiram got to his feet and stared at the woods. He didn't dare blink. They must be close. He needed to be ready for them. His hands worked, prepared to rip apart the first thing that moved. Behind him, the tops of three heads appeared from underwater. The zombies had walked across the floor of the pond heading for the shore. Each step brought them up a little more. They stared intently at their molester and killer. Chunks of their rotted flesh fell away as they rose past their chests. They stepped carefully onto the beach, fanning out, preparing to attack.

Kyle took the point. He had Hiram's hunting knife in his hand. He intended to use it on the farmer the same way Hiram had used it on him. The other two zombies followed his lead. The wind shifted in Hiram's direction. One whiff of the breeze and the farmer knew exactly where they were. Hiram spun around and caught Kyle by the wrist as his arm came down to strike. His eyes went insane. His face twisted with rage. He ripped the knife out of

Kyle's hand, drew back, and shoved it into his temple. Kyle stumbled back and yanked it out, howling. Stinking pus oozed down the side of his face.

"You monster!" Kyle spat. *"You can't kill me twice!"*

"Yeah?" Hiram shot back. "Come a little closer, MacGuire! I'll rip your stinking head off!"

One of the zombies dove and caught Hiram's ankle. Hiram recognized him. His name was Will Webber. He used to like to walk alone in the woods in Vernon. Johnny Mildaur was the other corpse, a runaway from East Windsor. He launched at the farmer's free ankle, but Hiram lifted his leg out of the way. Johnny flopped onto the sand. Hiram crushed his rotted head with his work boot.

Hiram hollered in triumph, *"Take that, you stinky-nasty little bastard!"*

Will bit into Hiram's calf. His holler turned into a cry of pain. Hiram bent down and grabbed the zombie by the hair. Will's scalp slipped off in his hand. Hiram's jaw dropped open. Kyle sprang up, grabbed the scalp, and jammed it into Hiram's mouth. He held his hand over it so the farmer couldn't spit it out. Hiram went ballistic as he struggled to breathe. He twisted Kyle's fingers back with all of his strength. He snapped the zombie's arm off at the elbow and beat him with the pus-covered end. He spat the chewed-up scalp into his face.

Kyle fell back. Hiram kicked Will off him and beat him, too. He went into a frenzy, tearing at their flesh, dismembering them, and tossing their body parts all over the beach. Hiram jumped up and down on them until they were slimy blobs of quivering muck.

"You lose!" he sang. He unzipped his fly and pulled out his penis. He urinated on their remains, laughing as he spelled out: **Hiram was here!** in big bold yellow letters.

Hiram zipped up and stumbled away, wiping his hands on his shirt. He needed shelter from the rain and a place to dry out. He needed to know if he was on the run. He had prepared for that possibility. He had a lot of money stashed in off-shore bank accounts. Hiram was a child molester, a mass murderer, and a lunatic, but he wasn't a moron. He couldn't go home, but he knew a nearby haven. Hiram was one of the few people in Lancaster who knew where Lyle Gibbons kept his spare garage key.

As soon as Hiram was gone, Frank Garrison stumbled out of the woods. He walked through the dismembered corpses, turning in circles, holding his head. A hand grabbed his ankle. He spun toward it.

Will glared at him. *"Traitor!"* he spat.

Frank ripped his leg away. "Screw you!" he cried, backing up. His voice sounded strange. He held his chest. He had no heartbeat or respiration. He was forcing the words out of his mouth with no breath. He choked back a sob. "The farmer didn't kill me, you did!" He thrust his arms out. "Look what you did to me, man! I'm a monster!"

"*He's not like us,*" Will said. "*Can you feel it? He's not connected to us through Jeremy.*"

"*Smells like the living,*" Kyle sneered. "*Living dead.*"

"Go to hell!"

"*Vengeance is ours, Frank,*" Kyle whispered. "*Help us kill them. They deserve to die!*"

"No!" Frank exclaimed. "I'm not a killer!" He ran toward the farm, his hands over his face as he wept. "I'll never help you! Never!"

"*Not yet,*" Will whispered, "*but you will get hungry.*"

"*Brains… brains!*" Kyle mocked.

Will and Kyle's eyes closed and they were silent.

*   *   *

Graham Shooter waited in his room until he felt the vibrations of his mother's footsteps tromping upstairs before he put his sneakers on. Connie would bathe now. It was a ritual that would last an hour. When she was finished, she would read for another hour, and then go to bed. After eighteen years of marriage to a police officer, she didn't wait up anymore. He wouldn't be back until tomorrow morning. Graham knew she wasn't worried. She only worried about *the knock.* Connie feared that more than anything. It was the middle of the night, patrolman on the doorstep *knock.* Graham shivered. Losing his father was the worst thing he could think of happening. It was bad enough he hadn't been around much this week. He couldn't imagine losing him forever.

Detective Calvin David Shooter, Sr. had worked every day since arriving in Lancaster leaving the unpacking to Graham, his mother, and his brother. Coco was a jerk most of the time, but they tried to have patience. He had just gotten out of ninety days of drug rehabilitation. He hadn't sworn off drinking or smoking pot, but at least he was off the harder drugs. Coco knew if he got caught with any drug at all, it was back to rehab for one-hundred-eighty days. So far that threat had kept him sober.

Graham's deafness wasn't a handicap in his house. The TVs had closed caption, the doorbell and phone had lights to signal him, and his family knew sign language. Coco wouldn't sign anymore. Graham hated that, but it didn't matter. It made him fight harder to become adept at lipreading. He was tired of Coco being able to bad mouth him in front of his hearing friends. The one thing his brother had done for him – and to be mean – gave him the chance to go to public school.

Graham liked deaf school well enough, but it was his social life he had in mind. He fully intended to go to Gallaudet University and become a teacher. In the meantime, Graham didn't want to be transported a million miles away each day to go to school. He was tired of being segregated from his neighbors. He couldn't hear, but he wasn't retarded. He wanted to make friends with kids who didn't live far away. School wouldn't be the center of his social circle anymore. He knew it would be hard. There would be problems with films without captions and teachers who taught with their backs to the class. Some of the kids might tease him because his voice was off-key, but Graham didn't care. He would find acceptance. He was through having friendships over the TTY, his Droid, or the Internet.

Graham put on his waterproof Patriots jacket, peeked out his bedroom door to make sure his mom wasn't lurking around, pocketed his Droid, and then hopped out of his window. He sucked in the clean wet country air and smiled as he pulled the screen back down. He left it open a crack for his return. He felt the thunder boom. The lightning filled him with glee.

I love the rain! Graham thought.

His mother would tan his behind if she caught him out in it, but it was worth the risk. His backside was no stranger to the paddle. He wasn't bad or anything, and he didn't get beaten often, but there were times he earned his spankings.

Graham grinned. *Like tonight!*

He reached down and patted the grass thanking it for being so close. He had chosen the only downstairs bedroom when his parents gave him first pick for this reason. He loved to sneak out and wander around. The lightning didn't scare him and neither did the dark. Sometimes he walked for miles in the middle of the night. He learned his way around most of Worcester. Why should he go through all of the trouble of climbing up and down trees to sneak out if he didn't have to? There weren't any close enough to this house to do that anyway, not like their old one. Coco was livid since he liked sneaking out, too, but that was just too bad for him.

So? Graham thought, taking the long way around his yard. *I'm a spoiled brat. Sue me!*

Graham crossed Mary Circle heading east. He wasn't a hundred yards into the woods before he was soaked, but he was in his glory. The summer rain was warm. His destination for the evening was Lancaster High School. It was on a hill overlooking the town. It promised a dynamite view of the area and the storm. His mother didn't want him to go to a crime scene with his dad tonight? Fine. He could watch the lights from up there. If he could find a way, he would get on the roof. He debated going to the cliffs, but decided against it. It was too risky in the dark until he became familiar with them.

Graham hoped to be able to do that with Mrs. Sturgess' sons and their friends. She had told him that out of all the boys he could meet in Lancaster, they were the best. She raved about the McKees, some boy named Matt, her sons Sandy and Ian, and the Ramirez brothers. Graham was dying to meet them all and to go to the farm. His mother had said no regarding that so far. There was unpacking to do. He agreed with her, but too easily. He hadn't known unpacking was going to take all week! He figured it would be worth the wait. He would've met with Susan again on Thursday, but she canceled to go to that poor kid's funeral. They rescheduled for Monday. Susan promised to bring her sons with her. Graham looked forward to that.

As he neared the top of a small hill overlooking the section of streets Susan called Rainbow West – Red Road, Orange Street, Brown Road, and Green Drive – a familiar scent hit his nose.

Graham frowned, shaking his auburn hair out. *That stench is the worst!* he thought.

He decided to find the source of the reek regardless of the consequences. He inhaled deeply through his mouth and climbed the rest of the way up the hill. He came over the crest dripping wet. The source of the scent was close. Up here, it was ten times as pungent. He scrunched up his nose. He looked around, rated the view, but elected to go on. There were too many trees in the way to see very much. He stepped through a mess of blown down branches feeling the force of the lightning exploding in the sky. He watched in awe. A few steps further, Graham found the source of the stench polluting the countryside.

"Oh, crap!" JT Keroack exclaimed. He slapped the blunt he and Keith were smoking out of his brother's hand. He grimaced, his braces glinting.

"Ow!" Keith cried, the burning head landing on his wrist. He slapped it out. "Careful, JT! You burned me!"

JT lifted his younger brother off the log he was sitting on and spun him around. Keith gasped when he saw Graham. He didn't know him, but he felt like he was in deep trouble just the same. Keith knew sneaking out was colossally stupid, but he couldn't resist. Getting stoned in a thunderstorm was the coolest. He was already grounded forever, so what did it matter? Keith hadn't worried about getting caught until now.

"Who are you?" JT asked. His parents ignored his pot smoking, but would wreck him if he got caught.

Graham walked over and looked closely at the taller boy's lips. The rain blurred his vision. He motioned for JT to repeat what he said.

JT rolled his hazel eyes. "What are you? Deaf?" he asked.

"Yes," Graham replied. "I'm Graham."

"His voice sounds funny," Keith remarked, relaxing a bit. He looked for the blunt and sighed when he found it. It was floating in a puddle.

"That's because he can't hear, man," JT remarked, introducing himself and his brother. He spoke very slowly.

Graham shook hands with them. "Just talk regular," he nodded. "I can read your lips. You don't have to talk slow."

"We thought you were a nark," Keith said.

"A nark?" Graham asked, cocking his head.

"A cop, or something," JT corrected.

"That's not me," Graham said. Now he knew why they looked so worried. "That's my dad."

JT and Keith gasped.

Graham laughed, "Don't worry. My older brother smokes pot. I don't, but I won't tell on you."

"Thank God!" Keith cried. "I'm in enough crap…"

A woman's scream pierced the darkness. They heard it over the thunder. The brothers looked at each other. JT hollered, "C'mon!" sprinting toward Mary Circle. Keith moved to follow. His brother's long legs were sure to leave him behind if he wasn't quick. Graham grabbed his arm. He asked what was wrong.

"A woman screamed!" Keith exclaimed. He started to run. He pulled Graham to come with him.

"That way?" he asked, nervously pointing toward his house. *Oh, God! It can't be the knock!*

"That way!" Keith replied, pointing farther down. "Let's go!"

They ran down the hill together. They could barely see JT up ahead. Graham took the lead. The sudden rush of adrenaline made Keith very lightheaded. He held on to the back of Graham's Patriots raincoat. They caught up to JT quickly. He was vomiting in the bushes. Keith thought it was the stink all around them that had made his brother sick. It smelled like a skunk squished in the middle of the road on a hot summer day. Graham's expression told Keith otherwise. His face turned white. Keith followed his gaze to the O'Connor's front door.

"I'm stoned," Keith whispered, his dinner threatening to come up.

Terry Greer was on the O'Connors' front porch, his eyes gouged out, his slashed throat wagging in the wind. He was stabbing Brandy O'Connor, an obese woman in her mid-thirties, repeatedly with a large kitchen knife. She was against the doorjamb trying to scream again, but Terry had severed her vocal cords. Two additional boys held her husband, Charles, Todd's father, on the sidewalk. Every time he struggled to move, the smaller boy punched him in the balls. Keith and Graham watched in horror as Terry rammed the knife into Brandy's stomach. She fell on the porch, her eyes wide with confusion, and died. Charles wailed.

"Shut up!" Terry screamed. *"Did you know Hiram Milliken's been molesting your son for years? Your wife did! Did you know the farmer murdered Todd tonight?"*

Terry kicked him in the face before they ran away leaving Charles alive. Keith watched, frozen in horror, as the dead kids dashed right past them. He took one look at Terry's destroyed face and puked in the bushes next to his brother. Graham held his nose. The stench of death nearly overwhelmed him. JT wiped his mouth. He stared at Charles shocked as he crawled up the steps toward his dead wife.

"C'mon!" JT cried, yanking at Graham and Keith. "We have to follow them!"

"Are you crazy!?" Keith cried, slapping his hand away. He spat to the side and asked, "Did you see his face?"

"Dead face!" Graham cried.

"Do you want to let them get away?" JT snapped, shaking his brother. "What if they get into Rainbow West, man? What about mom?"

"We have to," Graham insisted, terror making him shake, "so we can tell the police where they are. My dad's on a call tonight in town somewhere. It's probably because of them."

They ran after the zombies.

"Jesus, man!" Keith cried, tears threatening. He glanced back at the O'Connors' residence. "Look at all the blood!"

Graham hoped, as they followed the killers toward Wickett Avenue, that they weren't making the biggest mistake of their young lives.

*　　*　　*

The fourth ambulance to arrive on the scene at Mike's house was from Ellington. Stafford and Tolland were already there, the E.M.T.s helping Larry Singleton field dress the wounded. Robert was the only injured party to regain consciousness so far, but Shooter ordered him taken to the hospital with the others. There had to be something wrong with him, a head injury or maybe a concussion. Robert had convinced Shooter of this when he stumbled over to where he had been interrogating the boys. He fell into the detective's arms and said:

"Believe... them. It's... true."

Shooter held him up and called, "E.M.T! Get this man on a stretcher!" He thought, *Oh, the walking dead, right?*

Shooter couldn't believe they had attempted to insult his intelligence like that. The boys were handcuffed and locked in the back of his car. The redhead with the broken wrist had wailed and kicked, but he got no mercy. The unconscious one, the millionaire's son, was in the first ambulance. He was in bad shape, so Shooter let him go for the moment. There would be a complaint filed against him over the hot-tempered redhead, but Shooter didn't care. They were prime suspects in a multiple murder case especially with some of the weapons in their possession. Shooter wasn't taking any chances.

Hand grenades? Shooter angrily thought. *Kids today can get their hands on anything!*

They were involved and that was good enough for him. If they were even remotely capable of the carnage he had witnessed, they were a danger to public safety.

473

A barrage of shots rang out. The officers on the scene drew their weapons and sought cover next to the cars. Shooter waited, straining his ears to hear over the storm. It came again, automatic weapon fire. He pinpointed the direction. Ricci said the street was named Bog Dancer Drive. Shooter was a weapons expert. If those shots weren't coming from an M4A1 Carbine assault rifle, he would eat his Beretta. He opened his car door and ordered McMahon and Ricci to follow him. He glanced at the boys in the back seat, cursed, and slammed the car into gear.

"Stay down," Shooter barked, pointing at them in the mirror.

"What's going on?" Matt asked, straining to adjust his handcuffed arms.

"Gunshots," Ricardo replied, trying to scrunch lower in the seat. "It's Jack," he added, recognizing the sound. He glanced over at Derek who winced in pain and sobbed. He asked, "Are you okay?"

"No!" Derek hollered, his face contorting. His wrist felt like it was on fire. *"See if I ever tell the truth again!"*

"Shut up back there!" Shooter ordered, turning right onto Bog Dancer Drive.

"Drop dead!" Ricardo cried. "Let us out of this car before you get us killed!"

"No chance!" Shooter snapped, looking in the rearview mirror. "You're the only suspects I've got! You don't expect me to believe your bullshit story about…?"

"Look out!" Matt cried.

Shooter slammed on his brakes. The car slid sideways. Derek screamed as the other boys fell against him. The car stopped. They scrambled to get off him. The patrolmen following put their vehicles nose to nose blocking the road. They turned on their spotlights, their strobes flashing.

Shooter stared out the windshield. "Holy mother!" he gasped. "What the hell is that?"

"That," Ricardo replied, "is our bullshit story, estúpido."

Shooter couldn't believe his eyes. A little boy was standing in the middle of the road with an M4 Carbine assault rifle emptying his clip into another boy who danced a bullet-ridden jig on the front lawn of one of the houses. The victim fell lifeless onto the wet grass. An old woman was beating a boy with a broom handle raging volumes of profanity. Still, another was trying to hold on to a smaller kid who squirmed and twisted trying to get away.

"Teddy!" Chris exclaimed. "Stay with me!"

Shooter leaped out of the car. He leveled his pistol aiming at Jack. "Drop the rifle!" he ordered. *"Now!"*

Ricci opened Shooter's passenger door and aimed as McMahon radioed for back up.

"Are you crazy!?" Jack cried, glaring at Shooter. "Don't aim at me, moron! Aim at them!"

"Who?" Shooter snapped. "The kid you just shot to death? Put down the gun, little boy, before I blow your head off!"

The bullet-ridden dead boy on the lawn sat up. Shooter's heart leapt into his throat. Nancy continued to battle in her driveway. The zombie grabbed hold of the broom handle. She wrestled him for it, kicking him and biting his hand. It snapped from the stress. Kevin and Cynthia Mellon ran out of their house with Douggie behind them. Cynthia ordered him back, but he ignored her. The Mellons ran over to Nancy's driveway, but stopped short as the boy on the lawn climbed to his feet. He grinned at them, and then at Shooter and Ricci. Pus was leaking from the bullet holes in his chest. He looked down and shook his head.

"Let him keep his toy, officer," David Leech said. *"For all the good it will do him, or you!"*

Shooter and Ricci slowly adjusted their aim toward him.

McMahon screamed. They spun around in time to see him swarmed by four zombies who had come out of the woods. Shooter and Ricci ran back. McMahon was fighting as hard as he could, punching a boy repeatedly. Shooter grabbed the first zombie he came to and ripped him off the officer. It was Sam. Shooter gagged at the stinking pus-filled hole in his chest. He saw his heart. It wasn't beating. Sam tried to bite him. Shooter pressed his pistol to Sam's temple and pulled the trigger.

A chunk of his skull flew away. Pus and gore blasted out of the side of Sam's head. Sam laughed. Shooter shoved him, the world starting to spin. He grabbed McMahon and Ricci and dragged them back to his car. Cynthia screamed as Nancy plunged the broken end of the broom handle into her opponent's eye. He reached up, grabbed her by the throat, and pulled her down to the tar. He rolled on top of her and yanked the stick out of his head with a loud pop. He raised it into the air.

"No!" Jack screamed, running toward him.

David stepped into his path. Jack pulled the trigger on the assault rifle, but it was empty. He threw it away balling up his fists.

"Why stop us, Jack?" David asked, quickly holding his hand up.

"Jack?" Nancy asked, looking over. "Oh, my God! *Jackie!?"*

"Get away from her, you bastards!" Chris cried.

"Stay out of this, McKee!" Sam hollered. He walked past Shooter and the patrolmen. They gagged at his stench, but did nothing to stop him.

"Yeah!" the boy holding Nancy echoed. He sneered at Cynthia. *"You get back, too!"* He held the jagged end of the stick to Nancy's face. *"I'll kill her. Move!"*

Cynthia backed into her husband. Kevin wrapped his arms around her from behind. He was on the verge of a breakdown. Douggie stood next to Chris opposite Teddy, his arms locked around his leg.

"That's right," David nodded. One of his teeth fell out as he spoke. *"Nobody moves. This is Jack's big moment of truth."*

475

"Let go of my mother!" Jack spat.

David shoved him back. Jack snapped David's hand off trying to flip him. He looked at it dumbly and tossed it aside. It landed by Douggie who started to screech. Chris kicked it away and slapped his hand over Douggie's mouth, pulling him against Teddy. Derek was in the back of Shooter's car trying frantically to get his mother's attention. Cynthia was hysterical and couldn't hear him over the storm.

David held up his stump and shook his head. *"Look what you did, Jack,"* he sneered. *"I only wanted to tell you the truth."*

"About what?" Jack snapped, circling him, his hands working. *The gym bag is on the lawn if I can get to it.*

"About her," David replied. He gestured at Nancy. *"About Hiram. She knew, Jack. Did you know that? She knew what the farmer was doing to you and she didn't do a thing to stop him. She has to pay. Her, the farmer, and the witch. They're all to blame."*

"Liar!" Jack exclaimed. The bag was beneath his feet.

"Tell him!" the dead boy holding Nancy snapped, dragging the jagged edge of the broom handle against her cheek. Nancy cried out as the stick tore into her face. *"Tell him the truth or I'll cut your eyeball out!"*

"Leave her alone!" Cynthia screamed, diving toward him. Kevin grabbed her and yanked her back.

The dead boy spun around with the broken end of the handle. He dove off Nancy and stabbed it into Cynthia's chest. It went through her and into Kevin. Cynthia felt a flash of pain and slowly looked down. Her eyes grew wide with surprise. She felt Kevin go limp. His weight pulled them both over. They hit the ground sideways. Cynthia shuddered and stopped breathing. The Mellons died staked together on Nancy's front lawn.

"Oh, my God!" Teddy cried.

Derek and Douggie screamed, *"Mom!"*

Nancy rolled away, got to her feet, and ran toward the wide-mouthed officers. Jack grabbed a grenade, pulled the pin, and slammed it into David's pus-filled stomach.

He dove for cover screaming, *"Die!"*

Only it didn't go off. David pulled it out and dropped it on the ground. He was about to laugh when the officers broke their shock and opened fire. The dead boys scrambled for the woods behind Nancy's house.

"This isn't over, Dougan!" Sam called, his voice echoing all around them. *"We'll take the witch first! We'll come back for your mother! That's a promise!"*

"Go to hell!" Jack yelled, grabbing his rifle. "Do you hear me? All of you!"

Nancy looked at her son and started screaming. McMahon gently led her away. Shooter, his hands shaking like crazy, called Chris over. He handed him the keys to the handcuffs and motioned toward his car. Douggie held his leg, wailing. Teddy pulled him away and hugged him, his expression shocked and grieving. Chris opened the back door and set Matt free. Matt undid the others while Chris tried to help Teddy calm Douggie. Derek ran straight for his dead parents and threw his arms around them.

"Why did you stop her!?" he wailed, slapping his father's corpse.

Chris handed Teddy and Douggie to Ricardo and went to Derek. He reached out for him. Derek jumped into his arms. Chris held him in the rain, his cries louder than the thunder.

*　　*　　*

Max and Craig had been approaching Grady Lane when they heard the shots. They doubled their speed, running across the street to the barbed wire fence. They climbed over it, carefully. Max followed as Craig led him to Jeremy who was lying naked in the pasture surrounded by mooing cows. One of them was licking Jeremy's face. Max shooed her away. Craig knelt next to his best friend's head. Jeremy was as pale as a sheet.

"Is he all right?" Max asked, removing his basketball shorts. He was wearing Chicago Bulls boxers beneath them. Craig helped him put them on Jeremy.

"I'm not sure," Craig replied, wiping the rain from Jeremy's face.

The mind-link was alive with hundreds of whispering voices. Craig knew Jeremy was trying to keep him from hearing them, but this close it was impossible. They jumped hearing screams from Bog Dancer Drive. Max looked at Craig with urgency. Craig shook his unconscious friend.

"Jeremy? Wake up, okay?" Through the mind-link, Craig yelled, *"Jeremy!"*

"Ow!" Jeremy groaned, stirring. *"Not so... loud, Bullhorn-Dougan."*

"You're okay!" Max exclaimed, but then gasped when Jeremy opened his eyes. They were glowing with powerful midnight blue energy. *"¡Dios mío!"*

"Give me... a hand," Jeremy whispered, struggling to stand.

His voice boomed into the pasture and inside their heads at the same time. Max winced. It felt like Jeremy had reached into his skull. They helped him up.

"Lord, what happened to you?" Max asked, staring wide-eyed at him.

"Not... sure," Jeremy replied, appearing exhausted. He shook his head. *"Voices... in my head. Thoughts not... mine. Sleep. I'm making them... sleep... but... I'm trying to... get everyone. Missed the Mellons, damn it... There was... a little boy in... my dream. Giuseppe... the witch."*

"Ms. Adler?" Craig asked, getting under his arm to steady him.

"Yes," Jeremy said. He strained, concentrating. *"Get me... to... the road... no time."*

"Maybe you should rest, man," Max suggested, holding him steady.

"No!" Jeremy cried. Craig cringed at the volume. ***"The… road. There… isn't… time to argue."***

Max and Craig held him on either side and helped him walk. It took forever. Jeremy kept falling. His eyes glowed brighter the closer they got to Grady Lane. It guided them around the cow pies. The light grew even stronger as Jeremy reached out in every direction with his mind.

"Chris… Jack… Derek," Jeremy gasped, touching each of their minds with his power. ***"Detective Shooter… I need you… right now!"***

✻   ✻   ✻

Marianna sighed deliberately loudly as she placed a cold compress on Ms. Adler's forehead. Her husband didn't miss her disdain. José was standing by the kitchen sink looking out the side window. He paused and cringed before opening his beer. The first words out of his wife's mouth when he appeared at the door carrying their surprise houseguest were straight and to the point.

"Other husbands bring home stray dogs or cats! Mine brings home stray women!"

José set Ms. Adler on the sofa. Marianna insisted they call her a doctor. There was blood all over the back of her head and in her hair.

José shook his head. "She asked me not to," he replied.

"What do you suggest we do then?" Marianna snapped in Spanish. "Keep her here?"

José looked over her wounds and determined they weren't serious. He said, "What's the harm in letting the woman lie down? I'm sure she'll wake soon. I can convince her to go to the hospital. Why cause a fuss in the meantime?"

That reasoning seemed logical. It had come to him while he was helping Ms. Adler out of her car. He had been surprised enough to find her there. It was funny now that José thought about it. Ms. Adler had spoken to him in Spanish. He was glad it wasn't a service problem. He didn't want to do any mechanic work. It had been a dark day for every family in Lancaster with Thomas McKee's untimely death. It was a night to turn in early. As he carried Ms. Adler to his house, José had failed to notice Hiram Milliken. The farmer was watching them from the side of the garage.

Marianna mumbled something about Ms. Adler resting when she came into the kitchen. She sat at the table slicing plantains. She was making tostones and rice & beans for the boys' dinner tomorrow if they came home. She had decided to let them stay at the McKees longer if they wished. Chris and Jeremy were good friends to her children. She was thankful for them.

José gulped his beer and swallowed. He saw past the yard to their northwest property border. Marianna jumped when lightning exploded nearby.

478

José laughed a little, but made the sign of the cross. *That was awfully close,* he thought. *Too close for comfort.* He paused in mid-sip when the lightning flashed again. He leaned over the sink and peered through the glass. *Are my eyes deceiving me? No, there really are three boys coming into our yard! One of them looks like Mona Keroack's kid, Keith, I think. Oops! The tall one fell. I'll bet that smarted...*

Without warning, Terry Greer crashed through the kitchen window. José threw his hands up to shield himself from the glass. Terry landed on top of him knocking him backward. They hit the table. Marianna screamed and fell sideways onto the floor. José struck his head. He was stunned, but still conscious. Marianna felt something cold and clammy grab her wrist and slip the knife out of her hand. She looked into Terry's grinning ghoulish face. She gazed into his empty eye sockets and smelled his awful stench. Marianna was shocked, but she didn't scream until she saw his neck. His esophagus was hanging out wiggling. Her scream exploded right into his skeletal grin.

"Scared you!" Terry exclaimed, and burst out laughing.

"Stop screwing around, Greer!" Sam snapped, climbing through the shattered pane. *"Find the witch!"*

"No need," Ms. Adler said, from the kitchen doorway. Her eyes were glowing. She latched on to them with her telekinesis. *"I have found you!"*

José opened his eyes.

Ms. Adler whipped her hand to the side and smashed both zombies through the front wall. The wall blasted out into the storm. Debris and broken wood sailed everywhere as they cut through an electrical wire in the framing. The lights flickered and died.

Terry and Sam careened through the air. They smacked onto the pavement in the middle of Wickett Avenue. Ms. Adler sarcastically thanked José for his hospitality, her eyes shining in the darkness. She rose off the floor and floated out of the hole in the wall after them. She glided across the yard and settled in the road. The zombies jumped up. José pulled Marianna to him. They watched as more of the walking dead surrounded her.

"¡Ella es una bruja!" Marianna cried.

"No doubt about that," José whispered.

JT, Keith, and Graham were going to rush the house when they saw Terry smash through the window. They had agreed to try and stop them if they attacked anyone else. Their good intentions were put on hold when seconds later the killers crashed through the front wall and sailed into the street. The Hill Witch flew out after them. JT was glad for the death-stench permeating the area. A long-held family secret was his lack of bladder control. He even had an alarm on his nightstand that woke him up if he started to wet his bed. He just finished his junior year of high school and it was embarrassing, but when JT saw of Ms. Adler floating through the air? He had pissed his pants.

"Holy Jesus!" Keith cried. "That's the Hill Witch!"

"Who?" Graham asked, not sure he read those words correctly. *Did he say witch?*

"I'll tell you later," Keith replied, tugging his brother and Graham closer to the road. "C'mon, you guys! This I've got to see!"

Ms. Adler scowled at the dead boys, curling up her nose at their stink. She prepared for their imminent attack. She stayed in the middle of Wickett Avenue, spinning around in the pouring rain, keeping all of them in sight. She wasn't making that mistake again. Lightning exploded nearby. She cringed and prepared to deflect it if necessary. She sighed relief when it struck too far away to affect her. The boys snatched at her and retreated. They were taunting her. They howled and spat, screaming profanity over the thunder. The rain flowed off their bodies carrying their gore to the sides of the road. JT reached out to touch some of it, but Graham stopped him.

"Are you sure you want to do that?" he asked. "It smells terrible!"

"Yeah," Keith agreed, scrunching up his nose, "and on top of everything else, somebody reeks like piss."

Grrr! JT thought, his face flushing.

Ms. Adler turned toward the police cars flying up Grady Lane. There were three sets of flashing red and blue lights. They hung a left, tires squealing, and headed straight for her. They stopped ten yards away and blocked off the road, their spotlights blaring.

Graham silently cheered and cried, *"The Cavalry's here!"*

The doors flew open. Shooter jumped out leveling his pistol. Jack popped out of the passenger's side. He sighted in Ms. Adler with his assault rifle. McMahon joined him and Ricci joined Shooter. Matt, Max, Ricardo, Chris, Douggie, and Derek filed out of the patrol cars. Craig came out last helping Jeremy walk. Jeremy reached out for Derek to steady him. Derek's face contorted with terror. He slapped Jeremy's hand away.

"Don't touch me!" Derek screamed, his face bright red. "Do you hear me!? *Monster!* You're a monster!"

Max stepped angrily forward.

Jeremy stopped him. ***"It's okay, Max,"*** he sadly said and projected. ***"He's just scared. I would be, too."***

Chris grabbed Derek who fell into him, his knees buckling. Whatever he said had to be ignored right now. Derek had lost his entire world this week. He was entitled to vent some rage.

Shooter watched Craig help Jeremy walk out in front of them. He wasn't sure about what had happened over on Bog Dancer Drive, but this voice appeared in their heads. When it did, Derek went psycho. Chris had to hold him on the ground until it went away. Shooter knew what he had to do though and so did the others. They jumped into the patrol cars, picked up three other boys, and headed here. The Dougan woman stayed behind. She had run into her house and slammed the door when the mind-voice appeared. Shooter guessed he should be glad someone had a plan of action. It was against his better judgment, but he held his ground and waited for Jeremy to tell him what to do next. It scared him to feel so out of control, but the kid was the only one who seemed to know what he was doing.

"Is that Jeremy McKee?" JT asked, straining to see through the police spotlights.

Keith gasped, "Look at his eyes!"

Jeremy and Craig stopped a safe distance from the dead boys and Ms. Adler. They observed her cautiously. She sneered at them, her eyes narrowing. No one moved. The zombies shifted in indecision. Craig opened his mind to the information swimming in Jeremy's head. He found it easy to hate her. She snorted hearing that thought. She stepped toward them, but the dead boys blocked her path. She sighed, shaking her head.

"So," Ms. Adler sneered. *"Now you know."* She glanced around raising an eyebrow. *"I am surprised the whole town is not here beside you."*

"They're sleeping thanks," Jeremy said. His voice was venomous. **"Enough people are dead because of you."**

The inhabitants of every house in town were asleep. Stoves were shut off and showers interrupted, everyone filled with the overwhelming desire to take a nap. Jeremy had spared only those in imminent danger or people out in the storm. The zombies were draining his strength to function, so he could do precious little else. Jeremy had taken the time to learn what happened to him, what he was, and how to use the power. Ms. Adler was a fountain of information. He had picked her brain while she slept. He didn't care much for what he found out.

Jeremy leaned into Craig, **"And you're wrong. I don't know everything. Not yet."** He asked, **"Why did you do this to me?"**

Ms. Adler laughed. *"The creation demands answers from its creator?"*

"I can make you tell me," Jeremy said. **"You gave me the power. Telepathy, telekinetics, healing… I can kick some serious ass. Making it work is mostly instinct, like I always knew how, I just didn't have the power. I found your experience pretty helpful. I can kick the crap out of you if you make me."**

Jeremy was talking and mind-speaking in every direction at the same time. Everyone present felt his angry words in their heads.

"Really?" Ms. Adler cried, acting surprised. Lightning struck by the high school. She jumped.

So did Craig. *"I felt that!"* he cried, through the mind-link.

Jeremy nodded. He said to his former teacher, **"There are lots of people in town with interesting memories of you, especially the ones you manipulated. Bea Jones? Dr. Stone? Susan Sturgess? I let them have their memories back. It was pretty simple. I just imagined it happening and it did. I gave them back their pain. Do you know how hurt they're going to be when they wake up tomorrow? And Old Ted Collins? He's your godfather, right? I think he can say your name again."**

"Silence, you pitiful bastard!" Ms. Adler raged. *"Do not speak of that to me!"*

Jeremy ignored her. ***"I watched his memories of the day you murdered your father. I'd like to know why you did that."***

"Hah!" Ms. Adler spat. *"You know nothing!"*

"Maybe not," Jeremy shrugged. His eyes flashed with a pulse of pure thought energy. Everyone felt it ripple through the air. ***"Why don't you tell me. I know how to read you. You can't stop me."***

"Do not bet your life on it!" Ms. Adler exclaimed, balling up her fists. *"Power is no substitute for experience! Knowing how to use it and using it effectively are two different things! You may have gleaned experience from my mind, but you have yet to apply it! You... will... lose!"*

"Nobody move," Jeremy said, and projected to everyone in range. ***"She's mine."***

The dead boys froze as his eyes burst forth incredible brilliance. Ms. Adler stumbled back, her hands on the sides of her head.

She screamed, *"Get out of my mind!"*

"I want you to tell me why you did this to me!" Jeremy demanded. ***"I want to know why you made me a freak!"***

"I will tell you... nothing!" Ms. Adler cried, falling to one knee. *"Telepathy is not... my only power!"*

She reached out with both hands and lowered her head. The pavement started to bend and shift. It shook beneath them violently until they couldn't keep their footing. Everyone fell onto the blacktop except Jeremy and Craig. They were floating six inches above the ground.

Ms. Adler looked up and gasped.

Jeremy's eyes narrowed. ***"My turn."***

He balled up his fists and thrust them out in front of him. A shockwave exploded from his hands and tore into the street. Chunks of tar and dirt shot out as the wave plowed through the zombies and struck Ms. Adler. The zombies launched away from the epicenter. Ms. Adler cried out as the force sent her flying into one of Ramirezes' weeping willow trees. She crashed into it with a loud crack and fell to the ground, dazed. Everyone cheered.

Jeremy glared at his hands in amazement.

Craig did, too. "Wow," he said.

"No kidding," Jeremy agreed.

"Hey!" Craig exclaimed. "Make her a kid like you did to my dad!"

Jeremy frowned. ***"I can't do that anymore for some reason."***

"Duh," Sam said, the first zombie to recover. *"We're not inside you anymore. You can't add our strength to yours."* He laughed. *"What do you think having all of our spirits inside you did? It amped you up by a thousand. You're not that powerful by yourself."*

"Maybe," Jeremy shrugged.

He swung his arm in Sam's direction picturing a fist of telekinetic force in his mind. It shot forth, his thoughts becoming reality. He felt it as it struck Sam on the chin with a dull smack. Sam sailed into the side of Ms. Adler's Mercedes. He crushed in the driver's side door worse than it already was and shattered the window. He fell to the ground in a heap.

Jeremy nodded. *"I can still kick your ass, Stone."*

Ms. Adler levitated to the road, her face drawn back in a snarl. *"This is not over, boy!"*

She threw her hands out in a circle. The debris from Jeremy's shockwave rose up and flew straight for him and Craig. A hundred rock missiles charged toward their heads. Craig cried out. Jeremy made a lifting gesture. The blacktop tore up from the ground in front of them forming a ten-foot high wall, intercepting the attack. Jeremy lowered his hands. The road dropped with a crunch.

"Nice try," Jeremy said. *"I'm starting to get the hang of this."* He leaned toward her. *"Let's rumble! I want to know what you are!"*

Jeremy lashed out with his telepathy again, diving into her mind with his battering ram non-subtlety. There was no grace, no finesse, he simply crashed into her brain. Ms. Adler fought back, marshaling her psychic defenses, but Jeremy smashed through them with ease. She tried to force him out of her mind, but he only probed deeper. He ripped through her, digging for her memories. She was hiding them, but something was there, something she wanted. The closer he got to knowing, the harder she fought. She tried to flood his mind with horrific visions designed to make him withdraw. He witnessed each boy's death as Hiram murdered them. She made him feel their pain. Craig felt it, too, and fell to his knees. Jeremy threw them back at her magnified by a factor of ten. Ms. Adler screamed at the horror.

In the middle of his attack, Jeremy became confused. She was weakening, he could feel it, and she was furious, yet she was elated at the same time. She was in awe of him, but she wanted to crush him. Then something inexplicable happened. Jeremy heard a woman calling out, begging him to save her. He realized the truth as he absorbed Ms. Adler's life experience. He got it in a single blinding flash of revelation from the two distinctly different minds inside her body.

"Oh, man!" Jeremy cried. *"There's two of you in there!"*

A moment's distraction was all the time Ms. Adler needed. Her face tightened with supreme effort. *"You want memories?"* she cried. *"Take theirs, in spades!"*

She caught him off balance as she charged into his mind releasing the power within him like flipping a switch. Jeremy's telepathy roared to life, obeying her command. It reached out without any control. Jeremy and Craig fell to the ground, grabbing their heads. Jeremy felt a tidal wave of thoughts heading right for him from every direction. He tried desperately to stop them, but he couldn't. The power was a raging rabid wild animal.

Jeremy panicked as the mind-link with Craig overloaded and expanded. Instantly, he locked minds with Graham, JT, and Keith. Everything they knew, their secrets, everything about them flooded into him all at once. They cried out with him as their souls were ripped wide open. He locked on to Chris, Matt, Douggie... all of his friends, and then Jack. Their minds joined his and scrambled together inside him until he was a living mass of chaos. Jeremy couldn't tell what piece of which belonged to whom. He let out a bloodcurdling scream in his communal mind-voice. Shooter, José, Marianna, McMahon, and Ricci watched in horror as the kids fell to the ground. They rolled around, groveling and drooling. They twitched and convulsed, their eyes flashing wildly in all directions.

Ms. Adler lowered to the ground. *"Foolish child!"* she cried, throwing her head back and laughing. *"Your inexperience gives me victory!"*

José took a step forward from the porch.

Marianna grabbed his hand. She said, "Don't even think about it."

"Aren't you forgetting something?" Sam asked, tapping Ms. Adler on the shoulder.

The zombies swarmed her, ripping her skin, tearing at her hair. Terry bit her breast. Sam tried to strangle her. They felt drunk with the savagery, on the verge of revenge when she fought back.

"Get off me!" Ms. Adler cried, bucking up.

The zombies were thrown back by her telekinetics landing on the road. Terry got to his feet and charged her. She caught him one-handed by the throat.

"Do you really... think you can... stop us?" Terry choked.

"Child's play," Ms. Adler spat.

Her eyes beamed. Her power filled him. He expanded like a balloon. Terry's body puffed out from his head to his feet growing wider and wider.

"Oh, no!" he cried.

Terry exploded. Stinking guts and pus splashed onto the street. Ms. Adler watched comically as the storm washed him away. Jeremy felt the drain on his power cease a bit with Terry's destruction. Slowly, delicately, he reached out to his friends. He whispered soothing calm words and told them not to fight. He said to hold on to him. Everyone did except Derek. Jeremy forced him to having no time to argue. They opened themselves to him, found trust inside, and dared to risk everything. They felt him inside of them, too, fighting to keep them sane.

Ms. Adler turned toward the stunned zombies. Blood dripped down her forehead from a missing patch of hair. Her lips twisted back, grotesquely. She waved her hand and lifted them off the ground. They raged in protest, but she held them in the air, squishing them tightly together.

"You children smell terrible," she remarked. *"Time for a bath."*

She glanced toward the gas station. Hiram ducked down inside the repair bay. He fought hard to shut off his thoughts and hide from her, but he didn't have to. She wasn't even looking. The gas pump handle lifted snapping Carl Gibbons' padlock. The hose snaked through the air. Ms. Adler winked at it. The handle compressed. Gasoline shot out of the nozzle.

"Get in the house!" José cried, dragging Marianna through the doorway.

The pressure wasn't enough to spray across the street, so she helped it along. A river of fuel shot through the air dousing Sam first. She filled his mouth with it and soaked his clothes. She did the same with the others, lowering them to the ground as she drowned them in gasoline. They writhed and fought against her hold, but it was too strong. When the gas started saturating the ground, she released the handle and put it back into its carriage.

"We'll still be here!" Sam raged. *"This won't end it!"*

Ms. Adler shook her head and mentally drew an incendiary grenade out of Jack's gym bag. It flew through the air into her hand. She caught it, pulled the pin with her teeth, and spat it out.

"Goodbye, boys," Ms. Adler sneered. *"Have a delightful death."*

She tossed the grenade over her shoulder. The safety snapped free. The grenade landed right in Sam's crotch.

"No!" they screamed.

There was a flash of light and heat as they exploded into flame. A fireball shot into the night sky. It set nearby treetops on fire, but the torrential rain put them out quickly. Jeremy felt the drain on his power suddenly end as a rush of energy returned to him. His vision cleared and he saw Ms. Adler walking toward him. He heard the boys in his head cry out for him to stop her, but he couldn't, not yet. Their thoughts were entwined, their minds scrambled. If he didn't put them back together where they belonged, who knew what would happen? She was coming for him now. If he didn't stop her, he was dead.

Jeremy faced a choice, him or his friends. He chose his friends. Craig lent him every ounce of strength he had left, and so did the others. Jeremy took the mind damaged the worst first and repaired Graham Shooter. Graham cried inside. He knew the level of sacrifice being made for him by someone he didn't even know.

Ms. Adler reached down for Jeremy, grinning.

Shooter shot her through the heart.

Ms. Adler stumbled back, grabbing her chest, her eyes wide with surprise. A chunk of her back fell out of her shirt onto the wet ground.

"No way are you touching that kid!" Shooter cried, and shot her again.

McMahon and Ricci followed his lead. Ms. Adler fell, a bullet shattering her kneecap. She landed on top of Jeremy. Panic filled her as death approached. She thrust a desperate command into Jeremy's distracted mind. His hand latched on to her wrist. She forced his healing power to save her life. Shooter and the officers approached quickly, their guns level. Ms. Adler snapped her head up, her eyes wildly glowing. She broke all thirty of their fingers at once. They fell to their knees crying out in agony as their pistols dropped to the blacktop.

"Enough!" she screamed, thrusting her hand out. They flew away from her, careening off the hood of Shooter's car. She whirled around and grabbed Jeremy by the neck, hoisting him up. *"No more games! I want what is mine!"*

Graham shook his head as he struggled to stand. The witch was attacking Jeremy. Light bathed them as Jeremy jerked and spasmed frantically trying to save his friends before she finished him off. The other kids writhed and moaned all around. They were going to die if Jeremy couldn't get their minds pieced back together. Jeremy McKee, a kid he didn't even know, was sacrificing himself to save them all.

Graham's mind reeled from the terror of what had just happened. His entire life had been torn wide open for Jeremy to see, but he sensed Jeremy's soul throughout the experience. Graham felt his goodness, his love for his friends, his selflessness, and now he was going to die at the hands of the woman Keith had called the Hill Witch?

I'm not going to let that happen! Graham thought.

He didn't know what Jeremy and the witch were, but he knew enough to see who the bad guy was. He shoved his fear down. He dove into Ms. Adler, knocked her down, and landed on top of her trying to hold her. Ms. Adler glared up at him, her face twisting with outrage. Graham actually heard her screaming at him in his mind.

"You are going to wish you did not do that!"

"Oh, God," Shooter whispered, his fingers dangling. *"Graham!"*

Ms. Adler lifted Graham into the air with her telekinetics as she stood. He floated away from her toward the garage. Shooter charged them, but Ms. Adler slammed him face first onto the pavement. She turned back to Graham, following him as he glided backward through the air. Her eyes flashed. Graham screamed as his collarbones snapped. They shot upward, jagged and sharp, piercing his skin. Blood ran down his chest. Then she broke his legs. She broke his arms. She broke his face. She broke every bone in his body except his spine so he could feel everything. Blood flowed from his nose. She spat at him. Graham burst into tears at the incredible agony.

Ms. Adler whipped her hand to the side. Graham whipped through the air. He crashed through the garage bay door and landed at Hiram's feet, unconsciousness mercifully claiming him. Hiram reached out, his hand quivering as he touched Graham's bloody body. Ms. Adler drew Jeremy to her, dragging him across the ground. The pavement scraped his legs and chest with long wounds that healed instantly. He struggled desperately to finish with his friends before she killed him.

"Your friends are dead!" Ms. Adler snapped. She raised her hand and lifted him up with her power. He flipped over and hung in the air in front of her. *"I have waited a lifetime for this moment,"* she informed him, closing her eyes and concentrating. *"Let it end... at long last!"*

Jeremy felt a twinge like something had latched on to his essence. The slight tugging became a pull. Jeremy struggled against it realizing his danger. She was attempting to yank his spirit out of his body into hers.

"Why?" Jeremy gasped. *"Why... do you want... my soul?"*

Ms. Adler laughed. *"I never believed in the soul, child. I believed it was merely the energy of the mind. Of course, I have learned differently thanks to Hiram's little victims. It opens up a whole new world of research to me."* She squeezed her eyes closed tighter as she marshaled her will. *"As for you? I need to move you out of there. You are coming in here. I am going in there. There have been two of us inside this wretched female body long enough! I want out! I gave your body the power for my use, not yours. Günter Bremen will live again! Your body and the power inside it are mine!"*

Jeremy felt her mental energy building. He fought to hold himself and the others together, but he was losing. He couldn't concentrate on her without giving up on his friends, and he wouldn't do that. He couldn't! Ms. Adler focused the power she needed to rip his soul from his body. All of her years of planning had come down to this moment. In seconds, nothing would stop her from killing them all.

Jeremy scanned outward, desperately searching. *God? Help me! Please! Help me save my friends!*

His mind suddenly touched the vilest grotesque thoughts as he scanned Hiram. The farmer was leaning over Graham about to do unspeakable things to him.

Murderer! Jeremy thought, and knew he had found the answer.

Hiram reached down for Graham, his hands twitching. Jeremy latched on to his shoulders. He cried out, "What the...? *Let me go!"* as Jeremy pulled him through the air with his telekinetics. He sailed out of the garage bay. Ms. Adler opened her eyes prepared to claim what was hers, and Jeremy threw Hiram between them. Ms. Adler lashed out blindly, so desperate to finish this and so sure of her victory, she didn't bother to confirm whose soul she had grabbed. She screamed, *"Oh, no!"* as her power snagged Hiram's soul and tore it from his body. In a split second, she sucked him and everything he was into her.

Jeremy fell to the ground free from her hold. He scampered back dodging Hiram's limp form as it landed on its back. His dead eyes stared up at the sky in amazement. Jeremy looked at Ms. Adler. Her face contorted. Her eyes changed from brown to blue, to a paler shade of blue, and back again. She stumbled, grabbed her head, and cried out in three different voices.

"You fool! Don't...!

"What's going...?

"No! I am in control! I am...!

"Holy...! What did you do to me, you stupid...!

"Stop! You are setting her free!"

"You killed me? You idiot! I'll kill you!"

The dark blue eyes stayed. Margaret screamed and ran away, terrified. She ran through the garage parking lot and disappeared around the side of the building. Jeremy heard her cries getting farther away as Bremen and Hiram fought for control of her mind and body.

Jeremy brushed off and got shakily to his feet. He finished with his friends quickly now that he could focus, but the Herculean effort drained the remainder of his strength. He struggled to stay conscious. His friends groaned as they stood. Derek glared at him, terrified, but Jeremy ignored him. There was a more pressing task waiting for him in the garage bay. Graham Shooter, the real hero, was severely injured.

"Craig?" Jeremy asked, reaching out through the mind-link.

"Give me a second, okay?" Craig asked, his mind-voice shaky. *"I have to get my thoughts together."*

Jeremy nodded understanding. He stumbled toward the garage as he felt exhaustion claiming him. The world swam, images shifted, but he struggled on. Ambulances and cops were coming up Grady Lane, their sirens blaring. Jeremy scanned Graham as he approached him.

So brave, he thought sadly, touching his mind. *So loyal.*

Jeremy managed a weak smile before passing out and falling to the ground at Graham's feet.

*   *   *

Chris panicked as Jeremy's hand went limp in the back of the ambulance. Tears welled up in his eyes. Larry, who got one of the firemen to drive for him, checked his vital signs. Chris feared the worst. He didn't have any hope left in him. He didn't believe anything good could come from any of this.

Craig reached out and touched him on the forearm. "He's sleeping," he whispered.

Larry scowled. "Can I do my job, *doctor?"* he asked.

Jack was sitting next to Craig drowning in a sea of guilt. He accepted the blame for everything that had happened. A tear rolled down the side of his face. He looked away. He cursed his young body for its inability to hold in his emotions. One tear followed another. His whole body shook as he fought for control. It was a fight he lost.

Oh, God, Jack thought, the tears salty on his lips. The enormity of his new life was suddenly thrust upon him. *What did he do to me? What am I going to do now?*

Jack felt utterly alone. He was the twelve-year-old father of a fourteen-year-old boy. How would he get a job? Where would he go? With Mike? With his mother? Had she known about Hiram all of those years? Who would take care of Craig? In the beginning, it seemed like the best thing that ever happened to him. Would it end up the worst? It wasn't a blessing, was it? It was a punishment. Jack didn't know, but he felt genuine concern about his fate. David Leech's words about Nancy came back to him. He thrust them forcibly away.

Is it true? Did mom know?

"Jack?" Chris asked, sliding over next to him. "Are you all right?"

He's treating me like a kid, Jack thought. *And I am, but a boy with all of the life experiences of a grown man. I don't feel the same though!*

Everything Jack had experienced in his difficult life seemed like a scary movie he watched once. It wasn't part of him anymore, but it was close enough for him to touch. He didn't want to touch it. What a horrible man he had become! What a nightmare life he made for his son. He reached his arms around Chris and buried his face in his chest. He didn't want to be a man anymore. He wanted to be what he was, a boy who needed to be held very badly right now.

"Easy, Jack," Chris said, rubbing his back. "I'm here, okay? I'm here."

Craig was amazed at how easily his father slipped into Chris' arms, how desperately he needed to have the pain and fear hugged away. It was the part of his father he had always seen beneath the surface, the part of Jack he loved that everyone forgot was in there. It was the happy smiling boy in his grandmother's pictures, his deep green eyes so innocent. The boy who disappeared at the hands of a man who violated him. Hiram robbed the world and Craig of the Jack Dougan who might have been. Jeremy had given him back.

Craig would sacrifice everything for his father to have this new life. The affection Chris was showing him was genuine and unreserved. He thanked God for giving his family the gift of the McKees. It was as if they were created solely for making the Dougans whole. This was his sacrifice, to be the boy without a father. Like Jack, Craig wondered what would become of them now.

The rain fell harder. It partially obscured the ambulance behind them, its lights blurry in the darkness, its sirens silent. Robert Bigelow was back there with Teddy and Derek. Derek had refused to ride with Jeremy even after Chris asked him to. Craig frowned. He didn't share Derek's fear of Jeremy, but it was a fear shared by others. Max and Ricardo were frightened, too, but their friendship for Jeremy wouldn't let them abandon him. Matt – who had remained behind in Lancaster – had no fear, only a fascination with everything he had seen. Douggie rode with Ricardo and Max in the ambulance even farther back. It was the one they couldn't see through the storm any longer. Kate Pierce was there, too, with Graham Shooter.

That poor guy, Craig thought.

The pain wracking Graham from Ms. Adler's assault was almost more than he could take. He was holding on, but only barely.

"I guess I'm just a baby now, huh?" Jack sniffled, wiping his face with the back of his hand. It interrupted Craig's train of thought.

"No, Jack," Chris said. He thought about Sandy, his father, and the smoldering crater burning where his heart used to be. "Believe me, I need someone right now, too. You're going to need friends."

"Really?" Jack asked. "You want to be my friend? After everything I…?"

"I am your friend, Jack," Chris replied, "and don't worry, all right? We'll make it through this. The guy you used to be isn't here anymore."

Jack leaned his head against Chris' shoulder. "I can still hear him," he whispered, ominously.

"He'll go away," Chris said. "We'll make him."

Craig was startled as they barreled over a speed bump in the hospital driveway. He suddenly felt concern about Virginia. She was probably worried half out of her mind since they were no longer in their room. Jeremy stirred the instant that thought came into his best friend's mind. Craig assumed his friend had slipped from a peaceful sleep into a nightmare, but he didn't receive any images through the mind-link. That confused him. He glanced up and spotted the gaping hole in the top floor of the hospital. Sheets of plastic covering were flapping in the wind. Dread came over him. Craig closed his eyes and prayed as the ambulance came to a stop.

"Let's move it out," Larry said. "We have a long night ahead of us."

*　　*　　*

Nancy ran through the rain toward the Emergency Room door an hour later, holding her hand over the wound on her face. She passed a fresh line of ambulances unloading patients and corpses. The car accident that killed Thomas McKee had only been the beginning of their suffering today. She picked up her pace while the wind picked up her skirt. Her thoughts were paranoid and askew. She spotted Anna Bigelow coming toward her. She was dragging Teddy out of the hospital by his arm as he wailed in protest.

"I didn't call you to come and get me!" Teddy cried, pulling against her. "I called you so we could be here for dad! I want to stay with dad!"

Anna ignored him and dragged him toward the parking lot. Her face was black with anger. Teddy struggled until she finally stopped. She spun around and slapped him across the face. Teddy gasped and held his free hand to his cheek.

"I want to know everything that happened with Milliken," Anna snarled, jabbing her finger in his face. "You said something happened to you when you called me. I want to know what it is. Were you violated? Did he do something sexual to you? We're going home this instant and you're going to tell me! Now, get in the car!"

Tad watched fearfully from the backseat of his mother's pea green Toyota as she chucked Teddy in next to him. She climbed into the driver's seat, started the car, and pulled out, her face animated as she screamed at her son. Nancy felt a chill go down her spine as they disappeared out of the lot. She turned back toward the hospital, frightened.

Jack. Jesus, Lord, I have t' find Jack! It's th' only way I can prove I'm not insane!

Nancy reached the Emergency Room doors and entered. She immediately recognized the bleeding man on the stretcher inside and her breath caught in her throat. It was Robert Bigelow. Blood was flowing through the bandage on his head. Larry pushed him past and ordered her out of the way. She followed him in, unscathed by his rough tone. Her short stout frame waddled comically in her haste. She slowed to a walk when they crossed the threshold into the building. She stopped as the room began to spin.

It was a madhouse. Doctors were frantically barking orders. Their voices boomed over the din of nervous onlookers and those who had been in the waiting room before the Lancaster people began to arrive. Nurses, in a forced calm, their faces registering near hysteria, labored quickly to follow the doctors' directions. There was blood everywhere. It was on the floor, the counter, and stained the front of every blue-green hospital gown in sight. The injured filled each cubicle. Nancy heard their desperate moaning as she slipped through the chaos. She stared at their faces as she passed. She prayed this was a horrible dream. She remembered Wade, but then she quickly shut it out of her mind.

Nancy paused in the doorway to the last cubicle on the right. There were two beds in the room. Dr. Montclair was hunched over the one on the right hurriedly stitching a large gash in Mike's forehead. Her son was unconscious and as pale as a sheet. His blood gushed over the doctor's latex gloves and down the side of Mike's face. Adele looked over, the fear in her expression carrying the uncertainty of his condition. Nancy knew there must be noise around her, voices since their mouths were moving, but she heard nothing.

Sandra was standing behind the nurse, tears streaming down her cheeks. Nancy's mouth hung open loosely as her head turned toward the other bed. A group of boys including her grandson were desperately trying to hold Jeremy down. He was unconscious, but seizing. All of the sounds in the world came rushing back to her in Craig's desperate tone.

"Grandma?" he cried, his voice broken with sobs. "Oh, God, grandma! Help us!"

Nancy took a step forward becoming strong for them. Craig needed her. A thousand questions went through her mind: *What's goin' on? Why's Craig out of bed? Where's th' McKee boy's cast? Why aren't they in their room? Where's Virginia while her boy's sufferin'?*

Chris held his brother's shoulders to the mattress. Craig pleaded with Jeremy to hang on. The Puerto Rican brothers had his legs. They barked at Derek to help them. He shook his head, his eyes wide with fear, as he backed out the door. Another boy was holding Jeremy's arms down. Nancy gasped, clutching her chest. *It's him!* There was no doubt here in the light, out of the storm. He turned to her. Nancy felt an explosion of non-reality go off in her head.

I'm not insane. Oh, no, I've gone stark ravin' loony!

"Mom?" Jack asked, his child's eyes desperate.

Nancy didn't have the chance to scream. The door behind her slammed shut. Jeremy bolted upright. Some invisible force shoved the boys back, scattering them around the room. Jack slammed into a utility table spilling the doctor's tools. Ricardo went over the counter and shattered a row of glass containers. Cotton balls sailed into the air. Craig held on to the railing. Time stood still as every head in the room turned toward Jeremy.

Jeremy's eyes glowed with a deeper blue than before. They looked like pools of liquid energy. His face twisted and time resumed in slow motion. It was like still life, like flipping the pages on a homemade cartoon drawn on a pad of paper. Shock invaded the doctor, the nurse, Sandra, and Nancy, paralyzing them in the light flowing from the eyes of the boy floating several inches above his bed.

"Oh, my God!" Craig cried. *"Jeremy!"*

For a moment, it seemed Jeremy would scream, too. The power in the room was immense. Everyone felt its force. Jeremy turned to Nancy, his attention drawn to her overwhelming emotion. She held her hands out in a pleading gesture while beneath her skull invisible fingers dove into her brain.

"Uh, oh," Max whispered, stepping back.

Jeremy raged at Nancy, his words coming so fast it was impossible to understand him. She violently shook her head, begging him not to go any further. She felt him inside her mind rifling through her memories. Disbelief came over his features. Craig could see everything Jeremy did through their mind-link. He mentally retreated, denying his friend the stabling influence of his presence at the impossibility of what he was seeing. In that instant, Jeremy lost control reacting to Craig's sudden breakdown. His power reached out and linked every mind in the room with his and Nancy's. He frantically searched for someone to help him understand what it all meant. He needed to find stability. He had to control the buildup of power that was about to blow them and the room to smithereens. Jack fell to his knees.

She sacrificed her son to a madman in her desperation not to lose the husband she loved, and everything that's happened since? The children, the murders?

It barreled through their heads. Jeremy's rage grew. He lashed out at Nancy and showed her what she did. He showed her every death laying the blame for everything at her feet. Dr. Montclair grabbed a syringe, jabbed it into Jeremy's arm, and squeezed the plunger.

"No!" Jeremy cried, breaking the mind-link. Everyone dropped to the floor. *"My mom! I have to save...* my mom... Oh, God, no *godno..."*

Jeremy fell onto the bed. The boys, except for Jack and Chris, rushed toward him. Dr. Montclair backed away fighting the urge to vomit. He glared at Nancy and allowed himself a single moment to hate her. He didn't understand what had just happened, but Mike Dougan was dying. He was a doctor and Mike's only chance.

"Jackie?" Nancy asked, reaching for him.

"N… no…," Jack replied, his voice quivering.

He stood and moved slowly away, twitching, shaking his head. He backed up until he felt Chris behind him.

Chris wrapped his arms around him and held him. "I've got you, Jack," he said. He stared at Nancy in disbelief. "I've got you."

"Nurse Weissenberg!" Dr. Montclair bellowed.

Adele stared at Nancy, her mouth agape. She jumped at the volume of the doctor's voice. It forced every thought out of her mind.

"Jackie, please!" Nancy pleaded. "Let me explain, lad! Let me…!"

"No!" Jack cried. "Don't touch me!"

Nancy fell over on her side, crying. Chris' knees buckled. He slid down the wall to a seated position on the floor. Jack fell into his lap. He held on to Chris for his sanity as he joined his mother's sobbing. Chris gazed into the room, his mind finally shutting down.

Craig stared at Jeremy, his hands locked around his friend's wrist. If he broke contact with him now, he knew he would go crazy. Ricardo and Max joined Chris and Jack. Sandra stood motionless. Mike's unconscious hand had grabbed her the moment the mind-link was formed. She nearly fainted. She desperately held the bed's safety rail.

"Why in the world is this door closed?" Dr. Cameron Sativa exclaimed, as he flung it open. "What's going on in here?"

"Back off, Cameron!" Dr. Montclair barked. He glared at Nancy. "Do something constructive. Get that woman out of my Emergency Room."

"Orderlies?" Dr. Sativa called, motioning into the hall. Two college boys appeared in the doorway. He snapped his fingers twice and pointed at Nancy. "Remove her."

The orderlies dragged her away. Nancy begged for a chance to explain. She called out for Jack. Chris, Max, and Ricardo felt him tighten up each time she said his name. When Jack wouldn't answer, she called Craig. He refused to listen. It didn't matter how much he owed her or how much he loved her, Craig knew she had done so much for him not only because she loved him, but also for her guilt. His heart unraveled. He heard the administrator order her sedated when she got hysterical.

Craig nodded. *Good,* he thought. *I can't deal with this right now.*

"Craig?" Jeremy's voice appeared in his head. It was faint and far away.

"I'm here," Craig replied. There was a sharp edge in his mind-voice.

"Sorry," Jeremy thought-whispered. *"… so sorry…"*

"It isn't your fault, Jeremy," Craig sobbed, talking out loud. His façade of strength cracked. "It's okay."

"Craig?" Max asked. "Are you okay? Is Jeremy awake?"

Craig shook his head in answer to both questions. His lower lip quivered.

"Dr. Montclair?" Dr. Sativa asked. "Are you almost through here?"

"Almost," the doctor replied. "How are the others?"

Dr. Sativa had sent Robert Bigelow to the ICU. He had sustained a severe concussion. Lyle Gibbons was banged up, but was treated. Lisa was cut up pretty severely and had lost a lot of blood. There was a bite mark on the inside of her leg riddled with infection. He had prescribed I.V. antibiotics.

"Thank God," Dr. Sativa commented, "she didn't cut her face at all. She's such a pretty girl. Her father's with her in her room. Officer Kate Pierce also has a concussion although a mild one. She's been admitted overnight for observation. One of the residents set Derek Mellon's wrist. He's getting a cast. We're treating him for shock. Graham Shooter is having his bones set. Surgery's necessary for his face, but he's too weak, just not warranting ICU. He's assigned a room in Pediatrics."

Dr. Sativa moved in close. He whispered, "Dabney Copeland has been the victim of a savage assault. He has some internal hemorrhaging. I contacted his father, but he hung up on me. Can you imagine? We may have to take him to surgery, but his father refused to come in or sign any papers. I'll order it myself if it becomes life-threatening."

"Agreed," Dr. Montclair nodded, tying off Mike's stitches. "Nurse? Have Mr. Dougan taken to X-ray. I want to see the extent of his injuries. Type him and start an I.V. He's lost a lot of blood."

"Yes, doctor," Adele replied.

"He's… O positive, and I'm… going…," Sandra managed to say.

Dr. Montclair cut her off. "… to bed after the nurses patch you up. And get the McKee and Dougan boys back into a room. I haven't discharged them yet."

"Doctor?" Adele asked. "What happened up there? The room they were in this afternoon is… it's…"

"We'll discuss it when there's time," Dr. Montclair said. "Right now we have patients. Orderly! We need help in here!"

"Henry?" Dr. Sativa asked, side-stepping Adele. The orderlies came in to take Mike away. Another nurse wheeled Sandra down the hall in a wheelchair toward the adult ward. "About the McKee woman…"

"Mom?" Chris asked, his mind suddenly coming back to life. "Oh, my God! Where's my mom!"

"Stay there!" Dr. Montclair commanded, pointing at him.

Chris glared at the doctor.

"I mean it, Mr. McKee." he continued, squatting down. "She's in surgery. There was an accident. There's nothing you can do right now, do you understand?"

Chris opened his mouth to demand the doctor get out of his face and take him to his mother now!

Dr. Sativa tapped on Dr. Montclair's shoulder. "She's out of surgery," he said. "We have her in ICU."

"Where's that?" Chris demanded.

Jack stood up. He wiped his face and stuffed his emotions. He helped Chris to stand.

"Tell me! Where's my mother?"

"You can't see her just yet."

"The hell I can't!" Chris hollered, clenching his fist.

Jack placed his hand on Chris' chest and stood between them. "Please, Chris," he said. He slowly opened the fist and placed his hand in it. "We've been through so much already. No more tonight, okay?"

"He's right, Chris," Ricardo said, placing his hand on Chris' shoulder. "We need to hold together, man."

"Don't lose it now, McKee," Max agreed. He lifted Craig up and set him on the foot of Jeremy's bed. He looked him in the eye. Craig shook with every breath. "Your mom's okay, isn't she, doctor?"

Dr. Montclair nodded. He reached out to Chris. "I'll explain it later."

Chris pulled away from him.

"There are no visitors allowed in Intensive Care, Mr. McKee. I'm sorry. If you go home, I'm sure things will be better in the morning, and maybe…"

"Home?" they cried.

"Are you crazy?" Jack asked.

"We're not going anywhere, got it?" Max growled. "Lead us up to wherever you plan on putting Jeremy and Craig. We'll stay there, but none of us is leaving and that's the end of that!"

"I'm afraid that isn't possible, young man," Dr. Sativa said. "Hospital policy is clear on the matter of guests."

"Screw your policy!" Chris cried. "We're not leaving!"

"I could have security remove you."

"And I can kick your ass!" Max exclaimed.

"Enough!" Dr. Montclair yelled, sticking out his chest. "I'll not have any of that here. Stay if you must, but do not disturb the other patients."

"Henry?"

"No, Cameron," he said. "It's not worth fighting over. Let's get them up to Pediatrics and stop screwing around. Once we're through, there's a mountain of paperwork to fill out."

"I'll tell mom," Ricardo offered.

Max nodded, pointing toward the waiting room. "Tell her we need clothes. All of us."

Dr. Montclair took a moment and examined everyone. He wanted to ensure they were uninjured and not just being tough guys. He moved Jeremy's bed with help from Craig and Max into the hall toward the elevators. Ricardo returned with Keith and JT who had refused to call their mother. They talked one of the officers into doing it for them. They reached the elevator in time to climb in.

"I told mama to stay home," Ricardo nodded. "I promised to call if anything changed. Dad's bringing the clothes back."

The elevator went up quickly. The doors opened on the Pediatrics floor. Chris moaned at the dancing clowns lining the hallway walls.

"God, I hate those things!"

"I don't know, Chris," Jack shrugged. "I kind of like them."

The boys looked down at him.

"Most of the younger kids do," Dr. Montclair offered, coming to Jack's rescue.

Jack whispered, "Yeah, us younger kids."

"Oh, please," Max sighed. "Will you give me a break, old man?"

Dr. Montclair made a mental note of that odd statement as they pushed the bed out into the hall, but he said nothing. He was more concerned with what he had seen downstairs in the Emergency Room. He was intrigued the boys weren't mentioning it. That was strange. They weren't surprised at the ease in which their friend had violated Nancy Dougan's most intimate memories? Levitated above his bed? Barraged them with visions of things that should've remained forever unknown? He looked at Jack. It was odd a woman her age with a son so young. He bore an uncanny resemblance to Craig's father, the drunkard who caused a scene mere hours ago.

Jeremy's arm caught his attention. An icy chill ran down his spine. He grabbed it and scrutinized it. There was no visual evidence it had ever been broken or stitched. Something was going on here. Psychokinesis? Dr. Montclair never believed in such things. The boy had power though. He had seen it. He was sure Jeremy was behind the destruction of the room, too, not a freak bolt of lightning as they initially thought, but why would he injure his mother?

"There's a boy in the room named Mickey Downing," Dr. Montclair said. "He had been wandering the hospital and got caught in the incident up here. He's asleep now. Please don't wake him. His grandmother is very concerned. She's bringing the boy's parents."

"Mickey?" Craig asked. *The kid from the carnival?* He remembered Ezmerelda's words with absolute clarity.

"Your father won't beat you for much longer. You have an important part to play in this little drama. You have to be strong. Can you remember that? You must be. Jeremy needs your strength."

Craig patted Jeremy's shoulder and glanced at his father. *I guess she was right. Man, who is she?*

"We won't," Chris replied. He glanced into the destroyed room as they passed. He shook his head. *Did Jeremy do that? Oh, God, what's happening?*

"Chris?" Jack asked, tugging at his shirt.

"I'm okay, Jack," he said. "What about you?"

Jack shook his head. It was taking all of his strength to hold back his tears. He didn't want to cry in front of the doctor, but he knew he would. His new lease on life ached with the pain of a broken heart.

Max went into the room first. He backed through the door leading the bed. Craig let go of Jeremy's hand to let them pass, but quickly retook it and followed them to the empty spot by the window. It was a three-person room. Craig saw that it was Mickey from the carnival. Dr. Montclair motioned to Craig in a gesture that said, "Get in the empty bed." He shook his head refusing to leave Jeremy's side. Jeremy was softy mind-speaking to him. Craig nodded as he mentally answered.

Dr. Montclair took note of this action, too. He suddenly remembered the two boys screaming as Jeremy's arm was set. Both of them fainted as if they had both felt the pain. There was a lot he didn't understand. He requested that Chris get his brother into a hospital gown.

"Craig should take that as a hint as well." Dr. Montclair remarked, and left the room.

"What's his name again?" Keith asked, nodding toward Mickey.

"Mickey Downing," Chris replied. "That's what Montclair said."

"Where's he from?" JT asked, secretly glad for the hard rain that had washed the urine stink from his clothes.

"He's with the carnival," Craig said.

Ricardo asked, "How did he end up here? His timing must suck."

"I don't think he's here... by accident," Dabney said. He was standing in the doorway in a hospital gown. "There was something... he said at the carnival, right, Craig?" He swaggered back and forth. He looked like death warmed over.

"Dabney!" Chris exclaimed. He rushed over and grabbed him under the arm.

"Get the doctor!" Jack cried.

Max moved toward the door.

Dabney stopped him shaking his head. "No more doctors. They can't do anything... for me anyway. I'm bleeding on the inside. Hiram beat me up pretty bad. My... father won't sign... for my surgery and the doctor... can't override that... as long as it's not life-threatening. I have to... be almost dead first. Besides, they keep asking me... questions... and I'm sick of their damned questions!"

"Are you sure, man?" Max asked.

Dabney nodded leaning into Chris who led him to a chair next to Craig's bed. Chris sat drawing Dabney down with him. Craig burst into tears. So did Chris, the weight of the day finally taking its toll. It was a chain reaction. Soon they were all huddled together, the walls breaking down. Each knew today they had cried more, and had more reason to, than ever before.

"Hiram would've killed me," Dabney whispered. "Oh, God... he was beating me... and I couldn't stop him!"

Jeremy felt their pain. It was as great as his own. His power was alive even through the drug. He was fighting to wake up. He needed his friends. He was unwilling to draw any more strength from Craig who was feeling emotionally drained. They had fought the good fight, but they had lost. Too many people had gotten hurt. Too many people were dead. Some believed they were to blame.

Craig believed he was for not seeking help all those years his father beat him. A good counselor might have dragged the dirty secrets of Jack's past out of him and put an end to Hiram's killings. Jack thought he was for allowing his abuse to go on all those years out of shame. Chris did, too, for taking matters into his own hands. None of them realized this was all the Hill Witch's doing. She had used her telepathy to protect Hiram, influencing them and preventing the farmer's exposure. She needed him to kill for her. It wasn't their fault. How could he make them understand?

Dabney didn't tell either. He was in the most precarious spot of all. He had a long way to go before he would ever be all right again. On top of his abuse at Hiram's hands, his father despised him so much he willingly gave Dabney to Ms. Adler, without any mental coercion, knowing she was delivering him up to a murderer. The pain of his internal injuries paled when compared to the ache in Dabney's soul. Jeremy could see in his mind how he wished he hadn't survived, how worthless and guilty he felt, and how confused he was at the feelings growing in his heart for Chris. He rested his head against Chris' chest, holding him tighter. Chris kissed his forehead, gathering him into his lap. He didn't want to let him go. Part of him never did. He didn't understand why any more than Dabney did.

There was Jeremy, too. The deaths of the men Hiram molested when they were boys... and Sandy... and Henry Schwartz... killed by the spirits he had set free even though they were controlling him.

I could have fought harder, Jeremy despaired, *been stronger.*

Jeremy would live with that weakness for the rest of his life. Like Dabney, death sounded better. What about what he had done to Jack? Jeremy healed his soul, but he was twelve years old again. What if he couldn't cope with his new life and what he had learned about his mother? Should he have let Jack die when he wanted to? The point was moot. There was no going back now. Jeremy didn't have the power to reverse it. And the zombies? It was why he had been so weak. They used him to animate their dead flesh, drawing strength from him until the Hill Witch severed their link. They had used him and he couldn't stop them.

What about Günter Bremen, the author of this tragedy? He was gone. Hiram was inside Margaret's body with him now. Jeremy reached out with his power trying to find them. It saddened and infuriated him. He felt helpless. He had to find them. He had to stop them.

"We will, Jeremy," Craig sniffled, wiping his eyes with the back of his hand. "I swear to God we will."

"Will what?" Chris asked, drying his eyes on Dabney's hospital gown.

"Find Ms. Adler," Jeremy groaned, sitting up.

"Jeremy!" they cried, coming to his bedside.

"You're awake!" Chris added.

Dabney looked at him but remained where he was.

"Yeah," Jeremy yawned, shaking his head, "but it took me a while. Whatever Dr. Montclair gave me was some strong stuff. My body seems to heal automatically, just not instantly unless I help it along like I did with my arm. I wish I'd thought of that earlier. There's too much I don't know." He lowered his gaze. "God, guys... I've never been so scared in my life."

Jeremy looked at Dabney and his face filled with sadness. He motioned for him to come over.

"He's hurt," Chris said.

"In more ways than one," Jeremy softly said. He put his hand on Dabney's chest. "Hold on, okay? I'll take care of the pain. I'll take care of everything."

"You know, don't you?" Dabney sadly asked. "My father... tried to have me murdered."

"I know," Jeremy replied, his face darkening.

"I knew he hated me, but... Jesus, I don't ever want to see his face again!"

"You won't have to," Jeremy said. "You're staying with us now. You're part of our family, I promise. Now, hush. I can help you."

"You? How can...? Holy mother... *McKee!?*" Dabney gasped.

The boys stood back fearfully as Jeremy's eyes began to glow. The deep midnight blue light flowed through his hand into Dabney's body. Dabney felt Jeremy's presence inside of him as he fell into his lap. Jeremy held him, following the pain. He found his bleeding innards and healed them. The bruises on his face faded. Their nervous systems became one for an instant as Jeremy used his own body as a template to make Dabney's the way it should be. Dabney saw the real Jeremy then. He sensed his fear of what he had become.

Christ, he's terrified!

Jeremy struggled to maintain control of what he barely understood. Dabney found Craig in there, too, Jeremy's anchor to sanity. He knew they were two sides of the same coin now, the power and the restraint, each needing the other so desperately. Dabney longed to be loved that way. Jeremy linked him with them and loved him precisely the way he wanted. He gave Chris and Dabney a glimpse of what was growing within them. Dabney rested his head on Jeremy's chest and looked at Chris.

Chris took his hand and nodded. "Afraid?" he asked.

"No," Dabney replied. "You?"

"Never," Chris said.

Craig said, "I'm here, too, Dabney."

The light dimmed and it was over.

"Better?" Jeremy asked, into his mind.

Dabney nodded, not wanting to move.

"Good," Jeremy continued. *"Then listen to me carefully, Dabs. Don't even think about killing yourself, man, you hear? There's been enough death. So many people will miss you, like me. I need you, man."*

"You need me?" Dabney asked.

Jeremy said, *"You're one of the strongest people I know. This isn't over. More people are going to die if we don't stop Ms. Adler and the farmer. You know what we have to do."*

"I'm the chaos," Dabney nodded, remembering Ezmerelda's words.

"Dude, that was awesome!" JT exclaimed.

"No kidding!" Keith agreed.

"Is he better now?" Chris asked, patting Dabney on the shoulder as he stood.

"Good as new," Craig said.

Jeremy touched his face. *"God, Dougan,"* he said, looking at the tear-smudged dirt and dried blood lining his best friend's cheeks. *"Don't you ever wash?"*

"Oh, now that's funny!" Craig replied. "Like I've had time? *Excuse me, Ms. Adler! Don't rip my mind apart for a second! I need to shower so I won't be stinky!"*

The boys nervously laughed.

"Jeremy?" Chris asked. "Can you heal the others? Can you heal mom?"

"I think so," Jeremy said, with a pang of guilt. *"It's my fault she's like that."*

"That's bull," Jack interrupted. "If you're going to blame somebody, blame me."

"Look, you guys," Dabney said, holding his hand up. "There's only one person to blame and it's Günter Bremen."

"You know?" Jeremy asked.

Dabney nodded.

"You're right. Bremen did all of this. We're the ones who have to do something about it."

"You sound like you have an idea, man," Max said. "God, I'd like to kill that witch."

"I would, too" Jeremy agreed, *"but there are people in danger of dying right here, Max. They have to come first."*

"I know, amigo," Max whispered. "I'm just afraid of waiting."

"We all are," Chris agreed. "Man, Jeremy! We're not even sure what's happened to you!"

"*Trust me, bro,*" Jeremy pleaded. "*You'll know everything, I promise. It won't be much longer.*"

"Are you ready?" Craig asked.

"*I'm ready,*" Jeremy nodded. He looked at his friends. "*If I asked you to, would you guys help me?*"

Jeremy looked at them one by one. He waited for each of them to nod. At the same time, his mind touched Graham in the room down the hall. He brought him into the link he formed. He was unconscious, but still feeling his pain. He reached out for Derek, too, but pulled back.

"*No. He's too filled with rage. He's lost the most.*"

Max asked what they needed to do.

Jeremy frowned. "*My mom's in ICU,*" he said, his eyes glowing brightly. "*When I scanned her from the Emergency Room, it was like she was fading, slipping through my fingers.*"

Chris gasped.

Jeremy grabbed his arm. "*We'll help her, Chris, I promise, but I need your strength. Bremen was right about one thing. I have his knowledge of the power, but not his experience. Mom's in there somewhere. I need you to come with me into her mind and help me find her before she's gone completely.*"

Chris felt something that vaguely resembled an electric shock. Jeremy's midnight blue light passed through his body and branched into everyone else. Their minds went blank in a flash of blue brilliance as Jeremy amped up his power. They felt him tugging at their spirits. The hospital room vanished. Their vision blurred and went black. When their sight returned, they were flying down a long tunnel. They collectively gasped as they zipped through it following behind Jeremy. They reached the end falling out through the tunnel's mouth into an angry gray sky.

Jeremy lowered them carefully to the ground. They looked around, stunned to find themselves in the middle of a vast desert wasteland. The ground was dry and cracked. A hot wind whipped around them in a sandstorm. They struggled to keep from being blown over. The sky went black. Steel blue clouds shot over the horizon. Silent heat lightning flashed above them. They joined hands feeling as though they were in a dream. It was the most real dream any of them ever experienced.

Craig pointed at something. They fought their way through the storm, shielding their eyes, struggling to reach the only sign of refuge within sight. It was a mahogany brown door with a brilliant gold handle hanging in mid-air. Jeremy and Chris stood before it. They looked at the door, and then at each other with recognition on their faces.

"I know that door!" Chris yelled, hoping Jeremy could hear him over the wind.

"*So do I!*" Jeremy agreed. "*It's from mom's bedroom!*"

"Well? Open it, for God's sake!" Max cried, shielding his eyes from the sand. "We're getting blasted back here!"

It took both of them to turn the knob and all of them to push the door open. A rush of air blew them through the doorway into a grand circular hall. There were colossal marble pillars around the perimeter stretching up twenty-five feet to a solid gold-domed ceiling ornately carved with a lattice of grapevines. The vines became real at the edges of the dome and wound down along the pure white columns to the floor. The floor had an outer circle of black marble which spiraled into bright green, then yellow, and then turned black again.

The door slammed shut. Max helped his brother up. Chris helped Dabney who looked down, blushing. He was nude. They all were. Craig smirked. He wasn't the only one begging for puberty anymore. Jack, Keith, and Graham were right there with him. He told them that clothes were optional inside someone's mind. Keith helped Graham stand. He walked over to Jeremy and shook his hand.

"Nice to meet you," Graham nodded. His face drew back in surprise. "Hey! I can hear!"

"You can do anything you want in here, Graham," Jeremy said. *"You saved my life. I won't forget that."*

"I'm hurt pretty badly," Graham signed, out of habit. "My mom's probably scared to death."

"I scanned your body," Jeremy said. *"You won't die. After we save my mom, you're next to heal. I'm going to take care of everybody. I hope you don't mind that I brought you here. I couldn't leave you with all that pain."*

Graham nodded. He was glad to see he had made the right choice helping no matter how much it hurt him.

"This is better than getting stoned, man!" JT cried.

Jeremy rolled his eyes.

"Wow!" Ricardo exclaimed, spinning around with his arms out. "Will you look at this place?"

Jeremy frowned at their amazement as the others crooned. He wondered why everyone else had such beautiful mindscapes when his was so plain, so empty. Was that who he was? A plain and empty person? Superficial?

"No, man," Craig said, hearing his thoughts. "You've never had to paint your canvass, that's all. Some of us need a place inside, you know? For you, when you're lonely, you watch Star Trek, you read comics. Your world is on the outside."

"I guess you're right," Jeremy shrugged. *"I like your place the best."*

"I don't know," Craig replied. "This place is fantastic!"

Jack nudged Chris and pointed to a long red carpet that led to a set of double doors. There were gleaming life-sized silver statutes on either side of the doorway. Everyone walked toward them, curiously.

Craig and Ricardo laughed.

"What's so funny?" Max asked.

"The statues!" Ricardo cried, pointing at them. "It's Jeremy and Chris!"

"What?" Chris gasped. He looked at them and shook his head. *Oh, great! This is worse than the family pictures mom always brings out every time a new friend comes over!*

Jeremy was the statue to the left. He was standing tall, a knight in shining armor, his right hand over his brow searching for something, or someone. A long sword hung down from his left hand pointed at an angle toward the ground.

The Loyal Knight, Jeremy thought, *searching for his wandering King.* He felt a pang of loss.

Craig put his arm around him.

Chris' statue was Robin Hood. His bow was drawn back ready to steal from the rich to give to the poor. It was flattering, Jeremy supposed, but he could tell his brother was unhappy with the tights his statue was wearing. He knew that without having to read his thoughts.

"It's not that bad," Max said to Chris.

Chris put his hands on his hips. "Oh, sure! Jeremy is a knight in shining armor, and I'm *Robin Hood: Men in Tights?"*

"You could have been in a skirt, homo," Jeremy smiled.

"Homo?" Jack asked. He looked up at Chris who just sighed.

"He's gay, dad," Craig said.

"You're gay?" Jack whispered, as the others moved closer to the statues.

"What if he isn't alone?" Dabney asked.

"Is that a problem?" Chris asked.

"No!" Jack exclaimed. He whispered, "I think it's great you guys have the guts to admit it."

"I haven't admitted anything," Dabney corrected. His eyes met Chris'. He flashed a shy grin. "Yet."

They held hands. Everyone looked at them. No one said a word.

Chris whispered, "Jeeze, Dabs. What's happening here?"

"I have no idea," Dabney whispered back. He squeezed Chris' hand. "But I like it."

"Me, too," Chris said. He smiled.

The door on the left opened slightly. A short bald man slipped through before quickly closing it behind him. He was wearing a butler's outfit neatly pressed and a pair of sparkling white gloves. The boys heard a symphony of strings and brass playing. It was beautiful. It invited them to dance. The butler stopped in the middle of the boys, crossed his arms, and shook his head.

"This simply will not do," he said, arrogantly. "This is a formal occasion. You cannot come in like that. You must put some clothes on."

"Who says, cue-ball?" Jack asked.

"Why, the Lady of the Manor, Mister… er, *Master* Jack," the butler replied.

"Mom?" Chris asked. "She's here?"

"Of course, Master Christopher," he said. He looked at Chris as if he should know that already. "Where else would she be?"

"How do you know my brother's name?" Jeremy asked, touching the man's black sleeve. It felt icy cold. Jeremy pulled back, surprised.

"Come now, Jeremy," he smiled. "I've known you boys all of your lives. Now, you must get dressed. As I said, this is a formal occasion, black tie and all that. As soon as you are ready, I will announce you."

The butler turned and reached for the door handle.

Chris stopped him. "Wait! Who are you?"

"Come now, Master Christopher," the butler sighed. "Time is short. The Lady Virginia has an appointment with the light."

"The light?" Craig asked, panic in his voice. "Does he mean what I think he means?"

"I'm not sure, dude," Jeremy replied. ***"Let's just get dressed and get in there."***

In a flash, Jeremy and Craig appeared in black tuxedos. The other guys stared at them with anxious expressions.

Jeremy smiled. ***"It's easy,"*** he said. ***"Just concentrate."***

"That's easy for you to say," Max said. "You're the main mind-man around here!"

"No, Max," Craig said, changing his outfit three times in succession before returning to his tuxedo. "See? There's nothing to it! Just picture yourself dressed, that's all. You can do anything in here!"

They did as instructed. Ricardo and Max appeared in powder blue tuxes. Jack was in one a shade of green like his eyes. Dabney chose navy. JT selected new denim jeans with a white shirt and thin silk tie. Graham appeared in a white tux with a red bow tie. Keith wore a purple suit and tie with a black top hat. Chris' tux was black leather. His coat was down to his knees and open in the front. His cummerbund was a brilliant yellow. The butler scowled as the boys praised themselves, but nodded his approval. He turned and flung the doors open. When he did, they inhaled sharply.

Beyond the double doors was a grand ballroom twice the size of the room in which they stood, filled with people oddly familiar to Jeremy and Chris. They were people from their mother's past, people they had seen in photo albums. They danced in curt synchronization to the orchestra in the balcony. It was as if they had been transported in time back to the seventeen hundreds. A ten-foot banquet table sat beneath the balcony. It was covered with food and golden flasks filled with a sweet-smelling wine that made their mouths water. The butler rang a small silver bell hanging next to the door. The orchestra stopped playing. All eyes turned toward him.

The butler cleared his throat and announced, "Ladies and gentlemen! Master Christopher and Jeremy. Their associates Craig, Masters Max, Ricardo, Dabney, Graham, Keith, Jared, and Jack."

"Jared?" Jack whispered to JT.

"Eat me," JT snorted.

The room erupted in cheers and applause. The boys looked at each other and shrugged. The crowd on the dance floor opened so a woman with a giant powdered wig and a flowing blue gown could get through. An albino boy with crystal blue eyes walked with her daintily holding her hand. Jeremy, Craig, and Dabney recognized him immediately despite being in a black tuxedo with a bright red tie.

"Oh, my God!" they exclaimed. "It's you!"

"Who?" Chris asked.

"Yeah, man," Ricardo echoed. "Who?" He felt a chill then as recognition came over him. "Oh, wow!"

"Oh, my handsome boys!" the Lady Virginia crooned, holding her hands out to Jeremy and Chris. "I've been waiting for you all evening! Allow me to introduce you to my escort. Mickey Downing? May I present my sons."

Mickey smiled shyly. "Hi, Jeremy," he said, his voice soft and sweet. "Welcome to the ball."

*　　*　　*

Matt grabbed hold of the dashboard with both hands as Susan Sturgess barreled into Johnson Memorial's parking lot. He flew out of the seat when the wheels of the Cherokee hit the first speed bump and banged his head against the ceiling. He cried out. Susan slammed on the brakes. The Jeep slid slightly to one side on the rain-soaked pavement. She turned to him. Her expression made Matt's stomach churn.

Susan was always pale. She wasn't much of an outdoors person even in warm weather, but she was as white as sour cream now. There was a look of anguish etched in her features. She appeared to have aged ten years in the drive from Lancaster. Matt rubbed his head and nodded that he was okay. Susan continued to the parking lot more carefully this time. Matt decided never to ride with her again without a seatbelt.

"Jesus, Matt," Susan said, tightly gripping the steering wheel. Her sculpted nails dug into the leather covering. "Tell me this is a bad friggin' joke, okay?"

Matt looked out his window at the hospital room Jeremy had destroyed. The plastic covering rippled in the wind.

"I wish I could," he finally said, choking back a sob. "I'd give anything to be able to say that it was."

Susan pulled into a parking space in front of the Emergency Room door. She rested her head on the steering wheel trying to focus. She would be able

James Christopher

to if the world would stop spinning for a minute. It had to. She had to catch up. Somehow it had taken off without her on the day Ian disappeared. The situation was horrifying. She was barely holding it together. Before she had fallen asleep this evening – which was odd since she never went to bed early – she knew Ian was at camp. Now, she couldn't understand how a week could go by and no one realized Ian was missing. From the moment she heard Matt's voice on her voicemail, nothing made any sense at all.

"Mrs. Sturgess? This is Matt Gardner. I'm at Mike Dougan's house and I... really need somebody... right now. No one's answering the phone at my house and... *Please! Sandy's dead!* Jeremy's... oh, God, Mrs. Sturgess! You've got to come quick!"

Susan had been in bed when her cell phone rang. The television was still on in the living room. She heard the voices of the news channel crew. She wondered why Alex hadn't answered her phone. It was on the table next to him in the charger. She assumed he had fallen asleep in his recliner again. He said something about being tired and had planned on turning in early, too. It was a fair guess he hadn't made it judging from the space in their bed. Susan wasn't surprised. He had taken Thomas' death hard. They all had.

"... Please! Sandy's dead!"

The effort to get out of bed was Herculean. She stumbled into the living room and picked up her phone. There was one call and a voicemail message from Matt Gardner. She listened to it. The words played at the edge of her mind for what seemed an eternity. Her eyelids snapped open when Sean, awakened by the phone and standing in his bedroom doorway, began screaming. Alex was there almost immediately. He scooped Sean into his arms. It was hard enough for her to listen to the words Matt was rambling without Alex continually asking, "Sue? Where's Ian? Christ, Sue! Where could he be?"

Susan called Matt and told him to stay where he was. She would be right there. She dressed while she tried to tell her husband what Matt had told her.

It was a waste of time, Susan thought. *Alex didn't get past the "Sandy's dead!" part before he crumbled.*

She wasn't sure if he had heard her say Ian might be gone, too. Too much of what Matt had said didn't make any sense. She ran out the door without her jacket or her purse and leaped into the Cherokee.

"Are you...," Matt began. He swallowed hard and continued, "... okay, Mrs. Sturgess?"

"I'm not sure, Matt," Susan replied. "Is it true? Are my... boys really...?"

Matt laid his hand on her shoulder.

Susan sobbed once and gritted her teeth. "No!" she cried, choking back the tirade of emotions about to overwhelm her. She patted Matt's hand. "I won't... God damn it, I won't!"

"Mrs. Sturgess?"

"No, Matt," Susan said. "I'm not okay, all right?"

Matt drew his hand back as if stung.

Susan's face cracked down the middle. "Oh, God...," she gasped, watching a tear roll down his cheek. She wiped it away. "I'm sorry. Okay, honey? I'm sorry. I just... I can't believe this is happening."

"It's okay," Matt sniffled. "If I hadn't been there, I wouldn't believe it either."

Susan motioned for him to get out. If it was true and her boys were gone, she had the rest of her life to mourn. Right now, it was time to find out what was going on. As they stepped into the rain, her mind began to freefall. She wasn't sure what had happened down on Milliken Road or how the boys found themselves in the middle of everything, but whatever it was, it was terrible.

If the number of police cars and ambulances by the roadblock where she picked up Matt weren't enough to convince her, the burning bodies on Wickett Avenue were. The stench was awful. She thought, *Where is everybody?* There was an isolated person here and there, but in a town like Lancaster an event of this magnitude should have brought out the entire population. It was a good thing the officers at the roadblock wouldn't let her cross and go down to Mike's house. If Sandy's body was really down there?

My God, Susan shuddered. *What am I going to do?*

Lyle was watching through his daughter's window as Susan and Matt approached the Emergency Room. Lisa was next to him asleep in her bed. She breathed evenly. Her bandaged leg stuck out from under the covers. He looked at it. He felt the pain of her infected bite and her wounds. He shook his head. He wasn't going to leave her side for anything after the way he had failed her tonight. He read the look of fear on Susan's face and decided he needed to go. He had to offer comfort to one of the few people he called a friend. Susan must be devastated. He knew he would be.

Lyle had watched the safety catch of the grenade wedged between Ian and Sandy spring away. His heart blew into as many pieces as they did. When the car exploded and the black claimed him, Lyle went willingly. How could anyone blame him? It was madness down there.

The walking dead? Blood and bodies all over the place? Jack Dougan a kid? How could any of that be real?

Lyle should've taken Sandra's call more seriously, but how could he? Everything she said was preposterous, but when they got over there and that head crashed through Lisa's windshield? He just stood there gaping at it like a raw troop in his first firefight.

If it wasn't for Jack...

Lyle pinched the bridge of his nose. He kissed Lisa on the cheek. He touched the bandage on his forehead and winced. The spot was tender from a piece of shrapnel that had clipped off a chunk of his skin. He stepped into the hallway easing the door closed. He whispered a quiet prayer that his baby girl would stay asleep until he returned. The least he could do after his colossal failure was be there when her eyes opened. He would be on his knees begging her forgiveness. He also intended to find Jack. Regardless of whatever kind of insanity made him appear like a boy again, he had saved Lisa's life. If Jack was still a man? Lyle was going to shake his hand and give him anything he wanted. If he was a boy?

Christ, that's so nuts!

Lyle walked to the nurses' station

Adele nodded at Susan. "I don't see why you can't go up," she said, patting Susan's hand. "Dr. Sativa gave his consent for the boys to stay up there." She leaned over glancing left to right before continuing. "Confidentially, I don't think he had much choice. From the look on their faces, I think they would've put the doctor in a room if he had tried to force them to leave. Besides, the Downings went up about five minutes ago to sit with their son. He's in the same room."

"Thank you, Nurse Weissenberg," Susan replied. "Where's Virginia McKee?"

Adele's face sank. Susan felt the world beginning to spin all over again.

"She's in ICU, Sue," Lyle answered. "She was hurt pretty bad."

Susan threw her arms around him. Lyle held her fighting as hard as she was to not start bawling.

Matt stared at him with a stunned look. *Virginia's hurt? How?*

A janitor passed with a mop bucket filled with steaming hot water and bleach. Matt's eyes followed him until he pushed open the door to the examination room. He looked away immediately when he saw the blood covering everything. He shut his eyes trying to make the image go away. The snarling visage of Ian Sturgess the zombie replaced it. Matt's eyes snapped open.

"Jesus Christ, Lyle!" Susan exclaimed, pushing back from him. "What happened here?"

Lyle frowned, scratching his head. "I'm not sure," he replied. "I'm going to find out. When I do, someone's going to die."

"Too many people are dead already," Matt quietly remarked. He cringed. *What's wrong with me? Why am I all of a sudden saying the wrong things at the wrong time?* He lowered his eyes from Susan's stunned gaze. "I'm sorry. I don't know what's wrong with me."

"Gardner?" Lyle asked, leaning over eye to eye. "I was there, remember? For what you went through tonight, a half a dozen other men would've crapped their boxers."

Adele gasped.

Lyle ignored her. "You can go to combat with me anytime."

Matt nodded. "Let's just hope it isn't anytime soon."

"Amen," Lyle whispered. He stuck his arm out motioning toward the elevators. "C'mon," he said to Susan. "I'll walk you up."

"Hey!" Matt exclaimed. "Is Lisa…?"

"She's sleeping," Lyle interrupted, in a *drop the subject* tone.

Susan ignored it. "Lisa, too?"

"Yeah," he growled. "Lisa, too."

They walked to the elevators in silence. Matt strategically blocked Susan's view of the examination room. He knew his effort had been in vain when she gasped. Matt wished he was as fat as he was tall. Lyle pushed the call button shifting uncomfortably. He mumbled a string of curses when the elevator failed to appear instantly and headed for the stairwell. Susan and Matt dumbly followed ignoring the elevator doors as they opened.

Lyle paused in mid-step halfway up to Pediatrics. Matt peered around his ample buttocks. Derek was sitting on the steps holding his cast, sobbing. Douggie was dry-eyed, but looked very frightened. He was behind Derek having slipped away from the waiting room.

Matt squeezed around Lyle, dread enclosing his heart. *Did something else happen?* He remembered Kevin and Cynthia and almost started to cry with him.

"Derek?" Matt whispered.

Derek burst into violent sobs.

Matt looked at Lyle and Susan, his eyes tearing. "Kevin and Cynthia died, too," he whispered.

Susan placed her hand on her chest, shock invading her face. "Sweet mother of God!" she gasped. She drew Douggie to her holding him as he quietly wept.

They patiently waited while Derek fought for composure. Douggie stopped sobbing. Lyle picked Derek up and held him like a little boy. He looked like one in Lyle's tree trunk forearms. Derek wiped his eyes. His body shuddered with each deep breath.

"I… had a… nightmare," Derek sighed, stifling his emotions. "When I woke up, it was real."

"I know the feeling, son," Lyle said, squeezing him.

"No," Derek said. "You didn't see it all, Mr. Gibbons. Jeremy's a monster."

"Derek…," Matt began.

Derek cut him off his face flushing almost purple. "No!" he hollered, his face contorting. "He is a monster! You were there, Matt! You saw! I could feel him! He was in my mind!"

Matt opened his mouth to object, but closed it when Derek fell against Lyle's chest sobbing once more. Susan reached over, leaning with Douggie, and together they rubbed his back. They sat down on the stairs. Susan looked at Lyle first, but he only shrugged. She looked at Matt her eyes asking every question for her. He debated his answer before finally nodding his head and looking away.

"Oh, come on!" Susan cried, gently rocking Douggie. "You don't expect me to believe Jeremy's a monster, do you?"

"Oh?" Derek cried. He jumped off Lyle's lap. "Just wait! You'll see!"

He stomped his bare feet up the stairs angrily wiping his eyes. He heard them following. He entered the door for Pediatrics.

I'll show them! Derek thought.

When Derek woke up from his nightmare in the room down the hall, he had gone to find Chris. Now, he stood outside the same door he had opened ten minutes ago. He was terrified. Susan walked over to him with a questioning gaze.

"Open it," Derek whispered. "I can't."

Susan pushed open the door with her rear end. Their jaws fell open at the same time. Jeremy was floating cross-legged above his bed. His eyes were glowing midnight blue. Beneath him, scattered like leaves, were Max, Ricardo, Craig, Chris, Jack, Dabney, Keith, and JT.

"Come in and close the door," Carson Downing smiled. He was sitting on Mickey's bed holding his son's trembling hand.

Alberta smiled as they turned toward her husband's voice.

He said, "The Lord is at work in here."

*　　*　　*

"Where are they going?" Jack asked, watching Jeremy, Craig, and Mickey leaving the ball. His green eyes were concerned.

"I'm not sure," Max replied, "but I think we should do like the kid asked."

"Keep Mrs. McKee dancing?" Keith asked, nodding his head and scratching it.

"Exactly," Max said, bringing them to the Lady Virginia.

Jeremy and Craig walked with Mickey as he led them through the crowd. He went out a duplicate set of doors directly across from where the butler had announced their presence. Beyond them was a spectacular garden filled with bright green plants and a rainbow of flowers that stretched on forever. A large white marble fountain bubbled crystal clear water while a naked trumpet-playing cherub danced along the top. He paused his playing to wink at Jeremy and Craig before resuming. The music was melodic and otherworldly.

Mickey motioned for them to join him, carefully sitting on the fountain's edge. His expression was urgent. Jeremy watched the storm raging outside. It seemed unable, or unwilling, to touch the pretty garden. Giant swirling columns of sand ricocheted off some invisible barrier. Silent lightning stabbed down from the sky tearing up quarter-mile stretches of earth each place it struck.

Craig nodded at Jeremy sensing his friend's fear. "I know. It's frightening."

"I hope they can keep your mom dancing," Mickey sighed, running his fingers across the surface of the water. It was as crystal blue as his eyes. "They have to."

Jeremy and Craig glanced behind them. Chris and the others were taking turns waltzing with the Lady Virginia. She laughed and joked, more at ease than Jeremy had ever seen her.

Why is it so important to keep her dancing? Jeremy and Craig wondered.

Mickey seemed genuinely relieved when JT claimed he didn't know how to waltz and the Lady Virginia had offered to teach him. He studied their movements as she glided across the floor in her eldest son's arms. Chris was an accomplished dancer. Jeremy assumed it was in his gay gene. Craig grinned at the mental comment. Dabney laughed outright since he was an accomplished dancer, too, likewise contending with a budding gay gene. The guests looked at him, oddly. Chris threw his head back and ignored them. Jeremy dimmed their mind-link so there wouldn't be any more eavesdropping and only Craig could hear him.

The butler stood in the corner of the ballroom by a large round ornate door. He kept impatiently checking his gold pocket watch as if he was waiting for something. Jeremy and Craig turned to Mickey.

"Your mom's in danger," Mickey said, his eyes clouding. "I don't know if we can delay this much longer."

"Jesus, that bald guy gives me the creeps!" Craig exclaimed, pointing at the butler.

"Please don't take the Lord's name in vain, Craig," Mickey said. "It isn't a good thing to do, you know. Jesus is our friend. He loves you."

"Sorry," Craig replied, glancing nervously up at the sky. "The bald guy does bug me though."

"Me, too," Jeremy agreed, his power amplifying his voice.

He was speaking and projecting simultaneously. He couldn't seem to remember how not to do that. He wondered if maybe he couldn't separate the two inside his mother's mind.

"Mr. D makes a lot of people feel that way," Mickey offered.

"Mr. D?" Jeremy asked, raising an eyebrow. *"Is that his name? You sound like you know him."*

Mickey giggled, rocking his legs nervously. "I've known him as long as I can remember."

"How did you get in here?" Craig asked. The thought of the butler sent a chill down his spine. He wanted to change the subject. A gnawing sense of urgency was playing on his bladder, if he even had a bladder in here.

"The same way we did?" Jeremy asked.

"No," Mickey replied. "You came in the long way. I came in with your mom."

"With my mom?"

"But how?" Craig asked.

Mickey smiled. "I can see and hear things. My grandmother calls it Clairvoyance, but she says it's more than that. I have brief flashes of insight almost like her ability to see into the future, but for me it works best with simple things like games of chance, you know? Like with Dabney's werewolf? Sometimes, if the timing is right, I can go inside someone's mind like now. It has to be someone waiting for the light. My abilities are tied completely to the light." His expression darkened. "We came to help you. My grandmother's has searched for Günter Bremen for a very long time." He held his hand over Jeremy's head. "I can feel your power. It's very strong."

"Yours must be, too," Jeremy concluded, *"if you're here."*

"It was a gift from the Lord," Mickey said. "I have to help you destroy the evil one. There were others that needed help, too."

"Like Jeremy's mom?" Craig asked.

"I had to help her," Mickey replied. "It wasn't her time to go. Mr. D gets impatient sometimes and tries to bring people into the light before their time."

"Mr. D brings people…," Craig began.

"… into the light?"

"Of course," Mickey said. "It's his job. He gets impatient sometimes."

"What…? Craig started, and then swallowed, "… does *Mr. D* stand for?"

Mickey cocked his head. He gazed at Craig, oddly. "Death," he said.

"The butler is Death?" Jeremy cried, standing up.

"The Angel of Death," Mickey said. He grabbed his wrist and pulled him gently back down. "Here Gabriel's a butler. He comes as different things to different people. They don't even recognize him sometimes, but I do. He can't hide from me. It's part of my gift."

"He's after my mom?" Jeremy asked.

"We have to do something!" Craig exclaimed. "We have to stop him!"

"You can't," Mickey said. "No one can. We can cheat him, delay him, trick him even, but we can't stop him. He's part of the natural order. The rules are strict."

"Then how can we save my mom?" Jeremy asked.

"Well, that's been easy so far," Mickey frowned. "Mr. D had to convince her to go since it wasn't her time. She almost did, but I stopped her, by the grace of the Lord. We have to keep her busy until she heals enough that Mr. D goes away. It could be a long time…"

"… or it could be right now!" Jeremy exclaimed.

"Are you thinking what I hear you thinking?" Craig asked.

"You bet!" Jeremy exclaimed. *"I can heal her!"*

"Did you say you can heal, too?" Mickey asked. "The Lord must trust you a lot to give you so many of His gifts."

Jeremy growled, ***"The Lord had nothing to do with it, Mickey. Bremen gave me these powers and tried to steal my body. It didn't work."***

"See?" Mickey smiled. "The Lord trusted you enough to let you keep them. If you can heal your mom, Mr. D will go away."

"No problem," Craig said, his eyes filling with victory. "Jeremy healed me and I did die! Well, for about a second, but still."

Mickey looked at Craig, oddly. He reached out and touched his forehead. His irises vanished and his eyes glowed white for a moment. He raised an eyebrow and his crystal blue irises returned.

"Wow," Mickey whispered. "Many of His gifts, for sure."

The ground rumbled. Mickey looked at Mr. D. Jeremy and Craig watched in fear as the butler's face drew up in a sly smile. He dropped his white gloves on the floor. He flipped the latch on the door and it began to open.

"No!" Mickey cried, bolting back into the ballroom.

Jeremy and Craig ran after him. All of the guests in the room disappeared. The purest white light poured from the edges of the opening door.

"Hey!" Jack exclaimed. "Where did everybody go?"

The boys looked at each other.

"I'm sorry, gentlemen," Mr. D said, clearing his throat. "This affair has come to an end."

The door flung open the rest of the way with a loud bang. The warm light swirling within cascaded over them. It was brighter than the sun, but they could still look into it. Its warmth was amazing. Its promise of peace irresistible.

"Come, Virginia," Mr. D continued. "It's time for you dance with me now into the light."

Virginia turned toward the boys and smiled. Her grin was equally joyous as it was sad. "I have to go now, my darlings," she said, her eyes tearing. "I love you. Don't ever forget that, okay?"

Chris stared at her, dumbstruck. She turned away and walked toward the doorway. *What's she talking about?* he wondered, his hands on his hips. He wanted to dance some more, maybe with Dabney. *Where the hell does she think she's going?*

"Not there, Master Christopher, I assure you," Mr. D replied. "Come, Virginia. We mustn't keep Thomas waiting."

"Thomas?" Virginia whispered, drifting along as if entranced. "My darling Thomas."

"Wait, Mr. D, please!" Mickey cried. "Chris! Don't let her go into the light!"

The boys all moved at the same time. They grabbed hold of the back of Virginia's flowing gown and tugged on it. She slowed down, but she didn't stop. Their feet dragged across the floor as she drew them along with her.

They pulled with all of their strength, straining in their tug of war between life and death.

"This isn't fair, Mr. D!" Mickey pleaded.

"On the contrary, Mickey," Mr. D replied, holding his skeletal hand up. Ricardo screamed. Mr. D ignored him. "I may be impatient sometimes, but I am always fair."

"Mickey?" JT mused. "Not *Master* Mickey? Weird."

"It isn't her time!" Jeremy cried, his eyes glowing brighter as his anger grew. *"Leave her alone, damn it!"*

"Now, none of that, Jeremy!" Mr. D snapped, his expression darkening. "There is nothing damned about this."

"Jeremy?" JT softly asked. "Not *Master* Jeremy?"

"You let her go right now!" Jeremy raged. His feet left the floor as his power continued to build. *"I'll make you if I have to!"*

"Will you?"

Mr. D's immense voice filled the whole world. He sneered, his irises burning bright red. He shimmered, distorting, and when he focused again, the butler was gone. In his place stood a skeletal figure in a hooded black robe that reeked of decaying flesh. He looked exactly the way Jeremy had always thought he would.

"Do you believe you can fight Death?"

"Death?" Max cried. "Jeremy! ¿Estas loco?"

"Pull!" Chris cried, fighting the light as its warmth called to him, too. "Oh, God, pull you guys!"

"We're pulling!" Jack exclaimed.

"No, please," Virginia pleaded, struggling forward. "Thomas? Is that you, my love?"

"No!" Jeremy yelled.

Mickey jumped up and yanked him back down to the ground. Jeremy glared at him with surprise and anger.

"I told you, Jeremy," he scolded, shaking his finger. "You can't fight him. You can only trick him or cheat him. If the door is open again, your mom's body must be failing. If you can heal her, it has to be now."

"What about them?"

"Leave us here!" Chris cried, as he struggled to keep Virginia back. She inched closer to the doorway. "Go save mom!"

"All right!" Jeremy cried, closing his eyes. *"I'm out!"* He faded away.

"Wait!" Mickey cried, but it was too late.

"Help us, Mickey!" Chris begged.

Mickey shook his head. He ran over, grabbed a section of the gown, and pulled.

"Why did you try to stop him?" Craig asked, straining. "Is something wrong?"

"Well, I hate to say this, but… man, Jeremy needs to talk to my grandmother."

"What is it?" Ricardo asked. "What's wrong?"

Mickey replied, "Well, if Virginia dies while you're in here? You're all going to die with her."

The boys paused. They looked down at Mickey, shocked.

Mickey shrugged.

"Pull!"

＊　　＊　　＊

Susan pushed Derek into the room and carried in wide-eyed Douggie. Lyle and Matt closed the door. Susan's palms were sweating. Her heart threatened to pound out of her chest. Whatever was going on, she had the feeling it would be bad if the rest of the world saw it. Lyle stood motionless. Derek backed away in terror. Susan set Douggie down, slipped across the room, and dropped the shades.

"Good Lord!" Susan hissed, looking down at the boys lying askew on the bed. "Is he hurting them?"

"I don't believe so," Carson said, stroking Mickey's hand. He was wearing a pale brown three-piece suit that almost perfectly matched his hair and eyes. Behind his thick glasses and pearly smile, Carson looked like a televangelist.

"Our son is with him, too," Alberta said.

She touched Mickey's forehead with her finger. In addition to being an albino, it was apparent he carried a lot of his mother's genes. Her light blonde hair was done up with way too much hairspray. It glistened in the fluorescent light. Her pale blue eyes reflected a caring soul.

"We'd better not take the chance!" Lyle barked. He lunged at Jeremy.

"No!" Matt cried, knocking him onto the other bed. It felt like hitting a brick wall.

"Are you nuts, kid?" Lyle asked. As he stood up, he held Matt out in front of him. "What if he's killing them?"

"He's not!" Derek cried, tugging on Lyle's shirt.

"How do you know?"

"Because I'm not," Jeremy replied, lowering to the bed. His eyes slowly returned to normal. "Even though he's scared to death of me, Derek knows me better than that, Mr. Gibbons."

"Yeah?" Lyle snapped, setting Matt down. "Well, la-de-dah, Mr. Miracle!" He pointed at Max and Ricardo. "What are you doing to my godsons?"

Jeremy opened his mind to them. The glow returned to his eyes as he showed them exactly where Max, Ricardo, and the others were. Carson and Alberta began to pray.

Lyle stumbled back. "Sweet Mary, mother of God," he whispered, realizing what Jeremy needed to do. "You'll never make it in time!"

"I have to," Jeremy said. *"Will you help me?"*

"I will," Derek said. He sobbed as he gingerly reached out.

Jeremy leaned forward and embraced him.

"I'm sorry, Jeremy," Derek whispered. "I'm scared! My mom's… and…"

"I know, Derek," Jeremy replied. *"You're not alone, okay? I'll never let you be alone, I promise."*

"I'll… help, too," Susan choked, tentatively stepping forward. "Jesus, Jeremy… what happened to you?" She swallowed hard. "Are Sandy and Ian…?"

Susan didn't have to finish the question. She could tell by the look in his eyes what the answer was. She swore she heard her heart break.

Lyle snapped her back. "Let's do this then!" he exclaimed. "You take care of your mom! She's a good lady."

"I want to go, too!" Douggie insisted.

Derek looked at him like he was insane.

"Yeah, man," Matt nodded. "Me, too."

"What about me?" Susan asked, suddenly very frightened. "I… want to help, too, but… I… can't go in there."

"Fine," Jeremy replied. *"Come to ICU with me then. My mom's dying."*

Carson paused, looking sympathetic. "We'll pray for you, son," he nodded.

"I owe Mickey," Jeremy said.

"Nonsense," Alberta replied. "Mickey does the Lord's work. This is only the beginning, Jeremy." Her pleasant nature faded away with grim seriousness. "There's a war on the horizon. We're here to help prepare you."

Jeremy nodded and pointed to Craig's empty bed. *"I'd lay down if I were you,"* he said to the others. *"Once you're in, there won't be anything left behind to hold up your bodies."*

*　　*　　*

Mr. D, a butler again, laughed as Virginia inched closer to the light. The boys struggled, but were rapidly losing ground. Their strength began to fail. They felt Chris' anguish at the thought of losing his mother just hours after losing his father. His desperation fed their determination and they pulled harder. The fact that they were also about to die didn't make them feel like quitting.

"Hang on, boys!" a voice boomed throughout the ballroom. "The cavalry's here!"

"Lyle!" the Ramirez brothers cried, as he lumbered toward them.

Douggie, Derek, and Matt were right behind him.

"What are you doing here, Lyle?" Mr. D asked, his voice filled with disdain. "Put some clothes on! This is a formal occasion!"

"Hey!" Douggie cried, looking down. "Cool!"

"Lyle?" JT asked. "Not Mister Lyle? What's up with that?"

"You know him?" Ricardo asked.

Lyle's Marine dress blues appeared. Derek followed suit with his glistening white baseball uniform. On the back, in glistening red sequined letters, it read *Lobster Boy* with the number one. Matt appeared in white Dickies, a black top, and Hush Puppy shoes. Douggie refused to dress at all.

"Death and I go way back," Lyle said. He grabbed Virginia around the waist from the front and pushed her backward. "All the way to Afghanistan. I've cheated this bastard more times than I can count."

"Not this time, Lyle," Mr. D said. He grinned. "Would you like to see your wife? I can arrange it, you know. Just take a quick peek into the light." He cupped his hand to his mouth and called, "Oh, Marjorie!"

"Don't listen to him!" Mickey cried. "He's mean sometimes especially when he's losing!"

"Derek!" Chris exclaimed. "You're here, too? And Douggie?"

"He took my parents!" Derek cried. "He took Dan! He's not taking Virginia! Now, pull!"

"Your friends cheat, Mickey," Mr. D snorted. "This isn't fair at all. Come to me, Virginia," he beckoned. "Don't let these fools stop you!"

"Thomas?" Virginia smiled. "Oh, darling… I need you…"

*   *   *

Susan wasn't sure what kept her feet moving, but she was thankful for it. She was in such excruciating pain over her loss she barely remembered what mental command lifted her legs up or bent her knees. Jeremy walked in front of her holding her hand as he led her through the hallways. His skin was so soft, so warm, and felt charged with electricity. She could feel the power pulsating beneath his flesh. It rushed through his body with each heartbeat. Every fiber of her being wanted to yank him back, spin him around, and demand he tell her what was happening. Instead, like she was on autopilot, she followed him down the hallway.

Jeremy looked back at her and nodded hearing every thought. He knew her hunger for answers, but he also knew she couldn't handle them right now. She couldn't stand the strain of so many conflicting emotions. No human being could. It was the answer why he and Craig were still sane. His mind was no longer human. The power had changed him. It forced his mind to adapt and was dragging Craig along with him.

"Wait," Jeremy whispered, touching the door handle to ICU. It was locked.

"Now what?" Susan asked, trying the handle.

"This," Jeremy replied. His eyes flashed. There was a muffled click. The door swung open.

"Neat trick," Susan mumbled. "Remind me to call you the next time I lock my keys in the Jeep."

Jeremy nodded. "It's a deal." He went inside.

Susan followed him.

Every room on this floor had glass walls. Machines clicked and beeped breaking the grim silence at irregular intervals. A team of nurses and a staff physician sat at the station at the end of the hall closely watching the monitors. Jeremy planted a suggestion in their minds that they couldn't see him or Susan. It was a trick he had gleaned from the Hill Witch. He didn't dare put them to sleep reading their concern over some of the vital signs they were observing. Mike Dougan's vitals, for example, were stable, but dangerously low. They passed his room. Susan pointed at Sandra who had decided not to leave her husband's side. She had her head on Mike's stomach with her eyes closed as she drifted in and out of sleep. They snuck past saying nothing.

Jeremy promised he would take care of Mike and everyone else the moment he saved his mother. He'd read something in the doctor's mind about Virginia's vital signs being erratic. Her brainwave patterns were insanely wrong, too, as if several other patterns were overlapping hers. He was sure she wouldn't make it through the night. He was already formulating a strategy to set her up on life support if her vitals failed. Susan and Jeremy slipped into Virginia's room determined to make sure that didn't happen. They entered. Jeremy froze.

"Oh, my God!" Susan gasped, her hand over her mouth. "What happened to her?"

Virginia was sitting on an incline. Only a spot or two of her whole body didn't have a bandage. Her leg was suspended in the air in a large white cast. Her toes were sticking out of the end. They were bruised black and blue. So was her face. Her features were barely visible through the swelling. Her heart monitor was flashing erratically. The numbers counting the beats changed continuously going higher, lower, higher, lower. Jeremy felt her pain without even trying.

"I happened to her," Jeremy gulped, taking his hand from Susan and drifting to his mother. A single tear fell. His eyes narrowed. He said, "It wasn't my fault."

"Can you help her?" Susan whispered. *What an insane question!*

Jeremy let his hand drift across her cheek before laying it on her shoulder. His eyes exploded with brilliance as he channeled his power into her body. Susan took a step back in amazement.

"Just watch… huh?"

Virginia's body rejected his healing power. He tried again, his heartbeat quickening. Once more, the energy flowed over her and got sent back. Her body was refusing to allow him entry. Puzzled, he scanned her. Susan leaned over confused by the expression of desperation on his face. Jeremy reached out and grabbed Susan's hand. He forced his mother's feelings into Susan, mentally begging her to tell him what they meant. Susan sighed as she remembered the joy of the sensations flooding her.

"We might have a problem here," Susan whispered.

*　　*　　*

Graham let go of Lady Virginia's gown when he saw Keith's foot pass the threshold of the doorway. His straining expression faded. It became clear to Graham they were about to face keeping another person away from the light. He lunged forward, seized Keith by his hair and a belt loop, yanked him back, and threw him onto the ballroom floor. Lyle grabbed Graham by the shirt when he nearly fell inside next and tossed him away, too. He landed on top of Keith with a groan and rolled to one knee.

Keith shook his head struggling to stand. "What a rush!" he gasped.

"Dude," JT called, his heart starting again, "don't you dare do that again!"

"I won't!" Keith replied, helping Graham up.

They returned to Lady Virginia taking their places on her gown once again. Everyone was behind her pulling. Mickey alternated between pulling and slapping Mr. D's hand away each time he reached out to assist her through the doorway. Mr. D glared at him angrily, but said nothing. There was nothing he could say. Mickey's presence was causing him to follow the rules to the letter. There were times that child annoyed him beyond all words. Mr. D believed he might regret it when the time came to collect him. He smiled as Virginia slipped into the light. Another inch, maybe two, and victory would be his.

"Oh, crap!" Dabney cried, putting his foot up on the doorjamb. Using his legs, he pulled back with all of his might. "We're losing her!"

"No!" Chris cried, in a panic. "Pull harder!"

"We're trying, man!" Ricardo groaned.

"Try harder!" Derek exclaimed. "I'm not losing anybody else! I'm not!"

"That's a foolish statement, Master Derek," Mr. D sighed. He slipped his gloves back on as the Lady Virginia stepped into the light. "You are destined to lose more than you ever bargained for. All of you are. A piece of advice? If you don't wish to see me again anytime soon, I suggest you endeavor not to be separated. You have strength in your numbers. There's a hunter in the wilderness, children. He's coming for all of you."

"Hiram!" Craig cried. "He means Hiram!"

"Craig!" Jack exclaimed. "Look out!"

The material of Lady Virginia's flowing gown suddenly detached from her dress and sent her rescuers sprawling. Lyle hit the floor first. A landslide of teenage boys tumbled down on top of him. He grunted and groaned as he tried to break all of their falls. He only missed Ricardo who slammed flat on his back with a loud "*Oof!*" and a smack.

Graham, JT, Douggie, and Jack recovered first. They dove at the doorway, but Mr. D held up his hand freezing them in mid-air. Mickey stormed over to him with his crystal blue eyes filled with cold anger.

Mr. D shook his head. **"I'm sorry, Mickey,"** he whispered, his irises glowing red. **"It's over."**

"*Mom!*" Chris cried.

Max and Matt grabbed him from either side.

"No, Mr. D," Mickey replied, nodding at the doorway. "Not quite yet."

Mr. D glanced over, his brow furrowing. He was confused, and then irritated as Virginia backed out of the doorway. He frowned spotting a hand from the other side pushing her back. Whatever troublesome spirit it was interfering with his work would have an eternity to regret their actions. Mr. D opened his mouth to protest. Jeremy's giant glowing face appeared in the air.

Mr. D mumbled, **"It just isn't my day."**

"Jeremy!" the boys cried.

"It's about damned time!" Lyle bellowed.

Mickey stared at him, shaking his head. "Must you curse?"

Jeremy looked at his brother. Chris could tell by his expression something was wrong.

"Please!" Lady Virginia cried, struggling to get past the hand holding her back. "Let me by, okay? Thomas? Thomas, are you in there?"

"Who the heck is that?" Keith cried, pointing at the hand.

"Whoever it is," Jack said, "he's a friendly."

"Jeremy?" Chris asked. He gazed up at the *Great and Powerful Oz* visage of his little brother. "What's wrong? Why is the door still open?"

Jeremy's face clouded. *"I can't heal her,"* he said, his voice echoing loudly throughout the hall. *"Her body's in a state that won't let me interfere without her help. It keeps rejecting me."*

"State?" Dabney asked. He stepped up to steady Chris who looked like he was going to faint.

"What kinda state?" Lyle barked.

"She's pregnant," Jeremy replied, nodding at his mother. *"She… it's a girl."*

Lady Virginia suddenly spun around snapping out of her trance. When she did, the arm of the spirit holding her back lost its grip. Sandy Sturgess in a white tuxedo and tails tumbled out of the doorway and landed right at the feet of the friends who had watched him die. He looked up at them adjusting his glasses.

"*Um... hi, guys,*" he said, and smiled, shyly.

"Sandy!?" they cried. "Oh, my God! *Sandy!*"

"Wait!" Virginia cried, her gown disappearing along with her costumed hairdo and make-up. Blue jeans and a tee shirt replaced it. She ran away from the door directly under the image of her son. "Jeremy! Did you say I was...?"

Jeremy smiled feeling a rush of strength and renewed fight come into his mother's body. They all felt it and surrounded her, their fear fading away.

"Yeah, mom," Jeremy smiled. **"You're knocked up."**

"But how?" Virginia asked. "Your father and I were always so careful!"

"She-yeah!" the boys nervously exclaimed.

"Oh, cut that out!" Virginia groaned. She turned to Mr. D, shaking her head. "I'm not going, Gabriel."

"I know, my dear," he sighed, and the doorway slammed shut. **"I suppose it's just as well."** He smiled, mischievously. **"It was fun though, wasn't it? Until next time?"**

"*Wait!*" Sandy cried. "*Open the door! I have to go back!*"

Mr. D glared at him with his red irises burning. **"I think not!"**

His voice was like raging thunder. Sandy shrank back against Chris who grabbed him by the shoulders.

"You interfered where you had no place, Sanford. Let's see how you like being earthbound for a time. It might teach you some respect!"

"Sanford?" JT wondered. "Not Master Sanford? Seriously, I don't get it."

Mr. D turned to the others and bowed, curtly. **"Adieu,"** he said. He added, with a sly grin, **"For now."**

He vanished.

"*Oh, nuts,*" Sandy muttered. "*What am I supposed to do now?*"

"Come with us," Chris said, turning him around. His eyes filled with tears. "God, Sanford, I missed you. Do you know how much it hurt...?"

Sandy reached out and tenderly touched his friend's cheek. His eyes filled with sympathy. "*I know, I missed you, too, but it's not that simple, Chris. I'm dead, remember? I don't belong here anymore.*"

"But you do," Mickey interjected, taking Sandy's hand. "You overestimate Mr. D. He can't deny you entrance into the light. If you're still here, it's on a higher authority."

"*You're... right,*" Sandy nodded, his gaze faraway. "*I can sense that now that you mention it, but why?*"

"Maybe because we love you, too?" Max suggested, patting Sandy on the back.

Lyle rolled his eyes. "I doubt it, Max. Lots of people we love die and don't come back." He thought of Marjorie.

"No kidding," Derek mumbled.

"True," Mickey said.

"Then why is he here?" Craig asked.

"I think the Lord will let us know that when the time is right," Mickey said. "Jeremy? You can take your friends out now."

Jeremy nodded, looking down at his mother. ***"Mom? Are you okay?"***

Virginia smiled, weakly. "You go ahead. I'll be okay. You can heal me now." She turned and gathered together Dabney, Derek, Douggie, Jack, and Craig. She squatted down in front of them. "You boys listen to me, all right?" she asked, holding their hands together. "I know everything that's happened. When I stepped into the light, I saw it all. It's destiny, boys, do you understand? It's all destiny. Mourn for what you've lost, but don't despair. You're my boys now every one of you. You're part of my family. We'll get through this, I promise."

"We're going to live with you?" Derek asked.

"All of us?" echoed Dabney.

"All of you," Virginia smiled. She looked at the Mellon brothers. "Your grandmother will certainly agree. It's in your parents' Will. She was part of the decision making process when we planned for this. She would've taken you boys, but she felt she was too old to parent anymore." She held Derek's face lovingly, her eyes filled with sympathy and understanding. "You guys don't know everything we parents do," she said.

Derek choked back a sob.

"It's up to us to plan for every eventuality when it comes to raising our kids, even the worst ones we can imagine."

"What about me?" Dabney asked, lowering his eyes. "My father's a powerful man."

Lyle snapped, "Nuts, Copeland. You ain't seen powerful until this woman gets her panties in an uproar. Just ask Jack. He'll tell you."

"You got that right!" Jack grinned.

"What about it, boys?" Virginia asked, turning to Chris and Jeremy. "Is there room in our hearts for a family as big as this?"

Jeremy and Chris looked at each other, smiled, and turned to the boys. "Absolutely," they replied together.

Matt groaned, "Oh, no! Not that again! You guys give me the creeps when you do that!"

"Oh?" Jeremy smiled. ***"What about..."***

"... if we..." Chris continued.

"... do something..." Max added.

"... like this..." Keith said.

"... Gorilla Boy?" JT finished.

Matt was dizzy from following the sentence. "No!" he pleaded, holding his hands up. "I give!" He scowled. "Wait a minute! *Gorilla Boy?*"

Everyone turned to Graham. He smiled, sheepishly. "I saw him when he came in," he said, and signed. "He's really hairy."

They all laughed as they began to vanish. Sandy winked at Virginia. She mouthed, "Thank you," to him, and he disappeared.

Virginia closed her eyes once she was alone and made the guests from her party reappear. The music resumed. Outside the ballroom, the storm subsided and the sun shone brightly. Her hand rested gently on her belly. She danced in the presence of the husband she loved and somehow felt radiating all around her.

"Give me the damned password," Hiram growled.

He was in Ms. Adler's basement laboratory glaring at the computer screen. It read: **ENTER PASSWORD.**

"You do not need it," the voice within replied.

"The hell I don't, Bremen!" Hiram snapped. "I'm gettin' out of this body, and…!"

"… you want the secret of the power?"

Hiram smiled. "You're quick. Did you think I'd give it up after tasting it?"

"I will give it to you."

Hiram laughed, whirling around in the swivel chair. His breasts jiggled with each gasping breath.

"You want me to trust you?"

"Would you rather," Günter Bremen replied, *"spend the rest of your life with a vagina, Mein Herr?"*

Hiram frowned. He groped his crotch. "I see your point," he muttered. "Don't even think about double-crossing me, you got that? I control this body now. Just be glad I can't read you or I'd just take what I need. I'll be the one to choose which body I want, too."

"Done. You can have any body you want."

"Just like that?"

"I want a body for myself as well. We can do this simultaneously if you like. All we need…"

"… are enough brain samples, right?" Hiram interrupted, his heart skipping a beat. He smiled. "You let me worry about that. Margaret can't interfere with me the way she could with you."

They heard Margaret sobbing within, but just barely. They ignored her.

"And a lab. We cannot stay here. They will be coming."

"You know," Hiram said, standing up. "I hate your guts. You're sicker than I ever was."

"And I hate yours, you miscreant."

"Good," Hiram said. "We know where each other stands."

Hiram walked out of the lab, crossed the basement, and climbed the stairs. He made his way to the gardening shed out back. He secured a five-gallon gasoline can from next to the lawnmower and slipped back into the house.

"What about the lab?" Hiram asked, standing in the doorway.

"Burn it," Günter said. *"We will only need the computer. It is beneath the floor. We can access it by remote. It has its own power source, too. The fire will take care of the rest. We will have everything we need by the time they are finished sifting through the rubble."*

Hiram nodded. He saturated the lab and the basement with gasoline pouring a trail that led up the stairs into the kitchen. He opened all of the gas valves on the stove before leaving through the front door. He paused on the cliff overlooking Lancaster and grinned. The town was alive with flashing lights from police cars and ambulances. Every lamp in every house was burning. The people were awake from Jeremy's enforced sleep.

It was time to leave and get to the Mercedes while they still could. Not forever and not for long either. Hiram was coming back to finish what he'd started. He would give the *Gift* to every boy in Lancaster. It would be child's play once the power was his, even stronger than Jeremy's. He walked into the darkness, his throaty laughter echoing on the breeze.

Gasoline flowed out of the lab in a stream, pooling in the middle of the basement floor. The lab door slowly swung closed and sealed with an eerie sucking sound.

"Ye'll not be coverin' all your tracks today, bucko," Wade whispered. He faded away.

Giuseppe's giggle was barely audible until it, too, vanished.

A box of wooden stove matches fell from the windowsill in the kitchen onto the floor. It opened and they scattered all over the linoleum. One match jumped up, grew splintered arms and legs, and tenderly danced its way to the flint on the side of the box. It dragged its head against the rough surface. The flame came to life scarcely a second before the Adler house exploded into the night sky.

About the Author

James Christopher grew up in New England. He's created stories since childhood. He lives in Connecticut where he is working on his next book.

Made in the USA
Middletown, DE
13 February 2022